Agatha Christie
Miss Marple Omnibus

Volume One

BOOKS BY AGATHA CHRISTIE

The ABC Murders
The Adventure of the Christmas Pudding
After the Funeral
And Then There Were None
Appointment with Death
At Bertram's Hotel
The Big Four
The Body in the Library
By the Pricking of My Thumbs
Cards on the Table
A Caribbean Mystery
Cat Among the Pigeons
The Clocks
Crooked House
Curtain: Poirot's Last Case
Dead Man's Folly
Death Comes as the End
Death in the Clouds
Death on the Nile
Destination Unknown
Dumb Witness
Elephants Can Remember
Endless Night
Evil Under the Sun
Five Little Pigs
4.50 from Paddington
Hallowe'en Party
Hercule Poirot's Christmas
Hickory Dickory Dock
The Hollow
The Hound of Death
The Labours of Hercules
The Listerdale Mystery
Lord Edgware Dies
The Man in the Brown Suit
The Mirror Crack'd from Side to Side
Miss Marple's Final Cases
The Moving Finger
Mrs McGinty's Dead
The Murder at the Vicarage
Murder in Mesopotamia
Murder in the Mews
A Murder is Announced
Murder is Easy
The Murder of Roger Ackroyd
Murder on the Links
Murder on the Orient Express
The Mysterious Affair at Styles

The Mysterious Mr Quin
The Mystery of the Blue Train
Nemesis
N or M?
One, Two, Buckle My Shoe
Ordeal by Innocence
The Pale Horse
Parker Pyne Investigates
Partners in Crime
Passenger to Frankfurt
Peril at End house
A Pocket Full of Rye
Poirot Investigates
Poirot's Early Cases
Postern of Fate
Problem at Pollensa Bay
Sad Cypress
The Secret Adversary
The Secret of Chimneys
The Seven Dials Mystery
The Sittaford Mystery
Sleeping Murder
Sparkling Cyanide
Taken at the Flood
They Came to Baghdad
They Do It With Mirrors
Third Girl
The Thirteen Problems
Three-Act Tragedy
Towards Zero
Why Didn't They Ask Evans?

*Novels under the Nom de Plume
of 'Mary Westmacott'*

Absent in the Spring
The Burden
A Daughter's A Daughter
Giant's Bread
The Rose and the Yew Tree
Unfinished Portrait

*Books under the name of
Agatha Christie Mallowan*

Come Tell Me How You Live
Star Over Bethlehem

Autobiography

Agatha Christie: An Autobiography

Agatha Christie
Miss Marple Omnibus

Volume One

The Body in the Library

The Moving Finger

A Murder is Announced

4.50 from Paddington

HarperCollins*Publishers*

HarperCollins*Publishers*
77–85 Fulham Palace Road,
Hammersmith, London W6 8JB

This edition first published 1997

5 7 9 8 6

ISBN 0 00 649959 7

Set in Times by
Rowland Phototypesetting Ltd,
Bury St Edmunds, Suffolk

Printed and bound in Great Britain by
Omnia Books Ltd, Glasgow

CONTENTS

The Body in the Library

To My Friend Nan

AUTHOR'S FOREWORD

There are certain clichés belonging to certain types of fiction. The 'bold bad baronet' for melodrama, the 'body in the library' for the detective story. For several years I treasured up the possibility of a suitable 'Variation on a well-known Theme'. I laid down for myself certain conditions. The library in question must be a highly orthodox and conventional library. The body, on the other hand, must be a wildly improbable and highly sensational body. Such were the terms of the problem, but for some years they remained as such, represented only by a few lines of writing in an exercise book. Then, staying one summer for a few days at a fashionable hotel by the seaside I observed a family at one of the tables in the dining-room; an elderly man, a cripple, in a wheeled chair, and with him was a family party of a younger generation. Fortunately they left the next day, so that my imagination could get to work unhampered by any kind of knowledge. When people ask 'Do you put real people in your books?' the answer is that, for me, it is quite impossible to write about anyone I know, or have ever spoken to, or indeed have even heard about! For some reason, it kills them for me stone dead. But I can take a 'lay figure' and endow it with qualities and imaginings of my own.

So an elderly crippled man became the pivot of the story. Colonel and Mrs Bantry, those old cronies of my Miss Marple, had just the right kind of library. In the manner of a cookery recipe add the following ingredients: a tennis pro, a young dancer, an artist, a girl guide, a dance hostess, etc., and serve up *à la* Miss Marple!

Agatha Christie

CHAPTER ONE

Mrs Bantry was dreaming. Her sweet peas had just taken a First at the flower show. The vicar, dressed in cassock and surplice, was giving out the prizes in church. His wife wandered past, dressed in a bathing-suit, but as is the blessed habit of dreams this fact did not arouse the disapproval of the parish in the way it would assuredly have done in real life . . .

Mrs Bantry was enjoying her dream a good deal. She usually did enjoy those early-morning dreams that were terminated by the arrival of early-morning tea. Somewhere in her inner consciousness was an awareness of the usual early-morning noises of the household. The rattle of the curtain-rings on the stairs as the housemaid drew them, the noises of the second housemaid's dustpan and brush in the passage outside. In the distance the heavy noise of the front-door bolt being drawn back.

Another day was beginning. In the meantime she must extract as much pleasure as possible from the flower show — for already its dream-like quality was becoming apparent . . .

Below her was the noise of the big wooden shutters in the drawing-room being opened. She heard it, yet did not hear it. For quite half an hour longer the usual household noises would go on, discreet, subdued, not disturbing because they were so familiar. They would culminate in a swift, controlled sound of footsteps along the passage, the rustle of a print dress, the subdued chink of tea-things as the tray was deposited on the table outside, then the soft knock and the entry of Mary to draw the curtains.

In her sleep Mrs Bantry frowned. Something disturbing was penetrating through to the dream state, something out of its time. Footsteps along the passage, footsteps that were too hurried and too soon. Her ears listened unconsciously for the chink of china, but there was no chink of china.

The knock came at the door. Automatically from the depths of her dreams Mrs Bantry said: 'Come in.' The door opened — now there would be the chink of curtain-rings as the curtains were drawn back.

But there was no chink of curtain-rings. Out of the dim green light Mary's voice came – breathless, hysterical: 'Oh, ma'am, oh, ma'am, *there's a body in the library*.'

And then with a hysterical burst of sobs she rushed out of the room again.

II

Mrs Bantry sat up in bed.

Either her dream had taken a very odd turn or else – or else Mary had really rushed into the room and had said (incredible! fantastic!) that there was a body in the library.

'Impossible,' said Mrs Bantry to herself. 'I must have been dreaming.'

But even as she said it, she felt more and more certain that she had not been dreaming, that Mary, her superior self-controlled Mary, had actually uttered those fantastic words.

Mrs Bantry reflected a minute and then applied an urgent conjugal elbow to her sleeping spouse.

'Arthur, Arthur, wake up.'

Colonel Bantry grunted, muttered, and rolled over on his side.

'Wake up, Arthur. Did you hear what she said?'

'Very likely,' said Colonel Bantry indistinctly. 'I quite agree with you, Dolly,' and promptly went to sleep again.

Mrs Bantry shook him.

'You've got to listen. Mary came in and said that there was a body in the library.'

'Eh, what?'

'A *body* in the *library*.'

'Who said so?'

'Mary.'

Colonel Bantry collected his scattered faculties and proceeded to deal with the situation. He said:

'Nonsense, old girl; you've been dreaming.'

'No, I haven't. I thought so, too, at first. But I haven't. She really came in and said so.'

'Mary came in and said there was a body in the library?'

'Yes.'

'But there couldn't be,' said Colonel Bantry.

'No, no, I suppose not,' said Mrs Bantry doubtfully.

Rallying, she went on:

'But then why did Mary say there was?'

'She can't have.'

'She did.'

'You must have imagined it.'

'I didn't imagine it.'

Colonel Bantry was by now thoroughly awake and prepared to deal with the situation on its merits. He said kindly:

'You've been dreaming, Dolly, that's what it is. It's that detective story you were reading – *The Clue of the Broken Match*. You know – Lord Edgbaston finds a beautiful blonde dead on the library hearthrug. Bodies are always being found in libraries in books. I've never known a case in real life.'

'Perhaps you will now,' said Mrs Bantry. 'Anyway, Arthur, you've got to get up and see.'

'But really, Dolly, it *must* have been a dream. Dreams often do seem wonderfully vivid when you first wake up. You feel quite sure they're true.'

'I was having quite a different sort of dream – about a flower show and the vicar's wife in a bathing-dress – something like that.'

With a sudden burst of energy Mrs Bantry jumped out of bed and pulled back the curtains. The light of a fine autumn day flooded the room.

'I did *not* dream it,' said Mrs Bantry firmly. 'Get up at once, Arthur, and go downstairs and see about it.'

'You want me to go downstairs and ask if there's a body in the library? I shall look a damned fool.'

'You needn't ask anything,' said Mrs Bantry. 'If there *is* a body – and of course it's just possible that Mary's gone mad and thinks she sees things that aren't there – well, somebody will tell you soon enough. *You* won't have to say a word.'

Grumbling, Colonel Bantry wrapped himself in his dressing-gown and left the room. He went along the passage and down the staircase. At the foot of it was a little knot of huddled servants; some of them were sobbing. The butler stepped forward impressively.

'I'm glad you have come, sir. I have directed that nothing should be done until you came. Will it be in order for me to ring up the police, sir?'

'Ring 'em up about what?'

The butler cast a reproachful glance over his shoulder at the tall young woman who was weeping hysterically on the cook's shoulder.

'I understood, sir, that Mary had already informed you. She said she had done so.'

Mary gasped out:

'I was so upset I don't know what I said. It all came over me again and my legs gave way and my inside turned over. Finding it like that – oh, oh, oh!'

She subsided again on to Mrs Eccles, who said: 'There, there, my dear,' with some relish.

'Mary is naturally somewhat upset, sir, having been the one to make the gruesome discovery,' explained the butler. 'She went into the library as usual, to draw the curtains, and – almost stumbled over the body.'

'Do you mean to tell me,' demanded Colonel Bantry, 'that there's a dead body in my library – *my* library?'

The butler coughed.

'Perhaps, sir, you would like to see for yourself.'

III

'Hallo, 'allo, 'allo. Police station here. Yes, who's speaking?'

Police-Constable Palk was buttoning up his tunic with one hand while the other held the receiver.

'Yes, yes, Gossington Hall. Yes? Oh, good-morning, sir.' Police-Constable Palk's tone underwent a slight modification. It became less impatiently official, recognizing the generous patron of the police sports and the principal magistrate of the district.

'Yes, sir? What can I do for you? – I'm sorry, sir, I didn't quite catch – a *body*, did you say? – yes? – yes, if you please, sir – that's right, sir – young woman not known to you, you say? – quite, sir. Yes, you can leave it all to me.'

Police-Constable Palk replaced the receiver, uttered a long-drawn whistle and proceeded to dial his superior officer's number.

Mrs Palk looked in from the kitchen whence proceeded an appetizing smell of frying bacon.

'What is it?'

'Rummest thing you ever heard of,' replied her husband. 'Body of a young woman found up at the Hall. In the Colonel's library.'

'Murdered?'

'Strangled, so he says.'

'Who was she?'

'The Colonel says he doesn't know her from Adam.'

'Then what was she doing in 'is library?'

Police-Constable Palk silenced her with a reproachful glance and spoke officially into the telephone.

'Inspector Slack? Police-Constable Palk here. A report has just come in that the body of a young woman was discovered this morning at seven-fifteen —'

IV

Miss Marple's telephone rang when she was dressing. The sound of it flurried her a little. It was an unusual hour for her telephone to ring. So well ordered was her prim spinster's life that unforeseen telephone calls were a source of vivid conjecture.

'Dear me,' said Miss Marple, surveying the ringing instrument with perplexity. 'I wonder who that can be?'

Nine o'clock to nine-thirty was the recognized time for the village to make friendly calls to neighbours. Plans for the day, invitations and so on were always issued then. The butcher had been known to ring up just before nine if some crisis in the meat trade had occurred. At intervals during the day spasmodic calls might occur, though it was considered bad form to ring after nine-thirty at night. It was true that Miss Marple's nephew, a writer, and therefore erratic, had been known to ring up at the most peculiar times, once as late as ten minutes to midnight. But whatever Raymond West's eccentricities, early rising was not one of them. Neither he nor anyone of Miss Marple's acquaintance would be likely to ring up before eight in the morning. Actually a quarter to eight.

Too early even for a telegram, since the post office did not open until eight.

'It must be,' Miss Marple decided, 'a wrong number.'

Having decided this, she advanced to the impatient instrument and quelled its clamour by picking up the receiver. 'Yes?' she said.

'Is that you, Jane?'

Miss Marple was much surprised.

'Yes, it's Jane. You're up very early, Dolly.'

Mrs Bantry's voice came breathless and agitated over the wires.

'The most awful thing has happened.'

'Oh, my dear.'

'We've just found a body in the library.'

For a moment Miss Marple thought her friend had gone mad.

'You've found a *what*?'

'I know. One doesn't believe it, does one? I mean, I thought they only happened in books. I had to argue for hours with Arthur this morning before he'd even go down and see.'

Miss Marple tried to collect herself. She demanded breathlessly: 'But whose body is it?'

'It's a blonde.'

'A what?'

'A blonde. A beautiful blonde – like books again. None of us have ever seen her before. She's just lying there in the library, dead. That's why you've got to come up at once.'

'You want *me* to come up?'

'Yes, I'm sending the car down for you.'

Miss Marple said doubtfully:

'Of course, dear, if you think I can be of any comfort to you –'

'Oh, I don't want comfort. But you're so good at bodies.'

'Oh no, indeed. My little successes have been mostly theoretical.'

'But you're very good at murders. She's been murdered, you see, strangled. What I feel is that if one has got to have a murder actually happening in one's house, one might as well enjoy it, if you know what I mean. That's why I want you to come and help me find out who did it and unravel the mystery and all that. It really *is* rather thrilling, isn't it?'

'Well, of course, my dear, if I can be of any *help* to you.'

'Splendid! Arthur's being rather difficult. He seems to think I shouldn't enjoy myself about it at all. Of course, I do know it's very sad and all that, but then I don't know the girl – and when you've seen her you'll understand what I mean when I say she doesn't look *real* at all.'

V

A little breathless, Miss Marple alighted from the Bantrys' car, the door of which was held open for her by the chauffeur.

Colonel Bantry came out on the steps, and looked a little surprised.

'Miss Marple? – er – very pleased to see you.'

'Your wife telephoned to me,' explained Miss Marple.

'Capital, capital. She ought to have someone with her. She'll crack up otherwise. She's putting a good face on things at the moment, but you know what it is –'

At this moment Mrs Bantry appeared, and exclaimed:

'Do go back into the dining-room and eat your breakfast, Arthur. Your bacon will get cold.'

'I thought it might be the Inspector arriving,' explained Colonel Bantry.

'He'll be here soon enough,' said Mrs Bantry. 'That's why it's important to get your breakfast first. You need it.'

'So do you. Much better come and eat something. Dolly –'

'I'll come in a minute,' said Mrs Bantry. 'Go on, Arthur.'

Colonel Bantry was shooed back into the dining-room like a recalcitrant hen.

'*Now!*' said Mrs Bantry with an intonation of triumph. 'Come on.'

She led the way rapidly along the long corridor to the east of the house. Outside the library door Constable Palk stood on guard. He intercepted Mrs Bantry with a show of authority.

'I'm afraid nobody is allowed in, madam. Inspector's orders.'

'Nonsense, Palk,' said Mrs Bantry. 'You know Miss Marple perfectly well.'

Constable Palk admitted to knowing Miss Marple.

'It's very important that she should see the body,' said Mrs Bantry. 'Don't be stupid, Palk. After all, it's *my* library, isn't it?'

Constable Palk gave way. His habit of giving in to the gentry was lifelong. The Inspector, he reflected, need never know about it.

'Nothing must be touched or handled in any way,' he warned the ladies.

'Of course not,' said Mrs Bantry impatiently. 'We know *that*. You can come in and watch, if you like.'

Constable Palk availed himself of this permission. It had been his intention, anyway.

Mrs Bantry bore her friend triumphantly across the library to the big old-fashioned fireplace. She said, with a dramatic sense of climax: 'There!'

Miss Marple understood then just what her friend had meant when she said the dead girl wasn't real. The library was a room very typical of its owners. It was large and shabby and untidy. It had big sagging arm-chairs, and pipes and books and estate papers laid out on the big table. There were one or two good old family portraits on the walls, and some bad Victorian water-colours, and some would-be-funny hunting scenes. There was a big vase of Michaelmas daisies in the corner. The whole room was dim and mellow and casual. It spoke of long occupation and familiar use and of links with tradition.

And across the old bearskin hearthrug there was sprawled something new and crude and melodramatic.

The flamboyant figure of a girl. A girl with unnaturally fair hair dressed up off her face in elaborate curls and rings. Her thin body was dressed in a backless evening-dress of white spangled satin. The face was heavily made-up, the powder standing out grotesquely on its blue swollen surface, the mascara of the lashes lying thickly on the distorted cheeks, the scarlet of the lips looking like a gash. The finger-nails were enamelled in a deep blood-red and so were the toenails in their cheap silver sandal shoes. It was a cheap, tawdry, flamboyant figure – most incongruous in the solid old-fashioned comfort of Colonel Bantry's library.

Mrs Bantry said in a low voice:

'You see what I mean? It just isn't *true*!'

The old lady by her side nodded her head. She looked down long and thoughtfully at the huddled figure.

She said at last in a gentle voice:

'She's very young.'

'Yes – yes – I suppose she is.' Mrs Bantry seemed almost surprised – like one making a discovery.

Miss Marple bent down. She did not touch the girl. She looked at the fingers that clutched frantically at the front of the girl's dress, as though she had clawed it in her last frantic struggle for breath.

There was the sound of a car scrunching on the gravel outside. Constable Palk said with urgency:

'That'll be the Inspector . . .'

True to his ingrained belief that the gentry didn't let you down, Mrs Bantry immediately moved to the door. Miss Marple followed her. Mrs Bantry said:

'That'll be all right, Palk.'

Constable Palk was immensely relieved.

VI

Hastily downing the last fragments of toast and marmalade with a drink of coffee, Colonel Bantry hurried out into the hall and was relieved to see Colonel Melchett, the Chief Constable of the county, descending from a car with Inspector Slack in attendance. Melchett was a friend of the Colonel's. Slack he had never much taken to – an energetic man who belied his name and who accompanied his bustling manner with a good deal of disregard for the feelings of anyone he did not consider important.

'Morning, Bantry,' said the Chief Constable. 'Thought I'd better come along myself. This seems an extraordinary business.'

'It's – it's –' Colonel Bantry struggled to express himself. 'It's *incredible – fantastic!*'

'No idea who the woman is?'

'Not the slightest. Never set eyes on her in my life.'

'Butler know anything?' asked Inspector Slack.

'Lorrimer is just as taken aback as I am.'

'Ah,' said Inspector Slack. 'I wonder.'

Colonel Bantry said:

'There's breakfast in the dining-room, Melchett, if you'd like anything?'

'No, no – better get on with the job. Haydock ought to be here any minute now – ah, here he is.'

Another car drew up and big, broad-shouldered Doctor Haydock, who was also the police surgeon, got out. A second police car had disgorged two plain-clothes men, one with a camera.

'All set – eh?' said the Chief Constable. 'Right. We'll go along. In the library, Slack tells me.'

Colonel Bantry groaned.

'It's incredible! You know, when my wife insisted this morning that the housemaid had come in and said there was a body in the library, I just wouldn't believe her.'

'No, no, I can quite understand that. Hope your missus isn't too badly upset by it all?'

'She's been wonderful – really wonderful. She's got old Miss Marple up here with her – from the village, you know.'

'Miss Marple?' The Chief Constable stiffened. 'Why did she send for her?'

'Oh, a woman wants another woman – don't you think so?'

Colonel Melchett said with a slight chuckle:

'If you ask me, your wife's going to try her hand at a little amateur detecting. Miss Marple's quite the local sleuth. Put it over us properly once, didn't she, Slack?'

Inspector Slack said: 'That was different.'

'Different from what?'

'That was a local case, that was, sir. The old lady knows everything that goes on in the village, that's true enough. But she'll be out of her depth here.'

Melchett said dryly: 'You don't know very much about it yourself yet, Slack.'

'Ah, you wait, sir. It won't take me long to get down to it.'

VII

In the dining-room Mrs Bantry and Miss Marple, in their turn, were partaking of breakfast.

After waiting on her guest, Mrs Bantry said urgently:

'Well, Jane?'

Miss Marple looked up at her, slightly bewildered.

Mrs Bantry said hopefully:

'Doesn't it *remind* you of anything?'

For Miss Marple had attained fame by her ability to link up trivial village happenings with graver problems in such a way as to throw light upon the latter.

'No,' said Miss Marple thoughtfully, 'I can't say that it does – not at the moment. I was reminded a little of Mrs Chetty's youngest – Edie, you know – but I think that was just because this poor girl bit her nails and her front teeth stuck out a little. Nothing more than that. And, of course,' went on Miss Marple, pursuing the parallel further, 'Edie was fond of what I call cheap finery, too.'

'You mean her dress?' said Mrs Bantry.

'Yes, a very tawdry satin – poor quality.'

Mrs Bantry said:

'I know. One of those nasty little shops where everything is a guinea.' She went on hopefully:

'Let me see, what happened to Mrs Chetty's Edie?'

'She's just gone into her second place – and doing very well, I believe.'

Mrs Bantry felt slightly disappointed. The village parallel didn't seem to be exactly hopeful.

'What I can't make out,' said Mrs Bantry, 'is what she could possibly be doing in Arthur's study. The window was forced, Palk tells me. She might have come down here with a burglar and then they quarrelled – but that seems such nonsense, doesn't it?'

'She was hardly dressed for burglary,' said Miss Marple thoughtfully.

'No, she was dressed for dancing – or a party of some kind. But there's nothing of that kind down here – or anywhere near.'

'N-n-o,' said Miss Marple doubtfully.

Mrs Bantry pounced.

'Something's in your mind, Jane.'

'Well, I was just wondering –'

'Yes?'

'Basil Blake.'

Mrs Bantry cried impulsively: 'Oh, no!' and added as though in explanation, 'I know his mother.'

The two women looked at each other.

Miss Marple sighed and shook her head.

'I quite understand how you feel about it.'

'Selina Blake is the nicest woman imaginable. Her herbaceous borders are simply marvellous – they make me green with envy. And she's frightfully generous with cuttings.'

Miss Marple, passing over these claims to consideration on the part of Mrs Blake, said:

'All the same, you know, there has been a lot of *talk*.'

'Oh, I know — I know. And of course Arthur goes simply livid when he hears Basil Blake mentioned. He was really *very* rude to Arthur, and since then Arthur won't hear a good word for him. He's got that silly slighting way of talking that these boys have nowadays — sneering at people sticking up for their school or the Empire or that sort of thing. And then, of course, the *clothes* he wears!

'People say,' continued Mrs Bantry, 'that it doesn't matter what you wear in the country. I never heard such nonsense. It's just in the country that everyone notices.' She paused, and added wistfully: 'He was an adorable baby in his bath.'

'There was a lovely picture of the Cheviot murderer as a baby in the paper last Sunday,' said Miss Marple.

'Oh, but Jane, you don't think *he* —'

'No, no, dear. I didn't mean that at all. That would indeed be jumping to conclusions. I was just trying to account for the young woman's presence down here. St Mary Mead is such an unlikely place. And then it seemed to me that the only possible explanation was Basil Blake. He *does* have parties. People came down from London and from the studios — you remember last July? Shouting and singing — the most *terrible* noise — everyone very drunk, I'm afraid — and the mess and the broken glass next morning simply unbelievable — so old Mrs Berry told me — and a young woman asleep in the bath with practically *nothing on*!'

Mrs Bantry said indulgently:

'I suppose they were film people.'

'Very likely. And then — what I expect you've heard — several week-ends lately he's brought down a young woman with him — a platinum blonde.'

Mrs Bantry exclaimed:

'You don't think it's *this* one?'

'Well — I wondered. Of course, I've never seen her close to — only just getting in and out of the car — and once in the cottage garden when she was sunbathing with just some shorts and a brassière. I never really saw her *face*. And all these girls with their make-up and their hair and their nails look so alike.'

'Yes. Still, it *might* be. It's an idea, Jane.'

CHAPTER TWO

It was an idea that was being at that moment discussed by Colonel Melchett and Colonel Bantry.

The Chief Constable, after viewing the body and seeing his subordinates set to work on their routine tasks, had adjourned with the master of the house to the study in the other wing of the house.

Colonel Melchett was an irascible-looking man with a habit of tugging at his short red moustache. He did so now, shooting a perplexed sideways glance at the other man. Finally, he rapped out:

'Look here, Bantry, got to get this off my chest. Is it a fact that you don't know from Adam who this girl is?'

The other's answer was explosive, but the Chief Constable interrupted him.

'Yes, yes, old man, but look at it like this. Might be deuced awkward for you. Married man – fond of your missus and all that. But just between ourselves – if you *were* tied up with this girl in any way, better say so *now*. Quite natural to want to suppress the fact – should feel the same myself. But it won't do. Murder case. Facts bound to come out. Dash it all, I'm not suggesting *you* strangled the girl – not the sort of thing you'd do – *I* know that. But, after all, she came here – to this house. Put it she broke in and was waiting to see you, and some bloke or other followed her down and did her in. Possible, you know. See what I mean?'

'Damn it all, Melchett, I tell you I've never set eyes on that girl in my life! I'm not that sort of man.'

'That's all right, then. Shouldn't blame you, you know. Man of the world. Still, if you say so – Question is, what was she doing down here? She doesn't come from these parts – that's quite certain.'

'The whole thing's a nightmare,' fumed the angry master of the house.

'The point is, old man, what was she doing in your library?'

'How should I know? *I* didn't ask her here.'

'No, no. But she *came* here, all the same. Looks as though she wanted to see you. You haven't had any odd letters or anything?'

'No, I haven't.'

Colonel Melchett inquired delicately:

'What were you doing yourself last night?'

'I went to the meeting of the Conservative Association. Nine o'clock, at Much Benham.'

'And you got home when?'

'I left Much Benham just after ten — had a bit of trouble on the way home, had to change a wheel. I got back at a quarter to twelve.'

'You didn't go into the library?'

'No.'

'Pity.'

'I was tired. I went straight up to bed.'

'Anyone waiting up for you?'

'No. I always take the latchkey. Lorrimer goes to bed at eleven unless I give orders to the contrary.'

'Who shuts up the library?'

'Lorrimer. Usually about seven-thirty this time of year.'

'Would he go in there again during the evening?'

'Not with my being out. He left the tray with whisky and glasses in the hall.'

'I see. What about your wife?'

'I don't know. She was in bed when I got home and fast asleep. She may have sat in the library yesterday evening or in the drawing-room. I forgot to ask her.'

'Oh well, we shall soon know all the details. Of course, it's possible one of the servants may be concerned, eh?'

Colonel Bantry shook his head.

'I don't believe it. They're all a most respectable lot. We've had 'em for years.'

Melchett agreed.

'Yes, it doesn't seem likely that they're mixed up in it. Looks more as though the girl came down from town — perhaps with some young fellow. Though why they wanted to break into this house —'

Bantry interrupted.

'London. That's more like it. We don't have goings on down here — at least —'

'Well, what is it?'

'Upon my word!' exploded Colonel Bantry. 'Basil Blake!'

'Who's he?'

24

'Young fellow connected with the film industry. Poisonous young brute. My wife sticks up for him because she was at school with his mother, but of all the decadent useless young jackanapes! Wants his behind kicked! He's taken that cottage on the Lansham Road – you know – ghastly modern bit of building. He has parties there, shrieking, noisy crowds, and he has girls down for the weekend.'

'Girls?'

'Yes, there was one last week – one of these platinum blondes –'

The Colonel's jaw dropped.

'A platinum blonde, eh?' said Melchett reflectively.

'Yes. I say, Melchett, you don't think –'

The Chief Constable said briskly:

'It's a possibility. It accounts for a girl of this type being in St Mary Mead. I think I'll run along and have a word with this young fellow – Braid – Blake – what did you say his name was?'

'Blake. Basil Blake.'

'Will he be at home, do you know?'

'Let me see. What's today – Saturday? Usually gets here sometime Saturday morning.'

Melchett said grimly:

'We'll see if we can find him.'

II

Basil Blake's cottage, which consisted of all modern conveniences enclosed in a hideous shell of half timbering and sham Tudor, was known to the postal authorities, and to William Booker, builder, as 'Chatsworth'; to Basil and his friends as 'The Period Piece', and to the village of St Mary Mead at large as 'Mr Booker's new house'.

It was little more than a quarter of a mile from the village proper, being situated on a new building estate that had been bought by the enterprising Mr Booker just beyond the Blue Boar, with frontage on what had been a particularly unspoilt country lane. Gossington Hall was about a mile farther on along the same road.

Lively interest had been aroused in St Mary Mead when news went round that 'Mr Booker's new house' had been bought by a film star. Eager watch was kept for the first appearance of the legendary creature in the village, and it may be said that as far as appearances went Basil Blake was all that could be asked for. Little by little, however, the real facts leaked out. Basil Blake was *not* a film star – not even a film actor. He was a very junior person, rejoicing in the title of about fifteenth in the list of those responsible for Set Decorations at Lemville Studios, headquarters of British New Era Films. The village maidens lost interest, and the ruling class of censorious spinsters took exception to Basil Blake's way of life. Only the landlord of the Blue Boar continued to be enthusiastic about Basil and Basil's friends. The revenues of the Blue Boar had increased since the young man's arrival in the place.

The police car stopped outside the distorted rustic gate of Mr Booker's fancy, and Colonel Melchett, with a glance of distaste at the excessive half timbering of Chatsworth, strode up to the front door and attacked it briskly with the knocker.

It was opened much more promptly than he had expected. A young man with straight, somewhat long, black hair, wearing orange corduroy trousers and a royal-blue shirt, snapped out: 'Well, what do you want?'

'Are you Mr Basil Blake?'

'Of course I am.'

'I should be glad to have a few words with you, if I may, Mr Blake?'

'Who are you?'

'I am Colonel Melchett, the Chief Constable of the County.'

Mr Blake said insolently:

'You don't say so; how amusing!'

And Colonel Melchett, following the other in, understood what Colonel Bantry's reactions had been. The toe of his own boot itched.

Containing himself, however, he said with an attempt to speak pleasantly:

'You're an early riser, Mr Blake.'

'Not at all. I haven't been to bed yet.'

'Indeed.'

'But I don't suppose you've come here to inquire into my hours of bedgoing – or if you have it's rather a waste of the county's time and money. What is it you want to speak to me about?'

Colonel Melchett cleared his throat.

'I understand, Mr Blake, that last week-end you had a visitor – a – er – fair-haired young lady.'

Basil Blake stared, threw back his head and roared with laughter.

'Have the old cats been on to you from the village? About my morals? Damn it all, morals aren't a police matter. *You* know that.'

'As you say,' said Melchett dryly, 'your morals are no concern of mine. I have come to you because the body of a fair-haired young woman of slightly – er – exotic appearance has been found – murdered.'

'Strewth!' Blake stared at him. 'Where?'

'In the library at Gossington Hall.'

'At Gossington? At old Bantry's? I say, that's pretty rich. Old Bantry! The dirty old man!'

Colonel Melchett went very red in the face. He said sharply through the renewed mirth of the young man opposite him: 'Kindly control your tongue, sir. I came to ask you if you can throw any light on this business.'

'You've come round to ask me if I've missed a blonde? Is that it? Why should – hallo, 'allo, 'allo, what's this?'

A car had drawn up outside with a scream of brakes. Out of it tumbled a young woman dressed in flapping black-and-white pyjamas. She had scarlet lips, blackened eyelashes, and a platinum-blonde head. She strode up to the door, flung it open, and exclaimed angrily:

'Why did you run out on me, you brute?'

Basil Blake had risen.

'So there you are! Why shouldn't I leave you? I told you to clear out and you wouldn't.'

'Why the hell should I because you told me to? I was enjoying myself.'

'Yes – with that filthy brute Rosenberg. You know what *he's* like.'

'You were jealous, that's all.'

'Don't flatter yourself. I hate to see a girl I like who can't hold her drink and lets a disgusting Central European paw her about.'

'That's a damned lie. You were drinking pretty hard yourself – and going on with the black-haired Spanish bitch.'

'If I take you to a party I expect you to be able to behave yourself.'

'And I refuse to be dictated to, and that's that. You said we'd go to the party and come on down here afterwards. I'm not going to leave a party before I'm ready to leave it.'

'No – and that's why I left you flat. I was ready to come down here and I came. I don't hang round waiting for any fool of a woman.'

'Sweet, polite person you are!'

'You seem to have followed me down all right!'

'I wanted to tell you what I thought of you!'

'If you think you can boss me, my girl, you're wrong!'

'And if you think you can order me about, you can think again!'

They glared at each other.

It was at this moment that Colonel Melchett seized his opportunity, and cleared his throat loudly.

Basil Blake swung round on him.

'Hallo, I forgot you were here. About time you took yourself off, isn't it? Let me introduce you – Dinah Lee – Colonel Blimp of the County Police. And now, Colonel, that you've seen my blonde is alive and in good condition, perhaps you'll get on with the good work concerning old Bantry's little bit of fluff. Good-morning!'

Colonel Melchett said:

'I advise you to keep a civil tongue in your head, young man, or you'll let yourself in for trouble,' and stumped out, his face red and wrathful.

CHAPTER THREE

In his office at Much Benham, Colonel Melchett received and scrutinized the reports of his subordinates:

'. . . so it all seems clear enough, sir,' Inspector Slack was concluding: 'Mrs Bantry sat in the library after dinner and went to bed just before ten. She turned out the lights when she left the room and, presumably, no one entered the room afterwards. The servants went to bed at half-past ten and Lorrimer, after putting the drinks in the hall, went to bed at a quarter to eleven. Nobody heard anything out of the usual except the third housemaid, and she heard too much! Groans and a blood-curdling yell and sinister footsteps and I don't know what. The second housemaid who shares a room with her says the other girl slept all night through without a sound. It's those ones that make up things that cause us all the trouble.'

'What about the forced window?'

'Amateur job, Simmons says; done with a common chisel – ordinary pattern – wouldn't have made much noise. Ought to be a chisel about the house but nobody can find it. Still, that's common enough where tools are concerned.'

'Think any of the servants know anything?'

Rather unwillingly Inspector Slack replied:

'No, sir, I don't think they do. They all seemed very shocked and upset. I had my suspicions of Lorrimer – reticent, he was, if you know what I mean – but I don't think there's anything in it.'

Melchett nodded. He attached no importance to Lorrimer's reticence. The energetic Inspector Slack often produced that effect on people he interrogated.

The door opened and Dr Haydock came in.

'Thought I'd look in and give you the rough gist of things.'

'Yes, yes, glad to see you. Well?'

'Nothing much. Just what you'd think. Death was due to strangulation. Satin waistband of her own dress, which was passed round the neck and crossed at the back. Quite easy and simple to do. Wouldn't have needed great strength – that is, if the girl were taken by surprise. There are no signs of a struggle.'

'What about time of death?'

'Say, between ten o'clock and midnight.'

'You can't get nearer than that?'

Haydock shook his head with a slight grin.

'I won't risk my professional reputation. Not earlier than ten and not later than midnight.'

'And your own fancy inclines to which time?'

'Depends. There was a fire in the grate – the room was warm – all that would delay rigor and cadaveric stiffening.'

'Anything more you can say about her?'

'Nothing much. She was young – about seventeen or eighteen, I should say. Rather immature in some ways but well developed muscularly. Quite a healthy specimen. She was virgo intacta, by the way.'

And with a nod of his head the doctor left the room.

Melchett said to the Inspector:

'You're quite sure she'd never been seen before at Gossington?'

29

'The servants are positive of that. Quite indignant about it. They'd have remembered if they'd ever seen her about in the neighbourhood, they say.'

'I expect they would,' said Melchett. 'Anyone of that type sticks out a mile round here. Look at that young woman of Blake's.'

'Pity it wasn't her,' said Slack; 'then we should be able to get on a bit.'

'It seems to me this girl must have come down from London,' said the Chief Constable thoughtfully. 'Don't believe there will be any local leads. In that case, I suppose, we should do well to call in the Yard. It's a case for them, not for us.'

'Something must have brought her down here, though,' said Slack. He added tentatively: 'Seems to me, Colonel and Mrs Bantry *must* know something – of course, I know they're friends of yours, sir –'

Colonel Melchett treated him to a cold stare. He said stiffly:

'You may rest assured that I'm taking every possibility into account. *Every* possibility.' He went on: 'You've looked through the list of persons reported missing, I suppose?'

Slack nodded. He produced a typed sheet.

'Got 'em here. Mrs Saunders, reported missing a week ago, dark-haired, blue-eyed, thirty-six. 'Tisn't her – and, anyway, everyone knows except her husband that she's gone off with a fellow from Leeds – commercial. Mrs Barnard – she's sixty-five. Pamela Reeves, sixteen, missing from her home last night, had attended Girl Guide rally, dark-brown hair in pigtail, five feet five –'

Melchett said irritably:

'Don't go on reading idiotic details, Slack. This wasn't a school-girl. In my opinion –'

He broke off as the telephone rang. 'Hallo – yes – yes, Much Benham Police Headquarters – what? Just a minute –'

He listened, and wrote rapidly. Then he spoke again, a new tone in his voice:

'Ruby Keene, eighteen, occupation professional dancer, five feet four inches, slender, platinum-blonde hair, blue eyes, *retroussé* nose, believed to be wearing white diamanté evening-dress, silver sandal shoes. Is that right? What? Yes, not a doubt of it, I should say. I'll send Slack over at once.'

He rang off and looked at his subordinate with rising excitement. 'We've got it, I think. That was the Glenshire Police' (Glenshire was the adjoining county). 'Girl reported missing from the Majestic Hotel, Danemouth.'

'Danemouth,' said Inspector Slack. 'That's more like it.'

Danemouth was a large and fashionable watering-place on the coast not far away.

'It's only a matter of eighteen miles or so from here,' said the Chief Constable. 'The girl was a dance hostess or something at the Majestic. Didn't come on to do her turn last night and the management were very fed up about it. When she was still missing this morning one of the other girls got the wind up about her, or someone else did. It sounds a bit obscure. You'd better go over to Danemouth at once, Slack. Report there to Superintendent Harper, and co-operate with him.'

II

Activity was always to Inspector Slack's taste. To rush off in a car, to silence rudely those people who were anxious to tell him things, to cut short conversations on the plea of urgent necessity. All this was the breath of life to Slack.

In an incredibly short time, therefore, he had arrived at Danemouth, reported at police headquarters, had a brief interview with a distracted and apprehensive hotel manager, and, leaving the latter with the doubtful comfort of – 'got to make sure it *is* the girl, first, before we start raising the wind' – was driving back to Much Benham in company with Ruby Keene's nearest relative.

He had put through a short call to Much Benham before leaving Danemouth, so the Chief Constable was prepared for his arrival, though not perhaps for the brief introduction of: 'This is Josie, sir.'

Colonel Melchett stared at his subordinate coldly. His feeling was that Slack had taken leave of his senses.

The young woman who had just got out of the car came to the rescue.

'That's what I'm known as professionally,' she explained with a momentary flash of large, handsome white teeth. 'Raymond and Josie, my partner and I call ourselves, and, of course, all the hotel know me as Josie. Josephine Turner's my real name.'

Colonel Melchett adjusted himself to the situation and invited

Miss Turner to sit down, meanwhile casting a swift, professional glance over her.

She was a good-looking young woman of perhaps nearer thirty than twenty, her looks depending more on skilful grooming than actual features. She looked competent and good-tempered, with plenty of common sense. She was not the type that would ever be described as glamorous, but she had nevertheless plenty of attraction. She was discreetly made-up and wore a dark tailor-made suit. Though she looked anxious and upset she was not, the Colonel decided, particularly grief-stricken.

As she sat down she said: 'It seems too awful to be true. Do you really think it's Ruby?'

'That, I'm afraid, is what we've got to ask you to tell us. I'm afraid it may be rather unpleasant for you.'

Miss Turner said apprehensively:

'Does she – does she – look very terrible?'

'Well – I'm afraid it may be rather a shock to you.' He handed her his cigarette-case and she accepted one gratefully.

'Do – do you want me to look at her right away?'

'It would be best, I think, Miss Turner. You see, it's not much good asking you questions until we're sure. Best get it over, don't you think?'

'All right.'

They drove down to the mortuary.

When Josie came out after a brief visit, she looked rather sick.

'It's Ruby all right,' she said shakily. 'Poor kid! Goodness, I do feel queer. There isn't' – she looked round wistfully – 'any gin?'

Gin was not available, but brandy was, and after gulping a little down Miss Turner regained her composure. She said frankly:

'It gives you a turn, doesn't it, seeing anything like that? Poor little Rube! What swine men are, aren't they?'

'You believe it was a man?'

Josie looked slightly taken aback.

'Wasn't it? Well, I mean – I naturally thought –'

'Any special man you were thinking of?'

She shook her head vigorously.

'No – not me. I haven't the least idea. Naturally Ruby wouldn't have let on to me if –'

'If what?'

Josie hesitated.

'Well – if she'd been – going about with anyone.'

Melchett shot her a keen glance. He said no more until they were back at his office. Then he began:

'Now, Miss Turner, I want all the information you can give me.'

'Yes, of course. Where shall I begin?'

'I'd like the girl's full name and address, her relationship to you and all you know about her.'

Josephine Turner nodded. Melchett was confirmed in his opinion that she felt no particular grief. She was shocked and distressed but no more. She spoke readily enough.

'Her name was Ruby Keene – her professional name, that is. Her real name was Rosy Legge. Her mother was my mother's cousin. I've known her all my life, but not particularly well, if you know what I mean. I've got a lot of cousins – some in business, some on the stage. Ruby was more or less training for a dancer. She had some good engagements last year in panto and that sort of thing. Not really classy, but good provincial companies. Since then she's been engaged as one of the dancing partners at the Palais de Danse in Brixwell – South London. It's a nice respectable place and they look after the girls well, but there isn't much money in it.' She paused.

Colonel Melchett nodded.

'Now this is where I come in. I've been dance and bridge hostess at the Majestic in Danemouth for three years. It's a good job, well paid and pleasant to do. You look after people when they arrive – size them up, of course – some like to be left alone and others are lonely and want to get into the swing of things. You try to get the right people together for bridge and all that, and get the young people dancing with each other. It needs a bit of tact and experience.'

Again Melchett nodded. He thought that this girl would be good at her job; she had a pleasant, friendly way with her and was, he thought, shrewd without being in the least intellectual.

'Besides that,' continued Josie, 'I do a couple of exhibition dances every evening with Raymond. Raymond Starr – he's the tennis and dancing pro. Well, as it happens, this summer I slipped on the rocks bathing one day and gave my ankle a nasty turn.'

Melchett had noticed that she walked with a slight limp.

'Naturally that put the stop to dancing for a bit and it was rather

33

awkward. I didn't want the hotel to get someone else in my place. That's always a danger' – for a minute her good-natured blue eyes were hard and sharp; she was the female fighting for existence – 'that they may queer your pitch, you see. So I thought of Ruby and suggested to the manager that I should get her down. I'd carry on with the hostess business and the bridge and all that. Ruby would just take on the dancing. Keep it in the family, if you see what I mean?'

Melchett said he saw.

'Well, they agreed, and I wired to Ruby and she came down. Rather a chance for her. Much better class than anything she'd ever done before. That was about a month ago.'

Colonel Melchett said:

'I understand. And she was a success?'

'Oh, yes,' Josie said carelessly, 'she went down quite well. She doesn't dance as well as I do, but Raymond's clever and carried her through, and she was quite nice-looking, you know – slim and fair and baby-looking. Overdid the make-up a bit – I was always on at her about that. But you know what girls are. She was only eighteen, and at that age they always go and overdo it. It doesn't do for a good-class place like the Majestic. I was always ticking her off about it and getting her to tone it down.'

Melchett asked: 'People liked her?'

'Oh, yes. Mind you, Ruby hadn't got much comeback. She was a bit dumb. She went down better with the older men than with the young ones.'

'Had she got any special friend?'

The girl's eyes met his with complete understanding.

'Not in the way *you* mean. Or, at any rate, not that *I* knew about. But then, you see, she wouldn't tell me.'

Just for a moment Melchett wondered why not – Josie did not give the impression of being a strict disciplinarian. But he only said: 'Will you describe to me now when you last saw your cousin.'

'Last night. She and Raymond do two exhibition dances – one at 10.30 and the other at midnight. They finished the first one. After it, I noticed Ruby dancing with one of the young men staying in the hotel. I was playing bridge with some people in the lounge. There's a glass panel between the lounge and the ballroom. That's the last time I saw her. Just after midnight Raymond came up in a

34

terrible taking, said where was Ruby, she hadn't turned up, and it was time to begin. I *was* vexed, I can tell you! That's the sort of silly thing girls do and get the management's backs up and then they get the sack! I went up with him to her room, but she wasn't there. I noticed that she'd changed. The dress she'd been dancing in – a sort of pink, foamy thing with full skirts – was lying over a chair. Usually she kept the same dress on unless it was the special dance night – Wednesdays, that is.

'I'd no idea where she'd got to. We got the band to play one more foxtrot – still no Ruby, so I said to Raymond I'd do the exhibition dance with him. We chose one that was easy on my ankle and made it short – but it played up my ankle pretty badly all the same. It's all swollen this morning. Still Ruby didn't show up. We sat about waiting up for her until two o'clock. Furious with her, I was.'

Her voice vibrated slightly. Melchett caught the note of real anger in it. Just for a moment he wondered. The reaction seemed a little more intense than was justified by the facts. He had a feeling of something deliberately left unsaid. He said:

'And this morning, when Ruby Keene had not returned and her bed had not been slept in, you went to the police?'

He knew from Slack's brief telephone message from Danemouth that that was not the case. But he wanted to hear what Josephine Turner would say.

She did not hesitate. She said: 'No, *I* didn't.'

'Why not, Miss Turner?'

Her eyes met his frankly. She said:

'*You* wouldn't – in my place!'

'You think not?'

Josie said:

'I've got my job to think about. The one thing a hotel doesn't want is scandal – especially anything that brings in the police. I didn't think anything had happened to Ruby. Not for a minute! I thought she'd just made a fool of herself about some young man. I thought she'd turn up all right – and I was going to give her a good dressing down when she did! Girls of eighteen are such fools.'

Melchett pretended to glance through his notes.

'Ah, yes, I see it was a Mr Jefferson who went to the police. One of the guests staying at the hotel?'

35

Josephine Turner said shortly:

'Yes.'

Colonel Melchett asked:

'What made this Mr Jefferson do that?'

Josie was stroking the cuff of her jacket. There was a constraint in her manner. Again Colonel Melchett had a feeling that something was being withheld. She said rather sullenly:

'He's an invalid. He – he gets all het up rather easily. Being an invalid, I mean.'

Melchett passed on from that. He asked:

'Who was the young man with whom you last saw your cousin dancing?'

'His name's Bartlett. He'd been there about ten days.'

'Were they on very friendly terms?'

'Not specially, I should say. Not that *I* knew, anyway.'

Again a curious note of anger in her voice.

'What does he have to say?'

'Said that after their dance Ruby went upstairs to powder her nose.'

'That was when she changed her dress?'

'I suppose so.'

'And that is the last thing you know? After that she just –'

'Vanished,' said Josie. 'That's right.'

'Did Miss Keene know anybody in St Mary Mead? Or in this neighbourhood?'

'I don't know. She may have done. You see, quite a lot of young men come into Danemouth to the Majestic from all round about. I wouldn't know where they lived unless they happened to mention it.'

'Did you ever hear your cousin mention Gossington?'

'Gossington?' Josie looked patently puzzled.

'Gossington Hall.'

She shook her head.

'Never heard of it.' Her tone carried conviction. There was curiosity in it too.

'Gossington Hall,' explained Colonel Melchett, 'is where her body was found.'

'Gossington Hall?' She stared. 'How extraordinary!'

Melchett thought to himself: 'Extraordinary's the word!' Aloud he said:

'Do you know a Colonel or Mrs Bantry?'

Again Josie shook her head.

'Or a Mr Basil Blake?'

She frowned slightly.

'I think I've heard that name. Yes, I'm sure I have – but I don't remember anything about him.'

The diligent Inspector Slack slid across to his superior officer a page torn from his note-book. On it was pencilled:

'*Col. Bantry dined at Majestic last week.*'

Melchett looked up and met the Inspector's eye. The Chief Constable flushed. Slack was an industrious and zealous officer and Melchett disliked him a good deal. But he could not disregard the challenge. The Inspector was tacitly accusing him of favouring his own class – of shielding an 'old school tie.'

He turned to Josie.

'Miss Turner, I should like you, if you do not mind, to accompany me to Gossington Hall.'

Coldly, defiantly, almost ignoring Josie's murmur of assent, Melchett's eyes met Slack's.

CHAPTER FOUR

St Mary Mead was having the most exciting morning it had known for a long time.

Miss Wetherby, a long-nosed, acidulated spinster, was the first to spread the intoxicating information. She dropped in upon her friend and neighbour Miss Hartnell.

'Forgive me coming so early, dear, but I thought, perhaps, you mightn't have heard the *news*.'

'What news?' demanded Miss Hartnell. She had a deep bass voice and visited the poor indefatigably, however hard they tried to avoid her ministrations.

'About the body in Colonel Bantry's library – a *woman's* body –'

'In Colonel Bantry's *library?*'

'Yes. Isn't it *terrible?*'

'His poor wife.' Miss Hartnell tried to disguise her deep and ardent pleasure.

'Yes, indeed. I don't suppose she had any idea.'

Miss Hartnell observed censoriously:

'She thought too much about her garden and not enough about her husband. You've got to keep an eye on a man — all the time — all the time,' repeated Miss Hartnell fiercely.

'I know. I know. It's really too dreadful.'

'I wonder what Jane Marple will say. Do you think she knew anything about it? She's so sharp about these things.'

'Jane Marple has gone up to Gossington.'

'What? This morning?'

'Very early. Before breakfast.'

'But really! I do think! Well, I mean, I think that is carrying things *too* far. We all know Jane likes to poke her nose into things — but I call this indecent!'

'Oh, but Mrs Bantry sent for her.'

'Mrs Bantry *sent* for her?'

'Well, the car came — with Muswell driving it.'

'Dear me! How very peculiar . . .'

They were silent a minute or two digesting the news.

'Whose body?' demanded Miss Hartnell.

'You know that dreadful woman who comes down with Basil Blake?'

'That terrible peroxide blonde?' Miss Hartnell was slightly behind the times. She had not yet advanced from peroxide to platinum. 'The one who lies about in the garden with practically nothing on?'

'Yes, my dear. There she was — on the hearthrug — *strangled*!'

'But what do you mean — at *Gossington*?'

Miss Wetherby nodded with infinite meaning.

'Then — Colonel Bantry *too* —?'

Again Miss Wetherby nodded.

'Oh!'

There was a pause as the ladies savoured this new addition to village scandal.

'What a wicked woman!' trumpeted Miss Hartnell with righteous wrath.

'Quite, quite abandoned, I'm afraid!'

'And Colonel Bantry – such a nice quiet man –'

Miss Wetherby said zestfully:

'Those quiet ones are often the worst. Jane Marple always says so.'

II

Mrs Price Ridley was among the last to hear the news.

A rich and dictatorial widow, she lived in a large house next door to the vicarage. Her informant was her little maid Clara.

'A *woman*, you say, Clara? *Found dead on Colonel Bantry's hearthrug?*'

'Yes, mum. And they say, mum, as she hadn't anything on at all, mum, not a stitch!'

'That will do, Clara. It is not necessary to go into details.'

'No, mum, and they say, mum, that at first they thought it was Mr Blake's young lady – what comes down for the weekends with 'im to Mr Booker's new 'ouse. But now they say it's quite a different young lady. And the fishmonger's young man, he says he'd never have believed it of Colonel Bantry – not with him handing round the plate on Sundays and all.'

'There is a lot of wickedness in the world, Clara,' said Mrs Price Ridley. 'Let this be a warning to you.'

'Yes, mum. Mother, she never *will* let me take a place where there's a gentleman in the 'ouse.'

'That will *do*, Clara,' said Mrs Price Ridley.

III

It was only a step from Mrs Price Ridley's house to the vicarage.

Mrs Price Ridley was fortunate enough to find the vicar in his study.

The vicar, a gentle, middle-aged man, was always the last to hear anything.

'Such a *terrible* thing,' said Mrs Price Ridley, panting a little, because she had come rather fast. 'I felt I must have your advice, your counsel about it, dear vicar.'

Mr Clement looked mildly alarmed. He said:

'Has anything happened?'

'Has anything *happened*?' Mrs Price Ridley repeated the question dramatically. 'The most terrible scandal! None of us had any idea of it. An abandoned woman, completely unclothed, strangled on Colonel Bantry's hearthrug.'

The vicar stared. He said:

'You – you are feeling quite well?'

'No wonder you can't believe it! *I* couldn't at first. The hypocrisy of the man! All these years!'

'Please tell me exactly what all this is about.'

Mrs Price Ridley plunged into a full-swing narrative. When she had finished Mr Clement said mildly:

'But there is nothing, is there, to point to Colonel Bantry's being involved in this?'

'Oh, dear vicar, you are so unworldly! But I must tell you a little story. Last Thursday – or was it the Thursday before? well, it doesn't matter – I was going up to London by the cheap day train. Colonel Bantry was in the same carriage. He looked, I thought, very abstracted. And nearly the whole way he buried himself behind *The Times*. As though, you know, he didn't want to *talk*.'

The vicar nodded with complete comprehension and possible sympathy.

'At Paddington I said good-bye. He had offered to get me a taxi, but I was taking the bus down to Oxford Street – but he got into one, and I distinctly heard him tell the driver to go to – *where do you think*?'

Mr Clement looked inquiring.

'An address in *St John's Wood*!'

Mrs Price Ridley paused triumphantly.

The vicar remained completely unenlightened.

'That, I consider, *proves* it,' said Mrs Price Ridley.

IV

At Gossington, Mrs Bantry and Miss Marple were sitting in the drawing-room.

'You know,' said Mrs Bantry, 'I can't help feeling glad they've taken the body away. It's not *nice* to have a body in one's house.'

Miss Marple nodded.

'I know, dear. I know just how you feel.'

'You can't,' said Mrs Bantry; 'not until you've had one. I know you had one next door once, but that's not the same thing. I only hope,' she went on, 'that Arthur won't take a dislike to the library. We sit there so much. What are you doing, Jane?'

For Miss Marple, with a glance at her watch, was rising to her feet.

'Well, I was thinking I'd go home. If there's nothing more I can do for you?'

'Don't go yet,' said Mrs Bantry. 'The finger-print men and the photographers and most of the police have gone, I know, but I still feel something might happen. You don't want to miss anything.'

The telephone rang and she went off to answer. She returned with a beaming face.

'I told you more things would happen. That was Colonel Melchett. He's bringing the poor girl's cousin along.'

'I wonder why,' said Miss Marple.

'Oh, I suppose, to see where it happened and all that.'

'More than that, I expect,' said Miss Marple.

'What do you mean, Jane?'

'Well, I think — perhaps — he might want her to meet Colonel Bantry.'

Mrs Bantry said sharply:

'To see if she recognizes him? I suppose — oh, yes, I suppose they're bound to suspect Arthur.'

'I'm afraid so.'

'As though Arthur could have anything to do with it!'

Miss Marple was silent. Mrs Bantry turned on her accusingly.

'And don't quote old General Henderson — or some frightful old man who kept his housemaid — at me. Arthur isn't like that.'

'No, no, of course not.'

'No, but he *really* isn't. He's just — sometimes — a little silly about pretty girls who come to tennis. You know — rather fatuous and avuncular. There's no harm in it. And why shouldn't he? After all,' finished Mrs Bantry rather obscurely, 'I've got the garden.'

Miss Marple smiled.

'You must not worry, Dolly,' she said.

'No, I don't mean to. But all the same I do a little. So does Arthur. It's upset him. All these policemen prowling about. He's gone down to the farm. Looking at pigs and things always soothes him if he's been upset. Hallo, here they are.'

The Chief Constable's car drew up outside.

Colonel Melchett came in accompanied by a smartly dressed young woman.

'This is Miss Turner, Mrs Bantry. The cousin of the – er – victim.'

'How do you do,' said Mrs Bantry, advancing with outstretched hand. 'All this must be rather awful for you.'

Josephine Turner said frankly: 'Oh, it is. None of it seems *real*, somehow. It's like a bad dream.'

Mrs Bantry introduced Miss Marple.

Melchett said casually: 'Your good man about?'

'He had to go down to one of the farms. He'll be back soon.'

'Oh –' Melchett seemed rather at a loss.

Mrs Bantry said to Josie: 'Would you like to see where – where it happened? Or would you rather not?'

Josephine said after a moment's pause:

'I think I'd like to see.'

Mrs Bantry led her to her library with Miss Marple and Melchett following behind.

'She was there,' said Mrs Bantry, pointing dramatically; 'on the hearthrug.'

'Oh!' Josie shuddered. But she also looked perplexed. She said, her brow creased: 'I just *can't* understand it! I *can't*!'

'Well, *we* certainly can't,' said Mrs Bantry.

Josie said slowly:

'It isn't the sort of place –' and broke off.

Miss Marple nodded her head gently in agreement with the unfinished sentiment.

'That,' she murmured, 'is what makes it so very interesting.'

'Come now, Miss Marple,' said Colonel Melchett good-humouredly, 'haven't you got an explanation?'

'Oh yes, I've got an *explanation*,' said Miss Marple. 'Quite a feasible one. But of course it's only my own *idea*. Tommy Bond,' she continued, 'and Mrs Martin, our new schoolmistress. She went to wind up the clock and a frog jumped out.'

Josephine Turner looked puzzled. As they all went out of the room she murmured to Mrs Bantry: 'Is the old lady a bit funny in the head?'

'Not at all,' said Mrs Bantry indignantly.

Josie said: 'Sorry; I thought perhaps she thought she *was* a frog or something.'

Colonel Bantry was just coming in through the side door. Melchett hailed him, and watched Josephine Turner as he introduced them to each other. But there was no sign of interest or recognition in her face. Melchett breathed a sigh of relief. Curse Slack and his insinuations!

In answer to Mrs Bantry's questions Josie was pouring out the story of Ruby Keene's disappearance.

'Frightfully worrying for you, my dear,' said Mrs Bantry.

'I was more angry than worried,' said Josie. 'You see, I didn't know then that anything had happened to her.'

'And yet,' said Miss Marple, 'you went to the police. Wasn't that — excuse me — rather *premature*?'

Josie said eagerly:

'Oh, but I didn't. That was Mr Jefferson —'

Mrs Bantry said: 'Jefferson?'

'Yes, he's an invalid.'

'Not *Conway* Jefferson? But I know him well. He's an old friend of ours. Arthur, listen — Conway Jefferson. He's staying at the Majestic, and it was he who went to the police! Isn't that a coincidence?'

Josephine Turner said:

'Mr Jefferson was here last summer too.'

'Fancy! And we never knew. I haven't seen him for a long time.' She turned to Josie. 'How — how is he, nowadays?'

Josie considered.

'I think he's wonderful, really — quite wonderful. Considering, I mean. He's always cheerful — always got a joke.'

'Are the family there with him?'

'Mr Gaskell, you mean? And young Mrs Jefferson? And Peter? Oh, yes.'

There was something inhibiting Josephine Turner's usual attractive frankness of manner. When she spoke of the Jeffersons there was something not quite natural in her voice.

Mrs Bantry said: 'They're both very nice, aren't they? The young ones, I mean.'

Josie said rather uncertainly:

'Oh yes — yes, they are. I — we — yes, they are, *really*.'

V

'And what,' demanded Mrs Bantry as she looked through the window at the retreating car of the Chief Constable, 'did she mean by that? "They are, *really*." Don't you think, Jane, that there's something —'

Miss Marple fell upon the words eagerly.

'Oh, I do — indeed I do. It's quite *unmistakable*! Her manner changed *at once* when the Jeffersons were mentioned. She had seemed quite natural up to then.'

'But what do you think it *is*, Jane?'

'Well, my dear, *you* know them. All I feel is that there is *something*, as you say, about them which is worrying that young woman. Another thing, did you notice that when you asked her if she wasn't anxious about the girl being missing, she said that she was *angry*! And she *looked* angry — *really* angry! That strikes me as *interesting*, you know. I have a feeling — perhaps I'm wrong — that that's her main reaction to the fact of the girl's death. She didn't care for her, I'm sure. She's not grieving in any way. But I do think, very definitely, that the thought of that girl, Ruby Keene, makes her *angry*. And the interesting point is — *why*?'

'We'll find out!' said Mrs Bantry. 'We'll go over to Danemouth and stay at the Majestic — yes, Jane, you too. I need a change for my nerves after what has happened here. A few days at the Majestic — that's what we need. And you'll meet Conway Jefferson. He's a dear — a perfect dear. It's the saddest story imaginable. Had a son and daughter, both of whom he loved dearly. They were both married, but they still spent a lot of time at home. His wife, too, was the sweetest woman, and he was devoted to her. They were flying home one year from France and there was an accident. They were all killed: the pilot, Mrs Jefferson, Rosamund, and Frank. Conway had both legs so badly injured they had to be amputated. And he's been wonderful — his courage, his pluck! He was a very active man and now he's a helpless cripple, but he never complains. His daughter-in-law lives with him – she was a widow when Frank Jefferson married her and she had a son by her first marriage – Peter Carmody. They both live with Conway. And Mark Gaskell, Rosamund's husband, is there too most of the time. The whole thing was the most awful tragedy.'

'And now,' said Miss Marple, 'there's another tragedy –'

Mrs Bantry said: 'Oh yes – yes – but it's nothing to do with the Jeffersons.'

'Isn't it?' said Miss Marple. 'It was Mr Jefferson who went to the police.'

'So he did ... You know, Jane, that *is* curious ...'

CHAPTER FIVE

Colonel Melchett was facing a much annoyed hotel manager. With him was Superintendent Harper of the Glenshire Police and the inevitable Inspector Slack – the latter rather disgruntled at the Chief Constable's wilful usurpation of the case.

Superintendent Harper was inclined to be soothing with the almost tearful Mr Prestcott – Colonel Melchett tended towards a blunt brutality.

'No good crying over spilt milk,' he said sharply. 'The girl's dead – strangled. You're lucky that she wasn't strangled in your hotel. This puts the inquiry in a different county and lets your establishment down extremely lightly. But certain inquiries have got to be made, and the sooner we get on with it the better. You can trust us to be discreet and tactful. So I suggest you cut the cackle and come to the horses. Just what exactly do you know about the girl?'

'I knew nothing of her – nothing at all. Josie brought her here.'

'Josie's been here some time?'

'Two years – no, three.'

'And you like her?'

'Yes, Josie's a good girl – a nice girl. Competent. She gets on with people, and smooths over differences – bridge, you know, is a touchy sort of game –' Colonel Melchett nodded feelingly. His wife was a keen but an extremely bad bridge player. Mr Prestcott went on: 'Josie was very good at calming down unpleasantnesses. She could handle people well – sort of bright and firm, if you know what I mean.'

Again Melchett nodded. He knew now what it was Miss Josephine Turner had reminded him of. In spite of the make-up and the smart turnout there was a distinct touch of the nursery governess about her.

'I depend upon her,' went on Mr Prestcott. His manner became aggrieved. 'What does she want to go playing about on slippery rocks in that damn' fool way? We've got a nice beach here. Why couldn't she bathe from that? Slipping and falling and breaking her ankle. It wasn't fair on *me*! I pay her to dance and play bridge and keep people happy and amused – not to go bathing off rocks and breaking her ankle. Dancers ought to be careful of their ankles – not take risks. I was very annoyed about it. It wasn't fair to the hotel.'

Melchett cut the recital short.

'And then she suggested this girl – her cousin – coming down?'

Prestcott assented grudgingly.

'That's right. It sounded quite a good idea. Mind you, I wasn't going to pay anything extra. The girl could have her keep; but as for salary, that would have to be fixed up between her and Josie. That's the way it was arranged. *I* didn't know anything about the girl.'

'But she turned out all right?'

'Oh yes, there wasn't anything wrong with her – not to look at, anyway. She was very young, of course – rather cheap in style, perhaps, for a place of this kind, but nice manners – quiet and well-behaved. Danced well. People liked her.'

'Pretty?'

It had been a question hard to answer from a view of the blue swollen face.

Mr Prestcott considered.

'Fair to middling. Bit weaselly, if you know what I mean. Wouldn't have been much without make-up. As it was she managed to look quite attractive.'

'Many young men hanging about after her?'

'I know what you're trying to get at, sir.' Mr Prestcott became excited. '*I* never saw anything. Nothing special. One or two of the boys hung around a bit – but all in the day's work, so to speak. Nothing in the strangling line, I'd say. She got on well with the older people, too – had a kind of prattling way with her – seemed quite a kid, if you know what I mean. It amused them.'

Superintendent Harper said in a deep melancholy voice:

'Mr Jefferson, for instance?'

The manager agreed.

'Yes, Mr Jefferson was the one I had in mind. She used to sit with him and his family a lot. He used to take her out for drives sometimes. Mr Jefferson's very fond of young people and very good to them. I don't want to have any misunderstanding. Mr Jefferson's a cripple; he can't get about much – only where his wheel-chair will take him. But he's always keen on seeing young people enjoy themselves – watches the tennis and the bathing and all that – and gives parties for young people here. He likes youth – and there's nothing bitter about him as there well might be. A very popular gentleman and, I'd say, a very fine character.'

Melchett asked:

'And he took an interest in Ruby Keene?'

'Her talk amused him, I think.'

'Did his family share his liking for her?'

'They were always very pleasant to her.'

Harper said:

'And it was he who reported the fact of her being missing to the police?'

He contrived to put into the words a significance and a reproach to which the manager instantly responded.

'Put yourself in my place, Mr Harper. *I* didn't dream for a minute anything was wrong. Mr Jefferson came along to my office, storming, and all worked up. The girl hadn't slept in her room. She hadn't appeared in her dance last night. She must have gone for a drive and had an accident, perhaps. The police must be informed at once! Inquiries made! In a state, he was, and quite high-handed. He rang up the police station then and there.'

'Without consulting Miss Turner?'

'Josie didn't like it much. I could see that. She was very annoyed about the whole thing – annoyed with Ruby, I mean. But what could she say?'

'I think,' said Melchett, 'we'd better see Mr Jefferson. Eh, Harper?'

Superintendent Harper agreed.

II

Mr Prestcott went up with them to Conway Jefferson's suite. It was on the first floor, overlooking the sea. Melchett said carelessly:

'Does himself pretty well, eh? Rich man?'

'Very well off indeed, I believe. Nothing's ever stinted when he comes here. Best rooms reserved – food usually *à la carte*, expensive wines -- best of everything.'

Melchett nodded.

Mr Prestcott tapped on the outer door and a woman's voice said: 'Come in.'

The manager entered, the others behind him.

Mr Prestcott's manner was apologetic as he spoke to the woman who turned her head at their entrance from her seat by the window.

'I am so sorry to disturb you, Mrs Jefferson, but these gentlemen are -- from the police. They are very anxious to have a word with Mr Jefferson. Er – Colonel Melchett – Superintendent Harper, Inspector – er – Slack – Mrs Jefferson.'

Mrs Jefferson acknowledged the introduction by bending her head.

A plain woman, was Melchett's first impression. Then, as a slight smile came to her lips and she spoke, he changed his opinion. She had a singularly charming and sympathetic voice and her eyes, clear hazel eyes, were beautiful. She was quietly but not unbecomingly dressed and was, he judged, about thirty-five years of age.

She said:

'My father-in-law is asleep. He is not strong at all, and this affair has been a terrible shock to him. We had to have the doctor, and the doctor gave him a sedative. As soon as he wakes he will, I know, want to see you. In the meantime, perhaps I can help you? Won't you sit down?'

Mr Prestcott, anxious to escape, said to Colonel Melchett: 'Well – er – if that's all I can do for you?' and thankfully received permission to depart.

With his closing of the door behind him, the atmosphere took on a mellow and more social quality. Adelaide Jefferson had the power of creating a restful atmosphere. She was a woman who never seemed to say anything remarkable but who succeeded in stimulating other people to talk and setting them at their ease. She struck now the right note when she said:

'This business has shocked us all very much. We saw quite a lot of the poor girl, you know. It seems quite unbelievable. My father-in-law is terribly upset. He was very fond of Ruby.'

Colonel Melchett said:

'It was Mr Jefferson, I understand, who reported her disappearance to the police?'

He wanted to see exactly how she would react to that. There was a flicker – just a flicker – of – annoyance? concern? – he could not say what exactly, but there was *something*, and it seemed to him she had definitely to brace herself, as though to an unpleasant task, before going on.

She said:

'Yes, that is so. Being an invalid, he gets easily upset and worried. We tried to persuade him that it was all right, that there was some natural explanation, and that the girl herself would not like the police being notified. He insisted. Well' – she made a slight gesture – 'he was right and we were wrong.'

Melchett asked: 'Exactly how well did you know Ruby Keene, Mrs Jefferson?'

She considered.

'It's difficult to say. My father-in-law is very fond of young people and likes to have them round him. Ruby was a new type to him – he was amused and interested by her chatter. She sat with us a good deal in the hotel and my father-in-law took her out for drives in the car.'

Her voice was quite non-committal. Melchett thought to himself: 'She could say more if she chose.'

He said: 'Will you tell me what you can of the course of events last night?'

'Certainly, but there is very little that will be useful, I'm afraid. After dinner Ruby came and sat with us in the lounge. She remained even after the dancing had started. We had arranged to play bridge later, but we were waiting for Mark, that is Mark Gaskell, my brother-in-law – he married Mr Jefferson's daughter, you know –

who had some important letters to write, and also for Josie. She was going to make a fourth with us.'

'Did that often happen?'

'Quite frequently. She's a first-class player, of course, and very nice. My father-in-law is a keen bridge player and whenever possible liked to get hold of Josie to make the fourth instead of an outsider. Naturally, as she has to arrange the fours, she can't always play with us, but she does whenever she can, and as' — her eyes smiled a little — 'my father-in-law spends a lot of money in the hotel, the management are quite pleased for Josie to favour us.'

Melchett asked:

'You like Josie?'

'Yes, I do. She's always good-humoured and cheerful, works hard and seems to enjoy her job. She's shrewd, though not well educated, and — well — never pretends about anything. She's natural and unaffected.'

'Please go on, Mrs Jefferson.'

'As I say, Josie had to get her bridge fours arranged and Mark was writing, so Ruby sat and talked with us a little longer than usual. Then Josie came along, and Ruby went off to do her first solo dance with Raymond — he's the dance and tennis professional. She came back to us afterwards just as Mark joined us. Then she went off to dance with a young man and we four started our bridge.'

She stopped, and made a slight insignificant gesture of helplessness.

'And that's all I know! I just caught a glimpse of her once dancing, but bridge is an absorbing game and I hardly glanced through the glass partition at the ballroom. Then, at midnight, Raymond came along to Josie very upset and asked where Ruby was. Josie, naturally, tried to shut him up but —'

Superintendent Harper interrupted. He said in his quiet voice: 'Why "*naturally*," Mrs Jefferson?'

'Well' — she hesitated, looked, Melchett thought, a little put out — 'Josie didn't want the girl's absence made too much of. She considered herself responsible for her in a way. She said Ruby was probably up in her bedroom, said the girl had talked about having a headache earlier — I don't think that was true, by the way; Josie just said it by way of excuse. Raymond went off and telephoned up to Ruby's room, but apparently there was no answer, and he came back in rather a state – temperamental, you know. Josie went off with him and tried to soothe him down, and in the end she danced with him instead of Ruby. Rather plucky of her, because you could see afterwards it had hurt her ankle. She came back to us when the dance was over and tried to calm down Mr Jefferson. He had got worked up by then. We persuaded him in the end to go to bed, told him Ruby had probably gone for a spin in a car and that they'd had a puncture. He went to bed worried, and this morning he began to agitate at once.' She paused. 'The rest you know.'

'Thank you, Mrs Jefferson. Now I'm going to ask you if you've any idea who could have done this thing.'

She said immediately: 'No idea whatever. I'm afraid I can't help you in the slightest.'

He pressed her. 'The girl never said anything? Nothing about jealousy? About some man she was afraid of? Or intimate with?'

Adelaide Jefferson shook her head to each query.

There seemed nothing more that she could tell them.

The Superintendent suggested that they should interview young George Bartlett and return to see Mr Jefferson later. Colonel Melchett agreed, and the three men went out, Mrs Jefferson promising to send word as soon as Mr Jefferson was awake.

'Nice woman,' said the Colonel, as they closed the door behind them.

'A very nice lady indeed,' said Superintendent Harper.

III

George Bartlett was a thin, lanky youth with a prominent Adam's apple and an immense difficulty in saying what he meant. He was in such a state of dither that it was hard to get a calm statement from him.

'I say, it is awful, isn't it? Sort of thing one reads about in the Sunday papers – but one doesn't feel it really happens, don't you know?'

'Unfortunately there is no doubt about it, Mr Bartlett,' said the Superintendent.

'No, no, of course not. But it seems so rum somehow. And miles from here and everything – in some country house, wasn't it?

Awfully county and all that. Created a bit of a stir in the neighbourhood – what?'

Colonel Melchett took charge.

'How well did you know the dead girl, Mr Bartlett?'

George Bartlett looked alarmed.

'Oh, n-n-n-ot well at all, s-s-sir. No, hardly at all – if you know what I mean. Danced with her once or twice – passed the time of day – bit of tennis – *you* know.'

'You were, I think, the last person to see her alive last night?'

'I suppose I was – doesn't it sound awful? I mean, she was perfectly all right when I saw her – absolutely.'

'What time was that, Mr Bartlett?'

'Well, you know, I never know about time – wasn't very late, if you know what I mean.'

'You danced with her?'

'Yes – as a matter of fact – well, yes, I did. Early on in the evening, though. Tell you what, it was just after her exhibition dance with the pro. fellow. Must have been ten, half-past, eleven, I don't know.'

'Never mind the time. We can fix that. Please tell us exactly what happened.'

'Well, we danced, don't you know. Not that *I'm* much of a dancer.'

'How you dance is not really relevant, Mr Bartlett.'

George Bartlett cast an alarmed eye on the Colonel and stammered:

'No – er – n-n-n-o, I suppose it isn't. Well, as I say, we danced, round and round, and I talked, but Ruby didn't say very much and she yawned a bit. As I say, I don't dance awfully well, and so girls – well – inclined to give it a miss, if you know what I mean. She said she had a headache – I know where I get off, so I said righty ho, and that was that.'

'What was the last you saw of her?'

'She went off upstairs.'

'She said nothing about meeting anyone? Or going for a drive? Or – or – having a date?' The Colonel used the colloquial expression with a slight effort.

Bartlett shook his head.

'Not to me.' He looked rather mournful. 'Just gave me the push.'

52

'What was her manner? Did she seem anxious, abstracted, anything on her mind?'

George Bartlett considered. Then he shook his head.

'Seemed a bit bored. Yawned, as I said. Nothing more.'

Colonel Melchett said:

'And what did you do, Mr Bartlett?'

'Eh?'

'What did you do when Ruby Keene left you?'

George Bartlett gaped at him.

'Let's see now – what *did* I do?'

'We're waiting for you to tell us.'

'Yes, yes – of course. Jolly difficult, remembering things, what? Let me see. Shouldn't be surprised if I went into the bar and had a drink.'

'*Did* you go into the bar and have a drink?'

'That's just it. I *did* have a drink. Don't think it was just then. Have an idea I wandered out, don't you know? Bit of air. Rather stuffy for September. Very nice outside. Yes, that's it. I strolled around a bit, then I came in and had a drink and then I strolled back to the ballroom. Wasn't much doing. Noticed what's-her-name – Josie – was dancing again. With the tennis fellow. She'd been on the sick list – twisted ankle or something.'

'That fixes the time of your return at midnight. Do you intend us to understand that you spent over an hour walking about outside?'

'Well, I had a drink, you know. I was – well, I was thinking of things.'

This statement received more credulity than any other.

Colonel Melchett said sharply:

'What were you thinking about?'

'Oh, I don't know. Things,' said Mr Bartlett vaguely.

'You have a car, Mr Bartlett?'

'Oh, yes, I've got a car.'

'Where was it, in the hotel garage?'

'No, it was in the courtyard, as a matter of fact. Thought I might go for a spin, you see.'

'Perhaps you did go for a spin?'

'No – no, I didn't. Swear I didn't.'

'You didn't, for instance, take Miss Keene for a spin?'

'Oh, I say. Look here, what are you getting at? I didn't – I swear I didn't. Really, now.'

'Thank you, Mr Bartlett, I don't think there is anything more at present. *At present*,' repeated Colonel Melchett with a good deal of emphasis on the words.

They left Mr Bartlett looking after them with a ludicrous expression of alarm on his unintellectual face.

'Brainless young ass,' said Colonel Melchett. 'Or isn't he?'

Superintendent Harper shook his head.

'We've got a long way to go,' he said.

CHAPTER SIX

Neither the night porter nor the barman proved helpful. The night porter remembered ringing up to Miss Keene's room just after midnight and getting no reply. He had not noticed Mr Bartlett leaving or entering the hotel. A lot of gentlemen and ladies were strolling in and out, the night being fine. And there were side doors off the corridor as well as the one in the main hall. He was fairly certain Miss Keene had not gone out by the main door, but if she had come down from her room, which was on the first floor, there was a staircase next to it and a door out at the end of the corridor, leading on to the side terrace. She could have gone out of that unseen easily enough. It was not locked until the dancing was over at two o'clock.

The barman remembered Mr Bartlett being in the bar the preceding evening but could not say when. Somewhere about the middle of the evening, he thought. Mr Bartlett had sat against the wall and was looking rather melancholy. He did not know how long he was there. There were a lot of outside guests coming and going in the bar. He had noticed Mr Bartlett but he couldn't fix the time in any way.

As they left the bar, they were accosted by a small boy of about nine years old. He burst immediately into excited speech.

'I say, are you the detectives? I'm Peter Carmody. It was my grandfather, Mr Jefferson, who rang up the police about Ruby. Are you from Scotland Yard? You don't mind my speaking to you, do you?'

Colonel Melchett looked as though he were about to return a short answer, but Superintendent Harper intervened. He spoke benignly and heartily.

'That's all right, my son. Naturally interests you, I expect?'

'You bet it does. Do you like detective stories? I do. I read them all, and I've got autographs from Dorothy Sayers and Agatha Christie and Dickson Carr and H. C. Bailey. Will the murder be in the papers?'

'It'll be in the papers all right,' said Superintendent Harper grimly.

'You see, I'm going back to school next week and I shall tell them all that I knew her — really knew her *well*.'

'What did you think of her, eh?'

Peter considered.

'Well, I didn't like her much. I think she was rather a stupid sort of girl. Mum and Uncle Mark didn't like her much either. Only Grandfather. Grandfather wants to see you, by the way. Edwards is looking for you.'

Superintendent Harper murmured encouragingly:

'So your mother and your Uncle Mark didn't like Ruby Keene much? Why was that?'

'Oh, I don't know. She was always butting in. And they didn't like Grandfather making such a fuss of her. I expect,' said Peter cheerfully, 'that they're glad she's dead.'

Superintendent Harper looked at him thoughtfully. He said: 'Did you hear them — er — say so?'

'Well, not exactly. Uncle Mark said: "Well, it's one way out, anyway," and Mums said: "Yes, but such a horrible one," and Uncle Mark said it was no good being hypocritical.'

The men exchanged glances. At that moment a respectable, clean-shaven man, neatly dressed in blue serge, came up to them.

'Excuse me, gentlemen. I am Mr Jefferson's valet. He is awake now and sent me to find you, as he is very anxious to see you.'

Once more they went up to Conway Jefferson's suite. In the sitting-room Adelaide Jefferson was talking to a tall, restless man who was prowling nervously about the room. He swung round sharply to view the new-comers.

'Oh, yes. Glad you've come. My father-in-law's been asking for you. He's awake now. Keep him as calm as you can, won't you? His health's not too good. It's a wonder, really, that this shock didn't do for him.'

Harper said:

'I'd no idea his health was as bad as that.'

'He doesn't know it himself,' said Mark Gaskell. 'It's his heart, you see. The doctor warned Addie that he mustn't be over-excited or startled. He more or less hinted that the end might come any time, didn't he, Addie?'

Mrs Jefferson nodded. She said:

'It's incredible that he's rallied the way he has.'

Melchett said dryly:

'Murder isn't exactly a soothing incident. We'll be as careful as we can.'

He was sizing up Mark Gaskell as he spoke. He didn't much care for the fellow. A bold, unscrupulous, hawklike face. One of those men who usually get their own way and whom women frequently admire.

'But not the sort of fellow I'd trust,' the Colonel thought to himself.

Unscrupulous – that was the word for him.

The sort of fellow who wouldn't stick at anything . . .

III

In the big bedroom overlooking the sea, Conway Jefferson was sitting in his wheeled chair by the window.

No sooner were you in the room with him than you felt the power and magnetism of the man. It was as though the injuries which had left him a cripple had resulted in concentrating the vitality of his shattered body into a narrower and more intense focus.

He had a fine head, the red of the hair slightly grizzled. The face was rugged and powerful, deeply sun-tanned, and the eyes were a startling blue. There was no sign of illness or feebleness about him. The deep lines on his face were the lines of suffering, not the lines of weakness. Here was a man who would never rail against fate but accept it and pass on to victory.

He said: 'I'm glad you've come.' His quick eyes took them in. He said to Melchett: 'You're the Chief Constable of Radfordshire? Right. And you're Superintendent Harper? Sit down. Cigarettes on the table beside you.'

They thanked him and sat down. Melchett said:

'I understand, Mr Jefferson, that you were interested in the dead girl?'

A quick, twisted smile flashed across the lined face.

'Yes – they'll all have told you that! Well, it's no secret. How much has my family said to you?'

He looked quickly from one to the other as he asked the question.

It was Melchett who answered.

'Mrs Jefferson told us very little beyond the fact that the girl's chatter amused you and that she was by way of being a protégée. We have only exchanged half a dozen words with Mr Gaskell.'

Conway Jefferson smiled.

'Addie's a discreet creature, bless her. Mark would probably have been more outspoken. I think, Melchett, that I'd better tell you some facts rather fully. It's important, in order that you should understand my attitude. And, to begin with, it's necessary that I go back to the big tragedy of my life. Eight years ago I lost my wife, my son, and my daughter in an aeroplane accident. Since then I've been like a man who's lost half himself – and I'm not speaking of my physical plight! I was a family man. My daughter-in-law and my son-in-law have been very good to me. They've done all they can to take the place of my flesh and blood. But I've realized – especially of late, that they have, after all, their own lives to live.

'So you must understand that, essentially, I'm a lonely man. I like young people. I enjoy them. Once or twice I've played with the idea of adopting some girl or boy. During this last month I got very friendly with the child who's been killed. She was absolutely natural – completely naïve. She chattered on about her life and her experiences – in pantomime, with touring companies, with Mum and Dad as a child in cheap lodgings. Such a different life from any

I've known! Never complaining, never seeing it as sordid. Just a natural, uncomplaining, hard-working child, unspoilt and charming. Not a lady, perhaps, but, thank God, neither vulgar nor – abominable word – "lady-like".

'I got more and more fond of Ruby. I decided, gentlemen, to adopt her legally. She would become – by law – my daughter. That, I hope, explains my concern for her and the steps I took when I heard of her unaccountable disappearance.'

There was a pause. Then Superintendent Harper, his unemotional voice robbing the question of any offence, asked: 'May I ask what your son-in-law and daughter-in-law said to that?'

Jefferson's answer came back quickly:

'What could they say? They didn't, perhaps, like it very much. It's the sort of thing that arouses prejudice. But they behaved very well – yes, very well. It's not as though, you see, they were dependent on me. When my son Frank married I turned over half my worldly goods to him then and there. I believe in that. Don't let your children wait until you're dead. They want the money when they're young, not when they're middle-aged. In the same way when my daughter Rosamund insisted on marrying a poor man, I settled a big sum of money on her. That sum passed to him at her death. So, you see, that simplified the matter from the financial angle.'

'I see, Mr Jefferson,' said Superintendent Harper.

But there was a certain reserve in his tone. Conway Jefferson pounced upon it.

'But you don't agree, eh?'

'It's not for me to say, sir, but families, in my experience, don't always act reasonably.'

'I dare say you're right, Superintendent, but you must remember that Mr Gaskell and Mrs Jefferson aren't, strictly speaking, my *family*. They're not blood relations.'

'That, of course, makes a difference,' admitted the Superintendent.

For a moment Conway Jefferson's eyes twinkled. He said: 'That's not to say that they didn't think me an old fool! That *would* be the average person's reaction. But I wasn't being a fool. I know character. With education and polishing, Ruby Keene could have taken her place anywhere.'

Melchett said:

'I'm afraid we're being rather impertinent and inquisitive, but it's important that we should get at all the facts. You proposed to make full provision for the girl – that is, settle money upon her, but you hadn't already done so?'

Jefferson said:

'I understand what you're driving at – the possibility of someone's benefiting by the girl's death? But nobody could. The necessary formalities for legal adoption were under way, but they hadn't yet been completed.'

Melchett said slowly:

'Then, if anything happened to you –?'

He left the sentence unfinished, as a query. Conway Jefferson was quick to respond.

'Nothing's likely to happen to me! I'm a cripple, but I'm not an invalid. Although doctors *do* like to pull long faces and give advice about not overdoing things. Not overdoing things! I'm as strong as a horse! Still, I'm quite aware of the fatalities of life – my God, I've good reason to be! Sudden death comes to the strongest man – especially in these days of road casualties. But I'd provided for that. I made a new will about ten days ago.'

'Yes?' Superintendent Harper leaned forward.

'I left the sum of fifty thousand pounds to be held in trust for Ruby Keene until she was twenty-five, when she would come into the principal.'

Superintendent Harper's eyes opened. So did Colonel Melchett's. Harper said in an almost awed voice:

'That's a very large sum of money, Mr Jefferson.'

'In these days, yes, it is.'

'And you were leaving it to a girl you had only known a few weeks?'

Anger flashed into the vivid blue eyes.

'Must I go on repeating the same thing over and over again? I've no flesh and blood of my own – no nieces or nephews or distant cousins, even! I might have left it to charity. I prefer to leave it to an individual.' He laughed. 'Cinderella turned into a princess overnight! A fairy-godfather instead of a fairy-godmother. Why not? It's *my* money. *I* made it.'

Colonel Melchett asked: 'Any other bequests?'

'A small legacy to Edwards, my valet – and the remainder to Mark and Addie in equal shares.'

'Would – excuse me – the residue amount to a large sum?'

'Probably not. It's difficult to say exactly, investments fluctuate all the time. The sum involved, after death duties and expenses had been paid, would probably have come to something between five and ten thousand pounds net.'

'I see.'

'And you needn't think I was treating them shabbily. As I said, I divided up my estate at the time my children married. I left myself, actually, a very small sum. But after – after the tragedy – I wanted something to occupy my mind. I flung myself into business. At my house in London I had a private line put in connecting my bedroom with my office. I worked hard – it helped me not to think, and it made me feel that my – my mutilation had not vanquished me. I threw myself into work' – his voice took on a deeper note, he spoke more to himself than to his audience – 'and, by some subtle irony, everything I did prospered! My wildest speculations succeeded. If I gambled, I won. Everything I touched turned to gold. Fate's ironic way of righting the balance, I suppose.'

The lines of suffering stood out on his face again.

Recollecting himself, he smiled wryly at them.

'So you see, the sum of money I left Ruby was indisputably mine to do with as my fancy dictated.'

Melchett said quickly:

'Undoubtedly, my dear fellow, we are not questioning that for a moment.'

Conway Jefferson said: 'Good. Now I want to ask some questions in my turn, if I may. I want to hear – more about this terrible business. All I know is that she – that little Ruby was found strangled in a house some twenty miles from here.'

'That is correct. At Gossington Hall.'

Jefferson frowned.

'Gossington? But that's –'

'Colonel Bantry's house.'

'Bantry! *Arthur Bantry*? But I know him. Know him and his wife! Met them abroad some years ago. I didn't realize they lived in this part of the world. Why, it's –'

He broke off. Superintendent Harper slipped in smoothly:

'Colonel Bantry was dining in the hotel here Tuesday of last week. You didn't see him?'

'Tuesday? Tuesday? No, we were back late. Went over to Harden Head and had dinner on the way back.'

Melchett said:

'Ruby Keene never mentioned the Bantrys to you?'

Jefferson shook his head.

'Never. Don't believe she knew them. Sure she didn't. She didn't know anybody but theatrical folk and that sort of thing.' He paused and then asked abruptly:

'What's Bantry got to say about it?'

'He can't account for it in the least. He was out at a Conservative meeting last night. The body was discovered this morning. He says he's never seen the girl in his life.'

Jefferson nodded. He said:

'It certainly seems fantastic.'

Superintendent Harper cleared his throat. He said:

'Have you any idea at all, sir, who can have done this?'

'Good God, I wish I had!' The veins stood out on his forehead. 'It's incredible, unimaginable! I'd say it couldn't have happened, if it hadn't happened!'

'There's no friend of hers – from her past life – no man hanging about – or threatening her?'

'I'm sure there isn't. She'd have told me if so. She's never had a regular "boyfriend." She told me so herself.'

Superintendent Harper thought:

'Yes, I dare say that's what *she* told you! But that's as may be!'

Conway Jefferson went on:

'Josie would know better than anyone if there had been some man hanging about Ruby or pestering her. Can't she help?'

'She says not.'

Jefferson said, frowning:

'I can't help feeling it must be the work of some maniac – the brutality of the method – breaking into a country house – the whole thing so unconnected and senseless. There are men of that type, men outwardly sane, but who decoy girls – sometimes children – away and kill them. Sexual crimes really, I suppose.'

Harper said:

'Oh, yes, there are such cases, but we've no knowledge of anyone of that kind operating in this neighbourhood.'

Jefferson went on:

'I've thought over all the various men I've seen with Ruby. Guests here and outsiders – men she'd danced with. They all seem harmless enough – the usual type. She had no special friend of any kind.'

Superintendent Harper's face remained quite impassive, but unseen by Conway Jefferson there was still a speculative glint in his eye.

It was quite possible, he thought, that Ruby Keene might have had a special friend even though Conway Jefferson did not know about it.

He said nothing, however. The Chief Constable gave him a glance of inquiry and then rose to his feet. He said:

'Thank you, Mr Jefferson. That's all we need for the present.'

Jefferson said:

'You'll keep me informed of your progress?'

'Yes, yes, we'll keep in touch with you.'

The two men went out.

Conway Jefferson leaned back in his chair.

His eyelids came down and veiled the fierce blue of his eyes. He looked suddenly a very tired man.

Then, after a minute or two, the lids flickered. He called: 'Edwards!'

From the next room the valet appeared promptly. Edwards knew his master as no one else did. Others, even his nearest, knew only his strength. Edwards knew his weakness. He had seen Conway Jefferson tired, discouraged, weary of life, momentarily defeated by infirmity and loneliness.

'Yes, sir?'

Jefferson said:

'Get on to Sir Henry Clithering. He's at Melborne Abbas. Ask him, from me, to get here today if he can, instead of tomorrow. Tell him it's urgent.'

CHAPTER SEVEN

When they were outside Jefferson's door, Superintendent Harper said:

'Well, for what it's worth, we've got a motive, sir.'

'H'm,' said Melchett. 'Fifty thousand pounds, eh?'

'Yes, sir. Murder's been done for a good deal less than that.'

'Yes, but –'

Colonel Melchett left the sentence unfinished. Harper, however, understood him.

'You don't think it's likely in this case? Well, I don't either, as far as that goes. But it's got to be gone into all the same.'

'Oh, of course.'

Harper went on.

'If, as Mr Jefferson says, Mr Gaskell and Mrs Jefferson are already well provided for and in receipt of a comfortable income, well, it's not likely they'd set out to do a brutal murder.'

'Quite so. Their financial standing will have to be investigated, of course. Can't say I like the appearance of Gaskell much – looks a sharp, unscrupulous sort of fellow – but that's a long way from making him out a murderer.'

'Oh, yes, sir, as I say, I don't think it's *likely* to be either of them, and from what Josie said I don't see how it would have been humanly possible. They were both playing bridge from twenty minutes to eleven until midnight. No, to my mind there's another possibility much more likely.'

Melchett said: 'Boy friend of Ruby Keene's?'

'That's it, sir. Some disgruntled young fellow – not too strong in the head, perhaps. Someone, I'd say, she knew before she came here. This adoption scheme, if he got wise to it, may just have put the lid on things. He saw himself losing her, saw her being removed to a different sphere of life altogether, and he went mad and blind with rage. He got her to come out and meet him last night, had a row with her over it, lost his head completely and did her in.'

'And how did she come to be in Bantry's library?'

'I think that's feasible. They were out, say, in his car at the time. He came to himself, realized what he'd done, and his first thought was how to get rid of the body. Say they were near the gates of a big house at the time. The idea comes to him that if she's found there the hue and cry will centre round the house and its occupants and will leave him comfortably out of it. She's a little bit of a thing. He could easily carry her. He's got a chisel in the car. He forces a window and plops her down on the hearthrug. Being a strangling case, there's no blood or mess to give him away in the car. See what I mean, sir?'

'Oh, yes, Harper, it's all perfectly possible. But there's still one thing to be done. *Cherchez l'homme.*'

'What? Oh, very good, sir.'

Superintendent Harper tactfully applauded his superior's joke, although, owing to the excellence of Colonel Melchett's French accent he almost missed the sense of the words.

II

'Oh – er – I say – er – c-could I speak to you a minute?' It was George Bartlett who thus waylaid the two men. Colonel Melchett, who was not attracted to Mr Bartlett and who was anxious to see how Slack had got on with the investigation of the girl's room and the questioning of the chambermaids, barked sharply:

'Well, what is it – what is it?'

Young Mr Bartlett retreated a step or two, opening and shutting his mouth and giving an unconscious imitation of a fish in a tank.

'Well – er – probably isn't important, don't you know – thought I ought to tell you. Matter of fact, can't find my car.'

'What do you mean, can't find your car?'

Stammering a good deal, Mr Bartlett explained that what he meant was that he couldn't find his car.

Superintendent Harper said:

'Do you mean it's been stolen?'

George Bartlett turned gratefully to the more placid voice.

'Well, that's just it, you know. I mean, one can't tell, can one? I mean someone may just have buzzed off in it, not meaning any harm, if you know what I mean.'

'When did you last see it, Mr Bartlett?'

'Well, I was tryin' to remember. Funny how difficult it is to remember anything, isn't it?'

Colonel Melchett said coldly:

'Not, I should think, to a normal intelligence. I understood you to say just now that it was in the courtyard of the hotel last night –'

Mr Bartlett was bold enough to interrupt. He said:

'That's just it – was it?'

'What do you mean by "was it?" You said it *was*.'

'Well – I mean I *thought* it was. I mean – well, I didn't go out and look, don't you see?'

Colonel Melchett sighed. He summoned all his patience. He said:

'Let's get this quite clear. When was the last time you saw – actually *saw* your car? What make is it, by the way?'

'Minoan 14.'

'And you last saw it – when?'

George Bartlett's Adam's apple jerked convulsively up and down.

'Been trying to think. Had it before lunch yesterday. Was going for a spin in the afternoon. But somehow, you know how it is, went to sleep instead. Then, after tea, had a game of squash and all that, and a bathe afterwards.'

'And the car was then in the courtyard of the hotel?'

'Suppose so. I mean, that's where I'd put it. Thought, you see, I'd take someone for a spin. After dinner, I mean. But it wasn't my lucky evening. Nothing doing. Never took the old bus out after all.'

Harper said:

'But, as far as you knew, the car was still in the courtyard?'

'Well, naturally. I mean, I'd put it there – what?'

'Would you have noticed if it had *not* been there?'

Mr Bartlett shook his head.

'Don't think so, you know. Lots of cars going and coming and all that. Plenty of Minoans.'

Superintendent Harper nodded. He had just cast a casual glance out of the window. There were at that moment no less than eight Minoan 14s in the courtyard – it was the popular cheap car of the year.

'Aren't you in the habit of putting your car away at night?' asked Colonel Melchett.

'Don't usually bother,' said Mr Bartlett. 'Fine weather and all that, you know. Such a fag putting a car away in a garage.'

Glancing at Colonel Melchett, Superintendent Harper said: 'I'll join you upstairs, sir. I'll just get hold of Sergeant Higgins and he can take down particulars from Mr Bartlett.'

'Right, Harper.'

Mr Bartlett murmured wistfully:

'Thought I ought to let you know, you know. Might be important, what?'

III

Mr Prestcott had supplied his additional dancer with board and lodging. Whatever the board, the lodging was the poorest the hotel possessed.

Josephine Turner and Ruby Keene had occupied rooms at the extreme end of a mean and dingy little corridor. The rooms were small, faced north on to a portion of the cliff that backed the hotel, and were furnished with the odds and ends of suites that had once, some thirty years ago, represented luxury and magnificence in the best suites. Now, when the hotel had been modernized and the bedrooms supplied with built-in receptacles for clothes, these large Victorian oak and mahogany wardrobes were relegated to those rooms occupied by the hotel's resident staff, or given to guests in the height of the season when all the rest of the hotel was full.

As Melchett saw at once, the position of Ruby Keene's room was ideal for the purpose of leaving the hotel without being observed, and was particularly unfortunate from the point of view of throwing light on the circumstances of that departure.

At the end of the corridor was a small staircase which led down to an equally obscure corridor on the ground floor. Here there was a glass door which led out on to the side terrace of the hotel, an unfrequented terrace with no view. You could go from it to the main terrace in front, or you could go down a winding path and come out in a lane that eventually rejoined the cliff road farther along. Its surface being bad, it was seldom used.

Inspector Slack had been busy harrying chamber-maids and examining Ruby's room for clues. He had been lucky enough to find the room exactly as it had been left the night before.

Ruby Keene had not been in the habit of rising early. Her usual procedure, Slack discovered, was to sleep until about ten or half-past and then ring for breakfast. Consequently, since Conway Jefferson had begun his representations to the manager very early, the police had taken charge of things before the chambermaids had touched the room. They had actually not been down that corridor at all. The other rooms there, at this season of the year, were only opened and dusted once a week.

'That's all to the good as far as it goes,' Slack explained gloomily. 'It means that if there *were* anything to find we'd find it, but there isn't anything.'

The Glenshire police had already been over the room for finger-prints, but there were none unaccounted for. Ruby's own, Josie's, and the two chambermaids – one on the morning and one on the evening shift. There were also a couple of prints made by Raymond Starr, but these were accounted for by his story that he had come up with Josie to look for Ruby when she did not appear for the midnight exhibition dance.

There had been a heap of letters and general rubbish in the pigeon-holes of the massive mahogany desk in the corner. Slack had just been carefully sorting through them. But he had found nothing of a suggestive nature. Bills, receipts, theatre programmes, cinema stubs, newspaper cuttings, beauty hints torn from magazines. Of the letters there were some from 'Lil,' apparently a friend from the Palais de Danse, recounting various affairs and gossip, saying they 'missed Rube a lot. Mr Findeison asked after you ever so often! Quite put out, he is! Young Reg has taken up with May now you've gone. Barny asks after you now and then. Things going much as usual. Old Grouser still as mean as ever with us girls. He ticked off Ada for going about with a fellow.'

Slack had carefully noted all the names mentioned. Inquiries would be made – and it was possible some useful information might come to light. To this Colonel Melchett agreed; so did Superintendent Harper, who had joined them. Otherwise the room had little to yield in the way of information.

Across a chair in the middle of the room was the foamy pink dance frock Ruby had worn early in the evening with a pair of pink satin high-heeled shoes kicked off carelessly on the floor. Two sheer silk stockings were rolled into a ball and flung down. One had a ladder in it. Melchett recalled that the dead girl had had bare feet and legs. This, Slack learned, was her custom. She used make-up on her legs instead of stockings and only sometimes wore stockings for dancing, by this means saving expense. The wardrobe door was open and showed a variety of rather flashy evening dresses and a row of shoes below. There was some soiled underwear in the clothes-basket, some nail parings, soiled face-cleaning tissue and bits of cotton wool stained with rouge and nail-polish in the waste-paper basket – in fact, nothing out of the ordinary! The facts seemed plain to read. Ruby Keene had hurried upstairs, changed her clothes and hurried off again – *where*?

Josephine Turner, who might be supposed to know most of Ruby's life and friends, had proved unable to help. But this, as Inspector Slack pointed out, might be natural.

'If what you tell me is true, sir – about this adoption business, I mean – well, Josie would be all for Ruby breaking with any old friends she might have and who might queer the pitch, so to speak. As I see it, this invalid gentleman gets all worked up about Ruby Keene being such a sweet, innocent, childish little piece of goods. Now, supposing Ruby's got a tough boy friend – that won't go down so well with the old boy. So it's Ruby's business to keep that dark. Josie doesn't know much about the girl anyway – not about her friends and all that. But one thing she wouldn't stand for – Ruby's messing up things by carrying on with some undesirable fellow. So it stands to reason that Ruby (who, as I see it, was a sly little piece!) would keep very dark about seeing any old friend. She wouldn't let on to Josie anything about it – otherwise Josie would say: "No, you don't, my girl." But you know what girls are – especially young ones – always ready to make a fool of themselves over a tough guy. Ruby wants to see him. He comes down here, cuts up rough about the whole business, and wrings the girl's neck.'

'I expect you're right, Slack,' said Colonel Melchett, disguising his usual repugnance for the unpleasant way Slack had of putting things. 'If so, we ought to be able to discover this tough friend's identity fairly easily.'

'You leave it to me, sir,' said Slack with his usual confidence. 'I'll get hold of this "Lil" girl at that Palais de Danse place and turn her right inside out. We'll soon get at the truth.'

Colonel Melchett wondered if they would. Slack's energy and activity always made him feel tired.

'There's one other person you might be able to get a tip from, sir,' went on Slack, 'and that's the dance and tennis pro. fellow. He must have seen a lot of her and he'd know more than Josie would. Likely enough she'd loosen her tongue a bit to him.'

'I have already discussed that point with Superintendent Harper.'

'Good, sir. *I've* done the chambermaids pretty thoroughly! They don't know a thing. Looked down on these two, as far as I can make out. Scamped the service as much as they dared. Chambermaid was in here last at seven o'clock last night, when she turned down the bed and drew the curtains and cleared up a bit. There's a bathroom next door, if you'd like to see it?'

The bathroom was situated between Ruby's room and slightly larger room occupied by Josie. It was illuminating. Colonel Melchett silently marvelled at the amount of aids to beauty that women could use. Rows of jars of face cream, cleansing cream, vanishing cream, skin-feeding cream! Boxes of different shades of powder. An untidy heap of every variety of lipstick. Hair lotions and 'brightening' applications. Eyelash black, mascara, blue stain for under the eyes, at least twelve different shades of nail varnish, face tissues, bits of cotton wool, dirty powder-puffs. Bottles of lotions — astringent, tonic, soothing, etc.

'Do you mean to say,' he murmured feebly, 'that women use all these things?'

Inspector Slack, who always knew everything, kindly enlightened him.

'In private life, sir, so to speak, a lady keeps to one or two distinct shades, one for evening, one for day. They know what suits them and they keep to it. But these professional girls, they have to ring a change, so to speak. They do exhibition dances, and one night it's a tango and the next a crinoline Victorian dance and then a kind of Apache dance and then just ordinary ballroom, and, of course, the make-up varies a good bit.'

'Good lord!' said the Colonel. 'No wonder the people who turn out these creams and messes make a fortune.'

'Easy money, that's what it is,' said Slack. 'Easy money. Got to spend a bit in advertisement, of course.'

Colonel Melchett jerked his mind away from the fascinating and age-long problem of woman's adornments. He said to Harper, who had just joined them:

'There's still this dancing fellow. Your pigeon, Superintendent?'

'I suppose so, sir.'

As they went downstairs Harper asked:

'What did you think of Mr Bartlett's story, sir?'

'About his car? I think, Harper, that that young man wants watching. It's a fishy story. Supposing that he did take Ruby Keene out in that car last night, after all?'

IV

Superintendent Harper's manner was slow and pleasant and absolutely non-committal. These cases where the police of two counties had to collaborate were always difficult. He liked Colonel Melchett and considered him an able Chief Constable, but he was nevertheless glad to be tackling the present interview by himself. Never do too much at once, was Superintendent Harper's rule. Bare routine inquiry for the first time. That left the persons you were interviewing relieved and predisposed them to be more unguarded in the next interview you had with them.

Harper already knew Raymond Starr by sight. A fine-looking specimen, tall, lithe, and good-looking, with very white teeth in a deeply-bronzed face. He was dark and graceful. He had a pleasant, friendly manner and was very popular in the hotel.

'I'm afraid I can't help you much, Superintendent. I knew Ruby quite well, of course. She'd been here over a month and we had practised our dances together and all that. But there's really very little to say. She was quite a pleasant and rather stupid girl.'

'It's her friendships we're particularly anxious to know about. Her friendships with men.'

'So I suppose. Well, *I* don't know anything! She'd got a few young men in tow in the hotel, but nothing special. You see, she was nearly always monopolized by the Jefferson family.'

'Yes, the Jefferson family.' Harper paused meditatively. He shot a shrewd glance at the young man. 'What did you think of that business, Mr Starr?'

Raymond Starr said coolly: 'What business?'

Harper said: 'Did you know that Mr Jefferson was proposing to adopt Ruby Keene legally?'

This appeared to be news to Starr. He pursed up his lips and whistled. He said:

'The clever little devil! Oh, well, there's no fool like an old fool.'

'That's how it strikes you, is it?'

'Well – what else can one say? If the old boy wanted to adopt someone, why didn't he pick upon a girl of his own class?'

'Ruby Keene never mentioned the matter to you?'

'No, she didn't. I knew she was elated about something, but I didn't know what it was.'

'And Josie?'

'Oh, I think Josie must have known what was in the wind. Probably she was the one who planned the whole thing. Josie's no fool. She's got a head on her, that girl.'

Harper nodded. It was Josie who had sent for Ruby Keene. Josie, no doubt, who had encouraged the intimacy. No wonder she had been upset when Ruby had failed to show up for her dance that night and Conway Jefferson had begun to panic. She was envisaging her plans going awry.

He asked:

'Could Ruby keep a secret, do you think?'

'As well as most. She didn't talk about her own affairs much.'

'Did she ever say anything – anything at all – about some friend of hers – someone from her former life who was coming to see her here, or whom she had had difficulty with – you know the sort of thing I mean, no doubt.'

'I know perfectly. Well, as far as I'm aware, there was no one of the kind. Not by anything she ever said.'

'Thank you, Mr Starr. Now will you just tell me in your own words exactly what happened last night?'

'Certainly. Ruby and I did our ten-thirty dance together –'

'No signs of anything unusual about her then?'

Raymond considered.

'I don't think so. I didn't notice what happened afterwards. I had my own partners to look after. I do remember noticing she wasn't in the ballroom. At midnight she hadn't turned up. I was very annoyed and went to Josie about it. Josie was playing bridge with the Jeffersons. She hadn't any idea where Ruby was, and I think she got a bit of a jolt. I noticed her shoot a quick, anxious glance at Mr Jefferson. I persuaded the band to play another dance and I went to the office and got them to ring up to Ruby's room. There wasn't any answer. I went back to Josie. She suggested that Ruby was perhaps asleep in her room. Idiotic suggestion really, but it was meant for the Jeffersons, of course! She came away with me and said we'd go up together.'

'Yes, Mr Starr. And what did she say when she was alone with you?'

'As far as I can remember, she looked very angry and said: "Damned little fool. She can't do this sort of thing. It will ruin all her chances. Who's she with, do you know?"

'I said that I hadn't the least idea. The last I'd seen of her was dancing with young Bartlett. Josie said: "She wouldn't be with *him*. What *can* she be up to? She isn't with that film man, is she?"'

Harper said sharply; '*Film man?* Who was he?'

Raymond said: 'I don't know his name. He's never stayed here. Rather an unusual-looking chap – black hair and theatrical-looking. He has something to do with the film industry, I believe – or so he told Ruby. He came over to dine here once or twice and danced with Ruby afterwards, but I don't think she knew him at all well. That's why I was surprised when Josie mentioned him. I said I didn't think he'd been here tonight. Josie said: "Well, she must be out with *someone*. What on earth am I going to say to the Jeffersons?" I said what did it matter to the Jeffersons? And Josie said it *did* matter. And she said, too, that she'd never forgive Ruby if she went and messed things up.

'We'd got to Ruby's room by then. She wasn't there, of course, but she'd been there, because the dress she had been wearing was lying across a chair. Josie looked in the wardrobe and said she thought she'd put on her old white dress. Normally she'd have changed into a black velvet dress for our Spanish dance. I was pretty angry by this time at the way Ruby had let me down. Josie did her best to soothe me and said she'd dance herself so that old Prestcott shouldn't get after us all. She went away and changed her dress and we went down and did a tango – exaggerated style and quite showy but not really too exhausting upon the ankles. Josie was very plucky about it – for it hurt her, I could see. After that she asked me to help her soothe the Jeffersons down. She said it was important. So, of course, I did what I could.'

Superintendent Harper nodded. He said:

'Thank you, Mr Starr.'

To himself he thought: 'It was important, all right! Fifty thousand pounds!'

He watched Raymond Starr as the latter moved gracefully away. He went down the steps of the terrace, picking up a bag of tennis balls and a racquet on the way. Mrs Jefferson, also carrying a racquet, joined him and they went towards the tennis courts.

'Excuse me, sir.'

Sergeant Higgins, rather breathless, stood at Harper's side.

The Superintendent, jerked from the train of thought he was following, looked startled.

'Message just come through for you from headquarters, sir. Labourer reported this morning saw glare as of fire. Half an hour ago they found a burnt-out car in a quarry. Venn's Quarry – about two miles from here. Traces of a charred body inside.'

A flush came over Harper's heavy features. He said:

'What's come to Glenshire? An epidemic of violence? Don't tell me we're going to have a Rouse case now!'

He asked: 'Could they get the number of the car?'

'No, sir. But we'll be able to identify it, of course, by the engine number. A Minoan 14, they think it is.'

CHAPTER EIGHT

Sir Henry Clithering, as he passed through the lounge of the Majestic, hardly glanced at its occupants. His mind was preoccupied. Nevertheless, as is the way of life, something registered in his subconscious. It waited its time patiently.

Sir Henry was wondering as he went upstairs just what had induced the sudden urgency of his friend's message. Conway Jefferson was not the type of man who sent urgent summonses to anyone. Something quite out of the usual must have occurred, decided Sir Henry.

Jefferson wasted no time in beating about the bush. He said:

'Glad you've come. Edwards, get Sir Henry a drink. Sit down, man. You've not heard anything, I suppose? Nothing in the papers yet?'

Sir Henry shook his head, his curiosity aroused.

'What's the matter?'

'Murder's the matter. I'm concerned in it and so are your friends the Bantrys.'

'Arthur and Dolly Bantry?' Clithering sounded incredulous.

'Yes, you see, the body was found in their house.'

Clearly and succinctly, Conway Jefferson ran through the facts. Sir Henry listened without interrupting. Both men were accustomed to grasping the gist of a matter. Sir Henry, during his term as Commissioner of the Metropolitan Police, had been renowned for his quick grip on essentials.

'It's an extraordinary business,' he commented when the other had finished. 'How do the Bantrys come into it, do you think?'

'That's what worries me. You see, Henry, it looks to me as though possibly the fact that I know them might have a bearing on the case. That's the only connection I can find. Neither of them, I gather, ever saw the girl before. That's what they say, and there's no reason to disbelieve them. It's most unlikely they *should* know her. Then isn't it possible that she was decoyed away and her body deliberately left in the house of friends of mine?'

Clithering said:

'I think that's far-fetched.'

'It's possible, though,' persisted the other.

'Yes, but unlikely. What do you want *me* to do?'

Conway Jefferson said bitterly:

'I'm an invalid. I disguise the fact – refuse to face it – but now it comes home to me. I can't go about as I'd like to, asking questions, looking into things. I've got to stay here meekly grateful for such scraps of information as the police are kind enough to dole out to me. Do you happen to know Melchett, by the way, the Chief Constable of Radfordshire?'

'Yes, I've met him.'

Something stirred in Sir Henry's brain. A face and figure noted unseeingly as he passed through the lounge. A straight-backed old lady whose face was familiar. It linked up with the last time he had seen Melchett.

74

He said:

'Do you mean you want me to be a kind of amateur sleuth? That's not my line.'

Jefferson said:

'You're *not* an amateur, that's just it.'

'I'm not a professional any more. I'm on the retired list now.'

Jefferson said: 'That simplifies matters.'

'You mean that if I were still at Scotland Yard I couldn't butt in? That's perfectly true.'

'As it is,' said Jefferson, 'your experience qualifies you to take an interest in the case, and any co-operation you offer will be welcomed.'

Clithering said slowly:

'Etiquette permits, I agree. But what do you really want, Conway? To find out who killed this girl?'

'Just that.'

'You've no idea yourself?'

'None whatever.'

Sir Henry said slowly:

'You probably won't believe me, but you've got an expert at solving mysteries sitting downstairs in the lounge at this minute. Someone who's better than I am at it, and who in all probability *may* have some local dope.'

'What are you talking about?'

'Downstairs in the lounge, by the third pillar from the left, there sits an old lady with a sweet, placid spinsterish face, and a mind that has plumbed the depths of human iniquity and taken it as all in the day's work. Her name's Miss Marple. She comes from the village of St Mary Mead, which is a mile and a half from Gossington, she's a friend of the Bantrys – and where crime is concerned she's the goods, Conway.'

Jefferson stared at him with thick, puckered brows. He said heavily:

'You're joking.'

'No, I'm not. You spoke of Melchett just now. The last time I saw Melchett there was a village tragedy. Girl supposed to have drowned herself. Police quite rightly suspected that it wasn't suicide, but murder. They thought they knew who did it. Along to me comes old Miss Marple, fluttering and dithering. She's afraid, she says, they'll hang the wrong person. She's got no evidence, but she knows who did do it. Hands me a piece of paper with a name written on it. And, by God, Jefferson, she was right!'

Conway Jefferson's brows came down lower than ever. He grunted disbelievingly:

'Woman's intuition, I suppose,' he said sceptically.

'No, she doesn't call it that. Specialized knowledge is her claim.'

'And what does that mean?'

'Well, you know, Jefferson, *we* use it in police work. We get a burglary and we usually know pretty well who did it – of the regular crowd, that is. We know the sort of burglar who acts in a particular sort of way. Miss Marple has an interesting, though occasionally trivial, series of parallels from village life.'

Jefferson said sceptically:

'What is she likely to know about a girl who's been brought up in a theatrical milieu and probably never been in a village in her life?'

'I think,' said Sir Henry Clithering firmly, 'that she might have ideas.'

II

Miss Marple flushed with pleasure as Sir Henry bore down upon her.

'Oh, Sir Henry, this is indeed a great piece of luck meeting you here.'

Sir Henry was gallant. He said:

'To me it is a great pleasure.'

Miss Marple murmured, flushing: 'So kind of you.'

'Are you staying here?'

'Well, as a matter of fact, we are.'

'*We*?'

'Mrs Bantry's here too.' She looked at him sharply. 'Have you heard yet? Yes, I can see you have. It is terrible, is it not?'

'What's Dolly Bantry doing here? Is her husband here too?'

'No. Naturally, they both reacted quite differently. Colonel Bantry, poor man, just shuts himself up in his study, or goes down to one of the farms, when anything like this happens. Like tortoises, you know, they draw their heads in and hope nobody will notice them. Dolly, of course, is *quite* different.'

'Dolly, in fact,' said Sir Henry, who knew his old friend fairly well, 'is almost enjoying herself, eh?'

'Well – er – yes. Poor dear.'

'And she's brought you along to produce the rabbits out of the hat for her?'

Miss Marple said composedly:

'Dolly thought that a change of scene would be a good thing and she didn't want to come alone.' She met his eye and her own gently twinkled. 'But, of course, your way of describing it is quite true. It's rather embarrassing for me, because, of course, I am no use at all.'

'No ideas? No village parallels?'

'I don't know very much about it all yet.'

'I can remedy that, I think. I'm going to call you into consultation, Miss Marple.'

He gave a brief recital of the course of events. Miss Marple listened with keen interest.

'Poor Mr Jefferson,' she said. 'What a very sad story. These terrible accidents. To leave him alive, crippled, seems more cruel than if he had been killed too.'

'Yes, indeed. That's why all his friends admire him so much for the resolute way he's gone on, conquering pain and grief and physical disabilities.'

'Yes, it is splendid.'

'The only thing I can't understand is this sudden outpouring of affection for this girl. She may, of course, have had some remarkable qualities.'

'Probably not,' said Miss Marple placidly.

'You don't think so?'

'I don't think her qualities entered into it.'

Sir Henry said:

'He isn't just a nasty old man, you know.'

'Oh, no, no!' Miss Marple got quite pink. 'I wasn't implying that for a minute. What I was trying to say was – very badly, I know – that he was just looking for a nice bright girl to take his dead daughter's place – and then this girl saw her opportunity and played it for all she was worth! That sounds rather uncharitable, I know,

77

but I have seen so many cases of the kind. The young maidservant at Mr Harbottle's, for instance. A *very* ordinary girl, but quiet with nice manners. His sister was called away to nurse a dying relative and when she got back she found the girl completely above herself, sitting down in the drawing-room laughing and talking and not wearing her cap or apron. Miss Harbottle spoke to her very sharply and the girl was impertinent, and then old Mr Harbottle left her quite dumbfounded by saying that he thought she had kept house for him long enough and that he was making other arrangements.

'Such a scandal as it created in the village, but poor Miss Harbottle had to go and live *most* uncomfortably in rooms in Eastbourne. People *said* things, of course, but I believe there was no familiarity of any kind – it was simply that the old man found it much pleasanter to have a young, cheerful girl telling him how clever and amusing he was than to have his sister continually pointing out his faults to him, even if she *was* a good economical manager.'

There was a moment's pause, and then Miss Marple resumed.

'And there was Mr Badger who had the chemist's shop. Made a lot of fuss over the young lady who worked in his toilet section. Told his wife they must look on her as a daughter and have her to live in the house. Mrs Badger didn't see it that way at all.'

Sir Henry said: 'If she'd only been a girl in his own rank of life – a friend's child –'

Miss Marple interrupted him.

'Oh! but that wouldn't have been nearly as satisfactory from his point of view. It's like King Cophetua and the beggar maid. If you're really rather a lonely, tired old man, and if, perhaps, your own family have been neglecting you' – she paused for a second – 'well, to befriend someone who will be overwhelmed with your magnificence – (to put it rather melodramatically, but I hope you see what I mean) – well, that's much more interesting. It makes you feel a much greater person – a beneficent monarch! The recipient is more likely to be dazzled, and that, of course, is a pleasant feeling for you.' She paused and said: 'Mr Badger, you know, bought the girl in his shop some really fantastic presents, a diamond bracelet and a most expensive radio-gramophone. Took out a lot of his savings to do so. However, Mrs Badger, who was a much more astute woman than poor Miss Harbottle (marriage, of course, *helps*), took the trouble to find out a few things. And when Mr Badger discovered that the girl was carrying on with a *very* undesirable young man connected with the racecourses, and had actually pawned the bracelet to give him the money – well, he was completely disgusted and the affair passed over quite safely. And he gave Mrs Badger a diamond ring the following Christmas.'

Her pleasant, shrewd eyes met Sir Henry's. He wondered if what she had been saying was intended as a hint. He said:

'Are you suggesting that if there had been a young man in Ruby Keene's life, my friend's attitude towards her might have altered?'

'It probably would, you know. I dare say, in a year or two, he might have liked to arrange for her marriage himself – though more likely he wouldn't - gentlemen are usually rather selfish. But I certainly think that if Ruby Keene had had a young man she'd have been careful to keep very quiet about it.'

'And the young man might have resented that?'

'I suppose that *is* the most plausible solution. It struck me, you know, that her cousin, the young woman who was at Gossington this morning, looked definitely *angry* with the dead girl. What you've told me explains *why*. No doubt she was looking forward to doing very well out of the business.'

'Rather a cold-blooded character, in fact?'

'That's too harsh a judgment, perhaps. The poor thing has had to earn her living, and you can't expect her to sentimentalize because a well-to-do man and woman – as you have described Mr Gaskell and Mrs Jefferson – are going to be done out of a further large sum of money to which they have really no particular moral right. I should say Miss Turner was a hard-headed, ambitious young woman, with a good temper and considerable *joie de vivre*. A little,' added Miss Marple, 'like Jessie Golden, the baker's daughter.'

'What happened to her?' asked Sir Henry.

'She trained as a nursery governess and married the son of the house, who was home on leave from India. Made him a very good wife, I believe.'

Sir Henry pulled himself clear of these fascinating side issues. He said:

'Is there any reason, do you think, why my friend Conway Jefferson should suddenly have developed this "Cophetua complex," if you like to call it that?'

'There might have been.'

'In what way?'

Miss Marple said, hesitating a little:

'I should think – it's only a suggestion, of course – that perhaps his son-in-law and daughter-in-law *might* have wanted to get married again.'

'Surely he couldn't have objected to that?'

'Oh, no, not *objected*. But, you see, you must look at it from *his* point of view. He had a terrible shock and loss – so had they. The three bereaved people live together and the *link* between them is the loss they have all sustained. But Time, as my dear mother used to say, is a great healer. Mr Gaskell and Mrs Jefferson are young. Without knowing it themselves, they may have begun to feel restless, to resent the bonds that tied them to their past sorrow. And so, feeling like that, old Mr Jefferson would have become conscious of a sudden lack of sympathy without knowing its cause. It's usually that. Gentlemen so *easily* feel neglected. With Mr Harbottle it was Miss Harbottle going away. And with the Badgers it was Mrs Badger taking such an interest in Spiritualism and always going out to séances.'

'I must say,' said Sir Henry ruefully, 'that I dislike the way you reduce us all to a General Common Denominator.'

Miss Marple shook her head sadly.

'Human nature is very much the same anywhere, Sir Henry.'

Sir Henry said distastefully:

'Mr Harbottle! Mr Badger! And poor Conway! I hate to intrude the personal note, but have you any parallel for *my* humble self in your village?'

'Well, of course, there is Briggs.'

'Who's Briggs?'

'He was the head gardener up at Old Hall. *Quite* the best man they ever had. Knew *exactly* when the under-gardeners were slacking off – quite uncanny it was! He managed with only three men and a boy and the place was kept better than it had been with six. And took several firsts with his sweet peas. He's retired now.'

'Like me,' said Sir Henry.

'But he still does a little jobbing – if he likes the people.'

'Ah,' said Sir Henry. 'Again like me. That's what I'm doing now – jobbing – to help an old friend.'

'Two old friends.'

'Two?' Sir Henry looked a little puzzled.

Miss Marple said:

'I suppose you meant Mr Jefferson. But I wasn't thinking of him. I was thinking of Colonel and Mrs Bantry.'

'Yes – yes – I see –' He asked sharply: 'Was that why you alluded to Dolly Bantry as "poor dear" at the beginning of our conversation?'

'Yes. She hasn't begun to realize things yet. *I* know because I've had more experience. You see, Sir Henry, it seems to me that there's a great possibility of this crime being the kind of crime that never *does* get solved. Like the Brighton trunk murders. But if that happens it will be absolutely disastrous for the Bantrys. Colonel Bantry, like nearly all retired military men, is really *abnormally* sensitive. He reacts very quickly to public opinion. He won't notice it for some time, and then it will begin to go home to him. A slight here, and a snub there, and invitations that are refused, and excuses that are made – and then, little by little, it will dawn upon him and he'll retire into his shell and get terribly morbid and miserable.'

'Let me be sure I understand you rightly, Miss Marple. You mean that, because the body was found in his house, people will think that *he* had something to do with it?'

'Of course they will! I've no doubt they're saying so already. They'll say so more and more. And people will cold shoulder the Bantrys and avoid them. That's why the truth has got to be found out and why I was willing to come here with Mrs Bantry. An open accusation is one thing – and quite easy for a soldier to meet. He's indignant and he has a chance of fighting. But this other *whispering* business will break him – will break them both. So you see, Sir Henry, we've *got* to find out the truth.'

Sir Henry said:

'Any ideas as to why the body should have been found in his house? There must be an explanation of that. Some connection.'

'Oh, of course.'

'The girl was last seen here about twenty minutes to eleven. By midnight, according to the medical evidence, she was dead. Gossington's about eighteen miles from here. Good road for sixteen of those miles until one turns off the main road. A powerful car could do it in well under half an hour. Practically *any* car could average thirty-five. But why anyone should either kill her here and take her body out to Gossington or should take her out to Gossington and strangle her there, I don't know.'

'Of course you don't, because it didn't happen.'

'Do you mean that she was strangled by some fellow who took her out in a car and he then decided to push her into the first likely house in the neighbourhood?'

'I don't think anything of the kind. I think there was a very careful plan made. What happened was that the plan went wrong.'

Sir Henry stared at her.

'Why did the plan go wrong?'

Miss Marple said rather apologetically:

'Such curious things happen, don't they? If I were to say that this particular plan went wrong because human beings are so much more vulnerable and sensitive than anyone thinks, it wouldn't sound sensible, would it? But that's what I believe – and –'

She broke off. 'Here's Mrs Bantry now.'

CHAPTER NINE

Mrs Bantry was with Adelaide Jefferson. The former came up to Sir Henry and exclaimed: '*You*?'

'I, myself.' He took both her hands and pressed them warmly. 'I can't tell you how distressed I am at all this, Mrs B.'

Mrs Bantry said mechanically:

'*Don't call me Mrs B.*!' and went on: 'Arthur isn't here. He's taking it all rather seriously. Miss Marple and I have come here to sleuth. Do you know Mrs Jefferson?'

'Yes, of course.'

He shook hands. Adelaide Jefferson said:

'Have you seen my father-in-law?'

'Yes, I have.'

'I'm glad. We're anxious about him. It was a terrible shock.'

Mrs Bantry said:

'Let's come out on the terrace and have drinks and talk about it all.'

The four of them went out and joined Mark Gaskell, who was

sitting at the extreme end of the terrace by himself.

After a few desultory remarks and the arrival of the drinks Mrs Bantry plunged straight into the subject with her usual zest for direct action.

'We can talk about it, can't we?' she said. 'I mean, we're all old friends – except Miss Marple, and she knows all about crime. And she wants to help.'

Mark Gaskell looked at Miss Marple in a somewhat puzzled fashion. He said doubtfully:

'Do you – er – write detective stories?'

The most unlikely people, he knew, wrote detective stories. And Miss Marple, in her old-fashioned spinster's clothes, looked a singularly unlikely person.

'Oh no, I'm not clever enough for *that*.'

'She's wonderful,' said Mrs Bantry impatiently. 'I can't explain now, but she is. Now, Addie, I want to know all about things. What was she really like, this girl?'

'Well –' Adelaide Jefferson paused, glanced across at Mark, and half laughed. She said: 'You're so direct.'

'Did you like her?'

'No, of course I didn't.'

'What was she really like?' Mrs Bantry shifted her inquiry to Mark Gaskell. Mark said deliberately:

'Common or garden gold-digger. And she knew her stuff. She'd got her hooks into Jeff all right.'

Both of them called their father-in-law Jeff.

Sir Henry thought, looking disapprovingly at Mark:

'Indiscreet fellow. Shouldn't be so outspoken.'

He had always disapproved a little of Mark Gaskell. The man had charm but he was unreliable – talked too much, was occasionally boastful – not quite to be trusted, Sir Henry thought. He had sometimes wondered if Conway Jefferson thought so too.

'But couldn't you *do* something about it?' demanded Mrs Bantry.

Mark said dryly:

'We might have – if we'd realized it in time.'

He shot a glance at Adelaide and she coloured faintly. There had been reproach in that glance.

She said:

'Mark thinks I ought to have seen what was coming.'

'You left the old boy alone too much, Addie. Tennis lessons and all the rest of it.'

'Well, I had to have some exercise.' She spoke apologetically. 'Anyway, I never dreamed—'

'No,' said Mark, 'neither of us ever dreamed. Jeff has always been such a sensible, level-headed old boy.'

Miss Marple made a contribution to the conversation.

'Gentlemen,' she said with her old-maid's way of referring to the opposite sex as though it were a species of wild animal, 'are frequently not as level-headed as they seem.'

'I'll say you're right,' said Mark. 'Unfortunately, Miss Marple, we didn't realize that. We wondered what the old boy saw in that rather insipid and meretricious little bag of tricks. But we were pleased for him to be kept happy and amused. We thought there was no harm in her. No harm in her! I wish I'd wrung her neck!'

'Mark,' said Addie, 'you really *must* be careful what you say.'

He grinned at her engagingly.

'I suppose I must. Otherwise people will think I actually *did* wring her neck. Oh well, I suppose I'm under suspicion, anyway. If anyone had an interest in seeing that girl dead it was Addie and myself.'

'Mark,' cried Mrs Jefferson, half laughing and half angry, 'you really *mustn't*!'

'All right, all right,' said Mark Gaskell pacifically. 'But I do like speaking my mind. Fifty thousand pounds our esteemed father-in-law was proposing to settle upon that half-baked nitwitted little slypuss.'

'Mark, you mustn't — she's dead.'

'Yes, she's dead, poor little devil. And after all, why shouldn't she use the weapons that Nature gave her? Who am I to judge? Done plenty of rotten things myself in my life. No, let's say Ruby was entitled to plot and scheme and we were mugs not to have tumbled to her game sooner.'

Sir Henry said:

'What did you say when Conway told you he proposed to adopt the girl?'

Mark thrust out his hands.

'What could we say? Addie, always the little lady, retained her self-control admirably. Put a brave face upon it. I endeavoured to follow her example.'

'*I* should have made a fuss!' said Mrs Bantry.

'Well, frankly speaking, we weren't entitled to make a fuss. It was Jeff's money. We weren't his flesh and blood. He'd always been damned good to us. There was nothing for it but to bite on the bullet.' He added reflectively: 'But we didn't love little Ruby.'

Adelaide Jefferson said:

'If only it had been some other kind of girl. Jeff had two godchildren, you know. If it had been one of them – well, one would have *understood* it.' She added, with a shade of resentment: 'And Jeff's always seemed so fond of Peter.'

'Of course,' said Mrs Bantry. 'I always have known Peter was your first husband's child – but I'd quite forgotten it. I've always thought of him as Mr Jefferson's grandson.'

'So have I,' said Adelaide. Her voice held a note that made Miss Marple turn in her chair and look at her.

'It was Josie's fault,' said Mark. 'Josie brought her here.'

Adelaide said:

'Oh, but surely you don't think it was deliberate, do you? Why, you've always liked Josie so much.'

'Yes, I did like her. I thought she was a good sport.'

'It was sheer accident her bringing the girl down.'

'Josie's got a good head on her shoulders, my girl.'

'Yes, but she couldn't foresee –'

Mark said:

'No, she couldn't. I admit it. I'm not really accusing her of planning the whole thing. But I've no doubt she saw which way the wind was blowing long before we did and kept very quiet about it.'

Adelaide said with a sigh:

'I suppose one can't blame her for that.'

Mark said:

'Oh, we can't blame anyone for anything!'

Mrs Bantry asked:

'Was Ruby Keene very pretty?'

Mark stared at her. 'I thought you'd seen –'

Mrs Bantry said hastily:

'Oh yes, I saw her – her body. But she'd been strangled, you know, and one couldn't tell –' She shivered.

Mark said, thoughtfully:

'I don't think she was really pretty at all. She certainly wouldn't have been without any make-up. A thin ferrety little face, not much chin, teeth running down her throat, nondescript sort of nose –'

'It sounds revolting,' said Mrs Bantry.

'Oh no, she wasn't. As I say, with make-up she managed to give quite an effect of good looks, don't you think so, Addie?'

'Yes, rather chocolate-box, pink and white business. She had nice blue eyes.'

'Yes, innocent baby stare, and the heavily-blacked lashes brought out the blueness. Her hair was bleached, of course. It's true, when I come to think of it, that in colouring – artificial colouring, anyway – she had a kind of spurious resemblance to Rosamund – my wife, you know. I dare say that's what attracted the old man's attention to her.'

He sighed.

'Well, it's a bad business. The awful thing is that Addie and I can't help being glad, really, that she's dead –'

He quelled a protest from his sister-in-law.

'It's no good, Addie; I know what you feel. I feel the same. And I'm not going to pretend! But, at the same time, if you know what I mean, I really am most awfully concerned for Jeff about the whole business. It's hit him very hard. I –'

He stopped, and stared towards the doors leading out of the lounge on to the terrace.

'Well, well – see who's here. What an unscrupulous woman you are, Addie.'

Mrs Jefferson looked over her shoulder, uttered an exclamation and got up, a slight colour rising in her face. She walked quickly along the terrace and went up to a tall middle-aged man with a thin brown face, who was looking uncertainly about him.

Mrs Bantry said: 'Isn't that Hugo McLean?'

Mark Gaskell said:

'Hugo McLean it is. Alias William Dobbin.'

Mrs Bantry murmured:

'He's very faithful, isn't he?'

'Dog-like devotion,' said Mark. 'Addie's only got to whistle and Hugo comes trotting from any odd corner of the globe. Always hopes that some day she'll marry him. I dare say she will.'

Miss Marple looked beamingly after them. She said:

86

'I see. A romance?'

'One of the good old-fashioned kind,' Mark assured her. 'It's been going on for years. Addie's that kind of woman.'

He added meditatively: 'I suppose Addie telephoned him this morning. She didn't tell me she had.'

Edwards came discreetly along the terrace and paused at Mark's elbow.

'Excuse me, sir. Mr Jefferson would like you to come up.'

'I'll come at once.' Mark sprang up.

He nodded to them, said: 'See you later,' and went off.

Sir Henry leant forward to Miss Marple. He said:

'Well, what do you think of the principal beneficiaries of the crime?'

Miss Marple said thoughtfully, looking at Adelaide Jefferson as she stood talking to her old friend:

'I should think, you know, that she was a very devoted mother.'

'Oh, she is,' said Mrs Bantry. 'She's simply devoted to Peter.'

'She's the kind of woman,' said Miss Marple, 'that everyone likes. The kind of woman that could go on getting married again and again. I don't mean a *man's* woman – that's quite different.'

'I know what you mean,' said Sir Henry.

'What you both mean,' said Mrs Bantry, 'is that she's a good listener.'

Sir Henry laughed. He said:

'And Mark Gaskell?'

'Ah,' said Miss Marple, 'he's a downy fellow.'

'Village parallel, please?'

'Mr Cargill, the builder. He bluffed a lot of people into having things done to their houses they never meant to do. And how he charged them for it! But he could always explain his bills away plausibly. A downy fellow. He married money. So did Mr Gaskell, I understand.'

'You don't like him.'

'Yes, I do. Most women would. But he can't take me in. He's a very attractive person, I think. But a little unwise, perhaps, to *talk* as much as he does.'

'Unwise is the word,' said Sir Henry. 'Mark will get himself into trouble if he doesn't look out.'

A tall dark young man in white flannels came up the steps to the terrace and paused just for a minute, watching Adelaide Jefferson and Hugo McLean.

'And that,' said Sir Henry obligingly, 'is X, whom we might describe as an interested party. He is the tennis and dancing pro. – Raymond Starr, Ruby Keene's partner.'

Miss Marple looked at him with interest. She said:

'He's very nice-looking, isn't he?'

'I suppose so.'

'Don't be absurd, Sir Henry,' said Mrs Bantry; 'there's no supposing about it. He *is* good-looking.'

Miss Marple murmured:

'Mrs Jefferson has been taking tennis lessons, I think she said.'

'Do you mean anything by that, Jane, or don't you?'

Miss Marple had no chance of replying to this downright question. Young Peter Carmody came across the terrace and joined them. He addressed himself to Sir Henry:

'I say, are you a detective, too? I saw you talking to the Superintendent – the fat one is a superintendent, isn't he?'

'Quite right, my son.'

'And somebody told me you were a frightfully important detective from London. The head of Scotland Yard or something like that.'

'The head of Scotland Yard is usually a complete dud in books, isn't he?'

'Oh no, not nowadays. Making fun of the police is very old-fashioned. Do you know who did the murder yet?'

'Not yet, I'm afraid.'

'Are you enjoying this very much, Peter?' asked Mrs Bantry.

'Well, I am, rather. It makes a change, doesn't it? I've been hunting round to see if I could find any clues, but I haven't been lucky. I've got a souvenir, though. Would you like to see it? Fancy, Mother wanted me to throw it away. I do think one's parents are rather trying sometimes.'

He produced from his pocket a small matchbox. Pushing it open, he disclosed the precious contents.

'See, *it's a finger-nail. Her finger-nail!* I'm going to label it *Finger-nail of the Murdered Woman* and take it back to school. It's a good souvenir, don't you think?'

'Where did you get it?' asked Miss Marple.

'Well, it was a bit of luck, really. Because, of course, I didn't know she was going to be murdered *then*. It was before dinner last night. Ruby caught her nail in Josie's shawl and it tore it. Mums cut it off for her and gave it to me and said put it in the wastepaper basket, and I meant to, but I put it in my pocket instead, and this morning I remembered and looked to see if it was still there and it was, so now I've got it as a souvenir.'

'Disgusting,' said Mrs Bantry.

Peter said politely: 'Oh, do you think so?'

'Got any other souvenirs?' asked Sir Henry.

'Well, I don't know. I've got something that might be.'

'Explain yourself, young man.'

Peter looked at him thoughtfully. Then he pulled out an envelope. From the inside of it he extracted a piece of browny tapey substance.

'It's a bit of that chap George Bartlett's shoe-lace,' he explained. 'I saw his shoes outside the door this morning and I bagged a bit just in case.'

'In case what?'

'In case he should be the murderer, of course. He was the last person to see her and that's always frightfully suspicious, you know. Is it nearly dinner-time, do you think? I'm frightfully hungry. It always seems such a long time between tea and dinner. Hallo, there's Uncle Hugo. I didn't know Mums had asked *him* to come down. I suppose she sent for him. She always does if she's in a jam. Here's Josie coming. Hi, Josie!'

Josephine Turner, coming along the terrace, stopped and looked rather startled to see Mrs Bantry and Miss Marple.

Mrs Bantry said pleasantly:

'How d'you do, Miss Turner. We've come to do a bit of sleuthing!'

Josie cast a guilty glance round. She said, lowering her voice:

'It's awful. Nobody knows yet. I mean, it isn't in the papers yet. I suppose everyone will be asking me questions and it's so awkward. I don't know what I ought to say.'

Her glance went rather wistfully towards Miss Marple, who said:

'Yes, it will be a very difficult situation for you, I'm afraid.'

Josie warmed to this sympathy.

'You see, Mr Prestcott said to me: "Don't talk about it." And that's all very well, but everyone is sure to ask me, and you can't offend people, can you? Mr Prestcott said he hoped I'd feel able to carry on as usual – and he wasn't very nice about it, so of course I want to do my best. And I really don't see why it should all be blamed on me.'

Sir Henry said:

'Do you mind me asking you a frank question, Miss Turner?'

'Oh, do ask me anything you like,' said Josie, a little insincerely.

'Has there been any unpleasantness between you and Mrs Jefferson and Mr Gaskell over all this?'

'Over the murder, do you mean?'

'No, I don't mean the murder.'

Josie stood twisting her fingers together. She said rather sullenly:

'Well, there has and there hasn't, if you know what I mean. Neither of them have *said* anything. But I think they blamed it on me – Mr Jefferson taking such a fancy to Ruby, I mean. It wasn't my fault, though, was it? These things happen, and I never dreamt of such a thing happening beforehand, not for a moment. I – I was quite dumbfounded.'

Her words rang out with what seemed undeniable sincerity.

Sir Henry said kindly:

'I'm quite sure you were. But once it *had* happened?'

Josie's chin went up.

'Well, it was a piece of luck, wasn't it? Everyone's got the right to have a piece of luck sometimes.'

She looked from one to the other of them in a slightly defiant questioning manner and then went on across the terrace and into the hotel.

Peter said judicially:

'I don't think *she* did it.'

Miss Marple murmured:

'It's interesting, that piece of finger-nail. It had been worrying me, you know – how to account for her nails.'

'Nails?' asked Sir Henry.

'The dead girl's nails,' explained Mrs Bantry. 'They were quite *short*, and now that Jane says so, of course it *was* a little unlikely. A girl like that usually has absolute talons.'

Miss Marple said:

'But of course if she tore one off, then she might clip the others close, so as to match. Did they find nail parings in her room, I wonder?'

Sir Henry looked at her curiously. He said:

'I'll ask Superintendent Harper when he gets back.'

'Back from where?' asked Mrs Bantry. 'He hasn't gone over to Gossington, has he?'

Sir Henry said gravely:

'No. There's been another tragedy. Blazing car in a quarry –'

Miss Marple caught her breath.

'Was there someone in the car?'

'I'm afraid so – yes.'

Miss Marple said thoughtfully:

'I expect that will be the Girl Guide who's missing – Patience – no, Pamela Reeves.'

Sir Henry stared at her.

'Now why on earth do you think that, Miss Marple?'

Miss Marple got rather pink.

'Well, it was given out on the wireless that she was missing from her home – since last night. And her home was Daneleigh Vale; that's not very far from here. And she was last seen at the Girl-Guide Rally up on Danebury Downs. That's very close indeed. In fact, she'd have to pass through Danemouth to get home. So it does rather fit in, doesn't it? I mean, it looks as though she might have seen – or perhaps heard – something that no one was supposed to see and hear. If so, of course, she'd be a source of danger to the murderer and she'd have to be – removed. Two things like that *must* be connected, don't you think?'

Sir Henry said, his voice dropping a little:

'You think – a second murder?'

'Why not?' Her quiet placid gaze met his. 'When anyone has committed one murder, they don't shrink from another, do they? Nor even from a third.'

'A third? You don't think there will be a *third* murder?'

'I think it's just possible . . . Yes, I think it's highly possible.'

'Miss Marple,' said Sir Henry, 'you frighten me. Do you know who is going to be murdered?'

Miss Marple said: 'I've a very good idea.'

CHAPTER TEN

Superintendent Harper stood looking at the charred and twisted heap of metal. A burnt-up car was always a revolting object, even without the additional gruesome burden of a charred and blackened corpse.

Venn's Quarry was a remote spot, far from any human habitation. Though actually only two miles as the crow flies from Danemouth, the approach to it was by one of those narrow, twisted, rutted roads, little more than a cart track, which led nowhere except to the quarry itself. It was a long time now since the quarry had been worked, and the only people who came along the lane were the casual visitors in search of blackberries. As a spot to dispose of a car it was ideal. The car need not have been found for weeks but for the accident of the glow in the sky having been seen by Albert Biggs, a labourer, on his way to work.

Albert Biggs was still on the scene, though all he had to tell had been heard some time ago, but he continued to repeat the thrilling story with such embellishments as occurred to him.

'Why, dang my eyes, I said, whatever be that? Proper glow it was, up in the sky. Might be a bonfire, I says, but who'd be having bonfire over to Venn's Quarry? No, I says, 'tis some mighty big fire, to be sure. But whatever would it be, I says? There's no house or farm to that direction. 'Tis over by Venn's, I says, that's where it is, to be sure. Didn't rightly know what I ought to do about it, but seeing as Constable Gregg comes along just then on his bicycle, I tells him about it. 'Twas all died down by then, but I tells him just where 'twere. 'Tis over that direction, I says. Big glare in the sky, I says. Mayhap as it's a rick, I says. One of them tramps, as likely as not, set alight of it. But I did never think as how it might be a car — far less as someone was being burnt up alive in it. 'Tis a terrible tragedy, to be sure.'

The Glenshire police had been busy. Cameras had clicked and the position of the charred body had been carefully noted before the police surgeon had started his own investigation.

The latter came over now to Harper, dusting black ash off his hands, his lips set grimly together.

'A pretty thorough job,' he said. 'Part of one foot and shoe are about all that has escaped. Personally I myself couldn't say if the body was a man's or a woman's at the moment, though we'll get some indication from the bones, I expect. But the shoe is one of the black strapped affairs – the kind schoolgirls wear.'

'There's a schoolgirl missing from the next county,' said Harper; 'quite close to here. Girl of sixteen or so.'

'Then it's probably her,' said the doctor. 'Poor kid.'

Harper said uneasily: 'She wasn't alive when –?'

'No, no, I don't think so. No signs of her having tried to get out. Body was just slumped down on the seat – with the foot sticking out. She was dead when she was put there, I should say. Then the car was set fire to in order to try and get rid of the evidence.'

He paused, and asked:

'Want me any longer?'

'I don't think so, thank you.'

'Right. I'll be off.'

He strode away to his car. Harper went over to where one of his sergeants, a man who specialized in car cases, was busy.

The latter looked up.

'Quite a clear case, sir. Petrol poured over the car and the whole thing deliberately set light to. There are three empty cans in the hedge over there.'

A little farther away another man was carefully arranging small objects picked out of the wreckage. There was a scorched black leather shoe and with it some scraps of scorched and blackened material. As Harper approached, his subordinate looked up and exclaimed:

'Look at this, sir. This seems to clinch it.'

Harper took the small object in his hand. He said:

'Button from a Girl Guide's uniform?'

'Yes, sir.'

'Yes,' said Harper, 'that does seem to settle it.'

A decent, kindly man, he felt slightly sick. First Ruby Keene and now this child, Pamela Reeves.

He said to himself, as he had said before:

'What's come to Glenshire?'

His next move was first to ring up his own Chief Constable, and afterwards to get in touch with Colonel Melchett. The disappearance of Pamela Reeves had taken place in Radfordshire though her body had been found in Glenshire.

The next task set him was not a pleasant one. He had to break the news to Pamela Reeve's father and mother . . .

II

Superintendent Harper looked up consideringly at the façade of Braeside as he rang the front door bell.

Neat little villa, nice garden of about an acre and a half. The sort of place that had been built fairly freely all over the countryside in the last twenty years. Retired Army men, retired Civil Servants – that type. Nice decent folk; the worst you could say of them was that they might be a bit dull. Spent as much money as they could afford on their children's education. Not the kind of people you associated with tragedy. And now tragedy had come to them. He sighed.

He was shown at once into a lounge where a stiff man with a grey moustache and a woman whose eyes were red with weeping both sprang up. Mrs Reeves cried out eagerly:

'You have some news of Pamela?'

Then she shrank back, as though the Superintendent's commiserating glance had been a blow.

Harper said:

'I'm afraid you must prepare yourself for bad news.'

'Pamela –' faltered the woman.

Major Reeves said sharply:

'Something's happened – to the child?'

'Yes, sir.'

'Do you mean she's dead?'

Mrs Reeves burst out:

'Oh no, no,' and broke into a storm of weeping. Major Reeves put his arm round his wife and drew her to him. His lips trembled but he looked inquiringly at Harper, who bent his head.

'An accident?'

'Not exactly, Major Reeves. She was found in a burnt-out car

94

which had been abandoned in a quarry.'

'In a car? In a quarry?'

His astonishment was evident.

Mrs Reeves broke down altogether and sank down on the sofa, sobbing violently.

Superintendent Harper said:

'If you'd like me to wait a few minutes?'

Major Reeves said sharply:

'What does this mean? Foul play?'

'That's what it looks like, sir. That's why I'd like to ask you some questions if it isn't too trying for you.'

'No, no, you're quite right. No time must be lost if what you suggest is true. But I can't believe it. Who would want to harm a child like Pamela?'

Harper said stolidly:

'You've already reported to your local police the circumstances of your daughter's disappearance. She left here to attend a Guides rally and you expected her home for supper. That is right?'

'Yes.'

'She was to return by bus?'

'Yes.'

'I understand that, according to the story of her fellow Guides, when the rally was over Pamela said she was going into Danemouth to Woolworth's, and would catch a later bus home. That strikes you as quite a normal proceeding?'

'Oh yes, Pamela was very fond of going to Woolworth's. She often went into Danemouth to shop. The bus goes from the main road, only about a quarter of a mile from here.'

'And she had no other plans, so far as you know?'

'None.'

'She was not meeting anybody in Danemouth?'

'No, I'm sure she wasn't. She would have mentioned it if so. We expected her back for supper. That's why, when it got so late and she hadn't turned up, we rang up the police. It wasn't like her not to come home.'

'Your daughter had no undesirable friends – that is, friends that you didn't approve of?'

'No, there was never any trouble of that kind.'

Mrs Reeves said tearfully:

'Pam was just a child. She was very young for her age. She liked games and all that. She wasn't precocious in any way.'

'Do you know a Mr George Bartlett who is staying at the Majestic Hotel in Danemouth?'

Major Reeves stared.

'Never heard of him.'

'You don't think your daughter knew him?'

'I'm quite sure she didn't.'

He added sharply: 'How does he come into it?'

'He's the owner of the Minoan 14 car in which your daughter's body was found.'

Mrs Reeves cried: 'But then he must —'

Harper said quickly:

'He reported his car missing early today. It was in the courtyard of the Majestic Hotel at lunch time yesterday. Anybody might have taken the car.'

'But didn't someone see who took it?'

The Superintendent shook his head.

'Dozens of cars going in and out all day. And a Minoan 14 is one of the commonest makes.'

Mrs Reeves cried:

'But aren't you doing something? Aren't you trying to find the — the devil who did this? My little girl — oh, my little girl! She wasn't burnt alive, was she? Oh, Pam, Pam . . . !'

'She didn't suffer, Mrs Reeves. I assure you she was already dead when the car was set alight.'

Reeves asked stiffly:

'How was she killed?'

Harper gave him a significant glance.

'We don't know. The fire had destroyed all evidence of that kind.'

He turned to the distraught woman on the sofa.

'Believe me, Mrs Reeves, we're doing everything we can. It's a matter of checking up. Sooner or later we shall find someone who saw your daughter in Danemouth yesterday, and saw whom she was with. It all takes time, you know. We shall have dozens, hundreds of reports coming in about a Girl Guide who was seen here, there, and everywhere. It's a matter of selection and of patience — but we shall find out the truth in the end, never you fear.'

Mrs Reeves asked:

'Where — where is she? Can I go to her?'

Again Superintendent Harper caught the husband's eye. He said:

'The medical officer is attending to all that. I'd suggest that your husband comes with me now and attends to all the formalities. In the meantime, try and recollect anything Pamela may have said — something, perhaps, that you didn't pay attention to at the time but which might throw some light upon things. You know what I mean — just some chance word or phrase. That's the best way you can help us.'

As the two men went towards the door, Reeves said, pointing to a photograph:

'There she is.'

Harper looked at it attentively. It was a hockey group. Reeves pointed out Pamela in the centre of the team.

'A nice kid,' Harper thought, as he looked at the earnest face of the pigtailed girl.

His mouth set in a grim line as he thought of the charred body in the car.

He vowed to himself that the murder of Pamela Reeves should not remain one of Glenshire's unsolved mysteries.

Ruby Keene, so he admitted privately, might have asked for what was coming to her, but Pamela Reeves was quite another story. A nice kid, if he ever saw one. He'd not rest until he'd hunted down the man or woman who'd killed her.

CHAPTER ELEVEN

A day or two later Colonel Melchett and Superintendent Harper looked at each other across the former's big desk. Harper had come over to Much Benham for a consultation.

Melchett said gloomily:

'Well, we know where we are — or rather where we aren't!'

'Where we aren't expresses it better, sir.'

'We've got two deaths to take into account,' said Melchett. 'Two murders. Ruby Keene and the child Pamela Reeves. Not much to identify her by, poor kid, but enough. That shoe that escaped burning has been identified positively as hers by her father, and there's this button from her Girl Guide uniform. A fiendish business, Superintendent.'

Superintendent Harper said very quietly:

'I'll say you're right, sir.'

'I'm glad it's quite certain she was dead before the car was set on fire. The way she was lying, thrown across the seat, shows that. Probably knocked on the head, poor kid.'

'Or strangled, perhaps,' said Harper.

Melchett looked at him sharply.

'You think so?'

'Well, sir, there are murderers like that.'

'I know. I've seen the parents – the poor girl's mother's beside herself. Damned painful, the whole thing. The point for us to settle is – are the two murders connected?'

'I'd say definitely yes.'

'So would I.'

The Superintendent ticked off the points on his fingers.

'Pamela Reeves attended rally of Girl Guides on Danebury Downs. Stated by companions to be normal and cheerful. Did not return with three companions by the bus to Medchester. Said to them that she was going into Danemouth to Woolworth's and would take the bus home from there. The main road into Danemouth from the downs does a big round inland. Pamela Reeves took a short-cut over two fields and a footpath and lane which would bring her into Danemouth near the Majestic Hotel. The lane, in fact, actually passes the hotel on the west side. It's possible, therefore, that she overheard or saw something – something concerning Ruby Keene – which would have proved dangerous to the murderer – say, for instance, that she heard him arranging to meet Ruby Keene at eleven that evening. He realizes that this schoolgirl has overheard, and he has to silence her.'

Colonel Melchett said:

'That's presuming, Harper, that the Ruby Keene crime was premeditated – not spontaneous.'

Superintendent Harper agreed.

'I believe it was, sir. It looks as though it would be the other way – sudden violence, a fit of passion or jealousy – but I'm beginning to think that that's not so. I don't see otherwise how you can account for the death of the Reeves child. If she was a witness of the actual crime, it would be late at night, round about eleven p.m., and what would she be doing round about the Majestic at that time? Why, at nine o'clock her parents were getting anxious because she hadn't returned.'

'The alternative is that she went to meet someone in Danemouth unknown to her family and friends, and that her death is quite unconnected with the other death.'

'Yes, sir, and I don't believe that's so. Look how even the old lady, old Miss Marple, tumbled to it at once that there was a connection. She asked at once if the body in the burnt car was the body of the missing Girl Guide. Very smart old lady, that. These old ladies are sometimes. Shrewd, you know. Put their fingers on the vital spot.'

'Miss Marple has done that more than once,' said Colonel Melchett dryly.

'And besides, sir, there's the car. That seems to me to link up her death definitely with the Majestic Hotel. It was Mr George Bartlett's car.'

Again the eyes of the two men met. Melchett said:

'George Bartlett? Could be! What do you think?'

Again Harper methodically recited various points.

'Ruby Keene was last seen with George Bartlett. He says she went to her room (borne out by the dress she was wearing being found there), but did she go to her room and change *in order to go out with him*? Had they made a date to go out together earlier – discussed it, say, before dinner, and did Pamela Reeves happen to overhear?'

Melchett said: 'He didn't report the loss of his car until the following morning, and he was extremely vague about it then, pretended he couldn't remember exactly when he had last noticed it.'

'That might be cleverness, sir. As I see it, he's either a very clever gentleman pretending to be a silly ass, or else – well, he is a silly ass.'

'What we want,' said Melchett, 'is motive. As it stands, he had no motive whatever for killing Ruby Keene.'

'Yes – that's where we're stuck every time. Motive. All the reports from the Palais de Danse at Brixwell are negative, I understand?'

'Absolutely! Ruby Keene had no special boy friend. Slack's been into the matter thoroughly – give Slack his due, he *is* thorough.'

'That's right, sir. Thorough's the word.'

'If there was anything to ferret out, he'd have ferreted it out. But there's nothing there. He got a list of her most frequent dancing partners – all vetted and found correct. Harmless fellows, and all able to produce alibis for that night.'

'Ah,' said Superintendent Harper. 'Alibis. That's what we're up against.'

Melchett looked at him sharply. 'Think so? I've left that side of the investigation to you.'

'Yes, sir. It's been gone into – very thoroughly. We applied to London for help over it.'

'Well?'

'Mr Conway Jefferson may think that Mr Gaskell and young Mrs Jefferson are comfortably off, but that is not the case. They're both extremely hard up.'

'Is that true?'

'Quite true, sir. It's as Mr Conway Jefferson said, he made over considerable sums of money to his son and daughter when they married. That was over ten years ago, though. Mr Jefferson fancied himself as knowing good investments. He didn't invest in anything absolutely wild cat, but he was unlucky and showed poor judgment more than once. His holdings have gone steadily down. I should say the widow found it difficult to make both ends meet and send her son to a good school.'

'But she hasn't applied to her father-in-law for help?'

'No, sir. As far as I can make out she lives with him, and consequently has no household expenses.'

'And his health is such that he wasn't expected to live long?'

'That's right, sir. Now for Mr Mark Gaskell. He's a gambler, pure and simple. Got through his wife's money very soon. Has got himself tangled up rather critically just at present. He needs money badly – and a good deal of it.'

'Can't say I liked the looks of him much,' said Colonel Melchett. 'Wild-looking sort of fellow – what? And he's got a motive all right. Twenty-five thousand pounds it meant to him getting that girl out of the way. Yes, it's a motive all right.'

'They both had a motive.'

'I'm not considering Mrs Jefferson.'

'No, sir, I know you're not. And, anyway, the alibi holds for both of them. They *couldn't* have done it. Just that.'

'You've got a detailed statement of their movements that evening?'

'Yes, I have. Take Mr Gaskell first. He dined with his father-in-law and Mrs Jefferson, had coffee with them afterwards when Ruby Keene joined them. Then he said he had to write letters and left them. Actually he took his car and went for a spin down to the front. He told me quite frankly he couldn't stick playing bridge for a whole evening. The old boy's mad on it. So he made letters an excuse. Ruby Keene remained with the others. Mark Gaskell returned when she was dancing with Raymond. After the dance Ruby came and had a drink with them, then she went off with young Bartlett, and Gaskell and the others cut for partners and started their bridge. That was at twenty minutes to eleven – and he didn't leave the table until after midnight. That's quite certain, sir. Everyone says so. The family, the waiters, everyone. Therefore *he* couldn't have done it. And Mrs Jefferson's alibi is the same. She, too, didn't leave the table. They're out, both of them – out.'

Colonel Melchett leaned back, tapping the table with a paper cutter.

Superintendent Harper said:

'That is, assuming the girl was killed before midnight.'

'Haydock said she was. He's a very sound fellow in police work. If he says a thing, it's so.'

'There might be reasons – health, physical idiosyncrasy, or something.'

'I'll put it to him.' Melchett glanced at his watch, picked up the telephone receiver and asked for a number. He said: 'Haydock ought to be at home at this time. Now, assuming that she was killed *after* midnight?'

Harper said:

'Then there might be a chance. There was some coming and going afterwards. Let's assume that Gaskell had asked the girl to meet him outside somewhere – say at twenty past twelve. He slips away for a minute or two, strangles her, comes back and disposes of the body later – in the early hours of the morning.'

Melchett said:

'Takes her by car thirty-odd miles to put her in Bantry's library? Dash it all, it's not a likely story.'

'No, it isn't,' the Superintendent admitted at once.

The telephone rang. Melchett picked up the receiver.

'Hallo, Haydock, is that you? Ruby Keene. Would it be possible for her to have been killed *after* midnight?'

'I told you she was killed between ten and midnight.'

'Yes, I know, but one could stretch it a bit – what?'

'No, you couldn't stretch it. When I say she was killed before midnight I mean before midnight, and don't try to tamper with the medical evidence.'

'Yes, but couldn't there be some physiological whatnot? You know what I mean.'

'I know that you don't know what you're talking about. The girl was perfectly healthy and not abnormal in any way – and I'm not going to say she was just to help you fit a rope round the neck of some wretched fellow whom you police wallahs have got your knife into. Now don't protest. I know your ways. And, by the way, the girl wasn't strangled willingly – that is to say, she was drugged first. Powerful narcotic. She died of strangulation but she was drugged first.' Haydock rang off.

Melchett said gloomily: 'Well, that's that.'

Harper said:

'Thought I'd found another likely starter – but it petered out.'

'What's that? Who?'

'Strictly speaking, he's your pigeon, sir. Name of Basil Blake. Lives near Gossington Hall.'

'Impudent young jackanapes!' The Colonel's brow darkened as he remembered Basil Blake's outrageous rudeness. 'How's he mixed up in it?'

'Seems he knew Ruby Keene. Dined over at the Majestic quite often – danced with the girl. Do you remember what Josie said to Raymond when Ruby was discovered to be missing? "She's not with that film fellow, is she?" I've found out it was Blake, she meant. He's employed with the Lemville Studios, you know. Josie has nothing to go upon except a belief that Ruby was rather keen on him.'

'Very promising, Harper, very promising.'

'Not so good as it sounds, sir. Basil Blake was at a party at the studios that night. You know the sort of thing. Starts at eight with cocktails and goes on and on until the air's too thick to see through and everyone passes out. According to Inspector Slack, who's questioned him, he left the show round about midnight. At midnight Ruby Keene was dead.'

'Anyone bear out his statement?'

'Most of them, I gather, sir, were rather – er – far gone. The – er – young woman now at the bungalow – Miss Dinah Lee – says his statement is correct.'

'Doesn't mean a thing!'

'No, sir, probably not. Statements taken from other members of the party bear Mr Blake's statement out on the whole, though ideas as to time are somewhat vague.'

'Where are these studios?'

'Lemville, sir, thirty miles south-west of London.'

'H'm – about the same distance from here?'

'Yes, sir.'

Colonel Melchett rubbed his nose. He said in a rather dissatisfied tone:

'Well, it looks as though we could wash him out.'

'I think so, sir. There is no evidence that he was seriously attracted by Ruby Keene. In fact' – Superintendent Harper coughed primly – 'he seems fully occupied with his own young lady.'

Melchett said:

'Well, we are left with "X," an unknown murderer – so unknown Slack can't find a trace of him! Or Jefferson's son-in-law, who might have wanted to kill the girl – but didn't have a chance to do so. Daughter-in-law ditto. Or George Bartlett, who has no alibi – but unfortunately no motive either. Or with young Blake, who has an alibi and no motive. And that's the lot! No, stop, I suppose we ought to consider the dancing fellow – Raymond Starr. After all, he saw a lot of the girl.'

Harper said slowly:

'Can't believe he took much interest in her – or else he's a thundering good actor. And, for all practical purposes, he's got an alibi too. He was more or less in view from twenty minutes to eleven until midnight, dancing with various partners. I don't see that we can make a case against him.'

'In fact,' said Colonel Melchett, 'we can't make a case against anybody.'

'George Bartlett's our best hope. If we could only hit on a motive.'

'You've had him looked up?'

'Yes, sir. Only child. Coddled by his mother. Came into a good deal of money on her death a year ago. Getting through it fast. Weak rather than vicious.'

'May be mental,' said Melchett hopefully.

Superintendent Harper nodded. He said:

'Has it struck you, sir – that that may be the explanation of the whole case?'

'Criminal lunatic, you mean?'

'Yes, sir. One of those fellows who go about strangling young girls. Doctors have a long name for it.'

'That would solve all our difficulties,' said Melchett.

'There's only one thing I don't like about it,' said Superintendent Harper.

'What?'

'It's too easy.'

'H'm – yes – perhaps. So, as I said at the beginning where are we?'

'Nowhere, sir,' said Superintendent Harper.

CHAPTER TWELVE

Conway Jefferson stirred in his sleep and stretched. His arms were flung out, long, powerful arms into which all the strength of his body seemed to be concentrated since his accident.

Through the curtains the morning light glowed softly.

Conway Jefferson smiled to himself. Always, after a night of rest, he woke like this, happy, refreshed, his deep vitality renewed. Another day!

So for a minute he lay. Then he pressed the special bell by his hand. And suddenly a wave of remembrance swept over him.

Even as Edwards, deft and quiet-footed, entered the room, a groan was wrung from his master.

Edwards paused with his hand on the curtains. He said: 'You're not in pain, sir?'

Conway Jefferson said harshly:

'No. Go on, pull 'em.'

The clear light flooded the room. Edwards, understanding, did not glance at his master.

His face grim, Conway Jefferson lay remembering and thinking. Before his eyes he saw again the pretty, vapid face of Ruby. Only in his mind he did not use the adjective vapid. Last night he would have said innocent. A naïve, innocent child! And now?

A great weariness came over Conway Jefferson. He closed his eyes. He murmured below his breath:

'Margaret . . .'

It was the name of his dead wife . . .

II

'I like your friend,' said Adelaide Jefferson to Mrs Bantry.

The two women were sitting on the terrace.

'Jane Marple's a very remarkable woman,' said Mrs Bantry.

'She's nice too,' said Addie, smiling.

'People call her a scandalmonger,' said Mrs Bantry, 'but she isn't really.'

'Just a low opinion of human nature?'

'You could call it that.'

'It's rather refreshing,' said Adelaide Jefferson, 'after having had too much of the other thing.'

Mrs Bantry looked at her sharply.

Addie explained herself.

'So much high-thinking – idealization of an unworthy object!'

'You mean Ruby Keene?'

Addie nodded.

'I don't want to be horrid about her. There wasn't any harm in her. Poor little rat, she had to fight for what she wanted. She wasn't bad. Common and rather silly and quite good-natured, but a decided little gold-digger. I don't think she schemed or planned. It was just that she was quick to take advantage of a possibility. And she knew just how to appeal to an elderly man who was – lonely.'

'I suppose,' said Mrs Bantry thoughtfully, 'that Conway *was* lonely?'

Addie moved restlessly. She said:

'He was – this summer.' She paused and then burst out: 'Mark will have it that it was all my fault. Perhaps it was, I don't know.'

She was silent for a minute, then, impelled by some need to talk, she went on speaking in a difficult, almost reluctant way.

'I – I've had such an odd sort of life. Mike Carmody, my first husband, died so soon after we were married – it – it knocked me out. Peter, as you know, was born after his death. Frank Jefferson was Mike's great friend. So I came to see a lot of him. He was Peter's godfather – Mike had wanted that. I got very fond of him – and – oh! sorry for him too.'

'Sorry?' queried Mrs Bantry with interest.

'Yes, just that. It sounds odd. Frank had always had everything he wanted. His father and his mother couldn't have been nicer to him. And yet – how can I say it? – you see, old Mr Jefferson's personality is so strong. If you live with it, you can't somehow have a personality of your own. Frank felt that.

'When we were married he was very happy – wonderfully so. Mr Jefferson was very generous. He settled a large sum of money on Frank – said he wanted his children to be independent and not have to wait for his death. It was so nice of him – so generous. But it was much too sudden. He ought really to have accustomed Frank to independence little by little.

'It went to Frank's head. He wanted to be as good a man as his father, as clever about money and business, as far-seeing and successful. And, of course, he wasn't. He didn't exactly speculate with the money, but he invested in the wrong things at the wrong time. It's frightening, you know, how soon money goes if you're not clever about it. The more Frank dropped, the more eager he was to get it back by some clever deal. So things went from bad to worse.'

'But, my dear,' said Mrs Bantry, 'couldn't Conway have advised him?'

'He didn't want to be advised. The one thing he wanted was to do well on his own. That's why we never let Mr Jefferson know. When Frank died there was very little left – only a tiny income for me. And I – I didn't let his father know either. You see –'

She turned abruptly.

'It would have felt like betraying Frank to him. Frank would have hated it so. Mr Jefferson was ill for a long time. When he got well he assumed that I was a very well-off widow. I've never undeceived him. It's been a point of honour. He knows I'm very careful about money – but he approves of that, thinks I'm a thrifty sort of woman. And, of course, Peter and I have lived with him practically ever since, and he's paid for all our living expenses. So I've never had to worry.'

She said slowly:

'We've been like a family all these years – only – only – you see (or don't you see?) I've never been Frank's *widow* to him – I've been Frank's *wife*.'

Mrs Bantry grasped the implication.

'You mean he's never accepted their deaths?'

'No. He's been wonderful. But he's conquered his own terrible tragedy by refusing to recognize death. Mark is Rosamund's husband and I'm Frank's wife – and though Frank and Rosamund aren't exactly here with us – they are still existent.'

Mrs Bantry said softly:

'It's a wonderful triumph of faith.'

'I know. We've gone on, year after year. But suddenly – this summer – something went wrong in me. I felt – I felt rebellious. It's an awful thing to say, but I didn't want to think of Frank any more! All that was over – my love and companionship with him, and my grief when he died. It was something that had been and wasn't any longer.

'It's awfully hard to describe. It's like wanting to wipe the slate clean and start again. I wanted to be me – Addie, still reasonably young and strong and able to play games and swim and dance – just a *person*. Even Hugo – (you know Hugo McLean?) he's a dear and wants to marry me, but, of course, I've never really thought of it – but this summer I *did* begin to think of it – not seriously – only vaguely . . .'

She stopped and shook her head.

'And so I suppose it's true. I *neglected Jeff*. I don't mean *really* neglected him, but my mind and thoughts weren't with him. When Ruby, as I saw, amused him, I was rather glad. It left me freer to go and do my own things. I never dreamed – of course I never dreamed – that he would be so – so – *infatuated* by her!'

Mrs Bantry asked:

'And when you did find out?'

'I was dumbfounded – absolutely dumbfounded! And, I'm afraid, angry too.'

'*I*'d have been angry,' said Mrs Bantry.

'There was Peter, you see. Peter's whole future depends on Jeff. Jeff practically looked on him as a grandson, or so I thought, but, of course, he wasn't a grandson. He was no relation at all. And to think that he was going to be – disinherited!' Her firm, well-shaped hands shook a little where they lay in her lap. 'For that's what it felt like – and for a vulgar, gold-digging little simpleton – Oh! I could have killed her!'

She stopped, stricken. Her beautiful hazel eyes met Mrs Bantry's in a pleading horror. She said:

'*What an awful thing to say!*'

Hugo McLean, coming quietly up behind them, asked:

'What's an awful thing to say?'

'Sit down, Hugo. You know Mrs Bantry, don't you?'

McLean had already greeted the older lady. He said now in a low, persevering way:

'What was an awful thing to say?'

Addie Jefferson said:

'That I'd like to have killed Ruby Keene.'

Hugo McLean reflected a minute or two. Then he said:

'No, I wouldn't say that if I were you. Might be misunderstood.'

His eyes – steady, reflective, grey eyes – looked at her meaningly. He said:

'*You've got to watch your step, Addie.*'

There was a warning in his voice.

III

When Miss Marple came out of the hotel and joined Mrs Bantry a few minutes later, Hugo McLean and Adelaide Jefferson were walking down the path to the sea together.

Seating herself, Miss Marple remarked:

'He seems very devoted.'

'He's been devoted for years! One of those men.'

'I know. Like Major Bury. He hung round an Anglo-Indian widow for quite ten years. A joke among her friends! In the end she gave in – but unfortunately ten days before they were to have been married she ran away with the chauffeur! Such a nice woman, too, and usually so well balanced.'

'People do do very odd things,' agreed Mrs Bantry. 'I wish you'd been here just now, Jane. Addie Jefferson was telling me all about herself – how her husband went through all his money but they never let Mr Jefferson know. And then, this summer, things felt different to her –'

Miss Marple nodded.

'Yes. She rebelled, I suppose, against being made to live in the past? After all, there's a time for everything. You can't sit in the house with the blinds down for ever. I suppose Mrs Jefferson just pulled them up and took off her widow's weeds, and her father-in-law, of course, didn't like it. Felt left out in the cold, though I don't suppose for a minute he realized who put her up to it. Still, he certainly wouldn't like it. And so, of course, like old Mr Badger when his wife took up Spiritualism, he was just ripe for what happened. Any fairly nice-looking young girl who listened prettily would have done.'

'Do you think,' said Mrs Bantry, 'that that cousin, Josie, got her down here deliberately – that it was a family plot?'

Miss Marple shook her head.

'No, I don't think so at all. I don't think Josie has the kind of mind that could foresee people's reactions. She's rather dense in that way. She's got one of those shrewd, limited, practical minds that never do foresee the future and are usually astonished by it.'

'It seems to have taken everyone by surprise,' said Mrs Bantry. 'Addie – and Mark Gaskell too, apparently.'

Miss Marple smiled.

'I dare say he had his own fish to fry. A bold fellow with a roving eye! Not the man to go on being a sorrowing widower for years, no matter how fond he may have been of his wife. I should think they were both restless under old Mr Jefferson's yoke of perpetual remembrance.

'Only,' added Miss Marple cynically, 'it's easier for gentlemen, of course.'

At that very moment Mark was confirming this judgment on himself in a talk with Sir Henry Clithering.

With characteristic candour Mark had gone straight to the heart of things.

'It's just dawned on me,' he said, 'that I'm Favourite Suspect No. I to the police! They've been delving into my financial troubles. I'm broke, you know, or very nearly. If dear old Jeff dies according to schedule in a month or two, and Addie and I divide the dibs also according to schedule, all will be well. Matter of fact, I owe rather a lot . . . If the crash comes it will be a big one! If I can stave it off, it will be the other way round – I shall come out on top and be a very rich man.'

Sir Henry Clithering said:

'You're a gambler, Mark.'

'Always have been. Risk everything – that's my motto! Yes, it's a lucky thing for me that somebody strangled that poor kid. I didn't do it. I'm not a strangler. I don't really think I could ever murder anybody. I'm too easygoing. But I don't suppose I can ask the police to believe *that*! I must look to them like the answer to the criminal investigator's prayer! I had a motive, was on the spot, I am not burdened with high moral scruples! I can't imagine why I'm not in the jug already! That Superintendent's got a very nasty eye.'

'You've got that useful thing, an alibi.'

'An alibi is the fishiest thing on God's earth! No innocent person ever has an alibi! Besides, it all depends on the time of death, or something like that, and you may be sure if three doctors say the girl was killed at midnight, at least six will be found who will swear positively that she was killed at five in the morning – and where's my alibi then?'

'At any rate, you are able to joke about it.'

'Damned bad taste, isn't it?' said Mark cheerfully. 'Actually, I'm rather scared. One is – with murder! And don't think I'm not sorry for old Jeff. I am. But it's better this way – bad as the shock was – than if he'd found her out.'

'What do you mean, found her out?'

Mark winked.

'Where did she go off to last night? I'll lay you any odds you like she went to meet a man. Jeff wouldn't have liked that. He wouldn't have liked it at all. If he'd found she was deceiving him – that she wasn't the prattling little innocent she seemed – well – my father-in-law is an odd man. He's a man of great self-control, but that self-control can snap. And then – look out!'

Sir Henry glanced at him curiously.

'Are you fond of him or not?'

'I'm very fond of him – and at the same time I resent him. I'll try and explain. Conway Jefferson is a man who likes to control his surroundings. He's a benevolent despot, kind, generous, and affectionate – but his is the tune, and the others dance to his piping.'

Mark Gaskell paused.

'I loved my wife. I shall never feel the same for anyone else. Rosamund was sunshine and laughter and flowers, and when she was killed I felt just like a man in the ring who's had a knock-out blow. But the referee's been counting a good long time now. I'm a man, after all. I like women. I don't want to marry again – not in the least. Well, that's all right. I've had to be discreet – but I've had my good times all right. Poor Addie hasn't. Addie's a really nice woman. She's the kind of woman men want to marry, not to sleep with. Give her half a chance and she would marry again – and be very happy and make the chap happy too. But old Jeff saw her always as Frank's wife – and hypnotized her into seeing herself like that. He doesn't know it, but we've been in prison. I broke out, on the quiet, a long time ago. Addie broke out this summer – and it gave him a shock. It split up his world. Result – Ruby Keene.'

Irrepressibly he sang:

> 'But she is in her grave, and, oh,
> The difference to me!

'Come and have a drink, Clithering.'

It was hardly surprizing, Sir Henry reflected, that Mark Gaskell should be an object of suspicion to the police.

CHAPTER THIRTEEN

Dr Metcalf was one of the best-known physicians in Danemouth. He had no aggressive bedside manner, but his presence in the sick room had an invariably cheering effect. He was middle-aged, with a quiet pleasant voice.

He listened carefully to Superintendent Harper and replied to his questions with gentle precision.

Harper said:

'Then I can take it, Doctor Metcalf, that what I was told by Mrs Jefferson was substantially correct?'

'Yes, Mr Jefferson's health is in a precarious state. For several years now the man has been driving himself ruthlessly. In his determination to live like other men, he has lived at a far greater pace than the normal man of his age. He has refused to rest, to take things easy, to go slow – or any of the other phrases with which I and his other medical advisers have tendered our opinion. The result is that the man is an overworked engine. Heart, lungs, blood pressure – they're all overstrained.'

'You say Mr Jefferson has absolutely refused to listen?'

'Yes. I don't know that I blame him. It's not what I say to my patients, Superintendent, but a man may as well wear out as rust out. A lot of my colleagues do that, and take it from me it's not a bad way. In a place like Danemouth one sees most of the other thing: invalids clinging to life, terrified of over-exerting themselves, terrified of a breath of draughty air, of a stray germ, of an injudicious meal!'

'I expect that's true enough,' said Superintendent Harper. 'What it amounts to, then, is this: Conway Jefferson is strong enough, physically speaking – or, I suppose I mean, muscularly speaking. Just what can he do in the active line, by the way?'

'He has immense strength in his arms and shoulders. He was a powerful man before his accident. He is extremely dexterous in his handling of his wheeled chair, and with the aid of crutches he can move himself about a room – from his bed to the chair, for instance.'

'Isn't it possible for a man injured as Mr Jefferson was to have artificial legs?'

'Not in his case. There was a spine injury.'

'I see. Let me sum up again. Jefferson is strong and fit in the muscular sense. He feels well and all that?'

Metcalf nodded.

'But his heart is in a bad condition. Any overstrain or exertion, or a shock or a sudden fright, and he might pop off. Is that it?'

'More or less. Over-exertion is killing him slowly, because he won't give in when he feels tired. That aggravates the cardiac condition. It is unlikely that exertion would kill him suddenly. But a sudden shock or fright might easily do so. That is why I expressly warned his family.'

Superintendent Harper said slowly:

'But in actual fact a shock *didn't* kill him. I mean, doctor, that there couldn't have been a much worse shock than this business, and he's still alive?'

Dr Metcalf shrugged his shoulders.

'I know. But if you'd had my experience, Superintendent, you'd know that case history shows the impossibility of prognosticating accurately. People who *ought* to die of shock and exposure *don't* die of shock and exposure, etc., etc. The human frame is tougher than one can imagine possible. Moreover, in my experience, a *physical* shock is more often fatal than a *mental* shock. In plain language, a door banging suddenly would be more likely to kill Mr Jefferson than the discovery that a girl he was fond of had died in a particularly horrible manner.'

'Why is that, I wonder?'

'The breaking of a piece of bad news nearly always sets up a defence reaction. It numbs the recipient. They are unable – at first – to take it in. Full realization takes a little time. But the banged door, someone jumping out of a cupboard, the sudden onslaught of a motor as you cross a road – all those things are immediate in their action. The heart gives a terrified leap – to put it in layman's language.'

Superintendent Harper said slowly:

'But as far as anyone would know, Mr Jefferson's death might easily have been caused by the shock of the girl's death?'

'Oh, easily.' The doctor looked curiously at the other. 'You don't think –'

'I don't know what I think,' said Superintendent Harper vexedly.

II

'But you'll admit, sir, that the two things would fit in very prettily together,' he said a little later to Sir Henry Clithering. 'Kill two birds with one stone. First the girl – and the fact of her death takes off Mr Jefferson too – before he's had any opportunity of altering his will.'

'Do you think he will alter it?'

'You'd be more likely to know that, sir, than I would. What do you say?'

'I don't know. Before Ruby Keene came on the scene I happen to know that he had left his money between Mark Gaskell and Mrs Jefferson. I don't see why he should now change his mind about that. But of course he might do so. Might leave it to a Cats' Home, or to subsidize young professional dancers.'

Superintendent Harper agreed.

'You never know what bee a man is going to get in his bonnet – especially when he doesn't feel there's any moral obligation in the disposal of his fortune. No blood relations in this case.'

Sir Henry said:

'He is fond of the boy – of young Peter.'

'D'you think he regards him as a grandson? You'd know that better than I would, sir.'

Sir Henry said slowly:

'No, I don't think so.'

'There's another thing I'd like to ask you, sir. It's a thing I can't judge for myself. But they're friends of yours and so you'd know. I'd like very much to know just how fond Mr Jefferson is of Mr Gaskell and young Mrs Jefferson.'

Sir Henry frowned.

'I'm not sure if I understand you, Superintendent?'

'Well, it's this way, sir. How fond is he of them as *persons* – apart from his relationship to them?'

'Ah, I see what you mean.'

'Yes, sir. Nobody doubts that he was very attached to them both

– but he was attached to them, as I see it, because they were, respectively, the husband and the wife of his daughter and his son. But supposing, for instance, one of them had married again?'

Sir Henry reflected. He said:

'It's an interesting point you raise there. I don't know. I'm inclined to suspect – this is a mere opinion – that it would have altered his attitude a good deal. He would have wished them well, borne no rancour, but I think, yes, I rather think that he would have taken very little more interest in them.'

'In both cases, sir?'

'I think so, yes. In Mr Gaskell's, almost certainly, and I rather think in Mrs Jefferson's also, but that's not nearly so certain. I think he *was* fond of her for her own sake.'

'Sex would have something to do with that,' said Superintendent Harper sapiently. 'Easier for him to look on her as a daughter than to look on Mr Gaskell as a son. It works both ways. Women accept a son-in-law as one of the family easily enough, but there aren't many times when a woman looks on her son's wife as a daughter.'

Superintendent Harper went on:

'Mind if we walk along this path, sir, to the tennis court? I see Miss Marple's sitting there. I want to ask her to do something for me. As a matter of fact I want to rope you both in.'

'In what way, Superintendent?'

'To get at stuff that I can't get at myself. I want you to tackle Edwards for me, sir.'

'Edwards? What do you want from him?'

'Everything you can think of! Everything he knows and what he thinks! About the relations between the various members of the family, his angle on the Ruby Keene business. Inside stuff. He knows better than anyone the state of affairs – you bet he does! And he wouldn't tell *me*. But he'll tell *you*. And something *might* turn up from it. That is, of course, if you don't object?'

Sir Henry said grimly:

'I don't object. I've been sent for, urgently, to get at the truth. I mean to do my utmost.'

He added:

'How do you want Miss Marple to help you?'

'With some girls. Some of those Girl Guides. We've rounded up half a dozen or so, the ones who were most friendly with Pamela

Reeves. It's possible that they may know something. You see, I've been thinking. It seems to me that if that girl was really going to Woolworth's she would have tried to persuade one of the other girls to go with her. Girls usually like to shop with someone.'

'Yes, I think that's true.'

'So I think it's possible that Woolworth's was only an excuse. I want to know where the girl was really going. She may have let slip something. If so, I feel Miss Marple's the person to get it out of these girls. I'd say she knows a thing or two about girls – more than I do. And, anyway, they'd be scared of the police.'

'It sounds to me the kind of village domestic problem that is right up Miss Marple's street. She's very sharp, you know.'

The Superintendent smiled. He said:

'I'll say you're right. Nothing much gets past her.'

Miss Marple looked up at their approach and welcomed them eagerly. She listened to the Superintendent's request and at once acquiesced.

'I should like to help you very much, Superintendent, and I think that perhaps I *could* be of some use. What with the Sunday School, you know, and the Brownies, and our Guides, and the Orphanage quite near – I'm on the committee, you know, and often run in to have a little talk with Matron – and then *servants* – I usually have very young maids. Oh, yes, I've quite a lot of experience in when a girl is speaking the truth and when she is holding something back.'

'In fact, you're an expert,' said Sir Henry.

Miss Marple flashed him a reproachful glance and said:

'Oh, *please* don't laugh at me, Sir Henry.'

'I shouldn't dream of laughing at you. You've had the laugh of me too many times.'

'One does see so much evil in a village,' murmured Miss Marple in an explanatory voice.

'By the way,' said Sir Henry, 'I've cleared up one point you asked me about. The Superintendent tells me that there were nail clippings in Ruby's wastepaper basket.'

Miss Marple said thoughtfully:

'There were? Then that's that . . .'

'Why did you want to know, Miss Marple?' asked the Superintendent.

116

Miss Marple said:

'It was one of the things that – well, that seemed *wrong* when I looked at the body. The hands were wrong, somehow, and I couldn't at first think *why*. Then I realized that girls who are very much made-up, and all that, usually have very long finger-nails. Of course, I know that girls everywhere do bite their nails – it's one of those habits that are very hard to break oneself of. But vanity often does a lot to help. Still, I presumed that this girl *hadn't* cured herself. And then the little boy – Peter, you know – he said something which showed that her nails *had* been long, only she caught one and broke it. So then, of course, she might have trimmed off the rest to make an even appearance, and I asked about clippings and Sir Henry said he'd find out.'

Sir Henry remarked:

'You said just now, "*one* of the things that seemed wrong when you looked at the body." Was there something else?'

Miss Marple nodded vigorously.

'Oh yes!' she said. 'There was the dress. The dress was *all* wrong.'

Both men looked at her curiously.

'Now why?' said Sir Henry.

'Well, you see, it was an old dress. Josie said so, definitely, and I could see for myself that it was shabby and rather worn. Now that's all wrong.'

'I don't see why.'

Miss Marple got a little pink.

'Well, the idea is, isn't it, that Ruby Keene changed her dress and went off to meet someone on whom she presumably had what my young nephews call a "crush"?'

The Superintendent's eyes twinkled a little.

'That's the theory. She'd got a date with someone – a boy friend, as the saying goes.'

'Then why,' demanded Miss Marple, 'was she wearing an old dress?'

The Superintendent scratched his head thoughtfully. He said:

'I see your point. You think she'd wear a new one?'

'I think she'd wear her best dress. Girls do.'

Sir Henry interposed.

'Yes, but look here, Miss Marple. Suppose she was going outside to this *rendezvous*. Going in an open car, perhaps, or walking in some rough going. Then she'd not want to risk messing a new frock and she'd put on an old one.'

'That would be the sensible thing to do,' agreed the Superintendent.

Miss Marple turned on him. She spoke with animation.

'The sensible thing to do would be to change into trousers and a pullover, or into tweeds. That, of course (I don't want to be snobbish, but I'm afraid it's unavoidable), that's what a girl of – of our class would do.

'A well-bred girl,' continued Miss Marple, warming to her subject, 'is always very particular to wear the right clothes for the right occasion. I mean, however hot the day was, a well-bred girl would never turn up at a point-to-point in a silk flowered frock.'

'And the correct wear to meet a lover?' demanded Sir Henry.

'If she were meeting him inside the hotel or somewhere where evening dress was worn, she'd wear her best evening frock, of course – but *outside* she'd feel she'd look ridiculous in evening dress and she'd wear her most attractive sportswear.'

'Granted, Fashion Queen, but the girl Ruby –'

Miss Marple said:

'Ruby, of course, wasn't – well, to put it bluntly – Ruby *wasn't* a lady. She belonged to the class that wear their best clothes however unsuitable to the occasion. Last year, you know, we had a picnic outing at Scrantor Rocks. You'd be surprised at the unsuitable clothes the girls wore. Foulard dresses and patent shoes and quite elaborate hats, some of them. For climbing about over rocks and in gorse and heather. And the young men in their best suits. Of course, hiking's different again. That's practically a uniform – and girls don't seem to realize that shorts are very unbecoming unless they are very slender.'

The Superintendent said slowly:

'And you think that Ruby Keene –?'

'I think that she'd have kept on the frock she was wearing – her best pink one. She'd only have changed it if she'd had something newer still.'

Superintendent Harper said:

'And what's your explanation, Miss Marple?'

Miss Marple said:

'I haven't got one – yet. But I can't help feeling that it's important . . .'

III

Inside the wire cage, the tennis lesson that Raymond Starr was giving had come to an end.

A stout middle-aged woman uttered a few appreciative squeaks, picked up a sky-blue cardigan and went off towards the hotel.

Raymond called out a few gay words after her.

Then he turned towards the bench where the three onlookers were sitting. The balls dangled in a net in his hand, his racquet was under one arm. The gay, laughing expression on his face was wiped off as though by a sponge from a slate. He looked tired and worried.

Coming towards them, he said: '*That's* over.'

Then the smile broke out again, that charming, boyish, expressive smile that went so harmoniously with his suntanned face and dark lithe grace.

Sir Henry found himself wondering how old the man was. Twenty-five, thirty, thirty-five? It was impossible to say.

Raymond said, shaking his head a little:

'*She*'ll never be able to play, you know.'

'All this must be very boring for you,' said Miss Marple.

Raymond said simply:

'It is, sometimes. Especially at the end of the summer. For a time the thought of the pay buoys you up, but even that fails to stimulate imagination in the end!'

Superintendent Harper got up. He said abruptly:

'I'll call for you in half an hour's time, Miss Marple, if that will be all right?'

'Perfectly, thank you. I shall be ready.'

Harper went off. Raymond stood looking after him. Then he said: 'Mind if I sit here for a bit?'

'Do,' said Sir Henry. 'Have a cigarette?' He offered his case, wondering as he did so why he had a slight feeling of prejudice against Raymond Starr. Was it simply because he was a professional tennis coach and dancer? If so, it wasn't the tennis – it was the dancing. The English, Sir Henry decided, had a distrust for any man

119

who danced too well! This fellow moved with too much grace! Ramon – Raymond – which was his name? Abruptly, he asked the question.

The other seemed amused.

'Ramon was my original professional name. Ramon and Josie – Spanish effect, you know. Then there was rather a prejudice against foreigners – so I became Raymond – very British –'

Miss Marple said:

'And is your real name something quite different?'

He smiled at her.

'Actually my real name is Ramon. I had an Argentine grandmother, you see –' (And that accounts for that swing from the hips, thought Sir Henry parenthetically.) 'But my first name is Thomas. Painfully prosaic.'

He turned to Sir Henry.

'You come from Devonshire, don't you, sir? From Stane? My people lived down that way. At Alsmonston.'

Sir Henry's face lit up.

'Are you one of the Alsmonston Starrs? I didn't realize that.'

'No – I don't suppose you would.'

There was a slight bitterness in his voice.

Sir Henry said awkwardly:

'Bad luck – er – all that.'

'The place being sold up after it had been in the family for three hundred years? Yes, it was rather. Still, our kind have to go, I suppose. We've outlived our usefulness. My elder brother went to New York. He's in publishing – doing well. The rest of us are scattered up and down the earth. I'll say it's hard to get a job nowadays when you've nothing to say for yourself except that you've had a public-school education! Sometimes, if you're lucky, you get taken on as a reception clerk at an hotel. The tie and the manner are an asset there. The only job I could get was showman in a plumbing establishment. Selling superb peach and lemon-coloured porcelain baths. Enormous showrooms, but as I never knew the price of the damned things or how soon we could deliver them – I got fired.

'The only things I *could* do were dance and play tennis. I got taken on at an hotel on the Riviera. Good pickings there. I suppose I was doing well. Then I overheard an old Colonel, real old Colonel, incredibly ancient, British to the backbone and always talking about Poona. He went up to the manager and said at the top of his voice:

' "Where's the *gigolo*? I want to get hold of the *gigolo*. My wife and daughter want to dance, yer know. Where is the feller? What does he sting yer for? It's the *gigolo* I want." '

Raymond went on:

'Silly to mind – but I did. I chucked it. Came here. Less pay but pleasanter work. Mostly teaching tennis to rotund women who will never, never, never be able to play. That and dancing with the neglected wallflower daughters of rich clients. Oh well, it's life, I suppose. Excuse today's hard-luck story!'

He laughed. His teeth flashed out white, his eyes crinkled up at the corners. He looked suddenly healthy and happy and very much alive.

Sir Henry said:

'I'm glad to have a chat with you. I've been wanting to talk with you.'

'About Ruby Keene? I can't help you, you know. I don't know who killed her. I knew very little about her. She didn't confide in me.'

Miss Marple said: 'Did you like her?'

'Not particularly. I didn't dislike her.'

His voice was careless, uninterested.

Sir Henry said:

'So you've no suggestions to offer?'

'I'm afraid not . . . I'd have told Harper if I had. It just seems to me one of those things! Petty, sordid little crime – no clues, no motive.'

'Two people had a motive,' said Miss Marple.

Sir Henry looked at her sharply.

'Really?' Raymond looked surprised.

Miss Marple looked insistently at Sir Henry and he said rather unwillingly:

'Her death probably benefits Mrs Jefferson and Mr Gaskell to the amount of fifty thousand pounds.'

'What?' Raymond looked really startled – more than startled – upset. 'Oh, but that's absurd – absolutely absurd – Mrs Jefferson – neither of them – could have had anything to do with it. It would be incredible to think of such a thing.'

Miss Marple coughed. She said gently:

'I'm afraid, you know, you're rather an idealist.'

'I?' he laughed. 'Not me! I'm a hard-boiled cynic.'

'Money,' said Miss Marple, 'is a very powerful motive.'

'Perhaps,' Raymond said hotly. 'But that either of those two would strangle a girl in cold blood –' He shook his head.

Then he got up.

'Here's Mrs Jefferson now. Come for her lesson. She's late.' His voice sounded amused. 'Ten minutes late!'

Adelaide Jefferson and Hugo McLean were walking rapidly down the path towards them.

With a smiling apology for her lateness, Addie Jefferson went on to the court. McLean sat down on the bench. After a polite inquiry whether Miss Marple minded a pipe, he lit it and puffed for some minutes in silence, watching critically the two white figures about the tennis court.

He said at last:

'Can't see what Addie wants to have lessons for. Have a game, yes. No one enjoys it better than I do. But why *lessons*?'

'Wants to improve her game,' said Sir Henry.

'She's not a bad player,' said Hugo. 'Good enough, at all events. Dash it all, she isn't aiming to play at Wimbledon.'

He was silent for a minute or two. Then he said:

'Who *is* this Raymond fellow? Where do they come from, these pros? Fellow looks like a dago to me.'

'He's one of the Devonshire Starrs,' said Sir Henry.

'What? Not really?'

Sir Henry nodded. It was clear that this news was unpleasing to Hugo McLean. He scowled more than ever.

He said: 'Don't know why Addie sent for *me*. She seems not to have turned a hair over this business! Never looked better. Why send for me?'

Sir Henry asked with some curiosity:

'When did she send for you?'

'Oh – er – when all this happened.'

'How did you hear? Telephone or telegram?'

'Telegram.'

'As a matter of curiosity, when was it sent off?'

'Well – I don't know exactly.'

'What time did you receive it?'

'I didn't exactly receive it. It was telephoned on to me – as a matter of fact.'

'Why, where were you?'

'Fact is, I'd left London the afternoon before. I was staying at Danebury Head.'

'What – quite near here?'

'Yes, rather funny, wasn't it? Got the message when I got in from a round of golf and came over here at once.'

Miss Marple gazed at him thoughtfully. He looked hot and uncomfortable. She said: 'I've heard it's very pleasant at Danebury Head, and not very expensive.'

'No, it's not expensive. I couldn't afford it if it was. It's a nice little place.'

'We must drive over there one day,' said Miss Marple.

'Eh? What? Oh – er - yes, I should.' He got up. 'Better take some exercise – get an appetite.'

He walked away stiffly.

'Women,' said Sir Henry, 'treat their devoted admirers very badly.'

Miss Marple smiled but made no answer.

'Does he strike you as rather a dull dog?' asked Sir Henry. 'I'd be interested to know.'

'A little limited in his ideas, perhaps,' said Miss Marple. 'But with possibilities, I think – oh, definitely possibilities.'

Sir Henry in his turn got up.

'It's time for me to go and do my stuff. I see Mrs Bantry is on her way to keep you company.'

IV

Mrs Bantry arrived breathless and sat down with a gasp.

She said:

'I've been talking to chambermaids. But it isn't any good. I haven't found out a thing more! Do you think that girl can really have been carrying on with someone without everybody in the hotel knowing all about it?'

'That's a very interesting point, dear. I should say, definitely *not*.

Somebody knows, depend upon it, if it's true! But she must have been very clever about it.'

Mrs Bantry's attention had strayed to the tennis court. She said approvingly:

'Addie's tennis is coming on a lot. Attractive young man, that tennis pro. Addie's looking quite nice-looking. She's still an attractive woman – I shouldn't be at all surprised if she married again.'

'She'll be a rich woman, too, when Mr Jefferson dies,' said Miss Marple.

'Oh, don't always have such a nasty mind, Jane! Why haven't you solved this mystery yet? We don't seem to be getting on at all. I thought you'd know *at once*.' Mrs Bantry's tone held reproach.

'No, no, dear. I didn't know at once – not for some time.'

Mrs Bantry turned startled and incredulous eyes on her.

'You mean you know *now* who killed Ruby Keene?'

'Oh yes,' said Miss Marple, 'I know *that*!'

'But Jane, who is it? Tell me at once.'

Miss Marple shook her head very firmly and pursed up her lips.

'I'm sorry, Dolly, but that wouldn't do at all.'

'Why wouldn't it do?'

'Because you're so indiscreet. You would go round telling everyone – or, if you didn't tell, you'd *hint*.'

'No, I wouldn't. I wouldn't tell a soul.'

'People who use that phrase are always the last to live up to it. It's no good, dear. There's a long way to go yet. A great many things that are quite obscure. You remember when I was so against letting Mrs Partridge collect for the Red Cross, and I couldn't say *why*. The reason was that her nose had twitched in just the same way as that maid of mine, Alice, twitched *her* nose when I sent her out to pay the books. Always paid them a shilling or so short, and said "it could go on to the next week's account," which, of course, was *exactly* what Mrs Partridge did, only on a much larger scale. Seventy-five pounds it was *she* embezzled.'

'Never mind Mrs Partridge,' said Mrs Bantry.

'But I had to explain to you. And if you care I'll give you a *hint*. The trouble in this case is that everybody has been much too *credulous* and *believing*. You simply cannot *afford* to believe everything that people tell you. When there's anything fishy about, I never believe anyone at all! You see, I know human nature so well.'

Mrs Bantry was silent for a minute or two. Then she said in a different tone of voice:

'I told you, didn't I, that I didn't see why I shouldn't enjoy myself over this case. A real murder in my own house! The sort of thing that will never happen again.'

'I hope not,' said Miss Marple.

'Well, so do I, really. Once is enough. But it's *my* murder, Jane; I want to enjoy myself over it.'

Miss Marple shot a glance at her.

Mrs Bantry said belligerently:

'Don't you believe that?'

Miss Marple said sweetly:

'Of course, Dolly, if you tell me so.'

'Yes, but you never believe what people tell you, do you? You've just said so. Well, you're quite right.' Mrs Bantry's voice took on a sudden bitter note. She said: 'I'm not altogether a fool. You may think, Jane, that I don't know what they're saying all over St Mary Mead – all over the county! They're saying, one and all, that there's no smoke without fire, that if the girl was found in Arthur's library, then Arthur must know something about it. They're saying that the girl was Arthur's mistress – that she was his illegitimate daughter – that she was blackmailing him. They're saying anything that comes into their damned heads! And it will go on like that! Arthur won't realize it at first – he won't know what's wrong. He's such a dear old stupid that he'd never believe people would think things like that about him. He'll be cold-shouldered and looked at askance (whatever *that* means!) and it will dawn on him little by little and suddenly he'll be horrified and cut to the soul, and he'll fasten up like a clam and just *endure*, day after day, in misery.

'It's because of all that's going to happen to him that I've come here to ferret out every single thing about it that I can! This murder's *got* to be solved! If it isn't, then Arthur's whole life will be wrecked – and I won't have that happen. I won't! I won't! I won't!'

She paused for a minute and said:

'I *won't* have the dear old boy go through hell for something he didn't do. That's the only reason I came to Danemouth and left him alone at home – to find out the truth.'

'I know, dear,' said Miss Marple. 'That's why I'm here too.'

125

CHAPTER FOURTEEN

In a quiet hotel room Edwards was listening deferentially to Sir Henry Clithering.

'There are certain questions I would like to ask you, Edwards, but I want you first to understand quite clearly my position here. I was at one time Commissioner of Police at Scotland Yard. I am now retired into private life. Your master sent for me when this tragedy occurred. He begged me to use my skill and experience in order to find out the truth.'

Sir Henry paused.

Edwards, his pale intelligent eyes on the other's face, inclined his head. He said: 'Quite so, Sir Henry.'

Clithering went on slowly and deliberately:

'In all police cases there is necessarily a lot of information that is held back. It is held back for various reasons – because it touches on a family skeleton, because it is considered to have no bearing on the case, because it would entail awkwardness and embarrassment to the parties concerned.'

Again Edwards said:

'Quite so, Sir Henry.'

'I expect, Edwards, that by now you appreciate quite clearly the main points of this business. The dead girl was on the point of becoming Mr Jefferson's adopted daughter. Two people had a motive in seeing that this should not happen. Those two people are Mr Gaskell and Mrs Jefferson.'

The valet's eyes displayed a momentary gleam. He said: 'May I ask if they are under suspicion, sir?'

'They are in no danger of arrest, if that is what you mean. But the police are bound to be suspicious of them and will continue to be so *until the matter is cleared up*.'

'An unpleasant position for them, sir.'

'Very unpleasant. Now to get at the truth one must have *all* the facts of the case. A lot depends, *must* depend, on the reactions, the words and gestures, of Mr Jefferson and his family. How did they

126

feel, what did they show, what things were said? I am asking you, Edwards, for inside information — the kind of inside information that only you are likely to have. You know your master's moods. From observation of them you probably know what caused them. I am asking this, not as a policeman, but as a friend of Mr Jefferson's. That is to say, if anything you tell me is not, in my opinion, relevant to the case, I shall not pass it on to the police.'

He paused. Edwards said quietly:

'I understand you, sir. You want me to speak quite frankly — to say things that in the ordinary course of events I should not say — and that, excuse me, sir, *you* wouldn't dream of listening to.'

Sir Henry said:

'You're a very intelligent fellow, Edwards. That's exactly what I *do* mean.'

Edwards was silent for a minute or two, then he began to speak.

'Of course I know Mr Jefferson fairly well by now. I've been with him quite a number of years. And I see him in his "off" moments, not only in his "on" ones. Sometimes, sir, I've questioned in my own mind whether it's good for anyone to fight fate in the way Mr Jefferson has fought. It's taken a terrible toll of him, sir. If, sometimes, he could have given way, been an unhappy, lonely, broken old man — well, it might have been better for him in the end. But he's too proud for that! He'll go down fighting — that's his motto.

'But that sort of thing leads, Sir Henry, to a lot of nervous reaction. He looks a good-tempered gentleman. I've seen him in violent rages when he could hardly speak for passion. And the one thing that roused him, sir, was deceit . . .'

'Are you saying that for any particular reason, Edwards?'

'Yes, sir, I am. You asked me, sir, to speak quite frankly?'

'That is the idea.'

'Well, then, Sir Henry, in my opinion the young woman that Mr Jefferson was so taken up with wasn't worth it. She was, to put it bluntly, a common little piece. And she didn't care tuppence for Mr Jefferson. All that play of affection and gratitude was so much poppycock. I don't say there was any harm in her — but she wasn't, by a long way, what Mr Jefferson thought her. It was funny, that, sir, for Mr Jefferson was a shrewd gentleman; he wasn't often deceived over people. But there, a gentleman isn't himself in his judgment when it comes to a young woman being in question. Young Mrs Jefferson, you see, whom he'd always depended upon a lot for sympathy, had changed a good deal this summer. He noticed it and he felt it badly. He was fond of her, you see. Mr Mark he never liked much.'

Sir Henry interjected:

'And yet he had him with him constantly?'

'Yes, but that was for Miss Rosamund's sake. Mrs Gaskell that was. She was the apple of his eye. He adored her. Mr Mark was Miss Rosamund's husband. He always thought of him like that.'

'Supposing Mr Mark had married someone else?'

'Mr Jefferson, sir, would have been furious.'

Sir Henry raised his eyebrows. 'As much as that?'

'He wouldn't have shown it, but that's what it would have been.'

'And if Mrs Jefferson had married again?'

'Mr Jefferson wouldn't have liked that either, sir.'

'Please go on, Edwards.'

'I was saying, sir, that Mr Jefferson fell for this young woman. I've often seen it happen with the gentlemen I've been with. Comes over them like a kind of disease. They want to protect the girl, and shield her, and shower benefits upon her – and nine times out of ten the girl is very well able to look after herself and has a good eye to the main chance.'

'So you think Ruby Keene was a schemer?'

'Well, Sir Henry, she was quite inexperienced, being so young, but she had the makings of a very fine schemer indeed when she'd once got well into her swing, so to speak! In another five years she'd have been an expert at the game!'

Sir Henry said:

'I'm glad to have your opinion of her. It's valuable. Now do you recall any incident in which this matter was discussed between Mr Jefferson and his family?'

'There was very little discussion, sir. Mr Jefferson announced what he had in mind and stifled any protests. That is, he shut up Mr Mark, who was a bit outspoken. Mrs Jefferson didn't say much – she's a quiet lady – only urged him not to do anything in a great hurry.'

Sir Henry nodded.

'Anything else? What was the girl's attitude?'

With marked distaste the valet said:

'I should describe it, sir, as jubilant.'

'Ah – jubilant, you say? You had no reason to believe, Edwards, that' – he sought about for a phrase suitable to Edwards – 'that – er – her affections were engaged elsewhere?'

'Mr Jefferson was not proposing marriage, sir. He was going to adopt her.'

'Cut out the "elsewhere" and let the question stand.'

The valet said slowly: 'There *was* one incident, sir. I happened to be a witness of it.'

'That is gratifying. Tell me.'

'There is probably nothing in it, sir. It was just that one day the young woman, chancing to open her handbag, a small snapshot fell out. Mr Jefferson pounced on it and said: "Hallo, Kitten, who's this, eh?"

'It was a snapshot, sir, of a young man, a dark young man with rather untidy hair and his tie very badly arranged.

'Miss Keene pretended that she didn't know anything about it. She said: "I've no idea, Jeffie. No idea at all. I don't know how it could have got into my bag. *I* didn't put it there!"

'Now, Mr Jefferson, sir, wasn't quite a fool. That story wasn't good enough. He looked angry, his brows came down heavy, and his voice was gruff when he said:

' "Now then, Kitten, now then. *You* know who it is right enough."

'She changed her tactics quick, sir. Looked frightened. She said: "I do recognize him now. He comes here sometimes and I've danced with him. I don't know his name. The silly idiot must have stuffed his photo into my bag one day. These boys are too silly for anything!" She tossed her head and giggled and passed it off. But it wasn't a likely story, was it? And I don't think Mr Jefferson quite believed it. He looked at her once or twice after that in a sharp way, and sometimes, if she'd been out, he asked her where she'd been.'

Sir Henry said: 'Have you ever seen the original of the photo about the hotel?'

'Not to my knowledge, sir. Of course, I am not much downstairs in the public departments.'

Sir Henry nodded. He asked a few more questions, but Edwards could tell him nothing more.

In the police station at Danemouth, Superintendent Harper was interviewing Jessie Davis, Florence Small, Beatrice Henniker, Mary Price, and Lilian Ridgeway.

They were girls much of an age, differing slightly in mentality. They ranged from 'county' to farmers' and shopkeepers' daughters. One and all they told the same story — Pamela Reeves had been just the same as usual, she had said nothing to any of them except that she was going to Woolworth's and would go home by a later bus.

In the corner of Superintendent Harper's office sat an elderly lady. The girls hardly noticed her. If they did, they may have wondered who she was. She was certainly no police matron. Possibly they assumed that she, like themselves, was a witness to be questioned.

The last girl was shown out. Superintendent Harper wiped his forehead and turned round to look at Miss Marple. His glance was inquiring, but not hopeful.

Miss Marple, however, spoke crisply.

'I'd like to speak to Florence Small.'

The Superintendent's eyebrows rose, but he nodded and touched a bell. A constable appeared.

Harper said: 'Florence Small.'

The girl reappeared, ushered in by the constable. She was the daughter of a well-to-do farmer — a tall girl with fair hair, a rather foolish mouth, and frightened brown eyes. She was twisting her hands and looked nervous.

Superintendent Harper looked at Miss Marple, who nodded.

The Superintendent got up. He said:

'This lady will ask you some questions.'

He went out, closing the door behind him.

Florence shot an uneasy glance at Miss Marple. Her eyes looked rather like one of her father's calves.

Miss Marple said: 'Sit down, Florence.'

Florence Small sat down obediently. Unrecognized by herself, she felt suddenly more at home, less uneasy. The unfamiliar and terrorizing atmosphere of a police station was replaced by something more familiar, the accustomed tone of command of somebody whose business it was to give orders. Miss Marple said:

'You understand, Florence, that it's of the utmost importance that everything about poor Pamela's doings on the day of her death should be known?'

Florence murmured that she quite understood.

'And I'm sure you want to do your best to help?'

Florence's eyes were wary as she said, of course she did.

'To keep back any piece of information is a very serious offence,' said Miss Marple.

The girl's fingers twisted nervously in her lap. She swallowed once or twice.

'I can make allowances,' went on Miss Marple, 'for the fact that you are naturally alarmed at being brought into contact with the police. You are afraid, too, that you may be blamed for not having spoken sooner. Possibly you are afraid that you may also be blamed for not stopping Pamela at the time. But you've got to be a brave girl and make a clean breast of things. If you refuse to tell what you know now, it will be a very serious matter indeed – *very* serious – practically *perjury*, and for that, as you know, you can be sent to prison.'

'I – I don't –'

Miss Marple said sharply:

'Now don't prevaricate, Florence! Tell me all about it at once! Pamela wasn't going to Woolworth's, was she?'

Florence licked her lips with a dry tongue and gazed imploringly at Miss Marple like a beast about to be slaughtered.

'Something to do with the films, wasn't it?' asked Miss Marple.

A look of intense relief mingled with awe passed over Florence's face. Her inhibitions left her. She gasped:

'Oh, *yes*!'

'I thought so,' said Miss Marple. 'Now I want all the details, please.'

Words poured from Florence in a gush.

'Oh! I've been ever so worried. I promised Pam, you see, I'd never say a word to a soul. And then when she was found all burnt up in that car – oh! it was horrible and I thought I should *die* – I felt it was all my fault. I ought to have stopped her. Only I never thought, not for a minute, that it wasn't all right. And then I was asked if she'd been quite as usual that day and I said "Yes" before I'd had time to think. And not having said anything then I didn't see how I could say anything later. And, after all, I didn't know

131

anything – not really – only what Pam told me.'

'What did Pam tell you?'

'It was as we were walking up the lane to the bus – on the way to the rally. She asked me if I could keep a secret, and I said "Yes," and she made me swear not to tell. She was going into Danemouth for a film test after the rally! She'd met a film producer – just back from Hollywood, he was. He wanted a certain type, and he told Pam she was just what he was looking for. He warned her, though, not to build on it. You couldn't tell, he said, not until you saw a person photographed. It might be no good at all. It was a kind of Bergner part, he said. You had to have someone quite young for it. A schoolgirl, it was, who changes places with a revue artist and has a wonderful career. Pam's acted in plays at school and she's awfully good. He said he could see she could act, but she'd have to have some intensive training. It wouldn't be all beer and skittles, he told her, it would be damned hard work. Did she think she could stick it?'

Florence Small stopped for breath. Miss Marple felt rather sick as she listened to the glib rehash of countless novels and screen stories. Pamela Reeves, like most other girls, would have been warned against talking to strangers – but the glamour of the films would obliterate all that.

'He was absolutely businesslike about it all,' continued Florence. 'Said if the test was successful she'd have a contract, and he said that as she was young and inexperienced she ought to let a lawyer look at it before she signed it. But she wasn't to pass on that *he'd* said that. He asked her if she'd have trouble with her parents, and Pam said she probably would, and he said: "Well, of course, that's always a difficulty with anyone as young as you are, but I think if it was put to them that this was a wonderful chance that wouldn't happen once in a million times, they'd see reason." But, anyway, he said, it wasn't any good going into that until they knew the result of the test. She mustn't be disappointed if it failed. He told her about Hollywood and about Vivien Leigh – how she'd suddenly taken London by storm – and how these sensational leaps into fame did happen. He himself had come back from America to work with the Lemville Studios and put some pep into the English film companies.'

Miss Marple nodded.

Florence went on:

'So it was all arranged. Pam was to go into Danemouth after the rally and meet him at his hotel and he'd take her along to the studios (they'd got a small testing studio in Danemouth, he told her). She'd have her test and she could catch the bus home afterwards. She could say she'd been shopping, and he'd let her know the result of the test in a few days, and if it was favourable Mr Harmsteiter, the boss, would come along and talk to her parents.

'Well, of course, it sounded too wonderful! I was green with envy! Pam got through the rally without turning a hair – we always call her a regular poker face. Then, when she said she was going into Danemouth to Woolworth's she just winked at me.

'I saw her start off down the footpath.' Florence began to cry. 'I ought to have stopped her. I ought to have stopped her. I ought to have known a thing like that couldn't be true. I ought to have told someone. Oh dear, I wish I was *dead*!'

'There, there.' Miss Marple patted her on the shoulder. 'It's quite all right. No one will blame you. You've done the right thing in telling me.'

She devoted some minutes to cheering the child up.

Five minutes later she was telling the story to Superintendent Harper. The latter looked very grim.

'The clever devil!' he said. 'By God, I'll cook his goose for him. This puts rather a different aspect on things.'

'Yes, it does.'

Harper looked at her sideways.

'It doesn't surprise you?'

'I expected something of the kind.'

Superintendent Harper said curiously:

'What put you on to this particular girl? They all looked scared to death and there wasn't a pin to choose between them as far as I could see.'

Miss Marple said gently:

'You haven't had as much experience with girls telling lies as I have. Florence looked at you very straight, if you remember, and stood very rigid and just fidgeted with her feet like the others. But you didn't watch her as she went out of the door. I knew at once then that she'd got something to hide. They nearly always relax too soon. My little maid Janet always did. She'd explain quite convincingly that the mice had eaten the end of a cake and give herself away by smirking as she left the room.'

'I'm very grateful to you,' said Harper.

He added thoughtfully: 'Lemville Studios, eh?'

Miss Marple said nothing. She rose to her feet.

'I'm afraid,' she said, 'I must hurry away. So glad to have been able to help you.'

'Are you going back to the hotel?'

'Yes – to pack up. I must go back to St Mary Mead as soon as possible. There's a lot for me to do there.'

CHAPTER FIFTEEN

Miss Marple passed out through the french windows of her drawing-room, tripped down her neat garden path, through a garden gate, in through the vicarage garden gate, across the vicarage garden, and up to the drawing-room window, where she tapped gently on the pane.

The vicar was busy in his study composing his Sunday sermon, but the vicar's wife, who was young and pretty, was admiring the progress of her offspring across the hearthrug.

'Can I come in, Griselda?'

'Oh, do, Miss Marple. Just *look* at David! He gets so angry because he can only crawl in reverse. He wants to get to something and the more he tries the more he goes backwards into the coal-box!'

'He's looking very bonny, Griselda.'

'He's not bad, is he?' said the young mother, endeavouring to assume an indifferent manner. 'Of course I don't *bother* with him much. All the books say a child should be left alone as much as possible.'

'Very wise, dear,' said Miss Marple. 'Ahem, I came to ask if there was anything special you are collecting for at the moment.'

The vicar's wife turned somewhat astonished eyes upon her.

'Oh, heaps of things,' she said cheerfully. 'There always are.'

She ticked them off on her fingers.

'There's the Nave Restoration Fund, and St Giles's Mission, and our Sale of Work next Wednesday, and the Unmarried Mothers, and a Boy Scouts' Outing, and the Needlework Guild, and the Bishop's Appeal for Deep Sea Fishermen.'

'Any of them will do,' said Miss Marple. 'I thought I might make a little round – with a book, you know – if you would authorize me to do so.'

'Are you up to something? I believe you are. Of course I authorize you. Make it the Sale of Work; it would be lovely to get some real money instead of those awful sachets and comic pen-wipers and depressing children's frocks and dusters all done up to look like dolls.

'I suppose,' continued Griselda, accompanying her guest to the window, 'you wouldn't like to tell me what it's all about?'

'Later, my dear,' said Miss Marple, hurrying off.

With a sigh the young mother returned to the hearthrug and, by way of carrying out her principles of stern neglect, butted her son three times in the stomach so that he caught hold of her hair and pulled it with gleeful yells. Then they rolled over and over in a grand rough-and-tumble until the door opened and the vicarage maid announced to the most influential parishioner (who didn't like children):

'Missus is in here.'

Whereupon Griselda sat up and tried to look dignified and more what a vicar's wife should be.

II

Miss Marple, clasping a small black book with pencilled entries in it, walked briskly along the village street until she came to the crossroads. Here she turned to the left and walked past the Blue Boar until she came to Chatsworth, alias 'Mr Booker's new house.'

She turned in at the gate, walked up to the front door and knocked briskly.

The door was opened by the blonde young woman named Dinah Lee. She was less carefully made-up than usual, and in fact looked slightly dirty. She was wearing grey slacks and an emerald jumper.

'Good morning,' said Miss Marple briskly and cheerfully. 'May I just come in for a minute?'

She pressed forward as she spoke, so that Dinah Lee, who

was somewhat taken aback at the call, had no time to make up her mind.

'Thank you so much,' said Miss Marple, beaming amiably at her and sitting down rather gingerly on a 'period' bamboo chair.

'Quite warm for the time of year, is it not?' went on Miss Marple, still exuding geniality.

'Yes, rather. Oh, quite,' said Miss Lee.

At a loss how to deal with the situation, she opened a box and offered it to her guest. 'Er – have a cigarette?'

'Thank you so much, but I don't smoke. I just called, you know, to see if I could enlist your help for our Sale of Work next week.'

'Sale of Work?' said Dinah Lee, as one who repeats a phrase in a foreign language.

'At the vicarage,' said Miss Marple. 'Next Wednesday.'

'Oh!' Miss Lee's mouth fell open. 'I'm afraid I couldn't –'

'Not even a small subscription – half a crown perhaps?'

Miss Marple exhibited her little book.

'Oh – er – well, yes, I dare say I could manage that.'

The girl looked relieved and turned to hunt in her handbag.

Miss Marple's sharp eyes were looking round the room.

She said:

'I see you've no hearthrug in front of the fire.'

Dinah Lee turned round and stared at her. She could not but be aware of the very keen scrutiny the old lady was giving her, but it aroused in her no other emotion than slight annoyance. Miss Marple recognized that. She said:

'It's rather dangerous, you know. Sparks fly out and mark the carpet.'

'Funny old Tabby,' thought Dinah, but she said quite amiably if somewhat vaguely:

'There used to be one. I don't know where it's got to.'

'I suppose,' said Miss Marple, 'it was the fluffy, woolly kind?'

'Sheep,' said Dinah. 'That's what it looked like.'

She was amused now. An eccentric old bean, this.

She held out a half-crown. 'Here you are,' she said.

'Oh, thank you, my dear.'

Miss Marple took it and opened the little book.

'Er – what name shall I write down?'

Dinah's eyes grew suddenly hard and contemptuous.

136

'Nosey old cat,' she thought, 'that's all she came for – prying around for scandal!'

She said clearly and with malicious pleasure:

'Miss Dinah Lee.'

Miss Marple looked at her steadily.

She said:

'This is Mr Basil Blake's cottage, isn't it?'

'Yes, and *I*'m Miss Dinah Lee!'

Her voice rang out challengingly, her head went back, her blue eyes flashed.

Very steadily Miss Marple looked at her. She said:

'Will you allow me to give you some advice, even though you may consider it impertinent?'

'I *shall* consider it impertinent. You had better say nothing.'

'Nevertheless,' said Miss Marple, 'I am going to speak. I want to advise you, very strongly, not to continue using your maiden name in the village.'

Dinah stared at her. She said:

'What – what do you mean?'

Miss Marple said earnestly:

'In a very short time you may need all the sympathy and goodwill you can find. It will be important to your husband, too, that he shall be thought well of. There is a prejudice in old-fashioned country districts against people living together who are not married. It has amused you both, I dare say, to pretend that that is what you are doing. It kept people away, so that you weren't bothered with what I expect you would call "old frumps." Nevertheless, old frumps have their uses.'

Dinah demanded:

'How did you know we are married?'

Miss Marple smiled a deprecating smile.

'Oh, my dear,' she said.

Dinah persisted.

'No, but how *did* you know? You didn't – you didn't go to Somerset House?'

A momentary flicker showed in Miss Marple's eyes.

'Somerset House? Oh, no. But it was quite easy to *guess*. Everything, you know, gets round in a village. The – er – the kind of quarrels you have – typical of early days of marriage. Quite – *quite* unlike an illicit relationship. It has been said, you know (and, I think, quite truly), that you can only really get under anybody's skin if you are married to them. When there is no – no *legal* bond, people are much more careful, they have to keep assuring themselves how happy and halcyon everything is. They have, you see, to *justify* themselves. They dare not quarrel! Married people, I have noticed, quite enjoy their battles and the – er – appropriate reconciliations.'

She paused, twinkling benignly.

'Well, I –' Dinah stopped and laughed. She sat down and lit a cigarette. 'You're absolutely marvellous!' she said.

Then she went on:

'But why do you want us to own up and admit to respectability?'

Miss Marple's face was grave. She said:

'Because, any minute now, *your husband may be arrested for murder*.'

III

For several moments Dinah stared at her. Then she said incredulously:

'Basil? Murder? Are you joking?'

'No, indeed. Haven't you seen the papers?'

Dinah caught her breath.

'You mean – that girl at the Majestic Hotel. Do you mean they suspect Basil of killing her?'

'Yes.'

'But it's nonsense!'

There was the whir of a car outside, the bang of a gate. Basil Blake flung open the door and came in, carrying some bottles. He said:

'Got the gin and the vermouth. Did you –?'

He stopped and turned incredulous eyes on the prim, erect visitor.

Dinah burst out breathlessly:

'Is she mad? She says you're going to be arrested for the murder of that girl Ruby Keene.'

'Oh, God!' said Basil Blake. The bottles dropped from his arms on to the sofa. He reeled to a chair and dropped down in it and buried his face in his hands. He repeated: 'Oh, my God! Oh, my God!'

Dinah darted over to him. She caught his shoulders.

'Basil, look at me! It isn't true! I know it isn't true! I don't believe it for a moment!'

His hand went up and gripped hers.

'Bless you, darling.'

'But why should they think – You didn't even *know* her, did you?'

'Oh, yes, he knew her,' said Miss Marple.

Basil said fiercely:

'Be quiet, you old hag. Listen, Dinah darling, I hardly knew her at all. Just ran across her once or twice at the Majestic. That's all, I swear that's all.'

Dinah said, bewildered:

'I don't understand. Why should anyone suspect you, then?'

Basil groaned. He put his hands over his eyes and rocked to and fro.

Miss Marple said:

'What did you do with the hearthrug?'

His reply came mechanically:

'I put it in the dustbin.'

Miss Marple clucked her tongue vexedly.

'That was stupid – very stupid. People don't put good hearthrugs in dustbins. It had spangles in it from her dress, I suppose?'

'Yes, I couldn't get them out.'

Dinah cried: 'But what are you both talking about?'

Basil said sullenly:

'Ask her. She seems to know all about it.'

'I'll tell you what I think happened, if you like,' said Miss Marple. 'You can correct me, Mr Blake, if I go wrong. I think that after having had a violent quarrel with your wife at a party and after having had, perhaps, rather too much – er – to drink, you drove down here. I don't know what time you arrived –'

Basil Blake said sullenly:

'About two in the morning. I meant to go up to town first, then when I got to the suburbs I changed my mind. I thought Dinah might come down here after me. So I drove down here. The place was all dark. I opened the door and turned on the light and I saw — and I saw —'

He gulped and stopped. Miss Marple went on:

'You saw a girl lying on the hearthrug — a girl in a white evening dress — strangled. I don't know whether you recognized her then —'

Basil Blake shook his head violently.

'I couldn't look at her after the first glance — her face was all blue — swollen. She'd been dead some time and she was *there* — in *my* room!'

He shuddered.

Miss Marple said gently:

'You weren't, of course, quite yourself. You were in a fuddled state and your nerves are not good. You were, I think, panic-stricken. You didn't know what to do —'

'I thought Dinah might turn up any minute. And she'd find me there with a dead body — a girl's dead body — and she'd think I'd killed her. Then I got an idea — it seemed, I don't know why, a good idea at the time — I thought: I'll put her in old Bantry's library. Damned pompous old stick, always looking down his nose, sneering at me as artistic and effeminate. Serve the pompous old brute right, I thought. He'll look a fool when a dead lovely is found on his hearthrug.' He added, with a pathetic eagerness to explain: 'I was a bit drunk, you know, at the time. It really seemed positively *amusing* to me. Old Bantry with a dead blonde.'

'Yes, yes,' said Miss Marple. 'Little Tommy Bond had very much the same idea. Rather a sensitive boy with an inferiority complex, he said teacher was always picking on him. He put a frog in the clock and it jumped out at her.

'You were just the same,' went on Miss Marple, 'only of course, bodies are more serious matters than frogs.'

Basil groaned again.

'By the morning I'd sobered up. I realized what I'd done. I was scared stiff. And then the police came here — another damned pompous ass of a Chief Constable. I was scared of him — and the only way I could hide it was by being abominably rude. In the middle of it all Dinah drove up.'

Dinah looked out of the window.

She said:

'There's a car driving up now . . . there are men in it.'

'The police, I think,' said Miss Marple.

Basil Blake got up. Suddenly he became quite calm and resolute. He even smiled. He said:

'So I'm for it, am I? All right, Dinah sweet, keep your head. Get on to old Sims – he's the family lawyer – and go to Mother and tell her everything about our marriage. She won't bite. And don't worry. *I didn't do it.* So it's bound to be all right, see, sweetheart?'

There was a tap on the cottage door. Basil called 'Come in.' Inspector Slack entered with another man. He said:

'Mr Basil Blake?'

'Yes.'

'I have a warrant here for your arrest on the charge of murdering Ruby Keene on the night of September 21st last. I warn you that anything you say may be used at your trial. You will please accompany me now. Full facilities will be given you for communicating with your solicitor.'

Basil nodded.

He looked at Dinah, but did not touch her. He said:

'So long, Dinah.'

'Cool customer,' thought Inspector Slack.

He acknowledged the presence of Miss Marple with a half bow and a 'Good morning,' and thought to himself:

'Smart old Pussy, *she's* on to it! Good job we've got that hearthrug. That and finding out from the car-park man at the studio that he left that party at *eleven* instead of midnight. Don't think those friends of his meant to commit perjury. They were bottled and Blake told 'em firmly the next day it was twelve o'clock when he left and they believed him. Well, *his* goose is cooked good and proper! Mental, I expect! Broadmoor, not hanging. First the Reeves kid, probably strangled her, drove her out to the quarry, walked back into Danemouth, picked up his own car in some side lane, drove to this party, then back to Danemouth, brought Ruby Keene out here, strangled her, put her in old Bantry's library, then probably got the wind up about the car in the quarry, drove there, set it on fire, and got back here. Mad – sex and blood lust – lucky *this* girl's escaped. What they call recurring mania, I expect.'

Alone with Miss Marple, Dinah Blake turned to her. She said:

'I don't know who you are, but you've got to understand this – *Basil didn't do it.*'

Miss Marple said:

'I know he didn't. I know who *did* do it. But it's not going to be easy to prove. I've an idea that something you said – just now – may help. It gave me an idea – the *connection* I'd been trying to find – now what *was* it?'

CHAPTER SIXTEEN

'I'm home, Arthur!' declared Mrs Bantry, announcing the fact like a Royal Proclamation as she flung open the study door.

Colonel Bantry immediately jumped up, kissed his wife, and declared heartily: 'Well, well, that's splendid!'

The words were unimpeachable, the manner very well done, but an affectionate wife of as many years' standing as Mrs Bantry was not deceived. She said immediately:

'Is anything the matter?'

'No, of course not, Dolly. What should be the matter?'

'Oh, I don't know,' said Mrs Bantry vaguely. 'Things are so queer, aren't they?'

She threw off her coat as she spoke and Colonel Bantry picked it up as carefully and laid it across the back of the sofa.

All exactly as usual – yet not as usual. Her husband, Mrs Bantry thought, seemed to have shrunk. He looked thinner, stooped more; they were pouches under his eyes and those eyes were not ready to meet hers.

He went on to say, still with that affectation of cheerfulness:

'Well, how did you enjoy your time at Danemouth?'

'Oh! it was great fun. You ought to have come, Arthur.'

'Couldn't get away, my dear. Lot of things to attend to here.'

'Still, I think the change would have done you good. And you like the Jeffersons?'

'Yes, yes, poor fellow. Nice chap. All very sad.'

'What have you been doing with yourself since I've been away?'

'Oh, nothing much. Been over the farms, you know. Agreed that Anderson shall have a new roof – can't patch it up any longer.'

'How did the Radfordshire Council meeting go?'

'I – well – as a matter of fact I didn't go.'

'Didn't *go*? But you were taking the chair?'

''Well, as a matter of fact, Dolly – seems there was some mistake about that. Asked me if I'd mind if Thompson took it instead.'

'I *see*,' said Mrs Bantry.

She peeled off a glove and threw it deliberately into the wastepaper basket. Her husband went to retrieve it, and she stopped him, saying sharply:

'Leave it. I hate gloves.'

Colonel Bantry glanced at her uneasily.

Mrs Bantry said sternly:

'Did you go to dinner with the Duffs on Thursday?'

'Oh, that! It was put off. Their cook was ill.'

'Stupid people,' said Mrs Bantry. She went on: 'Did you go to the Naylors' yesterday?'

'I rang up and said I didn't feel up to it, hoped they'd excuse me. They quite understood.'

'They did, did they?' said Mrs Bantry grimly.

She sat down by the desk and absent-mindedly picked up a pair of gardening scissors. With them she cut off the fingers, one by one, of her second glove.

'What *are* you doing, Dolly?'

'Feeling destructive,' said Mrs Bantry.

She got up. 'Where shall we sit after dinner, Arthur? In the library?'

'Well – er – I don't think so – eh? Very nice in here – or the drawing-room.'

'I think,' said Mrs Bantry, 'that we'll sit in the library!'

Her steady eye met his. Colonel Bantry drew himself up to his full height. A sparkle came into his eye.

He said:

'You're right, my dear. We'll sit in the library!'

II

Mrs Bantry put down the telephone receiver with a sigh of annoyance. She had rung up twice, and each time the answer had been the same: Miss Marple was out.

Of a naturally impatient nature, Mrs Bantry was never one to acquiesce in defeat. She rang up in rapid succession the vicarage, Mrs Price Ridley, Miss Hartnell, Miss Wetherby, and, as a last resource, the fishmonger who, by reason of his advantageous geographical position, usually knew where everybody was in the village.

The fishmonger was sorry, but he had not seen Miss Marple at all in the village that morning. She had not been her usual round.

'Where *can* the woman be?' demanded Mrs Bantry impatiently aloud.

There was a deferential cough behind her. The discreet Lorrimer murmured:

'You were requiring Miss Marple, madam? I have just observed her approaching the house.'

Mrs Bantry rushed to the front door, flung it open, and greeted Miss Marple breathlessly:

'I've been trying to get you *everywhere*. Where have you been?' She glanced over her shoulder. Lorrimer had discreetly vanished. 'Everything's *too* awful! People are beginning to cold-shoulder Arthur. He looks *years* older. We *must* do something, Jane. *You* must do something!'

Miss Marple said:

'You needn't worry, Dolly,' in a rather peculiar voice.

Colonel Bantry appeared from the study door.

'Ah, Miss Marple. Good morning. Glad you've come. My wife's been ringing you up like a lunatic.'

'I thought I'd better bring you the news,' said Miss Marple, as she followed Mrs Bantry into the study.

'News?'

'Basil Blake has just been arrested for the murder of Ruby Keene.'

'Basil Blake?' cried the Colonel.

'But he didn't do it,' said Miss Marple.

Colonel Bantry took no notice of this statement. It is doubtful if he even heard it.

'Do you mean to say he strangled that girl and then brought her along and put her in *my* library?'

'He put her in your library,' said Miss Marple. 'But he didn't kill her.'

'Nonsense! If he put her in my library, of course he killed her! The two things go together.'

'Not necessarily. He found her dead in his own cottage.'

'A likely story,' said the Colonel derisively. 'If you find a body, why, you ring up the police – naturally – if you're an honest man.'

'Ah,' said Miss Marple, 'but we haven't all got such iron nerves as you have, Colonel Bantry. You belong to the old school. This younger generation is different.'

'Got no stamina,' said the Colonel, repeating a well-worn opinion of his.

'Some of them,' said Miss Marple, 'have been through a bad time. I've heard a good deal about Basil. He did ARP work, you know, when he was only eighteen. He went into a burning house and brought out four children, one after another. He went back for a dog, although they told him it wasn't safe. The building fell in on him. They got him out, but his chest was badly crushed and he had to lie in plaster for nearly a year and was ill for a long time after that. That's when he got interested in designing.'

'Oh!' The Colonel coughed and blew his nose. 'I – er – never knew that.'

'He doesn't talk about it,' said Miss Marple.

'Er – quite right. Proper spirit. Must be more in the young chap than I thought. Always thought he'd shirked the war, you know. Shows you ought to be careful in jumping to conclusions.'

Colonel Bantry looked ashamed.

'But, all the same' – his indignation revived – 'what did he mean trying to fasten a murder on *me*?'

'I don't think he saw it like that,' said Miss Marple. 'He thought of it more as a – as a joke. You see, he was rather under the influence of alcohol at the time.'

'Bottled, was he?' said Colonel Bantry, with an Englishman's sympathy for alcoholic excess. 'Oh, well, can't judge a fellow by what he does when he's drunk. When I was at Cambridge, I remember I put a certain utensil – well, well, never mind. Deuce of a row there was about it.'

He chuckled, then checked himself sternly. He looked piercingly at Miss Marple with eyes that were shrewd and appraising. He said: '*You* don't think he did the murder, eh?'

'I'm sure he didn't.'

'And you think you know who did?'

Miss Marple nodded.

Mrs Bantry, like an ecstatic Greek chorus, said: 'Isn't she wonderful?' to an unhearing world.

'Well, who was it?'

Miss Marple said:

'I was going to ask you to help me. I think, if we went up to Somerset House we should have a very good idea.'

CHAPTER SEVENTEEN

Sir Henry's face was very grave.

He said:

'I don't like it.'

'I am aware,' said Miss Marple, 'that it isn't what you call orthodox. But it *is* so important, isn't it, to be quite *sure* – "to make assurance doubly sure," as Shakespeare has it. I think, if Mr Jefferson would agree –?'

'What about Harper? Is he to be in on this?'

'It might be awkward for him to know too much. But there might be a hint from you. To watch certain persons – have them trailed, you know.'

Sir Henry said slowly:

'Yes, that would meet the case . . .'

II

Superintendent Harper looked piercingly at Sir Henry Clithering.

'Let's get this quite clear, sir. You're giving me a hint?'

Sir Henry said:

'I'm informing you of what my friend has just informed me – he didn't tell me in confidence – that he proposes to visit a solicitor in Danemouth tomorrow for the purpose of making a new will.'

The Superintendent's bushy eyebrows drew downwards over his steady eyes. He said:

'Does Mr Conway Jefferson propose to inform his son-in-law and daughter-in-law of that fact?'

'He intends to tell them about it this evening.'

'I see.'

The Superintendent tapped his desk with a pen-holder.

He repeated again: 'I see . . .'

Then the piercing eyes bored once more into the eyes of the other man. Harper said:

'So you're not satisfied with the case against Basil Blake?'

'Are you?'

The Superintendent's moustaches quivered. He said:

'Is Miss Marple?'

The two men looked at each other.

Then Harper said:

'You can leave it to me. I'll have men detailed. There will be no funny business, I can promise you that.'

Sir Henry said:

'There is one more thing. You'd better see this.'

He unfolded a slip of paper and pushed it across the table.

This time the Superintendent's calm deserted him. He whistled:

'So that's it, is it? That puts an entirely different complexion on the matter. How did you come to dig up this?'

'Women,' said Sir Henry, 'are eternally interested in marriages.'

'Especially,' said the Superintendent, 'elderly single women.'

III

Conway Jefferson looked up as his friend entered.

His grim face relaxed into a smile.

He said:

'Well, I told 'em. They took it very well.'

'What did you say?'

'Told 'em that, as Ruby was dead, I felt that the fifty thousand I'd originally left her should go to something that I could associate with her memory. It was to endow a hostel for young girls working as professional dancers in London. Damned silly way to leave your money – surprised they swallowed it. As though I'd do a thing like that!'

He added meditatively:

'You know, I made a fool of myself over that girl. Must be turning

147

into a silly old man. I can see it now. She was a pretty kid — but most of what I saw in her I put there myself. I pretended she was another Rosamund. Same colouring, you know. But not the same heart or mind. Hand me that paper — rather an interesting bridge problem.'

IV

Sir Henry went downstairs. He asked a question of the porter.

'Mr Gaskell, sir? He's just gone off in his car. Had to go to London.'

'Oh! I see. Is Mrs Jefferson about?'

'Mrs Jefferson, sir, has just gone up to bed.'

Sir Henry looked into the lounge and through to the ballroom. In the lounge Hugo McLean was doing a crossword puzzle and frowning a good deal over it. In the ballroom Josie was smiling valiantly into the face of a stout, perspiring man as her nimble feet avoided his destructive tread. The stout man was clearly enjoying his dance. Raymond, graceful and weary, was dancing with an anaemic-looking girl with adenoids, dull brown hair, and an expensive and exceedingly unbecoming dress.

Sir Henry said under his breath:

'*And so to bed*,' and went upstairs.

V

It was three o'clock. The wind had fallen, the moon was shining over the quiet sea.

In Conway Jefferson's room there was no sound except his own heavy breathing as he lay, half propped up on pillows.

There was no breeze to stir the curtains at the window, but they stirred . . . For a moment they parted, and a figure was silhouetted against the moonlight. Then they fell back into place. Everything was quiet again, but there was someone else inside the room.

Nearer and nearer to the bed the intruder stole. The deep breathing on the pillow did not relax.

There was no sound, or hardly any sound. A finger and thumb

were ready to pick up a fold of skin, in the other hand the hypodermic was ready.

And then, suddenly, out of the shadows a hand came and closed over the hand that held the needle, the other arm held the figure in an iron grasp.

An unemotional voice, the voice of the law, said:

'No, you don't. I want that needle!'

The light switched on and from his pillows Conway Jefferson looked grimly at the murderer of Ruby Keene.

CHAPTER EIGHTEEN

Sir Henry Clithering said:

'Speaking as Watson, I want to know your methods, Miss Marple.'

Superintendent Harper said:

'*I*'d like to know what put you on to it first.'

Colonel Melchett said:

'You've done it again, by Jove! I want to hear all about it from the beginning.'

Miss Marple smoothed the puce silk of her best evening gown. She flushed and smiled and looked very self-conscious.

She said: 'I'm afraid you'll think my "methods", as Sir Henry calls them, are terribly amateurish. The truth is, you see, that most people – and I don't exclude policemen – are far too trusting for this wicked world. They believe what is told them. I never do. I'm afraid I always like to prove a thing for myself.'

'That is the scientific attitude,' said Sir Henry.

'In this case,' continued Miss Marple, 'certain things were taken for granted from the first – instead of just confining oneself to the facts. The facts, as I noted them, were that the victim was quite young and that she bit her nails and that her teeth stuck out a little – as young girls' so often do if not corrected in time with a plate – (and children are very naughty about their plates and taking them out when their elders aren't looking).

'But that is wandering from the point. Where was I? Oh, yes, looking down at the dead girl and feeling sorry, because it is always sad to see a young life cut short, and thinking that whoever had done it was a very wicked person. Of course it was all very confusing her being found in Colonel Bantry's library, altogether too like a book to be *true*. In fact, it made the wrong pattern. It wasn't, you see, *meant*, which confused us a lot. The *real* idea had been to plant the body on poor young Basil Blake (a *much* more likely person), and his action in putting it in the Colonel's library delayed things considerably, and must have been a source of great annoyance to the *real* murderer.

'Originally, you see, Mr Blake would have been the first object of suspicion. They'd have made inquiries at Danemouth, found he knew the girl, then found he had tied himself up with another girl, and they'd have assumed that Ruby came to blackmail him, or something like that, and that he'd strangled her in a fit of rage. Just an ordinary, sordid, what I call *night-club* type of crime!

'But that, of course, *all went wrong*, and interest became focused much too soon on the Jefferson family – to the great annoyance of a *certain person*.

'As I've told you, I've got a very suspicious mind. My nephew Raymond tells me (in fun, of course, and quite affectionately) that I have a mind like a *sink*. He says that most Victorians have. All I can say is that the Victorians knew a good deal about human nature.

'As I say, having this rather insanitary – or surely *sanitary*? – mind, I looked at once at the *money* angle of it. Two people stood to benefit by this girl's death – you couldn't get away from that. Fifty thousand pounds is a lot of money – especially when you are in financial difficulties, as both these people were. Of course they both seemed very nice, agreeable people – they didn't seem *likely* people – but one never can tell, can one?

'Mrs Jefferson, for instance – everyone liked her. But it did seem clear that she had become very restless that summer, and that she was tired of the life she led, completely dependent on her father-in-law. She knew, because the doctor had told her, that he couldn't live long – so *that* was all right – to put it callously – or it *would* have been all right if Ruby Keene hadn't come along. Mrs Jefferson was passionately devoted to her son, and some women have a curious idea that crimes committed for the sake of their offspring are almost morally justified. I have come across that attitude once or twice in the village. "Well, 'twas all for Daisy, you see, miss," they say, and seem to think that that makes doubtful conduct quite all right. Very *lax* thinking.

'Mr Mark Gaskell, of course, was a much more likely starter, if I may use such a sporting expression. He was a gambler and had not, I fancied, a very high moral code. But, for certain reasons, I was of the opinion that a *woman* was concerned in this crime.

'As I say, with my eye on motive, the money angle seemed *very* suggestive. It was annoying, therefore, to find that both these people had alibis for the time when Ruby Keene, according to the medical evidence, had met her death.

'But soon afterwards there came the discovery of the burnt-out car with Pamela Reeves's body in it, and then the whole thing leaped to the eye. The alibis, of course, were worthless.

'I now had two *halves* of the case, and both quite convincing, but they did not fit. There must *be* a connection, but I could not find it. The one person whom I *knew* to be concerned in the crime hadn't got a motive.

'It was stupid of me,' said Miss Marple meditatively. 'If it hadn't been for Dinah Lee I shouldn't have thought of it – the most obvious thing in the world. Somerset House! Marriage! It wasn't a question of only Mr Gaskell or Mrs Jefferson – there were the further possibilities of *marriage*. If either of those two was married, or even was *likely* to marry, *then the other party to the marriage contract was involved too*. Raymond, for instance, might think he had a pretty good chance of marrying a rich wife. He had been very assiduous to Mrs Jefferson, and it was his charm, I think, that awoke her from her long widowhood. She had been quite content just being a daughter to Mr Jefferson – like Ruth and Naomi – only Naomi, if you remember, took a lot of trouble to arrange a suitable marriage for Ruth.

'Besides Raymond there was Mr McLean. She liked him very much and it seemed highly possible that she would marry him in the end. *He* wasn't well off – and he was not far from Danemouth on the night in question. So it seemed, didn't it,' said Miss Marple, 'as though *anyone* might have done it?

'But, of course, really, in my mind, I *knew*. You couldn't get away, could you, from those bitten nails?'

'Nails?' said Sir Henry. 'But she tore her nail and cut the others.'

'Nonsense,' said Miss Marple. '*Bitten* nails and close *cut* nails are quite different! Nobody could mistake them who knew anything about girl's nails — very ugly, bitten nails, as I always tell the girls in my class. Those nails, you see, were a *fact*. And they could only mean one thing. *The body in Colonel Bantry's library wasn't Ruby Keene at all*.

'And that brings you straight to the one person who must be concerned. *Josie!* Josie identified the body. She knew, she *must* have known, that it wasn't Ruby Keene's body. She said it was. She was puzzled, completely puzzled, at finding that body where it was. She practically betrayed that fact. Why? Because *she* knew, none better, where it ought to have been found! In Basil Blake's cottage. Who directed our attention to Basil? Josie, by saying to Raymond that Ruby might have been with the film man. And before that, by slipping a snapshot of him into Ruby's handbag. Who cherished such bitter anger against the dead girl that she couldn't hide it even when she looked down at her dead? Josie! Josie, who was shrewd, practical, hard as nails, and *all out for money*.

'That is what I meant about believing too readily. Nobody thought of disbelieving Josie's statement that the body was Ruby Keene's. Simply because it didn't seem at the time that she could have any motive for lying. Motive was always the difficulty — Josie was clearly involved, but Ruby's death seemed, if anything, contrary to her interests. It was not till Dinah Lee mentioned Somerset House that I got the connection.

'Marriage! If Josie and Mark Gaskell were actually married — then the whole thing was clear. As we know now, Mark and Josie were married a year ago. They were keeping it dark until Mr Jefferson died.

'It was really quite interesting, you know, tracing out the course of events — seeing exactly how the plan had worked out. Complicated and yet simple. First of all the selection of the poor child, Pamela, the approach to her from the film angle. A screen test — of course the poor child couldn't resist it. Not when it was put up to her as plausibly as Mark Gaskell put it. She comes to the hotel, he is waiting for her, he takes her in by the side door and introduces her to Josie — one of their make-up experts! That poor child, it makes me quite sick to think of it! Sitting in Josie's bathroom while Josie bleaches her hair and makes up her face and varnishes her finger-nails and toenails. During all this, the drug was given. In an icecream soda, very likely. She goes off into a coma. I imagine that they put her into one of the empty rooms opposite – they were only cleaned once a week, remember.

'After dinner Mark Gaskell went out in his car – to the sea-front, *he* said. That is when he took Pamela's body to the cottage dressed in one of Ruby's old dresses and arranged it on the hearthrug. She was still unconscious, but not dead, when he strangled her with the belt of the frock . . . Not nice, no – but I hope and pray she knew nothing about it. Really, I feel quite pleased to think of him being hanged . . . That must have been just after ten o'clock. Then he drove back at top speed and found the others in the lounge where Ruby Keene, *still alive*, was dancing her exhibition dance with Raymond.

'I should imagine that Josie had given Ruby instructions beforehand. Ruby was accustomed to doing what Josie told her. She was to change, go into Josie's room and wait. She, too, was drugged, probably in after-dinner coffee. She was yawning, remember, when she talked to young Bartlett.

'Josie came up later to "look for her" – *but nobody but Josie went into Josie's room*. She probably finished the girl off then – with an injection, perhaps, or a blow on the back of the head. She went down, danced with Raymond, debated with the Jeffersons where Ruby could be, and finally went to bed. In the early hours of the morning she dressed the girl in Pamela's clothes, carried the body down the side stairs – she was a strong muscular young woman – fetched George Bartlett's car, drove two miles to the quarry, poured petrol over the car and set it alight. Then she walked back to the hotel, probably timing her arrival there for eight or nine o'clock – up early in her anxiety about Ruby!'

'An intricate plot,' said Colonel Melchett.

'Not more intricate than the steps of a dance,' said Miss Marple.

'I suppose not.'

'She was very thorough,' said Miss Marple. 'She even foresaw the discrepancy of the nails. That's why she managed to break one of Ruby's nails on her shawl. It made an excuse for pretending that Ruby had clipped her nails close.'

Harper said: 'Yes, she thought of everything. And the only real proof you had, Miss Marple, was a schoolgirl's bitten nails.'

'More than that,' said Miss Marple. 'People *will* talk too much.

Mark Gaskell talked too much. He was speaking of Ruby and he said 'her teeth ran down her throat.' But the dead girl in Colonel Bantry's library had teeth that stuck *out*.'

Conway Jefferson said rather grimly:

'And was the last dramatic *finale* your idea, Miss Marple?'

Miss Marple confessed. 'Well, it *was*, as a matter of fact. It's so nice to be *sure*, isn't it?'

'Sure is the word,' said Conway Jefferson grimly.

'You see,' said Miss Marple, 'once Mark and Josie knew that you were going to make a new will, they'd *have* to do something. They'd already committed *two* murders on account of the money. So they might as well commit a third. Mark, of course, must be absolutely clear, so he went off to London and established an alibi by dining at a restaurant with friends and going on to a night club. Josie was to do the work. They still wanted Ruby's death to be put down to Basil's account, so Mr Jefferson's death must be thought due to his heart failing. There was digitalin, so the Superintendent tells me, in the syringe. Any doctor would think death from heart trouble quite natural in the circumstances. Josie had loosened one of the stone balls on the balcony and she was going to let it crash down afterwards. His death would be put down to the shock of the noise.'

Melchett said: 'Ingenious devil.'

Sir Henry said: 'So the third death you spoke of was to be Conway Jefferson?'

Miss Marple shook her head.

'Oh no — I meant Basil Blake. They'd have got him hanged if they could.'

'Or shut up in Broadmoor,' said Sir Henry.

Conway Jefferson grunted. He said:

'Always knew Rosamund had married a rotter. Tried not to admit it to myself. She was damned fond of him. Fond of a murderer! Well, he'll hang as well as the woman. I'm glad he went to pieces and gave the show away.'

Miss Marple said:

'She was always the strong character. It was her plan throughout. The irony of it is that she got the girl down here herself, never dreaming that she would take Mr Jefferson's fancy and ruin all her own prospects.'

Jefferson said:

'Poor lass. Poor little Ruby . . .'

Adelaide Jefferson and Hugo McLean came in. Adelaide looked almost beautiful tonight. She came up to Conway Jefferson and laid a hand on his shoulder. She said, with a little catch in her breath:

'I want to tell you something, Jeff. At once. I'm going to marry Hugo.'

Conway Jefferson looked up at her for a moment. He said gruffly:

'About time you married again. Congratulations to you both. By the way, Addie, I'm making a new will tomorrow.'

She nodded. 'Oh yes, I know.'

Jefferson said:

'No, you don't. I'm settling ten thousand pounds on you. Everything else I have goes to Peter when I die. How does that suit you, my girl?'

'Oh, *Jeff*!' Her voice broke. 'You're *wonderful*!'

'He's a nice lad. I'd like to see a good deal of him – in the time I've got left.'

'Oh, you shall!'

'Got a great feeling for crime, Peter has,' said Conway Jefferson meditatively. 'Not only has he got the fingernail of the murdered girl – one of the murdered girls, anyway – but he was lucky enough to have a bit of Josie's shawl caught in with the nail. So he's got a souvenir of the murderess too! That makes him *very* happy!'

II

Hugo and Adelaide passed by the ballroom. Raymond came up to them.

Adelaide said, rather quickly:

'I must tell you my news. We're going to be married.'

The smile on Raymond's face was perfect – a brave, pensive smile.

'I hope,' he said, ignoring Hugo and gazing into her eyes, 'that you will be very, very happy . . .'

They passed on and Raymond stood looking after them.

155

'A nice woman,' he said to himself. 'A very nice woman. And she would have had money too. The trouble I took to mug up that bit about the Devonshire Starrs ... Oh well, my luck's out. Dance, dance, little gentleman!'

And Raymond returned to the ballroom.

The Moving Finger

To my Friends
Sydney and Mary Smith

CHAPTER ONE

When at last I was taken out of the plaster, and the doctors had pulled me about to their hearts' content, and nurses had wheedled me into cautiously using my limbs, and I had been nauseated by their practically using baby talk to me, Marcus Kent told me I was to go and live in the country.

'Good air, quiet life, nothing to do — that's the prescription for you. That sister of yours will look after you. Eat, sleep and imitate the vegetable kingdom as far as possible.'

I didn't ask him if I'd ever be able to fly again. There are questions that you don't ask because you're afraid of the answers to them. In the same way during the last five months I'd never asked if I was going to be condemned to lie on my back all my life. I was afraid of a bright hypocritical reassurance from Sister. 'Come now, *what* a question to ask! We don't let our patients go talking in *that* way!'

So I hadn't asked — and it had been all right. I wasn't to be a helpless cripple. I could move my legs, stand on them, finally walk a few steps — and if I did feel rather like an adventurous baby learning to toddle, with wobbly knees and cotton wool soles to my feet — well, that was only weakness and disuse and would pass.

Marcus Kent, who is the right kind of doctor, answered what I hadn't said.

'You're going to recover completely,' he said. 'We weren't sure until last Tuesday when you had that final overhaul, but I can tell you so authoritatively now. But — it's going to be a long business. A long and, if I may so, a wearisome business. When it's a question of healing nerves and muscles, the brain must help the body. Any impatience, any fretting, will throw you back. And whatever you do, don't "will yourself to get well quickly". Anything of that kind and you'll find yourself back in a nursing home. You've got to take life slowly and easily, the *tempo* is marked *Legato*. Not only has your body got to recover, but your nerves have been weakened by the necessity of keeping you under drugs for so long.

'That's why I say, go down to the country, take a house, get interested in local politics, in local scandal, in village gossip. Take an inquisitive and violent interest in your neighbours. If I may make a suggestion, go to a part of the world where you haven't got any friends scattered about.'

I nodded. 'I had already,' I said, 'thought of that.'

I could think of nothing more insufferable than members of one's own gang dropping in full of sympathy and their own affairs.

'But Jerry, you're looking marvellous — isn't he? Absolutely. Darling, I must tell you — What do you think Buster has done now?'

No, none of that for me. Dogs are wise. They crawl away into a quiet corner and lick their wounds and do not rejoin the world until they are whole once more.

So it came about that Joanna and I, sorting wildly through house agents' glowing eulogies of properties all over the British Isles, selected Little Furze, Lymstock, as one of the 'possibles' to be viewed, mainly because we had never been to Lymstock, and knew no one in that neighbourhood.

And when Joanna saw Little Furze she decided at once that it was just the house we wanted.

It lay about half a mile out of Lymstock on the road leading up to the moors. It was a prim low white house, with a sloping Victorian veranda painted a faded green. It had a pleasant view over a slope of heather-covered land with the church spire of Lymstock down below to the left.

It had belonged to a family of maiden ladies, the Misses Barton, of whom only one was left, the youngest, Miss Emily.

Miss Emily Barton was a charming little old lady who matched her house in an incredible way. In a soft apologetic voice she explained to Joanna that she had never let her house before, indeed would never have thought of doing so, 'but you see, my dear, things are so different nowadays — *taxation*, of course, and then my stocks and shares, so *safe*, as I always imagined, and indeed the bank manager *himself* recommended some of them, but they seem to be paying *nothing at all* these days — *foreign*, of course! And really it makes it all so *difficult*. One does not (I'm sure you will understand me, my dear, and not take offence, you look so kind) *like* the idea of letting one's house to strangers — but something must be done, and really, having seen you, I shall be quite *glad* to think of you being here — it needs, you know, *young life*. And I must confess I

160

did shrink from the idea of having *Men* here!'

At this point, Joanna had to break the news of me. Miss Emily rallied well.

'Oh dear, I see. How sad! A flying accident? So brave, these young men. Still, your brother will be practically an invalid –'

The thought seemed to soothe the gentle little lady. Presumably I should not be indulging in those grosser masculine activities which Emily Barton feared. She inquired diffidently if I smoked.

'Like a chimney,' said Joanna. 'But then,' she pointed out, 'so do I.'

'Of course, of course. So stupid of me. I'm afraid, you know, I haven't moved with the times. My sisters were all older than myself, and my dear mother lived to be ninety-seven – just fancy! – and was most particular. Yes, yes, everyone smokes now. The only thing is, there are no ash-trays in the house.'

Joanna said that we would bring lots of ash-trays, and she added with a smile, 'We won't put down cigarette ends on your nice furniture, that I do promise you. Nothing makes me so mad myself as to see people do that.'

So it was settled and we took Little Furze for a period of six months, with an option of another three, and Emily Barton explained to Joanna that she herself was going to be very comfortable because she was going into rooms kept by an old parlourmaid, 'my faithful Florence', who had married 'after being with us for fifteen years. *Such* a nice girl, and her husband is in the building trade. They have a nice house in the High Street and two beautiful rooms on the top floor where I shall be *most* comfortable, and Florence so pleased to have me.'

So everything seemed to be most satisfactory, and the agreement was signed and in due course Joanna and I arrived and settled in, and Miss Emily Barton's maid Partridge having consented to remain, we were well looked after with the assistance of a 'girl' who came in every morning and who seemed to be half-witted but amiable.

Partridge, a gaunt dour female of middle age, cooked admirably, and though disapproving of late dinner (it having been Miss Emily's custom to dine lightly off a boiled egg) nevertheless accommodated herself to our ways and went so far as to admit that she could see I needed my strength building up.

When we had settled in and been at Little Furze a week Miss

Emily Barton came solemnly and left cards. Her example was followed by Mrs Symmington, the lawyer's wife, Miss Griffith, the doctor's sister, Mrs Dane Calthrop, the vicar's wife, and Mr Pye of Prior's End.

Joanna was very much impressed.

'I didn't know,' she said in an awestruck voice, 'that people really *called* – with *cards.*'

'That is because, my child,' I said, 'you know nothing about the country.'

'Nonsense. I've stayed away for heaps of week-ends with people.'

'That is not at all the same thing,' I said.

I am five years older than Joanna. I can remember as a child the big white shabby untidy house we had with the fields running down to the river. I can remember creeping under the nets of raspberry canes unseen by the gardener, and the smell of white dust in the stable yard and an orange cat crossing it, and the sound of horse hoofs kicking something in the stables.

But when I was seven and Joanna two, we went to live in London with an aunt, and thereafter our Christmas and Easter holidays were spent there with pantomimes and theatres and cinemas and excursions to Kensington Gardens with boats, and later to skating rinks. In August we were taken to an hotel by the seaside somewhere.

Reflecting on this, I said thoughtfully to Joanna, and with a feeling of compunction as I realized what a selfish, self-centred invalid I had become:

'This is going to be pretty frightful for you, I'm afraid. You'll miss everything so.'

For Joanna is very pretty and very gay, and she likes dancing and cocktails, and love affairs and rushing about in high-powered cars.

Joanna laughed and said she didn't mind at all.

'As a matter of fact, I'm glad to get away from it all. I really was fed up with the whole crowd, and although you won't be sympathetic, I was really very cut up about Paul. It will take me a long time to get over it.'

I was sceptical over this. Joanna's love affairs always run the same course. She has a mad infatuation for some completely spineless young man who is a misunderstood genius. She listens to his endless complaints and works like anything to get him recognition.

162

Then, when he is ungrateful, she is deeply wounded and says her heart is broken – until the next gloomy young man comes along, which is usually about three weeks later!

So I did not take Joanna's broken heart very seriously. But I did see that living in the country was like a new game to my attractive sister.

'At any rate,' she said, 'I look all right, don't I?'

I studied her critically and was not able to agree.

Joanna was dressed (by Mirotin) for *le Sport*. That is to say she was wearing a skirt of outrageous and preposterous checks. It was skin-tight, and on her upper half she had a ridiculous little short-sleeved jersey with a Tyrolean effect. She had sheer silk stockings and some irreproachable but brand new brogues.

'No,' I said, 'you're all wrong. You ought to be wearing a very old tweed skirt, preferably of dirty green or faded brown. You'd wear a nice cashmere jumper matching it, and perhaps a cardigan coat, and you'd have a felt hat and thick stockings and old shoes. Then, and only then, you'd sink into the background of Lymstock High Street, and not stand out as you do at present.' I added: 'Your face is all wrong, too.'

'What's wrong with that? I've got on my Country Tan Make-up No. 2.'

'Exactly,' I said. 'If you lived in Lymstock, you would have on just a little powder to take the shine off your nose, and possibly a *soupçon* of lipstick – not very well applied – and you would almost certainly be wearing all your eyebrows instead of only a quarter of them.'

Joanna gurgled and seemed much amused.

'Do you think they'll think I'm awful?' she said.

'No,' I said. 'Just queer.'

Joanna had resumed her study of the cards left by our callers. Only the vicar's wife had been so fortunate, or possibly unfortunate, as to catch Joanna at home.

Joanna murmured:

'It's rather like Happy Families, isn't it? Mrs Legal the lawyer's wife, Miss Dose the doctor's daughter, etc.' She added with enthusiasm: 'I do think this is a nice place, Jerry! So sweet and funny and old-world. You just can't think of anything nasty happening here, can you?'

163

And although I knew what she said was really nonsense, I agreed with her. In a place like Lymstock nothing nasty could happen. It is odd to think that it was just a week later that we got the first letter.

II

I see that I have begun badly. I have given no description of Lymstock and without understanding what Lymstock is like, it is impossible to understand my story.

To begin with, Lymstock has its roots in the past. Somewhere about the time of the Norman Conquest, Lymstock was a place of importance. That importance was chiefly ecclesiastical. Lymstock had a priory, and it had a long succession of ambitious and powerful priors. Lords and barons in the surrounding countryside made themselves right with Heaven by leaving certain of their lands to the priory. Lymstock Priory waxed rich and important and was a power in the land for many centuries. In due course, however, Henry the Eighth caused it to share the fate of its contemporaries. From then on a castle dominated the town. It was still important. It had rights and privileges and wealth.

And then, somewhere in seventeen hundred and something, the tide of progress swept Lymstock into a backwater. The castle crumbled. Neither railways nor main roads came near Lymstock. It turned into a little provincial market town, unimportant and forgotten, with a sweep of moorland rising behind it, and placid farms and fields ringing it round.

A market was held there once a week, on which day one was apt to encounter cattle in the lanes and roads. It had a small race meeting twice a year which only the most obscure horses attended. It had a charming High Street with dignified houses set flat back, looking slightly incongruous with their ground-floor windows displaying buns or vegetables or fruit. It had a long straggling draper's shop, a large and portentous iron-monger's, a pretentious post office, and a row of straggly indeterminate shops, two rival butchers and an International Stores. It had a doctor, a firm of solicitors, Messrs Galbraith, Galbraith and Symmington, a beautiful and unexpectedly large church dating from fourteen hundred and twenty, with some

Saxon remains incorporated in it, a new and hideous school, and two pubs.

Such was Lymstock, and urged on by Emily Barton, anybody who was anybody came to call upon us, and in due course Joanna, having bought a pair of gloves and assumed a velvet beret rather the worse for wear, sallied forth to return them.

To us, it was all quite novel and entertaining. We were not there for life. It was, for us, an interlude. I prepared to obey my doctor's instructions and get interested in my neighbours.

Joanna and I found it all great fun.

I remembered, I suppose, Marcus Kent's instructions to enjoy the local scandals. I certainly didn't suspect how these scandals were going to be introduced to my notice.

The odd part of it was that the letter, when it came, amused us more than anything else.

It arrived, I remember, at breakfast. I turned it over, in the idle way one does when time goes slowly and every event must be spun out to its full extent. It was, I saw, a local letter with a typewritten address.

I opened it before the two with London postmarks, since one of them was a bill and the other from a rather tiresome cousin.

Inside, printed words and letters had been cut out and gummed to a sheet of paper. For a minute or two I stared at the words without taking them in. Then I gasped.

Joanna, who was frowning over some bills, looked up.

'Hallo,' she said, 'what is it? You look quite startled.'

The letter, using terms of the coarsest character, expressed the writer's opinion that Joanna and I were not brother and sister.

'It's a particularly foul anonymous letter,' I said.

I was still suffering from shock. Somehow one didn't expect that kind of thing in the placid backwater of Lymstock.

Joanna at once displayed lively interest.

'*No?* What does it say?'

In novels, I have noticed, anonymous letters of a foul and disgusting character are never shown, if possible, to women. It is implied that women must at all cost be shielded from the shock it might give their delicate nervous systems.

I am sorry to say it never occurred to me not to show the letter to Joanna. I handed it to her at once.

She vindicated my belief in her toughness by displaying no emotion but that of amusement.

'What an awful bit of dirt! I've always heard about anonymous letters, but I've never seen one before. Are they always like this?'

'I can't tell you,' I said. 'It's my first experience, too.'

Joanna began to giggle.

'You must have been right about my make-up, Jerry. I suppose they think I just *must* be an abandoned female!'

'That,' I said, 'coupled with the fact that our father was a tall, dark lantern-jawed man and our mother a fair-haired blue-eyed little creature, and that I take after him and you take after her.'

Joanna nodded thoughtfully.

'Yes, we're not a bit alike. Nobody would take us for brother and sister.'

'Somebody certainly hasn't,' I said with feeling.

Joanna said she thought it was frightfully funny.

She dangled the letter thoughtfully by one corner and asked what we were to do with it.

'The correct procedure, I believe,' I said, 'is to drop it into the fire with a sharp exclamation of disgust.'

I suited the action to the word, and Joanna applauded.

'You did that beautifully,' she added. 'You ought to have been on the stage. It's lucky we still have fires, isn't it?'

'The waste-paper basket would have been much less dramatic,' I agreed. 'I could, of course, have set light to it with a match and slowly watched it burn – or watched it slowly burn.'

'Things never burn when you want them to,' said Joanna. 'They go out. You'd probably have had to strike match after match.'

She got up and went towards the window. Then, standing there, she turned her head sharply.

'I wonder,' she said, 'who wrote it?'

'We're never likely to know,' I said.

'No – I suppose not.' She was silent a moment, and then said: 'I don't know when I come to think of it that it is so funny after all. You know, I thought they – they *liked* us down here.'

'So they do,' I said. 'This is just some half-crazy brain on the borderline.'

'I suppose so. Ugh – Nasty!'

As she went out into the sunshine I thought to myself as I smoked my after-breakfast cigarette that she was quite right. It was nasty. Someone resented our coming here – someone resented Joanna's bright young sophisticated beauty – somebody wanted to *hurt*. To take it with a laugh was perhaps the best way – but deep down it wasn't funny . . .

Dr Griffith came that morning. I had fixed up for him to give me a weekly overhaul. I liked Owen Griffith. He was dark, ungainly, with awkward ways of moving and deft, very gentle hands. He had a jerky way of talking and was rather shy.

He reported progress to be encouraging. Then he added:

'You're feeling all right, aren't you. Is it my fancy, or are you a bit under the weather this morning?'

'Not really,' I said. 'A particularly scurrilous anonymous letter arrived with the morning coffee, and it's left rather a nasty taste in the mouth.'

He dropped his bag on the floor. His thin dark face was excited.

'Do you mean to say that *you've* had one of them?'

I was interested.

'They've been going about, then?'

'Yes. For some time.'

'Oh,' I said, 'I see. I was under the impression that our presence as strangers was resented here.'

'No, no, it's nothing to do with that. It's just –' He paused and then asked, 'What did it say? At least –' he turned suddenly red and embarrassed – 'perhaps I oughtn't to ask?'

'I'll tell you with pleasure,' I said. 'It just said that the fancy tart I'd brought down with me wasn't my sister – not 'alf! And that, I may say, is a Bowdlerized version.'

His dark face flushed angrily.

'How damnable! Your sister didn't – she's not upset, I hope?'

'Joanna,' I said, 'looks a little like the angel off the top of the Christmas tree, but she's eminently modern and quite tough. She found it highly entertaining. Such things haven't come her way before.'

'I should hope not, indeed,' said Griffith warmly.

'And anyway,' I said firmly. 'That's the best way to take it, I think. As something utterly ridiculous.'

'Yes,' said Owen Griffith. 'Only –'

'Quite so,' I said. 'Only is the word!'

'The trouble is,' he said, 'that this sort of thing, once it starts, grows.'

'So I should imagine.'

'It's pathological, of course.'

I nodded. 'Any idea who's behind it?' I asked.

'No, I wish I had. You see, the anonymous letter pest arises from one of two causes. Either it's *particular* – directed at one particular person or set of people, that is to say it's *motivated*, it's someone who's got a definite grudge (or thinks they have) and who chooses a particularly nasty and underhand way of working it off. It's mean and disgusting but it's not necessarily crazy, and it's usually fairly easy to trace the writer – a discharged servant, a jealous woman – and so on. But if it's *general*, and not particular, then it's more serious. The letters are sent indiscriminately and serve the purpose of working off some frustration in the writer's mind. As I say, it's definitely pathological. And the craze grows. In the end, of course, you track down the person in question – it's often someone extremely unlikely, and that's that. There was a bad outburst of the kind over the other side of the county last year – turned out to be the head of the millinery department in a big draper's establishment. Quiet, refined woman – had been there for years. I remember something of the same kind in my last practice up north – but that turned out to be purely personal spite. Still, as I say, I've seen something of this kind of thing, and, quite frankly, it frightens me!'

'Has it been going on long?' I asked.

'I don't think so. Hard to say, of course, because people who get these letters don't go round advertising the fact. They put them in the fire.'

He paused.

'I've had one myself. Symmington, the solicitor, he's had one. And one or two of my poorer patients have told me about them.'

'All much the same sort of thing?'

'Oh yes. A definite harping on the sex theme. That's always a feature.' He grinned. 'Symmington was accused of illicit relations with his lady clerk – poor old Miss Ginch, who's forty at least, with pince-nez and teeth like a rabbit. Symmington took it straight to the police. My letters accused me of violating professional decorum with my lady patients, stressing the details. They're all quite childish and absurd, but horribly venomous.' His face changed, grew grave. 'But all the same, I'm *afraid*. These things can be dangerous, you know.'

'I suppose they can.'

'You see,' he said, 'crude, childish spite though it is, sooner or later one of these letters will hit the mark. And then, God knows what may happen! I'm afraid, too, of the effect upon the slow, suspicious uneducated mind. If they see a thing written, they believe it's true. All sorts of complications may arise.'

'It was an illiterate sort of letter,' I said thoughtfully, 'written by somebody practically illiterate, I should say.'

'Was it?' said Owen, and went away.

Thinking it over afterwards, I found that 'Was it?' rather disturbing.

CHAPTER TWO

I am not going to pretend that the arrival of our anonymous letter did not leave a nasty taste in the mouth. It did. At the same time, it soon passed out of my mind. I did not, you see, at that point, take it seriously. I think I remember saying to myself that these things probably happen fairly often in out-of-the-way villages. Some hysterical woman with a taste for dramatizing herself was probably at the bottom of it. Anyway, if the letters were as childish and silly as the one we had got, they couldn't do much harm.

The next *incident*, if I may put it so, occurred about a week later, when Partridge, her lips set tightly together, informed me that Beatrice, the daily help, would not be coming today.

'I gather, sir,' said Partridge, 'that the girl has been Upset.'

I was not very sure what Partridge was implying, but I diagnosed (wrongly) some stomachic trouble to which Partridge was too delicate to allude more directly. I said I was sorry and hoped she would soon be better.

'The girl is perfectly well, sir,' said Partridge. 'She is Upset in her Feelings.'

'Oh,' I said rather doubtfully.

'Owing,' went on Partridge, 'to a letter she has received. Making, I understand, Insinuations.'

The grimness of Partridge's eye, coupled with the obvious capital I of Insinuations, made me apprehensive that the insinuations were concerned with me. Since I would hardly have recognized Beatrice by sight if I had met her in the town so unaware of her had I been – I felt a not unnatural annoyance. An invalid hobbling about on two sticks is hardly cast for the role of deceiver of village girls. I said irritably:

'What nonsense!'

'My very words, sir, to the girl's mother,' said Partridge. '"Goings On in this house," I said to her, "there never have been and never will be while I am in charge. As to Beatrice," I said, "girls are different nowadays, and as to Goings On elsewhere I can say nothing." But the truth is, sir, that Beatrice's friend from the garage as she walks out with got one of them nasty letters too, and he isn't acting reasonable at all.'

'I have never heard anything so preposterous in my life,' I said angrily.

'It's my opinion, sir,' said Partridge, 'that we're well rid of the girl. What I say is, she wouldn't take on so if there wasn't *something* she didn't want found out. No smoke without fire, that's what I say.'

I had no idea how horribly tired I was going to get of that particular phrase.

II

That morning, by way of adventure, I was to walk down to the village. (Joanna and I always called it the village, although technically we were incorrect, and Lymstock would have been annoyed to hear us.)

The sun was shining, the air was cool and crisp with the sweetness of spring in it. I assembled my sticks and started off, firmly refusing to permit Joanna to accompany me.

'No,' I said, 'I will not have a guardian angel teetering along beside me and uttering encouraging chirrups. A man travels fastest who travels alone, remember. I have much business to transact. I shall go to Galbraith, Galbraith and Symmington, and sign that transfer of shares, I shall call in at the baker's and complain about the currant loaf, and I shall return that book we borrowed. I have to go to the bank, too. Let me away, woman, the morning is all too short.'

It was arranged that Joanna should pick me up with the car and drive me back up the hill in time for lunch.

'That ought to give you time to pass the time of day with everyone in Lymstock.'

'I have no doubt,' I said, 'that I shall have seen anybody who is anybody by then.'

For morning in the High Street was a kind of rendezvous for shoppers, when news was exchanged.

I did not, after all, walk down to the town unaccompanied. I had gone about two hundred yards, when I heard a bicycle bell behind me, then a scrunching of brakes, and then Megan Hunter more or less fell off her machine at my feet.

'Hallo,' she said breathlessly as she rose and dusted herself off.

I rather liked Megan and always felt oddly sorry for her.

She was Symmington the lawyer's step-daughter, Mrs Symmington's daughter by a first marriage. Nobody talked much about Mr (or Captain) Hunter, and I gathered that he was considered best forgotten. He was reported to have treated Mrs Symmington very badly. She had divorced him a year or two after the marriage. She was a woman with means of her own and had settled down with her little daughter in Lymstock 'to forget', and had eventually married the only eligible bachelor in the place, Richard Symmington. There were two boys of the second marriage to whom their parents were devoted, and I fancied that Megan sometimes felt odd man out in the establishment. She certainly did not resemble her mother, who was a small anaemic woman, fadedly pretty, who talked in a thin melancholy voice of servant difficulties and her health.

Megan was a tall awkward girl, and although she was actually twenty, she looked more like a schoolgirlish sixteen. She had a shock of untidy brown hair, hazel green eyes, a thin bony face, and an unexpected charming one-sided smile. Her clothes were drab and unattractive and she usually had on lisle thread stockings with holes in them.

She looked, I decided this morning, much more like a horse than a human being. In fact she would have been a very nice horse with a little grooming.

She spoke, as usual, in a kind of breathless rush.

171

'I've been up to the farm — you know, Lasher's — to see if they'd got any duck's eggs. They've got an awfully nice lot of little pigs. Sweet! Do you like pigs? I even like the smell.'

'Well-kept pigs shouldn't smell,' I said.

'Shouldn't they? They all do round here. Are you walking down to the town? I saw you were alone, so I thought I'd stop and walk with you, only I stopped rather suddenly.'

'You've torn your stocking,' I said.

Megan looked rather ruefully at her right leg.

'So I have. But it's got two holes already, so it doesn't matter very much, does it?'

'Don't you ever mend your stockings, Megan?'

'Rather. When Mummy catches me. But she doesn't notice awfully what I do — so it's lucky in a way, isn't it?'

'You don't seem to realize you're grown up,' I said.

'You mean I ought to be more like your sister? All dolled up?'

I rather resented this description of Joanna.

'She looks clean and tidy and pleasing to the eye,' I said.

'She's awfully pretty,' said Megan. 'She isn't a bit like you, is she? Why not?'

'Brothers and sisters aren't always alike.'

'No. Of course. I'm not very like Brian or Colin. And Brian and Colin aren't like each other.' She paused and said, 'It's very rum, isn't it?'

'What is?'

Megan replied briefly: 'Families.'

I said thoughtfully, 'I suppose they are.'

I wondered just what was passing in her mind. We walked on in silence for a moment or two, then Megan said in a rather shy voice:

'You fly, don't you?'

'Yes.'

'That's how you got hurt?'

'Yes, I crashed.'

Megan said:

'Nobody down here flies.'

'No,' I said. 'I suppose not. Would you like to fly, Megan?'

'Me?' Megan seemed surprised. 'Goodness, no. I should be sick. I'm sick in a train even.'

She paused, and then asked with that directness which only a child usually displays:

'Will you get all right and be able to fly again, or will you always be a bit of a crock?'

'My doctor says I shall be quite all right.'

'Yes, but is he the kind of man who tells lies?'

'I don't think so,' I replied. 'In fact, I'm quite sure of it. I trust him.'

'That's all right then. But a lot of people do tell lies.'

I accepted this undeniable statement of fact in silence.

Megan said in a detached judicial kind of way:

'I'm glad. I was afraid you looked bad tempered because you were crocked up for life – but if it's just natural, it's different.'

'I'm not bad tempered,' I said coldly.

'Well, irritable, then.'

'I'm irritable because I'm in a hurry to get fit again – and these things can't be hurried.'

'Then why fuss?'

I began to laugh.

'My dear girl, aren't you ever in a hurry for things to happen?'

Megan considered the question. She said:

'No. Why should I be? There's nothing to be in a hurry about. Nothing ever happens.'

I was struck by something forlorn in the words. I said gently: 'What do you do with yourself down here?'

She shrugged her shoulders.

'What is there to do?'

'Haven't you got any hobbies? Do you play games? Have you got friends round about?'

'I'm stupid at games. And I don't like them much. There aren't many girls round here, and the ones there are I don't like. They think I'm awful.'

'Nonsense. Why should they?'

Megan shook her head.

'Didn't you go to school at all?'

'Yes, I came back a year ago.'

'Did you enjoy school?'

'It wasn't bad. They taught you things in an awfully silly way, though.'

173

'How do you mean?'

'Well — just bits and pieces. Chopping and changing from one thing to the other. It was a cheap school, you know, and the teachers weren't very good. They could never answer questions properly.'

'Very few teachers can,' I said.

'Why not? They ought to.'

I agreed.

'Of course I'm pretty stupid,' said Megan. 'And such a lot of things seem to me such rot. History, for instance. Why, it's quite different out of different books!'

'That is its real interest,' I said.

'And grammar,' went on Megan. 'And silly compositions. And all the blathering stuff Shelley wrote, twittering on about skylarks, and Wordsworth going all potty over some silly daffodils. And Shakespeare.'

'What's wrong with Shakespeare?' I inquired with interest.

'Twisting himself up to say things in such a difficult way that you can't get at what he means. Still, I like *some* Shakespeare.'

'He would be gratified to know that, I'm sure,' I said.

Megan suspected no sarcasm. She said, her face lighting up:

'I like Goneril and Regan, for instance.'

'Why these two?'

'Oh, I don't know. They're *satisfactory*, somehow. Why do you think they were like that?'

'Like what?'

'Like they were. I mean *something* must have made them like that?'

For the first time I wondered. I had always accepted Lear's elder daughters as two nasty bits of goods and had let it go at that. But Megan's demand for a first cause interested me.

'I'll think about it,' I said.

'Oh, it doesn't really matter. I just wondered. Anyway, it's only English Literature, isn't it?'

'Quite, quite. Wasn't there any subject you enjoyed?'

'Only Maths.'

'Maths?' I said, rather surprised.

Megan's face had lit up.

'I loved Maths. But it wasn't awfully well taught. I'd like to be

174

taught Maths really well. It's heavenly. I think there's something heavenly about numbers, anyway, don't you?'

'I've never felt it,' I said truthfully.

We were now entering the High street. Megan said sharply:

'Here's Miss Griffith. Hateful woman.'

'Don't you like her?'

'I loathe her. She's always at me to join her foul Guides. I hate Guides. Why dress yourself up and go about in clumps, and put badges on yourself for something you haven't really learnt to do properly? I think it's all rot.'

On the whole, I rather agreed with Megan. But Miss Griffith had descended on us before I could voice my assent.

The doctor's sister, who rejoined in the singularly inappropriate name of Aimée, had all the positive assurance that her brother lacked. She was a handsome woman in a masculine weather-beaten way, with a deep hearty voice.

'Hallo, you two,' she bayed at us. 'Gorgeous morning, isn't it? Megan, you're just the person I wanted to see. I want some help addressing envelopes for the Conservative Association.'

Megan muttered something elusive, propped up her bicycle against the kerb and dived in a purposeful way into the International Stores.

'Extraordinary child,' said Miss Griffith, looking after her. 'Bone lazy. Spends her time mooning about. Must be a great trial to poor Mrs Symmington. I know her mother's tried more than once to get her to take up something – shorthand-typing, you know, or cookery, or keeping Angora rabbits. She needs an *interest* in life.'

I thought that was probably true, but felt that in Megan's place I should have withstood firmly any of Aimée Griffith's suggestions for the simple reason that her aggressive personality would have put my back up.

'I don't believe in idleness,' went on Miss Griffith. 'And certainly not for young people. It's not as though Megan was pretty or attractive or anything like that. Sometimes I think the girl's half-witted. A great disappointment to her mother. The father, you know,' she lowered her voice slightly, 'was definitely a wrong 'un. Afraid the child takes after him. Painful for her mother. Oh, well, it takes all sorts to make a world, that's what I say.'

'Fortunately,' I responded.

Aimée Griffith gave a 'jolly' laugh.

'Yes, it wouldn't do if we were all made to one pattern. But I don't like to see anyone not getting all they can out of life. I enjoy life myself and I want everyone to enjoy it too. People say to me you must be bored to death living down there in the country all the year round. Not a bit of it, I say. I'm always busy, always happy! There's always something going on in the country. My time's taken up, what with my Guides, and the Institute and various committees — to say nothing of looking after Owen.'

At this minute, Miss Griffith saw an acquaintance on the other side of the street, and uttering a bay of recognition she leaped across the road, leaving me free to pursue my course to the bank.

I always found Miss Griffith rather overwhelming, though I admired her energy and vitality, and it was pleasant to see the beaming contentment with her lot in life which she always displayed, and which was a pleasant contrast to the subdued complaining murmurs of so many women.

My business at the bank transacted satisfactorily, I went on to the offices of Messrs Galbraith, Galbraith and Symmington. I don't know if there were any Galbraiths extant. I never saw any. I was shown into Richard Symmington's inner office which had the agreeable mustiness of a long-established legal firm.

Vast numbers of deed boxes, labelled Lady Hope, Sir Everard Carr, William Yatesby-Hoares, Esq., Deceased, etc., gave the required atmosphere of decorous county families and legitimate long-established business.

Studying Mr Symmington as he bent over the documents I had brought, it occurred to me that if Mrs Symmington had encountered disaster in her first marriage, she had certainly played safe in her second. Richard Symmington was the acme of calm respectability, the sort of man who would never give his wife a moment's anxiety. A long neck with a pronounced Adam's apple, a slightly cadaverous face and a long thin nose. A kindly man, no doubt, a good husband and father, but not one to set the pulses madly racing.

Presently Mr Symmington began to speak. He spoke clearly and slowly, delivering himself of much good sense and shrewd acumen. We settled the matter in hand and I rose to go, remarking as I did so:

'I walked down the hill with your step-daughter.'

For a moment Mr Symmington looked as though he did not know who his step-daughter was, then he smiled.

'Oh yes, of course, Megan. She – er – has been back from school some time. We're thinking about finding her something to do – yes, to do. But of course she's very young still. And backward for her age, so they say. Yes, so they tell me.'

I went out. In the outer office was a very old man on a stool writing slowly and laboriously, a small cheeky-looking boy and a middle-aged woman with frizzy hair and pince-nez who was typing with some speed and dash.

If this was Miss Ginch I agreed with Owen Griffith that tender passages between her and her employer were exceedingly unlikely.

I went into the baker's and said my piece about the currant loaf. It was received with the exclamation and incredulity proper to the occasion, and a new currant loaf was thrust upon me in replacement – 'fresh from the oven this minute' – as its indecent heat pressed against my chest proclaimed to be no less than truth.

I came out of the shop and looked up and down the street hoping to see Joanna with the car. The walk had tired me a good deal and it was awkward getting along with my sticks and the currant loaf.

But there was no sign of Joanna as yet.

Suddenly my eyes were held in glad and incredulous surprise.

Along the pavement towards me there came floating a goddess. There is really no other word for it.

The perfect features, the crisply curling golden hair, the tall exquisitely shaped body! And she walked like a goddess, without effort, seeming to swim nearer and nearer. A glorious, an incredible, a breath-taking girl!

In my intense excitement something had to go. What went was the currant loaf. It slipped from my clutches. I made a dive after it and lost my stick, which clattered to the pavement, and I slipped and nearly fell myself.

It was the strong arm of the goddess that caught and held me. I began to stammer:

'Th-thanks awfully, I'm f-f-frightfully sorry.'

She had retrieved the currant loaf and handed it to me together with the stick. And then she smiled kindly and said cheerfully:

'Don't mention it. No trouble, I assure you,' and the magic died completely before the flat, competent voice.

A nice healthy-looking well set-up girl, no more.

I fell to reflecting what would have happened if the Gods had given Helen of Troy exactly those flat accents. How strange that a girl could trouble your inmost soul so long as she kept her mouth shut, and that the moment she spoke the glamour could vanish as though it had never been.

I had known the reverse happen, though. I had seen a little sad monkey-faced woman whom no one would turn to look at twice. Then she opened her mouth and suddenly enchantment had lived and bloomed and Cleopatra had cast her spell anew.

Joanna had drawn up at the kerb beside me without my noticing her arrival. She asked if there was anything the matter.

'Nothing,' I said, pulling myself together. 'I was reflecting on Helen of Troy and others.'

'What a funny place to do it,' said Joanna. 'You looked *most* odd, standing there clasping currant bread to your breast with your mouth wide open.'

'I've had a shock,' I said. 'I have been transplanted to Ilium and back again.

'Do you know who that is?' I added, indicating a retreating back that was swimming gracefully away.

Peering after the girl Joanna said that it was the Symmingtons' nursery governess.

'Is that what struck you all of a heap?' she asked. 'She's good-looking, but a bit of a wet fish.'

'I know,' I said. 'Just a nice kind girl. And I'd been thinking her Aphrodite.'

Joanna opened the door of the car and I got in.

'It's funny, isn't it?' she said. 'Some people have lots of looks and absolutely no S.A. That girl has. It seems such a pity.'

I said that if she was a nursery governess it was probably just as well.

CHAPTER THREE

That afternoon we went to tea with Mr Pye.

Mr Pye was an extremely ladylike plump little man, devoted to his *petit point* chairs, his Dresden shepherdesses and his collection of bric-à-brac. He lived at Prior's Lodge in the grounds of which were the ruins of the old Priory.

Prior's Lodge was certainly a very exquisite house and under Mr Pye's loving care it showed to its best advantage. Every piece of furniture was polished and set in the exact place most suited to it. The curtains and cushions were of exquisite tone and colour, and of the most expensive silks.

It was hardly a man's house, and it did strike me that to live there would be rather like taking up one's abode in a period room at a museum. Mr Pye's principal enjoyment in life was taking people round his house. Even those completely insensitive to their surroundings could not escape. Even if you were so hardened as to consider the essentials of living a radio, a cocktail bar, a bath and a bed surrounded by the necessary walls, Mr Pye did not despair of leading you to better things.

His small plump hands quivered with sensibility as he described his treasures, and his voice rose to a falsetto squeak as he narrated the exciting circumstances under which he had brought his Italian bedstead home from Verona.

Joanna and I being both fond of antiquities and of period furniture, met with approval.

'It is really a pleasure, a great pleasure, to have such an acquisition to our little community. The dear good people down here, you know, so painfully bucolic – not to say *provincial*. They don't know anything. Vandals – absolute vandals! And the inside of their houses – it would make you weep, dear lady, I assure you it would make you weep. Perhaps it has done so?'

Joanna said that she hadn't gone quite as far as that.

'But you see what I mean? They mix things so terribly! I've seen with my own eyes a most delightful little Sheraton piece – delicate,

179

perfect – a collector's piece, absolutely – and next to it a Victorian occasional table, or quite possibly a fumed oak revolving bookcase – yes, even that – *fumed oak*.'

He shuddered – and murmured plaintively:

'Why are people so blind? You agree – I'm sure you agree, that beauty is the only thing worth living for.'

Hypnotized by his earnestness, Joanna said, yes, yes, that was so.

'Then why,' demanded Mr Pye, 'do people surround themselves with ugliness?'

Joanna said it was very odd.

'Odd? It's *criminal*! That's what I call it – criminal! And the excuses they give! They say something is *comfortable*. Or that it is *quaint*. Quaint! Such a horrible word.'

'The house you have taken,' went on Mr Pye, 'Miss Emily Barton's house. Now that is charming, and she has some quite nice pieces. Quite nice. One or two of them are really first class. And she has taste, too – although I'm not quite so sure of that as I was. Sometimes, I am afraid, I think it's really sentiment. She likes to keep things as they were – but not for *le bon motif* – not because of the resultant harmony – but because it is the way her mother had them.'

He transferred his attention to me, and his voice changed. It altered from that of the rapt artist to that of the born gossip.

'You didn't know the family at all? No, quite so – yes, through house agents. But, my dears, you *ought* to have known that family! When I came here the old mother was still alive. An incredible person – quite incredible! A *monster*, if you know what I mean. Positively a monster. The old-fashioned Victorian monster, devouring her young. Yes, that's what it amounted to. She was monumental, you know, must have weighed seventeen stone, and all the five daughters revolved round her. "The girls"! That's how she always spoke of them. The girls! And the eldest was well over sixty then. "Those stupid girls!" she used to call them sometimes. Black slaves, that's all they were, fetching and carrying and agreeing with her. Ten o'clock they had to go to bed and they weren't allowed a fire in their bedroom, and as for asking their own friends to the house, that would have been unheard of. She despised them, you know, for not getting married, and yet so arranged their lives that it was practically impossible for them to meet anybody. I believe

Emily, or perhaps it was Agnes, did have some kind of affair with a curate. But his family wasn't good enough and Mamma soon put a stop to *that*!'

'It sounds like a novel,' said Joanna.

'Oh, my dear, it was. And then the dreadful old woman died, but of course it was far too late *then*. They just went on living there and talking in hushed voices about what poor Mamma would have wished. Even repapering her bedroom they felt to be quite sacrilegious. Still they did enjoy themselves in the parish in a quiet way ... But none of them had much stamina, and they just died off one by one. Influenza took off Edith, and Minnie had an operation and didn't recover and poor Mabel had a stroke – Emily looked after her in the most devoted manner. Really that poor woman has done nothing but nursing for the last ten years. A charming creature, don't you think? Like a piece of Dresden. So sad for her having financial anxieties – but of course all investments have depreciated.'

'We feel rather awful being in her house,' said Joanna.

'No, no, my dear young lady. You mustn't feel that way. Her dear good Florence is devoted to her and she told me herself how happy she was to have got such nice tenants.' Here Mr Pye made a little bow. 'She told me she thought she had been most fortunate.'

'The house,' I said, 'has a very soothing atmosphere.'

Mr Pye darted a quick glance at me.

'Really? You feel that? Now, that's very interesting. I wondered, you know. Yes, I wondered.'

'What do you mean, Mr Pye?' asked Joanna.

Mr Pye spread out his plump hands.

'Nothing, nothing. One wondered, that is all. I do believe in atmosphere, you know. People's thoughts and feelings. They give their impression to the walls and the furniture.'

I did not speak for a moment or two. I was looking round me and wondering how I would describe the atmosphere of Prior's Lodge. It seemed to me that the curious thing was that it hadn't any atmosphere! That was really very remarkable.

I reflected on this point so long that I heard nothing of the conversation going on between Joanna and her host. I was recalled to myself, however, by hearing Joanna uttering farewell preliminaries. I came out of my dream and added my quota.

We all went out into the hall. As we came towards the front door

181

a letter came through the box and fell on the mat.

'Afternoon post,' murmured Mr Pye as he picked it up. 'Now, my dear young people, you will come again, won't you? Such a pleasure to meet some broader minds, if you understand me. Someone with an appreciation of Art. Really you know, these dear good people down here, if you mention the Ballet, it conveys to them pirouetting toes, and *tulle* skirts and old gentlemen with opera glasses in the Naughty Nineties. It does indeed. Fifty years behind the times – that's what I put them down, as. A wonderful country, England. It has *pockets*. Lymstock is one of them. Interesting from a collector's point of view – I always feel I have voluntarily put myself under a glass shade when I am here. The peaceful backwater where nothing ever happens.'

Shaking hands with us twice over, he helped me with exaggerated care into the car. Joanna took the wheel, she negotiated with some care the circular sweep round a plot of unblemished grass, then with a straight drive ahead, she raised a hand to wave goodbye to our host where he stood on the steps of the house. I leaned forward to do the same.

But our gesture of farewell went unheeded. Mr Pye had opened his mail.

He was standing staring down at the open sheet in his hand.

Joanna had described him once as a plump pink cherub. He was still plump, but he was not looking like a cherub now. His face was a dark congested purple, contorted with rage and surprise.

And at that moment I realized that there had been something familiar about the look of that envelope. I had not realized it at the time – indeed it had been one of those things that you note unconsciously without knowing that you do note them.

'Goodness,' said Joanna. 'What's bitten the poor pet?'

'I rather fancy,' I said, 'that it's the Hidden Hand again.'

She turned an astonished face towards me and the car swerved.

'Careful, wench,' I said.

Joanna refixed her attention on the road. She was frowning.

'You mean a letter like the one you got?'

'That's my guess.'

'What is this place?' asked Joanna. 'It looks the most innocent sleepy harmless little bit of England you can imagine –'

'Where to quote Mr Pye, nothing ever happens,' I cut in. 'He chose the wrong minute to say that. Something has happened.'

'But who writes these things, Jerry?'

I shrugged my shoulders.

'My dear girl, how should I know? Some local nitwit with a screw loose, I suppose.'

'But why? It seems so idiotic.'

'You must read Freud and Jung and that lot to find out. Or ask our Dr Owen.'

Joanna tossed her head.

'Dr Owen doesn't like me.'

'He's hardly seen you.'

'He's seen quite enough, apparently, to make him cross over if he sees me coming along the High Street.'

'A most unusual reaction,' I said sympathetically. 'And one you're not used to.'

Joanna was frowning again.

'No, but seriously, Jerry, why *do* people write anonymous letters?'

'As I say, they've got a screw loose. It satisfies some urge, I suppose. If you've been snubbed, or ignored, or frustrated, and your life's pretty drab and empty, I suppose you get a sense of power from stabbing in the dark at people who are happy and enjoying themselves.'

Joanna shivered. 'Not nice.'

'No, not nice. I should imagine the people in these country places tend to be inbred — and so you would get a fair amount of queers.'

'Somebody, I suppose, quite uneducated and inarticulate? With better education —'

Joanna did not finish her sentence, and I said nothing. I have never been able to accept the easy belief that education is a panacea for every ill.

As we drove through the town before climbing up the hill road, I looked curiously at the few figures abroad in the High Street. Was one of those sturdy country-women going about with a load of spite and malice behind her placid brow, planning perhaps even now a further outpouring of vindictive spleen?

But I still did not take the thing seriously.

Two days later we went to a bridge party at the Symmingtons.

It was a Saturday afternoon – the Symmingtons always had their bridge parties on a Saturday, because the office was shut then.

There were two tables. The players were the Symmingtons, ourselves, Miss Griffith, Mr Pye, Miss Barton and a Colonel Appleton whom we had not yet met and who lived at Combeacre, a village some seven miles distant. He was a perfect specimen of the Blimp type, about sixty years of age, liked playing what he called a 'plucky game' (which usually resulted in immense sums above the line being scored by his opponents) and was so intrigued by Joanna that he practically never took his eyes off her the whole afternoon.

I was forced to admit that my sister was probably the most attractive thing that had been seen in Lymstock for many a long day.

When we arrived, Elsie Holland, the children's governess, was hunting for some extra bridge scorers in an ornate writing desk. She glided across the floor with them in the same celestial way I had first noticed, but the spell could not be cast a second time. Exasperating that it should be so – a waste of a perfectly lovely form and face. But I noticed now only too clearly the exceptionally large white teeth like tombstones, and the way she showed her gums when she laughed. She was, unfortunately, one of your prattling girls.

'Are these the ones, Mrs Symmington? It's ever so stupid of me not to remember where we put them away last time. It's my fault, too, I'm afraid. I had them in my hand and then Brian called out his engine had got caught, and I ran out and what with one thing and another I must have just stuffed them in somewhere stupid. These aren't the right ones, I see now, they're a bit yellow at the edges. Shall I tell Agnes tea at five? I'm taking the kiddies to Long Barrow so there won't be any noise.'

A nice kind bright girl. I caught Joanna's eye. She was laughing. I stared at her coldly. Joanna always knows what is passing in my mind, curse her.

We settled down to bridge.

I was soon to know to a nicety the bridge status of everyone in Lymstock. Mrs Symmington was an exceedingly good bridge player and was quite a devotee of the game. Like many definitely unintellectual women, she was not stupid and had a considerable natural shrewdness. Her husband was a good sound player, slightly over-cautious. Mr Pye can best be described as brilliant. He had an uncanny flair for psychic bidding. Joanna and I, since the party was in our honour, played at a table with Mrs Symmington and Mr Pye. It was Symmington's task to pour oil on troubled waters and by the exercise of tact to reconcile the three other players at his table. Colonel Appleton, as I have said, was wont to play 'a plucky game'. Little Miss Barton was without exception the worst bridge player I have ever come across and always enjoyed herself enormously. She did manage to follow suit, but had the wildest ideas as to the strength of her hand, never knew the score, repeatedly led out of the wrong hand and was quite unable to count trumps and often forgot what they were. Aimée Griffith's play can be summed up in her own words. 'I like a good game of bridge with no nonsense – and I don't play any of these rubbishly conventions. I say what I mean. And no postmortems! After all, it's only a game!' It will be seen, therefore, that their host had not too easy a task.

Play proceeded fairly harmoniously, however, with occasional forgetfulness on the part of Colonel Appleton as he stared across at Joanna.

Tea was laid in the dining-room, round a big table. As we were finishing, two hot and excited little boys rushed in and were introduced, Mrs Symmington beaming with maternal pride, as was their father.

Then, just as we were finishing, a shadow darkened my plate, and I turned my head to see Megan standing in the french window.

'Oh,' said her mother. 'Here's Megan.'

Her voice held a faintly surprised note, as though she had forgotten that Megan existed.

The girl came in and shook hands, awkwardly and without any grace.

'I'm afraid I forgot about your tea, dear,' said Mrs Symmington. 'Miss Holland and the boys took theirs out with them, so there's no nursery tea today. I forgot you weren't with them.'

Megan nodded.

'That's all right. I'll go to the kitchen.'

She slouched out of the room. She was untidily dressed as usual and there were potatoes in both heels.

Mrs Symmington said with a little apologetic laugh:

'My poor Megan. She's just at that awkward age, you know. Girls are always shy and awkward when they've just left school before they're properly grown up.'

I saw Joanna's fair head jerk backwards in what I knew to be a warlike gesture.

'But Megan's twenty, isn't she?' she said.

'Oh, yes, yes. She is. But of course she's very young for her age. Quite a child still. It's so nice, I think, when girls don't grow up too quickly.' She laughed again. 'I expect all mothers want their children to remain babies.'

'I can't think why,' said Joanna. 'After all, it would be a bit awkward if one had a child who remained mentally six while his body grew up.'

'Oh, you mustn't take things so literally, Miss Burton,' said Mrs Symmington.

It occurred to me at that moment that I did not much care for Mrs Symmington. That anaemic, slighted, faded prettiness concealed, I thought, a selfish and grasping nature. She said, and I disliked her a little more still:

'My poor Megan. She's rather a difficult child, I'm afraid. I've been trying to find something for her to do – I believe there are several things one can learn by correspondence. Designing and dress-making – or she might try and learn shorthand and typing.'

The red glint was still in Joanna's eye. She said as we sat down again at the bridge table:

'I suppose she'll be going to parties and all that sort of thing. Are you going to give a dance for her?'

'A dance?' Mrs Symmington seemed surprised and amused. 'Oh, no, we don't do things like that down here.'

'I see. Just tennis parties and things like that.'

'Our tennis court has not been played on for years. Neither Richard nor I play. I suppose, later, when the boys grow up – Oh, Megan will find plenty to do. She's quite happy just pottering about, you know. Let me see, did I deal? Two No Trumps.'

As we drove home, Joanna said with a vicious pressure on the accelerator pedal that made the car leap forward:

'I feel awfully sorry for that girl.'

'Megan?'

'Yes. Her mother doesn't like her.'

'Oh, come now, Joanna, it's not as bad as that.'

'Yes, it is. Lots of mothers don't like their children. Megan, I should imagine, is an awkward sort of creature to have about the house. She disturbs the pattern – the Symmington pattern. It's a complete unit without her – and that's a most unhappy feeling for a sensitive creature to have – and she *is* sensitive.'

'Yes,' I said, 'I think she is.'

I was silent a moment.

Joanna suddenly laughed mischievously.

'Bad luck for you about the governess.'

'I don't know what you mean,' I said with dignity.

'Nonsense. Masculine chagrin was written on your face every time you looked at her. I agree with you. It is a waste.'

'I don't know what you're talking about.'

'But I'm delighted, all the same. It's the first sign of reviving life. I was quite worried about you at the nursing home. You never even looked at that remarkably pretty nurse you had. An attractive minx, too – absolutely God's gift to a sick man.'

'Your conversation, Joanna, I find definitely low.'

My sister continued without paying the least attention to my remarks.

'So I was much relieved to see you'd still got an eye for a nice bit of skirt. She *is* a good looker. Funny that the S.A. should have been left out completely. It is odd, you know, Jerry. What *is* the thing that some women have and others haven't. What is it makes one woman, even if she only says "Foul weather" so attractive that every man within range wants to come over and talk about the weather with her? I suppose Providence makes a mistake every now and then when sending out the parcel. One Aphrodite face and form, one temperament ditto. And something goes astray and the Aphrodite temperament goes to some little plain-faced creature, and then all the other women go simply mad and say, "I can't think what the men see in her. She isn't even good looking!" '

'Have you quite finished, Joanna?'

'Well, you do agree, don't you?'

I grinned. 'I'll admit to disappointment.'

'And I don't see who else there is here for you. You'll have to fall back upon Aimée Griffith.'

'God forbid,' I said.

'She's quite good looking, you know.'

'Too much of an Amazon for me.'

'She seems to enjoy her life, all right,' said Joanna. 'Absolutely disgustingly hearty, isn't she? I shouldn't be at all surprised if she had a cold bath every morning.'

'And what are you going to do for yourself?' I asked.

'Me?'

'Yes. You'll need a little distraction down here if I know you.'

'Who's being low now? Besides, you forget Paul.' Joanna heaved up a not very convincing sigh.

'I shan't forget him nearly as quickly as you will. In about ten days you'll be saying, "Paul? Paul Who? I never knew a Paul."'

'You think I'm completely fickle,' said Joanna.

'When people like Paul are in question, I'm only too glad that you should be.'

'You never did like him. But he really was a bit of genius.'

'Possibly, though I doubt it. Anyway, from all I've heard, geniuses are people to be heartily disliked. One thing, you won't find any geniuses down here.'

Joanna considered for a moment, her head on one side.

'I'm afraid not,' she said regretfully.

'You'll have to fall back upon Owen Griffith,' I said. 'He's the only unattached male in the place. Unless you count old Colonel Appleton. He was looking at you like a hungry bloodhound most of the afternoon.'

Joanna laughed.

'He was, wasn't he? It was quite embarrassing.'

'Don't pretend. You're never embarrassed.'

Joanna drove in silence through the gate and round to the garage. She said then:

'There may be something in that idea of yours.'

'What idea?'

Joanna replied:

'I don't see why any man should deliberately cross the street to avoid me. It's rude, apart from anything else.'

'I see,' I said. 'You're going to hunt the man down in cold blood.'

'Well, I don't like being avoided.'

I got slowly and carefully out of the car, and balanced my sticks. Then I offered my sister a piece of advice.

'Let me tell you this, my girl. Owen Griffith isn't any of your tame whining artistic young men. Unless you're careful you'll stir up a hornet's nest about your ears. That man could be dangerous.'

'Oo, do you think so?' demanded Joanna with every symptom of pleasure at the prospect.

'Leave the poor devil alone,' I said sternly.

'How dare he cross the street when he saw me coming?'

'All you women are alike. You harp on one theme. You'll have Sister Aimée gunning you, too, if I'm not mistaken.'

'She dislikes me already,' said Joanna. She spoke meditatively, but with a certain satisfaction.

'We have come down here,' I said sternly, 'for peace and quiet, and I mean to see we get it.'

But peace and quiet were the last things we were to have.

CHAPTER FOUR

It was, I think, about a week later, that Partridge informed me that Mrs Baker would like to speak to me for a minute or two if I would be so kind.

The name Mrs Baker conveyed nothing at all to me.

'Who is Mrs Baker?' I said bewildered – 'Can't she see Miss Joanna?'

But it appeared that I was the person with whom an interview was desired. It further transpired that Mrs Baker was the mother of the girl Beatrice.

I had forgotten Beatrice. For a fortnight now, I had been conscious of a middle-aged woman with wisps of grey hair, usually on her knees retreating crablike from bathroom and stairs and passages when I appeared, and I knew, I suppose, that she was our new Daily Woman. Otherwise the Beatrice complication had faded from my mind.

I could not very well refuse to see Beatrice's mother, especially as I learned that Joanna was out, but I was, I must confess, a little nervous at the prospect. I sincerely hoped that I was not going to

189

be accused of having trifled with Beatrice's affections. I cursed the mischievous activities of anonymous letter writers to myself at the same time as, aloud, I commanded that Beatrice's mother should be brought to my presence.

Mrs Baker was a big broad weather-beaten woman with a rapid flow of speech. I was relieved to notice no signs of anger or accusation.

'I hope, sir,' she said, beginning at once when the door had closed behind Partridge, 'that you'll excuse the liberty I've taken in coming to see you. But I thought, sir, as you was the proper person to come to, and I should be thankful if you could see your way to telling me what I ought to do in the circumstances, because in my opinion, sir, something ought to be done, and I've never been one to let the grass grow under my feet, and what I say is, no use moaning and groaning, but "Up and doing" as vicar said in his sermon only the week before last.'

I felt slightly bewildered and as though I had missed something essential in the conversation.

'Certainly,' I said. 'Won't you – er – sit down, Mrs Baker? I'm sure I shall be glad to – er help you in any way I can –'

I paused expectantly.

'Thank you, sir.' Mrs Baker sat down on the edge of a chair. 'It's very good of you, I'm sure. And glad I am that I came to you, I said to Beatrice, I said, and her howling and crying on her bed, Mr Burton will know what to do, I said, being a London gentleman. And something must be done, what with young men being so hot-headed and not listening to reason the way they are, and not listening to a word a girl says, and anyway, if it was *me*, I says to Beatrice I'd give him as good as I got, and what about that girl down at the mill?'

I felt more than ever bewildered.

'I'm sorry,' I said. 'But I don't quite understand. What has happened?'

'It's the letters, sir. Wicked letters – indecent, too, using such words and all. Worse than I've ever seen in the Bible, even.'

Passing over an interesting side-line here, I said desperately:

'Has your daughter been having more letters?'

'Not her, sir. She had just the one. That one as was the occasion of her leaving here.'

'There was absolutely no reason —' I began, but Mrs Baker firmly and respectfully interrupted me:

'There is no need to tell me, sir, that what was wrote was all wicked lies. I had Miss Partridge's word for that — and indeed I would have known it for myself. You aren't that type of gentleman, sir, that I well know, and you an invalid and all. Wicked untruthful lies it was, but all the same I says to Beatrice as she'd better leave because you know what talk is, sir. No smoke without fire, that's what people say. And a girl can't be too careful. And besides the girl herself felt bashful like after what had been written, so I says, "Quite right," to Beatrice when she said she wasn't coming up here again, though I'm sure we both regretted the inconvenience being such —'

Unable to find her way out of this sentence, Mrs Baker took a deep breath and began again.

'And that, I hoped, would be the end of any nasty talk. But now George, down at the garage, him what Beatrice is going with, he's got one of them. Saying awful things about our Beatrice, and how she's going on with Fred Ledbetter's Tom — and I can assure you, sir, the girl has been no more than civil to him and passing the time of day so to speak.'

My head was now reeling under this new complication of Mr Ledbetter's Tom.

'Let me get this straight,' I said. 'Beatrice's — er — young man has had an anonymous letter making accusations about her and another young man?'

'That's right, sir, and not nicely put at all — horrible words used, and it drove young George mad with rage, it did, and he came round and told Beatrice he wasn't going to put up with that sort of thing from her, and he wasn't going to have her go behind his back with other chaps — and she says it's all a lie — and he says no smoke without fire, he says, and rushes off being hot-like in his temper, and Beatrice she took on ever so, poor girl, and I said I'll put my hat on and come straight up to you, sir.'

Mrs Baker paused and looked at me expectantly, like a dog waiting for reward after doing a particularly clever trick.

'But why come to me?' I demanded.

'I understood, sir, that you'd had one of these nasty letters yourself, and I thought, sir, that being a London gentleman, you'd know what to do about them.'

'If I were you,' I said, 'I should go to the police. This sort of thing ought to be stopped.'

Mrs Baker looked deeply shocked.

'Oh, no, sir. I couldn't go to the police.'

'Why not?'

'I've never been mixed up with the police, sir. None of us ever have.'

'Probably not. But the police are the only people who can deal with this sort of thing. It's their business.'

'Go to Bert Rundle?'

Bert Rundle was the constable, I knew.

'There's a sergeant, or an inspector, surely, at the police station.'

'Me, go into the police station?'

Mrs Baker's voice expressed reproach and incredulity. I began to feel annoyed.

'That's the only advice I can give you.'

Mrs Baker was silent, obviously quite unconvinced. She said wistfully and earnestly:

'These letters ought to be stopped, sir, they did ought to be stopped. There'll be mischief done sooner or later.'

'It seems to me there is mischief done now,' I said.

'I meant *violence*, sir. These young fellows, they get violent in their feelings – and so do the older ones.'

I asked:

'Are a good many of these letters going about?'

Mrs Baker nodded.

'It's getting worse and worse, sir. Mr and Mrs Beadle at the Blue Boar – very happy they've always been – and now these letters comes and it sets him thinking things – things that aren't so, sir.'

I leaned forward:

'Mrs Baker,' I said, 'have you any idea, any idea at all, who is writing these abominable letters?'

To my great surprise she nodded her head.

'We've got our idea, sir. Yes, we've all got a very fair idea.'

'Who is it?'

I had fancied she might be reluctant to mention a name, but she replied promptly:

''Tis Mrs Cleat – that's what we all think, sir. 'Tis Mrs Cleat for sure.'

I had heard so many names this morning that I was quite bewildered. I asked:

'Who is Mrs Cleat?'

Mrs Cleat, I discovered, was the wife of an elderly jobbing gardener. She lived in a cottage on the road leading down to the Mill. My further questions only brought unsatisfactory answers. Questioned as to why Mrs Cleat should write these letters, Mrs Baker would only say vaguely that "Twould be like her.'

In the end I let her go, reiterating once more my advice to go to the police, advice which I could see Mrs Baker was not going to act upon. I was left with the impression that I had disappointed her.

I thought over what she had said. Vague as the evidence was, I decided that if the village was all agreed that Mrs Cleat was the culprit, then it was probably true. I decided to go and consult Griffith about the whole thing. Presumably he would know this Cleat woman. If he thought advisable, he or I might suggest to the police that she was at the bottom of this growing annoyance.

I timed my arrival for about the moment I fancied Griffith would have finished his 'Surgery'. When the last patient had left, I went into the surgery.

'Hallo, it's you, Burton.'

I outlined my conversation with Mrs Baker, and passed on to him the conviction that this Mrs Cleat was responsible. Rather to my disappointment, Griffith shook his head.

'It's not so simple as that,' he said.

'You don't think this Cleat woman is at the bottom of it?'

'She may be. But I should think it most unlikely.'

'Then why do they all think it is her?'

He smiled.

'Oh,' he said, 'you don't understand. Mrs Cleat is the local witch.'

'Good gracious!' I exclaimed.

'Yes, sounds rather strange nowadays, nevertheless that's what it amounts to. The feeling lingers, you know, that there are certain people, certain families, for instance, whom it isn't wise to offend. Mrs Cleat came from a family of "wise women". And I'm afraid she's taken pains to cultivate the legend. She's a queer woman with a bitter and sardonic sense of humour. It's been easy enough for her, if a child cut its finger, or had a bad fall, or sickened with mumps, to nod her head and say, "Yes, he stole my apples last

193

week'' or ''He pulled my cat's tail.'' Soon enough mothers pulled their children away, and other women brought honey or a cake they'd baked to give to Mrs Cleat so as to keep on the right side of her so that she shouldn't ''ill wish'' them. It's superstitious and silly, but it happens. So naturally, now, they think she's at the bottom of this.'

'But she isn't?'

'Oh, no. She isn't the type. It's — it's not so simple as that.'

'Have you any idea?' I looked at him curiously.

He shook his head, but his eyes were absent.

'No,' he said. 'I don't know at all. But I don't like it, Burton — some harm is going to come of this.'

II

When I got back to the house I found Megan sitting on the veranda steps, her chin resting on her knees.

She greeted me with her usual lack of ceremony.

'Hallo,' she said. 'Do you think I could come to lunch?'

'Certainly,' I said.

'If it's chops, or anything difficult like that and they won't go round, just tell me,' shouted Megan as I went round to apprise Partridge of the fact that there would be three to lunch.

I fancy that Partridge sniffed. She certainly managed to convey without saying a word of any kind, that she didn't think much of that Miss Megan.

I went back to the veranda.

'Is it quite all right?' asked Megan anxiously.

'Quite all right,' I said. 'Irish stew.'

'Oh well, that's rather like dogs' dinner anyway, isn't it? I mean it's mostly potato and flavour.'

'Quite,' I said.

I took out my cigarette case and offered it to Megan. She flushed.

'How nice of you.'

'Won't you have one?'

'No, I don't think I will, but it was very nice of you to offer it to me — just as though I was a real person.'

'Aren't you a real person?' I said amused.

Megan shook her head, then, changing the subject, she stretched out a long dusty leg for my inspection.

'I've darned my stockings,' she announced proudly.

I am not an authority on darning, but it did occur to me that the strange puckered blot of violently contrasting wool was perhaps not quite a success.

'It's much more uncomfortable than the hole,' said Megan.

'It looks as though it might be,' I agreed.

'Does your sister darn well?'

I tried to think if I had ever observed any of Joanna's handiwork in this direction.

'I don't know,' I had to confess.

'Well, what does she do when she gets a hole in her stocking?'

'I rather think,' I said reluctantly, 'that she throws them away and buys another pair.'

'Very sensible,' said Megan. 'But I can't do that. I get an allowance now — forty pounds a year. You can't do much on that.'

I agreed.

'If only I wore black stockings, I could ink my legs,' said Megan sadly. 'That's what I always did at school. Miss Batworthy, the mistress who looked after our mending was like her name — blind as a bat. It was awfully useful.'

'It must have been,' I said.

We were silent while I smoked my pipe. It was quite a companionable silence.

Megan broke it by saying suddenly and violently:

'I suppose you think I'm awful, like everyone else?'

I was so startled that my pipe fell out of my mouth. It was a meerschaum, just colouring nicely, and it broke. I said angrily to Megan:

'Now, see what you've done.'

That most unaccountable of children, instead of being upset, merely grinned broadly.

'I do like you,' she said.

It was a most warming remark. It is the remark that one fancies perhaps erroneously that one's dog would say if he could talk. It occurred to me that Megan, for all she looked like a horse, had the disposition of a dog. She was certainly not quite human.

'What did you say before the catastrophe?' I asked, carefully

195

picking up the fragments of my cherished pipe.

'I said I supposed you thought me awful,' said Megan, but not at all in the same tone she had said it before.

'Why should I?'

Megan said gravely:

'Because I am.'

I said sharply:

'Don't be stupid.'

Megan shook her head.

'That's just it. I'm not really stupid. People think I am. They don't know that inside I know just what they're like, and that all the time I'm hating them.'

'*Hating* them?'

'Yes,' said Megan.

Her eyes, those melancholy, unchildlike eyes, stared straight into mine, without blinking. It was a long mournful gaze.

'You would hate people if you were like me,' she said. 'If you weren't wanted.'

'Don't you think you're being rather morbid?' I asked.

'Yes,' said Megan. 'That's what people always say when you're saying the truth. And it is true. I'm not wanted and I can quite see why. Mummie doesn't like me a bit. I remind her, I think, of my father, who was cruel to her and pretty dreadful from all I can hear. Only mothers can't say they don't want their children and just go away. Or eat them. Cats eat the kittens they don't like. Awfully sensible, I think. No waste or mess. But human mothers have to keep their children, and look after them. It hasn't been so bad while I could be sent away to school – but you see, what Mummie would really like is to be just herself and my stepfather and the boys.'

I said slowly:

'I still think you're morbid, Megan, but accepting some of what you say as true, why don't you go away and have a life of your own?'

She gave me an unchildlike smile.

'You mean take up a career. Earn my living?'

'Yes.'

'What at?'

'You could train for something, I suppose. Shorthand typing – book-keeping.'

'I don't believe I could. I am stupid about doing things. And besides —'

'Well?'

She had turned her face away, now she turned it slowly back again. It was crimson and there were tears in her eyes. She spoke now with all the childishness back in her voice.

'Why should I go away? And be made to go away? They don't want me, but I'll *stay*. I'll stay and make everyone sorry. I'll make them all sorry. Hateful pigs! I hate everyone here in Lymstock. They all think I'm stupid and ugly. I'll show them. I'll show them. I'll —'

It was a childish, oddly pathetic rage.

I heard a step on the gravel round the corner of the house.

'Get up,' I said savagely. 'Go into the house through the drawing-room. Go up to the first floor to the bathroom. End of the passage. Wash your face. Quick.'

She sprang awkwardly to her feet and darted through the window as Joanna came round the corner of the house.

'Gosh, I'm hot,' she called out. She sat down beside me and fanned her face with the Tyrolean scarf that had been round her head. 'Still I think I'm educating these damned brogues now. I've walked miles. I've learnt one thing, you shouldn't have these fancy holes in your brogues. The gorse prickles go through. Do you know, Jerry, I think we ought to have a dog?'

'So do I,' I said. 'By the way, Megan is coming to lunch.'

'Is she? Good.'

'You like her?' I asked.

'I think she's a changeling,' said Joanna. 'Something left on a doorstep, you know, while the fairies take the right one away. It's very interesting to meet a changeling. Oof, I must go up and wash.'

'You can't yet,' I said, 'Megan is washing.'

'Oh, she's been foot-slogging too, has she?'

Joanna took out her mirror and looked at her face long and earnestly. 'I don't think I like this lipstick,' she announced presently.

Megan came out through the window. She was composed, moderately clean, and showed no signs of the recent storm. She looked doubtfully at Joanna.

'Hallo,' said Joanna, still preoccupied by her face. 'I'm so glad you've come to lunch. Good gracious, I've got a freckle on my nose. I must do something about it. Freckles are so earnest and Scottish.'

Partridge came out and said coldly that luncheon was served.

'Come on,' said Joanna, getting up. 'I'm starving.'

She put her arm through Megan's and they went into the house together.

CHAPTER FIVE

I see that there has been one omission in my story. So far I have made little or no mention of Mrs Dane Calthrop, or indeed of the Rev. Caleb Dane Calthrop.

And yet both the vicar and his wife were distinct personalities. Dane Calthrop himself was perhaps a being more remote from everyday life than anyone I have ever met. His existence was in his books and in his study, and in his intimate knowledge of early Church history. Mrs Dane Calthrop, on the other hand, was quite terrifyingly on the spot. I have perhaps purposely put off mentioning her, because I was from the first a little afraid of her. She was a woman of character and of almost Olympian knowledge. She was not in the least the typical vicar's wife – but that, as I set it down, makes me ask myself, what do I know of vicar's wives?

The only one I remember well was a quiet nondescript creature, devoted to a big strong husband with a magnetic way of preaching. She had so little general conversation that it was a puzzle to know how to sustain a conversation with her.

Otherwise I was depending on the fictional presentment of vicars' wives, caricatures of females poking their noses everywhere, and uttering platitudes. Probably no such type exists.

Mrs Dane Calthrop never poked her nose in anywhere, yet she had an uncanny power of knowing things and I soon discovered that almost everyone in the village was slightly afraid of her. She gave no advice and never interfered, yet she represented, to any uneasy conscience, the Deity personified.

I have never seen a woman more indifferent to her material surroundings. On hot days she would stride about clad in Harris tweed, and in rain or even sleet, I have seen her absent-mindedly race down the village street in a cotton dress of printed poppies. She had a long thin well-bred face like a greyhound, and a most devastating sincerity of speech.

She stopped me in the High Street the day after Megan had come to lunch. I had the usual feeling of surprise, because Mrs Dane Calthrop's progress resembled coursing more than walking, and her eyes were always fixed on the distant horizon so that you felt sure her real objective was about a mile and a half away.

'Oh,' she said. 'Mr Burton!'

She said it rather triumphantly, as someone might who had solved a particularly clever puzzle.

I admitted that I was Mr Burton and Mrs Dane Calthrop stopped focusing on the horizon and seemed to be trying to focus on me instead.

'Now what,' she said, 'did I want to see you about?'

I could not help her there. She stood frowning, deeply perplexed.

'Something rather nasty,' she said.

'I'm sorry about that,' I said, startled.

'Ah,' cried Mrs Dane Calthrop. 'I hate my love with an A. That's it. Anonymous letters! What's this story you've brought down here about anonymous letters?'

'I didn't bring it,' I said. 'It was here already.'

'Nobody got any until you came, though,' said Mrs Dane Calthrop accusingly.

'But they did, Mrs Dane Calthrop. The trouble had already started.'

'Oh dear,' said Mrs Dane Calthrop. 'I don't like that.'

She stood there, her eyes absent and far away again. She said:

'I can't help feeling it's all *wrong*. We're not like that here. Envy, of course, and malice, and all the mean spiteful little sins – but I didn't think there was anyone who would do that – No, I really didn't. And it distresses me, you see, because *I* ought to know.'

Her fine eyes came back from the horizon and met mine. They were worried, and seemed to hold the honest bewilderment of a child.

'How should you know?' I said.

'I usually do. I've always felt that's my function. Caleb preaches good sound doctrine and administers the sacraments. That's a priest's

199

duty, but if you admit marriage at all for a priest, then I think his wife's duty is to know what people are feeling and thinking, even if she can't do anything about it. And I haven't the least idea whose mind is –'

She broke off, adding absently:

'They are such silly letters, too.'

'Have you – er – had any yourself?'

I was a little diffident of asking, but Mrs Dane Calthrop replied perfectly naturally, her eyes opening a little wider:

'Oh yes, two – no, three. I forget exactly what they said. Something very silly about Caleb and the school-mistress, I think. Quite absurd, because Caleb has absolutely no taste for fornication. He never has had. So lucky, being a clergyman.'

'Quite,' I said. 'Oh quite.'

'Caleb would have been a saint,' said Mrs Dane Calthrop, 'if he hadn't been just a little too intellectual.'

I did not feel qualified to answer this criticism, and anyway Mrs Dane Calthrop went on, leaping back from her husband to the letters in rather a puzzling way.

'There are so many things the letters might say, but don't. That's what is so curious.'

'I should hardly have thought they erred on the side of restraint,' I said bitterly.

'But they don't seem to *know* anything. None of the real things.'

'You mean?'

Those fine vague eyes met mine.

'Well, of course. There's plenty of adultery here – and everything else. Any amount of shameful secrets. Why doesn't the writer use those?' She paused and then asked abruptly, 'What did they say in your letter?'

'They suggested that my sister wasn't my sister.'

'And she is?'

Mrs Dane Calthrop asked the question with unembarrassed friendly interest.

'Certainly Joanna is my sister.'

Mrs Dane Calthrop nodded her head.

'That just shows you what I mean. I dare say there are other things –'

Her clear uninterested eyes looked at me thoughtfully, and I suddenly understood why Lymstock was afraid of Mrs Dane Calthrop.

In everybody's life there are hidden chapters which they hope may never be known. I felt that Mrs Dane Calthrop knew them.

For once in my life, I was positively delighted when Aimée Griffith's hearty voice boomed out:

'Hallo, Maud. Glad I've just caught you. I want to suggest an alteration of date for the Sale of Work. Morning, Mr Burton.'

She went on:

'I must just pop into the grocer's and leave my order, then I'll come along to the Institute if that suits you?'

'Yes, yes, that will do quite well,' said Mrs Dane Calthrop.

Aimée Griffith went into the International Stores.

Mrs Dane Calthrop said: 'Poor thing.'

I was puzzled. Surely she could not be pitying Aimée?

She went on, however:

'You know, Mr Burton, I'm rather afraid —'

'About this letter business?'

'Yes, you see it means — it must mean —' She paused, lost in thought, her eyes screwed up. Then she said slowly, as one who solves a problem, 'Blind hatred . . . yes, blind hatred. But even a blind man might stab to the heart by pure chance . . . And what would happen then, Mr Burton?'

We were to know that before another day had passed.

II

It was Partridge who brought the news of the tragedy. Partridge enjoys calamity. Her nose always twitches ecstatically when she has to break bad news of any kind.

She came into Joanna's room with her nose working overtime, her eyes bright, and her mouth pulled down into an exaggerated gloom. 'There's terrible news, this morning, miss,' she observed as she drew up the blinds.

It takes a minute or two for Joanna, with her London habits, to become fully conscious in the morning. She said, 'Er ah,' and rolled over without real interest.

Partridge placed her early tea beside her and began again. 'Terrible

201

it is. Shocking! I couldn't hardly believe it when I heard.'

'What's terrible?' said Joanna, struggling into wakefulness.

'Poor Mrs Symmington.' She paused dramatically. 'Dead.'

'Dead?' Joanna sat up in bed, now wide awake.

'Yes, miss, yesterday afternoon, and what's worse, took her own life.'

'Oh no, Partridge?'

Joanna was really shocked – Mrs Symmington was not, somehow, the sort of person you associated with tragedies.

'Yes, miss, it's the truth. Did it deliberate. Not but what she was drove to it, poor soul.'

'Drove to it?' Joanna had an inkling of the truth then. 'Not –?'

Her eyes questioned Partridge and Partridge nodded.

'That's right, miss. One of them nasty letters!'

'What did it say?'

But that, to Partridge's regret, she had not succeeded in learning.

'They're beastly things,' said Joanna. 'But I don't see why they should make one want to kill oneself.'

Partridge sniffed and then said with meaning:

'Not unless they were *true*, miss.'

'Oh,' said Joanna.

She drank her tea after Partridge had left the room, then she threw on a dressing-gown and came in to me to tell me the news.

I thought of what Owen Griffith had said. Sooner or later the shot in the dark went home. It had done with Mrs Symmington. She, apparently the most unlikely of women, had had a secret . . . It was true, I reflected, that for all her shrewdness she was not a woman of much stamina. She was the anaemic clinging type that crumples easily.

Joanna nudged me and asked me what I was thinking about.

I repeated to her what Owen had said.

'Of course,' said Joanna waspishly, 'he would know all about it. That man thinks he knows everything.'

'He's clever,' I said.

'He's conceited,' said Joanna. She added, 'Abominably conceited!'

After a minute or two she said:

'How awful for her husband – and for the girl. What do you think Megan will feel about it?'

I hadn't the slightest idea and said so. It was curious that one could never gauge what Megan would think or feel.

Joanna nodded and said:

'No, one never does know with changelings.'

After a minute or two she said:

'Do you think — would you like — I wonder if she'd like to come and stay with us for a day or two? It's rather a shock for a girl that age.'

'We might go along and suggest it,' I agreed.

'The children are all right,' said Joanna. 'They've got that governess woman. But I expect she's just the sort of creature that would drive someone like Megan mad.'

I thought that was very possible. I could imagine Elsie Holland uttering platitude after platitude and suggesting innumerable cups of tea. A kindly creature, but not, I thought, the person for a sensitive girl.

I had thought myself of bringing Megan away, and I was glad that Joanna had thought of it spontaneously without prompting from me.

We went down to the Symmingtons' house after breakfast.

We were a little nervous, both of us. Our arrival might look like sheer ghoulish curiosity. Luckily we met Owen Griffith just coming out through the gate. He looked worried and preoccupied.

He greeted me, however, with some warmth.

'Oh, hallo, Burton. I'm glad to see you. What I was afraid would happen sooner or later has happened. A damnable business!'

'Good morning, Dr Griffith,' said Joanna, using the voice she keeps for one of our deafer aunts.

Griffith started and flushed.

'Oh — oh, good morning, Miss Burton.'

'I thought perhaps,' said Joanna, 'that you didn't see me.'

Owen Griffith got redder still. His shyness enveloped him like a mantle.

'I'm — I'm so sorry — preoccupied — I didn't.'

Joanna went on mercilessly: 'After all, I *am* life size.'

'Merely kit-kat,' I said in a stern aside to her. Then I went on:

'My sister and I, Griffith, wondered whether it would be a good thing if the girl came and stopped with us for a day or two? What do you think? I don't want to butt in — but it must be rather grim

203

for the poor child. What would Symmington feel about it, do you think?'

Griffith turned the idea over in his mind for a moment or two.

'I think it would be an excellent thing,' he said at last. 'She's a queer nervy sort of girl, and it would be good for her to get away from the whole thing. Miss Holland is doing wonders – she's an excellent head on her shoulders, but she really has quite enough to do with the two children and Symmington himself. He's quite broken up – bewildered.'

'It was –' I hesitated – 'suicide?'

Griffith nodded.

'Oh yes. No question of accident. She wrote, "I can't go on" on a scrap of paper. The letter must have come by yesterday afternoon's post. The envelope was down on the floor by her chair and the letter itself was screwed up into a ball and thrown into the fireplace.'

'What did –'

I stopped, rather horrified at myself.

'I beg your pardon,' I said.

Griffith gave a quick unhappy smile.

'You needn't mind asking. That letter will have to be read at the inquest. No getting out of it, more's the pity. It was the usual kind of thing – couched in the same foul style. The specific accusation was that the second boy, Colin, was not Symmington's child.'

'Do you think that was true?' I exclaimed incredulously.

Griffith shrugged his shoulders.

'I've no means of forming a judgment. I've only been here five years. As far as I've ever seen, the Symmingtons were a placid, happy couple devoted to each other and their children. It's true that the boy doesn't particularly resemble his parents – he's got bright red hair, for one thing – but a child often throws back in appearance to a grandfather or grandmother.'

'That lack of resemblance might have been what prompted the particular accusation. A foul and quite uncalled-for bow at a venture.'

'Very likely. In fact, probably. There's not been much accurate knowledge behind these poison pen letters, just unbridled spite and malice.'

'But it happened to hit the bull's eye,' said Joanna. 'After all, she wouldn't have killed herself otherwise, would she?'

Griffith said doubtfully:

'I'm not quite sure. She's been ailing in health for some time, neurotic, hysterical. I've been treating her for a nervous condition. It's possible, I think, that the shock of receiving such a letter, couched in those terms, may have induced such a state of panic and despondency that she may have decided to take her life. She may have worked herself up to feel that her husband might not believe her if she denied the story, and the general shame and disgust might have worked upon her so powerfully as to temporarily unbalance her judgment.'

'Suicide whilst of unsound mind,' said Joanna.

'Exactly. I shall be quite justified, I think, in putting forward that point of view at the inquest.'

'I see,' said Joanna.

There was something in her voice which made Owen say:

'Perfectly justified!' in an angry voice. He added, 'You don't agree, Miss Burton?'

'Oh yes, I do,' said Joanna. 'I'd do exactly the same in your place.'

Owen looked at her doubtfully, then moved slowly away down the street. Joanna and I went on into the house.

The front door was open and it seemed easier than ringing the bell, especially as we heard Elsie Holland's voice inside.

She was talking to Mr Symmington who, huddled in a chair, was looking completely dazed.

'No, but really, Mr Symmington, you must take something. You haven't had any breakfast, not what I call a proper breakfast, and nothing to eat last night, and what with the shock and all, you'll be getting ill yourself, and you'll need all your strength. The doctor said so before he left.'

Symmington said in a toneless voice:

'You're very kind, Miss Holland, but —'

'A nice cup of hot tea,' said Elsie Holland, thrusting the beverage on him firmly.

Personally I should have given the poor devil a stiff whisky and soda. He looked as though he needed it. However, he accepted the tea, and looking up at Elsie Holland:

'I can't thank you for all you've done and are doing, Miss Holland. You've been perfectly splendid.'

The girl flushed and looked pleased.

'It's nice of you to say that, Mr Symmington. You must let me do all I can to help. Don't worry about the children — I'll see to them, and I've got the servants calmed down, and if there's anything I can do, letter-writing or telephoning, don't hesitate to ask me.'

'You're very kind,' Symmington said again.

Elsie Holland, turning, caught sight of us and came hurrying out into the hall.

'Isn't it terrible?' she said in a hushed whisper.

I thought, as I looked at her, that she was really a very nice girl. Kind, competent, practical in an emergency. Her magnificent blue eyes were just faintly rimmed with pink, showing that she had been soft-hearted enough to shed tears for her employer's death.

'Can we speak to you a minute,' asked Joanna. 'We don't want to disturb Mr Symmington.'

Elsie Holland nodded comprehendingly and led the way into the dining-room on the other side of the hall.

'It's been awful for him,' she said. 'Such a shock. Who ever would have thought a thing like this could happen? But of course, I do realize now that she had been queer for some time. Awfully nervy and weepy. I thought it was her health, though Dr Griffith always said there was nothing really wrong with her. But she was snappy and irritable and some days you wouldn't know just how to take her.'

'What we really came for,' said Joanna, 'was to know whether we could have Megan for a few days — that is, if she'd like to come.'

Elsie Holland looked rather surprised.

'Megan?' she said doubtfully. 'I don't know, I'm sure. I mean, it's ever so kind of you, but she's such a queer girl. One never knows what she's going to say or feel about things.'

Joanna said rather vaguely:

'We thought it might be a help, perhaps.'

'Oh well, as far as that goes, it would. I mean, I've got the boys to look after (they're with Cook just now) and poor Mr Symmington — he really needs looking after as much as anyone, and such a lot to do and see to. I really haven't had time to see much to Megan. I think she's upstairs in the old nursery at the top of the house. She seems to want to get away from everyone. I don't know if—'

Joanna gave me the faintest of looks. I slipped quickly out of the room and upstairs.

The old nursery was at the top of the house. I opened the door and went in. The room downstairs had given on to the garden behind and the blinds had not been down there. But in this room which faced the road they were decorously drawn down.

Through a dim grey gloom I saw Megan. She was crouching on a divan set against the far wall, and I was reminded at once of some terrified animal, hiding. She looked petrified with fear.

'Megan,' I said.

I came forward, and unconsciously I adopted the tone one does adopt when you want to reassure a frightened animal. I'm really surprised I didn't hold out a carrot or a piece of sugar. I felt like that.

She stared at me, but she did not move, and her expression did not alter.

'Megan,' I said again. 'Joanna and I have come to ask you if you would like to come and stay with us for a little.'

Her voice came hollowly out of the dim twilight.

'Stay with you? In your house?'

'Yes.'

'You mean, you'll take me away from here?'

'Yes, my dear.'

Suddenly she began to shake all over. It was frightening and very moving.

'Oh, do take me away! Please do. It's so awful, being here, and feeling so wicked.'

I came over to her and her hands fastened on my coat sleeve.

'I'm an awful coward. I didn't know what a coward I was.'

'It's all right, funny face,' I said. 'These things are a bit shattering. Come along.'

'Can we go at once? Without waiting a minute?'

'Well, you'll have to put a few things together, I suppose.'

'What sort of things? Why?'

'My dear girl,' I said. 'We can provide you with a bed and a bath and the rest of it, but I'm damned if I lend you my toothbrush.'

She gave a very faint weak little laugh.

'I see. I think I'm stupid today. You mustn't mind. I'll go and pack some things. You – you won't go away? You'll wait for me?'

'I'll be on the mat.'

'Thank you. Thank you very much. I'm sorry I'm so stupid. But you see it's rather dreadful when your mother dies.'

'I know,' I said.

I gave her a friendly pat on the back and she flashed me a grateful look and disappeared into a bedroom. I went on downstairs.

'I found Megan,' I said. 'She's coming.'

'Oh now, that *is* a good thing,' exclaimed Elsie Holland. 'It will take her out of herself. She's rather a nervy girl, you know. Difficult. It will be a great relief to feel I haven't got her on my mind as well as everything else. It's very kind of you, Miss Burton. I hope she won't be a nuisance. Oh dear, there's the telephone. I must go and answer it. Mr Symmington isn't fit.'

She hurried out of the room. Joanna said:

'Quite the ministering angel!'

'You said that rather nastily,' I observed. 'She's a nice kind girl, and obviously most capable.'

'Most. And she knows it.'

'This is unworthy of you, Joanna,' I said.

'Meaning why shouldn't the girl do her stuff?'

'Exactly.'

'I never can stand seeing people pleased with themselves,' said Joanna. 'It arouses all my worst instincts. How did you find Megan?'

'Crouching in a darkened room looking rather like a stricken gazelle.'

'Poor kid. She was quite willing to come?'

'She leapt at it.'

A series of thuds out in the hall announced the descent of Megan and her suitcase. I went out and took it from her. Joanna, behind me, said urgently:

'Come on. I've already refused some nice hot tea twice.'

We went out to the car. It annoyed me that Joanna had to sling the suitcase in. I could get along with one stick now, but I couldn't do any athletic feats.

'Get in,' I said to Megan.

She got in. I followed her. Joanna started the car and we drove off.

We got to Little Furze and went into the drawing-room.

Megan dropped into a chair and burst into tears. She cried with the hearty fervour of a child – bawled, I think, is the right word. I left the room in search of a remedy. Joanna stood by feeling rather helpless, I think.

Presently I heard Megan say in a thick choked voice:

'I'm sorry for doing this. It seems idiotic.'

Joanna said kindly, 'Not at all. Have another handkerchief.'

I gather she supplied the necessary article. I re-entered the room and handed Megan a brimming glass.

'What is it?'

'A cocktail,' I said.

'Is it? Is it really?' Megan's tears were instantly dried. 'I've never drunk a cocktail.'

'Everything has to have a beginning,' I said.

Megan sipped her drink gingerly, then a beaming smile spread over her face, she tilted her head back and gulped it down at a draught.

'It's lovely,' she said. 'Can I have another?'

'No,' I said.

'Why not?'

'In about ten minutes you'll probably know.'

'Oh!'

Megan transferred her attention to Joanna.

'I really am awfully sorry for having made such a nuisance of myself howling away like that. I can't think why. It seems awfully silly when I'm so glad to be here.'

'That's all right,' said Joanna. 'We're very pleased to have you.'

'You can't be, really. It's just kindness on your part. But I am grateful.'

'Please don't be grateful,' said Joanna. 'It will embarrass me. I was speaking the truth when I said we should be glad to have you. Jerry and I have used up all our conversation. We can't think of any more things to say to each other.'

'But now,' I said, 'we shall be able to have all sorts of interesting discussions – about Goneril and Regan and things like that.'

Megan's face lit up.

'I've been thinking about that, and I think I know the answer. It was because that awful old father of theirs always insisted on such a lot of sucking up. When you've always got to be saying thank you and how kind and all the rest of it, it would make you go a bit rotten and queer inside, and you'd just long to be able to be beastly for a change – and when you got the chance, you'd probably find it went to your head and you'd go too far. Old Lear was pretty awful, wasn't he? I mean, he did deserve the snub Cordelia gave him.'

'I can see,' I said, 'that we are going to have many interesting discussions about Shakespeare.'

'I can see you two are going to be very highbrow,' said Joanna. 'I'm afraid I always find Shakespeare terribly dreary. All those long scenes where everybody is drunk and it's supposed to be funny.'

'Talking of drink,' I said turning to Megan. 'How are you feeling?'

'Quite all right, thank you.'

'Not at all giddy? You don't see two of Joanna or anything like that?'

'No. I just feel as though I'd like to talk rather a lot.'

'Splendid,' I said. 'Obviously you are one of our natural drinkers. That is to say, if that really was your first cocktail.'

'Oh, it was.'

'A good strong head is an asset to any human being,' I said.

Joanna took Megan upstairs to unpack.

Partridge came in, looking sour, and said she had made two cup custards for lunch and what should she do about it?

CHAPTER SIX

The inquest was held three days later. It was all done as decorously as possible, but there was a large attendance and, as Joanna observed, the beady bonnets were wagging.

The time of Mrs Symmington's death was put at between three and four o'clock. She was alone in the house, Symmington was at his office, the maids were having their day out, Elsie Holland and the children were out walking and Megan had gone for a bicycle ride.

The letter must have come by the afternoon post. Mrs Symmington must have taken it out of the box, read it – and then in a state of agitation she had gone to the potting shed, fetched some of the

210

cyanide kept there for taking wasps' nests, dissolved it in water and drunk it after writing those last agitated words, 'I can't go on . . .'

Owen Griffith gave medical evidence and stressed the view he had outlined to us of Mrs Symmington's nervous condition and poor stamina. The coroner was suave and discreet. He spoke with bitter condemnation of people who write those despicable things, anonymous letters. Whoever had written that wicked and lying letter was morally guilty of murder, he said. He hoped the police would soon discover the culprit and take action against him or her. Such a dastardly and malicious piece of spite deserved to be punished with the utmost rigour of the law. Directed by him, the jury brought in the inevitable verdict. Suicide whilst temporarily insane.

The coroner had done his best − Owen Griffith also, but afterwards, jammed in the crowd of eager village women, I heard the same hateful sibilant whisper I had begun to know so well, 'No smoke without fire, that's what *I* say!' 'Must 'a been something in it for certain sure. She wouldn't never have done it otherwise . . .'

Just for a moment I hated Lymstock and its narrow boundaries, and its gossiping whispering women.

II

It is difficult to remember things in their exact chronological order. The next landmark of importance, of course, was Superintendent Nash's visit. But it was before that, I think, that we received calls from various members of the community, each of which was interesting in its way and shed some light on the characters and personalities of the people involved.

Aimée Griffith came on the morning after the inquest. She was looking, as always, radiant with health and vigour and succeeded, also as usual, in putting my back up almost immediately. Joanna and Megan were out, so I did the honours.

'Good morning,' said Miss Griffith. 'I hear you've got Megan Hunter here?'

'We have.'

'Very good of you, I'm sure. It must be rather a nuisance to you. I came up to say she can come to us if you like. I dare say I can find ways of making her useful about the house.'

I looked at Aimée Griffith with a good deal of distaste.

'How kind of you,' I said. 'But we like having her. She potters about quite happily.'

'I dare say. Much too fond of pottering, that child. Still, I suppose she can't help it, being practically half-witted.'

'I think she's rather an intelligent girl,' I said.

Aimée Griffith gave me a hard stare.

'First time I've ever heard any one say that of her,' she remarked. 'Why, when you talk to her, she looks through you as though she doesn't understand what you are saying!'

'She probably just isn't interested,' I said.

'If so, she's extremely rude,' said Aimée Griffith.

'That may be. But not half-witted.'

Miss Griffith declared sharply:

'At best, it's wool-gathering. What Megan needs is good hard work — something to give her an interest in life. You've no idea what a difference that makes to a girl. I know a lot about girls. You'd be surprised at the difference even becoming a Guide makes to a girl. Megan's much too old to spend her time lounging about and doing nothing.'

'It's been rather difficult for her to do anything else so far,' I said. 'Mrs Symmington always seemed under the impression that Megan was about twelve years old.'

Miss Griffith snorted.

'I know. I had no patience with that attitude of hers. Of course she's dead now, poor woman, so one doesn't want to say much, but she was a perfect example of what I call the unintelligent domestic type. Bridge and gossip and her children — and even there that Holland girl did all the looking after them. I'm afraid I never thought very much of Mrs Symmington, although of course I never suspected the truth.'

'The truth?' I said sharply.

Miss Griffith flushed.

'I was terribly sorry for Dick Symmington, its all having to come out as it did at the inquest,' she said. 'It was awful for him.'

'But surely you heard him say that there was not a word of truth in that letter — that he was quite sure of that?'

'Of course he *said* so. Quite right. A man's got to stick up for his wife. Dick would.' She paused and then explained: 'You see,

212

I've known Dick Symmington a long time.'

I was a little surprised.

'Really?' I said. 'I understood from your brother that he only bought this practice a few years ago.'

'Oh yes, but Dick Symmington used to come and stay in our part of the world up north. I've known him for years.'

Women jump to conclusions that men do not. Nevertheless, the suddenly softened tone of Aimée Griffith's voice put, as our old nurse would have expressed it, ideas into my head.

I looked at Aimée curiously. She went on – still in that softened tone:

'I know Dick very well . . . He's a proud man, and very reserved. But he's the sort of man who could be very jealous.'

'That would explain,' I said deliberately, 'why Mrs Symmington was afraid to show him or tell him about the letter. She was afraid that, being a jealous man, he might not believe her denials.'

Miss Griffith looked at me angrily and scornfully.

'Good Lord,' she said, 'do you think any woman would go and swallow a lot of cyanide of potassium for an accusation that wasn't true?'

'The coroner seemed to think it was possible. Your brother, too –'

Aimée interrupted me.

'Men are all alike. All for preserving the decencies. But you don't catch *me* believing that stuff. If an innocent woman gets some foul anonymous letter, she laughs and chucks it away. That's what I –' she paused suddenly, and then finished, 'would do.'

But I had noticed the pause. I was almost sure that what she had been about to say was 'That's what I did.'

I decided to take the war into the enemy's country.

'I see,' I said pleasantly, 'so you've had one, too?'

Aimée Griffith was the type of woman who scorns to lie. She paused a minute – flushed, then said:

'Well, yes. But I didn't let it worry me!'

'Nasty?' I inquired sympathetically, as a fellow-sufferer.

'Naturally. These things always are. The ravings of a lunatic. I read a few words of it, realized what it was and chucked it straight into the waste-paper basket.'

'You didn't think of taking it to the police?'

'Not then. Least said soonest mended – that's what I felt.'

An urge came over me to say solemnly: 'No smoke without fire!' but I restrained myself. To avoid temptation I reverted to Megan.

'Have you any idea of Megan's financial position?' I asked. 'It's not idle curiosity on my part. I wondered if it would actually be necessary for her to earn her living.'

'I don't think it's strictly *necessary*. Her grandmother, her father's mother, left her a small income, I believe. And in any case Dick Symmington would always give her a home and provide for her, even if her mother hasn't left her anything outright. No, it's the *principle* of the thing.'

'What principle?'

'Work, Mr Burton. There's nothing like work, for men and women. The one unforgivable sin is idleness.'

'Sir Edward Grey,' I said, 'afterwards our foreign minister, was sent down from Oxford for incorrigible idleness. The Duke of Wellington, I have heard, was both dull and inattentive at his books. And has it ever occurred to you, Miss Griffith, that you would probably not be able to take a good express train to London if little Georgie Stephenson had been out with his youth movement instead of lolling about, bored, in his mother's kitchen until the curious behaviour of the kettle lid attracted the attention of his idle mind?'

Aimée merely snorted.

'It is a theory of mine,' I said, warming to my theme, 'that we owe most of our great inventions and most of the achievements of genius to idleness — either enforced or voluntary. The human mind prefers to be spoon-fed with the thoughts of others, but deprived of such nourishment it will, reluctantly, begin to think for itself — and such thinking, remember, is original thinking and may have valuable results.

'Besides,' I went on, before Aimée could get in another sniff, 'there is the artistic side.'

I got up and took from my desk where it always accompanied me a photograph of my favourite Chinese picture. It represents an old man sitting beneath a tree playing cat's cradle with a piece of string on his fingers and toes.

'It was in the Chinese exhibition,' I said. 'It fascinated me. Allow me to introduce you. It is called "Old Man enjoying the Pleasure of Idleness".'

Aimée Griffith was unimpressed by my lovely picture. She said:

'Oh well, we all know what the Chinese are like!'

'It doesn't appeal to you?' I asked.

'Frankly, no. I'm not very interested in art, I'm afraid. Your attitude, Mr Burton, is typical of that of most men. You dislike the idea of women working – of their competing –'

I was taken aback, I had come up against the Feminist. Aimée was well away, her cheeks flushed.

'It is incredible to you that women should want a career. It was incredible to my parents. I was anxious to study for a doctor. They would not hear of paying the fees. But they paid them readily for Owen. Yet I should have made a better doctor than my brother.'

'I'm sorry about that,' I said. 'It was tough on you. If one wants to do a thing –'

She went on quickly:

'Oh, I've got over it now. I've plenty of will-power. My life is busy and active. I'm one of the happiest people in Lymstock. Plenty to do. But I do go up in arms against the silly old-fashioned prejudice that women's place is always the home.'

'I'm sorry if I offended you,' I said. 'And that wasn't really my point. I don't see Megan in a domestic role at all.'

'No, poor child. She'll be a misfit anywhere, I'm afraid.' Aimée had calmed down. She was speaking quite normally again. 'Her father, you know –'

She paused and I said bluntly: 'I *don't* know. Everyone says "her father" and drops their voice, and that is that. What did the man *do*? Is he alive still?'

'I really don't know. And I'm rather vague myself, I'm afraid. But he was definitely a bad lot. Prison, I believe. And a streak of very strong abnormality. That's why it wouldn't surprise me if Megan was a bit "wanting".'

'Megan,' I said, 'is in full possession of her senses, and as I said before, I consider her an intelligent girl. My sister thinks so too. Joanna is very fond of her.'

Aimée said:

'I'm afraid your sister must find it very dull down here.'

And as she said it, I learnt something else. Aimée Griffith disliked my sister. It was there in the smooth conventional tones of her voice.

'We've all wondered how you could both bear to bury yourselves in such an out-of-the-way spot.'

It was a question and I answered it.

'Doctor's orders. I was to come somewhere very quiet where nothing ever happened.' I paused and added, 'Not quite true of Lymstock now.'

'No, no, indeed.'

She sounded worried and got up to go. She said then:

'You know – it's got to be put a stop to – all this beastliness! We can't have it going on.'

'Aren't the police doing anything?'

'I suppose so. But I think we ought to take it in hand *ourselves*.'

'We're not as well equipped as they are.'

'Nonsense! We probably have far more sense and intelligence! A little determination is all that is needed.'

She said goodbye abruptly and went away.

When Joanna and Megan came back from their walk I showed Megan my Chinese picture. Her face lighted up. She said, 'It's heavenly, isn't it?'

'That *is* rather my opinion.'

Her forehead was crinkling in the way I knew so well.

'But it would be difficult, wouldn't it?'

'To be idle?'

'No, not to be idle – but to enjoy the pleasures of it. You'd have to be very old –'

She paused. I said: 'He *is* an old man.'

'I don't mean old that way. Not *age*. I mean old in – in . . .'

'You mean,' I said, 'that one would have to attain a very high state of civilization for the thing to present itself to you in that way – a fine point of sophistication? I think I shall complete your education, Megan, by reading to you one hundred poems translated from the Chinese.'

III

I met Symmington in the town later in the day.

'Is it quite all right for Megan to stay on with us for a bit?' I asked. 'It's company for Joanna – she's rather lonely sometimes with none of her own friends.'

'Oh – er – Megan? Oh yes, very good of you.'

216

I took a dislike to Symmington then which I never quite overcame. He had so obviously forgotten all about Megan. I wouldn't have minded if he had actively disliked the girl – a man may sometimes be jealous of a first husband's child – but he didn't dislike her, he just hardly noticed her. He felt towards her much as a man who doesn't care much for dogs would feel about a dog in the house. You notice it when you fall over it and swear at it, and you give it a vague pat sometimes when it presents itself to be patted. Symmington's complete indifference to his step-daughter annoyed me very much.

I said, 'What are you planning to do with her?'

'With Megan?' He seemed rather startled. 'Well, she'll go on living at home. I mean, naturally, it is her home.'

My grandmother, of whom I had been very fond, used to sing old-fashioned songs to her guitar. One of them, I remembered, ended thus:

> *'Oh maid, most dear, I am not here*
> *I have no place, no part,*
> *No dwelling more, by sea nor shore,*
> *But only in your heart.'*

I went home humming it.

IV

Emily Barton came just after tea had been cleared away.

She wanted to talk about the garden. We talked garden for about half an hour. Then we turned back towards the house.

It was then that lowering her voice, she murmured:

'I do hope that that child – that she hasn't been too much *upset* by all this dreadful business?'

'Her mother's death, you mean?'

'That, of course. But I really meant, the – the unpleasantness *behind* it.'

I was curious. I wanted Miss Barton's reaction.

'What do you think about that? Was it true?'

'Oh, no, no, surely not. I'm quite sure that Mrs Symmington never

217

– that he wasn't' – little Emily Barton was pink and confused – 'I mean it's quite untrue – although of course it may have been a judgment.'

'A judgment?' I said, staring.

Emily Barton was very pink, very Dresden china shepherdess-like.

'I cannot help feeling that all these dreadful letters, all the sorrow and pain they have caused, may have been sent for a *purpose*.'

'They were sent for a purpose, certainly,' I said grimly.

'No, no, Mr Burton, you misunderstood me. I'm not talking of the misguided creature who wrote them – someone quite abandoned that must be. I mean that they have been permitted – by Providence! To awaken us to a sense of our shortcomings.'

'Surely,' I said, 'the Almighty could choose a less unsavoury weapon.'

Miss Emily murmured that God moved in a mysterious way.

'No,' I said. 'There's too much tendency to attribute to God the evils that man does of his own free will. I might concede you the Devil. God doesn't really need to punish us, Miss Barton. We're so very busy punishing ourselves.'

'What I can't make out is *why* should anyone want to do such a thing?'

I shrugged my shoulders.

'A warped mentality.'

'It seems very sad.'

'It doesn't seem to me sad. It seems to me just damnable. And I don't apologize for the word. I mean just that.'

The pink had gone out of Miss Barton's cheeks. They were very white.

'But why, Mr Burton, *why*? What pleasure can anyone get out of it?'

'Nothing you and I can understand, thank goodness.'

Emily Barton lowered her voice.

'They say that *Mrs Cleat* – but I really cannot believe it.'

I shook my head. She went on in an agitated manner:

'Nothing of this kind has ever happened before – never in my memory. It has been such a happy little community. What would my dear mother have said? Well, one must be thankful that she has been spared.'

I thought from all I had heard that old Mrs Barton had been

sufficiently tough to have taken anything, and would probably have enjoyed this sensation.

Emily went on:

'It distresses me deeply.'

'You've not – er – had anything yourself?'

She flushed crimson.

'Oh, no – oh, no, indeed. Oh! that would be dreadful.'

I apologized hastily, but she went away looking rather upset.

I went into the house. Joanna was standing by the drawing-room fire which she had just lit, for the evenings were still chilly.

She had an open letter in her hand.

She turned her head quickly as I entered.

'Jerry! I found this in the letter box – dropped in by hand. It begins, "You painted trollop . . ."'

'What else does it say?'

Joanna gave a wide grimace.

'Same old muck.'

She dropped it on to the fire. With a quick gesture that hurt my back I jerked it off again just before it caught.

'Don't,' I said. 'We may need it.'

'Need it?'

'For the police.'

V

Superintendent Nash came to see me the following morning. From the first moment I saw him I took a great liking to him. He was the best type of CID county superintendent. Tall, soldierly, with quiet reflective eyes and a straightforward unassuming manner.

He said: 'Good morning, Mr Burton, I expect you can guess what I've come to see you about.'

'Yes, I think so. This letter business.'

He nodded.

'I understand you had one of them?'

'Yes, soon after we got here.'

'What did it say exactly?'

I thought a minute, then conscientiously repeated the wording of the letter as closely as possible.

219

The superintendent listened with an immovable face, showing no signs of any kind of emotion. When I had finished, he said:

'I see. You didn't keep the letter, Mr Burton?'

'I'm sorry. I didn't. You see, I thought it was just an isolated instance of spite against newcomers to the place.'

The superintendent inclined his head comprehendingly.

He said briefly: 'A pity.'

'However,' I said, 'my sister got one yesterday. I just stopped her putting it in the fire.'

'Thank you, Mr Burton, that was thoughtful of you.'

'I went across to my desk and unlocked the drawer in which I had put it. It was not, I thought, very suitable for Partridge's eyes. I gave it to Nash.

He read it through. Then he looked up and asked me:

'Is this the same in appearance as the last one?'

'I think so — as far as I can remember.'

'The same difference between the envelope and the text?'

'Yes,' I said. 'The envelope was typed. The letter itself had printed words pasted on to a sheet of paper.'

Nash nodded and put it in his pocket. Then he said:

'I wonder, Mr Burton, if you would mind coming down to the station with me? We could have a conference there and it would save a good deal of time and overlapping.'

'Certainly,' I said.. 'You would like me to come now?'

'If you don't mind.'

There was a police car at the door. We drove down in it.

I said:

'Do you think you'll be able to get to the bottom of this?'

Nash nodded with easy confidence.

'Oh yes, we'll get to the bottom of it all right. It's a question of time and routine. They're slow, these cases, but they're pretty sure. It's a matter of narrowing things down.'

'Elimination?' I said.

'Yes. And general routine.'

'Watching post boxes, examining typewriters, fingerprints, all that?'

He smiled. 'As you say.'

At the police station I found Symmington and Griffith were already there. I was introduced to a tall lantern-jawed man in plain clothes, Inspector Graves.

'Inspector Graves,' explained Nash, 'has come down from London to help us. He's an expert on anonymous letter cases.'

Inspector Graves smiled mournfully. I reflected that a life spent in the pursuit of anonymous letter writers must be singularly depressing. Inspector Graves, however, showed a kind of melancholy enthusiasm.

'They're all the same, these cases,' he said in a deep lugubrious voice like a depressed bloodhound. 'You'd be surprised. The wording of the letters and the things they say.'

'We had a case just on two years ago,' said Nash. 'Inspector Graves helped us then.'

Some of the letters, I saw, were spread out on the table in front of Graves. He had evidently been examining them.

'Difficulty is,' said Nash, 'to get hold of the letters. Either people put them in the fire, or they won't admit to having received anything of the kind. Stupid, you see, and afraid of being mixed up with the police. They're a backward lot here.'

'Still we've got a fair amount to get on with,' said Graves. Nash took the letter I had given him from his pocket and tossed it over to Graves.

The latter glanced through it, laid it with the others and observed approvingly:

'Very nice — very nice indeed.'

It was not the way I should have chosen to describe the epistle in question, but experts, I suppose, have their own point of view. I was glad that that screed of vituperative and obscene abuse gave *somebody* pleasure.

'We've got enough, I think, to go on with,' said Inspector Graves, 'and I'll ask you gentlemen, if you should get any more, to bring them along at once. Also, if you hear of someone else getting one — (you, in particular, doctor, among your patients) do your best to get them to come along here with them. I've got —' he sorted with deft fingers among his exhibits, 'one to Mr Symmington, received as far back as two months ago, one to Dr Griffith, one to Miss Ginch, one written to Mrs Mudge, the butcher's wife, one to Jennifer Clark, barmaid at the Three Crowns, the one received by Mrs Symmington, this one now to Miss Burton — oh yes, and one from the bank manager.'

'Quite a representative collection,' I remarked.

'And not one I couldn't match from other cases! This one here is as near as nothing to one written by that milliner woman. This one is the dead spit of an outbreak we had up in Northumberland – written by a schoolgirl, they were. I can tell you, gentlemen, I'd like to see something *new* sometimes, instead of the same old treadmill.'

'There is nothing new under the sun,' I murmured.

'Quite so, sir. You'd know that if you were in our profession.'

Nash sighed and said, 'Yes, indeed.'

Symmington asked:

'Have you come to any definite opinion as to the writer?'

Graves cleared his throat and delivered a small lecture.

'There are certain similarities shared by all these letters. I shall enumerate them, gentlemen, in case they suggest anything to your minds. The text of the letters is composed of words made up from individual letters cut out of a printed book. It's an old book, printed, I should say, about the year 1830. This has obviously been done to avoid the risk of recognition through handwriting which is, as most people know nowadays, a fairly easy matter . . . the so-called disguising of a hand not amounting to much when faced with expert tests. There are no fingerprints on the letters and envelopes of a distinctive character. That is to say, they have been handled by the postal authorities, the recipient, and there are other stray fingerprints, but no set common to all, showing therefore that the person who put them together was careful to wear gloves. The envelopes are type-written by a Windsor 7 machine, well worn, with the a and the t out of alignment. Most of them have been posted locally, or put in the box of a house by hand. It is therefore evident that they are of local provenance. They were written by a woman, and in my opinion a woman of middle age or over, and probably, though not certainly, unmarried.'

We maintained a respectful silence for a minute or two. Then I said:

'The typewriter's your best bet, isn't it? That oughtn't to be difficult in a little place like this.'

Inspector Graves shook his head sadly and said:

'That's where you're wrong, sir.'

'The typewriter,' said Superintendent Nash, 'is unfortunately too easy. It is an old one from Mr Symmington's office, given by him to the Women's Institute where, I may say, it's fairly easy of access. The ladies here all often go into the Institute.'

'Can't you tell something definite from the – er – the touch, don't you call it?'

Again Graves nodded.

'Yes, that can be done – but these envelopes have all been typed by someone using one finger.'

'Someone, then, unused to the typewriter?'

'No, I wouldn't say that. Someone, say, who can type but doesn't want us to know the fact.'

'Whoever writes these things has been very cunning,' I said slowly.

'She is, sir, she is,' said Graves. 'Up to every trick of the trade.'

'I shouldn't have thought one of these bucolic women down here would have had the brains,' I said.

Graves coughed.

'I haven't made myself plain, I'm afraid. Those letters were written by an educated woman.'

'What, by a lady?'

The word slipped out involuntarily. I hadn't used the term 'lady' for years. But now it came automatically to my lips, re-echoed from days long ago, and my grandmother's faint unconsciously arrogant voice saying, 'Of course, she isn't a *lady*, dear.'

Nash understood at once. The word lady still meant something to him.

'Not necessarily a lady,' he said. 'But certainly not a village woman. They're mostly pretty illiterate down here, can't spell, and certainly can't express themselves with fluency.'

I was silent, for I had had a shock. The community was so small. Unconsciously I had visualized the writer of the letters as a Mrs Cleat or her like, some spiteful, cunning half-wit.

Symmington put my thoughts into words. He said sharply:

'But that narrows it down to about half a dozen to a dozen people in the whole place!'

'That's right.'

'I can't believe it.'

Then, with a slight effort, and looking straight in front of him as though the mere sound of his own words were distasteful he said:

'You have heard what I stated at the inquest. In case you may have thought that that statement was actuated by a desire to protect my wife's memory, I should like to repeat now that I am firmly convinced that the subject matter of the letter my wife received was absolutely false. I *know* it was false. My wife was a very sensitive woman, and – er – well, you might call it *prudish* in some respects. Such a letter would have been a great shock to her, and she was in poor health.'

Graves responded instantly.

'That's quite likely to be right, sir. None of these letters show any signs of intimate knowledge. They're just blind accusations. There's been no attempt to blackmail. And there doesn't seem to be any religious bias – such as we sometimes get. It's just sex and spite! And that's going to give us quite a good pointer towards the writer.'

Symmington got up. Dry and unemotional as the man was, his lips were trembling.

'I hope you find the devil who writes these soon. She murdered my wife as surely as if she'd put a knife into her.' He paused. 'How does she feel now, I wonder?'

He went out, leaving that question unanswered.

'How does she feel, Griffith?' I asked. It seemed to me the answer was in his province.

'God knows. Remorseful, perhaps. On the other hand, it may be that she's enjoying her power. Mrs Symmington's death may have fed her mania.'

'I hope not,' I said, with a slight shiver. 'Because if so, she'll –'

I hesitated and Nash finished the sentence for me.

'She'll try it again? That, Mr Burton, would be the best thing that could happen, for us. The pitcher goes to the well once too often, remember.'

'She'd be mad to go on with it,' I exclaimed.

'She'll go on,' said Graves. 'They always do. It's a vice, you know, they can't let it alone.'

I shook my head with a shudder. I asked if they needed me any longer, I wanted to get out into the air. The atmosphere seemed tinged with evil.

'There's nothing more, Mr Burton,' said Nash. 'Only keep your eyes open, and do as much propaganda as you can – that is to say, urge on everyone that they've got to report any letter they receive.'

I nodded.

'I should think everyone in the place has had one of the foul things by now,' I said.

'I wonder,' said Graves. He put his sad head a little on one side and asked, 'You don't know, definitely, of anyone who *hasn't* had a letter?'

'What an extraordinary question! The population at large isn't likely to take me into their confidence.'

'No, no, Mr Burton, I didn't mean that. I just wondered if you knew of any one person who quite definitely, to your certain knowledge, has not received an anonymous letter.'

'Well, as a matter of fact,' I hesitated, 'I do, in a way.'

And I repeated my conversation with Emily Barton and what she had said.

Graves received the information with a wooden face and said: 'Well, that may come in useful. I'll note it down.'

I went out into the afternoon sunshine with Owen Griffith. Once in the street, I swore aloud.

'What kind of place is this for a man to come to lie in the sun and heal his wounds? It's full of festering poison, this place, and it looks as peaceful and as innocent as the Garden of Eden.'

'Even there,' said Owen dryly, 'there was one serpent.'

'Look here, Griffith, do they know anything? Have they got any idea?'

'I don't know. They've got a wonderful technique, the police. They're seemingly so frank, and they tell you nothing.'

'Yes. Nash is a nice fellow.'

'And a very capable one.'

'If anyone's batty in this place, *you* ought to know it,' I said accusingly.

Griffith shook his head. He looked discouraged. But he looked more than that – he looked worried. I wondered if he had an inkling of some kind.

We had been walking along the High Street. I stopped at the door of the house agents.

'I believe my second instalment of rent is due – in advance. I've got a good mind to pay it and clear out with Joanna right away. Forfeit the rest of the tenancy.'

'Don't go,' said Owen.

'Why not?'

He didn't answer. He said slowly after a minute or two, 'After all – I dare say you're right. Lymstock isn't healthy just now. It might – it might harm you or – or your sister.'

'Nothing harms Joanna,' I said. 'She's tough. I'm the weakly one. Somehow this business makes me sick.'

'It makes *me* sick,' said Owen.

I pushed the door of the house agents half open.

'But I shan't go,' I said. 'Vulgar curiosity is stronger than pusillanimity. I want to know the solution.'

I went in.

A woman who was typing got up and came towards me. She had frizzy hair and simpered, but I found her more intelligent than the spectacled youth who had previously held sway in the outer office.

A minute or two later something familiar about her penetrated through to my consciousness. It was Miss Ginch, lately Symmington's lady clerk. I commented on the fact.

'You were with Galbraith and Symmington, weren't you?' I said.

'Yes. Yes, indeed. But I thought it was better to leave. This is quite a good post, though not quite so well paid. But there are things that are more valuable than money, don't you think so?'

'Undoubtedly,' I said.

'Those awful letters,' breathed Miss Ginch in a sibilant whisper. 'I got a dreadful one. About me and Mr Symmington – oh, terrible it was, saying the most *awful* things! I knew my duty and I took it to the police, though of course it wasn't exactly *pleasant* for me, was it?'

'No, no, most unpleasant.'

'But they thanked me and said I had done quite right. But I felt that, after that, if people were talking – and evidently they *must* have been, or where did the writer get the idea from? – then I must avoid even the appearance of evil, though there has never been anything at all *wrong* between me and Mr Symmington.'

I felt rather embarrassed.

'No, no, of course not.'

'But people have such evil minds. Yes, alas, such evil minds!'

Nervously trying to avoid it, I nevertheless met her eye, and I made a most unpleasant discovery.

Miss Ginch was thoroughly enjoying herself.

226

Already once today I had come across someone who reacted pleasurably to anonymous letters. Inspector Graves's enthusiasm was professional. Miss Ginch's enjoyment I found merely suggestive and disgusting.

An idea flashed across my startled mind.

Had Miss Ginch written these letters herself?

CHAPTER SEVEN

When I got home I found Mrs Dane Calthrop sitting talking to Joanna. She looked, I thought, grey and ill.

'This has been a terrible shock to me, Mr Burton,' she said. 'Poor thing, poor thing.'

'Yes,' I said. 'It's awful to think of someone being driven to the stage of taking their own life.'

'Oh, you mean Mrs Symmington?'

'Didn't you?'

Mrs Dane Calthrop shook her head.

'Of course one is sorry for her, but it would have been bound to happen anyway, wouldn't it?'

'Would it?' said Joanna dryly.

Mrs Dane Calthrop turned to her.

'Oh, I think so, dear. If suicide is your idea of escape from trouble then it doesn't very much matter what the trouble is. Whenever some very unpleasant shock had to be faced, she'd have done the same thing. What it really comes down to is that she was that kind of woman. Not that one would have guessed it. She always seemed to me a selfish rather stupid woman, with a good firm hold on life. Not the kind to panic, you would think – but I'm beginning to realize how little I really know anyone.'

'I'm still curious as to whom you meant when you said "Poor thing,"' I remarked.

She stared at me.

'The woman who wrote the letters, of course.'

'I don't think,' I said dryly, 'I shall waste sympathy on her.'

Mrs Dane Calthrop leaned forward. She laid a hand on my knee.

'But don't you realize – can't you *feel*? Use your imagination. Think how desperately, violently unhappy anyone must be to sit down and write these things. How lonely, how cut off from human kind. Poisoned through and through, with a dark stream of poison that finds its outlet in this way. That's why I feel so self-reproachful. Somebody in this town has been racked with that terrible unhappiness, and I've had no idea of it. I should have had. You can't interfere with actions – I never do. But that black inward unhappiness – like a septic arm physically, all black and swollen. If you could cut it and let the poison out it would flow away harmlessly. Yes, poor soul, poor soul.'

She got up to go.

I did not feel like agreeing with her. I had no sympathy for our anonymous letter writer whatsoever. But I did ask curiously:

'Have you any idea at all, Mrs Calthrop, who this woman is?'

She turned her fine perplexed eyes on me.

'Well, I can guess,' she said. 'But then I might be wrong, mightn't I?'

She went swiftly out through the door, popping her head back to ask:

'Do tell me, why have you never married, Mr Burton?'

In anyone else it would have been an impertinence, but with Mrs Dane Calthrop you felt that the idea had suddenly come into her head and she had really wanted to know.

'Shall we say,' I said, rallying, 'that I have never met the right woman?'

'We can say so,' said Mrs Dane Calthrop, 'but it wouldn't be a very good answer, because so many men have obviously married the wrong woman.'

This time she really departed.

Joanna said:

'You know I really do think she's mad. But I like her. The people in the village here are afraid of her.'

'So am I, a little.'

'Because you never know what's coming next?'

'Yes. And there's a careless brilliancy about her guesses.'

Joanna said slowly: 'Do you really think whoever wrote these letters is very unhappy?'

'I don't know what the damned hag is thinking or feeling! And

228

I don't care. It's her victims I'm sorry for.'

It seems odd to me now that in our speculations about Poison Pen's frame of mind, we missed the most obvious one. Griffith had pictured her as possibly exultant. I had envisaged her as remorseful – appalled by the result of her handiwork. Mrs Dane Calthrop had seen her as suffering.

Yet the obvious, the inevitable reaction we did not consider – or perhaps I should say, I did not consider. That reaction was Fear.

For with the death of Mrs Symmington, the letters had passed out of one category into another. I don't know what the legal position was – Symmington knew, I suppose, but it was clear that with a death resulting, the position of the writer of the letters was much more serious. There could now be no question of passing it off as a joke if the identity of the writer was discovered. The police were active, a Scotland Yard expert called in. It was vital now for the anonymous author to remain anonymous.

And granted that Fear was the principal reaction, other things followed. Those possibilities also I was blind to. Yet surely they should have been obvious.

II

Joanna and I came down rather late to breakfast the next morning. That is to say, late by the standards of Lymstock. It was nine-thirty, an hour at which, in London, Joanna was just unclosing an eyelid, and mine would probably be still tight shut. However when Partridge had said 'Breakfast at half-past eight, or nine o'clock?' neither Joanna nor I had had the nerve to suggest a later hour.

To my annoyance, Aimée Griffith was standing on the door-step talking to Megan.

She gave tongue with her usual heartiness at the sight of us.

'Hallo, there, slackers! I've been up for hours.'

That, of course, was her own business. A doctor, no doubt, has to have early breakfast, and a dutiful sister is there to pour out his tea, or coffee. But it is no excuse for coming and butting in on one's more somnolent neighbours. Nine-thirty is not the time for a morning call.

Megan slipped back into the house and into the dining-room,

where I gathered she had been interrupted in her breakfast.

'I said I wouldn't come in,' said Aimée Griffith – though why it is more of a merit to force people to come and speak to you on the doorstep, than to talk to them inside the house I do not know. 'I just wanted to ask Miss Burton if she'd any vegetables to spare for our Red Cross stall on the main road. If so, I'd get Owen to call for them in the car.'

'You're out and about very early,' I said.

'The early bird catches the worm,' said Aimée. 'You have a better chance of finding people in this time of day. I'm off to Mr Pye's next. Got to go over to Brenton this afternoon. Guides.'

'Your energy makes me quite tired,' I said, and at that moment the telephone rang and I retired to the back of the hall to answer it, leaving Joanna murmuring rather doubtfully something about rhubarb and french beans and exposing her ignorance of the vegetable garden.

'Yes?' I said into the telephone mouthpiece.

A confused noise of deep breathing came from the other end of the wire and a doubtful female voice said 'Oh!'

'Yes?' I said again encouragingly.

'Oh,' said the voice again, and then it inquired adenoidally, 'Is that – what I mean – is that Little Furze?'

'This is Little Furze.'

'Oh!' This was clearly a stock beginning to every sentence. The voice inquired cautiously: 'Could I speak to Miss Partridge just a minute?'

'Certainly,' I said. 'Who shall I say?'

'Oh. Tell her it's Agnes, would you? Agnes Waddle.'

'Agnes Waddle?'

'That's right.'

Resisting the temptation to say, 'Donald Duck to you,' I put down the telephone receiver and called up the stairs to where I could hear the sound of Partridge's activities overheard.

'Partridge. Partridge.'

Partridge appeared at the head of the stairs, a long mop in one hand, and a look of 'What is it *now*?' clearly discernible behind her invariably respectful manner.

'Yes, sir?'

'Agnes Waddle wants to speak to you on the telephone.'

230

'I beg your pardon, sir?'

I raised my voice. 'Agnes Waddle.'

I have spelt the name as it presented itself to my mind. But I will now spell it as it was actually written.

'Agnes Woddell — whatever can she want now?'

Very much put out of countenance, Partridge relinquished her mop and rustled down the stairs, her print dress crackling with agitation.

I beat an unobtrusive retreat into the dining-room where Megan was wolfing down kidneys and bacon. Megan, unlike Aimée Griffith, was displaying no 'glorious morning face'. In fact she replied very gruffly to my morning salutations and continued to eat in silence.

I opened the morning paper and a minute or two later Joanna entered looking somewhat shattered.

'Whew!' she said. 'I'm so tired. And I think I've exposed my utter ignorance of what grows when. Aren't there runner beans this time of year?'

'August,' said Megan.

'Well, one has them any time in London,' said Joanna defensively.

'Tins, sweet fool,' I said. 'And cold storage on ships from the far-flung limits of empire.'

'Like ivory, apes and peacocks?' asked Joanna.

'Exactly.'

'I'd rather have peacocks,' said Joanna thoughtfully.

'I'd like a monkey of my own as a pet,' said Megan.

Meditatively peeling an orange, Joanna said:

'I wonder what it would feel like to be Aimée Griffith, all bursting with health and vigour and enjoyment of life. Do you think she's ever tired, or depressed, or — or wistful?'

I said I was quite certain Aimée Griffith was never wistful, and followed Megan out of the open french window on to the veranda.

Standing there, filling my pipe, I heard Partridge enter the dining-room from the hall and heard her voice say grimly:

'Can I speak to you a minute, miss?'

'Dear me,' I thought. 'I hope Partridge isn't going to give notice. Emily Barton will be very annoyed with us if so.'

Partridge went on: 'I must apologize, miss, for being rung up on

231

the telephone. That is to say, the young person who did so should have known better. I have never been in the habit of using the telephone or of permitting my friends to ring me up on it, and I'm very sorry indeed that it should have occurred, and the master taking the call and everything.'

'Why, that's quite all right, Partridge,' said Joanna soothingly, 'why shouldn't your friends use the phone if they want to speak to you?'

Partridge's face, I could feel, though I could not see it, was more dour than ever as she replied coldly:

'It is not the kind of thing that has ever been done in this house. Miss Emily would never permit it. As I say, I am sorry it occurred, but Agnes Woddell, the girl who did it, was upset and she's young too, and doesn't know what's fitting in a gentleman's house.'

'That's one for you, Joanna,' I thought gleefully.

'This Agnes who rung me up, miss,' went on Partridge, 'she used to be in service here under me. Sixteen she was, then, and come straight from the orphanage. And you see, not having a home, or a mother or any relations to advise her, she's been in the habit of coming to me. I can tell her what's what, you see.'

'Yes?' said Joanna and waited. Clearly there was more to follow.

'So I am taking the liberty of asking you, miss, if you would allow Agnes to come here to tea this afternoon in the kitchen. It's her day out, you see, and she's got something on her mind she wants to consult me about. I wouldn't dream of suggesting such a thing in the usual way.'

Joanna said bewildered:

'But why shouldn't you have any one to tea with you?'

Partridge drew herself up at this, so Joanna said afterwards, and really looked most formidable, as she replied:

'It has never been the custom of This House, miss. Old Mrs Barton never allowed visitors in the kitchen, excepting as it should be our own day out, in which case we were allowed to entertain friends here instead of going out, but otherwise, on ordinary days, no. And Miss Emily she keeps to the old ways.'

Joanna is very nice to servants and most of them like her but she has never cut any ice with Partridge.

'It's no good, my girl,' I said when Partridge had gone and Joanna had joined me outside. 'Your sympathy and leniency are not appreciated. The good old overbearing ways for Partridge and things done the way they should be done in a gentleman's house.'

'I never heard of such tyranny as not allowing them to have their friends to see them,' said Joanna. 'It's all very well, Jerry, but they can't *like* being treated like black slaves.'

'Evidently they do,' I said. 'At least the Partridges of this world do.'

'I can't imagine why she doesn't like me. Most people do.'

'She probably despises you as an inadequate housekeeper. You never draw your hand across a shelf and examine it for traces of dust. You don't look under the mats. You don't ask what happened to the remains of the chocolate soufflé, and you never order a nice bread pudding.'

'Ugh!' said Joanna.

She went on sadly. 'I'm a failure all round today. Despised by our Aimée for ignorance of the vegetable kingdom. Snubbed by Partridge for being a human being. I shall now go out into the garden and eat worms.'

'Megan's there already,' I said.

For Megan had wandered away a few minutes previously and was now standing aimlessly in the middle of a patch of lawn looking not unlike a meditative bird waiting for nourishment.

She came back, however, towards us and said abruptly:

'I say, I must go home today.'

'What?' I was dismayed.

She went on, flushing, but speaking with nervous determination.

'It's been awfully good of you having me and I expect I've been a fearful nuisance, but I have enjoyed it awfully, only now I must go back, because after all, well, it's my home and one can't stay away for ever, so I think I'll go this morning.'

Both Joanna and I tried to make her change her mind, but she was quite adamant, and finally Joanna got out the car and Megan went upstairs and came down a few minutes later with her belongings packed up again.

The only person pleased seemed to be Partridge, who had almost a smile on her grim face. She had never liked Megan much.

I was standing in the middle of the lawn when Joanna returned. She asked me if I thought I was a sundial.

'Why?'

'Standing there like a garden ornament. Only one couldn't put on you the motto of only marking the sunny hours. You looked like thunder!'

'I'm out of humour. First Aimée Griffith – ("Gracious!" murmured Joanna in parenthesis, "I must speak about those vegetables!") and then Megan beetling off. I'd thought of taking her for a walk up to Legge Tor.'

'With a collar and lead, I suppose?' said Joanna.

'What?'

Joanna repeated loudly and clearly as she moved off round the corner of the house to the kitchen garden:

'I said, "With a collar and lead, I suppose?" Master's lost his dog, that's what's the matter with you!'

III

I was annoyed, I must confess, at the abrupt way in which Megan had left us. Perhaps she had suddenly got bored with us.

After all, it wasn't a very amusing life for a girl. At home she'd got the kids and Elsie Holland.

I heard Joanna returning and hastily moved in case she should make more rude remarks about sundials.

Owen Griffith called in his car just before lunch time, and the gardener was waiting for him with the necessary garden produce.

Whilst old Adams was stowing it in the car I brought Owen indoors for a drink. He wouldn't stay to lunch.

When I came in with the sherry I found Joanna had begun doing her stuff.

No signs of animosity now. She was curled up in the corner of the sofa and was positively purring, asking Owen questions about his work, if he liked being a GP, if he wouldn't rather have specialized? She thought, doctoring was one of the most fascinating things in the world.

Say what you will of her, Joanna is a lovely, a heaven-born listener. And after listening to so many would-be geniuses telling her how they had been unappreciated, listening to Owen Griffith was easy money. By the time we had got to the third glass of sherry, Griffith was telling her about some obscure reaction or lesion in such scientific terms that nobody could have understood a word of it except a fellow medico.

Joanna was looking intelligent and deeply interested.

I felt a moment's qualm. It was really too bad of Joanna. Griffith was too good a chap to be played fast and loose with. Women really were devils.

Then I caught a sideways view of Griffith, his long purposeful chin and the grim set of his lips, and I was not so sure that Joanna was going to have it her own way after all. And anyway, a man has no business to let himself be made a fool of by a woman. It's his own look-out if he does.

Then Joanna said:

'Do change your mind and stay to lunch with us, Dr Griffith,' and Griffith flushed a little and said he would, only his sister would be expecting him back –

'We'll ring her up and explain,' said Joanna quickly and went out into the hall and did so.

I thought Griffith looked a little uneasy, and it crossed my mind that he was probably a little afraid of his sister.

Joanna came back smiling and said that that was all right.

And Owen Griffith stayed to lunch and seemed to enjoy himself. We talked about books and plays and world politics, and about music and painting and modern architecture.

We didn't talk about Lymstock at all, or about anonymous letters, or Mrs Symmington's suicide.

We got right away from everything, and I think Owen Griffith was happy. His dark sad face lighted up, and he revealed an interesting mind.

When he had gone I said to Joanna:

'That fellow's too good for your tricks.'

Joanna said:

'That's what you say! You men all stick together!'

'Why were you out after his hide, Joanna? Wounded vanity?'

'Perhaps,' said my sister.

That afternoon we were to go to tea with Miss Emily Barton at her rooms in the village.

We strolled down there on foot, for I felt strong enough now to manage the hill back again.

We must actually have allowed too much time and got there early, for the door was opened to us by a tall rawboned fierce-looking woman who told us that Miss Barton wasn't in yet.

'But she's expecting you, I know, so if you'll come up and wait, please.'

This was evidently Faithful Florence.

We followed her up the stairs and she threw open a door and showed us into what was quite a comfortable sitting-room, though perhaps a little over-furnished. Some of the things, I suspected, had come from Little Furze.

The woman was clearly proud of her room.

'It's nice, isn't it?' she demanded.

'Very nice,' said Joanna warmly.

'I make her as comfortable as I can. Not that I can do for her as I'd like to and in the way she ought to have. She ought to be in her own house, properly, not turned out into rooms.'

Florence, who was clearly a dragon, looked from one to the other of us reproachfully. It was not, I felt, our lucky day. Joanna had been ticked off by Aimée Griffith and Partridge and now we were both being ticked off by the dragon Florence.

'Parlourmaid I was for fifteen years there,' she added.

Joanna, goaded by injustice, said:

'Well, Miss Barton wanted to let the house. She put it down at the house agents.'

'Forced to it,' said Florence. 'And she living so frugal and careful. But even then, the government can't leave her alone! Has to have its pound of flesh just the same.'

I shook my head sadly.

'Plenty of money there was in the old lady's time,' said Florence. 'And then they all died off one by one, poor dears. Miss Emily nursing of them one after the other. Wore herself out she did, and always so patient and uncomplaining. But it told on her, and then to have worry about money on top of it all! Shares not bringing in

236

what they used to, so she says, and why not, I should like to know? They ought to be ashamed of themselves. Doing down a lady like her who's got no head for figures and can't be up to their tricks.'

'Practically everyone has been hit that way,' I said, but Florence remained unsoftened.

'It's all right for some as can look after themselves, but not for *her*. She needs looking after, and as long as she's with me I'm going to see no one imposes on her or upsets her in any way. I'd do anything for Miss Emily.'

And glaring at us for some moments in order to drive that point thoroughly home, the indomitable Florence left the room, carefully shutting the door behind her.

'Do you feel like a blood-sucker, Jerry?' inquired Joanna. 'Because I do. What's the matter with us?'

'We don't seem to be going down very well,' I said. 'Megan gets tired of us, Partridge disapproves of you, faithful Florence disapproves of both of us.'

Joanna murmured, 'I wonder why Megan *did* leave?'

'She got bored.'

'I don't think she did at all. I wonder – do you think, Jerry, it could have been something that Aimée Griffith said?'

'You mean this morning, when they were talking on the doorstep.'

'Yes. There wasn't much time, of course, but –'

I finished the sentence.

'But that woman's got the tread of a cow elephant! She might have –'

The door opened and Miss Emily came in. She was pink and a little out of breath and seemed excited. Her eyes were very blue and shining.

She chirruped at us in quite a distracted manner.

'Oh dear, I'm so sorry I'm late. Just doing a little shopping in the town, and the cakes at the Blue Rose didn't seem to me quite fresh, so I went on to Mrs Lygon's. I always like to get my cakes the last thing, then one gets the newest batch just out of the oven, and one isn't put off with the day before's. But I am so distressed to have kept you waiting – really unpardonable –'

Joanna cut in.

'It's our fault, Miss Barton. We're early. We walked down and Jerry strides along so fast now that we arrive everywhere too soon.'

'Never too soon, dear. Don't say that. One cannot have too much of a good thing, you know.'

And the old lady patted Joanna affectionately on the shoulder.

Joanna brightened up. At last, so it seemed, she was being a success. Emily Barton extended her smile to include me, but with a slight timidity in it, rather as one might approach a man-eating tiger guaranteed for the moment harmless.

'It's very good of you to come to such a feminine meal as tea, Mr Burton.'

Emily Barton, I think, has a mental picture of men as interminably consuming whiskies and sodas and smoking cigars, and in the intervals dropping out to do a few seductions of village maidens, or to conduct a liaison with a married woman.

When I said this to Joanna later, she replied that it was probably wishful thinking, that Emily Barton would have liked to come across such a man, but alas had never done so.

In the meantime Miss Emily was fussing round the room, arranging Joanna and myself with little tables, and carefully providing ashtrays, and a minute later the door opened and Florence came in bearing a tray of tea with some fine Crown Derby cups on it which I gathered Miss Emily had brought with her. The tea was china and delicious and there were plates of sandwiches and thin bread and butter, and a quantity of little cakes.

Florence was beaming now, and looked at Miss Emily with a kind of maternal pleasure, as at a favourite child enjoying a doll's tea party.

Joanna and I ate far more than we wanted to, our hostess pressed us so earnestly. The little lady was clearly enjoying her tea party and I perceived that, to Emily Barton, Joanna and I were a big adventure, two people from the mysterious world of London and sophistication.

Naturally, our talk soon dropped into local channels. Miss Barton spoke warmly of Dr Griffith, his kindness and his cleverness as a doctor. Mr Symmington, too, was a very clever lawyer, and had helped Miss Barton to get some money back from the income tax which she would never have known about. He was so nice to his children, too, devoted to them and to his wife – she caught herself up. 'Poor Mrs Symmington, it's so dreadfully sad, with those young children left motherless. Never, perhaps, a very strong woman – and her health had been bad of late. A brain storm, that is what it must have been. I read about such a thing in the paper. People really do not know what they are doing under those circumstances. And she can't have known what she was doing or else she would have remembered Mr Symmington and the children.'

'That anonymous letter must have shaken her up very badly,' said Joanna.

Miss Barton flushed. She said, with a tinge of reproof in her voice:

'Not a very nice thing to discuss, do you think, dear? I know there have been – er – letters, but we won't talk about them. Nasty things. I think they are better just ignored.'

Well, Miss Barton might be able to ignore them, but for some people it wasn't so easy. However I obediently changed the subject and we discussed Aimée Griffith.

'Wonderful, quite wonderful,' said Emily Barton. 'Her energy and her organizing powers are really splendid. She's so good with girls too. And she's so practical and up-to-date in every way. She really runs this place. And absolutely devoted to her brother. It's very nice to see such devotion between brother and sister.'

'Doesn't he ever find her a little overwhelming?' asked Joanna.

Emily Barton stared at her in a startled fashion.

'She has sacrificed a great deal for his sake,' she said with a touch of reproachful dignity.

I saw a touch of Oh Yeay! in Joanna's eye and hastened to divert the conversation to Mr Pye.

Emily Barton was a little dubious about Mr Pye.

All she could say was, repeated rather doubtfully, that he was very kind – yes, very kind. Very well off, too, and most generous. He had very strange visitors sometimes, but then, of course, he had travelled a lot.

We agreed that travel not only broadened the mind, but occasionally resulted in the forming of strange acquaintances.

'I have often wished, myself, to go on a cruise,' said Emily Barton wistfully. 'One reads about them in the papers and they sound so attractive.'

'Why don't you go?' asked Joanna.

This turning of a dream into a reality seemed to alarm Miss Emily. 'Oh, no, no, that would be *quite* impossible.'

'But why? They're fairly cheap.'

239

'Oh, it's not only the expense. But I shouldn't like to go alone. Travelling alone would look very peculiar, don't you think?'

'No,' said Joanna.

Miss Emily looked at her doubtfully.

'And I don't know how I would manage about my luggage – and going ashore at foreign ports – and all the different currencies –'

Innumerable pitfalls seemed to rise up before the little lady's affrighted gaze, and Joanna hastened to calm her by a question about an approaching garden fête and sale of work. This led us quite naturally to Mrs Dane Calthrop.

A faint spasm showed for a minute on Miss Barton's face.

'You know, dear,' she said, 'she is really a very *odd* woman. The things she says sometimes.'

I asked what things.

'Oh, I don't know. Such very *unexpected* things. And the way she looks at you, as though you weren't there but somebody else was – I'm expressing it badly but it is so hard to convey the impression I mean. And then she won't – well, *interfere* at all. There are so many cases where a vicar's wife could advise and – perhaps *admonish*. Pull people up, you know, and make them mend their ways. Because people would listen to her, I'm sure of that, they're all quite in awe of her. But she insists on being aloof and far away, and has such a curious habit of feeling sorry for the most unworthy people.'

'That's interesting,' I said, exchanging a quick glance with Joanna.

'Still, she is a very well-bred woman. She was a Miss Farroway of Bellpath, very good family, but these old families sometimes *are* a little peculiar, I believe. But she is devoted to her husband who is a man of very fine intellect – wasted, I am sometimes afraid, in this country circle. A good man, and most sincere, but I always find his habit of quoting Latin a little confusing.'

'Hear, hear,' I said fervently.

'Jerry had an expensive public school education, so he doesn't recognize Latin when he hears it,' said Joanna.

This led Miss Barton to a new topic.

'The schoolmistress here is a most unpleasant young woman,' she said. 'Quite *Red*, I'm afraid.' She lowered her voice over the word 'Red.'

Later, as we walked home up the hill, Joanna said to me:

'She's rather sweet.'

At dinner that night, Joanna said to Partridge that she hoped her tea-party had been a success.

Partridge got rather red in the face and held herself even more stiffly.

'Thank you, miss, but Agnes never turned up after all.'

'Oh, I'm sorry.'

'It didn't matter to *me*,' said Partridge.

She was so swelling with grievance that she condescended to pour it out to us.

'It wasn't me who thought of asking her! She rang up herself, said she'd something on her mind and could she come here, it being her day off. And I said, yes, subject to your permission which I obtained. And after that, not a sound or sign of her! And no word of apology either, though I should hope I'll get a postcard tomorrow morning. These girls nowadays – don't know their place – no idea of how to behave.'

Joanna attempted to soothe Partridge's wounded feelings.

'She mayn't have felt well. You didn't ring up to find out?'

Partridge drew herself up again.

'No, I did *not*, Miss. No, indeed. If Agnes likes to behave rudely that's her look-out, but I shall give her a piece of my mind when we meet.'

Partridge went out of the room still stiff with indignation and Joanna and I laughed.

'Probably a case of "Advice from Aunt Nancy's Column",' I said. ' "*My boy is very cold in his manner to me, what shall I do about it?*" Failing Aunt Nancy, Partridge was to be applied to for advice, but instead there has been a reconciliation and I expect at this minute that Agnes and her boy are one of those speechless couples locked in each other's arms that you come upon suddenly standing by a dark hedge. They embarrass you horribly, but you don't embarrass them.'

Joanna laughed and said she expected that was it.

We began talking of the anonymous letters and wondered how Nash and the melancholy Graves were getting on.

'It's a week today exactly,' said Joanna, 'since Mrs Symmington's suicide. I should think they must have got on to something by now.

Fingerprints, or handwriting, or *something*.'

I answered her absently. Somewhere behind my conscious mind, a queer uneasiness was growing. It was connected in some way with the phrase that Joanna had used, 'a week exactly'.

I ought, I dare say, to have put two and two together earlier. Perhaps, unconsciously, my mind was already suspicious.

Anyway the leaven was working now. The uneasiness was growing – coming to a head.

Joanna noticed suddenly that I wasn't listening to her spirited account of a village encounter.

'What's the matter, Jerry?'

I did not answer because my mind was busy piecing things together.

Mrs Symmington's suicide . . . She was alone in the house that afternoon . . . Alone in the house *because the maids were having their day out*. . . A week ago exactly . . .

'Jerry, what –'

I interrupted.

'Joanna, maids have days out once a week, don't they?'

'And alternate Sundays,' said Joanna. 'What on –'

'Never mind Sundays. They go out the same day every week?'

'Yes. That's the usual thing.'

Joanna was staring at me curiously. Her mind had not taken the track mine had done.

I crossed the room and rang the bell. Partridge came.

'Tell me,' I said, 'this Agnes Woddell. She's in service?'

'Yes, sir. At Mrs Symmington's. At Mr Symmington's, I should say now.'

I drew a deep breath. I glanced at the clock. It was half-past ten.

'Would she be back now, do you think?'

Partridge was looking disapproving.

'Yes, sir. The maids have to be in by ten there. They're old-fashioned.'

I said: 'I'm going to ring up.'

I went out to the hall. Joanna and Partridge followed me. Partridge was clearly furious. Joanna was puzzled. She said, as I was trying to get the number:

'What are you going to do, Jerry?'

'I'd like to be sure that the girl has come in all right.'

242

Partridge sniffed. Just sniffed, nothing more. But I did not care twopence about Partridge's sniffs.

Elsie Holland answered the telephone the other end.

'Sorry to ring you up,' I said. 'This is Jerry Burton speaking. Is – has – your maid Agnes come in?'

It was not until after I had said it that I suddenly felt a bit of a fool. For if the girl had come in and it was all right, how on earth was I going to explain my ringing up and asking. It would have been better if I had let Joanna ask the question, though even that would need a bit of explaining. I foresaw a new trail of gossip started in Lymstock, with myself and the unknown Agnes Woddell at its centre.

Elsie Holland sounded, not unnaturally, very much surprised.

'Agnes? Oh, she's sure to be in by now.'

I felt a fool, but I went on with it.

'Do you mind just seeing if she has come in, Miss Holland?'

There is one thing to be said for a nursery governess; she is used to doing things when told. Hers not to reason why! Elsie Holland put down the receiver and went off obediently.

Two minutes later I heard her voice.

'Are you there, Mr Burton?'

'Yes.'

'Agnes isn't in yet, as a matter of fact.'

I knew then that my hunch had been right.

I heard a noise of voices vaguely from the other end, then Symmington himself spoke.

'Hallo, Burton, what's the matter?'

'Your maid Agnes isn't back yet?'

'No. Miss Holland has just been to see. What's the matter? There's not been an accident, has there?'

'Not an *accident*,' I said.

'Do you mean you have reason to believe something has happened to the girl?'

I said grimly: 'I shouldn't be surprised.'

CHAPTER EIGHT

I slept badly that night. I think that, even then, there were pieces of the puzzle floating about in my mind. I believe that if I had given my mind to it, I could have solved the whole thing then and there. Otherwise why did those fragments tag along so persistently?

How much do we know at any time? Much more, or so I believe, than we know we know! But we cannot break through to that subterranean knowledge. It is there, but we cannot reach it.

I lay on my bed, tossing uneasily, and only vague bits of the puzzle came to torture me.

There *was* a pattern, if only I could get hold of it. I ought to know who wrote those damned letters. There was a trail somewhere if only I could follow it ...

As I dropped off to sleep, words danced irritatingly through my drowsy mind.

'No smoke without fire.' No fire without smoke. Smoke ... Smoke? Smoke screen ... No, that was the war – a war phrase. War. Scrap of paper ... Only a scrap of paper. Belgium – Germany ...

I fell asleep. I dreamt that I was taking Mrs Dane Calthrop, who had turned into a greyhound, for a walk with a collar and lead.

II

It was the ringing of the telephone that roused me. A persistent ringing.

I sat up in bed, glanced at my watch. It was half-past seven. I had not yet been called. The telephone was ringing in the hall downstairs.

I jumped out of bed, pulled on a dressing-gown, and raced down. I beat Partridge coming through the back door from the kitchen by a short head. I picked up the receiver.

'Hallo?'

'Oh –' It was a sob of relief. 'It's *you*!' Megan's voice. Megan's voice indescribably forlorn and frightened. 'Oh, please do come – *do* come. Oh, please do! Will you?'

'I'm coming at once,' I said. 'Do you hear? *At once*.'

I took the stairs two at a time and burst in on Joanna.

'Look here, Jo, I'm going off to the Symmingtons'.'

Joanna lifted a curly blonde head from the pillow and rubbed her eyes like a small child.

'Why – what's happened?'

'I don't know. It was the child – Megan. She sounded all in.'

'What do you think it is?'

'The girl Agnes, unless I'm very much mistaken.'

As I went out of the door, Joanna called after me:

'Wait. I'll get up and drive you down.'

'No need. I'll drive myself.'

'You can't drive the car.'

'Yes, I can.'

I did, too. It hurt, but not too much. I'd washed shaved, dressed, got the car out and driven to the Symmingtons' in half an hour. Not bad going.

Megan must have been watching for me. She came out of the house at a run and clutched me. Her poor little face was white and twitching.

'Oh, you've come – you've *come*!'

'Hold up, funny face,' I said. 'Yes, I've come. Now what is it?'

She began to shake. I put my arm round her.

'I – I found her.'

'You found Agnes? Where?'

The trembling grew.

'Under the stairs. There's a cupboard there. It has fishing-rods and golf clubs and things. You know.'

I nodded. It was the usual cupboard.

Megan went on.

'She was there – all huddled up – and – and *cold* – horribly cold. She was – she was *dead*, you know!'

I asked curiously, 'What made you look there?'

'I – I don't know. You telephoned last night. And we all began wondering where Agnes was. We waited up some time, but she didn't come in, and at last we went to bed. I didn't sleep very well

245

and I got up early. There was only Rose (the cook, you know) about. She was very cross about Agnes not having come back. She said she'd been before somewhere when a girl did a flit like that. I had some milk and bread and butter in the kitchen – and then suddenly Rose came in looking queer and she said that Agnes's outdoor things were still in her room. Her best ones that she goes out in. And I began to wonder if – if she'd ever left the house, and I started looking round, and I opened the cupboard under the stairs and – and she was there . . .'

'Somebody's rung up the police, I suppose?'

'Yes, they're here now. My stepfather rang them up straightaway. And then I – I felt I couldn't bear it, and I rang *you* up. You don't mind?'

'No,' I said. 'I don't mind.'

I looked at her curiously.

'Did anybody give you some brandy, or some coffee, or some tea after – after you found her?'

Megan shook her head.

I cursed the whole Symmington *ménage*. That stuffed shirt, Symmington, thought of nothing but the police. Neither Elsie Holland nor the cook seemed to have thought of the effect on the sensitive child who had made that gruesome discovery.

'Come on, slabface,' I said. 'We'll go to the kitchen.'

We went round the house to the back door and into the kitchen. Rose, a plump pudding-faced woman of forty, was drinking strong tea by the kitchen fire. She greeted us with a flow of talk and her hand to her heart.

She'd come all over queer, she told me, awful the palpitations were! Just think of it, it might have been *her*, it might have been any of them, murdered in their beds they might have been.

'Dish out a good strong cup of that tea for Miss Megan,' I said. 'She's had a shock, you know. Remember it was she who found the body.'

The mere mention of a body nearly sent Rose off again, but I quelled her with a stern eye and she poured out a cup of inky fluid.

'There you are, young woman,' I said to Megan. 'You drink that down. You haven't got any brandy, I suppose, Rose?'

Rose said rather doubtfully that there was a drop of cooking brandy left over from the Christmas puddings.

'That'll do,' I said, and put a dollop of it into Megan's cup. I saw by Rose's eye that she thought it a good idea.

I told Megan to stay with Rose.

'I can trust you to look after Miss Megan?' I said, and Rose replied in a gratified way, 'Oh yes, sir.'

I went through into the house. If I knew Rose and her kind, she would soon find it necessary to keep her strength up with a little food, and that would be good for Megan too. Confound these people, why couldn't they look after the child?

Fuming inwardly I ran into Elsie Holland in the hall. She didn't seem surprised to see me. I suppose that the gruesome excitement of the discovery made one oblivious of who was coming and going. The constable, Bert Rundle, was by the front door.

Elsie Holland gasped out:

'Oh, Mr Burton, isn't it *awful*? Whoever can have done such a dreadful thing?'

'It *was* murder, then?'

'Oh, *yes*. She was struck on the back of the head. It's all blood and hair – oh! it's *awful* – and bundled into that cupboard. Who can have done such a wicked thing? And *why*? Poor Agnes, I'm sure she never did any one any harm.'

'No,' I said. 'Somebody saw to that pretty promptly.'

She stared at me. Not, I thought, a quick-witted girl. But she had good nerves. Her colour was, as usual, slightly heightened by excitement, and I even fancied that in a macabre kind of way, and in spite of a naturally kind heart, she was enjoying the drama.

She said apologetically: 'I must go up to the boys. Mr Symmington is so anxious that they shouldn't get a shock. He wants me to keep them right away.'

'Megan found the body, I hear,' I said. 'I hope somebody is looking after her?'

I will say for Elsie Holland that she looked conscience stricken.

'Oh dear,' she said. 'I forgot all about her. I do hope she's all right. I've been so rushed, you know, and the police and everything – but it was remiss of me. Poor girl, she must be feeling bad. I'll go and look for her at once.'

I relented.

'She's all right,' I said. 'Rose is looking after her. You get along to the kids.'

She thanked me with a flash of white tombstone teeth and hurried upstairs. After all, the boys were her job, and not Megan – Megan was nobody's job. Elsie was paid to look after Symmington's blinking brats. One could hardly blame her for doing so.

As she flashed round the corner of the stairs, I caught my breath. For a minute I caught a glimpse of a Winged Victory, deathless and incredibly beautiful, instead of a conscientious nursery governess.

Then a door opened and Superintendent Nash stepped out into the hall with Symmington behind him.

'Oh, Mr Burton,' he said. 'I was just going to telephone you. I'm glad you are here.'

He didn't ask me – then – why I was here.

He turned his head and said to Symmington:

'I'll use this room if I may.'

It was a small morning-room with a window on the front of the house.

'Certainly, certainly.'

Symmington's poise was pretty good, but he looked desperately tired. Superintendent Nash said gently:

'I should have some breakfast if I were you, Mr Symmington. You and Miss Holland and Miss Megan will feel much better after coffee and eggs and bacon. Murder is a nasty business on an empty stomach.'

He spoke in a comfortable family doctor kind of way.

Symmington gave a faint attempt at a smile and said:

'Thank you, superintendent, I'll take your advice.'

I followed Nash into the little morning-room and he shut the door. He said then:

'You've got here very quickly? How did you hear?'

I told him that Megan had rung me up. I felt well disposed towards Superintendent Nash. He, at any rate, had not forgotten that Megan, too, would be in need of breakfast.

'I hear that you telephoned last night, Mr Burton, asking about this girl? Why was that?'

I suppose it did seem odd. I told him about Agnes's telephone call to Partridge and her non-appearance. He said, 'Yes, I see . . .'

He said it slowly and reflectively, rubbing his chin.

Then he sighed:

'Well,' he said. 'It's murder now, right enough. Direct physical

248

action. The question is, what did the girl know? Did she say anything to this Partridge? Anything definite?'

'I don't think so. But you can ask her.'

'Yes. I shall come up and see her when I've finished here.'

'What happened exactly?' I asked. 'Or don't you know yet?'

'Near enough. It was the maids' day out –'

'Both of them?'

'Yes, it seems that there used to be two sisters here who liked to go out together, so Mrs Symmington arranged it that way. Then when these two came, she kept to the same arrangement. They used to leave cold supper laid out in the dining-room, and Miss Holland used to get tea.'

'I see.'

'It's pretty clear up to a point. The cook, Rose, comes from Nether Mickford, and in order to get there on her day out she has to catch the half-past two bus. So Agnes has to finish clearing up lunch always. Rose used to wash up the supper things in the evenings to even things up.

'That's what happened yesterday. Rose went off to catch the bus at two twenty-five, Symmington left for his office at five-and-twenty to three. Elsie Holland and the children went out at a quarter to three. Megan Hunter went out on her bicycle about five minutes later. Agnes would then be alone in the house. As far as I can make out, she normally left the house between three o'clock and half-past three.'

'The house being then left empty?'

'Oh, they don't worry about that down here. There's not much locking up done in these parts. As I say, at ten minutes to three Agnes was alone in the house. That she never left it is clear, for she was in her cap and apron still when we found her body.'

'I suppose you can tell roughly the time of death?'

'Doctor Griffith won't commit himself. Between two o'clock and four-thirty, is his official medical verdict.'

'How was she killed?'

'She was first stunned by a blow on the back of the head. Afterwards an ordinary kitchen skewer, sharpened to a fine point, was thrust in the base of the skull, causing instantaneous death.'

I lit a cigarette. It was not a nice picture.

'Pretty cold blooded,' I said.

249

'Oh yes, yes, that was indicated.'

I inhaled deeply.

'Who did it?' I said. 'And why?'

'I don't suppose,' said Nash slowly, 'that we shall ever know exactly why. But we can guess.'

'She knew something?'

'She knew something.'

'She didn't give any one here a hint?'

'As far as I can make out, no. She's been upset, so the cook says, ever since Mrs Symmington's death, and according to this Rose, she's been getting more and more worried, and kept saying she didn't know what she ought to do.'

He gave a short exasperated sigh.

'It's always the way. They won't come to us. They've got that deep-seated prejudice against "being mixed up with the police". If she'd come along and told us what was worrying her, she'd be alive today.'

'Didn't she give the other woman *any* hint?'

'No, or so Rose says, and I'm inclined to believe her. For if she had, Rose would have blurted it out at once with a good many fancy embellishments of her own.'

'It's maddening,' I said, 'not to know.'

'We can still guess, Mr Burton. To begin with, it can't be anything very definite. It's got to be the sort of thing that you think over, and as you think it over, your uneasiness grows. You see what I mean?'

'Yes.'

'Actually, I think I know what it was.'

I looked at him with respect.

'That's good work, superintendent.'

'Well, you see, Mr Burton, I know something that you don't. On the afternoon that Mrs Symmington committed suicide both maids were supposed to be out. It was their day out. But actually Agnes came back to the house.'

'You know that?'

'Yes. Agnes has a boy friend — young Rendell from the fish shop. Wednesday is early closing and he comes along to meet Agnes and they go for a walk, or to the pictures if it's wet. That Wednesday they had a row practically as soon as they met. Our letter writer had been active, suggesting that Agnes had other fish to fry, and young

250

Fred Rendell was all worked up. They quarrelled violently and Agnes bolted back home and said she wasn't coming out unless Fred said he was sorry.'

'Well?'

'Well, Mr Burton, the kitchen faces the back of the house but the pantry looks out where we are looking now. There's only one entrance gate. You come through it and either up to the front door, or else along the path at the side of the house to the back door.'

He paused.

'Now I'll tell you something. That letter that came to Mrs Symmington that afternoon *didn't come by post*. It had a used stamp affixed to it, and the postmark faked quite convincingly in lamp-black, so that it would seem to have been delivered by the postman with the afternoon letters. But actually *it had not been through the post*. You see what that means?'

I said slowly: 'It means that it was left by *hand*, pushed through the letter box some time before the afternoon post was delivered, so that it should be amongst the other letters.'

'Exactly. The afternoon post comes round about a quarter to four. My theory is this. The girl was in the pantry looking through the window (it's masked by shrubs but you can see through them quite well) watching out for her young man to turn up and apologize.'

I said: '*And she saw whoever it was deliver that note?*'

'That's my guess, Mr Burton. I may be wrong, of course.'

'I don't think you are ... It's simple – and convincing – and it means that Agnes knew *who the anonymous letter writer was*.'

'Yes.'

'But then why didn't she – ?'

I paused, frowning.

Nash said quickly:

'As I see it, the girl *didn't realize what she had seen*. Not at first. Somebody had left a letter at the house, yes – but that somebody was nobody she would dream of connecting with the anonymous letters. It was somebody, from that point of view, quite above suspicion.

'But the more she thought about it, the more uneasy she grew. Ought she, perhaps, to tell someone about it? In her perplexity she thinks of Miss Barton's Partridge who, I gather, is a somewhat dominant personality and whose judgment Agnes would accept unhesitatingly. She decides to ask Partridge what she ought to do.'

'Yes,' I said thoughtfully. 'It fits well enough. And somehow or other, Poison Pen found out. How did she find out, superintendent?'

'You're not used to living in the country, Mr Burton. It's a kind of miracle how things get round. First of all there's the telephone call. Who overheard it your end?'

I reflected.

'I answered the telephone originally. Then I called up the stairs to Partridge.'

'Mentioning the girl's name?'

'Yes – yes, I did.'

'Any one overhear you?'

'My sister or Miss Griffith might have done so.'

'Ah, Miss Griffith. What was she doing up there?'

I explained.

'Was she going back to the village?'

'She was going to Mr Pye first.'

Superintendent Nash sighed.

'That's two ways it could have gone all over the place.'

I was incredulous.

'Do you mean that either Miss Griffith or Mr Pye would bother to repeat a meaningless little bit of information like that?'

'Anything's news in a place like this. You'd be surprised. If the dressmaker's mother has got a bad corn everybody hears about it! And then there is this end. Miss Holland, Rose – they could have heard what Agnes said. And there's Fred Rendell. It may have gone round through him that Agnes went back to the house that afternoon.'

I gave a slight shiver. I was looking out of the window. In front of me was a neat square of grass and a path and the low prim gate.

Someone had opened the gate, had walked very correctly and quietly up to the house, and had pushed a letter through the letter box. I saw, hazily, in my mind's eye, that vague woman's shape. The face was blank – but it must be a face that I knew . . .

Superintendent Nash was saying:

'All the same, this narrows things down. That's always the way we get 'em in the end. Steady, patient elimination. There aren't so very many people it could be now.'

'You mean –?'

'It knocks out any women clerks who were at their work all yesterday afternoon. It knocks out the school-mistress. She was teaching. And the district nurse. I know where she was yesterday. Not that I ever thought it was any of *them*, but now we're *sure*. You see, Mr Burton, we've got two definite times now on which to concentrate – yesterday afternoon, and the week before. On the day of Mrs Symmington's death from, say, a quarter-past three (the earliest possible time at which Agnes could have been in the house after her quarrel) and four o'clock when the post must have come (but I can get that fixed more accurately with the postman). And yesterday from ten minutes to three (when Miss Megan Hunter left the house) until half-past three or more probably a quarter-past three as Agnes hadn't begun to change.'

'What do you think happened yesterday?'

Nash made a grimace.

'What do I think? I think a certain lady walked up to the front door and rang the bell, quite calm and smiling, the afternoon caller ... Maybe she asked for Miss Holland, or for Miss Megan, or perhaps she had brought a parcel. Anyway Agnes turns round to get a salver for cards, or to take the parcel in, and our ladylike caller bats her on the back of her unsuspecting head.'

'What with?'

Nash said:

'The ladies round here usually carry large sizes in handbags. No saying what mightn't be inside it.'

'And then stabs her through the back of the neck and bundles her into the cupboard? Wouldn't that be a hefty job for a woman?'

Superintendent Nash looked at me with rather a queer expression.

'The woman we're after isn't normal – not by a long way – and that type of mental instability goes with surprising strength. Agnes wasn't a big girl.'

He paused and then asked: 'What made Miss Megan Hunter think of looking in that cupboard?'

'Sheer instinct,' I said.

Then I asked: 'Why drag Agnes into the cupboard? What was the point?'

'The longer it was before the body was found, the more difficult it would be to fix the time of death accurately. If Miss Holland, for instance, fell over the body as soon as she came in, a doctor might be able to fix it within ten minutes or so – which might be awkward for our lady friend.'

I said, frowning:

'But if Agnes were suspicious of this person –'

Nash interrupted me.

'She wasn't. Not to the pitch of definite suspicion. She just thought it "queer". She was a slow-witted girl, I imagine, and she was only vaguely suspicious with a feeling that something was wrong. She certainly didn't suspect that she was up against a woman who would do murder.'

'Did you suspect that?' I asked.

Nash shook his head. He said, with feeling:

'I ought to have known. That suicide business, you see, frightened Poison Pen. She got the wind up. Fear, Mr Burton, is an incalculable thing.'

'Yes, fear. That was the thing we ought to have foreseen. Fear – in a lunatic brain . . .'

'You see,' said Superintendent Nash, and somehow his words made the whole thing seem absolutely horrible. 'We're up against someone who's respected and thought highly of – someone, in fact, of good social position!'

III

Presently Nash said that he was going to interview Rose once more. I asked him, rather diffidently, if I might come too. Rather to my surprise he assented cordially.

'I'm very glad of your co-operation, Mr Burton, if I may say so.'

'That sounds suspicious,' I said. 'In books when a detective welcomes someone's assistance, that someone is usually the murderer.'

Nash laughed shortly. He said: 'You're hardly the type to write anonymous letters, Mr Burton.'

He added: 'Frankly, you can be useful to us.'

'I'm glad, but I don't see how.'

'You're a stranger down here, that's why. You've got no preconceived ideas about the people here. But at the same time, you've got the opportunity of getting to know things in what I may call a social way.'

'The murderer is a person of good social position,' I murmured.

'Exactly.'

'I'm to be the spy within the gates?'

'Have you any objection?'

I thought it over.

'No,' I said, 'frankly I haven't. If there's a dangerous lunatic about driving inoffensive women to suicide and hitting miserable little maidservants on the head, then I'm not averse to doing a bit of dirty work to put that lunatic under restraint.'

'That's sensible of you, sir. And let me tell you, the person we're after is dangerous. She's about as dangerous as a rattlesnake and a cobra and a black mamba rolled into one.'

I gave a slight shiver. I said:

'In fact, we've got to make haste?'

'That's right. Don't think we're inactive in the force. We're not. We're working on several different lines.'

He said it grimly.

I had a vision of a fine far-flung spider's web . . .

Nash wanted to hear Rose's story again, so he explained to me, because she had already told him two different versions, and the more versions he got from her, the more likely it was that a few grains of truth might be incorporated.

We found Rose washing up breakfast, and she stopped at once and rolled her eyes and clutched her heart and explained again how she'd been coming over queer all the morning.

Nash was patient with her but firm. He'd been soothing the first time, so he told me, and peremptory the second, and he now employed a mixture of the two.

Rose enlarged pleasurably on the details of the past week, of how Agnes had gone about in deadly fear, and had shivered and said, 'Don't ask me,' when Rose had urged her to say what was the matter. 'It would be death if she told me,' that's what she said, finished Rose, rolling her eyes happily.

Had Agnes given no hint of what was troubling her?

No, except that she went in fear of her life.

Superintendent Nash sighed and abandoned the theme, contenting himself with extracting an exact account of Rose's own activities the preceding afternoon.

This, put baldly, was that Rose had caught the 2.30 bus and had spent the afternoon and evening with her family, returning by the 8.40 bus from Nether Mickford. The recital was complicated by the extraordinary presentiments of evil Rose had had all the afternoon and how her sister had commented on it and how she hadn't been able to touch a morsel of seed cake.

From the kitchen we went in search of Elsie Holland, who was superintending the children's lessons. As always, Elsie Holland was competent and obliging. She rose and said:

'Now, Colin, you and Brian will do these three sums and have the answers ready for me when I come back.'

She then led us into the night nursery. 'Will this do? I thought it would be better not to talk before the children.'

'Thank you, Miss Holland. Just tell me, once more, are you *quite* sure that Agnes never mentioned to you being worried over anything — since Mrs Symmington's death, I mean?'

'No, she never said anything. She was a very quiet girl, you know, and didn't talk much.'

'A change from the other one, then!'

'Yes, Rose talks much too much. I have to tell her not to be impertinent sometimes.'

'Now, will you tell me exactly what happened yesterday afternoon? Everything you can remember.'

'Well, we had lunch as usual. One o'clock, and we hurry just a little. I don't let the boys dawdle. Let me see. Mr Symmington went back to the office, and I helped Agnes by laying the table for supper — the boys ran out in the garden till I was ready to take them.'

'Where did you go?'

'Towards Combeacre, by the field path — the boys wanted to fish. I forgot their bait and had to go back for it.'

'What time was that?'

'Let me see, we started about twenty to three — or just after. Megan was coming but changed her mind. She was going out on her bicycle. She's got quite a craze for bicycling.'

'I mean what time was it when you went back for the bait? Did you go into the house?'

'No. I'd left it in the conservatory at the back. I don't know what time it was then — about ten minutes to three, perhaps.'

'Did you see Megan or Agnes?'

'Megan must have started, I think. No, I didn't see Agnes. I didn't see anyone.'

'And after that you went fishing?'

'Yes, we went along by the stream. We didn't catch anything. We hardly ever do, but the boys enjoy it. Brian got rather wet. I had to change his things when we got in.'

'You attend to tea on Wednesdays?'

'Yes. It's all ready in the drawing-room for Mr Symmington. I just make the tea when he comes in. The children and I have ours in the schoolroom – and Megan, of course. I have my own tea things and everything in the cupboard up there.'

'What time did you get in?'

'At ten minutes to five. I took the boys up and started to lay tea. Then when Mr Symmington came in at five I went down to make his but he said he would have it with us in the schoolroom. The boys were so pleased. We played Animal Grab afterwards. It seems so awful to think of now – with that poor girl in the cupboard all the time.'

'Would anybody go to that cupboard normally?'

'Oh no, it's only used for keeping junk. The hats and coats hang in the little cloakroom to the right of the front door as you come in. No one might have gone to the other cupboard for months.'

'I see. And you noticed nothing unusual, nothing abnormal at all when you came back?'

The blue eyes opened very wide.

'Oh no, inspector, nothing at all. Everything was just the same as usual. That's what was so awful about it.'

'And the week before?'

'You mean the day Mrs Symmington –'

'Yes.'

'Oh, that was terrible – terrible!'

'Yes, yes, I know. You were out all that afternoon also?'

'Oh yes, I always take the boys out in the afternoon – if it's fine enough. We do lessons in the morning. We went up on the moor, I remember – quite a long way. I was afraid I was late back because as I turned in at the gate I saw Mr Symmington coming from his office at the other end of the road, and I hadn't even put the kettle on, but it was just ten minutes to five.'

'You didn't go up to Mrs Symmington?'

'Oh no. I never did. She always rested after lunch. She had attacks of neuralgia — and they used to come on after meals. Dr Griffith had given her some cachets to take. She used to lie down and try to sleep.'

Nash said in a casual voice:

'So no one would take her up the post?'

'The afternoon post? No, I'd look in the letter box and put the letters on the hall table when I came in. But very often Mrs Symmington used to come down and get it herself. She didn't sleep all the afternoon. She was usually up again by four.'

'You didn't think anything was wrong because she wasn't up that afternoon?'

'Oh, no, I never dreamed of such a thing. Mr Symmington was hanging up his coat in the hall and I said, "Tea's not quite ready, but the kettle's nearly boiling," and he nodded and called out, "Mona, Mona!" — and then as Mrs Symmington didn't answer he went upstairs to her bedroom, and it must have been the most terrible shock to him. He called me and I came, and he said, "Keep the children away," and then he phoned Dr Griffith and we forgot all about the kettle and it burnt the bottom out! Oh dear, it *was* dreadful, and she'd been so happy and cheerful at lunch.'

Nash said abruptly: 'What is your own opinion of that letter she received, Miss Holland?'

Elsie Holland said indignantly:

'Oh, I think it was wicked — wicked!'

'Yes, yes, I don't mean that. Did you think it was true?'

Elsie Holland said firmly:

'No, indeed I don't. Mrs Symmington was very sensitive — very sensitive indeed. She had to take all sorts of things for her nerves. And she was very — well, *particular*.' Elsie flushed. 'Anything of that sort — *nasty*, I mean — would have given her a great shock.'

Nash was silent for a moment, then he asked:

'Have you had any of these letters, Miss Holland?'

'No. No, I haven't had any.'

'Are you sure? Please' — he lifted a hand — 'don't answer in a hurry. They're not pleasant things to get, I know. And sometimes people don't like to admit they've had them. But it's very important in this case that we should know. We're quite aware that the statements in them are just a tissue of lies, so you needn't feel embarrassed.'

'But I haven't, superintendent. Really I haven't. Not anything of the kind.'

She was indignant, almost tearful, and her denials seemed genuine enough.

When she went back to the children, Nash stood looking out of the window.

'Well,' he said, 'that's that! She says she hasn't received any of these letters. And she sounds as though she's speaking the truth.'

'She did certainly. I'm sure she was.'

'H'm,' said Nash. 'Then what I want to know is, why the devil hasn't she?'

He went on rather impatiently, as I stared at him.

'She's a pretty girl, isn't she?'

'Rather more than pretty.'

'Exactly. As a matter of fact, she's uncommonly good looking. And she's young. In fact she's just the meat an anonymous letter writer would like. Then why has she been left out?'

I shook my head.

'It's interesting, you know. I must mention it to Graves. He asked if we could tell him definitely of any one who hadn't had one.'

'She's the second person,' I said. 'There's Emily Barton, remember.'

Nash gave a faint chuckle.

'You shouldn't believe everything you're told, Mr Burton. Miss Barton had one all right – more than one.'

'How do you know?'

'That devoted dragon she's lodging with told me – her late parlourmaid or cook. Florence Elford. Very indignant she was about it. Would like to have the writer's blood.'

'Why did Miss Emily say she hadn't had any?'

'Delicacy. Their language isn't nice. Little Miss Barton has spent her life avoiding the coarse and unrefined.'

'What did the letters say?'

'The usual. Quite ludicrous in her case. And incidentally insinuated that she poisoned off her old mother and most of her sisters!'

I said incredulously:

'Do you mean to say there's really this dangerous lunatic going about and we can't spot her right away?'

'We'll spot her,' said Nash, and his voice was grim. 'She'll write just one letter too many.'

'But, my goodness, man, she won't go on writing these things – not now.'

He looked at me.

'Oh yes she will. You see, *she can't stop now*. It's a morbid craving. The letters will go on, make no mistake about that.'

CHAPTER NINE

I went and found Megan before leaving the house. She was in the garden and seemed almost back to her usual self. She greeted me quite cheerfully.

I suggested that she should come back to us again for a while, but after a momentary hesitation she shook her head.

'It's nice of you – but I think I'll stay here. After all, it is – well, I suppose, it's my home. And I dare say I can help with the boys a bit.'

'Well,' I said, 'it's as you like.'

'Then I think I'll stay. I could – I could –'

'Yes?' I prompted.

'If – if anything awful happened, I could ring you up, couldn't I, and you'd come.'

I was touched. 'Of course. But what awful thing do you think might happen?'

'Oh, I don't know.' She looked vague. 'Things seem rather like that just now, don't they?'

'For God's sake,' I said. 'Don't go nosing out any more bodies! It's not good for you.'

She gave me a brief flash of a smile.

'No, it isn't. It made me feel awfully sick.'

I didn't much like leaving her there, but after all, as she had said, it was her home. And I fancied that now Elsie Holland would feel more responsible for her.

Nash and I went up together to Little Furze. Whilst I gave Joanna an account of the morning's doings, Nash tackled Partridge. He rejoined us looking discouraged.

'Not much help there. According to this woman, the girl only said she was worried about something and didn't know what to do and that she'd like Miss Partridge's advice.'

'Did Partridge mention the fact to any one?' asked Joanna.

Nash nodded, looking grim.

'Yes, she told Mrs Emory — your daily woman — on the lines, as far as I can gather, that there were *some* young women who were willing to take advice from their elders and didn't think they could settle everything for themselves off-hand! Agnes mightn't be very bright, but she was a nice respectful girl and knew her manners.'

'Partridge preening herself, in fact,' murmured Joanna. 'And Mrs Emory could have passed it round the town?'

'That's right, Miss Burton.'

'There's one thing rather surprises me,' I said. 'Why were my sister and I included among the recipients of the anonymous letters? We were strangers down here — nobody could have had a grudge against us.'

'You're failing to allow for the mentality of a Poison Pen — all is grist that comes to their mill. Their grudge, you might say, is against humanity.'

'I suppose,' said Joanna thoughtfully, 'that that is what Mrs Dane Calthrop meant.'

Nash looked at her inquiringly, but she did not enlighten him. The superintendent said:

'I don't know if you happened to look closely at the envelope of the letter you got, Miss Burton. If so, you may have noticed that it was actually addressed to Miss Barton, and the *a* altered to a *u* afterwards.'

That remark, properly interpreted, ought to have given us a clue to the whole business. As it was, none of us saw any significance in it.

Nash went off, and I was left with Joanna. She actually said: 'You don't think that letter can really have been meant for Miss Emily, do you?'

'It would hardly have begun "You painted trollop,"' I pointed out, and Joanna agreed.

Then she suggested that I should go down to the town. 'You

261

ought to hear what everyone is saying. It will be *the* topic this morning!'

I suggested that she should come too, but rather to my surprise Joanna refused. She said she was going to mess about in the garden.

I paused in the doorway and said, lowering my voice:

'I suppose Partridge is all right?'

'Partridge!'

The amazement in Joanna's voice made me feel ashamed of my idea. I said apologetically: 'I just wondered. She's rather "queer" in some ways – a grim spinster – the sort of person who might have religious mania.'

'This isn't religious mania – or so you told me Graves said.'

'Well, sex mania. They're very closely tied up together, I understand. She's repressed and respectable, and has been shut up here with a lot of elderly women for years.'

'What put the idea into your head?'

I said slowly:

'Well, we've only her word for it, haven't we, as to what the girl Agnes said to her? Suppose Agnes asked Partridge to tell her why Partridge came and left a note that day – and Partridge said she'd call round that afternoon and explain.'

'And then camouflaged it by coming to us and asking if the girl could come here?'

'Yes.'

'But Partridge never went out that afternoon.'

'We don't know that. We were out ourselves, remember.'

'Yes, that's true. It's possible, I suppose.' Joanna turned it over in her mind. 'But I don't think so, all the same. I don't think Partridge has the mentality to cover her tracks over the letters. To wipe off fingerprints, and all that. It isn't only cunning you want – it's knowledge. I don't think she's got that. I suppose –' Joanna hesitated, then said slowly, 'they are sure it is a woman, aren't they?'

'You don't think it's a man?' I exclaimed incredulously.

'Not – not an ordinary man – but a certain kind of man. I'm thinking, really, of Mr Pye.'

'So Pye is your selection?'

'Don't you feel yourself that he's a possibility? He's the sort of person who might be lonely – and unhappy – and spiteful. Everyone, you see, rather laughs at him. Can't you see him secretly hating all

262

the normal happy people, and taking a queer perverse artistic pleasure in what he was doing?'

'Graves said a middle-aged spinster.'

'Mr Pye,' said Joanna, '*is* a middle-aged spinster.'

'A misfit,' I said slowly.

'Very much so. He's rich, but money doesn't help. And I do feel he might be unbalanced. He is, really, rather a *frightening* little man.'

'He got a letter himself, remember.'

'We don't know that,' Joanna pointed out. 'We only thought so. And anyway, he might have been putting on an act.'

'For our benefit?'

'Yes. He's clever enough to think of that – and not to overdo it.'

'He must be a first-class actor.'

'But of course, Jerry, whoever is doing this *must* be a first-class actor. That's partly where the pleasure comes in.'

'For God's sake, Joanna, don't speak so understandingly! You make me feel that you – that you understand the mentality.'

'I think I do. I can – just – get into the mood. If I weren't Joanna Burton, if I weren't young and reasonably attractive and able to have a good time, if I were – how shall I put it? – behind bars, watching other people enjoy life, would a black evil tide rise in me, making me want to hurt, to torture – even to destroy?'

'Joanna!' I took her by the shoulders and shook her. She gave a little sigh and shiver, and smiled at me.

'I frightened you, didn't I, Jerry? But I have a feeling that that's the right way to solve this problem. You've got to be the person, knowing how they feel and what makes them act, and then – and then perhaps you'll know what they're going to do next.'

'Oh, hell!' I said. 'And I came down here to be a vegetable and get interested in all the dear little local scandals. Dear little local scandals! Libel, vilification, obscene language and murder!'

II

Joanna was quite right. The High Street was full of interested groups. I was determined to get everyone's reactions in turn.

I met Griffith first. He looked terribly ill and tired. So much so

263

that I wondered. Murder is not, certainly, all in the day's work to a doctor, but his profession does equip him to face most things including suffering, the ugly side of human nature, and the fact of death.

'You look all in,' I said.

'Do I?' He was vague. 'Oh! I've had some worrying cases lately.'

'Including our lunatic at large?'

'That, certainly.' He looked away from me across the street. I saw a fine nerve twitching in his eyelid.

'You've no suspicions as to – *who*?'

'No. No. I wish to God I had.'

He asked abruptly after Joanna, and said, hesitatingly, that he had some photographs she'd wanted to see.

I offered to take them to her.

'Oh, it doesn't matter. I shall be passing that way actually later in the morning.'

I began to be afraid that Griffith had got it badly. Curse Joanna! Griffith was too good a man to be dangled as a scalp.

I let him go, for I saw his sister coming and I wanted, for once, to talk to her.

Aimée Griffith began, as it were, in the middle of a conversation.

'Absolutely shocking!' she boomed. 'I hear you were there – quite early?'

There was a question in the words, and her eyes glinted as she stressed the word 'early.' I wasn't going to tell her that Megan had rung me up. I said instead:

'You see, I was a bit uneasy last night. The girl was due to tea at our house and didn't turn up.'

'And so you feared the worst? Damned smart of you!'

'Yes,' I said. 'I'm quite the human bloodhound.'

'It's the first murder we've ever had in Lymstock. Excitement is terrific. Hope the police can handle it all right.'

'I shouldn't worry,' I said. 'They're an efficient body of men.'

'Can't even remember what the girl looked like, although I suppose she's opened the door to me dozens of times. Quiet, insignificant little thing. Knocked on the head and then stabbed through the back of the neck, so Owen tells me. Looks like a boy friend to me. What do you think?'

'That's your solution?'

'Seems the most likely one. Had a quarrel, I expect. They're very inbred round here — bad heredity, a lot of them.' She paused, and then went on, 'I hear Megan Hunter found the body? Must have given her a bit of a shock.'

I said shortly:

'It did.'

'Not too good for her, I should imagine. In my opinion she's not too strong in the head — and a thing like this might send her completely off her onion.'

I took a sudden resolution. I had to know something.

'Tell me, Miss Griffith, was it you who persuaded Megan to return home yesterday?'

'Well, I wouldn't say exactly persuaded.'

I stuck to my guns.

'But you did say something to her?'

Aimée Griffith planted her feet firmly and stared me in the eyes. She was, just slightly, on the defensive. She said:

'It's no good that young woman shirking her responsibilities. She's young and she doesn't know how tongues wag, so I felt it my duty to give her a hint.'

'Tongues — ?' I broke off because I was too angry to go on.

Aimée Griffith continued with that maddeningly complacent confidence in herself which was her chief characteristic:

'Oh, I dare say *you* don't hear all the gossip that goes round. I do! I know what people are saying. Mind you, I don't for a minute think there's anything in it — not for a minute! But you know what people are — if they can say something ill-natured, they do! And it's rather hard lines on the girl when she's got her living to earn.'

'Her living to earn?' I said, puzzled.

Aimée went on:

'It's a difficult position for her, naturally. And I think she did the right thing. I mean, she couldn't go off at a moment's notice and leave the children with no one to look after them. She's been splendid — absolutely splendid. I say so to everybody! But there it is, it's an invidious position, and people will talk.'

'Who are you talking about?' I asked.

'Elsie Holland, of course,' said Aimée Griffith impatiently. 'In my opinion, she's a thoroughly nice girl, and has only been doing her duty.'

'And what are people saying?'

Aimée Griffith laughed. It was, I thought, rather an unpleasant laugh.

'They're saying that she's already considering the possibility of becoming Mrs Symmington No. 2 – that she's all out to console the widower and make herself indispensable.'

'But, good God,' I said, shocked, 'Mrs Symmington's only been dead a week!'

Aimée Griffith shrugged her shoulders.

'Of course. It's absurd! But you know what people are! The Holland girl is young and she's good looking – that's enough. And mind you, being a nursery governess isn't much of a prospect for a girl. I wouldn't blame her if she wanted a settled home and a husband and was playing her cards accordingly.

'Of course,' she went on, 'poor Dick Symmington hasn't the least idea of all this! He's still completely knocked out by Mona Symmington's death. But you know what men are! If the girl is always there, making him comfortable, looking after him, being obviously devoted to the children – well, he gets to be dependent on her.'

I said quietly:

'So you do think that Elsie Holland is a designing hussy?'

Aimée Griffith flushed.

'Not at all. I'm sorry for the girl – with people saying nasty things! That's why I more or less told Megan that she ought to go home. It looks better than having Dick Symmington and the girl alone in the house.'

I began to understand things.

Aimée Griffith gave her jolly laugh.

'You're shocked, Mr Burton, at hearing what our gossiping little town thinks. I can tell you this – they always think the worst!'

She laughed and nodded and strode away.

III

I came upon Mr Pye by the church. He was talking to Emily Barton, who looked pink and excited.

Mr Pye greeted me with every evidence of delight.

'Ah, Burton, good morning, good morning! How is your charming sister?'

I told him that Joanna was well.

'But not joining our village parliament? We're all agog over the news. Murder! Real Sunday newspaper murder in our midst! Not the most interesting of crimes, I fear. Somewhat sordid. The brutal murder of a little serving maid. No finer points about the crime, but still undeniably, news.'

Miss Barton said tremulously:

'It is shocking — quite shocking.'

Mr Pye turned to her.

'But you enjoy it, dear lady, you enjoy it. Confess it now. You disapprove, you deplore, but there *is* the thrill. I insist, there *is* the thrill!'

'Such a nice girl,' said Emily Barton. 'She came to me from St Clotilde's Home. Quite a raw girl. But most teachable. She turned into such a nice little maid. Partridge was very pleased with her.'

I said quickly:

'She was coming to tea with Partridge yesterday afternoon.' I turned to Pye. 'I expect Aimée Griffith told you.'

My tone was quite casual. Pye responded apparently quite unsuspiciously: 'She did mention it, yes. She said, I remember, that it was something quite new for servants to ring up on their employers' telephones.'

'Partridge would never dream of doing such a thing,' said Miss Emily, 'and I am really surprised at Agnes doing so.'

'You are behind the times, dear lady,' said Mr Pye. 'My two terrors use the telephone constantly and smoked all over the house until I objected. But one daren't say too much. Prescott is a divine cook, though temperamental, and Mrs Prescott is an admirable house-parlourmaid.'

'Yes, indeed, we all think you're very lucky.'

I intervened, since I did not want the conversation to become purely domestic.

'The news of the murder has got round very quickly,' I said.

'Of course, of course,' said Mr Pye. 'The butcher, the baker, the candlestick maker. Enter Rumour, painted full of tongues! Lymstock, alas! is going to the dogs. Anonymous letters, murders, any amount of criminal tendencies.'

Emily Barton said nervously: 'They don't think – there's no idea – that – that the two are connected.'

Mr Pye pounced on the idea.

'An interesting speculation. The girl knew something, therefore she was murdered. Yes, yes, most promising. How clever of you to think of it.'

'I – I can't bear it.'

Emily Barton spoke abruptly and turned away, walking very fast.

Pye looked after her. His cherubic face was pursed up quizzically.

He turned back to me and shook his head gently.

'A sensitive soul. A charming creature, don't you think? Absolutely a period piece. She's not, you know, of her own generation, she's of the generation before that. The mother must have been a woman of a very strong character. She kept the family time ticking at about 1870, I should say. The whole family preserved under a glass case. I do like to come across that sort of thing.'

I did not want to talk about period pieces.

'What do you really think about all this business?' I asked.

'Meaning by that?'

'Anonymous letters, murder . . .'

'Our local crime wave? What do you?'

'I asked you first,' I said pleasantly.

Mr Pye said gently:

'I'm a student, you know, of abnormalities. They interest me. Such apparently unlikely people do the most fantastic things. Take the case of Lizzie Borden. There's not really a reasonable explanation of that. In this case, my advice to the police would be – study *character*. Leave your fingerprints and your measuring of handwriting and your microscopes. Notice instead what people do with their hands, and their little tricks of manner, and the way they eat their food, and if they laugh sometimes for no apparent reason.'

I raised my eyebrows. 'Mad?' I said.

'Quite, quite mad,' said Mr Pye, and added, 'but you'd never know it!'

'Who?'

His eyes met mine. He smiled.

'No, no, Burton, that would be slander. We can't add slander to all the rest of it.'

He fairly skipped off down the street.

IV

As I stood staring after him the church door opened and the Rev. Caleb Dane Calthrop came out.

He smiled vaguely at me.

'Good – good morning, Mr – er – er –'

I helped him. 'Burton.'

'Of course, of course, you mustn't think I don't remember you. Your name had just slipped my memory for the moment. A beautiful day.'

'Yes,' I said rather shortly.

He peered at me.

'But something – something – ah, yes, that poor unfortunate child who was in service at the Symmingtons'. I find it hard to believe, I must confess, that we have a murderer in our midst, Mr – er – Burton.'

'It does seem a bit fantastic,' I said.

'Something else has just reached my ears.' He leaned towards me. 'I learn that there have been anonymous letters going about. Have you heard any rumour of such things?'

'I have heard,' I said.

'Cowardly and dastardly things.' He paused and quoted an enormous stream of Latin. 'Those words of Horace are very applicable, don't you think?' he said.

'Absolutely,' I said.

V

There didn't seem anyone more I could profitably talk to, so I went home, dropping in for some tobacco and for a bottle of sherry, so as to get some of the humbler opinions on the crime.

'A narsty tramp,' seemed to be the verdict.

'Come to the door, they do, and whine and ask for money, and then if it's a girl alone in the house, they turn nasty. My sister Dora,

269

over to Combeacre, she had a narsty experience one day – Drunk, he was, and selling those little printed poems . . .'

The story went on, ending with the intrepid Dora courageously banging the door in the man's face and taking refuge and barricading herself in some vague retreat, which I gathered from the delicacy in mentioning it must be the lavatory. 'And there she stayed till her lady came home!'

I reached Little Furze just a few minutes before lunch time. Joanna was standing in the drawing-room window doing nothing at all and looking as though her thoughts were miles away.

'What have you been doing with yourself?' I asked.

'Oh, I don't know. Nothing particular.'

I went out on the veranda. Two chairs were drawn up to an iron table and there were two empty sherry glasses. On another chair was an object at which I looked with bewilderment for some time.

'What on earth is this?'

'Oh,' said Joanna, 'I think it's a photograph of a diseased spleen or something. Dr Griffith seemed to think I'd be interested to see it.'

I looked at the photograph with some interest. Every man has his own ways of courting the female sex. I should not, myself, choose to do it with photographs of spleens, diseased or otherwise. Still no doubt Joanna had asked for it!

'It looks most unpleasant,' I said.

Joanna said it did, rather.

'How was Griffith?' I asked.

'He looked tired and very unhappy. I think he's got something on his mind.'

'A spleen that won't yield to treatment?'

'Don't be silly. I mean something real.'

'I should say the man's got *you* on his mind. I wish you'd lay off him, Joanna.'

'Oh, do shut up. I haven't done anything.'

'Women always say that.'

Joanna whirled angrily out of the room.

The diseased spleen was beginning to curl up in the sun. I took it by one corner and brought it into the drawing-room. I had no affection for it myself, but I presumed it was one of Griffith's treasures.

I stooped down and pulled out a heavy book from the bottom shelf of the bookcase in order to press the photograph flat again between its leaves. It was a ponderous volume of somebody's sermons.

The book came open in my hand in rather a surprising way. In another minute I saw why. *From the middle of it a number of pages had been neatly cut out.*

VI

I stood staring at it. I looked at the title page. It had been published in 1840.

There could be no doubt at all. I was looking at the book from the pages of which the anonymous letters had been put together. Who had cut them out?

Well, to begin with, it could be Emily Barton herself. She was, perhaps, the obvious person to think of. Or it could have been Partridge.

But there were other possibilities. The pages could have been cut out by anyone who had been alone in this room, any visitor, for instance, who had sat there waiting for Miss Emily. Or even anyone who called on business.

No, that wasn't so likely. I had noticed that when, one day, a clerk from the bank had come to see me, Partridge had shown him into the little study at the back of the house. That was clearly the house routine.

A visitor, then? Someone 'of good social position'. Mr Pye? Aimée Griffith? Mrs Dane Calthrop?

VII

The gong sounded and I went in to lunch. Afterwards, in the drawing-room I showed Joanna my find.

We discussed it from every aspect. Then I took it down to the police station.

They were elated at the find, and I was patted on the back for what was, after all, the sheerest piece of luck.

Graves was not there, but Nash was, and rang up the other man. They would test the book for fingerprints, though Nash was not hopeful of finding anything. I may say that he did not. There were mine, Partridge's and nobody else's, merely showing that Partridge dusted conscientiously.

Nash walked back with me up the hill. I asked how he was getting on. 'We're narrowing it down, Mr Burton. We've eliminated the people it couldn't be.'

'Ah,' I said. 'And who remains?'

'Miss Ginch. She was to meet a client at a house yesterday afternoon by appointment. The house was situated not far along the Combeacre Road, that's the road that goes past the Symmingtons'. She would have to pass the house both going and coming . . . the week before, the day the anonymous letter was delivered, and Mrs Symmington committed suicide, was her last day at Symmington's office. Mr Symmington thought at first she had not left the office at all that afternoon. He had Sir Henry Lushington with him all the afternoon and rang several times for Miss Ginch. I find, however, that she did leave the office between three and four. She went out to get some high denomination of stamp of which they had run short. The office boy could have gone, but Miss Ginch elected to go, saying she had a headache and would like the air. She was not gone long.'

'But long enough?'

'Yes, long enough to hurry along to the other end of the village, slip the letter in the box and hurry back. I must say, however, that I cannot find anybody who saw her near the Symmingtons' house.'

'Would they notice?'

'They might and they might not.'

'Who else is in your bag?'

Nash looked very straight ahead of him.

'You'll understand that we can't exclude anybody — anybody at all.'

'No,' I said. 'I see that.'

He said gravely: 'Miss Griffith went to Brenton for a meeting of Girl Guides yesterday. She arrived rather late.'

'You don't think —'

'No, I don't think. But I don't *know*. Miss Griffith seems an eminently sane healthy-minded woman — but I say, I don't *know*.'

'What about the previous week? Could she have slipped the letter in the box?'

'It's possible. She was shopping in the town that afternoon.' He paused. 'The same applies to Miss Emily Barton. She was out shopping early yesterday afternoon and she went for a walk to see some friends on the road past the Symmingtons' house the week before.'

I shook my head unbelievingly. Finding the cut book in Little Furze was bound, I knew, to direct attention to the owner of that house, but when I remembered Miss Emily coming in yesterday so bright and happy and excited . . .

Damn it all — excited . . . Yes, excited — pink cheeks — shining eyes — surely not because — not because —

I said thickly: 'This business is bad for one! One sees things — one imagines things —'

'Yes, it isn't very pleasant to look upon the fellow creatures one meets as possible criminal lunatics.'

He paused for a moment, then went on:

'And there's Mr Pye —'

I said sharply: 'So you have considered him?'

Nash smiled.

'Oh, yes, we've considered him all right. A very curious character — not, I should say, a very nice character. He's got no alibi. He was in his garden, alone, on both occasions.'

'So you're not only suspecting women?'

'I don't think a man wrote the letters — in fact I'm sure of it — and so is Graves — always excepting our Mr Pye, that is to say, who's got an abnormally female streak in his character. But we've checked up on *everybody* for yesterday afternoon. That's a murder case, you see. *You're* all right,' he grinned, 'and so's your sister, and Mr Symmington didn't leave his office after he got there and Dr Griffith was on a round in the other direction, and I've checked up on his visits.'

He paused, smiled again, and said, 'You see, we *are* thorough.'

I said slowly, 'So your case is eliminated down to those four — Miss Ginch, Mr Pye, Miss Griffith and little Miss Barton?'

'Oh, no, no, we've got a couple more — besides the vicar's lady.'

'You've thought of *her*?'

'We've thought of *everybody*, but Mrs Dane Calthrop is a little too openly mad, if you know what I mean. Still, she *could* have

273

done it. She was in a wood watching birds yesterday afternoon – and the birds can't speak for her.'

He turned sharply as Owen Griffith came into the police station.

'Hallo, Nash. I heard you were round asking for me this morning. Anything important?'

'Inquest on Friday, if that suits you, Dr Griffith.'

'Right. Moresby and I are doing the P.M. tonight.'

Nash said:

'There's just one other thing, Dr Griffith. Mrs Symmington was taking some cachets, powders or something, that you prescribed for her –'

He paused. Owen Griffith said interrogatively:

'Yes?'

'Would an overdose of those cachets have been fatal?'

Griffith said dryly:

'Certainly not. Not unless she'd taken about twenty-five of them!'

'But you once warned her about exceeding the dose, so Miss Holland tells me.'

'Oh that, yes. Mrs Symmington was the sort of woman who would go and overdo anything she was given – fancy that to take twice as much would do her twice as much good, and you don't want anyone to overdo even phenacetin or aspirin – bad for the heart. And anyway there's absolutely no doubt about the cause of death. It was cyanide.'

'Oh, I know that – you don't get my meaning. I only thought that when committing suicide you'd prefer to take an overdose of a soporific rather than to feed yourself prussic acid.'

'Oh quite. On the other hand, prussic acid is more dramatic and is pretty certain to do the trick. With barbiturates, for instance, you can bring the victim round if only a short time has elapsed.'

'I see, thank you, Dr Griffith.'

Griffith departed, and I said goodbye to Nash. I went slowly up the hill home. Joanna was out – at least there was no sign of her, and there was an enigmatical memorandum scribbled on the telephone block presumably for the guidance of either Partridge or myself.

'*If Dr Griffith rings up, I can't go on Tuesday, but could manage Wednesday or Thursday.*'

I raised my eyebrows and went into the drawing-room. I sat down in the most comfortable armchair – (none of them were very

274

comfortable, they tended to have straight backs and were reminiscent of the late Mrs Barton) – stretched out my legs and tried to think the whole thing out.

With sudden annoyance I remembered that Owen's arrival had interrupted my conversation with the inspector, and that he had just mentioned two other people as being possibilities.

I wondered who they were.

Partridge, perhaps, for one? After all, the cut book had been found in this house. And Agnes could have been struck down quite unsuspecting by her guide and mentor. No, you couldn't eliminate Partridge.

But who was the other?

Somebody, perhaps, that I didn't know? Mrs Cleat? The original local suspect?

I closed my eyes. I considered four people, strangely unlikely people, in turn. Gentle, frail little Emily Barton? What points were there actually against her? A starved life? Dominated and repressed from early childhood? Too many sacrifices asked of her? Her curious horror of discussing anything 'not quite nice'? Was that actually a sign of inner preoccupation with just these themes? Was I getting too horribly Freudian? I remembered a doctor once telling me that the mutterings of gentle maiden ladies when going off under an anaesthetic were a revelation. 'You wouldn't think they knew such words!'

Aimée Griffith?

Surely nothing repressed or 'inhibited' about her. Cheery, mannish, successful. A full, busy life. Yet Mrs Dane Calthrop had said, 'Poor thing!'

And there was something – something – some remembrance . . . Ah! I'd got it. Owen Griffith saying something like, 'We had an outbreak of anonymous letters up North where I had a practice.'

Had that been Aimée Griffith's work too? Surely rather a coincidence. Two outbreaks of the same thing.

Stop a minute, they'd tracked down the author of those. Griffith had said so. A schoolgirl.

Cold it was suddenly – must be a draught, from the window. I turned uncomfortably in my chair. Why did I suddenly feel so queer and upset?

Go on thinking . . . Aimée Griffith? Perhaps it was Aimée Griffith, *not* that other girl? And Aimée had come down here and started her tricks again. And that was why Owen Griffith was looking so unhappy and hag ridden. He suspected. Yes, he suspected . . .

My Pye? Not, somehow, a very nice little man. I could imagine him staging the whole business . . . laughing . . .

That telephone message on the telephone pad in the hall . . . why did I keep thinking of it? Griffith and Joanna – he was falling for her . . . No, that wasn't why the message worried me. It was something else . . .

My senses were swimming, sleep was very near. I repeated idiotically to myself, 'No smoke without fire. No smoke without fire . . . That's it . . . it all links up together . . .'

And then I was walking down the street with Megan and Elsie Holland passed. She was dressed as a bride, and people were murmuring:

'She's going to marry Dr Griffith at last. Of course they've been engaged secretly for years . . .'

There we were, in the church, and Dane Calthrop was reading the service in Latin.

And in the middle of it Mrs Dane Calthrop jumped up and cried energetically:

'It's got to be stopped, I tell you. It's got to be stopped!'

For a minute or two I didn't know whether I was asleep or awake. Then my brain cleared, and I realized I was in the drawing-room of Little Furze and that Mrs Dane Calthrop had just come through the window and was standing in front of me saying with nervous violence:

'It has got to be *stopped*, I tell you.'

I jumped up. I said: 'I beg your pardon. I'm afraid I was asleep. What did you say?'

Mrs Dane Calthrop beat one fist fiercely on the palm of her other hand.

'It's got to be stopped. These letters! Murder! You can't go on having poor innocent children like Agnes Woddell *killed*!'

'You're quite right,' I said. 'But how do you propose to set about it?'

Mrs Dane Calthrop said:

'We've got to do something!'

I smiled, perhaps in rather a superior fashion.

'And what do you suggest that we should do?'

'Get the whole thing cleared up! I said this wasn't a wicked place. I was wrong. It is.'

I felt annoyed. I said, not too politely:

'Yes, my dear woman, but what are you going to *do*?'

Mrs Dane Calthrop said: 'Put a stop to it all, of course.'

'The police are doing their best.'

'If Agnes could be killed yesterday, their best isn't good enough.'

'So you know better than they do?'

'Not at all. *I* don't know anything at all. That's why I'm going to call in an expert.'

I shook my head.

'You can't do that. Scotland Yard will only take over on a demand from the chief constable of the county. Actually they *have* sent Graves.'

'I don't mean *that* kind of an expert. I don't mean someone who knows about anonymous letters or even about murder. I mean someone who knows *people*. Don't you see? We want someone who knows a great deal about *wickedness*!'

It was a queer point of view. But it was, somehow, stimulating.

Before I could say anything more, Mrs Dane Calthrop nodded her head at me and said in a quick, confident tone:

'I'm going to see about it right away.'

And she went out of the window again.

CHAPTER TEN

The next week, I think, was one of the queerest times I have ever passed through. It had an odd dream quality. Nothing seemed real.

The inquest on Agnes Woddell was held and the curious of Lymstock attended *en masse*. No new facts came to light and the only possible verdict was returned, 'Murder by person or persons unknown.'

So poor little Agnes Woddell, having had her hour of limelight, was duly buried in the quiet old churchyard and life in Lymstock went on as before.

No, that last statement is untrue. Not as before . . .

There was a half-scared, half-avid gleam in almost everybody's eye. Neighbour looked at neighbour. One thing had been brought out clearly at the inquest – it was most unlikely that any stranger had killed Agnes Woddell. No tramps nor unknown men had been noticed or reported in the district. Somewhere, then, in Lymstock, walking down the High Street, shopping, passing the time of day, was a person who had cracked a defenceless girl's skull and driven a sharp skewer home to her brain.

And no one knew who that person was.

As I say, the days went by in a kind of dream. I looked at everyone I met in a new light, the light of a possible murderer. It was not an agreeable sensation!

And in the evenings, with the curtain drawn, Joanna and I sat talking, talking, arguing, going over in turn all the various possibilities that still seemed so fantastic and incredible.

Joanna held firm to her theory of Mr Pye. I, after wavering a little, had gone back to my original suspect, Miss Ginch. But we went over the possible names again and again.

Mr Pye?

Miss Ginch?

Mrs Dane Calthrop?

Aimée Griffith?

Emily Barton?

Partridge?

And all the time, nervously, apprehensively, we waited for something to happen.

But nothing did happen. Nobody, so far as we knew, received any more letters. Nash made periodic appearances in the town but what he was doing and what traps the police were setting, I had no idea. Graves had gone again.

Emily Barton came to tea. Megan came to lunch. Owen Griffith went about his practice. We went and drank sherry with Mr Pye. And we went to tea at the vicarage.

I was glad to find Mrs Dane Calthrop displayed none of the militant ferocity she had shown on the occasion of our last meeting. I think she had forgotten all about it.

She seemed now principally concerned with the destruction of white butterflies so as to preserve cauliflower and cabbage plants.

278

Our afternoon at the vicarage was really one of the most peaceful we had spent. It was an attractive old house and had a big shabby comfortable drawing-room with faded rose cretonne. The Dane Calthrops had a guest staying with them, an amiable elderly lady who was knitting something with white fleecy wool. We had very good hot scones for tea, the vicar came in, and beamed placidly on us whilst he pursued his gentle erudite conversation. It was very pleasant.

I don't mean that we got away from the topic of the murder, because we didn't.

Miss Marple, the guest, was naturally thrilled by the subject. As she said apologetically: 'We have so little to talk about in the country!' She had made up her mind that the dead girl must have been just like her Edith.

'Such a nice little maid, and so willing, but sometimes just a *little* slow to take in things.'

Miss Marple also had a cousin whose niece's sister-in-law had had a great deal of annoyance and trouble over some anonymous letters, so the letters, also, were very interesting to the charming old lady.

'But tell me, dear,' she said to Mrs Dane Calthrop, 'what do the village people – I mean the townspeople – say? What do *they* think?'

'Mrs Cleat still, I suppose,' said Joanna.

'Oh no,' said Mrs Dane Calthrop. 'Not *now*.'

Miss Marple asked who Mrs Cleat was.

Joanna said she was the village witch.

'That's right, isn't it, Mrs Dane Calthrop?'

The vicar murmured a long Latin quotation about, I think, the evil power of witches, to which we all listened in respectful and uncomprehending silence.

'She's a very silly woman,' said his wife. 'Likes to show off. Goes out to gather herbs and things at the full of the moon and takes care that everybody in the place knows about it.'

'And silly girls go and consult her, I suppose?' said Miss Marple.

I saw the vicar getting ready to unload more Latin on us and I asked hastily: 'But why shouldn't people suspect her of the murder now? They thought the letters were her doing.'

Miss Marple said: 'Oh! But the girl was killed with a *skewer*, so I hear – (very unpleasant!). Well, naturally, that takes *all* suspicion away from this Mrs Cleat. Because, you see, she could ill-wish her, so that the girl would waste away and die from natural causes.'

'Strange how the old beliefs linger,' said the vicar. 'In early Christian times, local superstitions were wisely incorporated with Christian doctrines and their more unpleasant attributes gradually eliminated.'

'It isn't superstition we've got to deal with here,' said Mrs Dane Calthrop, 'but *facts*.'

'And very unpleasant facts,' I said.

'As you say, Mr Burton,' said Miss Marple. 'Now *you* – excuse me if I am being too personal – are a stranger here, and have a knowledge of the world and of various aspects of life. It seems to me that you ought to be able to find a solution to this distasteful problem.'

I smiled. 'The best solution I have had was a dream. In my dream it all fitted in and panned out beautifully. Unfortunately when I woke up the whole thing was nonsense!'

'How interesting, though. Do tell me how the nonsense went!'

'Oh, it all started with the silly phrase. "No smoke without fire." People have been saying that *ad nauseam*. And then I got it mixed up with war terms. Smoke screens, scrap of paper, telephone messages – No, that was another dream.'

'And what was that dream?'

The old lady was so eager about it, that I felt sure she was a secret reader of Napoleon's Book of Dreams, which had been the great stand-by of my old nurse.

'Oh! only Elsie Holland – the Symmingtons' nursery governess, you know, was getting married to Dr Griffith and the vicar here was reading the service in Latin – ("Very appropriate, dear," murmured Mrs Dane Calthrop to her spouse) and then Mrs Dane Calthrop got up and forbade the banns and said it had got to be stopped!'

'But that part,' I added with a smile, 'was true. I woke up and found you standing over me saying it.'

'And I was quite right,' said Mrs Dane Calthrop – but quite mildly, I was glad to note.

'But where did a telephone message come in?' asked Miss Marple, crinkling her brows.

'I'm afraid I'm being rather stupid. That wasn't in the dream. It was just before it. I came through the hall and noticed Joanna had written down a message to be given to someone if they rang up . . .'

Miss Marple leaned forward. There was a pink spot in each cheek. 'Will you think me *very* inquisitive and *very* rude if I ask just what that message was?' She cast a glance at Joanna. 'I *do* apologize, my dear.'

Joanna, however, was highly entertained.

'Oh, I don't mind,' she assured the old lady. 'I can't remember anything about it myself, but perhaps Jerry can. It must have been something quite trivial.'

Solemnly I repeated the message as best I could remember it, enormously tickled at the old lady's rapt attention.

I was afraid the actual words were going to disappoint her, but perhaps she had some sentimental idea of a romance, for she nodded her head and smiled and seemed pleased.

'I see,' she said. 'I thought it might be something like that.'

Mrs Dane Calthrop said sharply: 'Like what, Jane?'

'Something quite ordinary,' said Miss Marple.

She looked at me thoughtfully for a moment or two, then she said unexpectedly:

'I can see you are a very clever young man – but not quite enough confidence in yourself. You ought to have!'

Joanna gave a loud hoot.

'For goodness' sake don't encourage him to feel like that. He thinks quite enough of himself as it is.'

'Be quiet, Joanna,' I said. 'Miss Marple understands me.'

Miss Marple had resumed her fleecy knitting. 'You know,' she observed pensively. 'To commit a successful murder must be very much like bringing off a conjuring trick.'

'The quickness of the hand deceives the eye?'

'Not only that. You've got to make people look at the wrong thing and in the wrong place – Misdirection, they call it, I believe.'

'Well,' I remarked. 'So far everybody seems to have looked in the wrong place for our lunatic at large.'

'I should be inclined, myself,' said Miss Marple, 'to look for somebody very sane.'

'Yes,' I said thoughtfully. 'That's what Nash said. I remember he stressed respectability too.'

'Yes,' agreed Miss Marple. 'That's *very* important.'

Well, we all seemed agreed.

I addressed Mrs Calthrop. 'Nash thinks,' I said, 'that there will be more anonymous letters. What do you think?'

She said slowly: 'There may be, I suppose.'

'If the police think that, there will have to be, no doubt,' said Miss Marple.

I went on doggedly to Mrs Dane Calthrop.

'Are you still sorry for the writer?'

She flushed. 'Why not?'

I don't think I agree with you, dear,' said Miss Marple. 'Not in this case.'

I said hotly: 'They've driven one woman to suicide, and caused untold misery and heartburnings!'

'Have you had one, Miss Burton?' asked Miss Marple of Joanna.

Joanna gurgled, 'Oh yes! It said the most frightful things.'

'I'm afraid,' said Miss Marple, 'that the people who are young and pretty are apt to be singled out by the writer.'

'That's why I certainly think it's odd that Elsie Holland hasn't had any,' I said.

'Let me see,' said Miss Marple. 'Is that the Symmingtons' nursery governess – the one you dreamt about, Mr Burton?'

'Yes.'

'She's probably had one and won't say so,' said Joanna.

'No,' I said, 'I believe her. So does Nash.'

'Dear me,' said Miss Marple. 'Now that's *very* interesting. That's the most interesting thing I've heard yet.'

II

As we were going home Joanna told me that I ought not to have repeated what Nash said about letters coming.

'Why not?'

'Because Mrs Dane Calthrop might be It.'

'You don't really believe that!'

'I'm not sure. She's a queer woman.'

We began our discussion of probables all over again.

It was two nights later that I was coming back in the car from Exhampton. I had had dinner there and then started back and it was already dark before I got into Lymstock

Something was wrong with the car lights, and after slowing up and switching on and off, I finally got out to see what I could do. I was some time fiddling, but I managed to fix them up finally.

The road was quite deserted. Nobody in Lymstock is about after dark. The first few houses were just ahead, amongst them the ugly gabled building of the Women's Institute. It loomed up in the dim starlight and something impelled me to go and have a look at it. I don't know whether I had caught a faint glimpse of a stealthy figure flitting through the gate – if so, it must have been so indeterminate that it did not register in my conscious mind, but I did suddenly feel a kind of overweening curiosity about the place.

The gate was slightly ajar, and I pushed it open and walked in. A short path and four steps led up to the door.

I stood there a moment hesitating. What was I really doing there? I didn't know, and then, suddenly, just near at hand, I caught the sound of a rustle. It sounded like a woman's dress. I took a sharp turn and went round the corner of the building towards where the sound had come from.

I couldn't see anybody. I went on and again turned a corner. I was at the back of the house now and suddenly I saw, only two feet away from me, an open window.

I crept up to it and listened. I could hear nothing, but somehow or other I felt convinced that there was someone inside.

My back wasn't too good for acrobatics as yet, but I managed to hoist myself up and drop over the sill inside. I made rather a noise unfortunately.

I stood just inside the window listening. Then I walked forward, my hands outstretched. I heard then the faintest sound ahead of me to my right.

I had a torch in my pocket and I switched it on.

Immediately a low, sharp voice said: 'Put that out.'

I obeyed instantly, for in that brief second I had recognized Superintendent Nash.

I felt him take my arm and propel me through a door and into a passage. Here, where there was no window to betray our presence to anyone outside, he switched on a lamp and looked at me more in sorrow than in anger.

'You *would* have to butt in just that minute, Mr Burton.'

'Sorry,' I apologized. 'But I got a hunch that I was on to something.'

'And so you were probably. Did you see anyone?'

I hesitated. 'I'm not sure,' I said slowly. 'I've got a vague feeling I saw someone sneak in through the front gate but I didn't really *see* anyone. Then I heard a rustle round the side of the house.'

Nash nodded.

'That's right. Somebody came round the house before you. They hesitated by the window, then went on quickly – heard *you*, I expect.'

I apologized again. 'What's the big idea?' I asked.

Nash said:

'I'm banking on the fact that an anonymous letter writer can't stop writing letters. She may know it's dangerous, but she'll have to do it. It's like a craving for drink or drugs.'

I nodded.

'Now you see, Mr Burton, I fancy whoever it is will want to keep the letters looking the same as much as possible. She's got the cut-out pages of that book, and can go on using letters and words cut out of them. But the envelopes present a difficulty. She'll want to type them on the same machine. She can't risk using another typewriter or her own handwriting.'

'Do you really think she'll go on with the game?' I asked incredulously.

'Yes, I do. And I'll bet you anything you like she's full of confidence. They're always vain as hell, these people! Well, then, I figured out that whoever it was would come to the Institute after dark so as to get at the typewriter.'

'Miss Ginch,' I said.

'Maybe.'

'You don't know yet?'

'I don't *know*.'

'But you suspect?'

'Yes. But somebody's very cunning, Mr Burton. Somebody knows all the tricks of the game.'

I could imagine some of the network that Nash had spread abroad. I had no doubt that every letter written by a suspect and posted or left by hand was immediately inspected. Sooner or later the criminal would slip up, would grow careless.

For the third time I apologized for my zealous and unwanted presence.

'Oh well,' said Nash philosophically. 'It can't be helped. Better luck next time.'

I went out into the night. A dim figure was standing beside my car. To my astonishment I recognized Megan.

'Hallo!' she said. 'I thought this was your car. What have you been doing?'

'What are you doing is much more to the point?' I said.

'I'm out for a walk. I like walking at night. Nobody stops you and says silly things, and I like the stars, and things smell better, and everyday things look all mysterious.'

'All of that I grant you freely,' I said. 'But only cats and witches walk in the dark. They'll wonder about you at home.'

'No, they won't. They never wonder where I am or what *I'm* doing.'

'How are you getting on?' I asked.

'All right, I suppose.'

'Miss Holland look after you and all that?'

'Elsie's all right. She can't help being a perfect fool.'

'Unkind – but probably true,' I said. 'Hop in and I'll drive you home.'

It was not quite true that Megan was never missed.

Symmington was standing on the doorstep as we drove up.

He peered towards us. 'Hallo, is Megan there?'

'Yes,' I said. 'I've brought her home.'

Symmington said sharply:

'You mustn't go off like this without telling us, Megan. Miss Holland has been quite worried about you.'

Megan muttered something and went past him into the house. Symmington sighed.

'A grown-up girl is a great responsibility with no mother to look after her. She's too old for school, I suppose.'

He looked towards me rather suspiciously.

'I suppose you took her for a drive?'

I thought it best to leave it like that.

CHAPTER ELEVEN

On the following day I went mad. Looking back on it, that is really the only explanation I can find.

I was due for my monthly visit to Marcus Kent . . . I went up by train. To my intense surprise Joanna elected to stay behind. As a rule she was eager to come and we usually stayed up for a couple of days.

This time, however, I proposed to return the same day by the evening train, but even so I was astonished at Joanna. She merely said enigmatically that she'd got plenty to do, and why spend hours in a nasty stuffy train when it was a lovely day in the country?

That, of course, was undeniable, but sounded very unlike Joanna.

She said she didn't want the car, so I was to drive it to the station and leave it parked there against my return.

The station of Lymstock is situated, for some obscure reason known to railway companies only, quite half a mile from Lymstock itself. Half-way along the road I overtook Megan shuffling along in an aimless manner. I pulled up.

'Hallo, what are you doing?'

'Just out for a walk.'

'But not what is called a good brisk walk, I gather. You were crawling along like a dispirited crab.'

'Well, I wasn't going anywhere particular.'

'Then you'd better come and see me off at the station.'

I opened the door of the car and Megan jumped in.

'Where are you going?' she asked.

'London. To see my doctor.'

'Your back's not worse, is it?'

'No, it's practically all right again. I'm expecting him to be very pleased about it.'

Megan nodded.

We drew up at the station. I parked the car and went in and bought my ticket at the booking office. There were very few people on the platform and nobody I knew.

'You wouldn't like to lend me a penny, would you?' said Megan. 'Then I'd get a bit of chocolate out of the slot machine.'

'Here you are, baby,' I said, handing her the coin in question. 'Sure you wouldn't like some clear gums or some throat pastilles as well?'

'I like chocolate best,' said Megan without suspecting sarcasm.

She went off to the chocolate machine, and I looked after her with a feeling of mounting irritation.

She was wearing trodden over shoes, and coarse unattractive stockings and a particularly shapeless jumper and skirt. I don't know why all this should have infuriated me, but it did.

I said angrily as she came back:

'Why do you wear those disgusting stockings?'

Megan looked down at them, surprised.

'What's the matter with them?'

'Everything's the matter with them. They're loathsome. And why wear a pullover like a decayed cabbage?'

'It's all right, isn't it? I've had it for years.'

'So I should imagine. And why do you –'

At this minute the train came in and interrupted my angry lecture.

I got into an empty first-class carriage, let down the window and leaned out to continue the conversation.

Megan stood below me, her face upturned. She asked me why I was so cross.

'I'm not cross,' I said untruly. 'It just infuriates me to see you so slack, and not caring how you look.'

'I couldn't look nice, anyway, so what does it matter?'

'My God,' I said. 'I'd like to see you turned out properly. I'd like to take you to London and outfit you from tip to toe.'

'I wish you could,' said Megan.

The train began to move. I looked down into Megan's upturned, wistful face.

And then, as I have said, madness came upon me.

I opened the door, grabbed Megan with one arm and fairly hauled her into the carriage.

There was an outraged shout from a porter, but all he could do was dexterously to bang shut the door again. I pulled Megan up from the floor where my impetuous action had landed her.

'What on earth did you do that for?' she demanded, rubbing one knee.

'Shut up,' I said. 'You're coming to London with me and when I've done with you you won't know yourself. I'll show you what you can look like if you try. I'm tired of seeing you mooch about down at heel and all anyhow.'

'Oh!' said Megan in an ecstatic whisper.

The ticket collector came along and I bought Megan a return ticket. She sat in her corner looking at me in a kind of awed respect.

'I say,' she said when the man had gone. 'You are sudden, aren't you?'

'Very,' I said. 'It runs in our family.'

How to explain to Megan the impulse that had come over me? She had looked like a wistful dog being left behind. She now had on her face the incredulous pleasure of the dog who has been taken on the walk after all.

'I suppose you don't know London very well?' I said to Megan.

'Yes, I do,' said Megan. 'I always went through it to school. And I've been to the dentist there and to a pantomime.'

'This,' I said darkly, 'will be a different London.'

We arrived with half an hour to spare before my appointment in Harley Street.

I took a taxi and we drove straight to Mirotin, Joanna's dress-maker. Mirotin is, in the flesh, an unconventional and breezy woman of forty-five, Mary Grey. She is a clever woman and very good company. I have always liked her.

I said to Megan. 'You're my cousin.'

'Why?'

'Don't argue,' I said.

Mary Grey was being firm with a stout Jewess who was enamoured of a skin-tight powder-blue evening dress. I detached her and took her aside.

'Listen,' I said. 'I've brought a little cousin of mine along. Joanna was coming up but was prevented. But she said I could leave it all to you. You see what the girl looks like now?'

'My God, I do,' said Mary Grey with feeling.

'Well, I want her turned out right in every particular from head to foot. *Carte blanche*. Stockings, shoes, undies, everything! By the way, the man who does Joanna's hair is close round here, isn't he?'

'Antoine? Round the corner. I'll see to that too.'

'You're a woman in a thousand.'

'Oh, I shall enjoy it – apart from the money – and that's not to be sneezed at in these days – half my damned brutes of women never pay their bills. But as I say, I shall enjoy it.' She shot a quick professional glance at Megan standing a little way away. 'She's got a lovely figure.'

'You must have X-ray eyes,' I said. 'She looks completely shapeless to me.'

Mary Grey laughed.

'It's these schools,' she said. 'They seem to take a pride in turning out girls who preen themselves on looking like nothing on earth. They call it being sweet and unsophisticated. Sometimes it takes a whole season before a girl can pull herself together and look human. Don't worry, leave it all to me.'

'Right,' I said. 'I'll come back and fetch her about six.'

II

Marcus Kent was pleased with me. He told me that I surpassed his wildest expectations.

'You must have the constitution of an elephant,' he said, 'to make a come-back like this. Oh well, wonderful what country air and no late hours or excitements will do for a man if he can only stick it.'

'I grant you your first two,' I said. 'But don't think that the country is free from excitements. We've had a good deal in my part.'

'What sort of excitement?'

'Murder,' I said.

Marcus Kent pursed up his mouth and whistled.

'Some bucolic love tragedy? Farmer lad kills his lass?'

'Not at all. A crafty, determined lunatic killer.'

'I haven't read anything about it. When did they lay him by the heels?'

'They haven't, and it's a she!'

'Whew! I'm not sure that Lymstock's quite the right place for you, old boy.'

I said firmly:

'Yes, it is. And you're not going to get me out of it.'

Marcus Kent has a low mind. He said at once:

'So that's it! Found a blonde?'

'Not at all,' I said, with a guilty thought of Elsie Holland. 'It's merely that the psychology of crime interests me a good deal.'

'Oh, all right. It certainly hasn't done you any harm so far, but just make sure that your lunatic killer doesn't obliterate *you*.'

'No fear of that,' I said.

'What about dining with me this evening? You can tell me all about your revolting murder.'

'Sorry. I'm booked.'

'Date with a lady – eh? Yes, you're definitely on the mend.'

'I suppose you could call it that,' I said, rather tickled at the idea of Megan in the role.

I was at Mirotin's at six o'clock when the establishment was officially closing. Mary Grey came to meet me at the top of the stairs outside the showroom. She had a finger to her lips.

'You're going to have a shock! If I say it myself, I've put in a good bit of work.'

I went into the big showroom. Megan was standing looking at herself in a long mirror. I give you my word I hardly recognized her! For the minute it took my breath away. Tall and slim as a willow with delicate ankles and feet shown off by sheer silk stockings and well-cut shoes. Yes, lovely feet and hands, small bones – quality and distinction in every line of her. Her hair had been trimmed and shaped to her head and it was glowing like a glossy chestnut. They'd had the sense to leave her face alone. She was not made up, or if she was it was so light and delicate that it did not show. Her mouth needed no lipstick.

Moreover there was about her something that I had never seen before, a new innocent pride in the arch of her neck. She looked at me gravely with a small shy smile.

'I do look – rather nice, don't I?' said Megan.

'Nice?' I said. 'Nice isn't the word! Come on out to dinner and if every second man doesn't turn round to look at you I'll be surprised. You'll knock all the other girls into a cocked hat.'

Megan was not beautiful, but she was unusual and striking looking. She had personality. She walked into the restaurant ahead of me and, as the head waiter hurried towards us, I felt the thrill of idiotic pride that a man feels when he has got something out of the ordinary with him.

We had cocktails first and lingered over them. Then we dined. And later we danced. Megan was keen to dance and I didn't want to disappoint her, but for some reason or other I hadn't thought she would dance well. But she did. She was light as a feather in my arms, and her body and feet followed the rhythm perfectly.

'Gosh!' I said. 'You can dance!'

She seemed a little surprised. 'Well, of course I can. We had dancing class every week at school.'

'It takes more than dancing class to make a dancer,' I said.

We went back to our table.

'Isn't this food lovely?' said Megan. 'And everything!'

She heaved a delighted sigh.

'Exactly my sentiments,' I said.

It was a delirious evening. I was still mad. Megan brought me down to earth when she said doubtfully:

'Oughtn't we to be going home?'

My jaw dropped. Yes, definitely I was mad. I had forgotten everything! I was in a world divorced from reality, existing in it with the creature I had created.

'Good Lord!' I said.

I realized that the last train had gone.

'Stay there,' I said. 'I'm going to telephone.'

I rang up the Llewellyn Hire people and ordered their biggest and fastest car to come round as soon as possible.

I came back to Megan. 'The last train has gone,' I said. 'So we're going home by car.'

'Are we? What fun!'

What a nice child she was, I thought. So pleased with everything, so unquestioning, accepting all my suggestions without fuss or bother.

The car came, and it was large and fast, but all the same it was very late when we came into Lymstock.

Suddenly conscience-stricken, I said, 'They'll have been sending out search parties for you!'

But Megan seemed in an equable mood. She said vaguely:

'Oh, I don't think so. I often go out and don't come home for lunch.'

'Yes, my dear child, but you've been out for tea and dinner too.'

However, Megan's lucky star was in the ascendant. The house was dark and silent. On Megan's advice, we went round to the back and threw stones at Rose's window.

In due course Rose looked out and with many suppressed exclamations and palpitations came down to let us in.

'Well now, and I saying you were asleep in your bed. The master and Miss Holland' — (slight sniff after Miss Holland's name) — 'had early supper and went for a drive. I said I'd keep an eye to the boys. I thought I heard you come in when I was up in the nursery trying to quiet Colin, who was playing up, but you weren't about when I came down so I thought you'd gone to bed. And that's what I said when the master came in and asked for you.'

I cut short the conversation by remarking that that was where Megan had better go now.

'Good night,' said Megan, 'and thank you *awfully*. It's been the loveliest day I've ever had.'

I drove home slightly light-headed still, and tipped the chauffeur handsomely, offering him a bed if he liked. But he preferred to drive back through the night.

The hall door had opened during our colloquy and as he drove away it was flung wide open and Joanna said:

'So it's you at last, is it?'

'Were you worried about me?' I asked, coming in and shutting the door.

Joanna went into the drawing-room and I followed her. There was a coffee pot on the trivet and Joanna made herself coffee whilst I helped myself to a whisky and soda.

'Worried about you? No, of course not. I thought you'd decided to stay in town and have a binge.'

'I've had a binge — of a kind.'

I grinned and then began to laugh.

Joanna asked what I was laughing at and I told her.

'But Jerry, you must have been mad — quite mad!'

'I suppose I was.'

'But, my dear boy, you can't do things like that — not in a place like this. It will be all round Lymstock tomorrow.'

'I suppose it will. But, after all, Megan's only a child.'

'She isn't. She's twenty. You can't take a girl of twenty to London and buy her clothes without a most frightful scandal. Good gracious, Jerry, you'll probably have to marry the girl.'

Joanna was half-serious, half-laughing.

It was at that moment that I made a very important discovery. 'Damn it all,' I said. 'I don't mind if I do. In fact – I should like it.'

A very funny expression came over Joanna's face. She got up and said dryly, as she went towards the door:

'Yes, I've known that for some time . . .'

She left me standing, glass in hand, aghast at my new discovery.

CHAPTER TWELVE

I don't know what the usual reactions are of a man who goes to propose marriage.

In fiction his throat is dry and his collar feels too tight and he is in a pitiable state of nervousness.

I didn't feel at all like that. Having thought of a good idea I just wanted to get it all settled as soon as possible. I didn't see any particular need for embarrassment.

I went along to the Symmingtons' house about eleven o'clock. I rang the bell and when Rose came, I asked for Miss Megan. It was the knowing look that Rose gave me that first made me feel slightly shy.

She put me in the little morning-room and whilst waiting there I hoped uneasily that they hadn't been upsetting Megan.

When the door opened and I wheeled round, I was instantly relieved. Megan was not looking shy or upset at all. Her head was still like a glossy chestnut, and she wore that air of pride and self-respect that she had acquired yesterday. She was in her old clothes again but she had managed to make them look different. It's wonderful what knowledge of her own attractiveness will do for a girl. Megan, I realized suddenly, had grown up.

I suppose I must really have been rather nervous, otherwise I should not have opened the conversation by saying affectionately,

'Hallo, catfish!' It was hardly, in the circumstances, a lover-like greeting.

It seemed to suit Megan. She grinned and said, 'Hallo!'

'Look here,' I said. 'You didn't get into a row about yesterday, I hope?'

Megan said with assurance, 'Oh, *no*,' and then blinked, and said vaguely, 'Yes, I believe I did. I mean, they said a lot of things and seemed to think it had been very odd – but then you know what people are and what fusses they make all about nothing.'

I was relieved to find that shocked disapproval had slipped off Megan like water off a duck's back.

'I came round this morning,' I said, 'because I've a suggestion to make. You see I like you a lot, and I think you like me –'

'Frightfully,' said Megan with rather disquieting enthusiasm.

'And we get on awfully well together, so I think it would be a good idea if we got married.'

'Oh,' said Megan.

She looked surprised. Just that. Not startled. Not shocked. Just mildly surprised.

'You mean you really want to marry me?' she asked with the air of one getting a thing perfectly clear.

'More than anything in the world,' I said – and I meant it.

'You mean, you're in love with me?'

'I'm in love with you.'

Her eyes were steady and grave. She said:

'I think you're the nicest person in the world – but I'm not in love with you.'

'I'll make you love me.'

'That wouldn't do. I don't want to be *made*.'

She paused and then said gravely: 'I'm not the sort of wife for you. I'm better at hating than at loving.'

She said it with a queer intensity.

I said, 'Hate doesn't last. Love does.'

'Is that true?'

'It's what I believe.'

Again there was a silence. Then I said:

'So it's "No," is it?'

'Yes, it's no.'

'And you don't encourage me to hope?'

'What would be the good of that?'

'None whatever,' I agreed, 'quite redundant, in fact — because I'm going to hope whether you tell me to or not.'

17

Well, that was that. I walked away from the house feeling slightly dazed but irritatingly conscious of Rose's passionately interested gaze following me.

Rose had had a good deal to say before I could escape.

That she'd never felt the same since that awful day! That she wouldn't have stayed except for the children and being sorry for poor Mr Symmington. That she wasn't going to stay unless they got another maid quick — and they wouldn't be likely to do that when there had been a murder in the house! That it was all very well for that Miss Holland to say she'd do the housework in the meantime. Very sweet and obliging she was — Oh yes, but it was mistress of the house that she was fancying herself going to be one fine day! Mr Symmington, poor man, never saw anything — but one knew what a widower was, a poor helpless creature made to be the prey of a designing woman. And that it wouldn't be for want of trying if Miss Holland didn't step into the dead mistress's shoes!

I assented mechanically to everything, yearning to get away and unable to do so because Rose was holding firmly on to my hat whilst she indulged in her flood of spite.

I wondered if there was any truth in what she said. Had Elsie Holland envisaged the possibility of becoming the second Mrs Symmington? Or was she just a decent kind-hearted girl doing her best to look after a bereaved household?

The result would quite likely be the same in either case. And why not? Symmington's young children needed a mother — Elsie was a decent soul — beside being quite indecently beautiful — a point which a man might appreciate — even such a stuffed fish as Symmington!

I thought all this, I know, because I was trying to put off thinking about Megan.

You may say that I had gone to ask Megan to marry me in an absurdly complacent frame of mind and that I deserved what I got — but it was not really like that. It was because I felt so assured, so

295

certain, that Megan belonged to me – that she was my business, that to look after her and make her happy and keep her from harm was the only natural right way of life for me, that I had expected her to feel, too, that she and I belonged to each other.

But I was not giving up. Oh no! Megan was my woman and I was going to have her.

After a moment's thought, I went to Symmington's office. Megan might pay no attention to strictures on her conduct, but I would like to get things straight.

Mr Symmington was disengaged, I was told, and I was shown into his room. By a pinching of the lips, and an additional stiffness of manner, I gathered that I was not exactly popular at the moment.

'Good morning,' I said. 'I'm afraid this isn't a professional call, but a personal one. I'll put it plainly. I dare say you'll have realized that I'm in love with Megan. I've asked her to marry me and she has refused. But I'm not taking that as final.'

I saw Symmington's expression change, and I read his mind with ludicrous ease. Megan was a disharmonious element in his house. He was, I felt sure, a just and kindly man, and he would never have dreamed of not providing a home for his dead wife's daughter. But her marriage to me would certainly be a relief. The frozen halibut thawed. He gave me a pale cautious smile.

'Frankly, do you know, Burton, I had no idea of such a thing. I know you've taken a lot of notice of her, but we've always regarded her as such a child.'

'She's not a child,' I said shortly.

'No, no, not in years.'

'She can be her age any time she's allowed to be,' I said, still slightly angry. 'She's not twenty-one, I know, but she will be in a month or two. I'll let you have all the information about myself you want. I'm well off and have led quite a decent life. I'll look after her and do all I can to make her happy.'

'Quite – quite. Still, it's up to Megan herself.'

'She'll come round in time,' I said. 'But I just thought I'd like to get straight with you about it.'

He said he appreciated that, and we parted amicably.

I ran into Miss Emily Barton outside. She had a shopping basket on her arm.

'Good morning, Mr Burton, I hear you went to London yesterday.'

Yes, she had heard all right. Her eyes were, I thought, kindly, but full of curiosity, too.

'I went to see my doctor,' I said.

Miss Emily smiled.

That smile made little of Marcus Kent. She murmured:

'I hear Megan nearly missed the train. She jumped in when it was going.'

'Helped by me,' I said. 'I hauled her in.'

'How lucky you were there. Otherwise there might have been an accident.'

It is extraordinary how much of a fool one gentle inquisitive old maiden lady can make a man feel!

I was saved further suffering by the onslaught of Mrs Dane Calthrop. She had her own tame elderly maiden lady in tow, but she herself was full of direct speech.

'Good morning,' she said. 'I heard you've made Megan buy herself some decent clothes? Very sensible of you. It takes a man to think of something really practical like that. I've been worried about that girl for a long time. Girls with brains are so liable to turn into morons, aren't they?'

With which remarkable statement, she shot into the fish shop.

Miss Marple, left standing by me, twinkled a little and said:

'Mrs Dane Calthrop is a very remarkable woman, you know. She's nearly always right.'

'It makes her rather alarming,' I said.

'Sincerity has that effect,' said Miss Marple.

Mrs Dane Calthrop shot out of the fish shop again and rejoined us. She was holding a large red lobster.

'Have you ever seen anything so unlike Mr Pye?' she said – 'very virile and handsome, isn't it?'

I was a little nervous of meeting Joanna but I found when I got home that I needn't have worried. She was out and she did not return for lunch. This aggrieved Partridge a good deal, who said sourly as she proffered two loin chops in an entrée dish: 'Miss Burton said specially as she was going to be *in*.'

I ate both chops in an attempt to atone for Joanna's lapse. All the same, I wondered where my sister was. She had taken to be very mysterious about her doings of late.

It was half-past three when Joanna burst into the drawing-room. I had heard a car stop outside and I half expected to see Griffith, but the car drove on and Joanna came in alone.

Her face was very red and she seemed upset. I perceived that something had happened.

'What's the matter?' I asked.

Joanna opened her mouth, closed it again, sighed, plumped herself down in a chair and stared in front of her.

She said:

'I've had the most awful day.'

'What's happened?'

'I've done the most incredible thing. It was awful –'

'But what –'

'I just started out for a walk, an ordinary walk – I went up over the hill and on to the moor. I walked miles – I felt like it. Then I dropped down into a hollow. There's a farm there – A God-forsaken lonely sort of spot. I was thirsty and I wondered if they'd got any milk or something. So I wandered into the farmyard and then the door opened and Owen came out.'

'Yes?'

'He thought it might be the district nurse. There was a woman in there having a baby. He was expecting the nurse and he'd sent word to her to get hold of another doctor. It – things were going wrong.'

'Yes?'

'So he said – to *me*. "Come on, you'll do – better than nobody." I said I couldn't, and he said what did I mean? I said I'd never done anything like that, that I didn't know anything –

'He said what the hell did that matter? And then he was *awful*.

He turned on me. He said, "You're a woman, aren't you? I suppose you can do your durnedest to help another woman?" And he went on at me — said I'd talked as though I was interested in doctoring and had said I wished I was a nurse. "All pretty talk, I suppose! You didn't mean anything real by it, but this *is* real and you're going to behave like a decent human being and not like a useless ornamental nit-wit!"

'I've done the most incredible things, Jerry. Held instruments and boiled them and handed things. I'm so tired I can hardly stand up. It was dreadful. But he saved her — and the baby. It was born alive. He didn't think at one time he could save it. Oh dear!'

Joanna covered her face with her hands.

I contemplated her with a certain amount of pleasure and mentally took my hat off to Owen Griffith. He'd brought Joanna slap up against reality for once.

I said, 'There's a letter for you in the hall. From Paul, I think.'

'Eh?' She paused for a minute and then said, 'I'd no idea, Jerry, what doctors had to *do*. The nerve they've got to have!'

I went out into the hall and brought Joanna her letter. She opened it, glanced vaguely at its contents, and let it drop.

'He was — really — rather wonderful. The way he fought — the way he wouldn't be beaten! He was rude and horrible to *me* — but he *was* wonderful.'

I observed Paul's disregarded letter with some pleasure. Plainly, Joanna was cured of Paul.

CHAPTER THIRTEEN

Things never come when they are expected.

I was full of Joanna's and my personal affairs and was quite taken aback the next morning when Nash's voice said over the telephone: '*We've got her*, Mr Burton!'

I was so startled I nearly dropped the receiver.

'You mean the —'

He interrupted.

'Can you be overheard where you are?'

'No, I don't think so – well, perhaps –'

It seemed to me that the baize door to the kitchen had swung open a trifle.

'Perhaps you'd care to come down to the station?'

'I will. Right away.'

I was at the police station in next to no time. In an inner room Nash and Sergeant Parkins were together. Nash was wreathed in smiles.

'It's been a long chase,' he said. 'But we're there at last.'

He flicked a letter across the table. This time it was all typewritten. It was, of its kind, fairly mild.

'*It's no use thinking you're going to step into a dead woman's shoes. The whole town is laughing at you. Get out now. Soon it will be too late. This is a warning. Remember what happened to that other girl. Get out and stay out.*'

It finished with some mildly obscene language.

'That reached Miss Holland this morning,' said Nash.

'Thought it was funny she hadn't had one before,' said Sergeant Parkins.

'Who wrote it?' I asked.

Some of the exultation faded out of Nash's face.

He looked tired and concerned. He said soberly:

'I'm sorry about it, because it will hit a decent man hard, but there it is. Perhaps he's had his suspicions already.'

'Who wrote it?' I reiterated.

'Miss Aimée Griffith.'

II

Nash and Parkins went to the Griffiths' house that afternoon with a warrant.

By Nash's invitation I went with them.

'The doctor,' he said, 'is very fond of you. He hasn't many friends in this place. I think if it is not too painful to you, Mr Burton, that you might help him to bear up under the shock.'

I said I would come. I didn't relish the job, but I thought I might be some good.

We rang the bell and asked for Miss Griffith and we were shown into the drawing-room. Elsie Holland, Megan and Symmington were there having tea.

Nash behaved very circumspectly.

He asked Aimée if he might have a few words with her privately.

She got up and came towards us. I thought I saw just a faint hunted look in her eye. If so, it went again. She was perfectly normal and hearty.

'Want me? Not in trouble over my car lights again, I hope?'

She led the way out of the drawing-room and across the hall into a small study.

As I closed the drawing-room door, I saw Symmington's head jerk up sharply. I supposed his legal training had brought him in contact with police cases, and he had recognized something in Nash's manner. He half rose.

That is all I saw before I shut the door and followed the others.

Nash was saying his piece. He was very quiet and correct. He cautioned her and then told her that he must ask her to accompany him. He had a warrant for her arrest and he read out the charge –

I forget now the exact legal term. It was the letters, not murder yet.

Aimée Griffith flung up her head and bayed with laughter. She boomed out: 'What ridiculous nonsense! As though I'd write a packet of indecent stuff like that. You must be mad. I've never written a word of the kind.'

Nash had produced the letter to Elsie Holland. He said:

'Do you deny having written this, Miss Griffith?'

If she hesitated it was only for a split second.

'Of course I do. I've never seen it before.'

Nash said quietly: 'I must tell you, Miss Griffith, that you were observed to type that letter on the machine at the Women's Institute between eleven and eleven-thirty p.m. on the night before last. Yesterday you entered the post office with a bunch of letters in your hand –'

'I never posted this.'

'No, *you* did not. Whilst waiting for stamps, you dropped it inconspicuously on the floor, so that somebody should come along unsuspectingly and pick it up and post it.'

'I never –'

The door opened and Symmington came in. He said sharply: 'What's going on? Aimée, if there is anything wrong, you ought to be legally represented. If you wish me –'

She broke then. Covered her face with her hands and staggered to a chair. She said:

'Go away, Dick, go away. Not you! Not *you*!'

'You need a solicitor, my dear girl.'

'Not you. I – I – couldn't bear it. I don't want you to know – all this.'

He understood then, perhaps. He said quietly:

'I'll get hold of Mildmay, of Exhampton. Will that do?'

She nodded. She was sobbing now.

Symmington went out of the room. In the doorway he collided with Owen Griffith.

'What's this?' said Owen violently. 'My sister –'

'I'm sorry, Dr Griffith. Very sorry. But we have no alternative.'

'You think she – was responsible for those letters?'

'I'm afraid there is no doubt of it, sir,' said Nash – he turned to Aimée, 'You must come with us now, please, Miss Griffith – you shall have every facility for seeing a solicitor, you know.'

Owen cried: 'Aimée?'

She brushed past him without looking at him.

She said: 'Don't talk to me. Don't say anything. And for God's sake don't *look* at me!'

They went out. Owen stood like a man in a trance.

I waited a bit, then I came up to him.

'If there's anything I can do, Griffith, tell me.'

He said like a man in a dream:

'Aimée? I don't believe it.'

'It may be a mistake,' I suggested feebly.

He said slowly: 'She wouldn't take it like that if it were. But I would never have believed it. I *can't* believe it.'

He sank down on a chair. I made myself useful by finding a stiff drink and bringing it to him. He swallowed it down and it seemed to do him good.

He said: 'I couldn't take it in at first. I'm all right now. Thanks, Burton, but there's nothing you can do. Nothing *anyone* can do.'

The door opened and Joanna came in. She was very white.
She came over to Owen and looked at me.
She said: 'Get out, Jerry. This is my business.'
As I went out of the door, I saw her kneel down by his chair.

III

I can't tell you coherently the events of the next twenty-four hours.
Various incidents stand out, unrelated to other incidents.

I remember Joanna coming home, very white and drawn, and of
how I tried to cheer her up, saying:

'Now who's being a ministering angel?'

And of how she smiled in a pitiful twisted way and said:

'He says he won't have me, Jerry. He's very, *very* proud and
stiff!'

And I said: 'My girl won't have me, either . . .'

We sat there for a while, Joanna saying at last:

'The Burton family isn't exactly in demand at the moment!'

I said, 'Never mind, my sweet, we still have each other,' and
Joanna said, 'Somehow or other, Jerry, that doesn't comfort me
much just now . . .'

IV

Owen came the next day and rhapsodied in the most fulsome way
about Joanna. She was wonderful, marvellous! The way she'd come
to him, the way she was willing to marry him — at once if he liked.
But he wasn't going to let her do that. No, she was too good, too
fine to be associated with the kind of muck that would start as soon
as the papers got hold of the news.

I was fond of Joanna, and knew she was the kind who's all right
when standing by in trouble, but I got rather bored with all this
high-falutin' stuff. I told Owen rather irritably not to be so damned
noble.

I went down to the High Street and found everybody's tongues
wagging nineteen to the dozen. Emily Barton was saying that she
had never really trusted Aimée Griffith. The grocer's wife was saying

303

with gusto that she'd always thought Miss Griffith had a queer look in her eye –

They had completed the case against Aimée, so I learnt from Nash. A search of the house had brought to light the cut pages of Emily Barton's book – in the cupboard under the stairs, of all places, wrapped up in an old roll of wallpaper.

'And a jolly good place too,' said Nash appreciatively. 'You never know when a prying servant won't tamper with a desk or a locked drawer – but those junk cupboards full of last year's tennis balls and old wallpaper are never opened except to shove something more in.'

'The lady would seem to have had a *penchant* for that particular hiding-place,' I said.

'Yes. The criminal mind seldom has much variety. By the way, talking of the dead girl, we've got one fact to go upon. There's a large heavy pestle missing from the doctor's dispensary. I'll bet anything you like that's what she was stunned with.'

'Rather an awkward thing to carry about,' I objected.

'Not for Miss Griffith. She was going to the Guides that afternoon, but she was going to leave flowers and vegetables at the Red Cross stall on the way, so she'd got a whopping great basket with her.'

'You haven't found the skewer?'

'No, and I shan't. The poor devil may be mad, but she wasn't mad enough to keep a blood-stained skewer just to make it easy for us, when all she'd got to do was to wash it and return it to a kitchen drawer.'

'I suppose,' I conceded, 'that you can't have everything.'

The vicarage had been one of the last places to hear the news. Old Miss Marple was very much distressed by it. She spoke to me very earnestly on the subject.

'It isn't *true*, Mr Burton. I'm sure it isn't true.'

'It's true enough, I'm afraid. They were lying in wait, you know. They actually *saw* her type that letter.'

'Yes, yes – perhaps they did. Yes, I can understand *that*.'

'And the printed pages from which the letters were cut were found where she'd hidden them in her house.'

Miss Marple stared at me. Then she said, in a very low voice: 'But that is horrible – really *wicked*.'

Mrs Dane Calthrop came up with a rush and joined us and said: 'What's the matter, Jane?'

Miss Marple was murmuring helplessly:

'Oh dear, oh dear, what can one *do*?'

'What's upset you, Jane?'

Miss Marple said: 'There must be *something*. But I am so old and so ignorant, and I am afraid, so foolish.'

I felt rather embarrassed and was glad when Mrs Dane Calthrop took her friend away.

I was to see Miss Marple again that afternoon, however. Much later when I was on my way home.

She was standing near the little bridge at the end of the village, near Mrs Cleat's cottage, and talking to Megan of all people.

I wanted to see Megan. I had been wanting to see her all day. I quickened my pace. But as I came up to them, Megan turned on her heel and went off in the other direction.

It made me angry and I would have followed her, but Miss Marple blocked my way.

She said: 'I wanted to speak to you. No, don't go after Megan now. It wouldn't be wise.'

I was just going to make a sharp rejoinder when she disarmed me by saying:

'That girl has great courage – a very high order of courage.'

I still wanted to go after Megan, but Miss Marple said:

'Don't try and see her now. I do know what I am talking about. She must keep her courage intact.'

There was something about the old lady's assertion that chilled me. It was as though she knew something that I didn't.

I was afraid and didn't know why I was afraid.

I didn't go home. I went back into the High Street and walked up and down aimlessly. I don't know what I was waiting for, nor what I was thinking about . . .

I got caught by that awful old bore Colonel Appleton. He asked after my pretty sister as usual and then went on:

'What's all this about Griffith's sister being mad as a hatter? They say she's been at the bottom of this anonymous letter business that's been such a confounded nuisance to everybody? Couldn't believe it at first, but they say it's quite true.'

I said it was true enough.

'Well, well – I must say our police force is pretty good on the whole. Give 'em time, that's all, give 'em time. Funny business this anonymous letter stunt – these desiccated old maids are always the ones who go in for it – though the Griffith woman wasn't bad looking even if she was a bit long in the tooth. But there aren't any decent-looking girls in this part of the world – except that governess girl of the Symmingtons. She's worth looking at. Pleasant girl, too. Grateful if one does any little thing for her. Came across her having a picnic or something with those kids not long ago. They were romping about in the heather and she was knitting – ever so vexed she'd run out of wool. "Well," I said, "like me to run you into Lymstock? I've got to call for a rod of mine there. I shan't be more than ten minutes getting it, then I'll run you back again." She was a bit doubtful about leaving the boys. "They'll be all right," I said. "Who's to harm them?" Wasn't going to have the boys along, no fear! So I ran her in, dropped her at the wool shop, picked her up again later and that was that. Thanked me very prettily. Grateful and all that. Nice girl.'

I managed to get away from him.

It was after that, that I caught sight of Miss Marple for the third time. She was coming out of the police station.

V

Where do one's fears come from? Where do they shape themselves? Where do they hide before coming out into the open?

Just one short phrase. Heard and noted and never quite put aside: 'Take me away – it's so awful being here – feeling so wicked . . .'

Why had Megan said that? What had she to feel wicked about?

There could be nothing in Mrs Symmington's death to make Megan feel wicked.

Why had the child felt wicked? Why? Why?

Could it be because she felt responsible in any way?

Megan? Impossible! Megan couldn't have had anything to do with those letters – those foul obscene letters.

Owen Griffith had known a case up North – a schoolgirl . . .

What had Inspector Graves said?

Something about an *adolescent mind* . . .

Innocent middle-aged ladies on operating tables babbling words they hardly knew. Little boys chalking up things on walls.

No, no, not *Megan*.

Heredity? Bad blood? An unconscious inheritance of something abnormal? Her misfortune, not her fault, a curse laid upon her by a past generation?

'I'm not the wife for you. I'm better at hating than loving.'

Oh, my Megan, my little child. Not *that*! Anything but that. And that old Tabby is after you, she suspects. She says you have courage. Courage to do *what*?

It was only a brainstorm. It passed. But I wanted to see Megan – I wanted to see her badly.

At half-past nine that night I left the house and went down to the town and along to the Symmingtons'.

It was then that an entirely new idea came into my mind. The idea of a woman whom nobody had considered for a moment.

(Or had Nash considered her?)

Wildly unlikely, wildly improbable, and I would have said up to today impossible, too. But that was not so. No, not *impossible*.

I redoubled my pace. Because it was now even more imperative that I should see Megan straightaway.

I passed through the Symmingtons' gate and up to the house. It was a dark overcast night. A little rain was beginning to fall. The visibility was bad.

I saw a line of light from one of the windows. The little morning-room?

I hesitated a moment or two, then instead of going up to the front door, I swerved and crept very quietly up to the window, skirting a big bush and keeping low.

The light came from a chink in the curtains which were not quite drawn. It was easy to look through and see.

It was a strangely peaceful and domestic scene. Symmington in a big armchair, and Elsie Holland, her head bent, busily patching a boy's torn shirt.

I could hear as well as see for the window was open at the top. Elsie Holland was speaking.

'But I do think, really, Mr Symmington, that the boys are quite old enough to go to boarding school. Not that I shan't hate leaving them because I shall. I'm ever so fond of them both.'

Symmington said: 'I think perhaps you're right about Brian, Miss Holland. I've decided that he shall start next term at Winhays – my

307

old prep. school. But Colin is a little young yet. I'd prefer him to wait another year.'

'Well of course I see what you mean. And Colin is perhaps a little young for his age —'

Quiet domestic talk – quiet domestic scene – and a golden head bent over needlework.

Then the door opened and Megan came in.

She stood very straight in the doorway, and I was aware at once of something tense and strung up about her. The skin of her face was tight and drawn and her eyes were bright and resolute. There was no diffidence about her tonight and no childishness.

She said, addressing Symmington, but giving him no title (and I suddenly reflected that I never heard her call him anything. Did she address him as father or as Dick or what?)

'I would like to speak to you, please. Alone.'

Symmington looked surprised and, I fancied, not best pleased. He frowned, but Megan carried her point with a determination unusual in her.

She turned to Elsie Holland and said:

'Do you mind, Elsie?'

'Oh, of course not,' Elsie Holland jumped up. She looked startled and a little flurried.

She went to the door and Megan came farther in so that Elsie passed her.

Just for a moment Elsie stood motionless in the doorway looking over her shoulder.

Her lips were closed, she stood quite still, one hand stretched out, the other clasping her needlework to her.

I caught my breath, overwhelmed by her beauty.

When I think of her now, I always think of her like that – in arrested motion, with that matchless deathless perfection that belonged to ancient Greece.

Then she went out shutting the door.

Symmington said rather fretfully:

'Well, Megan, what is it? What do you want?'

Megan had come right up to the table. She stood there looking down at Symmington. I was struck anew by the resolute determination of her face and by something else – a hardness new to me.

Then she opened her lips and said something that startled me to the core.

'I want some money,' she said.

The request didn't improve Symmington's temper. He said sharply:

'Couldn't you have waited until tomorrow morning? What's the matter, do you think your allowance is inadequate?'

A fair man, I thought even then, open to reason, though not to emotional appeal.

Megan said: 'I want a good deal of money.'

Symmington sat up straight in his chair. He said coldly:

'You will come of age in a few months' time. Then the money left you by your grandmother will be turned over to you by the public trustee.'

Megan said:

'You don't understand. I want money from *you*.' She went on, speaking faster. 'Nobody's ever talked much to me about my father. They've not wanted me to know about him. But I do know that he went to prison and I know why. It was for blackmail!'

She paused.

'Well, I'm his daughter. And perhaps I take after him. Anyway, I'm asking you to give me money because – if you don't' – she stopped and then went on very slowly and evenly – 'if you don't – *I shall say what I saw you doing to the cachet that day in my mother's room.*'

There was a pause. Then Symmington said in a completely emotionless voice:

'I don't know what you mean.'

Megan said: 'I think you do.'

And she smiled. It was not a nice smile.

Symmington got up. He went over to the writing desk. He took a cheque-book from his pocket and wrote out a cheque. He blotted it carefully and then came back. He held it out to Megan.

'You're grown up now,' he said. 'I can understand that you may feel you want to buy something rather special in the way of clothes and all that. I don't know what you're talking about. I didn't pay attention. But here's a cheque.'

Megan looked at it, then she said:

'Thank you. That will do to go on with.'

She turned and went out of the room. Symmington stared after her and at the closed door, then he turned round and as I saw his face I made a quick uncontrolled movement forward.

It was checked in the most extraordinary fashion. The big bush that I had noticed by the wall stopped being a bush. Superintendent Nash's arms went round me and Superintendent Nash's voice just breathed in my ear:

'Quiet, Burton. For God's sake.'

Then, with infinite caution he beat a retreat, his arm impelling me to accompany him.

Round the side of the house he straightened himself and wiped his forehead.

'Of course,' he said, 'you *would* have to butt in!'

'That girl isn't safe,' I said urgently. 'You saw his face? We've got to get her out of here.'

Nash took a firm grip of my arm.

'Now, look here, Mr Burton, you've got to *listen*.'

VI

Well, I listened.

I didn't like it – but I gave in.

But I insisted on being on the spot and I swore to obey orders implicitly.

So that is how I came with Nash and Parkins into the house by the back door which was already unlocked.

And I waited with Nash on the upstairs landing behind the velvet curtain masking the window alcove until the clocks in the house struck two, and Symmington's door opened and he went across the landing and into Megan's room.

I did not stir or make a move for I knew that Sergeant Parkins was inside masked by the opening door, and I knew that Parkins was a good man and knew his job, and I knew that I couldn't have trusted myself to keep quiet and not break out.

And waiting there, with my heart thudding, I saw Symmington come out with Megan in his arms and carry her downstairs, with Nash and myself a discreet distance behind him.

He carried her through to the kitchen and he had just arranged her comfortably with her head in the gas oven and had turned on the gas when Nash and I came through the kitchen door and switched on the light.

And that was the end of Richard Symmington. He collapsed. Even while I was hauling Megan out and turning off the gas I saw the collapse. He didn't even try to fight. He knew he'd played and lost.

VII

Upstairs I sat by Megan's bed waiting for her to come round and occasionally cursing Nash.

'How do you know she's all right? It was too big a risk.'

Nash was very soothing.

'Just a soporific in the milk she always had by her bed. Nothing more. It stands to reason, he couldn't risk her being poisoned. As far as he's concerned the whole business is closed with Miss Griffith's arrest. He can't afford to have any mysterious death. No violence, no poison. But if a rather unhappy type of girl broods over her mother's suicide, and finally goes and puts her head in the gas oven – well, people just say that she was never quite normal and the shock of her mother's death finished her.'

I said, watching Megan:

'She's a long time coming round.'

'You heard what Dr Griffith said? Heart and pulse quite all right – she'll just sleep and wake naturally. Stuff he gives a lot of his patients, he says.'

Megan stirred. She murmured something.

Superintendent Nash unobtrusively left the room.

Presently Megan opened her eyes. 'Jerry.'

'Hallo, sweet.'

'Did I do it well?'

'You might have been blackmailing ever since your cradle!'

Megan closed her eyes again. Then she murmured:

'Last night – I was writing to you – in case anything went – went wrong. But I was too sleepy to finish. It's over there.'

I went across to the writing-table. In a shabby little blotter I found Megan's unfinished letter.

'My dear Jerry,' it began primly:

311

'I was reading my school Shakespeare and the sonnet that begins:
   "*So are you to my thoughts as food to life
      Or as sweet-season'd showers are to the ground.*"
and I see that I am in love with you after all, because that is what
I feel . . .'

CHAPTER FOURTEEN

'So you see,' said Mrs Dane Calthrop, 'I was quite right to call in
an expert.'

I stared at her. We were all at the vicarage. The rain was pouring
down outside and there was a pleasant log fire, and Mrs Dane
Calthrop had just wandered round, beat up a sofa cushion and put
it for some reason of her own on the top of the grand piano.

'But did you?' I said, surprised. 'Who was it? What did he do?'

'It wasn't a he,' said Mrs Dane Calthrop.

With a sweeping gesture she indicated Miss Marple. Miss Marple
had finished the fleecy knitting and was now engaged with a crochet
hook and a ball of cotton.

'That's my expert,' said Mrs Dane Calthrop. 'Jane Marple. Look
at her well. I tell you, that woman knows more about the different
kinds of human wickedness than anyone I've ever known.'

'I don't think you should put it quite like that, dear,' murmured
Miss Marple.

'But you do.'

'One sees a good deal of human nature living in a village all the
year round,' said Miss Marple placidly.

Then, seeming to feel it was expected of her, she laid down her
crochet, and delivered a gentle old-maidish dissertation on murder.

'The great thing is in these cases to keep an absolutely open mind.
Most crimes, you see, are so absurdly simple. This one was. Quite
sane and straightforward – and quite understandable – in an
unpleasant way, of course.'

'Very unpleasant!'

'The truth was really so very obvious. *You* saw it, you know, Mr
Burton.'

'Indeed I did not.'

'But you did. You indicated the whole thing to me. You saw perfectly the relationship of one thing to the other, but you just hadn't enough self-confidence to see what those feelings of yours meant. To begin with, that tiresome phrase "No smoke without fire." It irritated you, but you proceeded quite correctly to label it for what it was – a smoke screen. Misdirection, you see – everybody looking at the wrong thing – the anonymous letters, but the whole point was that there *weren't* any anonymous letters!'

'But my dear Miss Marple, I can assure you that there *were*. I had one.'

'Oh yes, but they weren't real at all. Dear Maud here tumbled to that. Even in peaceful Lymstock there are plenty of scandals, and I can assure you any *woman* living in the place would have known about them and used them. But a man, you see, isn't interested in gossip in the same way – especially a detached logical man like Mr Symmington. A genuine woman writer of those letters would have made her letters much more to the point.

'So you see that if you disregard the smoke and come to the fire you know where you are. You just come down to the actual facts of what happened. And putting aside the letters, just one thing happened – Mrs Symmington died.

'So then, naturally, one thinks of who might have wanted Mrs Symmington to die, and of course the very first person one thinks of in such a case is, I am afraid, the *husband*. And one asks oneself is there any *reason*? – any *motive*? – for instance, *another* woman?

'And the very first thing I hear is that there is a very attractive young governess in the house. So clear, isn't it? Mr Symmington, a rather dry repressed unemotional man, tied to a querulous and neurotic wife and then suddenly this radiant young creature comes along.

'I'm afraid, you know, that gentlemen, when they fall in love at a certain age, get the disease very badly. It's quite a madness. And Mr Symmington, as far as I can make out, was never actually a *good* man – he wasn't very kind or very affectionate or very sympathetic – his qualities were all negative – so he hadn't really the strength to fight his madness. And in a place like this, only his wife's death would solve his problem. He wanted to marry the girl, you see. She's very respectable and so is he. And besides, he's devoted to his children and didn't want to give them up. He wanted everything, his home, his children, his respectability and Elsie. And the price he would have to pay for that was murder.

'He chose, I do think, a very clever way. He knew so well from his experience of criminal cases how soon suspicion falls on the husband if a wife dies unexpectedly – and the possibility of exhumation in the case of poison. So he created a death which seemed only incidental to something else. He created a non-existent anonymous letter writer. And the clever thing was that the police were certain to suspect a *woman* – and they were quite right in a way. All the letters *were* a woman's letters; he cribbed them very cleverly from the letters in the case last year and from a case Dr Griffith told him about. I don't mean that he was so crude as to reproduce any letter verbatim, but he took phrases and expressions from them and mixed them up, and the net result was that the letters definitely represented a woman's mind – a half-crazed repressed personality.

'He knew all the tricks that the police use, handwriting, typewriting tests, etc. He's been preparing his crime for some time. He typed all the envelopes before he gave away the typewriter to the Women's Institute, and he cut the pages from the book at Little Furze probably quite a long time ago when he was waiting in the drawing-room one day. People don't open books of sermons much!

'And finally, having got his false Poison Pen well established, he staged the real thing. A fine afternoon when the governess and the boys and his step-daughter would be out, and the servants having their regular day out. He couldn't foresee that the little maid Agnes would quarrel with her boy and come back to the house.'

Joanna asked:

'But what did she *see*? Do you know that?'

'I don't *know*. I can only guess. My guess would be that she didn't see anything.'

'That it was all a mare's nest?'

'No, no, my dear, I mean that she stood at the pantry window all the afternoon waiting for the young man to come and make it up and that – quite literally – she saw *nothing*. That is, *no one* came to the house at all, not the postman, nor anybody else.

'It would take her some time, being slow, to realize that that was very odd – because apparently Mrs Symmington *had* received an anonymous letter that afternoon.'

'Didn't she receive one?' I asked, puzzled.

'But of course not! As I say, this crime is so simple. Her husband just put the cyanide in the top cachet of the ones she took in the afternoon when her sciatica came on after lunch. All Symmington had to do was to get home before, or at the same time as Elsie Holland, call his wife, get no answer, go up to her room, drop a spot of cyanide in the plain glass of water she had used to swallow the cachet, toss the crumpled-up anonymous letter into the grate, and put by her hand the scrap of paper with "*I can't go on*" written on it.'

Miss Marple turned to me.

'You were quite right about that, too, Mr Burton. A "scrap of paper" was all wrong. People don't leave suicide notes on small torn scraps of paper. They use a *sheet* of paper – and very often an envelope too. Yes, the scrap of paper was wrong and you knew it.'

'You are rating me too high,' I said. 'I knew nothing.'

'But you did, you really *did*, Mr Burton. Otherwise why were you immediately impressed by the message your sister left scribbled on the telephone pad?'

I repeated slowly, ' "Say that *I can't go on* Friday" – I see! *I can't go on*?'

Miss Marple beamed on me.

'Exactly. Mr Symmington came across such a message and saw its possibilities. He tore off the words he wanted for when the time came – a message genuinely in his wife's handwriting.'

'Was there any further brilliance on my part?' I asked.

Miss Marple twinkled at me.

'You put me on the track, you know. You assembled those facts together for me – in sequence – and on top of it you told me the most important thing of all – that Elsie Holland had never received any anonymous letters.'

'Do you know,' I said, 'last night I thought that *she* was the letter writer and that that was why there had been no letters written to her?'

'Oh dear, me, no ... The person who writes anonymous letters practically always sends them to herself as well. That's part of the – well, the excitement, I suppose. No, no, the fact interested me for *quite* another reason. It was really, you see, Mr Symmington's one weakness. He couldn't bring himself to write a foul letter to the

315

girl he loved. It's a very interesting sidelight on human nature – and a credit to him, in a way – but it's where he gave himself away.'

Joanna said:

'And he killed Agnes? But surely that was quite unnecessary?'

'Perhaps it was, but what you don't realize, my dear (not having killed any one), is that your judgment is distorted afterwards and everything seems exaggerated. No doubt he heard the girl telephoning to Partridge, saying she'd been worried ever since Mrs Symmington's death, that there was something she didn't understand. He can't take any chances – this stupid, foolish girl has seen *something*, knows something.'

'Yet apparently he was at his office all that afternoon?'

'I should imagine he killed her before he went. Miss Holland was in the dining-room and kitchen. He just went out into the hall, opened and shut the front door as though he had gone out, then slipped into the little cloakroom. When only Agnes was left in the house, he probably rang the front-door bell, slipped back into the cloakroom, came out behind her and hit her on the head as she was opening the front door, and then after thrusting the body into the cupboard, he hurried along to his office, arriving just a little late if anyone had happened to notice it, but they probably didn't. You see, no one was suspecting a *man*.'

'Abominable brute,' said Mrs Dane Calthrop.

'You're not sorry for him, Mrs Dane Calthrop?' I inquired.

'Not in the least. Why?'

'I'm glad to hear it, that's all.'

Joanna said:

'But why Aimée Griffith? I know that the police have found the pestle taken from Owen's dispensary – and the skewer too. I suppose it's not so easy for a man to return things to kitchen drawers. And guess where they were? Superintendent Nash only told me just now when I met him on my way here. In one of those musty old deed-boxes in his office. Estate of Sir Jasper Harrington-West, deceased.'

'Poor Jasper,' said Mrs Dane Calthrop. 'He was a cousin of mine. Such a correct old boy. He would have had a fit!'

'Wasn't it madness to keep them?' I asked.

'Probably madder to throw them away,' said Mrs Dane Calthrop. 'No one had any suspicions about Symmington.'

'He didn't strike her with the pestle,' said Joanna. 'There was a clock weight there too, with hair and blood on it. He pinched the pestle, they think, on the day Aimée was arrested, and hid the book pages in her house. And that brings me back to my original question. What about Aimée Griffith? The police actually *saw* her write that letter.'

'Yes, of course,' said Miss Marple. 'She did write *that* letter.'

'But why?'

'Oh, my dear, surely you have realized that Miss Griffith had been in love with Symmington all her life?'

'Poor thing!' said Mrs Dane Calthrop mechanically.

'They'd always been good friends, and I dare say she thought, after Mrs Symmington's death, that some day, perhaps – well –' Miss Marple coughed delicately. 'And then the gossip began spreading about Elsie Holland and I expect that upset her badly. She thought of the girl as a designing minx worming her way into Symmington's affections and quite unworthy of him. And so, I think, she succumbed to temptation. Why not add one more anonymous letter, and frighten the girl out of the place? It must have seemed quite safe to her and she took, as she thought, every precaution.'

'Well?' said Joanna. 'Finish the story.'

'I should imagine,' said Miss Marple slowly, 'that when Miss Holland showed that letter to Symmington he realized at once who had written it, and he saw a chance to finish the case once and for all, and make himself safe. Not very nice – no, not very nice, but he was frightened, you see. The police wouldn't be satisfied until they'd got the anonymous letter writer. When he took the letter down to the police and he found they'd actually seen Aimée writing it, he felt he'd got a chance in a thousand of finishing the whole thing.

'He took the family to tea there that afternoon and as he came from the office with his attaché case, he could easily bring the torn-out book pages to hide under the stairs and clinch the case. Hiding them under the stairs was a neat touch. It recalled the disposal of Agnes's body, and, from the practical point of view, it was very easy for him. When he followed Aimée and the police, just a minute or two in the hall passing through would be enough.'

'All the same,' I said, 'there's one thing I can't forgive you for, Miss Marple – roping in Megan.'

317

Miss Marple put down her crochet which she had resumed. She looked at me over her spectacles and her eyes were stern.

'My dear young man, *something* had to be done. There was no evidence against this very clever and unscrupulous man. I needed someone to help me, someone of high courage and good brains. I found the person I needed.'

'It was very dangerous for her.'

'Yes, it was dangerous, but we are not put into this world, Mr Burton, to avoid danger when an innocent fellow-creature's life is at stake. You understand me?'

I understood.

CHAPTER FIFTEEN

Morning in the High Street.

Miss Emily Barton comes out of the grocer's with her shopping bag. Her cheeks are pink and her eyes are excited.

'Oh, dear, Mr Burton, I really am in such a flutter. To think I really am going on a cruise at last!'

'I hope you'll enjoy it.'

'Oh, I'm sure I shall. I should never have dared to go by myself. It does seem so *providential* the way everything has turned out. For a long time I've felt that I ought to part with Little Furze, that my means were really *too* straitened but I couldn't bear the idea of *strangers* there. But now that you have bought it and are going to live there with Megan – it is quite different. And then dear Aimée, after her terrible ordeal, not quite knowing what to do with herself, and her brother getting married (how nice to think you have *both* settled down with us!) and agreeing to come with me. We mean to be away quite a long time. We might even' – Miss Emily dropped her voice – '*go round the world*! And Aimée is so splendid and so practical. I really do think, don't you, that everything turns out for the *best*?'

Just for a fleeting moment I thought of Mrs Symmington and Agnes Woddell in their graves in the churchyard and wondered if they would agree, and then I remembered that Agnes's boy hadn't been very fond of her and that Mrs Symmington hadn't been very nice to Megan and, what the hell? we've all got to die some time! And I agreed with happy Miss Emily that everything was for the best in the best of possible worlds.

I went along the High Street and in at the Symmingtons' gate and Megan came out to meet me.

It was not a romantic meeting because an out-size Old English sheepdog came out with Megan and nearly knocked me over with his ill-timed exuberance.

'Isn't he *adorable*?' said Megan.

'A little overwhelming. Is he ours?'

'Yes, he's a wedding present from Joanna. We *have* had nice wedding presents, haven't we? That fluffy woolly thing that we don't know what it's for from Miss Marple, and the lovely Crown Derby tea-set from Mr Pye, and Elsie has sent me a toast-rack –'

'How typical,' I interjected.

'And she's got a post with a dentist and is very happy. And – where was I?'

'Enumerating wedding presents. Don't forget if you change your mind you'll have to send them all back.'

'I shan't change my mind. What else have we got? Oh, yes, Mrs Dane Calthrop has sent an Egyptian scarab.'

'Original woman,' I said.

'Oh! Oh! but you don't know the best. *Partridge* has actually sent me a present. It's the most hideous teacloth you've ever seen. But I think she *must* like me now because she says she embroidered it all with her own hands.'

'In a design of sour grapes and thistles, I suppose?'

'No, true lovers' knots.'

'Dear, dear,' I said, 'Partridge *is* coming on.'

Megan had dragged me into the house.

She said:

'There's just one thing I can't make out. Besides the dog's own collar and lead, Joanna has sent an extra collar and lead. What do you think that's for?'

'That,' I said, 'is Joanna's little joke.'

A Murder is Announced

To Ralph and Anne Newman
at whose house I first tasted
'Delicious Death!'

CHAPTER ONE

A Murder is Announced

Between 7.30 and 8.30 every morning except Sundays, Johnnie Butt made the round of the village of Chipping Cleghorn on his bicycle, whistling vociferously through his teeth, and alighting at each house or cottage to shove through the letterbox such morning papers as had been ordered by the occupants of the house in question from Mr Totman, stationer, of the High Street. Thus, at Colonel and Mrs Easterbrook's he delivered *The Times* and the *Daily Graphic*; at Mrs Swettenham's he left *The Times* and the *Daily Worker*; at Miss Hinchliffe and Miss Murgatroyd's he left the *Daily Telegraph* and the *News Chronicle*; at Miss Blacklock's he left the *Telegraph, The Times* and the *Daily Mail*.

At all these houses, and indeed at practically every house in Chipping Cleghorn, he delivered every Friday a copy of the *North Benham News and Chipping Cleghorn Gazette*, known locally simply as 'the *Gazette*'.

Thus, on Friday mornings, after a hurried glance at the headlines in the daily paper (*International situation critical! UNO meets today! Bloodhounds seek blonde typist's killer! Three collieries idle. Twenty-three die of food poisoning in Seaside Hotel*, etc.) most of the inhabitants of Chipping Cleghorn eagerly opened the *Gazette* and plunged into the local news. After a cursory glance at Correspondence (in which the passionate hates and feuds of rural life found full play) nine out of ten subscribers then turned to the PERSONAL Column. Here were grouped together higgledy-piggledy articles For Sale or Wanted, frenzied appeals for Domestic Help, innumerable insertions regarding dogs, announcements concerning poultry and garden equipment; and various other items of an interesting nature to those living in the small community of Chipping Cleghorn.

This particular Friday, October 29th, was no exception to the rule —

Mrs Swettenham, pushing back the pretty little grey curls from her forehead, opened *The Times*; looked with a lacklustre eye at the left-hand centre page; decided that, as usual, if there *was* any exciting news *The Times* had succeeded in camouflaging it in an impeccable manner; took a look at the Births, Marriages and Deaths, particularly the latter; then, her duty done, she put aside *The Times* and eagerly seized the *Chipping Cleghorn Gazette*.

When her son Edmund entered the room a moment later, she was already deep in the Personal Column.

'Good morning, dear,' said Mrs Swettenham. 'The Smedleys are selling their Daimler. 1935 – that's rather a long time ago, isn't it?'

Her son grunted, poured himself out a cup of coffee, helped himself to a couple of kippers, sat down at the table and opened the *Daily Worker* which he propped up against the toast rack.

'*Bull mastiff puppies*,' read out Mrs Swettenham. 'I really don't know how people manage to feed big dogs nowadays – I really *don't* . . . H'm, Selina Lawrence is advertising for a cook again. I could tell her it's just a waste of time advertising in these days. She hasn't put her address, only a box number – that's *quite* fatal – I could have told her so – servants simply insist on knowing where they are going. They like a good address . . . *False teeth* – I can't think why false teeth are so popular. *Best prices paid* . . . *Beautiful bulbs. Our special selection.* They sound rather cheap . . . Here's a girl wants an "*Interesting post – Would travel.*" I dare say! Who wouldn't? . . . *Dachshunds* . . . I've never really cared for dachshunds myself – I don't mean because they're *German*, because we've got over all that – I just don't care for them, that's all. – Yes, Mrs Finch?'

The door had opened to admit the head and torso of a grim-looking female in an aged velvet beret.

'Good morning, Mum,' said Mrs Finch. 'Can I clear?'

'Not yet. We haven't finished,' said Mrs Swettenham. 'Not quite finished,' she added ingratiatingly.

Casting a look at Edmund and his paper, Mrs Finch sniffed, and withdrew.

'I've only just begun,' said Edmund, just as his mother remarked:

'I do wish you wouldn't read that horrid paper, Edmund. Mrs Finch doesn't like it *at all*.'

'I don't see what my political views have to do with Mrs Finch.'

'And it isn't,' pursued Mrs Swettenham, 'as though you *were* a worker. You don't do any work at all.'

'That's not in the least true,' said Edmund indignantly. 'I'm writing a book.'

'I meant *real* work,' said Mrs Swettenham. 'And Mrs Finch does matter. If she takes a dislike to us and won't come, who else could we get?'

'Advertise in the *Gazette*,' said Edmund, grinning.

'I've just told you that's no use. Oh dear me, nowadays unless one has an old Nannie in the family, who will go into the kitchen and do everything, one is simply *sunk*.'

'Well, why haven't we an old Nannie? How remiss of you not to have provided me with one. What were you thinking about?'

'You had an *ayah*, dear.'

'No foresight,' murmured Edmund.

Mrs Swettenham was once more deep in the Personal Column.

'*Second-hand Motor Mower for sale.* Now I wonder . . . Goodness, what a *price*! . . . More dachshunds . . . "*Do write or communicate desperate Woggles.*" What silly nicknames people have . . . *Cocker Spaniels* . . . Do you remember darling Susie, Edmund? She really was *human*. Understood every word you said to her . . . *Sheraton sideboard for sale. Genuine family antique. Mrs Lucas, Dayas Hall* . . . What a liar that woman is! Sheraton indeed . . . !'

Mrs Swettenham sniffed and then continued her reading:

'*All a mistake, darling. Undying love. Friday as usual − J* . . . I suppose they've had a lovers' quarrel − or do you think it's a code for burglars? . . . *More dachshunds*! Really, I do think people have gone a little crazy about breeding dachshunds. I mean, there *are* other dogs. Your Uncle Simon used to breed Manchester Terriers. Such graceful little things. I do like dogs with *legs* . . . *Lady going abroad will sell her navy two-piece suiting* . . . no measurements or price given . . . *A marriage is announced* − no, a *murder* . . . *What? Well*, I never! Edmund, *Edmund*, listen to this . . . *A murder is announced and will take place on Friday, October 29th at Little Paddocks at 6.30 p.m. Friends please accept this, the only intimation.* What an extraordinary thing. *Edmund!*'

'What's that?' Edmund looked up from his newspaper.

'Friday, October 29th . . . Why, that's *today*.'

'Let me see.' Her son took the paper from her.

'But what does it mean?' Mrs Swettenham asked with lively curiosity.

Edmund Swettenham rubbed his nose doubtfully.

'Some sort of party, I suppose. The Murder Game – that kind of thing.'

'Oh,' said Mrs Swettenham doubtfully. 'It seems a very odd way of doing it. Just sticking it in the advertisements like that. Not at all like Letitia Blacklock who always seems to me such a sensible woman.'

'Probably got up by the bright young things she has in the house.'

'It's very short notice. Today. Do you think we're just supposed to go?'

'It says "Friends please accept this, the only intimation," ' her son pointed out.

'Well, I think these new-fangled ways of giving invitations are very tiresome,' said Mrs Swettenham decidedly.

'All right, Mother, you needn't go.'

'No,' agreed Mrs Swettenham.

There was a pause.

'Do you really *want* that last piece of toast, Edmund?'

'I should have thought my being properly nourished mattered more than letting that old hag clear the table.'

'Sh, dear, she'll *hear* you . . . Edmund, what happens at a Murder Game?'

'I don't know, exactly . . . They pin pieces of paper upon you, or something . . . No, I think you draw them out of a hat. And some-body's the victim and somebody else is a detective – and then they turn the lights out and somebody taps you on the shoulder and then you scream and lie down and sham dead.'

'It sounds quite exciting.'

'Probably a beastly bore. I'm not going.'

'Nonsense, Edmund,' said Mrs Swettenham resolutely. '*I'm* going and *you're* coming with me. That's *settled*!'

'Archie,' said Mrs Easterbrook to her husband, 'listen to *this*.'

Colonel Easterbrook paid no attention, because he was already snorting with impatience over an article in *The Times*.

'Trouble with these fellows is,' he said, 'that none of them knows the first thing about India! Not the first thing!'

'I know, dear, I know.'

'If they did, they wouldn't write such piffle.'

'Yes, I know. Archie, do listen. *A murder is announced and will take place on Friday, October 29th* (that's today), *at Little Paddocks at 6.30 p.m. Friends please accept this, the only intimation.*'

She paused triumphantly. Colonel Easterbrook looked at her indulgently but without much interest.

'Murder Game,' he said.

'Oh.'

'That's all it is. Mind you' — he unbent a little — 'it can be very good fun if it's well done. But it needs good organizing by someone who knows the ropes. You draw lots. One person's the murderer, nobody knows who. Lights out. Murderer chooses his victim. The victim has to count twenty before he screams. Then the person who's chosen to be the detective takes charge. Questions everybody. Where they were, what they were doing, tries to trip the real fellow up. Yes, it's a good game — if the detective — er — knows something about police work.'

'Like you, Archie. You had all those interesting cases to try in your district.'

Colonel Easterbrook smiled indulgently and gave his moustache a complacent twirl.

'Yes, Laura,' he said. 'I dare say I could give them a hint or two.'
And he straightened his shoulders.

'Miss Blacklock ought to have asked you to help her in getting the thing up.'

The Colonel snorted.

'Oh, well, she's got that young cub staying with her. Expect this is his idea. Nephew or something. Funny idea, though, sticking it in the paper.'

'It was in the Personal Column. We might never have seen it. I suppose it *is* an invitation, Archie?'

'Funny kind of invitation. I can tell you one thing. They can count *me* out.'

'Oh, Archie.' Mrs Easterbrook's voice rose in a shrill wail.

'Short notice. For all they know I might be busy.'

'But you're not, are you, darling?' Mrs Easterbrook lowered her voice persuasively. 'And I do think, Archie, that you really *ought* to go — just to help poor Miss Blacklock out. I'm sure she's counting on you to make the thing a success. I mean, you know so much about police work and procedure. The whole thing will fall flat if you don't go and help to make it a success. After all, one must be *neighbourly*.'

Mrs Easterbrook put her synthetic blonde head on one side and opened her blue eyes very wide.

'Of course, if you put it like that, Laura . . .' Colonel Easterbrook twirled his grey moustache again, importantly, and looked with indulgence on his fluffy little wife. Mrs Easterbrook was at least thirty years younger than her husband.

'If you put it like *that*, Laura,' he said.

'I really do think it's your *duty*, Archie,' said Mrs Easterbrook solemnly.

IV

The *Chipping Cleghorn Gazette* had also been delivered at Boulders, the picturesque three cottages knocked into one inhabited by Miss Hinchliffe and Miss Murgatroyd.

'Hinch?'

'What is it, Murgatroyd?'

'Where are you?'

'Henhouse.'

'Oh.'

Paddling gingerly through the long wet grass, Miss Amy Murgatroyd approached her friend. The latter, attired in corduroy slacks and battledress tunic, was conscientiously stirring in handfuls of balancer meal to a repellently steaming basin full of cooked potato peelings and cabbage stumps.

She turned her head with its short man-like crop and weatherbeaten countenance towards her friend.

Miss Murgatroyd, who was fat and amiable, wore a checked tweed skirt and a shapeless pullover of brilliant royal blue. Her curly bird's nest of grey hair was in a good deal of disorder and she was slightly out of breath.

'In the *Gazette*,' she panted. 'Just listen -- what can it *mean*? *A murder is announced . . . and will take place on Friday, October 29th, at Little Paddocks at 6.30 p.m. Friends please accept this, the only intimation.*'

She paused, breathless, as she finished reading, and awaited some authoritative pronouncement.

'Daft,' said Miss Hinchliffe.

'Yes, but what do you think it *means*?'

'Means a drink, anyway,' said Miss Hinchliffe.

'You think it's a sort of invitation?'

'We'll find out what it means when we get there,' said Miss Hinchliffe. 'Bad sherry, I expect. You'd better get off the grass, Murgatroyd. You've got your bedroom slippers on still. They're soaked.'

'Oh dear.' Miss Murgatroyd looked down ruefully at her feet. 'How many eggs today?'

'Seven. That damned hen's still broody. I must get her into the coop.'

'It's a funny way of putting it, don't you think?' Amy Murgatroyd asked, reverting to the notice in the *Gazette*. Her voice was slightly wistful.

But her friend was made of sterner and more single-minded stuff. She was intent on dealing with recalcitrant poultry and no announcement in a paper, however enigmatic, could deflect her.

She squelched heavily through the mud and pounced upon a speckled hen. There was a loud and indignant squawking.

'Give me ducks every time,' said Miss Hinchliffe. '*Far* less trouble . . .'

V

'Oo, scrumptious!' said Mrs Harmon across the breakfast table to her husband, the Rev. Julian Harmon, 'there's going to be a murder at Miss Blacklock's.'

'A murder?' said her husband, slightly surprised. 'When?'

'This afternoon . . . at least, this evening. 6.30. Oh, bad luck, darling, you've got your preparations for confirmation then. It *is* a shame. And you do so love murders!'

'I don't really know what you're talking about, Bunch.'

Mrs Harmon, the roundness of whose form and face had early led to the soubriquet of 'Bunch' being substituted for her baptismal name of Diana, handed the *Gazette* across the table.

'There. All among the second-hand pianos, and the old teeth.'

'What a very extraordinary announcement.'

'Isn't it?' said Bunch happily. 'You wouldn't think that Miss Blacklock cared about murders and games and things, would you? I suppose it's the young Simmonses put her up to it – though I should have thought Julia Simmons would find murders rather crude. Still, there it is, and I do think, darling, it's a *shame* you can't be there. Anyway, I'll go and tell you all about it, though it's rather wasted on me, because I don't really like games that happen in the dark. They frighten me, and I *do* hope I shan't have to be the one who's murdered. If someone suddenly puts a hand on my shoulder and whispers, "You're dead," I know my heart will give such a big bump that perhaps it really *might* kill me! Do you think that's likely?'

'No, Bunch. I think you're going to live to be an old, old woman – with me.'

'And die on the same day and be buried in the same grave. That would be lovely.'

Bunch beamed from ear to ear at this agreeable prospect.

'You seem very happy, Bunch?' said her husband, smiling.

'Who'd *not* be happy if they were me?' demanded Bunch, rather confusedly. 'With you and Susan and Edward, and all of you fond of me and not caring if I'm stupid . . . And the sun shining! And this lovely big house to live in!'

The Rev. Julian Harmon looked round the big bare dining-room and assented doubtfully.

'Some people would think it was the last straw to have to live in this great rambling draughty place.'

'Well, I like big rooms. All the nice smells from outside can get in and stay there. And you can be untidy and leave things about and they don't clutter you.'

330

'No labour-saving devices or central heating? It means a lot of work for you, Bunch.'

'Oh, Julian, it doesn't. I get up at half-past six and light the boiler and rush around like a steam engine, and by eight it's all done. And I keep it nice, don't I? With beeswax and polish and big jars of autumn leaves. It's not really harder to keep a big house clean than a small one. You go round with mops and things much quicker, because your behind isn't always bumping into things like it is in a small room. And I like sleeping in a big cold room – it's so cosy to snuggle down with just the tip of your nose telling you what it's like up above. And whatever size of house you live in, you peel the same amount of potatoes and wash up the same amount of plates and all that. Think how nice it is for Edward and Susan to have a big empty room to play in where they can have railways and dolls' tea-parties all over the floor and never have to put them away. And then it's nice to have extra bits of the house that you can let people have to live in. Jimmy Symes and Johnnie Finch – they'd have had to live with their in-laws otherwise. And you know, Julian, it isn't nice living with your in-laws. You're devoted to Mother, but you wouldn't really have liked to start our married life living with her and Father. And I shouldn't have liked it, either. I'd have gone on feeling like a little girl.'

Julian smiled at her.

'You're rather like a little girl still, Bunch.'

Julian Harmon himself had clearly been a model designed by Nature for the age of sixty. He was still about twenty-five years short of achieving Nature's purpose.

'I know I'm stupid –'

'You're not stupid, Bunch. You're very clever.'

'No, I'm not. I'm not a bit intellectual. Though I do try... And I really love it when you talk to me about books and history and things. I think perhaps it wasn't an awfully good idea to read aloud Gibbon to me in the evenings, because if it's been a cold wind out, and it's nice and hot by the fire, there's something about Gibbon that does, rather, make you go to sleep.'

Julian laughed.

'But I do love listening to you, Julian. Tell me the story again about the old vicar who preached about Ahasuerus.'

'You know that by heart, Bunch.'

'Just tell it me again. *Please.*'

Her husband complied.

'It was old Scrymgour. Somebody looked into his church one day. He was leaning out of the pulpit and preaching fervently to a couple of old charwomen. He was shaking his finger at them and saying, "Aha! I know what you are thinking. *You* think that the Great Ahasuerus of the First Lesson was Artaxerxes the Second. But he *wasn't*!" And then with enormous triumph, "He was Artaxerxes the *Third*." '

It had never struck Julian Harmon as a particularly funny story himself, but it never failed to amuse Bunch.

Her clear laugh floated out.

'The old pet!' she exclaimed. 'I think you'll be exactly like that some day, Julian.'

Julian looked rather uneasy.

'I know,' he said with humility. 'I do feel very strongly that I can't always get the proper simple approach.'

'I shouldn't worry,' said Bunch, rising and beginning to pile the breakfast plates on a tray. 'Mrs Butt told me yesterday that Butt, who never went to church and used to be practically the local atheist, comes every Sunday now on purpose to hear you preach.'

She went on, with a very fair imitation of Mrs Butt's super-refined voice:

' "And Butt was saying only the other day, Madam, to Mr Timkins from Little Worsdale, that we'd got real *culture* here in Chipping Cleghorn. *Not* like Mr Goss, at Little Worsdale, who talks to the congregation as though they were children who hadn't had any education. Real culture, Butt said, that's what *we've* got. Our Vicar's a highly educated gentleman – Oxford, not Milchester – and he gives us the full benefit of his education. All about the Romans and the Greeks he knows, and the Babylonians and the Assyrians, too. And even the Vicarage cat, Butt says, is called after an Assyrian king!" So there's glory for you,' finished Bunch triumphantly. 'Goodness, I must get on with things or I shall never get done. Come along, Tiglath Pileser, you shall have the herring bones.'

Opening the door and holding it dexterously ajar with her foot, she shot through with the loaded tray, singing in a loud and not particularly tuneful voice, her own version of a sporting song.

> '*It's a fine murdering day* (sang Bunch)
> *And as balmy as May*
> *And the sleuths from the village are gone.*'

A rattle of crockery being dumped in the sink drowned the next lines, but as the Rev. Julian Harmon left the house, he heard the final triumphant assertion:

> '*And we'll all go a'murdering today!*'

CHAPTER TWO

Breakfast at Little Paddocks

At Little Paddocks also, breakfast was in progress.

Miss Blacklock, a woman of sixty-odd, the owner of the house, sat at the head of the table. She wore country tweeds -- and with them, rather incongruously, a choker necklace of large false pearls. She was reading Lane Norcott in the *Daily Mail*. Julia Simmons was languidly glancing through the *Telegraph*. Patrick Simmons was checking up on the crossword in *The Times*. Miss Dora Bunner was giving her attention wholeheartedly to the local weekly paper.

Miss Blacklock gave a subdued chuckle. Patrick muttered: '*Adherent* – not *adhesive* – that's where I went wrong.'

Suddenly a loud cluck, like a startled hen, came from Miss Bunner.

'Letty – *Letty* – have you seen this? Whatever *can* it mean?'

'What's the matter, Dora?'

'The most extraordinary advertisement. It says Little Paddocks quite distinctly. But whatever can it *mean*?'

'If you'd let me see, Dora dear –'

Miss Bunner obediently surrendered the paper into Miss Blacklock's outstretched hand, pointing to the item with a tremulous forefinger.

'Just look, Letty.'

Miss Blacklock looked. Her eyebrows went up. She threw a quick scrutinizing glance round the table. Then she read the advertisement out loud.

'*A murder is announced and will take place on Friday, October 29th, at Little Paddocks at 6.30 p.m. Friends please accept this, the only intimation.*'

Then she said sharply: 'Patrick, is this your idea?'

Her eyes rested searchingly on the handsome devil-may-care face of the young man at the other end of the table.

Patrick Simmons' disclaimer came quickly.

'No, indeed, Aunt Letty. Whatever put that idea into your head? Why should I know anything about it?'

'I wouldn't put it past you,' said Miss Blacklock grimly. 'I thought it might be your idea of a joke.'

'A joke? Nothing of the kind.'

'And you, Julia?'

Julia, looking bored, said: 'Of course not.'

Miss Bunner murmured: 'Do you think Mrs Haymes –' and looked at an empty place where someone had breakfasted earlier.

'Oh, I don't think our Phillipa would try and be funny,' said Patrick. 'She's a serious girl, she is.'

'But what's the idea, anyway?' said Julia, yawning. 'What does it mean?'

Miss Blacklock said slowly, 'I suppose – it's some silly sort of hoax.'

'But why?' Dora Bunner exclaimed. 'What's the point of it? It seems a very stupid sort of joke. And in very bad taste.'

Her flabby cheeks quivered indignantly, and her shortsighted eyes sparkled with indignation.

Miss Blacklock smiled at her.

'Don't work yourself up over it, Bunny,' she said. 'It's just somebody's idea of humour, but I wish I knew whose.'

'It says today,' pointed out Miss Bunner. 'Today at 6.30 p.m. What do you think is going to happen?'

'*Death!*' said Patrick in sepulchral tones. 'Delicious Death.'

'Be quiet, Patrick,' said Miss Blacklock as Miss Bunner gave a little yelp.

'I only meant the special cake that Mitzi makes,' said Patrick apologetically. 'You know we *always* call it Delicious Death.'

Miss Blacklock smiled a little absentmindedly.

Miss Bunner persisted: 'But, Letty, what do you really think —?'

Her friend cut across the words with reassuring cheerfulness.

'I know one thing that will happen at 6.30,' she said dryly. 'We'll have half the village up here, agog with curiosity. I'd better make sure we've got some sherry in the house.'

II

'You *are* worried, aren't you Lotty?'

Miss Blacklock started. She had been sitting at her writing-table, absentmindedly drawing little fishes on the blotting-paper. She looked up into the anxious face of her old friend.

She was not quite sure what to say to Dora Bunner. Bunny, she knew, mustn't be worried or upset. She was silent for a moment or two, thinking.

She and Dora Bunner had been at school together. Dora then had been a pretty, fair-haired, blue-eyed, rather stupid girl. Her being stupid hadn't mattered, because her gaiety and high spirits and her prettiness had made her an agreeable companion. She ought, her friend thought, to have married some nice Army officer, or a country solicitor. She had so many good qualities — affection, devotion, loyalty. But life had been unkind to Dora Bunner. She had had to earn her living. She had been painstaking but never competent at anything she undertook.

The two friends had lost sight of each other. But six months ago a letter had come to Miss Blacklock, a rambling, pathetic letter. Dora's health had given way. She was living in one room, trying to subsist on her old-age pension. She endeavoured to do needlework, but her fingers were stiff with rheumatism. She mentioned their schooldays — since then life had driven them apart — but could — possibly — her old friend help?

Miss Blacklock had responded impulsively. Poor Dora, poor pretty silly fluffy Dora. She had swooped down upon Dora, had carried her off, had installed her at Little Paddocks with the comforting fiction that 'the housework is getting too much for me. I need someone to help me run the house.' It was not for long — the doctor had told her that — but sometimes she found poor old Dora a sad trial. She muddled everything, upset the temperamental foreign 'help', miscounted the laundry, lost bills and letters – and sometimes reduced the competent Miss Blacklock to an agony of exasperation. Poor old muddle-headed Dora, so loyal, so anxious to help, so pleased and proud to think she was of assistance – and, alas, so completely unreliable.

She said sharply:

'Don't, Dora. You know I asked you –'

'Oh.' Miss Bunner looked guilty. 'I know. I forgot. But – but you *are*, aren't you?'

'Worried? No. At least,' she added truthfully, 'not exactly. You mean about that silly notice in the *Gazette*?'

'Yes – even if it's a joke, it seems to me it's a – a spiteful sort of joke.'

'Spiteful?'

'Yes. It seems to me there's *spite* there somewhere. I mean – it's not a *nice* kind of joke.'

Miss Blacklock looked at her friend. The mild eyes, the long obstinate mouth, the slightly upturned nose. Poor Dora, so maddening, so muddle-headed, so devoted and such a problem. A dear fussy old idiot and yet, in a queer way, with an instinctive sense of values.

'I think you're right, Dora,' said Miss Blacklock. 'It's not a nice joke.'

'I don't like it at all,' said Dora Bunner with unsuspected vigour. 'It frightens me.' She added, suddenly: 'And it frightens *you*, Letitia.'

'Nonsense,' said Miss Blacklock with spirit.

'It's *dangerous*. I'm sure it is. Like those people who send you bombs done up in parcels.'

'My dear, it's just some silly idiot trying to be funny.'

'But it *isn't* funny.'

It wasn't really very funny ... Miss Blacklock's face betrayed her thoughts, and Dora cried triumphantly, 'You see. You think so, too!'

'But, Dora my dear –'

She broke off. Through the door there surged a tempestuous young woman with a well-developed bosom heaving under a tight jersey. She had on a dirndl skirt of a bright colour and had greasy dark plaits wound round and round her head. Her eyes were dark and flashing.

She said gustily:

'I can speak to you, yes, please, no?'

Miss Blacklock sighed.

'Of course, Mitzi, what is it?'

Sometimes she thought it would be preferable to do the entire work of the house as well as the cooking rather than be bothered with the eternal nerve storms of her refugee 'lady help'.

'I tell you at once – it is in order, I hope? I give you my notices and I *go* – I go at *once*!'

'For what reason? Has somebody upset you?'

'Yes, I am upset,' said Mitzi dramatically. 'I do not wish to die! Already in Europe I escape. My family they all die – they are all killed – my mother, my little brother, my so sweet little niece – all, all they are killed. But me I run away – I hide. I get to England. I work. I do work that never – never would I do in my own country – I –'

'I know all that,' said Miss Blacklock crisply. It was, indeed, a constant refrain on Mitzi's lips. 'But why do you want to leave *now*?'

'Because again they come to kill me!'

'Who do?'

'My enemies. The Nazis! Or perhaps this time it is the Bolsheviks. They find out I am here. They come to kill me. I have read it – yes – it is in the newspaper!'

'Oh, you mean in the *Gazette*?'

'*Here*, it is written *here*.' Mitzi produced the *Gazette* from where she had been holding it behind her back. 'See – here it says a *murder*. At Little Paddocks. That is here, is it not? This evening at 6.30. Ah! I do not wait to be murdered – *no*.'

'But why should this apply to *you*? It's – we think it is a joke.'

'A *joke*? It is not a joke to murder someone.'

'No, of course not. But, my dear child, if anyone wanted to murder you, they wouldn't advertise the fact in the paper, would they?'

'You do not think they would?' Mitzi seemed a little shaken. 'You think, perhaps, they do not mean to murder anyone at all? Perhaps it is *you* they mean to murder, Miss Blacklock.'

'I certainly can't believe anyone wants to murder me,' said Miss Blacklock lightly. 'And really, Mitzi, I don't see why anyone should want to murder you. After all, why should they?'

'Because they are bad peoples ... Very bad peoples. I tell you, my mother, my little brother, my so sweet niece . . .'

'Yes, yes.' Miss Blacklock stemmed the flow, adroitly. 'But I cannot really believe *anyone* wants to murder you, Mitzi. Of course, if you want to go off like this at a moment's notice, I cannot possibly stop you. But I think you will be very silly if you do.'

She added firmly, as Mitzi looked doubtful:

'We'll have that beef the butcher sent stewed for lunch. It looks very tough.'

'I make you a goulash, a special goulash.'

'If you prefer to call it that, certainly. And perhaps you could use up that rather hard bit of cheese in making some cheese straws. I think some people may come in this evening for drinks.'

'This evening? What do you mean, this evening?'

'At half-past six.'

'But that is the time in the paper? Who should come then? *Why* should they come?'

'They're coming to the funeral,' said Miss Blacklock with a twinkle. 'That'll do now, Mitzi. I'm busy. Shut the door after you,' she added firmly.

'And that's settled *her* for the moment,' she said as the door closed behind a puzzled-looking Mitzi.

'You are so efficient, Letty,' said Miss Bunner admiringly.

CHAPTER THREE

At 6.30 p.m.

'Well, here we are, all set,' said Miss Blacklock. She looked round the double drawing-room with an appraising eye. The rose-patterned chintzes – the two bowls of bronze chrysanthemums, the small vase of violets and the silver cigarette-box on a table by the wall, the tray of drinks on the centre table.

Little Paddocks was a medium-sized house built in the early Victorian style. It had a long shallow veranda and green-shuttered windows. The long, narrow drawing-room which lost a good deal

338

of light owing to the veranda roof had originally had double doors at one end leading into a small room with a bay window. A former generation had removed the double doors and replaced them with portières of velvet. Miss Blacklock had dispensed with the portières so that the two rooms had become definitely one. There was a fireplace each end, but neither fire was lit although a gentle warmth pervaded the room.

'You've had the central heating lit,' said Patrick.

Miss Blacklock nodded.

'It's been so misty and damp lately. The whole house felt clammy. I got Evans to light it before he went.'

'The precious precious coke?' said Patrick mockingly.

'As you say, the precious coke. But otherwise there would have been the even more precious coal. You know the Fuel Office won't even let us have the little bit that's due to us each week − not unless we can say definitely that we haven't got any other means of cooking.'

'I suppose there was once heaps of coke and coal for everybody?' said Julia with the interest of one hearing about an unknown country.

'Yes, and cheap, too.'

'And anyone could go and buy as much as they wanted, without filling in anything, and there wasn't any shortage? There was lots of it there?'

'All kinds and qualities − and *not* all stones and slates like what we get nowadays.'

'It must have been a wonderful world,' said Julia, with awe in her voice.

Miss Blacklock smiled. 'Looking back on it, *I* certainly think so. But then I'm an old woman. It's natural for me to prefer my own times. But you young things oughtn't to think so.'

'I needn't have had a job then,' said Julia. 'I could just have stayed at home and done the flowers, and written notes ... Why did one write notes and who were they to?'

'All the people that you now ring up on the telephone,' said Miss Blacklock with a twinkle. 'I don't believe you even know *how* to write, Julia.'

'Not in the style of that delicious "Complete Letter Writer" I found the other day. Heavenly! It told you the correct way of refusing a proposal of marriage from a widower.'

'I doubt if you would have enjoyed staying at home as much as you think,' said Miss Blacklock. 'There were duties, you know.' Her voice was dry. 'However, I don't really know much about it. Bunny and I,' she smiled affectionately at Dora Bunner, 'went into the labour market early.'

'Oh, we did, we did *indeed*,' agreed Miss Bunner. 'Those naughty, naughty children. I'll never forget them. Of course, Letty was clever. She was a business woman, secretary to a big financier.'

The door opened and Phillipa Haymes came in. She was tall and fair and placid-looking. She looked round the room in surprise.

'Hallo,' she said. 'Is it a party? Nobody told me.'

'Of course,' cried Patrick. 'Our Phillipa doesn't know. The only woman in Chipping Cleghorn who doesn't, I bet.'

Phillipa looked at him inquiringly.

'Here you behold,' said Patrick dramatically, waving a hand, 'the scene of a murder!'

Phillipa Haymes looked faintly puzzled.

'Here,' Patrick indicated the two big bowls of chrysanthemums, 'are the funeral wreaths and these dishes of cheese straws and olives represent the funeral baked meats.'

Phillipa looked inquiringly at Miss Blacklock.

'Is it a joke?' she asked. 'I'm always terribly stupid at seeing jokes.'

'It's a very nasty joke,' said Dora Bunner with energy. 'I don't like it at all.'

'Show her the advertisement,' said Miss Blacklock. 'I *must* go and shut up the ducks. It's dark. They'll be in by now.'

'Let me do it,' said Phillipa.

'Certainly not, my dear. You've finished your day's work.'

'I'll do it, Aunt Letty,' offered Patrick.

'No, you won't,' said Miss Blacklock with energy. 'Last time you didn't latch the door properly.'

'I'll do it, Letty dear,' cried Miss Bunner. 'Indeed, I should love to. I'll just slip on my goloshes – and now where did I put my cardigan?'

But Miss Blacklock, with a smile, had already left the room.

'It's no good, Bunny,' said Patrick. 'Aunt Letty's so efficient that she can never bear anybody else to do things for her. She really much prefers to do everything herself.'

'She loves it,' said Julia.

'I didn't notice you making any offers of assistance,' said her brother.

Julia smiled lazily.

'You've just said Aunt Letty likes to do things herself,' she pointed out. 'Besides,' she held out a well-shaped leg in a sheer stocking, 'I've got my best stockings on.'

'Death in silk stockings?' declaimed Patrick.

'Not silk – nylons, you idiot.'

'That's not nearly such a good title.'

'Won't somebody please tell me,' cried Phillipa plaintively, 'why there is all this insistence on death?'

Everybody tried to tell her at once – nobody could find the *Gazette* to show her because Mitzi had taken it into the kitchen.

Miss Blacklock returned a few minutes later.

'There,' she said briskly, '*that's* done.' She glanced at the clock. 'Twenty-past six. Somebody ought to be here soon – unless I'm entirely wrong in my estimate of my neighbours.'

'I don't see why anybody should come,' said Phillipa, looking bewildered.

'Don't you, dear? . . . I dare say you wouldn't. But most people are rather more inquisitive than you are.'

'Phillipa's attitude to life is that she just isn't interested,' said Julia, rather nastily.

Phillipa did not reply.

Miss Blacklock was glancing round the room. Mitzi had put the sherry and three dishes containing olives, cheese straws and some little fancy pastries on the table in the middle of the room.

'You might move that tray – or the whole table if you like – round the corner into the bay window in the other room, Patrick, if you don't mind. After all, I am *not* giving a party! *I* haven't asked anyone. And I don't intend to make it obvious that I expect people to turn up.'

'You wish, Aunt Letty, to disguise your intelligent anticipation?'

'Very nicely put, Patrick. Thank you, my dear boy.'

'Now we can all give a lovely performance of a quiet evening at home,' said Julia, 'and be quite surprised when somebody drops in.'

Miss Blacklock had picked up the sherry bottle. She stood holding it uncertainly in her hand.

Patrick reassured her.

'There's quite half a bottle there. It ought to be enough.'

'Oh, yes – yes . . .' She hesitated. Then, with a slight flush, she said:

'Patrick, would you mind . . . there's a new bottle in the cupboard in the pantry . . . Bring it and a corkscrew. I – we – might as well have a new bottle. This – this has been opened some time.'

Patrick went on his errand without a word. He returned with the new bottle and drew the cork. He looked up curiously at Miss Blacklock as he placed it on the tray.

'Taking things seriously, aren't you, darling?' he asked gently.

'Oh,' cried Dora Bunner, shocked. 'Surely, Letty, you can't imagine –'

'Hush,' said Miss Blacklock quickly. 'That's the bell. You see, my intelligent anticipation is being justified.'

II

Mitzi opened the door of the drawing-room and admitted Colonel and Mrs Easterbrook. She had her own methods of announcing people.

'Here is Colonel and Mrs Easterbrook to see you,' she said conversationally.

Colonel Easterbrook was very bluff and breezy to cover some slight embarrassment.

'Hope you don't mind us dropping in,' he said. (A subdued gurgle came from Julia.) 'Happened to be passing this way – eh what? Quite a mild evening. Notice you've got your central heating on. We haven't started ours yet.'

'Aren't your chrysanthemums *lovely*?' gushed Mrs Easterbrook. '*Such* beauties!'

'They're rather scraggy, really,' said Julia.

Mrs Easterbrook greeted Phillipa Haymes with a little extra cordiality to show that she *quite* understood that Phillipa was not really an agricultural labourer.

'How is Mrs Lucas' garden getting on?' she asked. 'Do you think it will ever be straight again? Completely neglected all through the war – and then only that dreadful old man Ashe who simply did nothing but sweep up a few leaves and put in a few cabbage plants.'

'It's yielding to treatment,' said Phillipa. 'But it will take a little time.'

Mitzi opened the door again and said:

'Here are the ladies from Boulders.'

' 'Evening,' said Miss Hinchliffe, striding over and taking Miss Blacklock's hand in her formidable grip. 'I said to Murgatroyd: "Let's just drop in at Little Paddocks!" I wanted to ask you how your ducks are laying.'

'The evenings do draw in so quickly now, don't they?' said Miss Murgatroyd to Patrick in a rather fluttery way. 'What *lovely* chrysanthemums!'

'Scraggy!' said Julia.

'Why can't you be co-operative?' murmured Patrick to her in a reproachful aside.

'You've got your central heating on,' said Miss Hinchliffe. She said it accusingly. 'Very early.'

'The house gets so damp this time of year,' said Miss Blacklock.

Patrick signalled with his eyebrows: 'Sherry yet?' and Miss Blacklock signalled back: 'Not yet.'

She said to Colonel Easterbrook:

'Are you getting any bulbs from Holland this year?'

The door again opened and Mrs Swettenham came in rather guiltily, followed by a scowling and uncomfortable Edmund.

'Here we are!' said Mrs Swettenham gaily, gazing round her with frank curiosity. Then, feeling suddenly uncomfortable, she went on: 'I just thought I'd pop in and ask you if by any chance you wanted a kitten, Miss Blacklock? Our cat is just –'

'About to be brought to bed of the progeny of a ginger tom,' said Edmund. 'The result will, I think, be frightful. Don't say you haven't been warned!'

'She's a very good mouser,' said Mrs Swettenham hastily. And added: 'What *lovely* chrysanthemums!'

'You've got your central heating on, haven't you?' asked Edmund, with an air of originality.

'Aren't people just like gramophone records?' murmured Julia.

'I don't like the news,' said Colonel Easterbrook to Patrick, buttonholing him fiercely. 'I don't like it at all. If you ask me, war's inevitable – absolutely inevitable.'

'I never pay any attention to news,' said Patrick.

Once more the door opened and Mrs Harmon came in.

Her battered felt hat was stuck on the back of her head in a vague attempt to be fashionable and she had put on a rather limp frilly blouse instead of her usual pullover.

'Hallo, Miss Blacklock,' she exclaimed, beaming all over her round face. 'I'm not too late, am I? When does the murder begin?'

III

There was an audible series of gasps. Julia gave an approving little giggle, Patrick crinkled up his face and Miss Blacklock smiled at her latest guest.

'Julian is just frantic with rage that he can't be here,' said Mrs Harmon. 'He *adores* murders. That's really why he preached such a good sermon last Sunday – I suppose I oughtn't to say it was a good sermon as he's my husband – but it really was good, didn't you think? – so much better than his usual sermons. But as I was saying it was all because of *Death Does the Hat Trick*. Have you read it? The girl at Boots kept it for me specially. It's simply baffling. You keep thinking you know – and then the whole thing switches round – and there are a lovely lot of murders, four or five of them. Well, I left it in the study when Julian was shutting himself up there to do his sermon, and he just picked it up and simply *could not* put it down! And consequently he had to write his sermon in a frightful hurry and had to just put down what he wanted to say very simply – without any scholarly twists and bits and learned references – and naturally it was heaps better. Oh dear, I'm talking too much. But do tell me, when is the murder going to begin?'

Miss Blacklock looked at the clock on the mantelpiece.

'If it's going to begin,' she said cheerfully, 'it ought to begin soon. It's just a minute to the half hour. In the meantime, have a glass of sherry.'

Patrick moved with alacrity through the archway. Miss Blacklock went to the table by the archway where the cigarette-box was.

'I'd love some sherry,' said Mrs Harmon. 'But what do you mean by *if*?'

'Well,' said Miss Blacklock, 'I'm as much in the dark as you are. I don't know what –'

She stopped and turned her head as the little clock on the mantelpiece began to chime. It had a sweet silvery bell-like tone. Everybody was silent and nobody moved. They all stared at the clock.

It chimed a quarter – and then the half. As the last note died away all the lights went out.

IV

Delighted gasps and feminine squeaks of appreciation were heard in the darkness. 'It's beginning,' cried Mrs Harmon in an ecstasy. Dora Bunner's voice cried out plaintively, 'Oh, I don't like it!' Other voices said, 'How terribly terribly frightening!' 'It gives me the creeps.' 'Archie, where are you?' 'What do I have to *do*?' 'Oh dear – did I step on your foot? I'm so sorry.'

Then, with a crash, the door swung open. A powerful flashlight played rapidly round the room. A man's hoarse nasal voice, reminiscent to all of pleasant afternoons at the cinema, directed the company crisply to:

'Stick 'em up!

'Stick 'em up, I tell you!' the voice barked.

Delightedly, hands were raised willingly above heads.

'Isn't it wonderful?' breathed a female voice. 'I'm *so* thrilled.'

And then, unexpectedly, a revolver spoke. It spoke twice. The ping of two bullets shattered the complacency of the room. Suddenly the game was no longer a game. Somebody screamed . . .

The figure in the doorway whirled suddenly round, it seemed to hesitate, a third shot rang out, it crumpled and then it crashed to the ground. The flashlight dropped and went out.

There was darkness once again. And gently, with a little Victorian protesting moan, the drawing-room door, as was its habit when not propped open, swung gently to and latched with a click.

Inside the drawing-room there was pandemonium. Various voices spoke at once. 'Lights.' 'Can't you find the switch?' 'Who's got a lighter?' 'Oh, I don't like it, I don't *like* it.' 'But those shots were *real*!' 'It was a *real* revolver he had.' 'Was it a burglar?' 'Oh, Archie, I want to get out of here.' 'Please, has somebody got a lighter?'

And then, almost at the same moment, two lighters clicked and burned with small steady flames.

Everybody blinked and peered at each other. Startled face looked into startled face. Against the wall by the archway Miss Blacklock stood with her hand up to her face. The light was too dim to show more than that something dark was trickling over her fingers.

Colonel Easterbrook cleared his throat and rose to the occasion.

'Try the switches, Swettenham,' he ordered.

Edmund, near the door, obediently jerked the switch up and down.

'Off at the main, or a fuse,' said the Colonel. 'Who's making that awful row?'

A female voice had been screaming steadily from somewhere beyond the closed door. It rose now in pitch and with it came the sound of fists hammering on a door.

Dora Bunner, who had been sobbing quietly, called out:

'It's Mitzi. Somebody's murdering Mitzi . . .'

Patrick muttered: 'No such luck.'

Miss Blacklock said: 'We must get candles. Patrick, will you –?'

The Colonel was already opening the door. He and Edmund, their lighters flickering, stepped into the hall. They almost stumbled over a recumbent figure there.

'Seems to have knocked him out,' said the Colonel. 'Where's that woman making that hellish noise?'

'In the dining-room,' said Edmund.

The dining-room was just across the hall. Someone was beating on the panels and howling and screaming.

'She's locked in,' said Edmund, stooping down. He turned the key and Mitzi came out like a bounding tiger.

The dining-room light was still on. Silhouetted against it Mitzi presented a picture of insane terror and continued to scream. A touch of comedy was introduced by the fact that she had been engaged in cleaning silver and was still holding a chamois leather and a large fish slice.

'Be quiet, Mitzi,' said Miss Blacklock.

'Stop it,' said Edmund, and as Mitzi showed no disposition to stop screaming, he leaned forward and gave her a sharp slap on the cheek. Mitzi gasped and hiccuped into silence.

'Get some candles,' said Miss Blacklock. 'In the kitchen cupboard. Patrick, you know where the fusebox is?'

'The passage behind the scullery? Right, I'll see what I can do.'

Miss Blacklock had moved forward into the light thrown from the dining-room and Dora Bunner gave a sobbing gasp. Mitzi let out another full-blooded scream.

'The blood, the *blood*!' she gasped. 'You are shot – Miss Blacklock, you bleed to death.'

'Don't be so stupid,' snapped Miss Blacklock. 'I'm hardly hurt at all. It just grazed my ear.'

'But, Aunt Letty,' said Julia, 'the blood.'

And indeed Miss Blacklock's white blouse and pearls and her hands were a horrifyingly gory sight.

'Ears always bleed,' said Miss Blacklock. 'I remember fainting in the hairdresser's when I was a child. The man had only just snipped my ear. There seemed to be a basin of blood at once. But we *must* have some light.'

'I get the candles,' said Mitzi.

Julia went with her and they returned with several candles stuck into saucers.

'Now let's have a look at our malefactor,' said the Colonel. 'Hold the candles down low, will you, Swettenham? As many as you can.'

'I'll come the other side,' said Phillipa.

With a steady hand she took a couple of saucers. Colonel Easterbrook knelt down.

The recumbent figure was draped in a roughly made black cloak with a hood to it. There was a black mask over the face and he wore black cotton gloves. The hood had slipped back disclosing a ruffled fair head.

Colonel Easterbrook turned him over, felt the pulse, the heart . . . then drew away his fingers with an exclamation of distaste, looking down on them. They were sticky and red.

'Shot himself,' he said.

'Is he badly hurt?' asked Miss Blacklock.

'H'm. I'm afraid he's dead ... May have been suicide – or he may have tripped himself up with that cloak thing and the revolver went off as he fell. If I could see better –'

At that moment, as though by magic, the lights came on again.

With a queer feeling of unreality those inhabitants of Chipping Cleghorn who stood in the hall of Little Paddocks realized that they stood in the presence of violent and sudden death. Colonel Easterbrook's hand was stained red. Blood was still trickling down Miss Blacklock's neck over her blouse and coat, and the grotesquely sprawled figure of the intruder lay at their feet ...

Patrick, coming from the dining-room, said, 'It seemed to be just one fuse gone ...' He stopped.

Colonel Easterbrook tugged at the small black mask.

'Better see who the fellow is,' he said. 'Though I don't suppose it's anyone we know ...'

He detached the mask. Necks were craned forward. Mitzi hiccuped and gasped, but the others were very quiet.

'He's quite young,' said Mrs Harmon with a note of pity in her voice.

And suddenly Dora Bunner cried out excitedly:

'Letty, Letty, it's the young man from the Spa Hotel in Medenham Wells. The one who came out here and wanted you to give him money to get back to Switzerland and you refused. I suppose the whole thing was just a pretext – to spy out the house ... Oh dear – he might easily have killed you ...'

Miss Blacklock, in command of the situation, said incisively:

'Phillipa, take Bunny into the dining-room and give her a half-glass of brandy. Julia dear, just run up to the bathroom and bring me the sticking plaster out of the bathroom cupboard – it's so messy bleeding like a pig. Patrick, will you ring up the police at once?'

CHAPTER FOUR

The Royal Spa Hotel

George Rydesdale, Chief Constable of Middleshire, was a quiet man. Of medium height, with shrewd eyes under rather bushy brows, he was in the habit of listening rather than talking. Then, in his unemotional voice, he would give a brief order – and the order was obeyed.

He was listening now to Detective-Inspector Dermot Craddock. Craddock was now officially in charge of the case. Rydesdale had recalled him last night from Liverpool where he had been sent to make certain inquiries in connection with another case. Rydesdale had a good opinion of Craddock. He not only had brains and imagination, he had also, which Rydesdale appreciated even more, the self-discipline to go slow, to check and examine each fact, and to keep an open mind until the very end of a case.

'Constable Legg took the call, sir,' Craddock was saying. 'He seems to have acted very well, with promptitude and presence of mind. And it can't have been easy. About a dozen people all trying to talk at once, including one of those Mittel Europas who go off at the deep end at the mere sight of a policeman. Felt sure she was going to be locked up, and fairly screamed the place down.'

'Deceased has been identified?'

'Yes, sir. Rudi Scherz. Swiss Nationality. Employed at the Royal Spa Hotel, Medenham Wells, as a receptionist. If you agree, sir, I thought I'd take the Royal Spa Hotel first, and go out to Chipping Cleghorn afterwards. Sergeant Fletcher is out there now. He'll see the bus people and then go on to the house.'

Rydesdale nodded approval.

The door opened, and the Chief Constable looked up.

'Come in, Henry,' he said. 'We've got something here that's a little out of the ordinary.'

Sir Henry Clithering, ex-Commissioner of Scotland Yard, came in with slightly raised eyebrows. He was a tall, distinguished-looking elderly man.

'It may appeal to even your blasé palate,' went on Rydesdale.

'I was never blasé,' said Sir Henry indignantly.

'The latest idea,' said Rydesdale, 'is to advertise one's murders beforehand. Show Sir Henry that advertisement, Craddock.'

'The *North Benham News and Chipping Cleghorn Gazette*,' said Sir Henry. 'Quite a mouthful.' He read the half inch of print indicated by Craddock's finger. 'H'm, yes, somewhat unusual.'

'Any line on who inserted this advertisement?' asked Rydesdale.

'By the description, sir, it was handed in by Rudi Scherz himself – on Wednesday.'

'Nobody questioned it? The person who accepted it didn't think it odd?'

'The adenoidal blonde who receives the advertisements is quite incapable of thinking, I should say, sir. She just counted the words and took the money.'

'What was the idea?' asked Sir Henry.

'Get a lot of the locals curious,' suggested Rydesdale. 'Get them all together at a particular place at a particular time, then hold them up and relieve them of their spare cash and valuables. As an idea, it's not without originality.'

'What sort of a place is Chipping Cleghorn?' asked Sir Henry.

'A large sprawling picturesque village. Butcher, baker, grocer, quite a good antique shop – two tea-shops. Self-consciously a beauty spot. Caters for the motoring tourist. Also highly residential. Cottages formerly lived in by agricultural labourers now converted and lived in by elderly spinsters and retired couples. A certain amount of building done round about in Victorian times.'

'I know,' said Sir Henry. 'Nice old Pussies and retired Colonels. Yes, if they noticed that advertisement they'd all come sniffing round at 6.30 to see what was up. Lord, I wish I had my own particular old Pussy here. Wouldn't she like to get her nice ladylike teeth into this. Right up her street, it would be.'

'Who's your own particular Pussy, Henry? An aunt?'

'No,' Sir Henry sighed. 'She's no relation.' He said reverently: 'She's just the finest detective God ever made. Natural genius cultivated in a suitable soil.'

He turned upon Craddock.

'Don't you despise the old Pussies in this village of yours, my boy,' he said. 'In case this turns out to be a high-powered mystery, which I don't suppose for a moment it will, remember that an elderly unmarried woman who knits and gardens is streets ahead of any detective sergeant. She can tell you what might have happened and what ought to have happened and even what actually *did* happen! And she can tell you *why* it happened!'

'I'll bear that in mind, sir,' said Detective-Inspector Craddock in his most formal manner, and nobody would have guessed that Dermot Eric Craddock was actually Sir Henry's godson and was on easy and intimate terms with his godfather.

Rydesdale gave a quick outline of the case to his friend.

'They'd all turn up at 6.30, I grant you that,' he said. 'But would that Swiss fellow know they would? And another thing – would they be likely to have much loot on them to be worth the taking?'

'A couple of old-fashioned brooches, a string of seed pearls – a little loose change, perhaps a note or two – not more,' said Sir Henry, thoughtfully. 'Did this Miss Blacklock keep much money in the house?'

'She says not, sir. Five pounds odd, I understand.'

'Mere chicken feed,' said Rydesdale.

'What you're getting at,' said Sir Henry, 'is that this fellow liked to playact – it wasn't the loot, it was the fun of playing and acting the hold-up. Cinema stuff? Eh? It's quite possible. How did he manage to shoot himself?'

Rydesdale drew a paper towards him.

'Preliminary medical report. The revolver was discharged at close range – singeing ... h'm ... nothing to show whether accident or suicide. Could have been done deliberately, or he could have tripped and fallen and the revolver which he was holding close to him could have gone off ... Probably the latter.' He looked at Craddock. 'You'll have to question the witnesses very carefully and make them say exactly what they saw.'

Detective-Inspector Craddock said sadly: 'They'll all have seen something different.'

'It's always interested me,' said Sir Henry, 'what people do see at a moment of intense excitement and nervous strain. What they do see and, even more interesting, what they don't see.'

'Where's the report on the revolver?'

'Foreign make – fairly common on the Continent – Scherz did not hold a permit for it – and did not declare it on coming into England.'

'Bad lad,' said Sir Henry.

'Unsatisfactory character all round. Well, Craddock, go and see what you can find out about him at the Royal Spa Hotel.'

II

At the Royal Spa Hotel, Inspector Craddock was taken straight to the Manager's office.

The Manager, Mr Rowlandson, a tall florid man with a hearty manner, greeted Inspector Craddock with expansive geniality.

'Glad to help you in any way we can, Inspector,' he said. 'Really a most surprising business. I'd never have credited it – never. Scherz seemed a very ordinary, pleasant young chap – not at all my idea of a hold-up man.'

'How long has he been with you, Mr Rowlandson?'

'I was looking that up just before you came. A little over three months. Quite good credentials, the usual permits, etc.'

'And you found him satisfactory?'

Without seeming to do so, Craddock marked the infinitesimal pause before Rowlandson replied.

'Quite satisfactory.'

Craddock made use of a technique he had found efficacious before now.

'No, no, Mr Rowlandson,' he said, gently shaking his head. 'That's not really quite the case, is it?'

'We-ll –' The Manager seemed slightly taken aback.

'Come now, there was something wrong. What was it?'

'That's just it. I don't know.'

'But you *thought* there was something wrong?'

'Well – yes – I did ... But I've nothing really to go upon. I shouldn't like my conjectures to be written down and quoted against me.'

Craddock smiled pleasantly.

'I know just what you mean. You needn't worry. But I've got to get some idea of what this fellow, Scherz, was like. You suspected him of – what?'

Rowlandson said, rather reluctantly:

'Well, there was trouble, once or twice, about the bills. Items charged that oughtn't to have been there.'

'You mean you suspected that he charged up certain items which didn't appear in the hotel records, and that he pocketed the difference when the bill was paid?'

'Something like that . . . Put it at the best, there was gross carelessness on his part. Once or twice quite a big sum was involved. Frankly, I got our accountant to go over his books, suspecting that he was – well, a wrong 'un, but though there were various mistakes and a good deal of slipshod method, the actual cash was quite correct. So I came to the conclusion that I must be mistaken.'

'Supposing you hadn't been wrong? Supposing Scherz had been helping himself to various small sums here and there, he could have covered himself, I suppose, by making good the money?'

'Yes, if he *had* the money. But people who help themselves to "small sums" as you put it – are usually hard up for those sums and spend them offhand.'

'So, if he wanted money to replace missing sums, he would have had to get money – by a hold-up or other means?'

'Yes. I wonder if this is his first attempt . . .'

'Might be. It was certainly a very amateurish one. Is there anyone else he could have got money from? Any women in his life?'

'One of the waitresses in the Grill. Her name's Myrna Harris.'

'I'd better have a talk with her.'

III

Myrna Harris was a pretty girl with a glorious head of red hair and a pert nose.

She was alarmed and wary, and deeply conscious of the indignity of being interviewed by the police.

'I don't know a thing about it, sir. Not a thing,' she protested. 'If I'd known what he was like I'd never have gone out with Rudi at all. Naturally, seeing as he worked in Reception here, I thought he was all right. Naturally I did. What I say is the hotel ought to be more careful when they employ people – especially foreigners. Because you never know where you are with foreigners. I suppose he might have been in with one of these gangs you read about?'

'We think,' said Craddock, 'that he was working quite on his own.'

'Fancy – and him so quiet and respectable. You'd never think. Though there have been things missed – now I come to think of it. A diamond brooch – and a little gold locket, I believe. But I never dreamed that it could have been Rudi.'

'I'm sure you didn't,' said Craddock. 'Anyone might have been taken in. You knew him fairly well?'

'I don't know that I'd say *well*.'

'But you were friendly?'

'Oh, we were friendly – that's all, just friendly. Nothing serious at all. I'm always on my guard with foreigners, anyway. They've often got a way with them, but you never know, do you? Some of those Poles during the war! And even some of the Americans! Never let on they're married men until it's too late. Rudi talked big and all that – but I always took it with a grain of salt.'

Craddock seized on the phrase.

'Talked big, did he? That's very interesting, Miss Harris. I can see you're going to be a lot of help to us. In what way did he talk big?'

'Well, about how rich his people were in Switzerland – and how important. But that didn't go with his being as short of money as he was. He always said that because of the money regulation he couldn't get money from Switzerland over here. That might be, I suppose, but his things weren't expensive. His clothes, I mean. They weren't really class. I think, too, that a lot of the stories he used to tell me were so much hot air. About climbing in the Alps, and saving people's lives on the edge of a glacier. Why, he turned quite giddy just going along the edge of Boulter's Gorge. Alps, indeed!'

'You went out with him a good deal?'

'Yes – well – yes, I did. He had awfully good manners and he knew how to – to look after a girl. The best seats at the pictures, always. And even flowers he'd buy me, sometimes. And he was just a lovely dancer – lovely.'

'Did he mention this Miss Blacklock to you at all?'

'She comes in and lunches here sometimes, doesn't she? And she's stayed here once. No, I don't think Rudi ever mentioned her. I didn't know he knew her.'

'Did he mention Chipping Cleghorn?'

He thought a faintly wary look came into Myrna Harris's eyes but he couldn't be sure.

'I don't think so . . . I think he did once ask about buses – what time they went – but I can't remember if that was Chipping Cleghorn or somewhere else. It wasn't just lately.'

He couldn't get more out of her. Rudi Scherz had seemed just as usual. She hadn't seen him the evening before. She'd no idea – no idea *at all* – she stressed the point, that Rudi Scherz was a crook.

And probably, Craddock thought, that was quite true.

CHAPTER FIVE

Miss Blacklock and Miss Bunner

Little Paddocks was very much as Detective-Inspector Craddock had imagined it to be. He noted ducks and chickens and what had been until lately an attractive herbaceous border and in which a few late Michaelmas daisies showed a last dying splash of purple beauty. The lawn and the paths showed signs of neglect.

Summing up, Detective-Inspector Craddock thought: 'Probably not much money to spend on gardeners – fond of flowers and a good eye for planning and massing a border. House needs painting. Most houses do, nowadays. Pleasant little property.'

As Craddock's car stopped before the front door, Sergeant Fletcher came round the side of the house. Sergeant Fletcher looked like a guardsman, with an erect military bearing, and was able to impart several different meanings to the one monosyllable: 'Sir.'

'So there you are, Fletcher.'

'Sir,' said Sergeant Fletcher.

'Anything to report?'

'We've finished going over the house, sir. Scherz doesn't seem to have left any fingerprints anywhere. He wore gloves, of course. No signs of any of the doors or windows being forced to effect an entrance. He seems to have come out from Medenham on the bus, arriving here at six o'clock. Side door of the house was locked at 5.30, I understand. Looks as though he must have walked in through the front door. Miss Blacklock states that that door isn't usually locked until the house is shut up for the night. The maid, on the other hand, states that the front door was locked all the afternoon – but she'd say anything: Very temperamental you'll find her. Mittel Europa refugee of some kind.'

'Difficult, is she?'

'Sir!' said Sergeant Fletcher, with intense feeling.

Craddock smiled.

Fletcher resumed his report.

'Lighting system is quite in order everywhere. We haven't spotted yet how he operated the lights. It was just the one circuit went. Drawing-room and hall. Of course, nowadays the wall brackets and lamps wouldn't all be on one fuse – but this is an old-fashioned installation and wiring. Don't see how he could have tampered with the fusebox because it's out by the scullery and he'd have had to go through the kitchen, so the maid would have seen him.'

'Unless she was in it with him?'

'That's very possible. Both foreigners – and I wouldn't trust her a yard – not a yard.'

Craddock noticed two enormous frightened black eyes peering out of a window by the front door. The face, flattened against the pane, was hardly visible.

'That her there?'

'That's right, sir.'

The face disappeared.

Craddock rang the front-door bell.

After a long wait the door was opened by a good-looking young woman with chestnut hair and a bored expression.

'Detective-Inspector Craddock,' said Craddock.

The young woman gave him a cool stare out of very attractive hazel eyes and said:

'Come in. Miss Blacklock is expecting you.'

The hall, Craddock noted, was long and narrow and seemed almost incredibly full of doors.

The young woman threw open a door on the left, and said: 'Inspector Craddock, Aunt Letty. Mitzi wouldn't go to the door. She's shut herself up in the kitchen and she's making the most marvellous moaning noises. I shouldn't think we'll get *any* lunch.'

She added in an explanatory manner to Craddock: 'She doesn't like the police,' and withdrew, shutting the door behind her.

Craddock advanced to meet the owner of Little Paddocks.

He saw a tall active-looking woman of about sixty. Her grey hair had a slight natural wave and made a distinguished setting for an intelligent, resolute face. She had keen grey eyes and a square determined chin. There was a surgical dressing on her left ear. She wore no make-up and was plainly dressed in a well-cut tweed coat and skirt and pullover. Round the neck of the latter she wore, rather unexpectedly, a set of old-fashioned cameos — a Victorian touch which seemed to hint at a sentimental streak not otherwise apparent.

Close beside her, with an eager round face and untidy hair escaping from a hairnet, was a woman of about the same age whom Craddock had no difficulty in recognizing as the 'Dora Bunner — companion' of Constable Legg's notes — to which the latter had added an off-the-record commentary of 'Scatty!'

Miss Blacklock spoke in a pleasant well-bred voice.

'Good morning, Inspector Craddock. This is my friend, Miss Bunner, who helps me run the house. Won't you sit down? You won't smoke, I suppose?'

'Not on duty, I'm afraid, Miss Blacklock.'

'What a shame!'

Craddock's eyes took in the room with a quick, practised glance. Typical Victorian double drawing-room. Two long windows in this room, built-out bay window in the other ... chairs ... sofa ... centre table with a big bowl of chrysanthemums — another bowl in window — all fresh and pleasant without much originality. The only incongruous note was a small silver vase with dead violets in it on a table near the archway into the further room. Since he could not imagine Miss Blacklock tolerating dead flowers in a room, he imagined it to be the only indication that something out of the way had occurred to distract the routine of a well-run household.

He said:

'I take it, Miss Blacklock, that this is the room in which the — incident occurred?'

'Yes.'

'And you should have seen it last night,' Miss Bunner exclaimed. 'Such a *mess*. Two little tables knocked over, and the leg off one — people barging about in the dark — and someone put down a lighted cigarette and burnt one of the best bits of furniture. People — young people especially — are so careless about these things ... Luckily none of the china got broken —'

Miss Blacklock interrupted gently but firmly:

'Dora, all these things, vexatious as they may be, are only trifles. It will be best, I think, if we just answer Inspector Craddock's questions.'

'Thank you, Miss Blacklock. I shall come to what happened last night presently. First of all I want you to tell me when you first saw the dead man — Rudi Scherz.'

'Rudi Scherz?' Miss Blacklock looked slightly surprised. 'Is that his name? Somehow, I thought . . . Oh, well, it doesn't matter. My first encounter with him was when I was in Medenham Spa for a day's shopping about — let me see, about three weeks ago. We — Miss Bunner and I — were having lunch at the Royal Spa Hotel. As we were just leaving after lunch, I heard my name spoken. It was this young man. He said: "It is Miss Blacklock, is it not?" And went on to say that perhaps I did not remember him, but that he was the son of the proprietor of the Hotel des Alpes at Montreux where my sister and I had stayed for nearly a year during the war.'

'The Hotel des Alpes, Montreux,' noted Craddock. 'And did you remember him, Miss Blacklock?'

'No, I didn't. Actually I had no recollection of ever having seen him before. These boys at hotel reception desks all look exactly alike. We had had a very pleasant time at Montreux and the proprietor there had been extremely obliging, so I tried to be as civil as possible and said I hoped he was enjoying being in England, and he said, yes, that his father had sent him over for six months to learn the hotel business. It all seemed quite natural.'

'And your next encounter?'

'About — yes, it must have been ten days ago, he suddenly turned up here. I was very surprised to see him. He apologized for troubling me, but said I was the only person he knew in England. He told me that he urgently needed money to return to Switzerland as his mother was dangerously ill.'

'But Letty didn't give it to him,' Miss Bunner put in breathlessly.

'It was a thoroughly fishy story,' said Miss Blacklock, with vigour. 'I made up my mind that he was definitely a wrong 'un. That story about wanting the money to return to Switzerland was *nonsense*. His father could easily have wired for arrangements to have been made in this country. These hotel people are all in with each other. I suspected that he'd been embezzling money or something of that

358

kind.' She paused and said dryly: 'In case you think I'm hard-hearted, I was secretary for many years to a big financier and one becomes wary about appeals for money. I know simply all the hard-luck stories there are.

'The only thing that did surprise me,' she added thoughtfully, 'was that he gave in so easily. He went away at once without any more argument. It's as though he had never expected to get the money.'

'Do you think now, looking back on it, that his coming was really by way of a pretext to spy out the land?'

Miss Blacklock nodded her head vigorously.

'That's exactly what I do think – now. He made certain remarks as I let him out – about the rooms. He said, "You have a very nice dining-room" (which of course it isn't – it's a horrid dark little room) just as an excuse to look inside. And then he sprang forward and unfastened the front door, said, "Let me." I think now he wanted to have a look at the fastening. Actually, like most people round here, we never lock the front door until it gets dark. *Anyone* could walk in.'

'And the side door? There is a side door to the garden, I understand?'

'Yes. I went out through it to shut up the ducks not long before the people arrived.'

'Was it locked when you went out?'

Miss Blacklock frowned.

'I can't remember . . . I think so. I certainly locked it when I came in.'

'That would be about quarter-past six?'

'Somewhere about then.'

'And the front door?'

'That's not usually locked until later.'

'Then Scherz could have walked in quite easily that way. Or he could have slipped in whilst you were out shutting up the ducks. He'd already spied out the lie of the land and had probably noted various places of concealment – cupboards, etc. Yes, that all seems quite clear.'

'I beg your pardon, it isn't at all clear,' said Miss Blacklock. 'Why on earth should anyone take all that elaborate trouble to come and burgle this house and stage that silly sort of hold-up?'

'Do you keep much money in the house, Miss Blacklock?'

'About five pounds in that desk there, and perhaps a pound or two in my purse.'

'Jewellery?'

'A couple of rings and brooches and the cameos I'm wearing. You must agree with me, Inspector, that the whole thing's absurd.'

'It wasn't burglary at all,' cried Miss Bunner. 'I've told you so, Letty, all along. It was *revenge*! Because you wouldn't give him that money! He deliberately shot at you – twice.'

'Ah,' said Craddock. 'We'll come now to last night. What happened exactly, Miss Blacklock? Tell me in your own words as nearly as you can remember.'

Miss Blacklock reflected a moment.

'The clock struck,' she said. 'The one on the mantelpiece. I remember saying that if anything were going to happen it would have to happen soon. And then the clock struck. We all listened to it without saying anything. It chimes, you know. It chimed the two quarters and then, quite suddenly, the lights went out.'

'What lights were on?'

'The wall brackets in here and the further room. The standard lamp and the two small reading lamps weren't on.'

'Was there a flash first, or a noise when the lights went out?'

'I don't think so.'

'I'm sure there *was* a flash,' said Dora Bunner. '*And* a crackling noise. Dangerous!'

'And then, Miss Blacklock?'

'The door opened –'

'Which door? There are two in the room.'

'Oh, this door in here. The one in the other room doesn't open. It's a dummy. The door opened and there he was – a masked man with a revolver. It just seemed too fantastic for words, but of course at the time I just thought it was a silly joke. He said something – I forget what –'

'"Hands up or I shoot!"' supplied Miss Bunner, dramatically.

'Something like that,' said Miss Blacklock, rather doubtfully.

'And you all put your hands up?'

'Oh, *yes*,' said Miss Bunner. 'We all did. I mean, it was *part* of it.'

'*I* didn't,' said Miss Blacklock, crisply. 'It seemed so utterly silly. And I was annoyed by the whole thing.'

'And then?'

'The flashlight was right in my eyes. It dazzled me. And then, quite incredibly, I heard a bullet whizz past me and hit the wall by my head. Somebody shrieked and then I felt a burning pain in my ear and heard the second report.'

'It was *terrifying*,' put in Miss Bunner.

'And what happened next, Miss Blacklock?'

'It's difficult to say — I was so staggered by the pain and the surprise. The — the figure turned away and seemed to stumble and then there was another shot and his torch went out and everybody began pushing and calling out. All banging into each other.'

'Where were you standing, Miss Blacklock?'

'She was over by the table. She'd got that vase of violets in her hand,' said Miss Bunner breathlessly.

'I was over here.' Miss Blacklock went over to the small table by the archway. 'Actually it was the cigarette-box I'd got in my hand.'

Inspector Craddock examined the wall behind her. The two bullet holes showed plainly. The bullets themselves had been extracted and had been sent for comparison with the revolver.

He said quietly:

'You had a very near escape, Miss Blacklock.'

'He *did* shoot at her,' said Miss Bunner. 'Deliberately *at* her! I saw him. He turned the flash round on everybody until he found her and then he held it right at her and just fired at *her*. He meant to kill *you*, Letty.'

'Dora dear, you've just got that into your head from mulling the whole thing over and over.'

'He shot at *you*,' repeated Dora stubbornly. 'He meant to shoot you and when he'd missed, he shot himself. I'm *certain* that's the way it was!'

'I don't think he meant to shoot himself for a minute,' said Miss Blacklock. 'He wasn't the kind of man who shoots himself.'

'You tell me, Miss Blacklock, that until the revolver was fired you thought the whole business was a joke?'

'Naturally. What else could I think it was?'

'Who do you think was the author of this joke?'

'You thought Patrick had done it at first,' Dora Bunner reminded her.

'Patrick?' asked the Inspector sharply.

'My young cousin, Patrick Simmons,' Miss Blacklock continued sharply, annoyed with her friend. 'It did occur to me when I saw this advertisement that it might be some attempt at humour on his part, but he denied it absolutely.'

'And then you were worried, Letty,' said Miss Bunner. 'You *were* worried, although you pretended not to be. And you were quite right to be worried. It said a murder is announced – and it *was* announced – *your* murder! And if the man hadn't missed, you *would* have been murdered. And then where should we all be?'

Dora Bunner was trembling as she spoke. Her face was puckered up and she looked as though she were going to cry.

Miss Blacklock patted her on the shoulder.

'It's all right, Dora dear – don't get excited. It's so bad for you. Everything's quite all right. We've had a nasty experience, but it's over now.' She added, 'You must pull yourself together for my sake, Dora. I rely on you, you know, to keep the house going. Isn't it the day for the laundry to come?'

'Oh, dear me, Letty, how *fortunate* you reminded me! I wonder if they'll return that missing pillowcase. I must make a note in the book about it. I'll go and see to it at once.'

'And take those violets away,' said Miss Blacklock. 'There's nothing I hate more than dead flowers.'

'What a pity. I picked them fresh yesterday. They haven't lasted at all – oh dear, I must have forgotten to put any water in the vase. Fancy that! I'm always forgetting things. Now I must go and see about the laundry. They might be here any moment.'

She bustled away, looking quite happy again.

'She's not very strong,' said Miss Blacklock, 'and excitements are bad for her. Is there anything more you want to know, Inspector?'

'I just want to know exactly how many people make up your household here and something about them.'

'Yes, well, in addition to myself and Dora Bunner, I have two young cousins living here at present, Patrick and Julia Simmons.'

'Cousins? Not a nephew and niece?'

'No. They call me Aunt Letty, but actually they are distant cousins. Their mother was my second cousin.'

'Have they always made their home with you?'

'Oh dear, no, only for the last two months. They lived in the South of France before the war. Patrick went into the Navy and Julia, I believe, was in one of the Ministries. She was at Llandudno. When the war was over their mother wrote and asked me if they could possibly come to me as paying guests – Julia is training as a dispenser in Milchester General Hospital, Patrick is studying for an engineering degree at Milchester University. Milchester, as you know, is only fifty minutes by bus, and I was very glad to have them here. This house is really too large for me. They pay a small sum for board and lodging and it all works out very well.' She added with a smile, 'I like having somebody young about the place.'

'Then there is a Mrs Haymes, I believe?'

'Yes. She works as an assistant gardener at Dayas Hall, Mrs Lucas's place. The cottage there is occupied by the old gardener and his wife and Mrs Lucas asked if I could billet her here. She's a very nice girl. Her husband was killed in Italy, and she has a boy of eight who is at a prep school and whom I have arranged to have here in the holidays.'

'And by way of domestic help?'

'A jobbing gardener comes in on Tuesdays and Fridays. A Mrs Huggins from the village comes up five mornings a week and I have a foreign refugee with a most unpronounceable name as a kind of lady cook help. You will find Mitzi rather difficult, I'm afraid. She has a kind of persecution mania.'

Craddock nodded. He was conscious in his own mind of yet another of Constable Legg's invaluable commentaries. Having appended the word 'Scatty' to Dora Bunner, and 'All right' to Letitia Blacklock, he had embellished Mitzi's record with the one word 'Liar'.

As though she had read his mind Miss Blacklock said:

'Please don't be too prejudiced against the poor thing because she's a liar. I do really believe that, like so many liars, there is a real substratum of truth behind her lies. I mean that though, to take an instance, her atrocity stories have grown and grown until every kind of unpleasant story that has ever appeared in print has happened to her or her relations personally, she did have a bad shock initially and did see one, at least, of her relations killed. I think a lot of these displaced persons feel, perhaps justly, that their claim to our notice

363

and sympathy lies in their atrocity value and so they exaggerate and invent.'

She added: 'Quite frankly, Mitzi is a maddening person. She exasperates and infuriates us all, she is suspicious and sulky, is perpetually having "feelings" and thinking herself insulted. But, in spite of it all, I really am sorry for her.' She smiled. 'And also, when she wants to, she can cook very nicely.'

'I'll try not to ruffle her more than I can help,' said Craddock soothingly. 'Was that Miss Julia Simmons who opened the door to me?'

'Yes. Would you like to see her now? Patrick has gone out. Phillipa Haymes you will find working at Dayas Hall.'

'Thank you, Miss Blacklock. I'd like to see Miss Simmons now if I may.'

CHAPTER SIX

Julia, Mitzi and Patrick

Julia, when she came into the room, and sat down in the chair vacated by Letitia Blacklock, had an air of composure that Craddock for some reason found annoying. She fixed a limpid gaze on him and waited for his questions.

Miss Blacklock had tactfully left the room.

'Please tell me about last night, Miss Simmons.'

'Last night?' murmured Julia with a blank stare. 'Oh, we all slept like logs. Reaction, I suppose.'

'I mean last night from six o'clock onwards.'

'Oh, I see. Well, a lot of tiresome people came –'

'They were?'

She gave him another limpid stare.

'Don't you know all this already?'

'I'm asking the questions, Miss Simmons,' said Craddock pleasantly.

'My mistake. I always find repetitions so dreary. Apparently you don't . . . Well, there was Colonel and Mrs Easterbrook, Miss Hinchliffe and Miss Murgatroyd, Mrs Swettenham and Edmund Swetten-ham, and Mrs Harmon, the Vicar's wife. They arrived in that order, and if you want to know what they said — they all said the same things in turn. "I see you've got your central heating on" and "What *lovely* chrysanthemums!"'

Craddock bit his lip. The mimicry was good.

'The exception was Mrs Harmon. She's rather a pet. She came in with her hat falling off and her shoelaces untied and she asked straight out when the murder was going to happen. It embarrassed everybody because they'd all been pretending they'd dropped in by chance. Aunt Letty said in her dry way that it was due to happen quite soon. And then that clock chimed and just as it finished the lights went out, the door was flung open and a masked figure said, "Stick 'em up, guys," or something like that. It was exactly like a bad film. Really quite ridiculous. And then he fired two shots at Aunt Letty and suddenly it wasn't ridiculous any more.'

'Where was everybody when this happened?'

'When the lights went out? Well, just standing about, you know. Mrs Harmon was sitting on the sofa — Hinch (that's Miss Hinchliffe) had taken up a manly stance in front of the fireplace.'

'You were all in this room, or the far room?'

'Mostly, I think, in this room. Patrick had gone into the other to get the sherry. I think Colonel Easterbrook went after him, but I don't really know. We were — well — as I said, just standing about.'

'Where were you yourself?'

'I think I was over by the window. Aunt Letty went to get the cigarettes.'

'On that table by the archway?'

'Yes — and then the lights went out and the bad film started.'

'The man had a powerful torch. What did he do with it?'

'Well, he shone it on us. Horribly dazzling. It just made you blink.'

'I want you to answer this very carefully, Miss Simmons. Did he hold the torch steady, or did he move it about?'

Julia considered. Her manner was now definitely less weary.

'He moved it,' she said slowly. 'Like a spotlight in a dance hall. It was full in my eyes and then it went on round the room and then the shots came. Two shots.'

'And then?'

'He whirled round – and Mitzi began to scream like a siren from somewhere and his torch went out and there was another shot. And then the door closed (it does, you know, slowly, with a whining noise – quite uncanny) and there we were all in the dark, not knowing what to do, and poor Bunny squealing like a rabbit and Mitzi going all out across the hall.'

'Would it be your opinion that the man shot himself deliberately, or do you think he stumbled and the revolver went off accidentally?'

'I haven't the faintest idea. The whole thing was so stagey. Actually I thought it was still some silly joke – until I saw the blood from Letty's ear. But even if you were actually going to fire a revolver to make the thing more real, you'd be careful to fire it well above someone's head, wouldn't you?'

'You would indeed. Do you think he could see clearly who he was firing at? I mean, was Miss Blacklock clearly outlined in the light of the torch?'

'I've no idea. I wasn't looking at her. I was looking at the man.'

'What I'm getting at is – do you think the man was deliberately aiming at her – at her in particular, I mean?'

Julia seemed a little startled by the idea.

'You mean deliberately picking on Aunt Letty? Oh, I shouldn't think so . . . After all, if he wanted to take a pot shot at Aunt Letty, there would be heaps of more suitable opportunities. There would be no point in collecting all the friends and neighbours just to make it more difficult. He could have shot her from behind a hedge in the good old Irish fashion any day of the week, and probably got away with it.'

And that, thought Craddock, was a very complete reply to Dora Bunner's suggestion of a deliberate attack on Letitia Blacklock.

He said with a sigh, 'Thank you, Miss Simmons. I'd better go and see Mitzi now.'

'Mind her fingernails,' warned Julia. 'She's a tartar!'

II

Craddock, with Fletcher in attendance, found Mitzi in the kitchen. She was rolling pastry and looked up suspiciously as he entered.

Her black hair hung over her eyes; she looked sullen, and the purple jumper and brilliant green skirt she wore were not becoming to her pasty complexion.

'What do you come in my kitchen for, Mr Policeman? You are police, yes? Always, always there is persecution – ah! I should be used to it by now. They say it is different here in England, but no, it is just the same. You come to torture me, yes, to make me say things, but I shall say *nothing*. You will tear off my fingernails, and put lighted matches on my skin – oh, yes, and worse than that. But I will not speak, do you hear? I shall say nothing – nothing at all. And you will send me away to a concentration camp, and I shall not care.'

Craddock looked at her thoughtfully, selecting what was likely to be the best method of attack. Finally he sighed and said:

'OK, then, get your hat and coat.'

'What is that you say?' Mitzi looked startled.

'Get your hat and coat and come along. I haven't got my nail-pulling apparatus and the rest of the bag of tricks with me. We keep all that down at the station. Got the handcuffs handy, Fletcher?'

'Sir!' said Sergeant Fletcher with appreciation.

'But I do not want to come,' screeched Mitzi, backing away from him.

'Then you'll answer civil questions civilly. If you like, you can have a solicitor present.'

'A lawyer? I do not like a lawyer. I do not want a lawyer.'

She put the rolling pin down, dusted her hands on a cloth and sat down.

'What do you want to know?' she asked sulkily.

'I want your account of what happened here last night.'

'You know very well what happened.'

'I want your account of it.'

'I tried to go away. Did she tell you that? When I saw that in the paper saying about murder. I wanted to go away. She would not let me. She is very hard – not at all sympathetic. She made me stay. But *I* knew – *I* knew what would happen. *I* knew I should be murdered.'

'Well, you weren't murdered, were you?'

'No,' admitted Mitzi grudgingly.

'Come now, tell me what happened.'

'I was nervous. Oh, I was nervous. All that evening. I hear things.

367

People moving about. Once I think someone is in the hall moving stealthily – but it is only that Mrs Haymes coming in through the side door (so as not to dirty the front steps, *she* says. Much *she* cares!). She is a Nazi herself, that one, with her fair hair and her blue eyes, so superior and looking at me and thinking that I – I am only dirt –'

'Never mind Mrs Haymes.'

'Who does she think *she* is? Has she had expensive university education like I have? Has she a degree in Economics? No, she is just a paid labourer. She digs and mows grass and is paid so much every Saturday. Who is she to call herself a lady?'

'Never mind Mrs Haymes, I said. Go on.'

'I take the sherry and the glasses, and the little pastries that I have made so nice into the drawing-room. Then the bell rings and I answer the door. Again and again I answer the door. It is degrading – but I do it. And then I go back into the pantry and I start to polish the silver, and I think it will be very handy, that, because if someone comes to kill me, I have there close at hand the big carving knife, all sharp.'

'Very foresighted of you.'

'And then, suddenly – I hear shots. I think: "It has come – it is happening." I run through the dining-room (the other door – it will not open). I stand a moment to listen and then there comes another shot and a big thud, out there in the hall, and I turn the door handle, but it is locked outside. I am shut in there like a rat in a trap. And I go mad with fear. I scream and I scream and I beat upon the door. And at last – at last – they turn the key and let me out. And then I bring candles, many many candles – and the lights go on, and I see blood – blood! Ach, Gott in Himmel, the blood! It is not the first time I have seen blood. My little brother – I see him killed before my eyes – I see blood in the street – people shot, dying – I –'

'Yes,' said Inspector Craddock. 'Thank you very much.'

'And now', said Mitzi dramatically, 'you can arrest me and take me to prison!'

'Not today,' said Inspector Craddock.

As Craddock and Fletcher went through the hall to the front door it was flung open and a tall handsome young man almost collided with them.

'Sleuths, as I live,' cried the young man.

'Mr Patrick Simmons?'

'Quite right, Inspector. You're the Inspector, aren't you, and the other's the Sergeant?'

'You are quite right, Mr Simmons. Can I have a word with you, please?'

'I am innocent, Inspector. I swear I am innocent.'

'Now then, Mr Simmons, don't play the fool. I've a good many other people to see and I don't want to waste time. What's this room? Can we go in here?'

'It's the so-called study — but nobody studies.'

'I was told that you were studying,' said Craddock.

'I found I couldn't concentrate on mathematics, so I came home.'

In a businesslike manner Inspector Craddock demanded full name, age, details of war service.

'And now, Mr Simmons, will you describe what happened last night?'

'We killed the fatted calf, Inspector. That is, Mitzi set her hand to making savoury pastries, Aunt Letty opened a new bottle of sherry —'

Craddock interrupted.

'A new bottle? Was there an old one?'

'Yes. Half full. But Aunt Letty didn't seem to fancy it.'

'Was she nervous, then?'

'Oh, not really. She's extremely sensible. It was old Bunny, I think, who had put the wind up her — prophesying disaster all day.'

'Miss Bunner was definitely apprehensive, then?'

'Oh, yes, she enjoyed herself thoroughly.'

'She took the advertisement seriously?'

'It scared her into fits.'

'Miss Blacklock seems to have thought, when she first read that advertisement, that you had had something to do with it. Why was that?'

'Ah, sure, I get blamed for everything round here!'

'You *didn't* have anything to do with it, did you, Mr Simmons?'

'Me? Never in the world.'

'Had you ever seen or spoken to this Rudi Scherz?'

'Never seen him in my life.'

'It was the kind of joke you might have played, though?'

'Who's been telling you that? Just because I once made Bunny an apple-pie bed – and sent Mitzi a postcard saying the Gestapo was on her track –'

'Just give me your account of what happened.'

'I'd just gone into the small drawing-room to fetch the drinks when, Hey Presto, the lights went out. I turned round and there's a fellow standing in the doorway saying, "Stick your hands up," and everybody gasping and squealing, and just when I'm thinking Can I rush him? he starts firing a revolver and then crash down he goes and his torch goes out and we're in the dark again, and Colonel Easterbrook starts shouting orders in his barrack-room voice. "Lights," he says, and will my lighter go on? No, it won't, as is the way of those cussed inventions.'

'Did it seem to you that the intruder was definitely aiming at Miss Blacklock?'

'Ah, how could I tell? I should say he just loosed off his revolver for the fun of the thing – and then found, maybe, he'd gone too far.'

'And shot himself?'

'It could be. When I saw the face of him, he looked like the kind of little pasty thief who might easily lose his nerve.'

'And you're sure you had never seen him before?'

'Never.'

'Thank you, Mr Simmons. I shall want to interview the other people who were here last night. Which would be the best order in which to take them?'

'Well, our Phillipa – Mrs Haymes – works at Dayas Hall. The gates of it are nearly opposite this gate. After that, the Swettenhams are the nearest. Anyone will tell you.'

CHAPTER SEVEN

Among Those Present

Dayas Hall had certainly suffered during the war years. Couch grass grew enthusiastically over what had once been an asparagus bed, as evidenced by a few waving tufts of asparagus foliage. Groundsel, bindweed and other garden pests showed every sign of vigorous growth.

A portion of the kitchen garden bore evidence of having been reduced to discipline and here Craddock found a sour-looking old man leaning pensively on a spade.

'It's Mrs 'Aymes you want? I couldn't say where you'd find 'er. 'As 'er own ideas, she 'as, about what she'll do. Not one to take advice. I could show her — show 'er willing — but what's the good, won't listen these young ladies won't! Think they know everything because they've put on breeches and gone for a ride on a tractor. But it's *gardening* that's needed here. And that isn't learned in a day. *Gardening*, that's what this place needs.'

'It looks as though it does,' said Craddock.

The old man chose to take this remark as an aspersion.

'Now look here, mister, what do you suppose I can do with a place this size? Three men and a boy, that's what it used to 'ave. And that's what it wants. There's not many men could put in the work on it that I do. 'Ere sometimes I am till eight o'clock at night. Eight o'clock.'

'What do you work by? An oil lamp?'

'Naterally I don't mean this time o' year. Naterally. *Summer* evenings I'm talking about.'

'Oh,' said Craddock. 'I'd better go and look for Mrs Haymes.'

The rustic displayed some interest.

'What are you wanting 'er for? Police, aren't you? She been in trouble, or is it the do there was up to Little Paddocks? Masked men bursting in and holding up a roomful of people with a revolver. An' that sort of thing wouldn't 'ave 'appened afore the war. Deserters, that's what it is. Desperate men roaming the countryside. Why don't the military round 'em up?'

'I've no idea,' said Craddock. 'I suppose this hold-up caused a lot of talk?'

'That it did. What's us coming to? That's what Ned Barker said. Comes of going to the pictures so much, he said. But Tom Riley he says it comes of letting these furriners run about loose. And depend on it, he says, that girl as cooks up there for Miss Blacklock and 'as such a nasty temper – *she's* in it, he said. She's a communist or worse, he says, and we don't like that sort 'ere. And Marlene, who's behind the bar, you understand, she will 'ave it that there must be something very valuable up at Miss Blacklock's. Not that you'd think it, she says, for I'm sure Miss Blacklock goes about as plain as plain, except for them great rows of false pearls she wears. And then she says "Supposin' as them pearls is *real*," and Florrie (what's old Bellamy's daughter) *she* says, "Nonsense," she says – "*noovo ar* – that's what they are – costume jewellery," she says. Costume jewellery – that's a fine way of labelling a string of false pearls. Roman pearls, the gentry used to call 'em once – and Parisian diamonds – my wife was a lady's maid and I know. But what does it all mean – just glass! I suppose it's "costume jewellery" that young Miss Simmons wears – gold ivy leaves and dogs and such like. 'Tisn't often you see a real bit of gold nowadays – even wedding rings they make of this grey plattinghum stuff. Shabby, I call it – for all that it costs the earth.'

Old Ashe paused for breath and then continued:

' "Miss Blacklock don't keep much money in the 'ouse, that I do know," says Jim Huggins, speaking up. He should know, for it's his wife as goes up and does for 'em at Little Paddocks, and she's a woman as knows most of what's going on. Nosey, if you take me.'

'Did he say what Mrs Huggins' view was?'

'That Mitzi's mixed up in it, that's what she thinks. Awful temper she 'as, and the airs she gives herself! Called Mrs Huggins a working woman to her face the other morning.'

Craddock stood a moment, checking over in his orderly mind the substance of the old gardener's remarks. It gave him a good cross-section of rural opinion in Chipping Cleghorn, but he didn't think there was anything to help him in his task. He turned away and the old man called after him grudgingly:

'Maybe you'd find her in the apple orchard. She's younger than I am for getting the apples down.'

And sure enough in the apple orchard Craddock found Phillipa Haymes. His first view was a pair of nice legs encased in breeches sliding easily down the trunk of a tree. Then Phillipa, her face flushed, her fair hair ruffled by the branches, stood looking at him in a startled fashion.

'Make a good Rosalind,' Craddock thought automatically, for Detective-Inspector Craddock was a Shakespeare enthusiast and had played the part of the melancholy Jaques with great success in a performance of *As You Like It* for the Police Orphanage.

A moment later he amended his view. Phillipa Haymes was too wooden for Rosalind, her fairness and her impassivitywere intensely English, but English of the twentieth rather than of the sixteenth century. Well-bred, unemotional English, without a sparkle of mischief.

'Good morning, Mrs Haymes. I'm sorry if I startled you. I'm Detective-Inspector Craddock of the Middleshire Police. I wanted to have a word with you.'

'About last night?'

'Yes.'

'Will it take long? Shall we —?'

She looked about her rather doubtfully.

Craddock indicated a fallen tree trunk.

'Rather informal,' he said pleasantly, 'but I don't want to interrupt your work longer than necessary.'

'Thank you.'

'It's just for the record. You came in from work at what time last night?'

'At about half-past five. I'd stayed about twenty minutes later in order to finish some watering in the greenhouse.'

'You came in by which door?'

'The side door. One cuts across by the ducks and the henhouse from the drive. It saves you going round, and besides it avoids dirtying up the front porch. I'm in rather a mucky state sometimes.'

'You always come in that way?'

'Yes.'

'The door was unlocked?'

'Yes. During the summer it's usually wide open. This time of the year it's shut but not locked. We all go out and in a good deal that way. I locked it when I came in.'

'Do you always do that?'

'I've been doing it for the last week. You see, it gets dark at six. Miss Blacklock goes out to shut up the ducks and the hens some time in the evening, but she very often goes out through the kitchen door.'

'And you are quite sure you did lock the side door this time?'

'I really am quite sure about that.'

'Quite so, Mrs Haymes. And what did you do when you came in?'

'Kicked off my muddy footwear and went upstairs and had a bath and changed. Then I came down and found that a kind of party was in progress. I hadn't known anything about this funny advertisement until then.'

'Now please describe just what occurred when the hold-up happened.'

'Well, the lights went out suddenly –'

'Where were you?'

'By the mantelpiece. I was searching for my lighter which I thought I had put down there. The lights went out – and everybody giggled. Then the door was flung open and this man shone a torch on us and flourished a revolver and told us to put our hands up.'

'Which you proceeded to do?'

'Well, I didn't, actually. I thought it was just fun, and I was tired and I didn't think I needed really to put them up.'

'In fact, you were bored by the whole thing?'

'I was, rather. And then the revolver went off. The shots sounded deafening and I was really frightened. The torch went whirling round and dropped and went out, and then Mitzi started screaming. It was just like a pig being killed.'

'Did you find the torch very dazzling?'

'No, not particularly. It was quite a strong one, though. It lit up Miss Bunner for a moment and she looked quite like a turnip ghost – you know, all white and staring with her mouth open and her eyes starting out of her head.'

'The man moved the torch?'

'Oh, yes, he played it all round the room.'

'As though he were looking for someone?'

'Not particularly, I should say.'

'And after that, Mrs Haymes?'

374

Phillipa Haymes frowned.

'Oh, it was all a terrible muddle and confusion. Edmund Swetten-ham and Patrick Simmons switched on their lighters and they went out into the hall and we followed, and someone opened the dining-room door – the lights hadn't fused there – and Edmund Swettenham gave Mitzi a terrific slap on the cheek and brought her out of her screaming fit, and after that it wasn't so bad.'

'You saw the body of the dead man?'

'Yes.'

'Was he known to you? Had you ever seen him before?'

'Never.'

'Have you any opinion as to whether his death was accidental, or do you think he shot himself deliberately?'

'I haven't the faintest idea.'

'You didn't see him when he came to the house previously?'

'No. I believe it was in the middle of the morning and I shouldn't have been there. I'm out all day.'

'Thank you, Mrs Haymes. One thing more. You haven't any valuable jewellery? Rings, bracelets, anything of that kind?'

Phillipa shook her head.

'My engagement ring – a couple of brooches.'

'And as far as you know there was nothing of particular value in the house?'

'No. I mean there is some quite nice silver – but nothing out of the ordinary.'

'Thank you, Mrs Haymes.'

II

As Craddock retraced his steps through the kitchen garden he came face to face with a large red-faced lady, carefully corseted.

'Good morning,' she said belligerently. 'What do you want here?'

'Mrs Lucas? I am Detective-Inspector Craddock.'

'Oh, that's who you are. I beg your pardon. I don't like strangers forcing their way into my garden wasting the gardeners' time. But I quite understand you have to do your duty.'

'Quite so.'

'May I ask if we are to expect a repetition of that outrage last night at Miss Blacklock's? Is it a gang?'

'We are satisfied, Mrs Lucas, that it was *not* the work of a gang.'

'There are far too many robberies nowadays. The police are getting slack.' Craddock did not reply. 'I suppose you've been talking to Phillipa Haymes?'

'I wanted her account as an eye-witness.'

'You couldn't have waited until one o'clock, I suppose? After all, it would be fairer to question her in *her* time, rather than in *mine* . . .'

'I'm anxious to get back to headquarters.'

'Not that one expects consideration nowadays. Or a decent day's work. On duty late, half an hour's pottering. A break for elevenses at ten o'clock. No work done at all the moment the rain starts. When you want the lawn mown there's always something wrong with the mower. And off duty five or ten minutes before the proper time.'

'I understood from Mrs Haymes that she left here at twenty minutes past five yesterday instead of five o'clock.'

'Oh, I dare say she did. Give her her due, Mrs Haymes is quite keen on her work, though there have been days when I have come out here and not been able to find her anywhere. She is a lady by birth, of course, and one feels it's one's duty to do something for these poor young war widows. Not that it isn't very inconvenient. Those long school holidays, and the arrangement is that she has extra time off then. I told her that there are really excellent camps nowadays where children can be sent and where they have a delightful time and enjoy it far more than wandering about with their parents. They need practically not come home at all in the summer holidays.'

'But Mrs Haymes didn't take kindly to that idea?'

'She's as obstinate as a mule, that girl. Just the time of year when I want the tennis court mowed and marked nearly every day. Old Ashe gets the lines crooked. But *my* convenience is never considered!'

'I presume Mrs Haymes takes a smaller salary than is usual.'

'Naturally. What else could she expect?'

'Nothing, I'm sure,' said Craddock. 'Good morning, Mrs Lucas.'

'It was dreadful,' said Mrs Swettenham happily. 'Quite – quite – dreadful, and what I say is that they ought to be far more careful what advertisements they accept at the *Gazette* office. At the time, when I read it, I thought it was very odd. I said so, didn't I, Edmund?'

'Do you remember just what you were doing when the lights went out, Mrs Swettenham?' asked the Inspector.

'How that reminds me of my old Nannie! *Where was Moses when the light went out?* The answer, of course, was "In the dark". Just like us yesterday evening. All standing about and wondering what was going to happen. And then, you know, the *thrill* when it suddenly went pitch black. And the door opening – just a dim figure standing there with a revolver and that blinding light and a menacing voice saying "Your money or your life!" Oh, I've never enjoyed anything so much. And then a minute later, of course, it was all *dreadful*. *Real* bullets, just *whistling* past our ears! It must have been just like the Commandos in the war.'

'Whereabouts were you standing or sitting at the time, Mrs Swettenham?'

'Now let me see, where was I? Who was I talking to, Edmund?'

'I really haven't the least idea, Mother.'

'Was it Miss Hinchliffe I was asking about giving the hens cod liver oil in the cold weather? Or was it Mrs Harmon – no, she'd only just arrived. I think I was just saying to Colonel Easterbrook that I thought it was really very dangerous to have an atom research station in England. It ought to be on some lonely island in case the radio-activity gets loose.'

'You don't remember if you were sitting or standing?'

'Does it really matter, Inspector? I was somewhere over by the window or near the mantelpiece, because I know I was *quite* near the clock when it struck. Such a thrilling moment! Waiting to see if anything might be going to happen.'

'You describe the light from the torch as blinding. Was it turned full on to you?'

'It was right in my eyes. I couldn't see a thing.'

'Did the man hold it still, or did he move it about, from person to person?'

'Oh, I don't really know. Which did he do, Edmund?'

'It moved rather slowly over us all, so as to see what we were all doing, I suppose, in case we should try and rush him.'

'And where exactly in the room were *you*, Mr Swettenham?'

'I'd been talking to Julia Simmons. We were both standing up in the middle of the room – the long room.'

'Was everyone in that room, or was there anyone in the far room?'

'Phillipa Haymes had moved in there, I think. She was over by that far mantelpiece. I think she was looking for something.'

'Have you any idea as to whether the third shot was suicide or an accident?'

'I've no idea at all. The man seemed to swerve round very suddenly and then crumple up and fall – but it was all very confused. You must realize that you couldn't really see anything. And then that refugee girl started yelling the place down.'

'I understand it was you who unlocked the dining-room door and let her out?'

'Yes.'

'The door was definitely locked on the outside?'

Edmund looked at him curiously.

'Certainly it was. Why, you don't imagine –'

'I just like to get my facts quite clear. Thank you, Mr Swettenham.'

IV

Inspector Craddock was forced to spend quite a long time with Colonel and Mrs Easterbrook. He had to listen to a long disquisition on the psychological aspect of the case.

'The psychological approach – that's the only thing nowadays,' the Colonel told him. 'You've got to understand your criminal. Now the whole set-up here is quite plain to a man who's had the wide experience that I have. Why does this fellow put that advert in? Psychology. He wants to advertise himself – to focus attention on himself. He's been passed over, perhaps despised as a foreigner by the other employees at the Spa Hotel. A girl has turned him down, perhaps. He wants to rivet her attention on him. Who is the idol of the cinema nowadays – the gangster – the tough guy? Very well, he will be a tough guy. Robbery with violence. A mask? A revolver? But he wants an audience – he must have an audience. So he arranges for an audience. And then, at the supreme moment, his part runs away with him – he's more than a burglar. He's a killer. He shoots – blindly –'

Inspector Craddock caught gladly at a word:

'You say "blindly", Colonel Easterbrook. You didn't think that he was firing deliberately at one particular object – at Miss Blacklock, that is to say?'

'No, no. He just loosed off, as I say, blindly. And that's what brought him to himself. The bullet hit someone – actually it was only a graze, but he didn't know that. He comes to himself with a bang. All this – this make-believe he's been indulging in – is *real*. He's shot at someone – perhaps killed someone . . . It's all up with him. And so in blind panic he turns the revolver on himself.'

Colonel Easterbrook paused, cleared his throat appreciatively and said in a satisfied voice, 'Plain as a pikestaff, that's what it is, plain as a pikestaff.'

'It really is wonderful,' said Mrs Easterbrook, 'the way you know exactly what happened, Archie.'

Her voice was warm with admiration.

Inspector Craddock thought it was wonderful, too, but he was not quite so warmly appreciative.

'Exactly where were you in the room, Colonel Easterbrook, when the actual shooting business took place?'

'I was standing with my wife – near a centre table with some flowers on it.'

'I caught hold of your arm, didn't I, Archie, when it happened? I was simply scared to death. I just had to hold on to you.'

'Poor little kitten,' said the Colonel playfully.

V

The Inspector ran Miss Hinchliffe to earth by a pigsty.

'Nice creatures, pigs,' said Miss Hinchliffe, scratching a wrinkled pink back. 'Coming on well, isn't he? Good bacon round about Christmas time. Well, what do you want to see me about? I told your people last night I hadn't the least idea who the man was. Never seen him anywhere in the neighbourhood snooping about or anything of that sort. Our Mrs Mopp says he came from one of the big hotels in Medenham Wells. Why didn't he hold up someone there if he wanted to? Get a much better haul.'

That was undeniable. Craddock proceeded with his inquiries.

'Where were you exactly when the incident took place?'

'Incident! Reminds me of my ARP days. Saw some incidents then, I can tell you. Where was I when the shooting started? That what you want to know?'

'Yes.'

'Leaning up against the mantelpiece hoping to God someone would offer me a drink soon,' replied Miss Hinchliffe promptly.

'Do you think that the shots were fired blindly, or aimed carefully at one particular person?'

'You mean aimed at Letty Blacklock? How the devil should I know? Damned hard to sort out what your impressions really were or what really happened after it's all over. All I know is the lights went out, and that torch went whirling round dazzling us all, and then the shots were fired and I thought to myself, "If that damned young fool Patrick Simmons is playing his jokes with a loaded revolver somebody will get hurt." '

'You thought it was Patrick Simmons?'

'Well, it seemed likely. Edmund Swettenham is intellectual and writes books and doesn't care for horseplay, and old Colonel Easterbrook wouldn't think that sort of thing funny. But Patrick's a wild boy. However, I apologize to him for the idea.'

'Did your friend think it might be Patrick Simmons?'

'Murgatroyd? You'd better talk to her yourself. Not that you'll get any sense out of her. She's down the orchard. I'll yell for her if you like.'

Miss Hinchliffe raised her stentorian voice in a powerful bellow:

'Hi-youp, Murgatroyd . . .'

'Coming . . .' floated back a thin cry.

'Hurry up – Polieece,' bellowed Miss Hinchliffe.

Miss Murgatroyd arrived at a brisk trot very much out of breath. Her skirt was down at the hem and her hair was escaping from an inadequate hair net. Her round, good-natured face beamed.

'Is it Scotland Yard?' she asked breathlessly. 'I'd no idea. Or I wouldn't have left the house.'

'We haven't called in Scotland Yard yet, Miss Murgatroyd. I'm Inspector Craddock from Milchester.'

'Well, that's very nice, I'm sure,' said Miss Murgatroyd vaguely. 'Have you found any clues?'

'Where were you at the time of the crime, that's what he wants to know, Murgatroyd?' said Miss Hinchliffe. She winked at Craddock.

'Oh dear,' gasped Miss Murgatroyd. 'Of course. I ought to have been prepared. *Alibis*, of course. Now, let me see, I was just with everybody else.'

'You weren't with me,' said Miss Hinchliffe.

'Oh, dear, Hinch, wasn't I? No, of course, I'd been admiring the chrysanthemums. Very poor specimens, really. And then it all happened – only I didn't really know it had happened – I mean I didn't know that anything like that had happened. I didn't imagine for a moment that it was a real revolver – and all so awkward in the dark, and that dreadful screaming. I got it all wrong, you know. I thought *she* was being murdered – I mean the refugee girl. I thought she was having her throat cut across the hall somewhere. I didn't know it was *him* – I mean, I didn't even know there was a man. It was really just a voice, you know, saying, "Put them up, please."'

' "Stick 'em up!" ' Miss Hinchliffe corrected. 'And no suggestion of "please" about it.'

'It's so terrible to think that until that girl started screaming I was actually enjoying myself. Only being in the dark was very awkward and I got a knock on my corn. Agony, it was. Is there anything more you want to know, Inspector?'

'No,' said Inspector Craddock, eyeing Miss Murgatroyd speculatively. 'I don't really think there is.'

Her friend gave a short bark of laughter.

'He's got you taped, Murgatroyd.'

'I'm sure, Hinch,' said Miss Murgatroyd, 'that I'm only too willing to say anything I can.'

'He doesn't want that,' said Miss Hinchliffe.

She looked at the Inspector. 'If you're doing this geographically I suppose you'll go to the Vicarage next. You might get something there. Mrs Harmon looks as vague as they make them – but I sometimes think she's got brains. Anyway, she's got something.'

As they watched the Inspector and Sergeant Fletcher stalk away, Amy Murgatroyd said breathlessly:

'Oh, Hinch, was I very awful? I do get so flustered!'

'Not at all,' Miss Hinchliffe smiled. 'On the whole, I should say you did very well.'

VI

Inspector Craddock looked round the big shabby room with a sense of pleasure. It reminded him a little of his own Cumberland home. Faded chintz, big shabby chairs, flowers and books strewn about, and a spaniel in a basket. Mrs Harmon, too, with her distraught air, and her general disarray and her eager face, he found sympathetic.

But she said at once, frankly, 'I shan't be any help to you. Because I shut my eyes. I hate being dazzled. And then there were shots and I screwed them up tighter than ever. And I did wish, oh, I did wish, that it had been a *quiet* murder. I don't like bangs.'

'So you didn't see anything.' The Inspector smiled at her. 'But you heard —?'

'Oh, my goodness, yes, there was plenty to *hear*. Doors opening and shutting, and people saying silly things and gasping and old Mitzi screaming like a steam engine — and poor Bunny squealing like a trapped rabbit. And everyone pushing and falling over everyone else. However, when there really didn't seem to be any more bangs coming, I opened my eyes. Everyone was out in the hall then, with candles. And then the lights came on and suddenly it was all as usual — I don't mean really as usual, but we were ourselves again, not just — people in the dark. People in the dark are quite different, aren't they?'

'I think I know what you mean, Mrs Harmon.'

Mrs Harmon smiled at him.

'And there he was,' she said. 'A rather weaselly-looking foreigner — all pink and surprised-looking — lying there dead — with a revolver beside him. It didn't — oh, it didn't seem to make *sense*, somehow.'

It did not make sense to the Inspector, either . . .

The whole business worried him.

CHAPTER EIGHT
Enter Miss Marple

Craddock laid the typed transcript of the various interviews before the Chief Constable. The latter had just finished reading the wire received from the Swiss police.

'So he had a police record all right,' said Rydesdale. 'H'm – very much as one thought.'

'Yes, sir.'

'Jewellery . . . h'm, yes . . . falsified entries . . . yes . . . cheque . . . Definitely a dishonest fellow.'

'Yes, sir – in a small way.'

'Quite so. And small things lead to large things.'

'I wonder, sir.'

The Chief Constable looked up.

'Worried, Craddock?'

'Yes, sir.'

'Why? It's a straightforward story. Or isn't it? Let's see what all these people you've been talking to have to say.'

He drew the report towards him and read it through rapidly.

'The usual thing – plenty of inconsistencies and contradictions. Different people's accounts of a few moments of stress never agree. But the main picture seems clear enough.'

'I know, sir – but it's an unsatisfactory picture. If you know what I mean – it's the wrong picture.'

'Well, let's take the facts. Rudi Scherz took the 5.20 bus from Medenham to Chipping Cleghorn arriving there at six o'clock. Evidence of conductor and two passengers. From the bus stop he walked away in the direction of Little Paddocks. He got into the house with no particular difficulty – probably through the front door. He held up the company with a revolver, he fired two shots, one of which slightly wounded Miss Blacklock, he then killed himself with a third shot, whether accidentally or deliberately there is not sufficient evidence to show. The reasons *why* he did all this are profoundly unsatisfactory, I agree. But *why* isn't really a question we are called upon to answer. A Coroner's jury may bring it in suicide – or accidental death. Whichever verdict it is, it's the same as far as we're concerned. We can write *finis*.'

'You mean we can always fall back upon Colonel Easterbrook's psychology,' said Craddock gloomily.

Rydesdale smiled.

'After all, the Colonel's probably had a good deal of experience,' he said. 'I'm pretty sick of the psychological jargon that's used so glibly about everything nowadays – but we can't really rule it out.'

'I still feel the picture's all wrong, sir.'

'Any reason to believe that somebody in the set-up at Chipping Cleghorn is lying to you?'

Craddock hesitated.

'I think the foreign girl knows more than she lets on. But that may be just prejudice on my part.'

'You think she might possibly have been in it with this fellow? Let him into the house? Put him up to it?'

'Something of the kind. I wouldn't put it past her. But that surely indicates that there really was something valuable, money or jewellery, in the house, and that doesn't seem to have been the case. Miss Blacklock negatived it quite decidedly. So did the others. That leaves us with the proposition that there was something valuable in the house that nobody knew about –'

'Quite a best-seller plot.'

'I agree it's ridiculous, sir. The only other point is Miss Bunner's certainty that it was a definite attempt by Scherz to murder Miss Blacklock.'

'Well, from what you say, and from her statement, this Miss Bunner –'

'Oh, I agree, sir,' Craddock put in quickly, 'she's an utterly unreliable witness. Highly suggestible. Anyone could put a thing into her head – but the interesting thing is that this is quite her own theory – no one *has* suggested it to her. Everybody else negatives it. For once she's *not* swimming with the tide. It definitely *is* her own impression.'

'And why should Rudi Scherz want to kill Miss Blacklock?'

'There you are, sir. I don't know. Miss Blacklock doesn't know – unless she's a much better liar than I think she is. Nobody knows. So presumably it isn't true.'

He sighed.

'Cheer up, Craddock,' said the Chief Constable. 'I'm taking you off to lunch with Sir Henry and myself. The best that the Royal Spa Hotel in Medenham Wells can provide.'

'Thank you, sir.' Craddock looked slightly surprised.

'You see, we received a letter –' He broke off as Sir Henry Clithering entered the room. 'Ah, there you are, Henry.'

Sir Henry, informal this time, said, 'Morning, Dermot.'

'I've got something for you, Henry,' said the Chief Constable.

'What's that?'

'Authentic letter from an old Pussy. Staying at the Royal Spa Hotel. Something she thinks we might like to know in connection with this Chipping Cleghorn business.'

'The old Pussies,' said Sir Henry triumphantly. 'What did I tell you? They hear everything. They see everything. And, unlike the famous adage, they speak all evil. What's this particular one got hold of?'

Rydesdale consulted the letter.

'Writes just like my old grandmother,' he complained. 'Spiky. Like a spider in the ink bottle, and all underlined. A good deal about how she hopes it won't be taking up our valuable time, but might possibly be of some slight assistance, etc, etc. What's her name? Jane – something – Murple – no, Marple, Jane Marple.'

'Ye Gods and Little Fishes,' said Sir Henry, 'can it be? George, it's my own particular, one and only, four-starred Pussy. The super Pussy of all old Pussies. And she has managed somehow to be at Medenham Wells, instead of peacefully at home at St Mary Mead, just at the right time to be mixed up in a murder. Once more a murder is announced – for the benefit and enjoyment of Miss Marple.'

'Well, Henry,' said Rydesdale sardonically, 'I'll be glad to see your paragon. Come on! We'll lunch at the Royal Spa and we'll interview the lady. Craddock, here, is looking highly sceptical.'

'Not at all, sir,' said Craddock politely.

He thought to himself that sometimes his godfather carried things a bit far.

Miss Jane Marple was very nearly, if not quite, as Craddock had pictured her. She was far more benignant than he had imagined and a good deal older. She seemed indeed very old. She had snow-white hair and a pink crinkled face and very soft innocent blue eyes, and she was heavily enmeshed in fleecy wool. Wool round her shoulders in the form of a lacy cape and wool that she was knitting and which turned out to be a baby's shawl.

She was all incoherent delight and pleasure at seeing Sir Henry, and became quite flustered when introduced to the Chief Constable and Detective-Inspector Craddock.

'But really, Sir Henry, how fortunate . . . how very fortunate. So long since I have seen you . . . Yes, my rheumatism. Very bad of late. Of course I couldn't have afforded this hotel (really fantastic what they charge nowadays) but Raymond – my nephew, Raymond West, you may remember him—?'

'Everyone knows *his* name.'

'Yes, the dear boy has been so successful with his clever books – he prides himself upon never writing about anything pleasant. The dear boy insisted on paying all my expenses. And his dear wife is making a name for herself too, as an artist. Mostly jugs of dying flowers and broken combs on windowsills. I never dare tell her, but I still admire Blair Leighton and Alma-Tadema. Oh, but I'm chattering. And the Chief Constable himself – indeed I never expected – so afraid I shall be taking up his time –'

'Completely ga-ga,' thought the disgusted Detective-Inspector Craddock.

'Come into the Manager's private room,' said Rydesdale. 'We can talk better there.'

When Miss Marple had been disentangled from her wool, and her spare knitting pins collected, she accompanied them, fluttering and protesting, to Mr Rowlandson's comfortable sitting-room.

'Now, Miss Marple, let's hear what you have to tell us,' said the Chief Constable.

Miss Marple came to the point with unexpected brevity.

'It was a cheque,' she said. 'He altered it.'

'He?'

'The young man at the desk here, the one who is supposed to

have staged that hold-up and shot himself.'

'He altered a cheque, you say?'

Miss Marple nodded.

'Yes. I have it here.' She extracted it from her bag and laid it on the table. 'It came this morning with my others from the Bank. You can see it was for seven pounds, and he altered it to seventeen. A stroke in front of the 7, and *teen* added after the word *seven* with a nice artistic little blot just blurring the whole word. Really very nicely done. A certain amount of *practice*, I should say. It's the same ink, because I wrote the cheque actually at the desk. I should think he'd done it quite often before, wouldn't you?'

'He picked the wrong person to do it to, this time,' remarked Sir Henry.

Miss Marple nodded agreement.

'Yes. I'm afraid he would never have gone very far in crime. I was quite the wrong person. Some busy young married woman, or some girl having a love affair — that's the kind who write cheques for all sorts of different sums and don't really look through their passbooks carefully. But an old woman who has to be careful of the pennies, and who has formed habits — that's quite the wrong person to choose. Seventeen pounds is a sum I *never* write a cheque for. Twenty pounds, a round sum, for the monthly wages and books. And as for my personal expenditure, I usually cash seven — it used to be five, but everything has gone up so.'

'And perhaps he reminded you of someone?' prompted Sir Henry, mischief in his eye.

Miss Marple smiled and shook her head at him.

'You are very naughty, Sir Henry. As a matter of fact he *did*. Fred Tyler, at the fish shop. Always slipped an extra 1 in the shillings column. Eating so much fish as we do nowadays, it made a long bill, and lots of people never added it up. Just ten shillings in his pocket every time, not much but enough to get himself a few neckties and take Jessie Spragge (the girl in the draper's) to the pictures. Cut a splash, that's what these young fellows want to do. Well, the very first week I was here, there was a mistake in my bill. I pointed it out to the young man and he apologized very nicely and looked very much upset, but I thought to myself then: "You've got a shifty eye, young man."

'What I mean by a shifty eye,' continued Miss Marple, 'is the kind that looks very straight at you and never looks away or blinks.'

Craddock gave a sudden movement of appreciation. He thought to himself "Jim Kelly to the life" remembering a notorious swindler he had helped to put behind bars not long ago.

'Rudi Scherz was a thoroughly unsatisfactory character,' said Rydesdale. 'He's got a police record in Switzerland, we find.'

'Made the place too hot for him, I suppose, and came over here with forged papers?' said Miss Marple.

'Exactly,' said Rydesdale.

'He was going about with the little red-haired waitress from the dining-room,' said Miss Marple. 'Fortunately I don't think her heart's affected at all. She just liked to have someone a bit "different", and he used to give her flowers and chocolates which the English boys don't do much. Has she told you all she knows?' she asked, turning suddenly to Craddock. 'Or not quite all yet?'

'I'm not absolutely sure,' said Craddock cautiously.

'I think there's a little to come,' said Miss Marple. 'She's looking very worried. Brought me kippers instead of herrings this morning, and forgot the milk jug. Usually she's an excellent waitress. Yes, she's worried. Afraid she might have to give evidence or something like that. But I expect' – her candid blue eyes swept over the manly proportions and handsome face of Detective-Inspector Craddock with truly feminine Victorian appreciation – 'that *you* will be able to persuade her to tell you all she knows.'

Detective-Inspector Craddock blushed and Sir Henry chuckled.

'It might be important,' said Miss Marple. 'He may have told her who it was.'

Rydesdale stared at her.

'Who what was?'

'I express myself so badly. Who it was who put him up to it, I mean.'

'So you think someone put him up to it?'

Miss Marple's eyes widened in surprise.

'Oh, but surely – I mean . . . Here's a personable young man – who filches a little bit here and a little bit there – alters a small cheque, perhaps helps himself to a small piece of jewellery if it's left lying around, or takes a little money from the till – all sorts of small petty thefts. Keeps himself going in ready money so that he can dress well, and take a girl about – all that sort of thing. And then suddenly he goes off with a revolver and holds up a room full of people, and shoots at someone. He'd *never* have done a thing like that — not for a moment! He wasn't that kind of person. It doesn't make *sense*.'

Craddock drew in his breath sharply. That was what Letitia Blacklock had said. What the Vicar's wife had said. What he himself felt with increasing force. *It didn't make sense.* And now Sir Henry's old Pussy was saying it, too, with complete certainty in her fluting old lady's voice.

'Perhaps you'll tell us, Miss Marple,' he said, and his voice was suddenly aggressive, 'what did happen, then?'

She turned on him in surprise.

'But how should I know what happened? There was an account in the paper — but it says so little. One can make conjectures, of course, but one has no accurate information.'

'George,' said Sir Henry, 'would it be very unorthodox if Miss Marple were allowed to read the notes of the interviews Craddock had with these people at Chipping Cleghorn?'

'It may be unorthodox,' said Rydesdale, 'but I've not got where I am by being orthodox. She can read them. I'd be curious to hear what she has to say.'

Miss Marple was all embarrassment.

'I'm afraid you've been listening to Sir Henry. Sir Henry is always too kind. He thinks too much of any little observations I may have made in the past. Really, I have no gifts — no gifts at all — except perhaps a certain knowledge of human nature. People, I find, are apt to be far too trustful. I'm afraid that I have a tendency always to believe the *worst*. Not a nice trait. But so often justified by subsequent events.'

'Read these,' said Rydesdale, thrusting the typewritten sheets upon her. 'They won't take you long. After all, these people are your kind — you must know a lot of people like them. You may be able to spot something that we haven't. The case is just going to be closed. Let's have an amateur's opinion on it before we shut up the files. I don't mind telling you that Craddock here isn't satisfied. He says, like you, that it doesn't make sense.'

There was silence whilst Miss Marple read. She put the typewritten sheets down at last.

'It's very interesting,' she said with a sigh. 'All the different things that people say – and think. The things they see – or think that they see. And all so complex, nearly all so trivial, and if one thing isn't trivial it's so hard to spot which one – like a needle in a haystack.'

Craddock felt a twinge of disappointment. Just for a moment or two, he had wondered if Sir Henry might be right about this funny old lady. She might have put her finger on something – old people were often very sharp. He'd never, for instance, been able to conceal anything from his own great-aunt Emma. She had finally told him that his nose twitched when he was about to tell a lie.

But just a few fluffy generalities, that was all that Sir Henry's famous Miss Marple could produce. He felt annoyed with her and said rather curtly:

'The truth of the matter is that the facts are indisputable. Whatever conflicting details these people give, they all saw one thing. They saw a masked man with a revolver and a torch open the door and hold them up, and whether they think he said "Stick 'em up" or "Your money or your life," or whatever phrase is associated with a hold-up in their minds, they *saw* him.'

'But surely,' said Miss Marple gently, 'they couldn't – actually – have seen anything at all . . .'

Craddock caught his breath. She'd got it! She was sharp, after all. He was testing her by that speech of his, but she hadn't fallen for it. It didn't actually make any difference to the facts, or to what happened, but she'd realized, as he'd realized, that those people who had seen a masked man holding them up couldn't really have *seen* him at all.

'If I understand rightly,' Miss Marple had a pink flush on her cheeks, her eyes were bright and pleased as a child's, 'there wasn't any light in the hall outside – and not on the landing upstairs either?'

'That's right,' said Craddock.

'And so, if a man stood in the doorway and flashed a powerful torch into the room, *nobody could see anything but the torch*, could they?'

'No, they couldn't. I tried it out.'

'And so when some of them say they saw a masked man, etc., they are really, though they don't realize it, recapitulating from what they saw *afterwards* – when the lights came on. So it really all fits in very well, doesn't it, on the assumption that Rudi Scherz was the

– I think "fall guy" is the expression I mean?'

Rydesdale stared at her in such surprise that she grew pinker still.

'I may have got the term wrong,' she murmured. 'I am not very clever about Americanisms – and I understand they change very quickly. I got it from one of Mr Dashiel Hammett's stories. (I understand from my nephew Raymond that he is considered at the top of the tree in what is called the "tough" style of literature.) A "*fall guy*", if I understand it rightly, means someone who will be blamed for a crime really committed by someone else. This Rudi Scherz seems to me exactly the right type for that. Rather stupid really, you know, but full of cupidity and probably extremely credulous.'

Rydesdale said, smiling tolerantly:

'Are you suggesting that he was persuaded by someone to go out and take pot shots at a room full of people? Rather a tall order.'

'I think he was told that it was a *joke*,' said Miss Marple. 'He was paid for doing it, of course. Paid, that is, to put an advertisement in the newspaper, to go out and spy out the household premises, and then, on the night in question, he was to go there, assume a mask and a black cloak and throw open a door, brandishing a torch, and cry "Hands up!" '

'And fire off a revolver?'

'No, no,' said Miss Marple. 'He never had a revolver.'

'But everyone says –' began Rydesdale, and stopped.

'Exactly,' said Miss Marple. 'Nobody could possibly have *seen* a revolver even if he had one. And I don't think he had. I think that after he'd called "Hands up" somebody came up quietly behind him in the darkness and fired those two shots over his shoulder. It frightened him to death. He swung round and, as he did so, that other person shot him and then let the revolver drop beside him . . .'

The three men looked at her. Sir Henry said softly:

'It's a possible theory.'

'But who is Mr X who came up in the darkness?' asked the Chief Constable.

Miss Marple coughed.

'You'll have to find out from Miss Blacklock who wanted to kill her.'

Good for old Dora Bunner, thought Craddock. Instinct against intelligence every time.

'So you think it was a deliberate attempt on Miss Blacklock's life,' asked Rydesdale.

'It certainly has that appearance,' said Miss Marple. 'Though there are one or two difficulties. But what I was really wondering about was whether there mightn't be a short cut. I've no doubt that whoever arranged this with Rudi Scherz took pains to tell him to keep his mouth shut about it, but if he talked to anybody it would probably be to that girl, Myrna Harris. And he may – he just may – have dropped some hint as to the kind of person who'd suggested the whole thing.'

'I'll see her now,' said Craddock, rising.

Miss Marple nodded.

'Yes, do, Inspector Craddock. I'll feel happier when you have. Because once she's told you anything she knows she'll be much safer.'

'Safer? . . . Yes, I see.'

He left the room. The Chief Constable said doubtfully, but tactfully:

'Well, Miss Marple, you've certainly given us something to think about.'

III

'I'm sorry about it, I am really,' said Myrna Harris. 'It's ever so nice of you not to be ratty about it. But, you see, Mum's the sort of person who fusses like anything. And it did look as though I'd – what's the phrase? – been an accessory before the fact' (the words ran glibly off her tongue). 'I mean, I was afraid you'd never take my word for it that I only thought it was just a bit of fun.'

Inspector Craddock repeated the reassuring phrase with which he had broken down Myrna's resistance.

'I will. I'll tell you *all* about it. But you will keep me out of it if you can because of Mum? It all started with Rudi breaking a date with me. We were going to the pictures that evening and then he said he wouldn't be able to come and I was a bit stand-offish with him about it – because, after all, it had been his idea and I don't fancy being stood up by a foreigner. And he said it wasn't his fault,

392

and I said that was a likely story, and then he said he'd got a bit of a lark on that night – and that he wasn't going to be out of pocket by it and how would I fancy a wrist-watch? So I said, what do you mean by a lark? And he said not to tell anyone, but there was to be a party somewhere and he was to stage a sham hold-up. Then he showed me the advertisement he'd put in and I had to laugh. He was a bit scornful about it all. Said it was kid's stuff really – but that was just like the English. They never really grew up – and, of course, I said what did he mean by talking like that about Us – and we had a bit of an argument, but we made it up. Only you can understand, can't you, sir, that when I read all about it, and it hadn't been a joke at all and Rudi had shot someone and then shot himself – why, I didn't know *what* to do. I thought if I said I knew about it beforehand, it would look as though I were in on the whole thing. But it really did seem like a joke when he told me about it. I'd have sworn he meant it that way. I didn't even know he'd got a revolver. He never said anything about taking a revolver with him.'

Craddock comforted her and then asked the most important question.

'Who did he say it was who had arranged this party?'

But there he drew a blank.

'He never said who it was that was getting him to do it. I suppose nobody was, really. It was all his own doing.'

'He didn't mention a name? Did he say *he* – or *she*?'

'He didn't say anything except that it was going to be a scream. "I shall laugh to see all their faces." That's what he said.'

He hadn't had long to laugh, Craddock thought.

IV

'It's only a theory,' said Rydesdale as they drove back to Medenham. 'Nothing to support it, nothing at all. Put it down as old maid's vapourings and let it go, eh?'

'I'd rather not do that, sir.'

'It's all very improbable. A mysterious X appearing suddenly in the darkness behind our Swiss friend. Where did he come from? Who was he? Where had he been?'

'He could have come in through the side door,' said Craddock, 'just as Scherz came. Or', he added slowly, 'he could have come from the kitchen.'

'*She* could have come from the kitchen, you mean?'

'Yes, sir, it's a possibility. I've not been satisfied about that girl all along. She strikes me as a nasty bit of goods. All that screaming and hysterics – it could have been put on. She could have worked on this young fellow, let him in at the right moment, rigged the whole thing, shot him, bolted back into the dining-room, caught up her bit of silver and her chamois and started her screaming act.'

'Against that we have the fact that – er – what's his name? – oh, yes, Edmund Swettenham definitely says the key was turned on the outside of the door, and that he turned it to release her. Any other door into that part of the house?'

'Yes, there's a door to the back stairs and kitchen just under the stairs, but it seems the handle came off three weeks ago and nobody's come to put it on yet. In the meantime you can't open the door. I'm bound to say that story seems correct. The spindle and the two handles were on a shelf outside the door in the hall and they were thickly coated with dust, but of course a professional would have ways of opening that door all right.'

'Better look up the girl's record. See if her papers are in order. But it seems to me the whole thing is very theoretical.'

Again the Chief Constable looked inquiringly at his subordinate. Craddock replied quietly:

'I know, sir, and of course if you think the case ought to be closed, it must be. But I'd appreciate it if I could work on it for just a little longer.'

Rather to his surprise the Chief Constable said quietly and approvingly:

'Good lad.'

'There's the revolver to work on. If this theory is correct, it wasn't Scherz's revolver and certainly nobody so far has been able to say that Scherz ever had a revolver.'

'It's a German make.'

'I know, sir. But this country's absolutely full of continental makes of guns. All the Americans brought them back and so did our chaps. You can't go by that.'

'True enough. Any other lines of inquiry?'

'There's got to be a motive. If there's anything in this theory at all, it means that last Friday's business wasn't a mere joke and wasn't an ordinary hold-up, it was a cold-blooded attempt at murder. *Somebody tried to murder Miss Blacklock*. Now *why*? It seems to me that if anyone knows the answer to that it must be Miss Blacklock herself.'

'I understand she rather poured cold water on that idea?'

'She poured cold water on the idea that *Rudi Scherz* wanted to murder her. And she was quite right. And there's another thing, sir.'

'Yes?'

'Somebody might try again.'

'That would certainly prove the truth of the theory,' said the Chief Constable dryly. 'By the way, look after Miss Marple, won't you?'

'Miss Marple? Why?'

'I gather she is taking up residence at the Vicarage in Chipping Cleghorn and coming into Medenham Wells twice a week for her treatments. It seems that Mrs What's-her-name is the daughter of an old friend of Miss Marple's. Good sporting instincts, that old bean. Oh, well, I suppose she hasn't much excitement in her life and sniffing round after possible murderers gives her a kick.'

'I wish she wasn't coming,' said Craddock seriously.

'Going to get under your feet?'

'Not that, sir, but she's a nice old thing. I shouldn't like anything to happen to her . . . always supposing, I mean, that there's anything *in* this theory.'

CHAPTER NINE

Concerning a Door

'I'm sorry to bother you again, Miss Blacklock –'

'Oh, it doesn't matter. I suppose, as the inquest was adjourned for a week, you're hoping to get more evidence?'

Detective-Inspector Craddock nodded.

'To begin with, Miss Blacklock, Rudi Scherz was not the son of the proprietor of the Hotel des Alpes at Montreux. He seems to have started his career as an orderly in a hospital at Berne. A good many of the patients missed small pieces of jewellery. Under another name he was a waiter at one of the small winter-sports places. His speciality there was making out duplicate bills in the restaurant with items on one that didn't appear on the other. The difference, of course, went into his pocket. After that he was in a department store in Zürich. Their losses from shoplifting were rather above the average whilst he was with them. It seems likely that the shoplifting wasn't entirely due to customers.'

'He was a picker-up of unconsidered trifles, in fact?' said Miss Blacklock dryly. 'Then I was right in thinking that I had not seen him before?'

'You were quite right – no doubt you were pointed out to him at the Royal Spa Hotel and he pretended to recognize you. The Swiss police had begun to make his own country rather too hot for him, and he came over here with a very nice set of forged papers and took a job at the Royal Spa.'

'Quite a good hunting ground,' said Miss Blacklock dryly. 'It's extremely expensive and very well-off people stay there. Some of them are careless about their bills, I expect.'

'Yes,' said Craddock. 'There were prospects of a satisfactory harvest.'

Miss Blacklock was frowning.

'I see all that,' she said. 'But why come to Chipping Cleghorn? What does he think we've got here that could possibly be better than the rich Royal Spa Hotel?'

'You stick to your statement that there's nothing of especial value in the house?'

'Of course there isn't. *I* should know. I can assure you, Inspector, we've not got an unrecognized Rembrandt or anything like that.'

'Then it looks, doesn't it, as though your friend Miss Bunner was right? He came here to attack *you*.'

('There, Letty, what did I tell you!'

'Oh, nonsense, Bunny.')

'But is it nonsense?' said Craddock. 'I think, you know, that it's true.'

Miss Blacklock stared very hard at him.

'Now, let's get this straight. You really believe that this young man came out here – having previously arranged by means of an advertisement that half the village would turn up agog at that particular time –'

'But he mayn't have meant *that* to happen,' interrupted Miss Bunner eagerly. 'It may have been just a horrid sort of warning – to *you*, Letty – that's how I read it at the time – "*A murder is announced*" – I felt in my bones that it was sinister – if it had all gone as planned he would have shot you and got away – and how would anyone have ever known who it was?'

'That's true enough,' said Miss Blacklock. 'But –'

'I knew that advertisement wasn't a joke, Letty. I said so. And look at Mitzi – *she* was frightened, too!'

'Ah,' said Craddock, 'Mitzi. I'd like to know rather more about that young woman.'

'Her permit and papers are quite in order.'

'I don't doubt that,' said Craddock dryly. 'Scherz's papers appeared to be quite correct, too.'

'But why should this Rudi Scherz want to murder me? That's what you don't attempt to explain, Inspector Craddock.'

'There may have been someone behind Scherz,' said Craddock slowly. 'Have you thought of that?'

He used the words metaphorically though it flashed across his mind that if Miss Marple's theory was correct, the words would also be true in a literal sense. In any case they made little impression on Miss Blacklock, who still looked sceptical.

'The point remains the same,' she said. 'Why on earth should anyone want to murder *me*?'

'It's the answer to that that I want *you* to give me, Miss Blacklock.'

'Well, I can't! That's flat. I've no enemies. As far as I'm aware I've always lived on perfectly good terms with my neighbours. I don't know any guilty secrets about anyone. The whole idea is ridiculous! And if what you're hinting is that Mitzi has something to do with this, that's absurd, too. As Miss Bunner has just told you, she was frightened to death when she saw that advertisement in the *Gazette*. She actually wanted to pack up and leave the house then and there.'

'That may have been a clever move on her part. She may have known you'd press her to stay.'

'Of course, if you've made up your mind about it, you'll find an answer to everything. But I can assure you that if Mitzi had taken an unreasoning dislike to me, she might conceivably poison my food, but I'm sure she wouldn't go in for all this elaborate rigmarole.

'The whole idea's absurd. I believe you police have got an anti-foreigner complex. Mitzi may be a liar but she's *not* a cold-blooded murderer. Go and bully her if you must. But when she's departed in a whirl of indignation, or shut herself up howling in her room, I've a good mind to make *you* cook the dinner. Mrs Harmon is bringing some old lady who is staying with her to tea this afternoon and I wanted Mitzi to make some little cakes – but I suppose you'll upset her completely. Can't you *possibly* go and suspect somebody else?'

II

Craddock went out to the kitchen. He asked Mitzi questions that he had asked her before and received the same answers.

Yes, she had locked the front door soon after four o'clock. No, she did not always do so, but that afternoon she had been nervous because of 'that dreadful advertisement'. It was no good locking the side door because Miss Blacklock and Miss Bunner went out that way to shut up the ducks and feed the chickens and Mrs Haymes usually came in that way from work.

'Mrs Haymes says she locked the door when she came in at 5.30.'

'Ah, and you believe her – oh, yes, you believe her . . .'

'Do you think we shouldn't believe her?'

'What does it matter what I think? You will not believe *me*.'

'Supposing you give us a chance. You think Mrs Haymes didn't lock that door?'

'I thinking she was very careful not to lock it.'

'What do you mean by that?' asked Craddock.

'That young man, he does not work alone. No, he knows *where* to come, he knows that *when* he comes a door will be left open for him – oh, very conveniently open!'

'What are you trying to say?'

'What is the use of what I say? You will not listen. You say I am a poor refugee girl who tells lies. You say that a fair-haired English lady, oh, no, *she* does not tell lies – she is so British – so honest. So you believe her and not me. But I could tell you. Oh, yes, I could tell you!'

She banged down a saucepan on the stove.

Craddock was in two minds whether to take notice of what might be only a stream of spite.

'We note everything we are told,' he said.

'I shall not tell you anything at all. Why should I? You are all alike. You persecute and despise poor refugees. If I say to you that when, a week before, that young man come to ask Miss Blacklock for money and she sends him away, as you say, with a flea in the ear – if I tell you that after that I hear him talking with Mrs Haymes – yes, out there in the summerhouse – all you say is that I make it up!'

And so you probably are making it up, thought Craddock. But he said aloud:

'You couldn't hear what was said out in the summerhouse.'

'There you are wrong,' screamed Mitzi triumphantly. 'I go out to get nettles – it makes very nice vegetables, nettles. They do not think so, but I cook it and not tell them. And I hear them talking in there. He say to her "But where can I hide?" And she say "I will show you" – and then she say, "At a quarter-past six," and I think, "Ach so! That is how you behave, my fine lady! After you come back from work, you go out to meet a man. You bring him into the house." Miss Blacklock, I think, she will not like that. She will turn you out. I will watch, I think, and listen and then I will tell Miss Blacklock. But I understand now I was wrong. It was not love she planned with him, it was to rob and to murder. But you will say I make all this up. Wicked Mitzi, you will say. I will take her to prison.'

Craddock wondered. She might be making it up. But possibly she might not. He asked cautiously:

'You are sure it was this Rudi Scherz she was talking to?'

'Of course I am sure. He just leave and I see him go from the drive across to the summerhouse. And presently,' said Mitzi defiantly, 'I go out to see if there are any nice young green nettles.'

Would there, the Inspector wondered, be any nice young green nettles in October? But he appreciated that Mitzi had had to produce a hurried reason for what had undoubtedly been nothing more than plain snooping.

'You didn't hear any more than what you have told me?'

Mitzi looked aggrieved.

'That Miss Bunner, the one with the long nose, she call and call me. Mitzi! Mitzi! So I have to go. Oh, she is irritating. Always interfering. Says she will teach me to cook. *Her* cooking! It tastes, yes, everything she does, of water, water, *water*!'

'Why didn't you tell me this the other day?' asked Craddock sternly.

'Because I did not remember – I did not think . . . Only afterwards do I say to myself, it was planned then – planned with *her*.'

'You are quite sure it was Mrs Haymes?'

'Oh, yes, I am sure. Oh, yes, I am very sure. She is a thief, that Mrs Haymes. A thief and the associate of thieves. What she gets for working in the garden, it is not enough for such a fine lady, no. She has to rob Miss Blacklock who has been kind to her. Oh, she is bad, bad, bad, that one!'

'Supposing,' said the Inspector, watching her closely, 'that someone was to say that *you* had been seen talking to Rudi Scherz?'

The suggestion had less effect than he had hoped for. Mitzi merely snorted and tossed her head.

'If anyone say they see me talking to him, that is lies, lies, lies, lies,' she said contemptuously. 'To tell lies about anyone, that is easy, but in England you have to prove them true. Miss Blacklock tell me that, and it is true, is it not? I do not speak with murderers and thieves. And no English policeman shall say I do. And how can I do cooking for lunch if you are here, talk, talk, talk? Go out of my kitchens, please. I want now to make a very careful sauce.'

Craddock went obediently. He was a little shaken in his suspicions of Mitzi. Her story about Phillipa Haymes had been told with great conviction. Mitzi might be a liar (he thought she was), but he fancied that there might be some substratum of truth in this particular tale. He resolved to speak to Phillipa on the subject. She had seemed to him when he questioned her a quiet, well-bred young woman. He had had no suspicion of her.

Crossing the hall, in his abstraction, he tried to open the wrong door. Miss Bunner, descending the staircase, hastily put him right.

'Not that door,' she said. 'It doesn't open. The next one to the left. Very confusing, isn't it? So many doors.'

'There are a good many,' said Craddock, looking up and down the narrow hall.

Miss Bunner amiably enumerated them for him.

'First the door to the cloakroom, and then the cloaks-cupboard door and then the dining-room – that's on that side. And on this side, the dummy door that you were trying to get through and then there's the drawing-room door proper, and then the china cupboard and the door of the little flower room, and at the end the side door. Most confusing. Especially these two being so near together. I've often tried the wrong one by mistake. We used to have the hall table against it, as a matter of fact, but then we moved it along against the wall there.'

Craddock had noted, almost mechanically, a thin line horizontally across the panels of the door he had been trying to open. He realized now it was the mark where the table had been. Something stirred vaguely in his mind as he asked, 'Moved? How long ago?'

In questioning Dora Bunner there was fortunately no need to give a reason for any question. Any query on any subject seemed perfectly natural to the garrulous Miss Bunner who delighted in the giving of information, however trivial.

'Now let me see, really quite recently – ten days or a fortnight ago.'

'Why was it moved?'

'I really can't remember. Something to do with the flowers. I think Phillipa did a big vase – she arranges flowers quite beautifully – all autumn colouring and twigs and branches, and it was so big it caught your hair as you went past, and so Phillipa said, "Why not move the table along and, anyway, the flowers would look much better against the bare wall than against the panels of the door." Only we had to take down "Wellington at Waterloo". Not a print I'm really very fond of. We put it under the stairs.'

'It's not really a dummy, then?' Craddock asked, looking at the door.

'Oh, no, it's a *real* door, if that's what you mean. It's the door of the small drawing-room, but when the rooms were thrown into one, one didn't need two doors, so this one was fastened up.'

'Fastened up?' Craddock tried it again, gently. 'You mean it's nailed up? Or just locked?'

'Oh, locked, I think, and bolted too.'

He saw the bolt at the top and tried it. The bolt slid back easily – too easily . . .

'When was it last open?' he asked Miss Bunner.

'Oh, years and years ago, I imagine. It's never been opened since I've been here, I know that.'

'You don't know where the key is?'

'There are a lot of keys in the hall drawer. It's probably among those.'

Craddock followed her and looked at a rusty assortment of old keys pushed far back in the drawer. He scanned them and selected one that looked different from the rest and went back to the door. The key fitted and turned easily. He pushed and the door slid open noiselessly.

'Oh, do be careful,' cried Miss Bunner. 'There may be something resting against it inside. We never open it.'

'Don't you?' said the Inspector.

His face now was grim. He said with emphasis:

'This door's been opened quite recently, Miss Bunner. The lock's been oiled and the hinges.'

She stared at him, her foolish face agape.

'But who could have done that?' she asked.

'That's what I mean to find out,' said Craddock grimly. He thought: 'X from outside? No – X was here – in this house – X was in the drawing-room that night . . .'

CHAPTER TEN

Pip and Emma

Miss Blacklock listened to him this time with more attention. She was an intelligent woman, as he had known, and she grasped the implications of what he had to tell her.

'Yes,' she said quietly. 'That does alter things . . . No one had any right to meddle with that door. Nobody *has* meddled with it to my knowledge.'

'You see what it means,' the Inspector urged. 'When the lights went out, *anybody in this room the other night* could have slipped out of that door, come up behind Rudi Scherz and fired at you.'

'Without being seen or heard or noticed?'

'Without being seen or heard or noticed. Remember when the lights went out people moved, exclaimed, bumped into each other. And after that all that could be seen was the blinding light of the electric torch.'

Miss Blacklock said slowly, 'And you believe that one of those people – one of my nice commonplace neighbours – slipped out and tried to murder me? *Me*? But *why*? For goodness' sake, why?'

'I've a feeling that you *must* know the answer to that question, Miss Blacklock.'

'But I don't, Inspector. I can assure you, I don't.'

'Well, let's make a start. Who gets your money if you were to die?'

Miss Blacklock said rather reluctantly:

'Patrick and Julia. I've left the furniture in this house and a small annuity to Bunny. Really, I've not much to leave. I had holdings in German and Italian securities which became worthless, and what with taxation, and the lower percentages that are now paid on invested capital, I can assure you I'm not worth murdering – I put most of my money into an annuity about a year ago.'

'Still, you *have* some income, Miss Blacklock, and your nephew and niece would come into it.'

'And so Patrick and Julia would plan to murder me? I simply don't believe it. They're not desperately hard up or anything like that.'

'Do you know that for a fact?'

'No. I suppose I only know it from what they've told me . . . But I really refuse to suspect them. *Some* day I *might* be worth murdering, but not now.'

'What do you mean by some day you might be worth murdering, Miss Blacklock?' Inspector Craddock pounced on the statement.

'Simply that one day – possibly quite soon – I *may* be a very rich woman.'

'That sounds interesting. Will you explain?'

'Certainly. You may not know it, but for more than twenty years I was secretary to and closely associated with Randall Goedler.'

Craddock was interested. Randall Goedler had been a big name in the world of finance. His daring speculations and the rather theatrical publicity with which he surrounded himself had made him a personality not quickly forgotten. He had died, if Craddock remembered rightly, in 1937 or 1938.

'He's rather before your time, I expect,' said Miss Blacklock. 'But you've probably heard of him.'

'Oh, yes. He was a millionaire, wasn't he?'

'Oh, several times over – though his finances fluctuated. He always risked most of what he made on some new *coup*.'

She spoke with a certain animation, her eyes brightened by memory.

'Anyway, he died a very rich man. He had no children. He left his fortune in trust for his wife during her lifetime and after her death to me absolutely.'

A vague memory stirred in the Inspector's mind.

IMMENSE FORTUNE TO COME TO FAITHFUL SECRETARY – something of that kind.

'For the last twelve years or so,' said Miss Blacklock with a slight twinkle, '*I've* had an excellent motive for murdering Mrs Goedler – but that doesn't help you, does it?'

'Did – excuse me for asking this – did Mrs Goedler resent her husband's disposition of his fortune?'

Miss Blacklock was now looking frankly amused.

'You needn't be so very discreet. What you really mean is, was I Randall Goedler's mistress? No, I wasn't. I don't think Randall ever gave me a sentimental thought, and I certainly didn't give him one. He was in love with Belle (his wife), and remained in love with her until he died. I think in all probability it was gratitude on his part that prompted his making his will. You see, Inspector, in the very early days, when Randall was still on an insecure footing, he came very near to disaster. It was a question of just a few thousands of actual cash. It was a big *coup*, and a very exciting one; daring, as all his schemes were; but he just hadn't got that little bit of cash to tide him over. I came to the rescue. I had a little money of my own. I believed in Randall. I sold every penny I had out and gave it to him. It did the trick. A week later he was an immensely wealthy man.

'After that, he treated me more or less as a junior partner. Oh!

they were exciting days.' She sighed. 'I enjoyed it all thoroughly. Then my father died, and my only sister was left a hopeless invalid. I had to give it all up and go and look after her. Randall died a couple of years later. I had made quite a lot of money during our association and I didn't really expect him to leave me anything, but I was very touched, yes, and very proud to find that if Belle predeceased me (and she was one of those delicate creatures whom everyone always says won't live long) I was to inherit his entire fortune. I think really the poor man didn't know who to leave it to. Belle's a dear, and she was delighted about it. She's really a very sweet person. She lives up in Scotland. I haven't seen her for years – we just write at Christmas. You see, I went with my sister to a sanatorium in Switzerland just before the war. She died of consumption out there.'

She was silent for a moment or two, then said:

'I only came back to England just over a year ago.'

'You said you might be a rich woman very soon . . . How soon?'

'I heard from the nurse attendant who looks after Belle Goedler that Belle is sinking rapidly. It may be – only a few weeks.'

She added sadly:

'The money won't mean much to me now. I've got quite enough for my rather simple needs. Once I should have enjoyed playing the markets again – but now . . . Oh, well, one grows old. Still, you do see, Inspector, don't you, that if Patrick and Julia wanted to kill me for a financial reason they'd be crazy not to wait for another few weeks.'

'Yes, Miss Blacklock, but what happens if you should predecease Mrs Goedler? Who does the money go to then?'

'D'you know, I've never really thought. Pip and Emma, I suppose . . .'

Craddock stared and Miss Blacklock smiled.

'Does that sound rather crazy? I believe, if I predecease Belle, the money would go to the legal offspring – or whatever the term is – of Randall's only sister, Sonia. Randall had quarrelled with his sister. She married a man whom he considered a crook and worse.'

'And was he a crook?'

'Oh, definitely, I should say. But, I believe, a very attractive person to women. He was a Greek or a Romanian or something – what was his name now? – Stamfordis, Dmitri Stamfordis.'

405

'Randall Goedler cut his sister out of his will when she married this man?'

'Oh, Sonia was a very wealthy woman in her own right. Randall had already settled packets of money on her, as far as possible in a way so that her husband couldn't touch it. But I believe that when the lawyers urged him to put in someone in case I predeceased Belle, he reluctantly put down Sonia's offspring, simply because he couldn't think of anyone else and he wasn't the sort of man to leave money to charities.'

'And there were children of the marriage?'

'Well, there are Pip and Emma.' She laughed. 'I know it sounds ridiculous. All I know is that Sonia wrote once to Belle after her marriage, telling her to tell Randall that she was extremely happy and that she had just had twins and was calling them Pip and Emma. As far as I know she never wrote again. But Belle, of course, may be able to tell you more.'

Miss Blacklock had been amused by her own recital. The Inspector did not look amused.

'It comes to this,' he said. 'If you had been killed the other night, there are presumably at least two people in the world who would have come into a very large fortune. You are wrong, Miss Blacklock, when you say that there is no one who has a motive for desiring your death. There are two people, at least, who are vitally interested. How old would this brother and sister be?'

Miss Blacklock frowned.

'Let me see . . . 1922 . . . no – it's difficult to remember . . . I suppose about twenty-five or twenty-six.' Her face had sobered. 'But you surely don't think –?'

'I think somebody shot at you with the intent to kill you. I think it possible that that same person or persons might try again. I would like you, if you will, to be very *very* careful, Miss Blacklock. One murder has been arranged and did not come off. I think it possible that another murder may be arranged very soon.'

Phillipa Haymes straightened her back and pushed back a tendril of hair from her damp forehead. She was cleaning a flower border.

'Yes, Inspector?'

She looked at him inquiringly. In return he gave her a rather closer scrutiny than he had done before. Yes, a good-looking girl, a very English type with her pale ash-blonde hair and her rather long face. An obstinate chin and mouth. Something of repression — of tautness about her. The eyes were blue, very steady in their glance, and told you nothing at all. The sort of girl, he thought, who would keep a secret well.

'I'm sorry always to bother you when you're at work, Mrs Haymes,' he said, 'but I didn't want to wait until you came back for lunch. Besides, I thought it might be easier to talk to you here, away from Little Paddocks.'

'Yes, Inspector?'

No emotion and little interest in the voice. But was there a note of wariness — or did he imagine it?

'A certain statement has been made to me this morning. This statement concerns you.'

Phillipa raised her eyebrows very slightly.

'You told me, Mrs Haymes, that this man, Rudi Scherz, was quite unknown to you?'

'Yes.'

'That when you saw him there, dead, it was the first time you had set eyes on him. Is that so?'

'Certainly. I had never seen him before.'

'You did not, for instance, have a conversation with him in the summerhouse of Little Paddocks?'

'In the *summer*house?'

He was almost sure he caught a note of fear in her voice.

'Yes, Mrs Haymes.'

'*Who* says so?'

'I am told that you had a conversation with this man, Rudi Scherz, and that he asked you where he could hide and you replied that you would show him, and that a time, a quarter-past six, was definitely mentioned. It would be a quarter-past six, roughly, when Scherz would get here from the bus stop on the evening of the hold-up.'

There was a moment's silence. Then Phillipa gave a short scornful laugh. She looked amused.

'I don't know who told you that,' she said. 'At least I can guess. It's a very silly, clumsy story — spiteful, of course. For some reason Mitzi dislikes me even more than she dislikes the rest of us.'

'You deny it?'

'Of course it's not true . . . I never met or saw Rudi Scherz in my life, and I was nowhere near the house that morning. I was over here, working.'

Inspector Craddock said very gently:

'Which morning?'

There was a momentary pause. Her eyelids flickered.

'Every morning. I'm here every morning. I don't get away until one o'clock.'

She added scornfully:

'It's no good listening to what Mitzi tells you. She tells lies all the time.'

'And that's that,' said Craddock when he was walking away with Sergeant Fletcher. 'Two young women whose stories flatly contradict each other. Which one am I to believe?'

'Everyone seems to agree that this foreign girl tells whoppers,' said Fletcher. 'It's been my experience in dealing with aliens that lying comes more easy than truth-telling. Seems to be clear she's got a spite against this Mrs Haymes.'

'So, if you were me, you'd believe Mrs Haymes?'

'Unless you've got reason to think otherwise, sir.'

And Craddock hadn't, not really — only the remembrance of a pair of over-steady blue eyes and the glib enunciation of the words *that morning*. For to the best of his recollection he hadn't said whether the interview in the summerhouse had taken place in the morning or the afternoon.

Still, Miss Blacklock or, if not Miss Blacklock, certainly Miss Bunner might have mentioned the visit of the young foreigner who had come to cadge his fare back to Switzerland. And Phillipa Haymes might have therefore assumed that the conversation was supposed to have taken place on that particular morning.

But Craddock still thought that there had been a note of fear in her voice as she asked:

'In the *summer*house?'

He decided to keep an open mind on the subject.

III

It was very pleasant in the Vicarage garden. One of those sudden spells of autumn warmth had descended upon England. Inspector Craddock could never remember if it was St Martin's or St Luke's Summer, but he knew that it was very pleasant – and also very enervating. He sat in a deck chair provided for him by an energetic Bunch, just on her way to a Mothers' Meeting, and, well protected with shawls and a large rug round her knees, Miss Marple sat knitting beside him. The sunshine, the peace, the steady click of Miss Marple's knitting needles, all combined to produce a soporific feeling in the Inspector. And yet, at the same time, there was a nightmarish feeling at the back of his mind. It was like a familiar dream where an undertone of menace grows and finally turns Ease into Terror . . .

He said abruptly, 'You oughtn't to be here.'

Miss Marple's needles stopped clicking for a moment. Her placid china-blue eyes regarded him thoughtfully.

She said, 'I know what you mean. You're a very conscientious boy. But it's perfectly all right. Bunch's father (he was vicar of our parish, a very fine scholar) and her mother (who is a most remarkable woman – real spiritual power) are very old friends of mine. It's the most natural thing in the world that when I'm at Medenham I should come on here to stay with Bunch for a little.'

'Oh, perhaps,' said Craddock. 'But – but don't snoop around . . . I've a feeling – I have really – that it isn't *safe*.'

Miss Marple smiled a little.

'But I'm afraid,' she said, 'that we old women always do snoop. It would be very odd and much more noticeable if I didn't. Questions about mutual friends in different parts of the world and whether they remember so and so, and do they remember who it was that Lady Somebody's daughter married? All that helps, doesn't it?'

'Helps?' said the Inspector, rather stupidly.

'Helps to find out if people are who they say they are,' said Miss Marple.

She went on:

'Because that's what's worrying you, isn't it? And that's really the particular way the world has changed since the war. Take this place, Chipping Cleghorn, for instance. It's very much like St Mary Mead where I live. Fifteen years ago one *knew* who everybody was. The Bantrys in the big house – and the Hartnells and the Price Ridleys and the Weatherbys ... They were people whose fathers and mothers and grandfathers and grandmothers, or whose aunts and uncles, had lived there before them. If somebody new came to live there, they brought letters of introduction, or they'd been in the same regiment or served on the same ship as someone there already. If anybody new – really new – really a stranger – came, well, they stuck out – everybody wondered about them and didn't rest till they found out.'

She nodded her head gently.

'But it's not like that any more. Every village and small country place is full of people who've just come and settled there without any ties to bring them. The big houses have been sold, and the cottages have been converted and changed. And people just come – and all you know about them is what they say of themselves. They've come, you see, from all over the world. People from India and Hong Kong and China, and people who used to live in France and Italy in little cheap places and odd islands. And people who've made a little money and can afford to retire. But nobody *knows* any more who anyone is. You can have Benares brassware in your house and talk about *tiffin* and *chota Hazri* – and you can have pictures of Taormina and talk about the English church and the library – like Miss Hinchliffe and Miss Murgatroyd. You can come from the South of France, or have spent your life in the East. People take you at your own valuation. They don't wait to call until they've had a letter from a friend saying that the So-and-So's are delightful people and she's known them all their lives.'

And that, thought Craddock, was exactly what *was* oppressing him. He didn't *know*. They were just faces and personalities and they were backed up by ration books and identity cards – nice neat identity cards with numbers on them, without photographs or fingerprints. Anybody who took the trouble could have a suitable identity card – and partly because of that, the subtler links that had held together English social rural life had fallen apart. In a town nobody expected to know his neighbour. In the country now nobody knew his neighbour either, though possibly he still thought he did . . .

Because of the oiled door, Craddock knew that there had been somebody in Letitia Blacklock's drawing-room who was not the pleasant friendly country neighbour he or she pretended to be . . .

And because of that he was afraid for Miss Marple who was frail and old and who noticed things . . .

He said: 'We can, to a certain extent, check up on these people . . .' But he knew that that wasn't so easy. India and China and Hong Kong and the South of France . . . It wasn't as easy as it would have been fifteen years ago. There were people, as he knew only too well, who were going about the country with borrowed identities — borrowed from people who had met sudden death by 'incidents' in the cities. There were organizations who bought up identities, who faked identity and ration cards — there were a hundred small rackets springing into being. You *could* check up — but it would take time — and time was what he hadn't got, because Randall Goedler's widow was very near death.

It was then that, worried and tired, lulled by the sunshine, he told Miss Marple about Randall Goedler and about Pip and Emma.

'Just a couple of names,' he said. 'Nicknames at that! They mayn't exist. They may be respectable citizens living in Europe somewhere. On the other hand, one, or both, of them may be here in Chipping Cleghorn.'

Twenty-five years old approximately — Who filled that description? He said, thinking aloud:

'That nephew and niece of hers — or cousins or whatever they are . . . I wonder when she saw them last —'

Miss Marple said gently: 'I'll find out for you, shall I?'

'Now, please, Miss Marple, don't —'

'It will be quite simple, Inspector, you really need not worry. And it won't be noticeable if I do it, because, you see, it won't be official. If there is anything wrong you don't want to put them on their guard.'

Pip and Emma, thought Craddock, Pip and Emma? He was getting obsessed by Pip and Emma. That attractive dare-devil young man, the good-looking girl with the cool stare . . .

He said: 'I may find out more about them in the next forty-eight hours. I'm going up to Scotland. Mrs Goedler, if she's able to talk,

411

may know a good deal more about them.'

'I think that's a very wise move.' Miss Marple hesitated. 'I hope', she murmured, 'that you have warned Miss Blacklock to be careful?'

'I've warned her, yes. And I shall leave a man here to keep an unobtrusive eye on things.'

He avoided Miss Marple's eye which said plainly enough that a policeman keeping an eye on things would be little good if the danger was in the family circle . . .

'And remember,' said Craddock, looking squarely at her, 'I've warned *you*.'

'I assure you, Inspector,' said Miss Marple, 'that I can take care of myself.'

CHAPTER ELEVEN

Miss Marple Comes to Tea

If Letitia Blacklock seemed slightly absentminded when Mrs Harmon came to tea and brought a guest who was staying with her, Miss Marple, the guest in question, was hardly likely to notice the fact since it was the first time she had met her.

The old lady was very charming in her gentle gossipy fashion. She revealed herself almost at once to be one of those old ladies who have a constant preoccupation with burglars.

'They can get in anywhere, my dear,' she assured her hostess, 'absolutely *anywhere* nowadays. So many new American methods. I myself pin my faith to a very old-fashioned device. *A cabin hook and eye*. They can pick locks and draw back bolts but a brass hook and eye defeats them. Have you ever tried that?'

'I'm afraid we're not very good at bolts and bars,' said Miss Blacklock cheerfully. 'There's really nothing much to burgle.'

'A chain on the front door,' Miss Marple advised. 'Then the maid need only open it a crack and see who is there and they can't force their way in.'

'I expect Mitzi, our Mittel European, would love that.'

'The hold-up you had must have been very, very frightening,' said Miss Marple. 'Bunch has been telling me all about it.'

'I was scared stiff,' said Bunch.

'It was an alarming experience,' admitted Miss Blacklock.

'It really seems like Providence that the man tripped himself up and shot himself. These burglars are so *violent* nowadays. How did he get in?'

'Well, I'm afraid we don't lock our doors much.'

'Oh, Letty,' exclaimed Miss Bunner. 'I forgot to tell you the Inspector was most peculiar this morning. He insisted on opening the second door – you know – the one that's never been opened – the one over there. He hunted for the key and everything and said the door had been oiled. But I can't see why because –'

Too late she got Miss Blacklock's signal to be quiet, and paused open-mouthed.

'Oh, Lotty, I'm so – sorry – I mean, oh, I *do* beg your pardon, Letty – oh dear, how stupid I am.'

'It doesn't matter,' said Miss Blacklock, but she was annoyed. 'Only I don't think Inspector Craddock wants that talked about. I didn't know you had been there when he was experimenting, Dora. You do understand, don't you, Mrs Harmon?'

'Oh, yes,' said Bunch. 'We won't breathe a word, will we, Aunt Jane? But I wonder *why* he –'

She relapsed into thought. Miss Bunner fidgeted and looked miserable, bursting out at last: 'I always say the wrong thing – Oh dear, I'm nothing but a trial to you, Letty.'

Miss Blacklock said quickly, 'You're my great comfort, Dora. And anyway in a small place like Chipping Cleghorn, there aren't really any secrets.'

'Now that is very true,' said Miss Marple. 'I'm afraid, you know, that things do get round in the most extraordinary way. Servants, of course, and yet it can't only be that, because one has so few servants nowadays. Still, there are the daily women and perhaps they are worse, because they go to everybody in turn and pass the news round.'

'Oh!' said Bunch Harmon suddenly. 'I've got it! Of course, if that door could open too, someone might have gone out of here in the dark and done the hold-up – only of course they didn't – because it was the man from the Royal Spa Hotel. Or wasn't it? . . . No, I don't see after all . . .' She frowned.

'Did it all happen in this room then?' asked Miss Marple, adding apologetically: 'I'm afraid you must think me sadly *curious*, Miss Blacklock – but it really is so very exciting – just like something one reads about in the paper – and actually to have happened to someone one knows . . . I'm just longing to hear all about it and to picture it all, if you know what I mean –'

Immediately Miss Marple received a confused and voluble account from Bunch and Miss Bunner – with occasional emendations and corrections from Miss Blacklock.

In the middle of it Patrick came in and good-naturedly entered into the spirit of the recital – going so far as to enact himself the part of Rudi Scherz.

'And Aunt Letty was there – in the corner by the archway . . . Go and stand there, Aunt Letty.'

Miss Blacklock obeyed, and then Miss Marple was shown the actual bullet holes.

'What a marvellous – what a providential escape,' she gasped.

'I was just going to offer my guests cigarettes –' Miss Blacklock indicated the big silver box on the table.

'People are so careless when they smoke,' said Miss Bunner disapprovingly. 'Nobody really respects good furniture as they used to do. Look at the horrid burn somebody made on this beautiful table by putting a cigarette down on it. *Disgraceful.*'

Miss Blacklock sighed.

'Sometimes, I'm afraid, one thinks too much of one's possessions.'

'But it's such a lovely table, Letty.'

Miss Bunner loved her friend's possessions with as much fervour as though they had been her own. Bunch Harmon had always thought it was a very endearing trait in her. She showed no sign of envy.

'It is a lovely table,' said Miss Marple politely. 'And what a very pretty china lamp on it.'

Again it was Miss Bunner who accepted the compliment as though she and not Miss Blacklock was the owner of the lamp.

'Isn't it delightful? Dresden. There is a pair of them. The other's in the spare room, I think.'

'You know where everything in this house is, Dora – or you think you do,' said Miss Blacklock, good-humouredly. 'You care far more about my things than I do.'

Miss Bunner flushed.

'I *do* like nice things,' she said. Her voice was half defiant — half wistful.

'I must confess,' said Miss Marple, 'that my own few possessions are very dear to me, too — so many *memories*, you know. It's the same with photographs. People nowadays have so few photographs about. Now I like to keep all the pictures of my nephews and nieces as babies — and then as children — and so on.'

'You've got a horrible one of me, aged three,' said Bunch. 'Holding a fox terrier and squinting.'

'I expect your aunt has many photographs of you,' said Miss Marple, turning to Patrick.

'Oh, we're only distant cousins,' said Patrick.

'I believe Elinor did send me one of you as a baby, Pat,' said Miss Blacklock. 'But I'm afraid I didn't keep it. I'd really forgotten how many children she'd had or what their names were until she wrote me about you two being over here.'

'Another sign of the times,' said Miss Marple. 'Nowadays one so often doesn't know one's younger relations *at all*. In the old days, with all the big family reunions, that would have been impossible.'

'I last saw Pat and Julia's mother at a wedding thirty years ago,' said Miss Blacklock. 'She was a very pretty girl.'

'That's why she has such handsome children,' said Patrick with a grin.

'You've got a marvellous old album,' said Julia. 'Do you remember, Aunt Letty, we looked through it the other day. The hats!'

'And how smart we thought ourselves,' said Miss Blacklock with a sigh.

'Never mind, Aunt Letty,' said Patrick, 'Julia will come across a snapshot of herself in about thirty years' time — and won't she think she looks a guy!'

'Did you do that on purpose?' said Bunch, as she and Miss Marple were walking home. 'Talk about photographs, I mean?'

'Well, my dear, it *is* interesting to know that Miss Blacklock didn't know either of her two young relatives by sight . . . Yes — I think Inspector Craddock will be interested to hear that.'

CHAPTER TWELVE

Morning Activities in Chipping Cleghorn

Edmund Swetenham sat down rather precariously on a garden roller.

'Good morning, Phillipa,' he said.

'Hallo.'

'Are you very busy?'

'Moderately.'

'What are you doing?'

'Can't you see?'

'No. I'm not a gardener. You seem to be playing with earth in some fashion.'

'I'm pricking out winter lettuce.'

'Pricking out? What a curious term! Like *pinking*. Do you know what pinking is? I only learnt the other day. I always thought it was a term for professional duelling.'

'Do you want anything particular?' asked Phillipa coldly.

'Yes. I want to see you.'

Phillipa gave him a quick glance.

'I wish you wouldn't come here like this. Mrs Lucas won't like it.'

'Doesn't she allow you to have followers?'

'Don't be absurd.'

'*Followers*. That's another nice word. It describes my attitude perfectly. Respectful – at a distance – but firmly pursuing.'

'Please go away, Edmund. You've no business to come here.'

'You're wrong,' said Edmund triumphantly. 'I *have* business here. Mrs Lucas rang up my mamma this morning and said she had a good many vegetable marrows.'

'Masses of them.'

'And would we like to exchange a pot of honey for a vegetable marrow or so.'

'That's not a fair exchange at all! Vegetable marrows are quite unsaleable at the moment – everybody has such a lot.'

'Naturally. That's why Mrs Lucas rang up. Last time, if I remember rightly, the exchange suggested was some skim milk – *skim* milk, mark you – in exchange for some lettuces. It was then very early in the season for lettuces. They were about a shilling each.'

Phillipa did not speak.

Edmund tugged at his pocket and extracted a pot of honey.

'So here,' he said, 'is my alibi. Used in a loose and quite indefensible meaning of the term. If Mrs Lucas pops her bust round the door of the potting shed, I'm here in quest of vegetable marrows. There is absolutely no question of dalliance.'

'I see.'

'Do you ever read Tennyson?' inquired Edmund conversationally.

'Not very often.'

'You should. Tennyson is shortly going to make a comeback in a big way. When you turn on your wireless in the evening it will be the *Idylls of the King* you will hear and not interminable Trollope. I always thought the Trollope pose was the most unbearable affectation. Perhaps a little of Trollope, but not to drown in him. But, speaking of Tennyson, have you read *Maud*?'

'Once, long ago.'

'It's got some points about it.' He quoted softly: ' "Faultily faultless, icily regular, splendidly null." That's you, Phillipa.'

'Hardly a compliment!'

'No, it wasn't meant to be. I gather Maud got under the poor fellow's skin just like you've got under mine.'

'Don't be absurd, Edmund.'

'Oh, hell, Phillipa, why are you like you are? What goes on behind your splendidly regular features? What do you think? What do you *feel*? Are you happy, or miserable, or frightened, or what? There must be *something*.'

Phillipa said quietly:

'What I feel is my own business.'

'It's mine, too. I want to make you talk. I want to know what goes on in that quiet head of yours. I've a *right* to know. I have really. I didn't want to fall in love with you. I wanted to sit quietly and write my book. Such a nice book, all about how miserable the world is. It's frightfully easy to be clever about how miserable everybody is. And it's all a habit, really. Yes, I've suddenly become convinced of that. After reading a life of Burne-Jones.'

Phillipa had stopped pricking out. She was staring at him with a puzzled frown.

'What has Burne-Jones got to do with it?'

'Everything. When you've read all about the Pre-Raphaelites you realize just what fashion is. They were all terrifically hearty and slangy and jolly, and laughed and joked, and everything was fine and wonderful. That was fashion, too. They weren't any happier or heartier than we are. And we're not any more miserable than they were. It's all fashion, I tell you. After the last war, we went in for sex. Now it's all frustration. None of it matters. Why are we talking about all this? I started out to talk about *us*. Only I got cold feet and shied off. Because you won't help me.'

'What do you want me to do?'

'*Talk!* Tell me things. Is it your husband? Do you adore him and he's dead and so you've shut up like a clam? Is that it? All right, you adored him, and he's dead. Well, other girls' husbands are dead – lots of them – and some of the girls loved their husbands. They tell you so in bars, and cry a bit when they're drunk enough, and then want to go to bed with you so that they'll feel better. It's one way of getting over it, I suppose. You've got to get over it, Phillipa. You're young – and you're extremely lovely – and I love you like Hell. Talk about your damned husband, tell me about him.'

'There's nothing to tell. We met and got married.'

'You must have been very young.'

'Too young.'

'Then you weren't happy with him? Go *on*, Phillipa.'

'There's nothing to go on about. We were married. We were as happy as most people are, I suppose. Harry was born. Ronald went overseas. He – he was killed in Italy.'

'And now there's Harry?'

'And now there's Harry.'

'I like Harry. He's a really nice kid. He likes me. We get on. What about it, Phillipa? Shall we get married? You can go on gardening and I can go on writing my book and in the holidays we'll leave off working and enjoy ourselves. We can manage, with tact, not to have to live with Mother. She can fork out a bit to support her adored son. I sponge, I write tripey books, I have defective eyesight and I talk too much. That's the worst. Will you try it?'

Phillipa looked at him. She saw a tall rather solemn young man

418

with an anxious face and large spectacles. His sandy head was rumpled and he was regarding her with a reassuring friendliness.

'No,' said Phillipa.

'Definitely – no?'

'Definitely no.'

'Why?'

'You don't know anything about me.'

'Is that all?'

'No, you don't know anything about anything.'

Edmund considered.

'Perhaps not,' he admitted. 'But who does? Phillipa, my adored one –' He broke off.

A shrill and prolonged yapping was rapidly approaching.

> *'Pekes in the high hall garden* (said Edmund)
> *When twilight was falling* (only it's eleven a.m.)
> *Phil, Phil, Phil, Phil,*
> *They were crying and calling*

'Your name doesn't lend itself to the rhythm, does it? Sounds like an Ode to a Fountain Pen. Have you got another name?'

'Joan. *Please* go away. That's Mrs Lucas.'

'*Joan, Joan, Joan, Joan.* Better, but still not good. *While greasy Joan doth keel the pot* – that's not a nice picture of married life, either.'

'Mrs Lucas is –'

'Oh *hell!*' said Edmund. 'Get me a blasted vegetable marrow.'

II

Sergeant Fletcher had the house at Little Paddocks to himself.

It was Mitzi's day off. She always went by the eleven o'clock bus into Medenham Wells. By arrangement with Miss Blacklock, Sergeant Fletcher had the run of the house. She and Dora Bunner had gone down to the village.

Fletcher worked fast. Someone in the house had oiled and prepared that door, and whoever had done it had done it in order to be able to leave the drawing-room unnoticed as soon as the lights went out.

419

That ruled out Mitzi who wouldn't have needed to use the door.

Who was left? The neighbours, Fletcher thought, might also be ruled out. He didn't see how they could have found an opportunity to oil and prepare the door. That left Patrick and Julia Simmons, Phillipa Haymes, and possibly Dora Bunner. The young Simmonses were in Milchester. Phillipa Haymes was at work. Sergeant Fletcher was free to search out any secrets he could. But the house was disappointingly innocent. Fletcher, who was an expert on electricity, could find nothing suggestive in the wiring or appurtenances of the electric fixtures to show how the lights had been fused. Making a rapid survey of the household bedrooms he found an irritating normality. In Phillipa Haymes' room were photographs of a small boy with serious eyes, an earlier photo of the same child, a pile of schoolboy letters, a theatre programme or two. In Julia's room there was a drawer full of snapshots of the South of France. Bathing photos, a villa set amidst mimosa. Patrick's held some souvenirs of naval days. Dora Bunner's held few personal possessions and they seemed innocent enough.

And yet, thought Fletcher, someone in the house must have oiled that door.

His thoughts broke off at a sound below stairs. He went quickly to the top of the staircase and looked down.

Mrs Swettenham was crossing the hall. She had a basket on her arm. She looked into the drawing-room, crossed the hall and went into the dining-room. She came out again without the basket.

Some faint sound that Fletcher made, a board that creaked unexpectedly under his feet, made her turn her head. She called up:

'Is that you, Miss Blacklock?'

'No, Mrs Swettenham, it's me,' said Fletcher.

Mrs Swettenham gave a faint scream.

'Oh! how you startled me. I thought it might be another burglar.'

Fletcher came down the stairs.

'This house doesn't seem very well protected against burglars,' he said. 'Can anybody always walk in and out just as they like?'

'I just brought up some of my quinces,' explained Mrs Swettenham. 'Miss Blacklock wants to make quince jelly and she hasn't got a quince tree here. I left them in the dining-room.'

Then she smiled.

'Oh, I see, you mean how did I get in? Well, I just came in

through the side door. We all walk in and out of each other's houses, Sergeant. Nobody dreams of locking a door until it's dark. I mean, it would be so awkward, wouldn't it, if you brought things and couldn't get in to leave them? It's not like the old days when you rang a bell and a servant always came to answer it.' Mrs Swettenham sighed. 'In India, I remember,' she said mournfully, 'we had eighteen servants – eighteen. Not counting the *ayah*. Just as a matter of course. And at home, when I was a girl, we always had three – although Mother always felt it was terribly poverty-stricken not to be able to afford a kitchen-maid. I must say that I find life very odd nowadays, Sergeant, though I know one mustn't complain. So much worse for the miners always getting psittacosis (or is that parrot disease?) and having to come out of the mines and try to be gardeners though they don't know weeds from spinach.'

She added, as she tripped towards the door, 'I mustn't keep you. I expect you're very busy. Nothing else is going to happen, is it?'

'Why should it, Mrs Swettenham?'

'I just wondered, seeing you here. I thought it might be a *gang*. You'll tell Miss Blacklock about the quinces, won't you?'

Mrs Swettenham departed. Fletcher felt like a man who has received an unexpected jolt. He had been assuming – erroneously, he now perceived – that it must have been someone in the house who had done the oiling of the door. He saw now that he was wrong. An outsider had only to wait until Mitzi had departed by bus and Letitia Blacklock and Dora Bunner were both out of the house. Such an opportunity must have been simplicity itself. That meant that he couldn't rule out anybody who had been in the drawing-room that night.

III

'Murgatroyd!'

'Yes, Hinch?'

'I've been doing a bit of thinking.'

'Have you, Hinch?'

'Yes, the great brain has been working. You know, Murgatroyd, the whole set-up the other evening was decidedly fishy.'

'Fishy?'

'Yes. Tuck your hair up, Murgatroyd, and take this trowel. Pretend it's a revolver.'

'Oh,' said Miss Murgatroyd, nervously.

'All right. It won't bite you. Now come along to the kitchen door. You're going to be the burglar. You stand *here*. Now you're going into the kitchen to hold up a lot of nitwits. Take the torch. Switch it on.'

'But it's broad daylight!'

'Use your imagination, Murgatroyd. Switch it on.'

Miss Murgatroyd did so, rather clumsily, shifting the trowel under one arm while she did so.

'Now then,' said Miss Hinchliffe, 'off you go. Remember the time you played Hermia in *A Midsummer Night's Dream* at the Women's Institute? Act. Give it all you've got. "Stick 'em up!" Those are your lines – and don't ruin them by saying "Please".'

Obediently, Miss Murgatroyd raised her torch, flourished the trowel and advanced on the kitchen door.

Transferring the torch to her right hand she swiftly turned the handle and stepped forward, resuming the torch in her left hand.

'Stick 'em up!' she fluted, adding vexedly: 'Dear me, this is very difficult, Hinch.'

'Why?'

'The door. It's a swing door, it keeps coming back and I've got both hands full.'

'Exactly,' boomed Miss Hinchliffe. 'And the drawing-room door at Little Paddocks always swings to. It isn't a swing door like this, but it won't stay open. That's why Letty Blacklock bought that absolutely delectable heavy glass doorstop from Elliot's in the High Street. I don't mind saying I've never forgiven her for getting in ahead of me there. I was beating the old brute down from eight guineas to six pound ten, and then Blacklock comes along and buys the damned thing. I'd never seen as attractive a doorstop; you don't often get those glass bubbles in that big size.'

'Perhaps the burglar put the doorstop against the door to keep it open,' suggested Miss Murgatroyd.

'Use your common sense, Murgatroyd. What does he do? Throw the door open, say "Excuse me a moment," stoop and put the stop into position and then resume business by saying "Hands up?" Try holding the door with your shoulder.'

'It's still very awkward,' complained Miss Murgatroyd.

'Exactly,' said Miss Hinchliffe. 'A revolver, a torch and a door to hold open – a bit too much, isn't it? So what's the answer?'

Miss Murgatroyd did not attempt to supply an answer. She looked inquiringly and admiringly at her masterful friend and waited to be enlightened.

'We know he'd got a revolver, because he fired it,' said Miss Hinchliffe. 'And we know he had a torch because we all saw it – that is unless we're all the victims of mass hypnotism like explanations of the Indian Rope Trick (what a bore that old Easterbrook is with his Indian stories) – so the question is, did someone hold that door open for him?'

'But who could have done that?'

'Well, *you* could have, for one, Murgatroyd. As far as I remember, you were standing directly behind it when the lights went out.' Miss Hinchliffe laughed heartily. 'Highly suspicious character, aren't you, Murgatroyd? But who'd think it to look at you? Here, give me that trowel – thank heavens it isn't really a revolver. You'd have shot yourself by now!'

IV

'It's a most extraordinary thing,' muttered Colonel Easterbrook. 'Most extraordinary. Laura.'

'Yes, darling?'

'Come into my dressing-room a moment.'

'What is it, darling?'

Mrs Easterbrook appeared through the open door.

'Remember my showing you that revolver of mine?'

'Oh, yes, Archie, a nasty horrid black thing.'

'Yes. Hun souvenir. Was in this drawer, wasn't it?'

'Yes, it was.'

'Well, it's not there now.'

'Archie, how *extraordinary*!'

'You haven't moved it or anything?'

'Oh, no, I'd never dare to touch the horrid thing.'

'Think old mother what's-her-name did?'

'Oh, I shouldn't think so, for a minute. Mrs Butt would never do a thing like that. Shall I ask her?'

'No – no, better not. Don't want to start a lot of talk. Tell me, do you remember when it was I showed it to you?'

'Oh, about a week ago. You were grumbling about your collars and the laundry and you opened this drawer wide and there it was at the back and I asked you what it was.'

'Yes, that's right. About a week ago. You don't remember the date?'

Mrs Easterbrook considered, eyelids down over her eyes, a shrewd brain working.

'Of course,' she said. 'It was Saturday. The day we were to have gone in to the pictures, but we didn't.'

'H'm – sure it wasn't before that? Wednesday? Thursday? Or even the week before that again?'

'No, dear,' said Mrs Easterbrook. 'I remember *quite* distinctly. It was Saturday the 30th. It just seems a long time because of all the trouble there's been. And I can tell you *how* I remember. It's because it was the day after the hold-up at Miss Blacklock's. Because when I saw your revolver it reminded me of the shooting the night before.'

'Ah,' said Colonel Easterbrook, 'then that's a great load off my mind.'

'Oh, Archie, why?'

'Just because if that revolver had disappeared before the shooting – well, it might possibly have been my revolver that was pinched by that Swiss fellow.'

'But how would he have known you had one?'

'These gangs have a most extraordinary communication service. They get to know everything about a place and who lives there.'

'What a lot you do know, Archie.'

'Ha. Yes. Seen a thing or two in my time. Still, as you definitely remember seeing my revolver *after* the hold-up – well, that settles it. The revolver that Swiss fellow used can't have been mine, can it?'

'Of course it can't.'

'A great relief. I should have had to go to the police about it. And they ask a lot of awkward questions. Bound to. As a matter of fact I never took out a licence for it. Somehow, after a war, one forgets these peacetime regulations. I looked on it as a war souvenir, not as a firearm.'

'Yes, I see. Of course.'

'But all the same – where on earth can the damned thing be?'

'Perhaps Mrs Butt took it. She's always seemed quite honest, but perhaps she felt nervous after the hold-up and thought she'd like to – to have a revolver in the house. Of course, she'll never admit doing that. I shan't even ask her. She might be offended. And what should we do then? This is such a big house – I simply couldn't –'

'Quite so,' said Colonel Easterbrook. 'Better not say anything.'

CHAPTER THIRTEEN

Morning Activities in Chipping Cleghorn (Continued)

Miss Marple came out of the Vicarage gate and walked down the little lane that led into the main street.

She walked fairly briskly with the aid of the Rev. Julian Harmon's stout ashplant stick.

She passed the Red Cow and the butcher's and stopped for a brief moment to look into the window of Mr Elliot's antique shop. This was cunningly situated next door to the Bluebird Tearooms and Café so that rich motorists, after stopping for a nice cup of tea and somewhat euphemistically named 'Home Made Cakes' of a bright saffron colour, could be tempted by Mr Elliot's judiciously planned shop window.

In this antique bow frame, Mr Elliot catered for all tastes. Two pieces of Waterford glass reposed on an impeccable wine-cooler. A walnut bureau made up of various bits and pieces proclaimed itself a Genuine Bargain, and on a table in the window itself were a nice assortment of cheap doorknockers and quaint pixies, a few chipped bits of Dresden, a couple of sad-looking bead necklaces, a mug with 'A Present from Tunbridge Wells' on it, and some tit-bits of Victorian silver.

Miss Marple gave the window her rapt attention, and Mr Elliot, an elderly obese spider, peeped out of his web to appraise the possibilities of this new fly.

But just as he decided that the charms of the Present from Tunbridge Wells were about to be too much for the lady who was staying at the Vicarage (for of course Mr Elliot, like everybody else, knew exactly who she was), Miss Marple saw out of the corner of her eye Miss Dora Bunner entering the Bluebird Café, and immediately decided that what she needed to counteract the cold wind was a nice cup of morning coffee.

Four or five ladies were already engaged in sweetening their morning shopping by a pause for refreshment. Miss Marple, blinking a little in the gloom of the interior of the Bluebird, and hovering artistically, was greeted by the voice of Dora Bunner at her elbow.

'Oh, good morning, Miss Marple. Do sit down here. I'm all alone.'

'Thank you.'

Miss Marple subsided gratefully on to the rather angular little blue-painted armchair which the Bluebird affected.

'Such a sharp wind,' she complained. 'And I can't walk very fast because of my rheumatic leg.'

'Oh, I know. I had sciatica one year – and, really, most of the time I was in *agony*.'

The two ladies talked rheumatism, sciatica and neuritis for some moments with avidity. A sulky-looking girl in a pink overall with a flight of bluebirds down the front of it took their order for coffee and cakes with a yawn and an air of weary patience.

'The cakes,' Miss Bunner said in a conspiratorial whisper, 'are really *quite* good here.'

'I was so interested in that very pretty girl I met as we were coming away from Miss Blacklock's the other day,' said Miss Marple. 'I think she said she does gardening. Or is she on the land? Hynes – was that her name?'

'Oh, yes, Phillipa Haymes. Our "Lodger", as we call her.' Miss Bunner laughed at her own humour. 'Such a nice quiet girl. A *lady*, if you know what I mean.'

'I wonder now. I knew a Colonel Haymes – in the Indian cavalry. Her father perhaps?'

'She's *Mrs* Haymes. A widow. Her husband was killed in Sicily or Italy. Of course, it might be *his* father.'

'I wondered, perhaps, if there might be a little romance on the way?' Miss Marple suggested roguishly. 'With that tall young man?'

'With Patrick, do you mean? Oh, I don't –'

'No, I meant a young man with spectacles. I've seen him about.'

'Oh, of course, Edmund Swettenham. Sh! That's his mother, Mrs Swettenham, over in the corner. I don't know, I'm sure. You think he admires her? He's such an odd young man – says the most disturbing things sometimes. He's supposed to be *clever*, you know,' said Miss Bunner with frank disapproval.

'Cleverness isn't everything,' said Miss Marple, shaking her head. 'Ah, here is our coffee.'

The sulky girl deposited it with a clatter. Miss Marple and Miss Bunner pressed cakes on each other.

'I was so interested to hear you were at school with Miss Blacklock. Yours is indeed an old friendship.'

'Yes, indeed.' Miss Bunner sighed. 'Very few people would be as loyal to their old friends as dear Miss Blacklock is. Oh dear, those days seem a long time ago. Such a pretty girl and enjoyed life so much. It all seemed so *sad*.'

Miss Marple, though with no idea of what had seemed so sad, sighed and shook her head.

'Life is indeed hard,' she murmured.

'*And sad affliction bravely borne,*' murmured Miss Bunner, her eyes suffusing with tears. 'I always think of that verse. True patience; true resignation. Such courage and patience *ought* to be rewarded, that is what I say. What I feel is that *nothing* is too good for dear Miss Blacklock and, whatever good things come to her, she truly *deserves* them.'

'Money,' said Miss Marple, 'can do a lot to ease one's path in life.'

She felt herself safe in this observation since she judged that it must be Miss Blacklock's prospects of future affluence to which her friend referred.

The remark, however, started Miss Bunner on another train of thought.

'Money!' she exclaimed with bitterness. 'I don't believe, you know, that until one has really experienced it, one can know what money or, rather, the lack of it, *means*.'

Miss Marple nodded her white head sympathetically.

Miss Bunner went on rapidly, working herself up, and speaking with a flushed face:

'I've heard people say so often "I'd rather have flowers on the table than a meal without them." But how many meals have those people ever missed? They don't know what it is — nobody knows who hasn't been through it — to be really *hungry*. Bread, you know, and a jar of meat paste, and a scrape of margarine. Day after day, and how one longs for a good plate of meat and two vegetables. And the *shabbiness*. Darning one's clothes and hoping it won't show. And applying for jobs and always being told you're too old. And then perhaps getting a job and after all one isn't strong enough. One faints. And you're back again. It's the *rent* — always the *rent* — that's *got* to be paid — otherwise you're out in the street. And in these days it leaves so little over. One's old-age pension doesn't go far — indeed it doesn't.'

'I know,' said Miss Marple gently. She looked with compassion at Miss Bunner's twitching face.

'I wrote to Letty. I just happened to see her name in the paper. It was a luncheon in aid of Milchester Hospital. There it was in black and white, Miss Letitia Blacklock. It brought the past back to me. I hadn't heard of her for years and years. She'd been secretary, you know, to that very rich man, Goedler. She was always a clever girl — the kind that gets on in the world. Not so much looks — as *character*. I thought — well, I thought — perhaps she'll remember me — and she's one of the people I *could* ask for a little help. I mean someone you've known as a girl — been at school with — well, they do *know* about you — they know you're not just a — begging-letter writer —'

Tears came into Dora Bunner's eyes.

'And then Lotty came and took me away — said she needed someone to help her. Of course, I was very surprised — *very* surprised — but then newspapers do get things wrong. How kind she was — and how *sympathetic*. And remembering all the old days so well . . . I'd do anything for her — I really would. And I try *very* hard, but I'm afraid sometimes I muddle things — my head's not what it was. I make mistakes. And I forget and say foolish things. She's very patient. What's so nice about her is that she always pretends that I *am* useful to her. That's real kindness, isn't it?'

Miss Marple said gently: 'Yes, that's real kindness.'

'I used to worry, you know, even after I came to Little Paddocks – about what would become of me if – if anything were to happen to Miss Blacklock. After all, there are so many accidents – these motors dashing about – one never knows, does one? But naturally I never *said* anything – but she must have guessed. Suddenly, one day she told me that she'd left me a small annuity in her will – and – what I value far more – all her beautiful furniture. I was quite *overcome* . . . But she said nobody else would value it as I should – and that is quite true – I can't bear to see some lovely piece of china smashed – or wet glasses put down on a table and leaving a mark. I do really look after her things. Some people – some people especially, are so terribly careless – and sometimes worse than careless!

'I'm not really as stupid as I look,' Miss Bunner continued with simplicity. 'I can see, you know, when Letty's being imposed upon. Some people – I won't name names – but they take *advantage*. Dear Miss Blacklock is, perhaps, just a shade too *trusting*.'

Miss Marple shook her head.

'*That's* a mistake.'

'Yes, it is. You and I, Miss Marple, know the world. Dear Miss Blacklock –' She shook her head.

Miss Marple thought that as the secretary of a big financier Miss Blacklock might be presumed to know the world too. But probably what Dora Bunner meant was that Letty Blacklock had always been comfortably off, and that the comfortably off do not know the deeper abysses of human nature.

'That Patrick!' said Miss Bunner with a suddenness and an asperity that made Miss Marple jump. 'Twice, at least, to my knowledge, he's got money out of her. Pretending he's hard up. Run into debt. All that sort of thing. She's far too generous. All she said to me when I remonstrated with her was: "The boy's young, Dora. Youth is the time to have your fling." '

'Well, that's true enough,' said Miss Marple. 'Such a handsome young man, too.'

'Handsome is as handsome does,' said Dora Bunner. 'Much too fond of poking fun at people. And a lot of going-on with girls, I expect. I'm just a figure of fun to him – that's all. He doesn't seem to realize that people have their feelings.'

'Young people *are* rather careless that way,' said Miss Marple.

Miss Bunner leaned forward suddenly with a mysterious air.

'You won't breathe a word, will you, my dear?' she demanded. 'But I can't help feeling that he *was* mixed up in this dreadful business. I think he knew that young man – or else Julia did. I daren't hint at such a thing to dear Miss Blacklock – at least I did, and she just snapped my head off. And, of course, it's *awkward* – because he's her nephew – or at any rate her *cousin* – and if the Swiss young man shot himself Patrick might be held morally responsible, mightn't he? If he'd put him up to it, I mean. I'm really terribly confused about the whole thing. Everyone making such a fuss about that other door into the drawing-room. That's another thing that worries me – the detective saying it had been oiled. Because, you see, I saw –'

She came to an abrupt stop.

Miss Marple paused to select a phrase.

'Most difficult for you,' she said sympathetically. 'Naturally you wouldn't want anything to get round to the police.'

'That's just it,' Dora Bunner cried. 'I lie awake at nights and worry . . . because, you see, I came upon Patrick in the shrubbery the other day. I was looking for eggs – one hen lays out – and there he was holding a feather and a cup – an oily cup. And he jumped most guiltily when he saw me and he said: "I was just wondering what this was doing here." Well, of course, he's a quick thinker. I should say he thought that up quickly when I startled him. And how did he come to find a thing like that in the shrubbery unless he was looking for it, knowing perfectly well it was there? Of course, I didn't *say* anything.'

'No, no, of course not.'

'But I gave him a *look*, if you know what I mean.'

Dora Bunner stretched out her hand and bit abstractedly into a lurid salmon-coloured cake.

'And then another day I happened to overhear him having a very curious conversation with Julia. They seemed to be having a kind of quarrel. He was saying: "If I thought you had anything to do with a thing like that!" and Julia (she's always so calm, you know) said: "Well, little brother, what would you do about it?" And then, *most* unfortunately, I trod on that board that always squeaks, and they saw me. So I said, quite gaily, "You two having a quarrel?" and Patrick said, "I'm warning Julia not to go in for these black market deals.'' Oh, it was all very slick, but I don't believe they were talking about anything of the sort! And, if you ask me, I believe Patrick had tampered with that lamp in the drawing-room – to make the lights go out, because I remember distinctly that it was the shepherdess – *not* the shepherd. And the next day –'

She stopped and her face grew pink. Miss Marple turned her head to see Miss Blacklock, standing behind them – she must just have come in.

'Coffee and gossip, Bunny?' said Miss Blacklock with quite a shade of reproach in her voice. 'Good morning, Miss Marple. Cold, isn't it?'

'We were just talking,' said Miss Bunner, hurriedly. 'So many rules and regulations nowadays. One really doesn't know where one is.'

The doors flew open with a clang and Bunch Harmon came into the Bluebird with a rush.

'Hallo,' she said, 'am I too late for coffee?'

'No, dear,' said Miss Marple. 'Sit down and have a cup.'

'We must get home,' said Miss Blacklock. 'Done your shopping, Bunny?'

Her tone was indulgent once more, but her eyes still held a slight reproach.

'Yes – yes, thank you, Letty. I must just pop into the chemist's in passing and get some aspirin and some cornplasters.'

As the doors of the Bluebird swung to behind them, Bunch asked: 'What were you talking about?'

Miss Marple did not reply at once. She waited whilst Bunch gave the order, then she said:

'Family solidarity is a very strong thing. Very strong. Do you remember some famous case – I really can't remember what it was. They said the husband poisoned his wife. In a glass of wine. Then, at the trial, the daughter said she'd drunk half her mother's glass – so that knocked the case against her father to pieces. They do say – but that may be just rumour – that she never spoke to her father or lived with him again. Of course, a father is one thing – and a nephew or a distant cousin is another. But still there it is – no one wants a member of their own family hanged, do they?'

'No,' said Bunch, considering. 'I shouldn't think they would.'

Miss Marple leaned back in her chair. She murmured under her breath, 'People are really very alike, everywhere.'

'Who am I like?'

'Well, really, dear, you are very much like yourself. I don't know that you remind me of anyone in particular. Except perhaps –'

'Here it comes,' said Bunch.

'I was just thinking of a parlourmaid of mine, dear.'

'A parlourmaid? I should make a terrible parlourmaid.'

'Yes, dear, so did she. She was no good at all at waiting at table. Put everything on the table crooked, mixed up the kitchen knives with the dining-room ones, and her cap (this was a long time ago, dear) her cap was *never* straight.'

Bunch adjusted her hat automatically.

'Anything else?' she demanded anxiously.

'I kept her because she was so pleasant to have about the house – and because she used to make me laugh. I liked the way she said things straight out. Came to me one day, "Of course, I don't know, ma'am," she says, "but Florrie, the way she sits down, it's just like a married woman." And sure enough poor Florrie was in trouble – the gentlemanly assistant at the hairdresser's. Fortunately it was in good time, and I was able to have a little talk with him, and they had a very nice wedding and settled down quite happily. She was a good girl, Florrie, but inclined to be taken in by a gentlemanly appearance.'

'She didn't do a murder, did she?' asked Bunch. 'The parlourmaid, I mean.'

'No, indeed,' said Miss Marple. 'She married a Baptist minister and they had a family of five.'

'Just like me,' said Bunch. 'Though I've only got as far as Edward and Susan up to date.'

She added, after a minute or two:

'Who are you thinking about now, Aunt Jane?'

'Quite a lot of people, dear, quite a lot of people,' said Miss Marple, vaguely.

'In St Mary Mead?'

'Mostly . . . I was really thinking about Nurse Ellerton – really an excellent kindly woman. Took care of an old lady, seemed really fond of her. Then the old lady died. And another came and *she* died. Morphia. It all came out. Done in the kindest way, and the shocking thing was that the woman herself really couldn't see that she'd done anything wrong. They hadn't long to live in any case, she said, and one of them had cancer and quite a lot of pain.'

'You mean – it was a mercy killing?'

'No, *no*. They signed their money away to her. She liked money, you know . . .

'And then there was that young man on the liner – Mrs Pusey at the paper shop, *her* nephew. Brought home stuff he'd stolen and got her to dispose of it. Said it was things that he'd bought abroad. She was quite taken in. And then when the police came round and started asking questions, he tried to bash her on the head, so that she shouldn't be able to give him away . . . Not a nice young man – but very good-looking. Had two girls in love with him. He spent a lot of money on one of them.'

'The nastiest one, I suppose,' said Bunch.

'Yes, dear. And there was Mrs Cray at the wool shop. Devoted to her son, spoilt him of course. He got in with a very queer lot. Do you remember Joan Croft, Bunch?'

'N-no, I don't think so.'

'I thought you might have seen her when you were with me on a visit. Used to stalk about smoking a cigar or a pipe. We had a Bank hold-up once, and Joan Croft was in the Bank at the time. She knocked the man down and took his revolver away from him. She was congratulated on her courage by the Bench.'

Bunch listened attentively. She seemed to be learning by heart.

'And –?' she prompted.

'That girl at St Jean des Collines that summer. Such a quiet girl – not so much quiet as silent. Everybody liked her, but they never got to know her much better . . . We heard afterwards that her husband was a *forger*. It made her feel cut off from people. It made her, in the end, a little queer. Brooding does, you know.'

'Any Anglo-Indian colonels in your reminiscences, darling?'

'Naturally, dear. There was Major Vaughan at The Larches and Colonel Wright at Simla Lodge. Nothing wrong with either of them. But I do remember Mr Hodgson, the Bank Manager, went on a cruise and married a woman young enough to be his daughter. No idea of where she came from – except what she told him of course.'

'And that wasn't true?'

'No, dear, it definitely wasn't.'

'Not bad,' said Bunch nodding, and ticking people off on her

433

fingers. 'We've had devoted Dora, and handsome Patrick, and Mrs Swettenham and Edmund, and Phillipa Haymes, and Colonel Easterbrook and Mrs Easterbrook – and if you ask me, I should say you're absolutely right about *her*. But there wouldn't be any reason for her murdering Letty Blacklock.'

'Miss Blacklock, of course, might know something about her that she didn't want known.'

'Oh, darling, that old Tanqueray stuff? Surely that's dead as the hills.'

'It might not be. You see, Bunch, you are not the kind that minds much about what people think of you.'

'I see what you mean,' said Bunch suddenly. 'If you'd been up against it, and then, rather like a shivering stray cat, you'd found a home and cream and a warm stroking hand and you were called Pretty Pussy and somebody thought the world of you . . . You'd do a lot to keep that . . . Well, I must say, you've presented me with a very complete gallery of people.'

'You didn't get them all right, you know,' said Miss Marple, mildly.

'Didn't I? Where did I slip up? Julia? *Julia, pretty Julia is peculiar.*'

'Three and sixpence,' said the sulky waitress, materializing out of the gloom.

'And,' she added, her bosom heaving beneath the bluebirds, 'I'd like to know, Mrs Harmon, why you call me peculiar. I had an aunt who joined the Peculiar People, but I've always been good Church of England myself, as the late Rev. Hopkinson can tell you.'

'I'm terribly sorry,' said Bunch. 'I was just quoting a song. I didn't mean you at all. I didn't know your name was Julia.'

'Quite a coincidence,' said the sulky waitress, cheering up. 'No offence, I'm sure, but hearing my name, as I thought – well, naturally if you think someone's talking about you, it's only human nature to listen. Thank you.'

She departed with her tip.

'Aunt Jane,' said Bunch, 'don't look so upset. What is it?'

'But surely,' murmured Miss Marple, 'that couldn't be so. There's no *reason* –'

'Aunt Jane!'

Miss Marple sighed and then smiled brightly.

'It's nothing, dear,' she said.

'Did you think you knew who did the murder?' asked Bunch. 'Who was it?'

'I don't know at all,' said Miss Marple. 'I got an idea for a moment – but it's gone. I wish I did know. Time's so short. So terribly short.'

'What do you mean, *short*?'

'That old lady up in Scotland may die any moment.'

Bunch said, staring:

'Then you really do believe in Pip and Emma. You think it was them – and that they'll try again?'

'Of course they'll try again,' said Miss Marple, almost absent-mindedly. 'If they tried once, they'll try again. If you've made up your mind to murder someone, you don't stop because the first time it didn't come off. Especially if you're fairly sure you're not suspected.'

'But if it's Pip and Emma,' said Bunch, 'there are only two people it *could* be. It *must* be Patrick and Julia. They're brother and sister and they're the only ones who are the right age.'

'My dear, it isn't nearly as simple as that. There are all sorts of ramifications and combinations. There's Pip's wife if he's married, or Emma's husband. There's their mother – she's an interested party even if she doesn't inherit direct. If Letty Blacklock hasn't seen her for thirty years, she'd probably not recognize her now. One elderly woman is very like another. You remember Mrs Wotherspoon drew her own and Mrs Bartlett's Old Age Pension although Mrs Bartlett had been dead for years. Anyway, Miss Blacklock's shortsighted. Haven't you noticed how she peers at people? And then there's the father. Apparently he was a real bad lot.'

'Yes, but he's a foreigner.'

'By birth. But there's no reason to believe he speaks broken English and gesticulates with his hands. I dare say he could play the part of – of an Anglo-Indian colonel as well as anybody else.'

'Is *that* what you think?'

'No, I don't. I don't indeed, dear. I just think that there's a great deal of money at stake, a great deal of money. And I'm afraid I know only too well the really terrible things that people will do to lay their hands on a lot of money.'

435

'I suppose they will,' said Bunch. 'It doesn't really do them any good, does it? Not in the end?'

'No – but they don't usually know that.'

'I can understand it.' Bunch smiled suddenly, her sweet, rather crooked smile. 'One feels it would be different for oneself . . . Even I feel that.' She considered: 'You pretend to yourself that you'd do a lot of good with all that money. Schemes . . . Homes for Unwanted Children . . . Tired Mothers . . . A lovely rest abroad somewhere for elderly women who have worked too hard . . .'

Her face grew sombre. Her eyes were suddenly dark and tragic.

'I know what you're thinking,' she said to Miss Marple. 'You're thinking that I'd be the worst kind. Because I'd kid myself. If you just wanted the money for selfish reasons you'd at any rate *see* what you were like. But once you began to pretend about doing good with it, you'd be able to persuade yourself, perhaps, that it wouldn't very much matter killing someone . . .'

Then her eyes cleared.

'But I shouldn't,' she said. 'I shouldn't really kill anyone. Not even if they were old, or ill, or doing a lot of harm in the world. Not even if they were blackmailers or – or absolute *beasts*.' She fished a fly carefully out of the dregs of the coffee and arranged it on the table to dry. 'Because people like living, don't they? So do flies. Even if you're old and in pain and you can just crawl out in the sun. Julian says those people like living even more than young strong people do. It's harder, he says, for them to die, the struggle's greater. I like living myself – not just being happy and enjoying myself and having a good time. I mean *living* – waking up and feeling, all over me, that I'm *there* – ticking over.'

She blew on the fly gently; it waved its legs, and flew rather drunkenly away.

'Cheer up, darling Aunt Jane,' said Bunch. '*I*'d never kill anybody.'

CHAPTER FOURTEEN

Excursion into the Past

After a night in the train, Inspector Craddock alighted at a small station in the Highlands. It struck him for a moment as strange that the wealthy Mrs Goedler – an invalid – with a choice of a London house in a fashionable square, an estate in Hampshire, and a villa in the South of France, should have selected this remote Scottish home as her residence. Surely she was cut off here from many friends and distractions. It must be a lonely life – or was she too ill to notice or care about her surroundings?

A car was waiting to meet him. A big old-fashioned Daimler with an elderly chauffeur driving it. It was a sunny morning and the Inspector enjoyed the twenty-mile drive, though he marvelled anew at this preference for isolation. A tentative remark to the chauffeur brought partial enlightenment.

'It's her own home as a girl. Ay, she's the last of the family. And she and Mr Goedler were always happier here than anywhere, though it wasn't often he could get away from London. But when he did they enjoyed themselves like a couple of bairns.'

When the grey walls of the old keep came in sight, Craddock felt that time was slipping backwards. An elderly butler received him, and after a wash and shave he was shown into a room with a huge fire burning in the grate, and breakfast was served to him.

After breakfast, a tall middle-aged woman in nurse's dress, with a pleasant and competent manner, came in and introduced herself as Sister McClelland.

'I have my patient all ready for you, Mr Craddock. She is, indeed, looking forward to seeing you.'

'I'll do my best not to excite her,' Craddock promised.

'I had better warn you of what will happen. You will find Mrs Goedler apparently quite normal. She will talk and enjoy talking and then – quite suddenly – her powers will fail. Come away at once, then, and send for me. She is, you see, kept almost entirely under the influence of morphia. She drowses most of the time. In preparation for your visit, I have given her a strong stimulant. As

437

soon as the effect of the stimulant wears off, she will relapse into semi-consciousness.'

'I quite understand, Miss McClelland. Would it be in order for you to tell me exactly what the state of Mrs Goedler's health is?'

'Well, Mr Craddock, she is a dying woman. Her life cannot be prolonged for more than a few weeks. To say that she should have been dead years ago would strike you as odd, yet it is the truth. What has kept Mrs Goedler alive is her intense enjoyment and love of being alive. That sounds, perhaps, an odd thing to say of someone who has lived the life of an invalid for many years and has not left her home here for fifteen years, but it is true. Mrs Goedler has never been a strong woman – but she has retained to an astonishing degree the will to live.' She added with a smile, 'She is a very charming woman, too, as you will find.'

Craddock was shown into a large bedroom where a fire was burning and where an old lady lay in a large canopied bed. Though she was only about seven or eight years older than Letitia Blacklock, her fragility made her seem older than her years.

Her white hair was carefully arranged, a froth of pale blue wool enveloped her neck and shoulders. There were lines of pain on the face, but lines of sweetness, too. And there was, strangely enough, what Craddock could only describe as a roguish twinkle in her faded blue eyes.

'Well, this is interesting,' she said. 'It's not often I receive a visit from the police. I hear Letitia Blacklock wasn't much hurt by this attempt on her? How is my dear Blackie?'

'She's very well, Mrs Goedler. She sent you her love.'

'It's a long time since I've seen her . . . For many years now, it's been just a card at Christmas. I asked her to come up here when she came back to England after Charlotte's death, but she said it would be painful after so long and perhaps she was right . . . Blackie always had a lot of sense. I had an old school friend to see me about a year ago, and, lor!' – she smiled – 'we bored each other to death. After we'd finished all the "Do you remembers?" there wasn't anything to say. *Most* embarrassing.'

Craddock was content to let her talk before pressing his questions. He wanted, as it were, to get back into the past, to get the feel of the Goedler–Blacklock ménage.

'I suppose,' said Belle shrewdly, 'that you want to ask about the

438

money? Randall left it all to go to Blackie after my death. Really, of course, Randall never dreamed that I'd outlive him. He was a big strong man, never a day's illness, and I was always a mass of aches and pains and complaints and doctors coming and pulling long faces over me.'

'I don't think complaints would be the right word, Mrs Goedler.'

The old lady chuckled.

'I didn't mean it in the complaining sense. I've never been *too* sorry for myself. But it was always taken for granted that I, being the weakly one, would go first. It didn't work out that way. No — it didn't work out that way . . .'

'Why, exactly, did your husband leave his money the way he did?'

'You mean, why did he leave it to Blackie? Not for the reason you've probably been thinking.' The roguish twinkle was very apparent. 'What minds you policemen have! Randall was never in the least in love with her and she wasn't with him. Letitia, you know, has really got a man's mind. She hasn't any feminine feelings or weaknesses. I don't believe she was ever in love with any man. She was never particularly pretty and she didn't care for clothes. She used a little make-up in deference to prevailing custom, but not to make herself look prettier.' There was pity in the old voice as she went on: 'She never knew any of the fun of being a woman.'

Craddock looked at the frail little figure in the big bed with interest. Belle Goedler, he realized, *had* enjoyed — still enjoyed — being a woman. She twinkled at him.

'I've always thought,' she said, 'it must be terribly dull to be a man.'

Then she said thoughtfully:

'I think Randall looked on Blackie very much as a kind of younger brother. He relied on her judgement which was always excellent. She kept him out of trouble more than once, you know.'

'She told me that she came to his rescue once with money?'

'That, yes, but I meant more than that. One can speak the truth after all these years. Randall couldn't really distinguish between what was crooked and what wasn't. His conscience wasn't sensitive. The poor dear really didn't know what was just smart — and what was dishonest. Blackie kept him straight. That's one thing about Letitia Blacklock, she's absolutely dead straight. She would never

439

do anything that was dishonest. She's a very fine character, you know. I've always admired her. They had a terrible girlhood, those girls. The father was an old country doctor – terrifically pig-headed and narrow-minded – the complete family tyrant. Letitia broke away, came to London, and trained herself as a chartered accountant. The other sister was an invalid, there was a deformity of kinds and she never saw people or went out. That's why, when the old man died, Letitia gave up everything to go home and look after her sister. Randall was wild with her – but it made no difference. If Letitia thought a thing was her duty she'd do it. And you couldn't move her.'

'How long was that before your husband died?'

'A couple of years, I think. Randall made his will before she left the firm, and he didn't alter it. He said to me: "We've no one of our own." (Our little boy died, you know, when he was two years old.) "After you and I are gone, Blackie had better have the money. She'll play the markets and make 'em sit up."'

'You see,' Belle went on, 'Randall enjoyed the whole money-making game so much – it wasn't just the money – it was the adventure, the risks, the excitement of it all. And Blackie liked it too. She had the same adventurous spirit and the same judgement. Poor darling, she'd never had any of the usual fun – being in love, and leading men on and teasing them – and having a home and children and all the real fun of life.'

Craddock thought it was odd, the real pity and indulgent contempt felt by this woman, a woman whose life had been hampered by illness, whose only child had died, whose husband had died, leaving her to a lonely widowhood, and who had been a hopeless invalid for years.

She nodded her head at him.

'I know what you're thinking. But I've *had* all the things that make life worth while – they may have been taken from me – but I have had them. I was pretty and gay as a girl, I married the man I loved, and he never stopped loving me ... My child died, but I had him for two precious years ... I've had a lot of physical pain – but if you have pain, you know how to enjoy the exquisite pleasure of the times when pain stops. And everyone's been kind to me, always ... I'm a lucky woman, really.'

Craddock seized upon an opening in her former remarks.

'You said just now, Mrs Goedler, that your husband left his fortune to Miss Blacklock because he had no one else to leave it to. But that's not strictly true, is it? He had a sister.'

'Oh, Sonia. But they quarrelled years ago and made a clean break of it.'

'He disapproved of her marriage?'

'Yes, she married a man called — now what was his name —?'

'Stamfordis.'

'That's it. Dmitri Stamfordis. Randall always said he was a crook. The two men didn't like each other from the first. But Sonia was wildly in love with him and quite determined to marry him. And I really never saw why she shouldn't. Men have such odd ideas about these things. Sonia wasn't a mere girl — she was twenty-five, and she knew exactly what she was doing. He was a crook, I dare say — I mean really a crook. I believe he had a criminal record — and Randall always suspected the name he was passing under here wasn't his own. Sonia knew all that. The point was, which of course Randall couldn't appreciate, that Dmitri was really a wildly attractive person to women. And he was just as much in love with Sonia as she was with him. Randall insisted that he was just marrying her for her money — but that wasn't true. Sonia was very handsome, you know. And she had plenty of spirit. If the marriage had turned out badly, if Dmitri had been unkind to her or unfaithful to her, she would just have cut her losses and walked out on him. She was a rich woman and could do as she chose with her life.'

'The quarrel was never made up?'

'No. Randall and Sonia never had got on very well. She resented his trying to prevent the marriage. She said, "Very well. You're quite impossible! This is the last you hear of me!" '

'But it was not the last you heard of her?'

Belle smiled.

'No, I got a letter from her about eighteen months afterwards. She wrote from Budapest, I remember, but she didn't give an address. She told me to tell Randall that she was extremely happy and that she'd just had twins.'

'And she told you their names?'

Again Belle smiled. 'She said they were born just after midday — and she intended to call them Pip and Emma. That may have been just a joke, of course.'

'Didn't you hear from her again?'

'No. She said she and her husband and the babies were going to America on a short stay. I never heard any more . . .'

'You don't happen, I suppose, to have kept that letter?'

'No, I'm afraid not . . . I read it to Randall and he just grunted: "She'll regret marrying that fellow one of these days." That's all he ever said about it. We really forgot about her. She went right out of our lives . . .'

'Nevertheless Mr Goedler left his estate to her children in the event of Miss Blacklock predeceasing you?'

'Oh, that was my doing. I said to him, when he told me about the will: "And suppose Blackie dies before I do?" He was quite surprised. I said, "Oh, I know Blackie is as strong as a horse and I'm a delicate creature – but there's such a thing as accidents, you know, and there's such a thing as creaking gates . . ." And he said, "There's no one – absolutely no one." I said, "There's Sonia." And he said at once, "And let that fellow get hold of my money? No – indeed!" I said, "Well, her children then. Pip and Emma, and there may be lots more by now" – and so he grumbled, but he did put it in.'

'And from that day to this,' Craddock said slowly, 'you've heard nothing of your sister-in-law or her children?'

'Nothing – they may be dead – they may be – anywhere.'

They may be in Chipping Cleghorn, thought Craddock.

As though she read his thoughts, a look of alarm came into Belle Goedler's eyes. She said, 'Don't let them hurt Blackie. Blackie's *good* – really good – you mustn't let harm come to –'

Her voice trailed off suddenly. Craddock saw the sudden grey shadows round her mouth and eyes.

'You're tired,' he said. 'I'll go.'

She nodded.

'Send Mac to me,' she whispered. 'Yes, tired . . .' She made a feeble motion of her hand. 'Look after Blackie . . . Nothing must happen to Blackie . . . look after her . . .'

'I'll do my very best, Mrs Goedler.' He rose and went to the door.

Her voice, a thin thread of sound, followed him . . .

'Not long now – until I'm dead – dangerous for her – take care . . .'

Sister McClelland passed him as he went out. He said, uneasily:

442

'I hope I haven't done her harm.'

'Oh, I don't think so, Mr Craddock. I told you she would tire quite suddenly.'

Later, he asked the nurse:

'The only thing I hadn't time to ask Mrs Goedler was whether she had any old photographs? If so, I wonder –'

She interrupted him.

'I'm afraid there's nothing of that kind. All her personal papers and things were stored with their furniture from the London house at the beginning of the war. Mrs Goedler was desperately ill at the time. Then the storage depository was blitzed. Mrs Goedler was very upset at losing so many personal souvenirs and family papers. I'm afraid there's nothing of that kind.'

So that was that, Craddock thought.

Yet he felt his journey had not been in vain. Pip and Emma, those twin wraiths, were not quite wraiths.

Craddock thought, 'Here's a brother and sister brought up somewhere in Europe. Sonia Goedler was a rich woman at the time of her marriage, but money in Europe hasn't remained money. Queer things have happened to money during these war years. And so there are two young people, the son and daughter of a man who had a criminal record. Suppose they came to England, more or less penniless. What would they do? Find out about any rich relatives. Their uncle, a man of vast fortune, is dead. Possibly the first thing they'd do would be to look up that uncle's will. See if by any chance money had been left to them or to their mother. So they go to Somerset House and learn the contents of his will, and then, perhaps, they learn of the existence of Miss Letitia Blacklock. Then they make inquiries about Randall Goedler's widow. She's an invalid, living up in Scotland, and they find out she hasn't long to live. *If this Letitia Blacklock dies before her*, they will come into a vast fortune. What then?'

Craddock thought, 'They wouldn't go to Scotland. They'd find out where Letitia Blacklock is living now. And they'd go there – but not as themselves . . . They'd go together – or separately? Emma . . . I wonder? . . . Pip and Emma . . . I'll eat my hat if Pip, or Emma, or both of them, aren't in Chipping Cleghorn now . . .'

CHAPTER FIFTEEN

Delicious Death

In the kitchen at Little Paddocks, Miss Blacklock was giving instructions to Mitzi.

'Sardine sandwiches as well as the tomato ones. And some of those little scones you make so nicely. And I'd like you to make that special cake of yours.'

'Is it a party then, that you want all these things?'

'It's Miss Bunner's birthday, and some people will be coming to tea.'

'At her age one does not have birthdays. It is better to forget.'

'Well, she doesn't want to forget. Several people are bringing her presents – and it will be nice to make a little party of it.'

'That is what you say last time – and see what happened!'

Miss Blacklock controlled her temper.

'Well, it won't happen this time.'

'How do you know what may happen in this house? All day long I shiver and at night I lock my door and I look in the wardrobe to see no one is hidden there.'

'That ought to keep you nice and safe,' said Miss Blacklock, coldly.

'The cake that you want me to make, it is the –?' Mitzi uttered a sound that to Miss Blacklock's English ear sounded like Schwitzebzr or alternatively like cats spitting at each other.

'That's the one. The rich one.'

'Yes. It is rich. For it I have *nothing*! Impossible to make such a cake. I need for it chocolate and much butter, and sugar and raisins.'

'You can use this tin of butter that was sent us from America. And some of the raisins we were keeping for Christmas. And here is a slab of chocolate and a pound of sugar.'

Mitzi's face suddenly burst into radiant smiles.

'So I make him for you good – good,' she cried, in an ecstasy. 'It will be rich, rich, of a melting richness! And on top I will put the icing – chocolate icing – I make him so nice – and write on it *Good Wishes*. These English people with their cakes that tastes of

444

sand, never *never* will they have tasted such a cake. Delicious, they will say – delicious –'

Her face clouded again.

'Mr Patrick. He called it Delicious Death. My cake! I will not have my cake called that!'

'It was a compliment really,' said Miss Blacklock. 'He meant it was worth dying to eat such a cake.'

Mitzi looked at her doubtfully.

'Well, I do not like that word – *death*. They are not dying because they eat my cake, no, they feel much much better . . .'

'I'm sure we all shall.'

Miss Blacklock turned away and left the kitchen with a sigh of relief at the successful ending of the interview. With Mitzi one never knew.

She ran into Dora Bunner outside.

'Oh, Letty, shall I run in and tell Mitzi just how to cut the sandwiches?'

'No,' said Miss Blacklock, steering her friend firmly into the hall. 'She's in a good mood now and I don't want her disturbed.'

'But I could just show her –'

'Please don't show her *anything*, Dora. These central Europeans don't *like* being shown. They hate it.'

Dora looked at her doubtfully. Then she suddenly broke into smiles.

'Edmund Swettenham just rang up. He wished me many happy returns of the day and said he was bringing me a pot of honey as a present this afternoon. Isn't it kind? I can't imagine how he knew it was my birthday.'

'Everybody seems to know. You must have been talking about it, Dora.'

'Well, I did just happen to mention that today I should be fifty-nine.'

'You're sixty-four,' said Miss Blacklock with a twinkle.

'And Miss Hinchliffe said, "You don't look it. What age do you think *I* am?" Which was rather awkward because Miss Hinchliffe always looks so peculiar that she might be any age. She said she was bringing me some eggs, by the way. I said our hens hadn't been laying very well, lately.'

'We're not doing so badly out of your birthday,' said Miss Blacklock. 'Honey, eggs – a magnificent box of chocolates from Julia –'

'I don't know where she gets such things.'

'Better not ask. Her methods are probably strictly illegal.'

'And your lovely brooch.' Miss Bunner looked down proudly at her bosom on which was pinned a small diamond leaf.

'Do you like it? I'm glad. I never cared for jewellery.'

'I love it.'

'Good. Let's go and feed the ducks.'

II

'Ha,' cried Patrick dramatically, as the party took their places round the dining-room table. 'What do I see before me? *Delicious Death*.'

'Hush,' said Miss Blacklock. 'Don't let Mitzi hear you. She objects to your name for her cake very much.'

'Nevertheless, Delicious Death it is! Is it Bunny's birthday cake?'

'Yes, it is,' said Miss Bunner. 'I really am having the most wonderful birthday.'

Her cheeks were flushed with excitement and had been ever since Colonel Easterbrook had handed her a small box of sweets and declaimed with a bow, 'Sweets to the Sweet!'

Julia had turned her head away hurriedly, and had been frowned at by Miss Blacklock.

Full justice was done to the good things on the tea table and they rose from their seats after a round of crackers.

'I feel slightly sick,' said Julia. 'It's that cake. I remember I felt just the same last time.'

'It's worth it,' said Patrick.

'These foreigners certainly understand confectionery,' said Miss Hinchliffe. 'What they can't make is a plain boiled pudding.'

Everybody was respectfully silent, though it seemed to be hovering on Patrick's lips to ask if anyone really *wanted* a plain boiled pudding.

'Got a new gardener?' asked Miss Hinchliffe of Miss Blacklock as they returned to the drawing-room.

'No, why?'

'Saw a man snooping round the henhouse. Quite a decent-looking Army type.'

'Oh, *that*,' said Julia. 'That's our detective.'

Mrs Easterbrook dropped her handbag.

'Detective?' she exclaimed. 'But – but – why?'

'I don't know,' said Julia. 'He prowls about and keeps an eye on the house. He's protecting Aunt Letty, I suppose.'

'Absolute nonsense,' said Miss Blacklock. 'I can protect myself, thank you.'

'But surely it's all over now,' cried Mrs Easterbrook. 'Though I meant to ask you, why did they adjourn the inquest?'

'Police aren't satisfied,' said her husband. 'That's what that means.'

'But aren't satisfied of what?'

Colonel Easterbrook shook his head with the air of a man who could say a good deal more if he chose. Edmund, who disliked the Colonel, said, 'The truth of it is, we're all under suspicion.'

'But suspicion of *what*?' repeated Mrs Easterbrook.

'Never mind, kitten,' said her husband.

'Loitering with intent,' said Edmund. 'The intent being to commit murder upon the first opportunity.'

'Oh, don't, please don't, Mr Swettenham.' Dora Bunner began to cry. 'I'm sure nobody here could possibly want to kill dear, dear Letty.'

There was a moment of horrible embarrassment. Edmund turned scarlet, murmured, 'Just a joke.' Phillipa suggested in a high clear voice that they might listen to the six o'clock news and the suggestion was received with enthusiastic assent.

Patrick murmured to Julia: 'We need Mrs Harmon here. She'd be sure to say in that high clear voice of hers, "But I suppose somebody *is* still waiting for a good chance to murder you, Miss Blacklock?" '

'I'm glad she and that old Miss Marple couldn't come,' said Julia. 'That old woman is the prying kind. And a mind like a sink, I should think. Real Victorian type.'

Listening to the news led easily into a pleasant discussion on the horrors of atomic warfare. Colonel Easterbrook said that the real menace to civilization was undoubtedly Russia, and Edmund said that he had several charming Russian friends – which announcement was coldly received.

The party broke up with renewed thanks to the hostess.

'Enjoy yourself, Bunny?' asked Miss Blacklock, as the last guest was sped.

'Oh, I did. But I've got a terrible headache. It's the excitement, I think.'

'It's the cake,' said Patrick. 'I feel a bit liverish myself. And you've been nibbling chocolates all the morning.'

'I'll go and lie down, I think,' said Miss Bunner. 'I'll take a couple of aspirins and try and have a nice sleep.'

'That would be a very good plan,' said Miss Blacklock.

Miss Bunner departed upstairs.

'Shall I shut up the ducks for you, Aunt Letty?'

Miss Blacklock looked at Patrick severely.

'If you'll be sure to latch that door properly.'

'I will. I swear I will.'

'Have a glass of sherry, Aunt Letty,' said Julia. 'As my old nurse used to say, "It will settle your stomach." A revolting phrase – but curiously apposite at this moment.'

'Well, I dare say it might be a good thing. The truth is one isn't used to rich things. Oh, Bunny, how you made me jump. What is it?'

'I can't find my aspirin,' said Miss Bunner disconsolately.

'Well, take some of mine, dear, they're by my bed.'

'There's a bottle on my dressing-table,' said Phillipa.

'Thank you – thank you very much. If I can't find mine – but I know I've got it *somewhere*. A new bottle. Now where could I have put it?'

'There's heaps in the bathroom,' said Julia impatiently. 'This house is chock-full of aspirin.'

'It vexes me to be so careless and mislay things,' replied Miss Bunner, retreating up the stairs again.

'Poor old Bunny,' said Julia, holding up her glass. 'Do you think we ought to have given her some sherry?'

'Better not, I think,' said Miss Blacklock. 'She's had a lot of excitement today, and it isn't really good for her. I'm afraid she'll be the worse for it tomorrow. Still, I really do think she has enjoyed herself!'

'She's loved it,' said Phillipa.

'Let's give Mitzi a glass of sherry,' suggested Julia. 'Hi, Pat,' she called as she heard him entering the side door. 'Fetch Mitzi.'

So Mitzi was brought in and Julia poured her out a glass of sherry.

'Here's to the best cook in the world,' said Patrick.

Mitzi was gratified – but felt nevertheless that a protest was due.

'That is not so. I am not really a cook. In my country I do intellectual work.'

'Then you're wasted,' said Patrick. 'What's intellectual work compared to a *chef d'œuvre* like Delicious Death?'

'Oo – I say to you I do not like –'

'Never mind what you like, my girl,' said Patrick. 'That's my name for it and here's to it. Let's all drink to Delicious Death and to hell with the after effects.'

III

'Phillipa my dear, I want to talk to you.'

'Yes, Miss Blacklock?'

Phillipa Haymes looked up in slight surprise.

'You're not worrying about anything, are you?'

'Worrying?'

'I've noticed that you've looked worried lately. There isn't anything wrong, is there?'

'Oh no, Miss Blacklock. Why should there be?'

'Well – I wondered. I thought, perhaps, that you and Patrick –?'

'Patrick?' Phillipa looked really surprised.

'It's not so, then. Please forgive me if I've been impertinent. But you've been thrown together a lot – and, although Patrick is my cousin, I don't think he's the type to make a satisfactory husband. Not for some time to come, at all events.'

Phillipa's face had frozen into a hard immobility.

'I shan't marry again,' she said.

'Oh, yes, you will some day, my child. You're young. But we needn't discuss that. There's no other trouble. You're not worried about – money, for instance?'

'No, I'm quite all right.'

'I know you get anxious sometimes about your boy's education. That's why I want to tell you something. I drove into Milchester

449

this afternoon to see Mr Beddingfeld, my lawyer. Things haven't been very settled lately and I thought I would like to make a new will – in view of certain eventualities. Apart from Bunny's legacy, everything goes to you, Phillipa.'

'What?' Phillipa spun round. Her eyes stared. She looked dismayed, almost frightened.

'But I don't want it – really I don't ... Oh, I'd rather not ... And, anyway, why? Why to *me*?'

'Perhaps,' said Miss Blacklock in a peculiar voice, 'because there's no one else.'

'But there's Patrick and Julia.'

'Yes, there's Patrick and Julia.' The odd note in Miss Blacklock's voice was still there.

'They are your relations.'

'Very distant ones. They have no claim on me.'

'But I – I haven't, either – I don't know what you think ... Oh, I don't want it.'

Her gaze held more hostility than gratitude. There was something almost like fear in her manner.

'I know what I'm doing, Phillipa. I've become fond of you – and there's the boy ... You won't get very much if I should die now – but in a few weeks' time it might be different.'

Her eyes met Phillipa's steadily.

'But you're not going to die!' Phillipa protested.

'Not if I can avoid it by taking due precautions.'

'Precautions?'

'Yes. Think it over ... And don't worry any more.'

She left the room abruptly. Phillipa heard her speaking to Julia in the hall.

Julia entered the drawing-room a few moments later.

There was a slightly steely glitter in her eyes.

'Played your cards rather well, haven't you, Phillipa? I see you're one of those quiet ones ... a dark horse.'

'So you heard –?'

'Yes, I heard. I rather think I was meant to hear.'

'What do you mean?'

'Our Letty's no fool ... Well, anyway, you're all right, Phillipa. Sitting pretty, aren't you?'

'Oh, Julia – I didn't mean – I never meant –'

'Didn't you? Of course you did. You're fairly up against things, aren't you? Hard up for money. But just remember this – if anyone bumps off Aunt Letty now, *you'll* be suspect No. 1.'

'But I shan't be. It would be idiotic if I killed her now when – if I waited –'

'So you *do* know about old Mrs What's-her-name dying up in Scotland? I wondered . . . Phillipa, I'm beginning to believe you're a very dark horse indeed.'

'I don't want to do you and Patrick out of anything.'

'Don't you, my dear? I'm sorry – but I don't believe you.'

CHAPTER SIXTEEN
Inspector Craddock Returns

Inspector Craddock had had a bad night on his night journey home. His dreams had been less dreams than nightmares. Again and again he was racing through the grey corridors of an old-world castle in a desperate attempt to get somewhere, or to prevent something, in time. Finally he dreamt that he awoke. An enormous relief surged over him. Then the door of his compartment slid slowly open, and Letitia Blacklock looked in at him with blood running down her face, and said reproachfully: 'Why didn't you save me? You could have if you'd tried.'

This time he really awoke.

Altogether, the Inspector was thankful finally to reach Milchester. He went straight away to make his report to Rydesdale who listened carefully.

'It doesn't take us much further,' he said. 'But it confirms what Miss Blacklock told you. Pip and Emma – h'm, I wonder.'

'Patrick and Julia Simmons are the right age, sir. If we could establish that Miss Blacklock hadn't seen them since they were children –'

With a very faint chuckle, Rydesdale said: 'Our ally, Miss Marple, has established that for us. Actually Miss Blacklock had never seen either of them at all until two months ago.'

'Then, surely, sir —'

'It's not so easy as all that, Craddock. We've been checking up. On what we've got, Patrick and Julia seem definitely to be out of it. His naval record is genuine – quite a good record bar a tendency to "insubordination". We've checked with Cannes, and an indignant Mrs Simmons says of course her son and daughter are at Chipping Cleghorn with her cousin Letitia Blacklock. So that's that!'

'And Mrs Simmons *is* Mrs Simmons?'

'She's been Mrs Simmons for a very long time, that's all I can say,' said Rydesdale dryly.

'That seems clear enough. Only – those two fitted. Right age. Not known to Miss Blacklock, personally. If we wanted Pip and Emma – well, there they were.'

The Chief Constable nodded thoughtfully, then he pushed across a paper to Craddock.

'Here's a little something we've dug up on Mrs Easterbrook.'

The Inspector read with lifted eyebrows.

'Very interesting,' he remarked. 'Hoodwinked that old ass pretty well, hasn't she? It doesn't tie in with this business, though, as far as I can see.'

'Apparently not. And here's an item that concerns Mrs Haymes.'

Again Craddock's eyebrows rose.

'I think I'll have another talk with the lady,' he said.

'You think this information might be relevant?'

'I think it might be. It would be a long shot, of course . . .'

The two men were silent for a moment or two.

'How has Fletcher got on, sir?'

'Fletcher has been exceedingly active. He's made a routine search of the house by agreement with Miss Blacklock – but he didn't find anything significant. Then he's been checking up on who could have had the opportunity of oiling that door. Checking who was up at the house on the days that that foreign girl was out. A little more complicated than we thought, because it appears she goes for a walk most afternoons. Usually down to the village where she has a cup of coffee at the Bluebird. So that when Miss Blacklock and Miss Bunner are out – which is most afternoons – they go blackberrying – the coast is clear.'

'And the doors are always left unlocked?'

'They used to be. I don't suppose they are now.'

'What are Fletcher's results? Who's known to have been in the house when it was left empty?'

'Practically the whole lot of them.'

Rydesdale consulted a page in front of him.

'Miss Murgatroyd was there with a hen to sit on some eggs. (Sounds complicated but that's what she says.) Very flustered about it all and contradicts herself, but Fletcher thinks that's temperamental and not a sign of guilt.'

'Might be,' Craddock admitted. 'She flaps.'

'Then Mrs Swettenham came up to fetch some horse meat that Miss Blacklock had left for her on the kitchen table, because Miss Blacklock had been in to Milchester in the car that day and always gets Mrs Swettenham's horse meat for her. That make sense to you?'

Craddock considered.

'Why didn't Miss Blacklock leave the horse meat when she passed Mrs Swettenham's house on her way back from Milchester?'

'I don't know, but she didn't. Mrs Swettenham says she (Miss B.) always leaves it on the kitchen table, and she (Mrs S.) likes to fetch it when Mitzi isn't there because Mitzi is sometimes so rude.'

'Hangs together quite well. And the next?'

'Miss Hinchliffe. Says she wasn't there at all lately. But she was. Because Mitzi saw her coming out of the side door one day and so did a Mrs Butt (she's one of the locals). Miss H. then admitted she might have been there but had forgotten. Can't remember what she went for. Says she probably just dropped in.'

'That's rather odd.'

'So was her manner, apparently. Then there's Mrs Easterbrook. She was exercising the dear dogs out that way and she just popped in to see if Miss Blacklock would lend her a knitting pattern but Miss Blacklock wasn't in. She says she waited a little.'

'Just so. Might be snooping round. Or might be oiling a door. And the Colonel?'

'Went there one day with a book on India that Miss Blacklock had expressed a desire to read.'

'Had she?'

'Her account is that she tried to get out of having to read it, but it was no use.'

'And that's fair enough,' sighed Craddock. 'If anyone is really determined to lend you a book, you never can get out of it!'

'We don't know if Edmund Swettenham was up there. He's extremely vague. Said he did drop in occasionally on errands for his mother, but thinks not lately.'

'In fact, it's all inconclusive.'

'Yes.'

Rydesdale said, with a slight grin:

'Miss Marple has also been active. Fletcher reports that she had morning coffee at the Bluebird. She's been to sherry at Boulders, and to tea at Little Paddocks. She's admired Mrs Swettenham's garden – and dropped in to see Colonel Easterbrook's Indian curios.'

'She may be able to tell us if Colonel Easterbrook's a pukka colonel or not.'

'She'd know, I agree – he seems all right. We'd have to check with the Far Eastern authorities to get certain identification.'

'And in the meantime' – Craddock broke off – 'do you think Miss Blacklock would consent to go away?'

'Go away from Chipping Cleghorn?'

'Yes. Take the faithful Bunner with her, perhaps, and leave for an unknown destination. Why shouldn't she go up to Scotland and stay with Belle Goedler? It's a pretty unget-at-able place.'

'Stop there and wait for her to die? I don't think she'd do that. I don't think any nice-natured woman would like that suggestion.'

'If it's a matter of saving her life –'

'Come now, Craddock, it isn't quite so easy to bump someone off as you seem to think.'

'Isn't it, sir?'

'Well – in one way – it's easy enough, I agree. Plenty of methods. Weed-killer. A bash on the head when she's out shutting up the poultry, a pot shot from behind a hedge. All quite simple. But to bump someone off and not be suspected of bumping them off – that's not quite so easy. And they must realize by now that they're all under observation. The original carefully planned scheme failed. Our unknown murderer has got to think up something else.'

'I know that, sir. But there's the time element to consider. Mrs Goedler's a dying woman – she might pop off any minute. That means that our murderer can't afford to wait.'

'True.'

'And another thing, sir. He – or she – must know that we're checking up on everybody.'

'And that takes time,' said Rydesdale with a sigh. 'It means checking with the East, with India. Yes, it's a long tedious business.'

'So that's another reason for – hurry. I'm sure, sir, that the danger is very real. It's a very large sum that's at stake. If Belle Goedler dies –'

He broke off as a constable entered.

'Constable Legg on the line from Chipping Cleghorn, sir.'

'Put him through here.'

Inspector Craddock, watching the Chief Constable, saw his features harden and stiffen.

'Very good,' barked Rydesdale. 'Detective-Inspector Craddock will be coming out immediately.'

He put the receiver down.

'Is it –?' Craddock broke off.

Rydesdale shook his head.

'No,' he said. 'It's Dora Bunner. She wanted some aspirin. Apparently she took some from a bottle beside Letitia Blacklock's bed. There were only a few tablets left in the bottle. She took two and left one. The doctor's got that one and is sending it to be analysed. He says it's definitely *not* aspirin.'

'She's dead?'

'Yes, found dead in her bed this morning. Died in her sleep, doctor says. He doesn't think it was natural, though her health was in a bad state. Narcotic poisoning, that's his guess. Autopsy's fixed for tonight.'

'Aspirin tablets by Letitia Blacklock's bed. The clever clever devil. Patrick told me Miss Blacklock threw away a half-bottle of sherry – opened a new one. I don't suppose she'd have thought of doing that with an open bottle of aspirin. Who had been in the house this time – within the last day or two? The tablets can't have been there long.'

Rydesdale looked at him.

'All our lot were there yesterday,' he said. 'Birthday party for Miss Bunner. Any of them could have nipped upstairs and done a neat little substitution. Or of course anyone living in the house could have done it any time.'

CHAPTER SEVENTEEN

The Album

Standing by the Vicarage gate, well wrapped up, Miss Marple took the note from Bunch's hand.

'Tell Miss Blacklock,' said Bunch, 'that Julian is terribly sorry he can't come up himself. He's got a parishioner dying out at Locke Hamlet. He'll come up after lunch if Miss Blacklock would like to see him. The note's about the arrangements for the funeral. He suggests Wednesday if the inquest's on Tuesday. Poor old Bunny. It's so typical of her, somehow, to get hold of poisoned aspirin meant for someone else. Goodbye, darling. I hope the walk won't be too much for you. But I've simply got to get that child to hospital at once.'

Miss Marple said the walk wouldn't be too much for her, and Bunch rushed off.

Whilst waiting for Miss Blacklock, Miss Marple looked round the drawing-room, and wondered just exactly what Dora Bunner had meant that morning in the Bluebird by saying that she believed Patrick had 'tampered with the lamp' to 'make the lights go out'. What lamp? And how had he 'tampered' with it?

She must, Miss Marple decided, have meant the small lamp that stood on the table by the archway. She had said something about a shepherdess or a shepherd – and this was actually a delicate piece of Dresden china, a shepherd in a blue coat and pink breeches holding what had originally been a candlestick and had now been adapted to electricity. The shade was of plain vellum and a little too big so that it almost masked the figure. What else was it that Dora Bunner had said? 'I remember distinctly that it was the shepherdess. And the next day –' Certainly it was a shepherd now.

Miss Marple remembered that when she and Bunch had come to tea, Dora Bunner had said something about the lamp being one of a *pair*. Of course – a shepherd and a shepherdess. And it had been the shepherdess on the day of the hold-up – and the next morning it had been the *other* lamp – the lamp that was here now, the shepherd. The lamps had been changed over during the night. And

456

Dora Bunner had had reason to believe (or had believed without reason) that it was Patrick who had changed them.

Why? Because, if the original lamp were examined, it would show just how Patrick had managed to 'make the lights go out'. How had he managed? Miss Marple looked earnestly at the lamp in front of her. The flex ran along the table over the edge and was plugged into the wall. There was a small pear-shaped switch half-way along the flex. None of it suggested anything to Miss Marple because she knew very little about electricity.

Where was the shepherdess lamp? she wondered. In the 'spare room' or thrown away, or – where was it Dora Bunner had come upon Patrick Simmons with a feather and an oily cup? In the shrubbery? Miss Marple made up her mind to put all these points to Inspector Craddock.

At the very beginning Miss Blacklock had leaped to the conclusion that her nephew Patrick had been behind the insertion of that advertisement. That kind of instinctive belief was often justified, or so Miss Marple believed. Because, if you knew people fairly well, you knew the kind of things they thought of . . .

Patrick Simmons . . .

A handsome young man. An engaging young man. A young man whom women liked, both young women and old women. The kind of man, perhaps, that Randall Goedler's sister had married. Could Patrick Simmons be 'Pip'? But he'd been in the Navy during the war. The police could soon check up on that.

Only – sometimes – the most amazing impersonations *did* happen.

You could get away with a great deal if you had enough audacity . . .

The door opened and Miss Blacklock came in. She looked, Miss Marple thought, many years older. All the life and energy had gone out of her.

'I'm very sorry, disturbing you like this,' said Miss Marple. 'But the Vicar had a dying parishioner and Bunch had to rush a sick child to hospital. The Vicar wrote you a note.'

She held it out and Miss Blacklock took it and opened it.

'Do sit down, Miss Marple,' she said. 'It's very kind of you to have brought this.'

She read the note through.

'The Vicar's a very understanding man,' she said quietly. 'He doesn't offer one fatuous consolation . . . Tell him that these arrangements will do very well. Her – her favourite hymn was *Lead, Kindly Light*.'

Her voice broke suddenly.

Miss Marple said gently:

'I am only a stranger, but I am so very very sorry.'

And suddenly, uncontrollably, Letitia Blacklock wept. It was a piteous overmastering grief, with a kind of hopelessness about it. Miss Marple sat quite still.

Miss Blacklock sat up at last. Her face was swollen and blotched with tears.

'I'm sorry,' she said. 'It – it just came over me. What I've lost. She – she was the only link with the past, you see. The only one who – who *remembered*. Now that she's gone I'm quite alone.'

'I know what you mean,' said Miss Marple. 'One *is* alone when the last one who *remembers* is gone. I have nephews and nieces and kind friends – but there's no one who knew me as a young girl – no one who belongs to the old days. I've been alone for quite a long time now.'

Both women sat silent for some moments.

'You understand very well,' said Letitia Blacklock. She rose and went over to her desk. 'I must write a few words to the Vicar.' She held the pen rather awkwardly and wrote slowly.

'Arthritic,' she explained. 'Sometimes I can hardly write at all.'

She sealed up the envelope and addressed it.

'If you wouldn't mind taking it, it would be very kind.'

Hearing a man's voice in the hall she said quickly:

'That's Inspector Craddock.'

She went to the mirror over the fireplace and applied a small powder puff to her face.

Craddock came in with a grim, angry face.

He looked at Miss Marple with disapprobation.

'Oh,' he said. 'So *you're* here.'

Miss Blacklock turned from the mantelpiece.

'Miss Marple kindly came up with a note from the Vicar.'

Miss Marple said in a flurried manner:

'I am going at once – at once. Please don't let me hamper you in *any* way.'

'Were you at the tea party here yesterday afternoon?'

Miss Marple said, nervously:

'No – no, I wasn't. Bunch drove me over to call on some friends.'

'Then there's nothing you can tell me.' Craddock held the door open in a pointed manner, and Miss Marple scuttled out in a somewhat abashed fashion.

'Nosey Parkers, these old women,' said Craddock.

'I think you're being unfair to her,' said Miss Blacklock. 'She really did come with a note from the Vicar.'

'I bet she did.'

'I don't think it was idle curiosity.'

'Well, perhaps you're right, Miss Blacklock, but my own diagnosis would be a severe attack of Nosey Parkeritis . . .'

'She's a very harmless old creature,' said Miss Blacklock.

'Dangerous as a rattlesnake if you only knew,' the Inspector thought grimly. But he had no intention of taking anyone into his confidence unnecessarily. Now that he knew definitely there was a killer at large, he felt that the less said the better. He didn't want the next person bumped off to be Jane Marple.

Somewhere – a killer . . . Where?

'I won't waste time offering sympathy, Miss Blacklock,' he said. 'As a matter of fact I feel pretty bad about Miss Bunner's death. We ought to have been able to prevent it.'

'I don't see what you could have done.'

'No – well, it wouldn't have been easy. But now we've got to work fast. Who's doing this, Miss Blacklock? Who's had two shots at killing you, and will probably, if we don't work fast enough, soon have another?'

Letitia Blacklock shivered. 'I don't know, Inspector – I don't know *at all*!'

'I've checked up with Mrs Goedler. She's given me all the help she can. It wasn't very much. There are just a few people who would definitely profit by your death. First Pip and Emma. Patrick and Julia Simmons are the right age, but their background seems clear enough. Anyway, we can't concentrate on these two alone. Tell me, Miss Blacklock, would you recognize Sonia Goedler if you saw her?'

'Recognize Sonia? Why, of course –' she stopped suddenly. 'No,' she said slowly, 'I don't know that I would. It's a long time. Thirty years . . . She'd be an elderly woman now.'

'What was she like when you remember her?'

'Sonia?' Miss Blacklock considered for some moments. 'She was rather small, dark . . .'

'Any special peculiarities? Mannerisms?'

'No – no, I don't think so. She was gay – very gay.'

'She mayn't be so gay now,' said the Inspector. 'Have you got a photograph of her?'

'Of Sonia? Let me see – not a proper photograph. I've got some old snapshots – in an album somewhere – at least, I think there's one of her.'

'Ah. Can I have a look at it?'

'Yes, of course. Now where did I put that album?'

'Tell me, Miss Blacklock, do you consider it remotely possible that Mrs Swettenham might be Sonia Goedler?'

'*Mrs Swettenham?*' Miss Blacklock looked at him in lively astonishment. 'But her husband was in the Government Service – in India first, I think, and then in Hong Kong.'

'What you mean is, that that's the story she's told you. You don't, as we say in the courts, know it of your own knowledge, do you?'

'No,' said Miss Blacklock slowly. 'When you put it like that, I don't . . . But Mrs Swettenham? Oh, it's absurd!'

'Did Sonia Goedler ever do any acting? Amateur theatricals?'

'Oh, yes. She was good.'

'There you are! Another thing, Mrs Swettenham wears a wig. At least,' the Inspector corrected himself, 'Mrs Harmon says she does.'

'Yes – yes, I suppose it might be a wig. All those little grey curls. But I still think it's absurd. She's really very nice and exceedingly funny sometimes.'

'Then there's Miss Hinchliffe and Miss Murgatroyd. Could either of them be Sonia Goedler?'

'Miss Hinchliffe is too tall. She's as tall as a man.'

'Miss Murgatroyd then?'

'Oh, but – oh, no, I'm sure Miss Murgatroyd couldn't be Sonia.'

'You don't see very well, do you, Miss Blacklock?'

'I'm short-sighted; is that what you mean?'

'Yes. What I'd like to see is a snapshot of this Sonia Goedler, even if it's a long time ago and not a good likeness. We're trained, you know, to pick out resemblances, in a way no amateur can ever do.'

'I'll try and find it for you.'

'Now?'

'What, at once?'

'I'd prefer it.'

'Very well. Now, let me see. I saw that album when we were tidying a lot of books out of the cupboard. Julia was helping me. She laughed, I remember, at the clothes we used to wear in those days . . . The books we put in the shelf in the drawing-room. Where did we put the albums and the big bound volumes of the *Art Journal*? What a wretched memory I have! Perhaps Julia will remember. She's at home today.'

'I'll find her.'

The Inspector departed on his quest. He did not find Julia in any of the downstairs rooms. Mitzi, asked where Miss Simmons was, said crossly that it was not her affair.

'Me! I stay in my kitchen and concern myself with the lunch. And nothing do I eat that I have not cooked myself. Nothing, do you hear?'

The Inspector called up the stair 'Miss Simmons,' and, getting no response, went up.

He met Julia face to face just as he turned the corner of the landing. She had just emerged from a door that showed behind it a small twisty staircase.

'I was up in the attic,' she explained. 'What is it?'

Inspector Craddock explained.

'Those old photograph albums? Yes, I remember them quite well. We put them in the big cupboard in the study, I think. I'll find them for you.'

She led the way downstairs and pushed open the study door. Near the window there was a large cupboard. Julia pulled it open and disclosed a heterogeneous mass of objects.

'Junk,' said Julia. 'All junk. But elderly people simply will *not* throw things away.'

The Inspector knelt down and took a couple of old-fashioned albums from the bottom shelf.

'Are these they?'

'Yes.'

Miss Blacklock came in and joined them.

'Oh, so *that's* where we put them. I couldn't remember.'

Craddock had the books on the table and was turning the pages.

Women in large cartwheel hats, women with dresses tapering down to their feet so that they could hardly walk. The photos had captions neatly printed underneath them, but the ink was old and faded.

'It would be in this one,' said Miss Blacklock. 'On about the second or third page. The other book is after Sonia had married and gone away.' She turned a page. 'It ought to be here.' She stopped.

There were several empty spaces on the page. Craddock bent down and deciphered the faded writing. 'Sonia . . . Self . . . R.G.' A little farther along, 'Sonia and Belle on beach'. And again, on the opposite page, 'Picnic at Skeyne'. He turned over another page: 'Charlotte, Self, Sonia. R.G.'

Craddock stood up. His lips were grim.

'*Somebody has removed these photographs* – not long ago, I should say.'

'There weren't any blank spaces when we looked at them the other day. Were there, Julia?'

'I didn't look very closely – only at some of the dresses. But no . . . you're right, Aunt Letty, there *weren't* any blank spaces.'

Craddock looked grimmer still.

'Somebody,' he said, 'has removed every photo of Sonia Goedler from this album.'

CHAPTER EIGHTEEN

The Letters

'Sorry to worry you again, Mrs Haymes.'

'It doesn't matter,' said Phillipa coldly.

'Shall we go into this room here?'

'The study? Yes, if you like, Inspector. It's very cold. There's no fire.'

'It doesn't matter. It's not for long. And we're not so likely to be overheard here.'

'Does that matter?'

'Not to me, Mrs Haymes. It might to you.'

'What do you mean?'

'I think you told me, Mrs Haymes, that your husband was killed fighting in Italy?'

'Well?'

'Wouldn't it have been simpler to have told me the truth – that he was a deserter from his regiment?'

He saw her face grow white, and her hands close and unclose themselves.

She said bitterly:

'Do you have to rake up *everything*?'

Craddock said dryly:

'We expect people to tell us the truth about themselves.'

She was silent. Then she said:

'Well?'

'What do you mean by "Well?", Mrs Haymes?'

'I mean, what are you going to do about it? Tell everybody? Is that necessary – or fair – or kind?'

'Does nobody know?'

'Nobody here. Harry' – her voice changed – 'my son, he doesn't know. I don't want him to know. I don't want him to know – ever.'

'Then let me tell you that you're taking a very big risk, Mrs Haymes. When the boy is old enough to understand, tell him the truth. If he finds out by himself some day – it won't be good for him. If you go on stuffing him up with tales of his father dying like a hero –'

'I don't do that. I'm not completely dishonest. I just don't talk about it. His father was – killed in the war. After all, that's what it amounts to – for us.'

'But your husband is still alive?'

'Perhaps. How should I know?'

'When did you see him last, Mrs Haymes?'

Phillipa said quickly:

'I haven't seen him for years.'

'Are you quite sure that's true? You didn't, for instance, see him about a fortnight ago?'

'What are you suggesting?'

'It never seemed to me very likely that you met Rudi Scherz in the summerhouse here. But Mitzi's story was very emphatic. I suggest, Mrs Haymes, that the man you came back from work to meet that morning was your husband.'

'I didn't meet anybody in the summerhouse.'

'He was hard up for money, perhaps, and you supplied him with some?'

'I've not seen him, I tell you. I didn't meet anybody in the summerhouse.'

'Deserters are often rather desperate men. They often take part in robberies, you know. Hold-ups. Things of that kind. *And they have foreign revolvers very often that they've brought back from abroad.*'

'I don't know where my husband is. I haven't seen him for years.'

'Is that your last word, Mrs Haymes?'

'I've nothing else to say.'

II

Craddock came away from his interview with Phillipa Haymes feeling angry and baffled.

'Obstinate as a mule,' he said to himself angrily.

He was fairly sure that Phillipa was lying, but he hadn't succeeded in breaking down her obstinate denials.

He wished he knew a little more about ex-Captain Haymes. His information was meagre. An unsatisfactory Army record, but nothing to suggest that Haymes was likely to turn criminal.

And anyway Haymes didn't fit in with the oiled door.

Someone in the house had done that, or someone with easy access to it.

He stood looking up the staircase, and suddenly he wondered what Julia had been doing up in the attic. An attic, he thought, was an unlikely place for the fastidious Julia to visit.

What had she been doing up there?

He ran lightly up to the first floor. There was no one about. He opened the door out of which Julia had come and went up the narrow stairs to the attic.

There were trunks there, old suitcases, various broken articles of furniture, a chair with a leg off, a broken china lamp, part of an old dinner service.

464

He turned to the trunks and opened the lid of one.

Clothes. Old-fashioned, quite good quality women's clothes. Clothes belonging, he supposed, to Miss Blacklock, or to her sister who had died.

He opened another trunk.

Curtains.

He passed to a small attaché-case. It had papers in it and letters. Very old letters, yellowed with time.

He looked at the outside of the case which had the initials C.L.B. on it. He deduced correctly that it had belonged to Letitia's sister Charlotte. He unfolded one of the letters. It began *Dearest Charlotte. Yesterday Belle felt well enough to go for a picnic. R.G. also took a day off. The Asvogel flotation has gone splendidly, R.G. is terribly pleased about it. The Preference shares are at a premium.*

He skipped the rest and looked at the signature:

Your loving sister, Letitia.

He picked up another.

Darling Charlotte. I wish you would sometimes make up your mind to see people. You do exaggerate, you know. It isn't nearly as bad as you think. And people really don't mind things like that. It's not the disfigurement you think it is.

He nodded his head. He remembered Belle Goedler saying that Charlotte Blacklock had a disfigurement or deformity of some kind. Letitia had, in the end, resigned her job, to go and look after her sister. These letters all breathed the anxious spirit of her affection and love for an invalid. She had written her sister, apparently, long accounts of everyday happenings, of any little detail that she thought might interest the sick girl. And Charlotte had kept these letters. Occasionally odd snapshots had been enclosed.

Excitement suddenly flooded Craddock's mind. Here, it might be, he would find a clue. In these letters there would be written down things that Letitia Blacklock herself had long forgotten. Here was a faithful picture of the past, and somewhere amongst it there might be a clue that would help him to identify the unknown. Photographs, too. There might, just possibly, be a photograph of Sonia Goedler here that the person who had taken the other photos out of the album did not know about.

Inspector Craddock packed the letters up again, carefully, closed the case, and started down the stairs.

Letitia Blacklock, standing on the landing below, looked at him in amazement.

'Was that you up in the attic? I heard footsteps. I couldn't imagine who –'

'Miss Blacklock, I have found some letters here, written by you to your sister Charlotte many years ago. Will you allow me to take them away and read them?'

She flushed angrily.

'Must you do a thing like that? Why? What good can they be to you?'

'They might give me a picture of Sonia Goedler, of her character – there may be some allusion – some incident – that will help.'

'They are private letters, Inspector.'

'I know.'

'I suppose you will take them anyway . . . You have the power to do so, I suppose, or you can easily get it. Take them – take them! But you'll find very little about Sonia. She married and went away only a year or two after I began to work for Randall Goedler.'

Craddock said obstinately:

'There may be *something*.' He added, 'We've got to try everything. I assure you the danger is very real.'

She said, biting her lips:

'I know. Bunny is dead – from taking an aspirin tablet that was meant for me. It may be Patrick, or Julia, or Phillipa, or Mitzi next – somebody young with their life in front of them. Somebody who drinks a glass of wine that is poured out for me, or eats a chocolate that is sent to me. Oh! take the letters – take them away. And afterwards burn them. They don't mean anything to anyone but me and Charlotte. It's all over – gone – past. Nobody remembers now . . .'

Her hand went up to the choker of false pearls she was wearing. Craddock thought how incongruous it looked with her tweed coat and skirt.

She said again:

'Take the letters.'

It was the following afternoon that the Inspector called at the Vicarage.

It was a dark gusty day.

Miss Marple had her chair pulled close to the fire and was knitting. Bunch was on hands and knees, crawling about the floor, cutting out material to a pattern.

She sat back and pushed a mop of hair out of her eyes, looking up expectantly at Craddock.

'I don't know if it's a breach of confidence,' said the Inspector, addressing himself to Miss Marple, 'but I'd like you to look at this letter.'

He explained the circumstances of his discovery in the attic.

'It's rather a touching collection of letters,' he said. 'Miss Black-lock poured out everything in the hopes of sustaining her sister's interest in life and keeping her health good. There's a very clear picture of an old father in the background – old Dr Blacklock. A real old pig-headed bully, absolutely set in his ways, and convinced that everything he thought and said was right. Probably killed thousands of patients through obstinacy. He wouldn't stand for any new ideas or methods.'

'I don't really know that I blame him there,' said Miss Marple. 'I always feel that the young doctors are only too anxious to experiment. After they've whipped out all our teeth, and administered quantities of very peculiar glands, and removed bits of our insides, they then confess that nothing can be done for us. I really prefer the old-fashioned remedy of big black bottles of medicine. After all, one can always pour those down the sink.'

She took the letter that Craddock handed her.

He said: 'I want you to read it because I think that that generation is more easily understood by you than by me. I don't know really quite how these people's minds worked.'

Miss Marple unfolded the fragile paper.

Dearest Charlotte,

I've not written for two days because we've been having the most terrible domestic complications. Randall's sister Sonia (you remember her? She came to take you out in the car that day? How

I wish you would go out more*), Sonia has declared her intention of marrying one Dmitri Stamfordis. I have only seen him once. Very attractive – not to be trusted, I should say. R.G. raves against him and says he is a crook and a swindler. Belle, bless her, just smiles and lies on her sofa. Sonia, who though she looks so impassive has really a terrific temper, is simply wild with R.G. I really thought yesterday she was going to murder him!*

I've done my best. I've talked to Sonia and I've talked to R.G. and I've got them both into a more reasonable frame of mind and then they come together and it all starts over again! You've no idea how tiring it is. R.G. has been making enquiries – and it does really seem as though this Stamfordis man was thoroughly undesirable.

In the meantime business is being neglected. I carry on at the office and in a way it's rather fun because R.G. gives me a free hand. He said to me yesterday: 'Thank Heaven, there's one sane person in the world. You're never likely to fall in love with a crook, Blackie, are you?' I said I didn't think I was likely to fall in love with anybody. R.G. said: 'Let's start a few new hares in the City.' He's really rather a mischievous devil sometimes and he sails terribly near the wind. 'You're quite determined to keep me on the straight and narrow path, aren't you, Blackie?' he said the other day. And I shall too! I can't understand how people can't see when a thing's dishonest – but RG really and truly doesn't. He only knows what is actually against the law.

Belle only laughs at all this. She thinks the fuss about Sonia is all nonsense. 'Sonia has her own money,' she said. 'Why shouldn't she marry this man if she wants to?' I said it might turn out to be a terrible mistake and Belle said, 'It's never a mistake to marry a man you want to marry – even if you regret it.' And then she said, 'I suppose Sonia doesn't want to break with Randall because of money. Sonia's very fond of money.'

No more now. How is Father? I won't say Give him my love. But you can if you think it's better to do so. Have you seen more people? You really must not be morbid, darling.

Sonia asks to be remembered to you. She has just come in and is closing and unclosing her hands like an angry cat sharpening its claws. I think she and R.G. have had another row. Of course Sonia can be very *irritating. She stares you down with that cool stare of hers.*

Lots of love, darling, and buck up. This iodine treatment may make a lot of difference. I've been enquiring about it and it really does seem to have good results.

Your loving sister,
Letitia

Miss Marple folded the letter and handed it back. She looked abstracted.

'Well, what do you think about her?' Craddock urged. 'What picture do you get of her?'

'Of Sonia? It's difficult, you know, to see anyone through another person's mind . . . Determined to get her own way – that, definitely, I think. And wanting the best of two worlds . . .'

'*Closing and unclosing her hands like an angry cat*,' murmured Craddock. 'You know, that reminds me of someone . . .'

He frowned.

'Making inquiries . . .' murmured Miss Marple.

'If we could get hold of the result of those inquiries,' said Craddock.

'Does that letter remind you of anything in St Mary Mead?' asked Bunch, rather indistinctly since her mouth was full of pins.

'I really can't say it does, dear . . . Dr Blacklock is, perhaps, a little like Mr Curtiss the Wesleyan minister. He wouldn't let his child wear a plate on her teeth. Said it was the Lord's Will if her teeth stuck out. "After all," I said to him, "you do trim your beard and cut your hair. It might be the Lord's Will that your hair should grow out." He said that was quite different. So like a man. But that doesn't help us with our present problem.'

'We've never traced that revolver, you know. It wasn't Rudi Scherz. If I knew who had had a revolver in Chipping Cleghorn –'

'Colonel Easterbrook has one,' said Bunch. 'He keeps it in his collar drawer.'

'How do you know, Mrs Harmon?'

'Mrs Butt told me. She's my daily. Or, rather, my twice-weekly. Being a military gentleman, she said, he'd naturally have a revolver and very handy it would be if burglars were to come along.'

'When did she tell you this?'

'Ages ago. About six months ago, I should think.'

'Colonel Easterbrook?' murmured Craddock.

'It's like those pointer things at fairs, isn't it?' said Bunch, still speaking through a mouthful of pins. 'Go round and round and stop at something different every time.'

'You're telling me!' said Craddock and groaned. 'Colonel Easterbrook was up at Little Paddocks to leave a book there one day. He could have oiled that door then. He was quite straightforward about being there though. Not like Miss Hinchliffe.'

Miss Marple coughed gently. 'You must make allowances for the times we live in, Inspector,' she said.

Craddock looked at her, uncomprehendingly.

'After all,' said Miss Marple, 'you *are* the Police, aren't you? People can't say everything they'd like to say to the Police, can they?'

'I don't see why not,' said Craddock. 'Unless they've got some criminal matter to conceal.'

'She means butter,' said Bunch, crawling actively round a table leg to anchor a floating bit of paper. 'Butter and corn for hens, and sometimes cream – and sometimes, even, a side of bacon.'

'Show him that note from Miss Blacklock,' said Miss Marple. 'It's some time ago now, but it reads like a first-class mystery story.'

'What have I done with it? Is this the one you mean, Aunt Jane?'

Miss Marple took it and looked at it.

'Yes,' she said with satisfaction. 'That's the one.'

She handed it to the Inspector.

'*I have made inquiries – Thursday is the day,*' Miss Blacklock had written. '*Any time after three. If there is any for me leave it in the usual place.*'

Bunch spat out her pins and laughed. Miss Marple was watching the Inspector's face.

The Vicar's wife took it upon herself to explain.

'Thursday is the day one of the farms round here makes butter. They let anybody they like have a bit. It's usually Miss Hinchliffe who collects it. She's very much in with all the farmers – because of her pigs, I think. But it's all a bit hush-hush, you know, a kind of local scheme of barter. One person gets butter, and sends along cucumbers, or something like that – and a little something when a pig's killed. And now and then an animal has an accident and has to be destroyed. Oh, you know the sort of thing. Only one can't, very well, say it right out to the Police. Because, I suppose, quite a lot of this barter is illegal – only nobody really knows because it's all so complicated. But I expect Hinch had slipped into Little Paddocks with a pound of butter or something and had put it in the *usual place*. That's a flour bin under the dresser, by the way. It doesn't have flour in it.'

Craddock sighed.

'I'm glad I came here to you ladies,' he said.

'There used to be clothing coupons, too,' said Bunch. 'Not usually bought – that wasn't considered honest. No money passes. But people like Mrs Butt or Mrs Finch or Mrs Huggins like a nice woollen dress or a winter coat that hasn't seen too much wear, and they pay for it with coupons instead of money.'

'You'd better not tell me any more,' said Craddock. 'It's all against the law.'

'Then there oughtn't to be such silly laws,' said Bunch, filling her mouth up with pins again. '*I* don't do it, of course, because Julian doesn't like me to, so I don't. But I know what's going on, of course.'

A kind of despair was coming over the Inspector.

'It all sounds so pleasant and ordinary,' he said. 'Funny and petty and simple. And yet one woman and a man have been killed, and another woman may be killed before I can get anything definite to go on. I've left off worrying about Pip and Emma for the moment. I'm concentrating on Sonia. I wish I knew what she looked like. There was a snapshot or two in with these letters, but none of the snaps could have been of her.'

'How do you know it couldn't have been her? Do you know what she looked like?'

'She was small and dark, Miss Blacklock said.'

'Really,' said Miss Marple, 'that's *very* interesting.'

'There was one snap that reminded me vaguely of someone. A tall fair girl with her hair all done up on top of her head. I don't know who she could have been. Anyway, it can't have been Sonia. Do you think Mrs Swettenham could have been dark when she was a girl?'

'Not very dark,' said Bunch. 'She's got blue eyes.'

'I hoped there might be a photo of Dmitri Stamfordis – but I suppose that was too much to hope for . . . Well' – he took up the letter – 'I'm sorry this doesn't suggest anything to you, Miss Marple.'

'Oh! but it does,' said Miss Marple. 'It suggests a good deal. Just read it through again, Inspector – especially where it says that Randall Goedler was making inquiries about Dmitri Stamfordis.'

Craddock stared at her.

The telephone rang.

Bunch got up from the floor and went out into the hall where, in accordance with the best Victorian traditions, the telephone had originally been placed and where it still was.

She re-entered the room to say to Craddock:

'It's for you.'

Slightly surprised, the Inspector went out to the instrument – carefully shutting the door of the living-room behind him.

'Craddock? Rydesdale here.'

'Yes, sir.'

'I've been looking through your report. In the interview you had with Phillipa Haymes I see she states positively that she hasn't seen her husband since his desertion from the Army?'

'That's right, sir – she was most emphatic. But in my opinion she wasn't speaking the truth.'

'I agree with you. Do you remember a case about ten days ago – man run over by a lorry – taken to Milchester General with concussion and a fractured pelvis?'

'The fellow who snatched a child practically from under the wheels of a lorry, and got run down himself?'

'That's the one. No papers of any kind on him and nobody came forward to identify him. Looked as though he might be on the run. He died last night without regaining consciousness. But he's been identified – deserter from the Army – Ronald Haymes, ex-Captain in the South Loamshires.'

'Phillipa Haymes' husband?'

'Yes. He'd got an old Chipping Cleghorn bus ticket on him, by the way – and quite a reasonable amount of money.'

'So he did get money from his wife? I always thought he was the man Mitzi overheard talking to her in the summerhouse. She denied it flatly, of course. But surely, sir, that lorry accident was before –'

Rydesdale took the words out of his mouth.

'Yes, he was taken to Milchester General on the 28th. The hold-up at Little Paddocks was on the 29th. That lets him out of any possible connection with it. But his wife, of course, knew nothing about the accident. She may have been thinking all along that he *was* concerned in it. She'd hold her tongue – naturally – after all he *was* her husband.'

'It was a fairly gallant bit of work, wasn't it, sir?' said Craddock slowly.

'Rescuing that child from the lorry? Yes. Plucky. Don't suppose it was cowardice that made Haymes desert. Well, all that's past history. For a man who'd blotted his copybook, it was a good death.'

'I'm glad for her sake,' said the Inspector. 'And for that boy of theirs.'

'Yes, he needn't be too ashamed of his father. And the young woman will be able to marry again now.'

Craddock said slowly:

'I was thinking of that, sir . . . It opens up – possibilities.'

'You'd better break the news to her as you're on the spot.'

'I will, sir. I'll push along there now. Or perhaps I'd better wait until she's back at Little Paddocks. It may be rather a shock – and there's someone else I rather want to have a word with first.'

CHAPTER NINETEEN

Reconstruction of the Crime

'I'll put on a lamp by you before I go,' said Bunch. 'It's so dark in here. There's going to be a storm, I think.'

She lifted the small reading lamp to the other side of the table where it would throw light on Miss Marple's knitting as she sat in a wide high-backed chair.

As the flex pulled across the table, Tiglath Pileser the cat leapt upon it and bit and clawed it violently.

'No, Tiglath Pileser, you mustn't . . . He really is awful. Look, he's nearly bitten it through – it's all frayed. Don't you understand, you idiotic puss, that you may get a nasty electric shock if you do that?'

473

'Thank you, dear,' said Miss Marple, and put out a hand to turn on the lamp.

'It doesn't turn on there. You have to press that silly little switch half-way along the flex. Wait a minute. I'll take these flowers out of the way.'

She lifted a bowl of Christmas roses across the table. Tiglath Pileser, his tail switching, put out a mischievous paw and clawed Bunch's arm. She spilled some of the water out of the vase. It fell on the frayed area of flex and on Tiglath Pileser himself, who leapt to the floor with an indignant hiss.

Miss Marple pressed the small pear-shaped switch. Where the water had soaked the frayed flex there was a flash and a crackle.

'Oh dear,' said Bunch. 'It's fused. Now I suppose all the lights in here are off.' She tried them. 'Yes, they are. So stupid being all on the same thingummibob. And it's made a burn on the table, too. Naughty Tiglath Pileser — it's all his fault. Aunt Jane — what's the matter? Did it startle you?'

'It's nothing, dear. Just something I saw quite suddenly which I ought to have seen before . . .'

'I'll go and fix the fuse and get the lamp from Julian's study.'

'No, dear, don't bother. You'll miss your bus. I don't want any more light. I just want to sit quietly and — think about something. Hurry dear, or you won't catch your bus.'

When Bunch had gone, Miss Marple sat quite still for about two minutes. The air of the room was heavy and menacing with the gathering storm outside.

Miss Marple drew a sheet of paper towards her.

She wrote first: *Lamp?* and underlined it heavily.

After a moment or two, she wrote another word.

Her pencil travelled down the paper, making brief cryptic notes . . .

II

In the rather dark living-room of Boulders with its low ceiling and latticed window panes, Miss Hinchliffe and Miss Murgatroyd were having an argument.

'The trouble with you, Murgatroyd,' said Miss Hinchliffe, 'is that you won't *try*.'

'But I tell you, Hinch, I can't remember a thing.'

'Now look here, Amy Murgatroyd, we're going to do some constructive thinking. So far we haven't shone on the detective angle. I was quite wrong over that door business. You didn't hold the door open for the murderer after all. You're cleared, Murgatroyd!'

Miss Murgatroyd gave a rather watery smile.

'It's just our luck to have the only silent cleaning woman in Chipping Cleghorn,' continued Miss Hinchliffe. 'Usually I'm thankful for it, but this time it means we've got off to a bad start. Everybody else in the place knows about that second door in the drawing-room being used – and we only heard about it yesterday –'

'I still don't quite understand how –'

'It's perfectly simple. Our original premises were quite right. You can't hold open a door, wave a torch and shoot with a revolver all at the same time. We kept in the revolver and the torch and cut out the door. Well, we were wrong. It was the revolver we ought to have cut out.'

'But he *did* have a revolver,' said Miss Murgatroyd. 'I saw it. It was there on the floor beside him.'

'When he was dead, yes. It's all quite clear. *He* didn't fire that revolver –'

'Then who did?'

'That's what we're going to find out. But whoever did it, the same person put a couple of poisoned aspirin tablets by Letty Blacklock's bed – and thereby bumped off poor Dora Bunner. And that couldn't have been Rudi Scherz, because he's as dead as a doornail. It was someone who was in the room that night of the hold-up and probably someone who was at the birthday party, too. And the only person *that* lets out is Mrs Harmon.'

'You think someone put those aspirins there the day of the birthday party?'

'Why not?'

'But how could they?'

'Well, we all went to the loo, didn't we?' said Miss Hinchliffe coarsely. 'And I washed my hands in the bathroom because of that sticky cake. And little Sweetie Easterbrook powdered her grubby little face in Blacklock's bedroom, didn't she?'

'Hinch! Do you think *she* –?'

'I don't know yet. Rather obvious, if she did. I don't think if you were going to plant some tablets, that you'd want to be seen in the bedroom at all. Oh, yes, there were plenty of opportunities.'

'The men didn't go upstairs.'

'There are back stairs. After all, if a man leaves the room, you don't follow him to see if he really is going where you think he is going. It wouldn't be delicate! Anyway, don't *argue*, Murgatroyd. I want to get back to the original attempt on Letty Blacklock. Now, to begin with, get the facts firmly into your head, because it's all going to depend upon you.'

Miss Murgatroyd looked alarmed.

'Oh dear, Hinch, you know what a muddle I get into!'

'It's not a question of your brains, or the grey fluff that passes for brains with you. It's a question of *eyes*. It's a question of what you *saw*.'

'But I didn't see *anything*.'

'The trouble with you is, Murgatroyd, as I said just now, that you won't *try*. Now pay attention. This is what happened. Whoever it is that's got it in for Letty Blacklock was there in that room that evening. He (I say *he* because it's easier, but there's no reason why it should be a man more than a woman except, of course, that men are dirty dogs), well, he has previously oiled that second door that leads out of the drawing-room and which is supposed to be nailed up or something. Don't ask me *when* he did it, because that confuses things. Actually, by choosing my time, I could walk into any house in Chipping Cleghorn and do anything I liked there for half an hour or so and with no one being the wiser. It's just a question of working out where the daily women are and when the occupiers are out and exactly where they've gone and how long they'll be. Just good staff work. Now, to continue. He's oiled that second door. It will open without a sound. Here's the set-up: Lights go out, door A (the regular door) opens with a flourish. Business with torch and hold-up lines. In the meantime, while we're all goggling, X (that's the best term to use) slips quietly out by door B into the dark hall, comes up behind that Swiss idiot, takes a couple of shots at Letty Blacklock and then shoots the Swiss. Drops the revolver, where lazy thinkers like you will assume it's evidence that the Swiss did the shooting, and nips back into the room again by the time that someone gets a lighter going. Got it?'

'Yes – ye-es, but who was it?'

'Well, if *you* don't know, Murgatroyd, nobody does!'

'*Me?*' Miss Murgatroyd fairly twittered in alarm. 'But I don't know anything *at all*. I don't *really*, Hinch!'

'Use that fluff of yours you call a brain. To begin with, where was everybody when the lights went out?'

'I don't know.'

'Yes, you do. You're maddening, Murgatroyd. You know where *you* were, don't you? You were behind the door.'

'Yes – yes, I was. It knocked against my corn when it flew open.'

'Why don't you go to a proper chiropodist instead of messing about yourself with your feet? You'll give yourself blood poisoning one of these days. Come on, now – *you're* behind the door. *I'm* standing against the mantelpiece with my tongue hanging out for a drink. Letty Blacklock is by the table near the archway, getting the cigarettes. Patrick Simmons had gone through the archway into the small room where Letty Blacklock has had the drinks put. Agreed?'

'Yes, yes, I remember all that.'

'Good, now somebody else followed Patrick into that room or was just starting to follow him. One of the men. The annoying thing is that I can't remember whether it was Easterbrook or Edmund Swettenham. Do you remember?'

'No, I don't.'

'You wouldn't! And there was someone else who went through to the small room: Phillipa Haymes. I remember that distinctly because I remember noticing what a nice flat back she has, and I thought to myself "That girl would look well on a horse." I was watching her and thinking just that. She went over to the mantelpiece in the other room. I don't know what it was she wanted there, because at that moment the lights went out.

'So that's the position. In the far drawing-room are Patrick Simmons, Phillipa Haymes, and *either* Colonel Easterbrook or Edmund Swettenham – we don't know which. Now, Murgatroyd, pay attention. The most probable thing is that it was *one of those three* who did it. If anyone wanted to get out of that far door, they'd naturally take care to put themselves in a convenient place when the lights went out. So, as I say, in all probability, it's one of those three. And in that case, Murgatroyd, there's not a thing you can do about it!'

Miss Murgatroyd brightened perceptibly.

'On the other hand,' continued Miss Hinchliffe, 'there's the possibility that it *wasn't* one of those three. And that's where you come in, Murgatroyd.'

'But how should *I* know anything about it?'

'As I said before, if you don't nobody does.'

'But I don't! I really *don't*! I couldn't see anything *at all*!'

'Oh, yes, you could. You're the only person who *could* see. You were standing behind the door. You couldn't look *at* the torch – because the door was between you and it. You were facing the other way, the same way as the torch was pointing. The rest of us were just dazzled. But *you* weren't dazzled.'

'No – no, perhaps not, but I didn't *see* anything, the torch went round and round –'

'Showing you *what*? It rested on *faces*, didn't it? And on tables? And on chairs?'

'Yes – yes, it did . . . Miss Bunner, her mouth wide open and her eyes popping out of her head, staring and blinking.'

'That's the stuff!' Miss Hinchliffe gave a sigh of relief. 'The difficulty there is in making you use that grey fluff of yours! Now then, keep it up.'

'But I didn't see any more, I didn't, really.'

'You mean you saw an empty room? Nobody standing about? Nobody sitting down?'

'No, of course not *that*. Miss Bunner with her mouth open and Mrs Harmon was sitting on the arm of a chair. She had her eyes tight shut and her knuckles all doubled up to her face – like a child.'

'Good, that's Mrs Harmon and Miss Bunner. Don't you see yet what I'm getting at? The difficulty is that I don't want to put ideas into your head. But when we've eliminated who you *did* see – we can get on to the important point which is, was there anyone you *didn't* see. Got it? Besides the tables and chairs and the chrysanthemums and the rest of it, there were certain people: Julia Simmons, Mrs Swettenham, Mrs Easterbrook – *either* Colonel Easterbrook or Edmund Swettenham – Dora Bunner and Bunch Harmon. All right, you saw Bunch Harmon and Dora Bunner. Cross them off. Now *think*, Murgatroyd, *think*, was there one of those people who definitely *wasn't* there?'

Miss Murgatroyd jumped slightly as a branch knocked against the open window. She shut her eyes. She murmured to herself . . .

'The flowers ... on the table ... the big armchair ... the torch didn't come round as far as you, Hinch – Mrs Harmon, yes ...'

The telephone rang sharply. Miss Hinchliffe went to it.

'Hallo, yes? The station?'

The obedient Miss Murgatroyd, her eyes closed, was reliving the night of the 29th. The torch, sweeping slowly round ... a group of people ... the windows ... the sofa ... Dora Bunner ... the wall ... the table with lamp ... the archway ... the sudden spat of the revolver ...

'... but that's *extraordinary*!' said Miss Murgatroyd.

'What?' Miss Hinchliffe was barking angrily into the telephone. 'Been there since this morning? What time? Damn and blast you, and you only ring me up *now*? I'll set the SPCA after you. An oversight? Is *that* all you've got to say?'

She banged down the receiver.

'It's that dog,' she said. 'The red setter. Been at the station since this morning – since this morning at eight o'clock! Without a drop of water! And the idiots only ring me up now. I'm going to get her right away.'

She plunged out of the room, Miss Murgatroyd squeaking shrilly in her wake.

'But listen, Hinch, a most extraordinary thing ... I don't understand it ...'

Miss Hinchliffe had dashed out of the door and across to the shed which served as a garage.

'We'll go on with it when I come back,' she called. 'I can't wait for you to come with me. You've got your bedroom slippers on as usual.'

She pressed the starter of the car and backed out of the garage with a jerk. Miss Murgatroyd skipped nimbly sideways.

'But listen, Hinch, I *must* tell you –'

'When I come back ...'

The car jerked and shot forward. Miss Murgatroyd's voice came faintly after it on a high excited note.

'But, Hinch, *she wasn't there* ...'

Overhead, the clouds had been gathering thick and blue. As Miss Murgatroyd stood looking after the retreating car, the first big drops began to fall.

In an agitated fashion, Miss Murgatroyd plunged across to a line of string on which she had, some hours previously, hung out a couple of jumpers and a pair of woollen combinations to dry.

She was murmuring under her breath:

'Really *most* extraordinary ... Oh dear, I shall never get these down in time ... And they were nearly dry ...'

She struggled with a recalcitrant clothes peg, then turned her head as she heard someone approaching.

Then she smiled a pleased welcome.

'Hallo – do go inside, you'll get wet.'

'Let me help you.'

'Oh, if you don't mind ... so annoying if they all get soaked again. I really ought to let down the line, but I think I can just reach.'

'Here's your scarf. Shall I put it round your neck?'

'Oh, thank you ... Yes, perhaps ... If I could just reach this peg ...'

The woollen scarf was slipped round her neck and then, suddenly, pulled tight ...

Miss Murgatroyd's mouth opened, but no sound came except a small choking gurgle.

And the scarf was pulled tighter still ...

IV

On her way back from the station, Miss Hinchliffe stopped the car to pick up Miss Marple who was hurrying along the street.

'Hallo,' she shouted. 'You'll get very wet. Come and have tea with us. I saw Bunch waiting for the bus. You'll be all alone at the Vicarage. Come and join us. Murgatroyd and I are doing a bit of reconstruction of the crime. I rather think we're just getting somewhere. Mind the dog. She's rather nervous.'

'What a beauty.'

'Yes, lovely bitch, isn't she? Those fools kept her at the station since this morning without letting me know. I told them off, the lazy b——s. Oh! excuse my language. I was brought up by grooms at home in Ireland.'

The little car turned with a jerk into the small backyard of Boulders.

A crowd of eager ducks and fowls encircled the two ladies as they descended.

'Curse Murgatroyd,' said Miss Hinchliffe, 'she hasn't given 'em their corn.'

'Is it difficult to get corn?' Miss Marple inquired.

Miss Hinchliffe winked.

'I'm in with most of the farmers,' she said.

Shooing away the hens, she escorted Miss Marple towards the cottage.

'Hope you're not too wet?'

'No, this is a very good mackintosh.'

'I'll light the fire if Murgatroyd hasn't lit it. Hiyah, Murgatroyd? Where is the woman? Murgatroyd! Where's that dog? *She's* disappeared now.'

A slow dismal howl came from outside.

'Curse the silly bitch.' Miss Hinchliffe tramped to the door and called:

'Hyoup, Cutie – Cutie. Damn' silly name but that's what they called her apparently. We must find her another name. Hiyah, Cutie.'

The red setter was sniffing at something lying below the taut string where a row of garments swirled in the wind.

'Murgatroyd's not even had the sense to bring the washing in. Where *is* she?'

Again the red setter nosed at what seemed to be a pile of clothes, and raised her nose high in the air and howled again.

'What's the *matter* with the dog?'

Miss Hinchliffe strode across the grass.

And quickly, apprehensively, Miss Marple ran after her. They stood there, side by side, the rain beating down on them and the older woman's arm went round the younger one's shoulders.

She felt the muscles go stiff and taut as Miss Hinchliffe stood looking down on the thing lying there, with the blue congested face and the protruding tongue.

'I'll kill whoever did this,' said Miss Hinchliffe in a low quiet voice, 'if I once get my hands on her . . .'

Miss Marple said questioningly:

'*Her?*'

Miss Hinchliffe turned a ravaged face towards her.

'Yes. I know who it is — near enough . . . That is, it's one of three possibles.'

She stood for another moment, looking down at her dead friend, and then turned towards the house. Her voice was dry and hard.

'We must ring up the police,' she said. 'And while we're waiting for them, I'll tell you. My fault, in a way, that Murgatroyd's lying out there. I made a game of it . . . Murder isn't a game . . .'

'No,' said Miss Marple. 'Murder isn't a game.'

'You know something about it, don't you?' said Miss Hinchliffe as she lifted the receiver and dialled.

She made a brief report and hung up.

'They'll be here in a few minutes . . . Yes, I heard that you'd been mixed up in this sort of business before . . . I think it was Edmund Swettenham told me so . . . Do you want to hear what we were doing, Murgatroyd and I?'

Succinctly she described the conversation held before her departure for the station.

'She called after me, you know, just as I was leaving . . . That's how I know it's a woman and not a man . . . If I'd waited — if only I'd *listened*! God dammit, the dog could have stopped where she was for another quarter of an hour.'

'Don't blame yourself, my dear. That does no good. One can't foresee.'

'No, one can't . . . Something tapped against the window, I remember. Perhaps *she* was outside there, then — yes, of course, she must have been . . . coming to the house . . . and there were Murgatroyd and I shouting to each other. Top of our voices . . . She heard . . . She heard it all . . .'

'You haven't told me yet what your friend said.'

'Just one sentence! "*She wasn't there.*" ' She paused. 'You see? There were three women we hadn't eliminated. Mrs Swettenham, Mrs Easterbrook, Julia Simmons. And one of those three — *wasn't there* . . . She wasn't there in the drawing-room because she had slipped out through the other door and was out in the hall.'

'Yes,' said Miss Marple, 'I see.'

'It's *one* of those three women. I don't know which. But I'll find out!'

'Excuse me,' said Miss Marple. 'But did she – did Miss Murgatroyd, I mean, say it exactly as you said it?'

'How d'you mean – as I said it?'

'Oh dear, how can I explain? You said it like this. *She-wasn't-there*. An equal emphasis on every word. You see, there are three ways you could say it. You could say, "*She* wasn't there." Very personal. Or again, "She *wasn't* there." Confirming some suspicion already held. Or else you could say (and this is nearer to the way you said it just now), "She wasn't *there* . . ." quite blankly – with the emphasis, if there was emphasis – on the *there*.'

'I don't know.' Miss Hinchliffe shook her head. 'I can't remember . . . How the hell can I remember? I think, yes, surely she'd say "*She* wasn't there"? That would be the natural way, I should think. But I simply don't know. Does it make any difference?'

'Yes,' said Miss Marple, thoughtfully. 'I think so. It's a very *slight* indication, of course, but I think it *is* an indication. Yes, I should think it makes a lot of difference . . .'

CHAPTER TWENTY
Miss Marple Is Missing

The postman, rather to his disgust, had lately been given orders to make an afternoon delivery of letters in Chipping Cleghorn as well as a morning one.

On this particular afternoon he left three letters at Little Paddocks at exactly ten minutes to five.

One was addressed to Phillipa Haymes in a schoolboy's hand; the other two were for Miss Blacklock. She opened them as she and Phillipa sat down at the tea table. The torrential rain had enabled Phillipa to leave Dayas Hall early today, since once she had shut up the greenhouses there was nothing more to do.

Miss Blacklock tore open her first letter which was a bill for repairing the kitchen boiler. She snorted angrily.

'Dymond's prices are *preposterous* – quite preposterous. Still, I suppose all the other people are just as bad.'

She opened the second letter which was in a handwriting quite unknown to her.

Dear Cousin Letty (it said),

I hope it will be all right for me to come to you on Tuesday? I wrote to Patrick two days ago but he hasn't answered. So I presume it's all right. Mother is coming to England next month and hopes to see you then.

My train arrives at Chipping Cleghorn at 6.15 if that's convenient?
Yours affectionately,
Julia Simmons

Miss Blacklock read the letter once with astonishment pure and simple, and then again with a certain grimness. She looked up at Phillipa who was smiling over her son's letter.

'Are Julia and Patrick back, do you know?'

Phillipa looked up.

'Yes, they came in just after I did. They went upstairs to change. They were wet.'

'Perhaps you'd not mind going and calling them.'

'Of course I will.'

'Wait a moment – I'd like you to read this.'

She handed Phillipa the letter she had received.

Phillipa read it and frowned. 'I don't understand . . .'

'Nor do I, quite . . . I think it's about time I did. Call Patrick and Julia, Phillipa.'

Phillipa called from the bottom of the stairs:

'Patrick! Julia! Miss Blacklock wants you.'

Patrick came running down the stairs and entered the room.

'Don't go, Phillipa,' said Miss Blacklock.

'Hallo, Aunt Letty,' said Patrick cheerfully. 'Want me?'

'Yes, I do. Perhaps you'll give me an explanation of *this*?'

Patrick's face showed an almost comical dismay as he read.

'I meant to telegraph her! What an ass I am!'

'This letter, I presume, is from your sister Julia?'

'Yes – yes, it is.'

Miss Blacklock said grimly:

'*Then who, may I ask, is the young woman whom you brought here as Julia Simmons,* and whom I was given to understand was your sister and my cousin?'

'Well – you see – Aunt Letty – the fact of the matter is – I can explain it all – I know I oughtn't to have done it – but it really seemed more of a lark than anything else. If you'll just let me explain –'

'I am waiting for you to explain. *Who is this young woman?*'

'Well, I met her at a cocktail party soon after I got demobbed. We got talking and I said I was coming here and then – well, we thought it might be rather a good wheeze if I brought her along ... You see, Julia, the real Julia, was mad to go on the stage and Mother had seven fits at the idea – however, Julia got a chance to join a jolly good repertory company up in Perth or somewhere and she thought she'd give it a try – but she thought she'd keep Mum calm by letting Mum think that she was here with me studying to be a dispenser like a good little girl.'

'I still want to know who this other young woman *is*.'

Patrick turned with relief as Julia, cool and aloof, came into the room.

'The balloon's gone up,' he said.

Julia raised her eyebrows. Then, still cool, she came forward and sat down.

'OK,' she said. 'That's that. I suppose you're very angry?' She studied Miss Blacklock's face with almost dispassionate interest. 'I should be if I were you.'

'*Who are you?*'

Julia sighed.

'I think the moment's come when I make a clean breast of things. Here we go. I'm one half of the Pip and Emma combination. To be exact, my christened name is Emma Jocelyn Stamfordis – only Father soon dropped the Stamfordis. I think he called himself De Courcy next.

'My father and mother, let me tell you, split up about three years after Pip and I were born. Each of them went their own way. And they split us up. I was Father's part of the loot. He was a bad parent on the whole, though quite a charming one. I had various desert spells of being educated in convents – when Father hadn't any money, or was preparing to engage in some particularly nefarious deal. He used to pay the first term with every sign of affluence and then depart and leave me on the nuns' hands for a year or two. In the intervals, he and I had some very good times together, moving in cosmopolitan society. However, the war separated us completely. I've no idea of what's happened to him. I had a few adventures myself. I was with the French Resistance for a time. Quite exciting. To cut a long story short, I landed up in London and began to think about my future. I knew that Mother's brother, with whom she'd had a frightful row, had died a very rich man. I looked up his will to see if there was anything for me. There wasn't – not directly, that is to say. I made a few inquiries about his widow – it seemed she was quite gaga and kept under drugs and was dying by inches. Frankly, it looked as though *you* were my best bet. You were going to come into a hell of a lot of money, and from all I could find out you didn't seem to have anyone much to spend it on. I'll be quite frank. It occurred to me that if I could get to know you in a friendly kind of way, and if you took a fancy to me – well, after all, conditions have changed a bit, haven't they, since Uncle Randall died? I mean, any money we ever had has been swept away in the cataclysm of Europe. I thought you might pity a poor orphan girl, all alone in the world, and make her, perhaps, a small allowance.'

'Oh, you did, did you?' said Miss Blacklock grimly.

'Yes. Of course, I hadn't seen you then . . . I visualized a kind of sob-stuff approach . . . Then, by a marvellous stroke of luck, I met Patrick here – and he turned out to be your nephew or your cousin, or something. Well, that struck me as a marvellous chance. I went bullheaded for Patrick and he fell for me in a most gratifying way. The real Julia was all wet about this acting stuff and I soon persuaded her it was her duty to Art to go and fix herself up in some uncomfortable lodgings in Perth and train to be the new Sarah Bernhardt.

'You mustn't blame Patrick too much. He felt awfully sorry for me, all alone in the world – and he soon thought it would be a really marvellous idea for me to come here as his sister and do my stuff.'

'And he also approved of your continuing to tell a tissue of lies to the police?'

'Have a heart, Letty. Don't you see that when that ridiculous hold-up business happened – or, rather, after it happened – I began

486

to feel I was in a bit of a spot. Let's face it, I've got a perfectly good motive for putting you out of the way. You've only got my word for it now that I wasn't the one who tried to do it. You can't expect me deliberately to go and incriminate myself. Even Patrick got nasty ideas about me from time to time, and if even *he* could think things like that, what on earth would the police think? That Detective-Inspector struck me as a man of singularly sceptical mind. No, I figured out the only thing for me to do was to sit tight as Julia and just fade away when term came to an end.

'How was I to know that fool Julia, the real Julia, would go and have a row with the producer, and fling the whole thing up in a fit of temperament? She writes to Patrick and asks if she can come here, and instead of wiring her "Keep away" he goes and forgets to do anything at all!' She cast an angry glance at Patrick. 'Of all the utter *idiots*!'

She sighed.

'You don't know the straits I've been put to in Milchester! Of course, I haven't been to the hospital at all. But I had to go *somewhere*. Hours and hours I've spent in the pictures seeing the most frightful films over and over again.'

'*Pip and Emma,*' murmured Miss Blacklock. 'I never believed, somehow, in spite of what the Inspector said, that they were *real* –'

She looked searchingly at Julia.

'You're Emma,' she said. 'Where's Pip?'

Julia's eyes, limpid and innocent, met hers.

'I don't know,' she said. 'I haven't the least idea.'

'I think you're lying, Julia. When did you see him last?'

Was there a momentary hesitation before Julia spoke?

She said clearly and deliberately:

'I haven't seen him since we were both three years old – when my mother took him away. I haven't seen either him or my mother. I don't know where they are.'

'And that's all you have to say?'

Julia sighed.

'I could say I was sorry. But it wouldn't really be true; because actually I'd do the same thing again – though not if I'd known about this murder business, of course.'

'Julia,' said Miss Blacklock, 'I call you that because I'm used to it. You were with the French Resistance, you say?'

'Yes. For eighteen months.'

'Then I suppose you learned to shoot?'

Again those cool blue eyes met hers.

'I can shoot all right. I'm a first-class shot. I didn't shoot at you, Letitia Blacklock, though you've only got my word for that. But I can tell you this, that if *I* had shot at you, I wouldn't have been likely to miss.'

II

The sound of a car driving up to the door broke through the tenseness of the moment.

'Who can that be?' asked Miss Blacklock.

Mitzi put a tousled head in. She was showing the whites of her eyes.

'It is the police come again,' she said. 'This, it is persecution! Why will they not leave us alone? I will not bear it. I will write to the Prime Minister. I will write to your King.'

Craddock's hand put her firmly and not too kindly aside. He came in with such a grim set to his lips that they all looked at him apprehensively. This was a new Inspector Craddock.

He said sternly:

'Miss Murgatroyd has been murdered. She was strangled – not more than an hour ago.' His eyes singled out Julia. 'You – Miss Simmons – where have you been all day?'

Julia said warily:

'In Milchester. I've just got in.'

'And you?' The eye went on to Patrick.

'Yes.'

'Did you both come back here together?'

'Yes – yes, we did,' said Patrick.

'No,' said Julia. 'It's no good, Patrick. That's the kind of lie that will be found out at once. The bus people know us well. I came back on the earlier bus, Inspector – the one that gets here at four o'clock.'

'And what did you do then?'

'I went for a walk.'

'In the direction of Boulders?'

'No, I went across the fields.'

He stared at her. Julia, her face pale, her lips tense, stared back. Before anyone could speak, the telephone rang.

Miss Blacklock, with an inquiring glance at Craddock, picked up the receiver.

'Yes. Who? Oh, Bunch. What? No. No, she hasn't. I've no idea ... Yes, he's here now.'

She lowered the instrument and said:

'Mrs Harmon would like to speak to you, Inspector. Miss Marple has not come back to the Vicarage and Mrs Harmon is worried about her.'

Craddock took two strides forward and gripped the telephone.

'Craddock speaking.'

'I'm worried, Inspector.' Bunch's voice came through with a childish tremor in it. 'Aunt Jane's out somewhere – and I don't know where. And they say that Miss Murgatroyd's been killed. Is it true?'

'Yes, it's true, Mrs Harmon. Miss Marple was there with Miss Hinchliffe when they found the body.'

'Oh, so *that's* where she is.' Bunch sounded relieved.

'No – no, I'm afraid she isn't. Not now. She left there about – let me see – half an hour ago. She hasn't got home?'

'No – she hasn't. It's only ten minutes' walk. Where can she be?'

'Perhaps she's called in on one of your neighbours?'

'I've rung them up – *all of them*. She's not there. I'm frightened, Inspector.'

'So am *I*,' thought Craddock.

He said quickly:

'I'll come round to you – at once.'

'Oh, *do* – there's a piece of paper. She was writing on it before she went out. I don't know if it means anything ... It just seems gibberish to me.'

Craddock replaced the receiver.

Miss Blacklock said anxiously:

'Has something happened to Miss Marple? Oh, I hope not.'

'I hope not, too.' His mouth was grim.

'She's so old – and frail.'

'I know.'

Miss Blacklock, standing with her hand pulling at the choker of pearls round her neck, said in a hoarse voice:

'It's getting worse and worse. Whoever's doing these things must be mad, Inspector – quite mad . . .'

'I wonder.'

The choker of pearls round Miss Blacklock's neck broke under the clutch of her nervous fingers. The smooth white globules rolled all over the room.

Letitia cried out in an anguished tone.

'My pearls – my *pearls* –' The agony in her voice was so acute that they all looked at her in astonishment. She turned, her hand to her throat, and rushed sobbing out of the room.

Phillipa began picking up the pearls.

'I've never seen her so upset over anything,' she said. 'Of course – she always wears them. Do you think, perhaps, that someone special gave them to her? Randall Goedler, perhaps?'

'It's possible,' said the Inspector slowly.

'They're not – they couldn't be – *real* by any chance?' Phillipa asked from where, on her knees, she was still collecting the white shining globes.

Taking one in his hand, Craddock was just about to reply contemptuously, 'Real? Of course not!' when he suddenly stifled the words.

After all, *could* the pearls be real?

They were so large, so even, so white that their falseness seemed palpable, but Craddock remembered suddenly a police case where a string of real pearls had been bought for a few shillings in a pawnbroker's shop.

Letitia Blacklock had assured him that there was no jewellery of value in the house. If these pearls were, by any chance, genuine, they must be worth a fabulous sum. And if Randall Goedler had given them to her – then they might be worth any sum you cared to name.

They looked false – they *must* be false, but – if they were real?

Why not? She might herself be unaware of their value. Or she might choose to protect her treasure by treating it as though it were a cheap ornament worth a couple of guineas at most. What would they be worth if real? A fabulous sum . . . Worth doing murder for – *if anybody knew about them*.

With a start, the Inspector wrenched himself away from his

490

speculations. Miss Marple was missing. He must go to the Vicarage.

III

He found Bunch and her husband waiting for him, their faces anxious and drawn.

'She hasn't come back,' said Bunch.

'Did she say she was coming back here when she left Boulders?' asked Julian.

'She didn't actually say so,' said Craddock slowly, throwing his mind back to the last time he had seen Jane Marple.

He remembered the grimness of her lips and the severe frosty light in those usually gentle blue eyes.

Grimness, an inexorable determination ... to do what? To go where?

'She was talking to Sergeant Fletcher when I last saw her,' he said. 'Just by the gate. And then she went through it and out. I took it she was going straight home to the Vicarage. I would have sent her in the car – but there was so much to attend to, and she slipped away very quietly. Fletcher may know something! Where's Fletcher?'

But Sergeant Fletcher, it seemed, as Craddock learned when he rang up Boulders, was neither to be found there nor had he left any message where he had gone. There was some idea that he had returned to Milchester for some reason.

The Inspector rang up headquarters in Milchester, but no news of Fletcher was to be found there.

Then Craddock turned to Bunch as he remembered what she had told him over the telephone.

'Where's that paper? You said she'd been writing something on a bit of paper.'

Bunch brought it to him. He spread it out on the table and looked down on it. Bunch leant over his shoulder and spelled it out as he read. The writing was shaky and not easy to read:

Lamp?

Then came the word *Violets.*

Then after a space:

Where is bottle of aspirin?

491

The next item in this curious list was more difficult to make out. '*Delicious Death*,' Bunch read. 'That's Mitzi's cake.'

'*Making enquiries*,' read Craddock.

'Inquiries? What about, I wonder. What's this? *Severe affliction bravely borne* . . . What on earth –!'

'*Iodine*,' read the Inspector. '*Pearls*. Ah, pearls.'

'And then *Lotty* – no, *Letty*. Her *e*'s look like *o*'s. And then *Berne*. And what's this? *Old Age Pension* . . .'

They looked at each other in bewilderment.

Craddock recapitulated swiftly:

'Lamp. Violets. Where is bottle of aspirin? Delicious Death. Making enquiries. Severe affliction bravely borne. Iodine. Pearls. Letty. Berne. Old Age Pension.'

Bunch asked: 'Does it mean anything? Anything at all? I can't see any connection.'

Craddock said slowly: 'I've just a glimmer – but I don't see. It's odd that she should have put down that about pearls.'

'What about pearls? What does it mean?'

'Does Miss Blacklock always wear that three-tier choker of pearls?'

'Yes, she does. We laugh about it sometimes. They're so dreadfully false-looking, aren't they? But I suppose she thinks it's fashionable.'

'There might be another reason,' said Craddock slowly.

'You don't mean that they're *real*. Oh! they *couldn't* be!'

'How often have you had an opportunity of seeing real pearls of that size, Mrs Harmon?'

'But they're so glassy.'

Craddock shrugged his shoulders.

'Anyway, they don't matter now. It's Miss Marple that matters. We've got to find her.'

They'd got to find her before it was too late – but perhaps it was already too late? Those pencilled words showed that she was on the track . . . But that was dangerous – horribly dangerous. And where the hell was Fletcher?

Craddock strode out of the Vicarage to where he'd left his car. Search – that was all he could do – search.

A voice spoke to him out of the dripping laurels.

'Sir!' said Sergeant Fletcher urgently. '*Sir* . . .'

CHAPTER TWENTY-ONE

Three Women

Dinner was over at Little Paddocks. It had been a silent and uncomfortable meal.

Patrick, uneasily aware of having fallen from grace, only made spasmodic attempts at conversation – and such as he did make were not well received. Phillipa Haymes was sunk in abstraction. Miss Blacklock herself had abandoned the effort to behave with her normal cheerfulness. She had changed for dinner and had come down wearing her necklace of cameos, but for the first time fear showed from her darkly circled eyes, and betrayed itself by her twitching hands.

Julia alone had maintained her air of cynical detachment throughout the evening.

'I'm sorry, Letty,' she said, 'that I can't pack my bag and go. But I presume the police wouldn't allow it. I don't suppose I'll darken your roof – or whatever the expression is – for long. I should imagine that Inspector Craddock will be round with a warrant and the handcuffs any moment. In fact, I can't imagine why something of the kind hasn't happened already.'

'He's looking for the old lady – for Miss Marple,' said Miss Blacklock.

'Do you think she's been murdered, too?' Patrick asked with scientific curiosity. 'But why? What could she know?'

'I don't know,' said Miss Blacklock dully. 'Perhaps Miss Murgatroyd told her something.'

'If she's been murdered too,' said Patrick, 'there seems to be logically only one person who could have done it.'

'Who?'

'Hinchliffe, of course,' said Patrick triumphantly. 'That's where she was last seen alive – at Boulders. My solution would be that she never left Boulders.'

'My head aches,' said Miss Blacklock in a dull voice. She pressed her fingers to her forehead. 'Why should Hinch murder Miss Marple? It doesn't make sense.'

'It would if Hinch had really murdered Murgatroyd,' said Patrick triumphantly.

Phillipa came out of her apathy to say:

'Hinch wouldn't murder Murgatroyd.'

Patrick was in an argumentative mood.

'She might have if Murgatroyd had blundered on something to show that she — Hinch — was the criminal.'

'Anyway, Hinch was at the station when Murgatroyd was killed.'

'She could have murdered Murgatroyd before she left.'

Startling them all, Letitia Blacklock suddenly screamed out:

'Murder, murder, *murder* —! Can't you talk of *anything* else? I'm frightened, don't you understand? I'm frightened. I wasn't before. I thought I could take care of myself ... But what can you do against a murderer who's waiting — and watching — and biding his time! Oh, God!'

She dropped her head forward on her hands. A moment later she looked up and apologized stiffly.

'I'm sorry. I — I lost control.'

'That's all right, Aunt Letty,' said Patrick affectionately. 'I'll look after you.'

'You?' was all Letitia Blacklock said, but the disillusionment behind the word was almost an accusation.

That had been shortly before dinner, and Mitzi had then created a diversion by coming and declaring that she was not going to cook the dinner.

'I do not do anything more in this house. I go to my room. I lock myself in. I stay there until it is daylight. I am afraid — people are being killed — that Miss Murgatroyd with her stupid English face — who would want to kill *her*? Only a maniac! Then it is a maniac that is about! And a maniac does not care *who* he kills. But me, I do not want to be killed! There are shadows in that kitchen — and I hear noises — I think there is someone out in the yard and then I think I see a shadow by the larder door and then it is footsteps I hear. So I go now to my room and I lock the door and perhaps even I put the chest of drawers against it. And in the morning I tell that cruel hard policeman that I go away from here. And if he will not let me I say: ''I scream and I scream and I scream until you have to let me go!'' '

Everybody, with a vivid recollection of what Mitzi could do in the screaming line, shuddered at the threat.

'So I go to my room,' said Mitzi, repeating the statement once more to make her intentions quite clear. With a symbolic action she cast off the cretonne apron she had been wearing. 'Good night, Miss Blacklock. Perhaps in the morning, you may not be alive. So in case that is so, I say goodbye.'

She departed abruptly and the door, with its usual gentle little whine, closed softly after her.

Julia got up.

'I'll see to dinner,' she said in a matter-of-fact way. 'Rather a good arrangement – less embarrassing for you all than having me sit down at table with you. Patrick (since he's constituted himself your protector, Aunt Letty) had better taste every dish first. I don't want to be accused of poisoning you on top of everything else.'

So Julia had cooked and served a really excellent meal.

Phillipa had come out to the kitchen with an offer of assistance but Julia had said firmly that she didn't want any help.

'Julia, there's something I want to say . . .'

'This is no time for girlish confidences,' said Julia firmly. 'Go on back in the dining-room, Phillipa.'

Now dinner was over and they were in the drawing-room with coffee on the small table by the fire – and nobody seemed to have anything to say. They were waiting – that was all.

At 8.30 Inspector Craddock rang up.

'I shall be with you in about a quarter of an hour's time,' he announced. 'I'm bringing Colonel and Mrs Easterbrook and Mrs Swettenham and her son with me.'

'But really, Inspector . . . I can't cope with people tonight –'

Miss Blacklock's voice sounded as though she were at the end of her tether.

'I know how you feel, Miss Blacklock. I'm sorry. But this is urgent.'

'Have you – found Miss Marple?'

'No,' said the Inspector and rang off.

Julia took the coffee tray out to the kitchen where, to her surprise, she found Mitzi contemplating the piled-up dishes and plates by the sink.

Mitzi burst into a torrent of words.

'See what you do in my so nice kitchen! That frying pan – only,

only for omelettes do I use it! And you, what have you used it for?'

'Frying onions.'

'Ruined – *ruined*. It will have now to be *washed* and never – *never* – do I wash my omelette pan. I rub it carefully over with a greasy newspaper, that is all. And this saucepan here that you have used – that one, I use him only for milk –'

'Well, I don't know what pans you use for what,' said Julia crossly. 'You chose to go to bed, and why on earth you've chosen to get up again I can't imagine. Go away again and leave me to wash up in peace.'

'No, I will not let you use my kitchen.'

'Oh, Mitzi, you *are* impossible!'

Julia stalked angrily out of the kitchen and at that moment the door-bell rang.

'I do not go to the door,' Mitzi called from the kitchen. Julia muttered an impolite Continental expression under her breath and stalked to the front door.

It was Miss Hinchliffe.

' 'Evening,' she said in her gruff voice. 'Sorry to barge in. Inspector's rung up, I expect?'

'He didn't tell us you were coming,' said Julia, leading the way to the drawing-room.

'He said I needn't come unless I liked,' said Miss Hinchliffe. 'But I do like.'

Nobody offered Miss Hinchliffe sympathy or mentioned Miss Murgatroyd's death. The ravaged face of the tall vigorous woman told its own tale, and would have made any expression of sympathy an impertinence.

'Turn all the lights on,' said Miss Blacklock. 'And put more coal on the fire. I'm cold – horribly cold. Come and sit here by the fire, Miss Hinchliffe. The Inspector said he would be here in a quarter of an hour. It must be nearly that now.'

'Mitzi's come down again,' said Julia.

'Has she? Sometimes I think that girl's mad – quite mad. But then perhaps we're all mad.'

'I've no patience with this saying that all people who commit crimes are mad,' barked Miss Hinchliffe. 'Horribly and intelligently sane – that's what I think a criminal is!'

The sound of a car was heard outside and presently Craddock

came in with Colonel and Mrs Easterbrook and Edmund and Mrs Swettenham.

They were all curiously subdued.

Colonel Easterbrook said in a voice that was like an echo of his usual tones:

'Ha! A good fire.'

Mrs Easterbrook wouldn't take off her fur coat and sat down close to her husband. Her face, usually pretty and rather vapid, was like a little pinched weasel face. Edmund was in one of his furious moods and scowled at everybody. Mrs Swettenham made what was evidently a great effort, and which resulted in a kind of parody of herself.

'It's awful – isn't it?' she said conversationally. 'Everything, I mean. And really the less one says, the better. Because one doesn't know *who* next – like the Plague. Dear Miss Blacklock, don't you think you ought to have a little brandy? Just half a wineglass even? I always think there's nothing like brandy – such a wonderful stimulant. I – it seems so terrible of us – forcing our way in here like this, but Inspector Craddock *made* us come. And it seems so terrible – she hasn't been found, you know. That poor old thing from the Vicarage, I mean. Bunch Harmon is nearly frantic. Nobody knows *where* she went instead of going home. She didn't come to us. I've not even seen her today. And I should know if she *had* come to the house because I was in the drawing-room – at the back, you know, and Edmund was in his study writing – and that's at the front – so if she'd come either way we *should* have seen. And, oh, I do hope and pray that nothing has happened to that dear sweet old thing – all her faculties still and *everything*.'

'Mother,' said Edmund in a voice of acute suffering, 'can't you shut up?'

'I'm sure, dear, I don't want to say a *word*,' said Mrs Swettenham, and sat down on the sofa by Julia.

Inspector Craddock stood near the door. Facing him, almost in a row, were the three women. Julia and Mrs Swettenham on the sofa. Mrs Easterbrook on the arm of her husband's chair. He had not brought about this arrangement, but it suited him very well.

Miss Blacklock and Miss Hinchliffe were crouching over the fire. Edmund stood near them. Phillipa was far back in the shadows.

Craddock began without preamble.

497

'You all know that Miss Murgatroyd's been killed,' he began. 'We've reason to believe that the person who killed her was a woman. And for certain other reasons we can narrow it down still more. I'm about to ask certain ladies here to account for what they were doing between the hours of four and four-twenty this afternoon. I have already had an account of her movements from – from the young lady who has been calling herself Miss Simmons. I will ask her to repeat that statement. At the same time, Miss Simmons, I must caution you that you need not answer if you think your answers may incriminate you, and anything you say will be taken down by Constable Edwards and may be used as evidence in court.'

'You have to say that, don't you?' said Julia. She was rather pale, but still composed. 'I repeat that between four and four-thirty I was walking along the field leading down to the brook by Compton Farm. I came back to the road by that field with three poplars in it. I didn't meet anyone as far as I can remember. I did not go near Boulders.'

'Mrs Swettenham?'

Edmund said, 'Are you cautioning all of us?'

The Inspector turned to him.

'No. At the moment only Miss Simmons. I have no reason to believe that any other statement made will be incriminating, but anyone, of course, is entitled to have a solicitor present and to refuse to answer questions unless he *is* present.'

'Oh, but that would be very silly and a complete waste of time,' cried Mrs Swettenham. 'I'm sure I can tell you at once exactly what I was doing. That's what you want, isn't it? Shall I begin now?'

'Yes, please, Mrs Swettenham.'

'Now, let me see.' Mrs Swettenham closed her eyes, opened them again. 'Of course I had nothing *at all* to do with killing Miss Murgatroyd. I'm sure *everybody* here knows *that*. But I'm a woman of the world, I know quite well that the police have to ask all the most unnecessary questions and write the answers down very carefully, because it's all for what they call "the record". That's it, isn't it?' Mrs Swettenham flashed the question at the diligent Constable Edwards and added graciously, 'I'm not going too fast for you, I hope?'

Constable Edwards, a good shorthand writer, but with little social *savoir-faire*, turned red to the ears and replied:

'It's quite all right, madam. Well, perhaps a *little* slower would be better.'

Mrs Swettenham resumed her discourse with emphatic pauses where she considered a comma or a full stop might be appropriate.

'Well, of course it's difficult to say – exactly – because I've not got, really, a very good sense of time. And ever since the war quite half our clocks haven't gone at all, and the ones that do go are often either fast or slow or stop because we haven't wound them up.' Mrs Swettenham paused to let this picture of confused time sink in and then went on earnestly. 'What I *think* I was doing at four o'clock was turning the heel of my sock (and for some extraordinary reason I was going round the wrong way – in purl, you know, not plain) but if I *wasn't* doing that, I must have been outside snipping off the dead chrysanthemums – no, that was earlier – before the rain.'

'The rain,' said the Inspector, 'started at 4.10 exactly.'

'Did it now? That helps a lot. Of course, I was upstairs putting a wash basin in the passage where the rain always comes through. And it was coming through so fast that I guessed at once that the gutter was stopped up again. So I came down and got my mackintosh and rubber boots. I called Edmund, but he didn't answer, so I thought perhaps he'd got to a very important place in his novel and I wouldn't disturb him, and I've done it quite often myself before. With the broom handle, you know, tied on to that long thing you push up windows with.'

'You mean,' said Craddock, noting bewilderment on his subordinate's face, 'that you were cleaning out the gutter?'

'Yes, it was all choked up with leaves. It took a long time and I got rather wet, but I got it clear at last. And then I went in and got changed and washed – so *smelly*, dead leaves – and then I went into the kitchen and put the kettle on. It was 6.15 by the kitchen clock.'

Constable Edwards blinked.

'Which means,' finished Mrs Swettenham triumphantly, 'that it was exactly twenty minutes to five.

'Or near enough,' she added.

'Did anybody see what you were doing whilst you were out cleaning the gutter?'

'No, indeed,' said Mrs Swettenham. 'I'd soon have roped them in to help if they had! It's a most difficult thing to do single-handed.'

'So, by your own statement, you were outside, in a mackintosh and boots, at the time when the rain was coming down and, according to you, you were employed during that time in cleaning out a gutter but you have no one who can substantiate that statement?'

'You can look at the gutter,' said Mrs Swettenham. 'It's beautifully clear.'

'Did you hear your mother call to you, Mr Swettenham?'

'No,' said Edmund. 'I was fast asleep.'

'Edmund,' said his mother reproachfully, 'I thought you were *writing*.'

Inspector Craddock turned to Mrs Easterbrook.

'Now, Mrs Easterbrook?'

'I was sitting with Archie in his study,' said Mrs Easterbrook, fixing wide innocent eyes on him. 'We were listening to the wireless together, weren't we, Archie?'

There was a pause. Colonel Easterbrook was very red in the face. He took his wife's hand in his.

'You don't understand these things, kitten,' he said. 'I – well, I must say, Inspector, you've rather sprung this business on us. My wife, you know, has been terribly upset by all this. She's nervous and highly strung and doesn't appreciate the importance of – of taking due consideration before she makes a statement.'

'Archie,' cried Mrs Easterbrook reproachfully, 'are you going to say you weren't with me?'

'Well, I wasn't, was I, my dear? I mean, one's got to stick to the facts. Very important in this sort of inquiry. I was talking to Lampson, the farmer at Croft End, about some chicken netting. That was about a quarter to four. I didn't get home until after the rain had stopped. Just before tea. A quarter to five. Laura was toasting the scones.'

'And had *you* been out also, Mrs Easterbrook?'

The pretty face looked more like a weasel's than ever. Her eyes had a trapped look.

'No – no, I just sat listening to the wireless. I didn't go out. Not then. I'd been out earlier. About – about half-past three. Just for a little walk. Not far.'

She looked as though she expected more questions, but Craddock said quietly:

'That's all, Mrs Easterbrook.'

He went on: 'These statements will be typed out. You can read them and sign them if they are substantially correct.'

Mrs Easterbrook looked at him with sudden venom.

'Why don't you ask the others where they were? That Haymes woman? And Edmund Swettenham? How do you know he *was* asleep indoors? Nobody saw him.'

Inspector Craddock said quietly:

'Miss Murgatroyd, before she died, made a certain statement. On the night of the hold-up here, *someone* was absent from this room. Someone who was supposed to have been in the room all the time. Miss Murgatroyd told her friend the names of the people she *did* see. By a process of elimination, she made the discovery that there was someone she did *not* see.'

'Nobody could see anything,' said Julia.

'Murgatroyd could,' said Miss Hinchliffe, speaking suddenly in her deep voice. 'She was over there behind the door, where Inspector Craddock is now. She was the only person who could see anything of what was happening.'

'*Aha! That is what you think, is it!*' demanded Mitzi.

She made one of her dramatic entrances, flinging open the door and almost knocking Craddock sideways. She was in a frenzy of excitement.

'Ah, you do not ask Mitzi to come in here with the others, do you, you stiff policeman? I am only Mitzi! Mitzi in the kitchen! Let her stay in the kitchen where she belongs! But I tell you that Mitzi, as well as anyone else, and perhaps better, yes, better, can see things. Yes, I see things. I see something the night of the burglary. I see something and I do not quite believe it, and I hold my tongue till now. I think to myself I will not tell what it is I have seen, not yet. I will wait.'

'And when everything had calmed down, you meant to ask for a little money from a certain person, eh?' said Craddock.

Mitzi turned on him like an angry cat.

'And why not? Why look down your nose? Why should I not be paid for it if I have been so generous as to keep silence? Especially if some day there will be money – much *much* money. Oh! I have heard things – I know what goes on. I know this Pippemmer – this secret society of which *she*' – she flung a dramatic finger towards Julia – 'is an agent. Yes, I would have waited and asked for money – but now I am afraid. I would rather be *safe*. For soon, perhaps, someone will kill *me*. So I will tell what I know.'

'All right then,' said the Inspector sceptically. 'What *do* you know?'

'I tell you.' Mitzi spoke solemnly. 'On that night I am *not* in the pantry cleaning silver as I say – I am already in the dining-room when I hear the gun go off. I look through the keyhole. The hall it is black, but the gun go off again and the torch it falls – and it swings round as it falls – and I see *her*. I see *her* there close to him, with the gun in her hand. I see Miss Blacklock.'

'Me?' Miss Blacklock sat up in astonishment. 'You must be mad!'

'But that's impossible,' cried Edmund. 'Mitzi couldn't have seen Miss Blacklock –'

Craddock cut in and his voice had the corrosive quality of a deadly acid.

'*Couldn't she, Mr Swettenham? And why not?* Because it *wasn't* Miss Blacklock who was standing there with the gun? It was *you*, wasn't it?'

'I – of course not – what the *hell*!'

'*You* took Colonel Easterbrook's revolver. *You* fixed up the business with Rudi Scherz – as a good joke. You had followed Patrick Simmons into the far room and when the lights went out you slipped out through the carefully oiled door. You shot at Miss Blacklock and then you killed Rudi Scherz. A few seconds later you were back in the drawing-room clicking your lighter.'

For a moment Edmund seemed at a loss for words, then he spluttered out:

'The whole idea is *monstrous*. Why *me*? What earthly motive had *I* got?'

'If Miss Blacklock dies before Mrs Goedler, two people inherit, remember. The two we know of as Pip and Emma. Julia Simmons has turned out to be Emma –'

'And you think I'm Pip?' Edmund laughed. 'Fantastic – absolutely *fantastic*! I'm about the right age – nothing else. And I can prove to you, you damned fool, that I *am* Edmund Swettenham. Birth certificate, schools, university – everything.'

'He isn't Pip.' The voice came from the shadows in the corner. Phillipa Haymes came forward, her face pale. '*I'm Pip*, Inspector.'

'*You*, Mrs Haymes?'

'Yes. Everybody seems to have assumed that Pip was a boy –

502

Julia knew, of course, that her twin was another girl – I don't know why she didn't say so this afternoon –'

'Family solidarity,' said Julia. 'I suddenly realized who you were. I'd had no idea till that moment.'

'I'd had the same idea as Julia did,' said Phillipa, her voice trembling a little. 'After I – lost my husband and the war was over, I wondered what I was going to do. My mother died many years ago. I found out about my Goedler relations. Mrs Goedler was dying and at her death the money would go to a Miss Blacklock. I found out where Miss Blacklock lived and I – I came here. I took a job with Mrs Lucas. I hoped that, since this Miss Blacklock was an elderly woman without relatives, she might, perhaps, be willing to help. Not me, because I could work, but help with Harry's education. After all, it *was* Goedler money and she'd no one particular of her own to spend it on.

'And then,' Phillipa spoke faster, it was as though, now her long reserve had broken down, she couldn't get the words out fast enough – 'that hold-up happened and I began to be frightened. Because it seemed to me that the only possible person with a motive for killing Miss Blacklock was *me*. I hadn't the least idea who Julia was – we aren't identical twins and we're not much alike to look at. No, it seemed as though I was the only one bound to be suspected.'

She stopped and pushed her fair hair back from her face, and Craddock suddenly realized that the faded snapshot in the box of letters must have been a photograph of Phillipa's mother. The likeness was undeniable. He knew too why that mention of closing and unclosing hands had seemed familiar – Phillipa was doing it now.

'Miss Blacklock has been good to me. Very *very* good to me – I didn't try to kill her. I never thought of killing her. But, all the same, I'm Pip.' She added, 'You see, you needn't suspect Edmund any more.'

'Needn't I?' said Craddock. Again there was that acid biting tone in his voice. 'Edmund Swettenham's a young man who's fond of money. A young man, perhaps, who would like to marry a rich wife. But she wouldn't be a rich wife *unless Miss Blacklock died before Mrs Goedler*. And since it seemed almost certain that Mrs Goedler would die before Miss Blacklock, well – he had to do something about it – *didn't you, Mr Swettenham*?'

'It's a damned lie!' Edmund shouted.

And then, suddenly, a sound rose on the air. It came from the kitchen – a long unearthly shriek of terror.

'That isn't Mitzi!' cried Julia.

'No,' said Inspector Craddock, 'it's someone who's murdered three people . . .'

CHAPTER TWENTY-TWO

The Truth

When the Inspector turned on Edmund Swettenham, Mitzi had crept quietly out of the room and back to the kitchen. She was running water into the sink when Miss Blacklock entered.

Mitzi gave her a shamefaced sideways look.

'What a liar you are, Mitzi,' said Miss Blacklock pleasantly. 'Here – that isn't the way to wash up. The silver first, and fill the sink right up. You can't wash up in about two inches of water.'

Mitzi turned the taps on obediently.

'You are not angry at what I say, Miss Blacklock?' she asked.

'If I were to be angry at all the lies you tell, I should never be out of a temper,' said Miss Blacklock.

'I will go and say to the Inspector that I make it all up, shall I?' asked Mitzi.

'He knows that already,' said Miss Blacklock, pleasantly.

Mitzi turned off the taps and as she did so two hands came up behind her head and with one swift movement forced it down into the water-filled sink.

'Only *I* know that you're telling the truth for once,' said Miss Blacklock viciously.

Mitzi thrashed and struggled but Miss Blacklock was strong and her hands held the girl's head firmly under water.

Then, from somewhere quite close behind her, Dora Bunner's voice rose piteously on the air:

'*Oh Lotty – Lotty – don't do it . . . Lotty.*'

Miss Blacklock screamed. Her hands flew up in the air, and Mitzi, released, came up choking and spluttering.

Miss Blacklock screamed again and again. For there was no one, except Mitzi, there in the kitchen with her . . .

'*Dora, Dora, forgive me. I had to . . . I had to* – '

She rushed distractedly towards the scullery door – and the bulk of Sergeant Fletcher barred her way, just as Miss Marple stepped, flushed and triumphant, out of the broom cupboard.

'I could always mimic people's voices,' said Miss Marple.

'You'll have to come with me, madam,' said Sergeant Fletcher. 'I was a witness of your attempt to drown this girl. And there will be other charges. I must warn you, Letitia Blacklock –'

'Charlotte Blacklock,' corrected Miss Marple. 'That's who she is, you know. Under that choker of pearls she always wears you'll find a scar of the operation.'

'Operation?'

'Operation for goitre.'

Miss Blacklock, quite calm now, looked at Miss Marple.

'So you know all about it?' she said.

'Yes, I've known for some time.'

Charlotte Blacklock sat down by the table and began to cry.

'You shouldn't have done that,' she said. 'Not made Dora's voice come. I loved Dora. I really loved Dora.'

Inspector Craddock and the others had crowded in the doorway.

Constable Edwards, who added a knowledge of first-aid and artificial respiration to his other accomplishments, was busy with Mitzi. As soon as Mitzi could speak she was lyrical with self-praise.

'I do that good, do I not? I am clever! And I am brave! Oh, I am brave! Very very nearly was *I* murdered, too. But I am so brave I risk *everything*.'

With a rush Miss Hinchliffe thrust aside the others and leapt upon the weeping figure of Charlotte Blacklock by the table.

It took all Sergeant Fletcher's strength to hold her off.

'Now then –' he said. 'Now then – no, no, Miss Hinchliffe –'

Between clenched teeth Miss Hinchliffe was muttering:

'Let me get at her. Just let me get at her. It was she who killed Amy Murgatroyd.'

Charlotte Blacklock looked up and sniffed.

'I didn't want to kill her. I didn't want to kill anybody – I had to – but it's Dora I mind about – after Dora was dead, I was all alone – ever since she died – I've been alone – oh, Dora – Dora –'

And once again she dropped her head on her hands and wept.

CHAPTER TWENTY-THREE

Evening at the Vicarage

Miss Marple sat in the tall armchair. Bunch was on the floor in front of the fire with her arms round her knees.

The Reverend Julian Harmon was leaning forward and was for once looking more like a schoolboy than a man foreshadowing his own maturity. And Inspector Craddock was smoking his pipe and drinking a whisky and soda and was clearly very much off duty. An outer circle was composed of Julia, Patrick, Edmund and Phillipa.

'I think it's your story, Miss Marple,' said Craddock.

'Oh no, my dear boy. I only just helped a little, here and there. *You* were in charge of the whole thing, and conducted it all, and you know so much that I don't.'

'Well, tell it together,' said Bunch impatiently. 'Bit each. Only let Aunt Jane start because I like the muddly way her mind works. When did you first think that the whole thing was a put-up job by Blacklock?'

'Well, my dear Bunch, it's hard to say. Of course, right at the very beginning, it did seem as though the ideal person – or, rather, the *obvious* person, I should say – to have arranged the hold-up *was* Miss Blacklock herself. She was the only person who was known to have been in contact with Rudi Scherz, and how much easier to arrange something like that when it's your own house. The central heating, for instance. No fires – because that would have meant light in the room. But the only person who could have arranged *not* to have a fire was the mistress of the house herself.

'Not that I thought of all that at the time – it just seemed to me that it was a pity it *couldn't* be as simple as that! Oh, no, I was taken in like everyone else, I thought that someone really did want to kill Letitia Blacklock.'

'I think I'd like to get clear first on what really happened,' said Bunch. 'Did this Swiss boy recognize her?'

'Yes. He'd worked in –'

She hesitated and looked at Craddock.

'In Dr Adolf Koch's clinic in Berne,' said Craddock. 'Koch was a world-famous specialist on operations for goitre. Charlotte Blacklock went there to have her goitre removed and Rudi Scherz was one of the orderlies. When he came to England he recognized in the hotel a lady who had been a patient and on the spur of the moment he spoke to her. I dare say he mightn't have done that if he'd paused to think, because he left the place under a cloud, but that was some time after Charlotte had been there, so she wouldn't know anything about it.'

'So he never said anything to her about Montreux and his father being a hotel proprietor?'

'Oh, no, she made that up to account for his having spoken to her.'

'It must have been a great shock to her,' said Miss Marple, thoughtfully. 'She felt reasonably safe – and then the almost impossible mischance of somebody turning up who had known her – not as one of the two Miss Blacklocks – she was prepared for *that* – but definitely as *Charlotte* Blacklock, a patient who'd been operated on for goitre.

'But you wanted to go through it all from the beginning. Well, the beginning, I think – if Inspector Craddock agrees with me – was when Charlotte Blacklock, a pretty, light-hearted, affectionate girl, developed that enlargement of the thyroid gland that's called a goitre. It ruined her life, because she was a very sensitive girl. A girl, too, who had always set a lot of stress on her personal appearance. And girls just at that age, in their teens, are particularly sensitive about themselves. If she'd had a mother, or a reasonable father, I don't think she would have got into the morbid state she undoubtedly did get into. She had no one, you see, to take her out of herself, and force her to see people and lead a normal life and not think too much about her infirmity. And, of course, in a different household, she might have been sent for an operation many years earlier.

'But Dr Blacklock, I think, was an old-fashioned, narrow-minded, tyrannical and obstinate man. He didn't believe in these operations. Charlotte must take it from him that nothing could be done – apart from dosage with iodine and other drugs. Charlotte *did* take it from him, and I think her sister also placed more faith in Dr Blacklock's powers as a physician than he deserved.

'Charlotte was devoted to her father in a rather weak and soppy way. She thought, definitely, that her father knew best. But she shut herself up more and more as the goitre became larger and more unsightly, and refused to see people. She was actually a kindly, affectionate creature.'

'That's an odd description of a murderess,' said Edmund.

'I don't know that it is,' said Miss Marple. 'Weak and kindly people are often very treacherous. And if they've got a grudge against life it saps the little moral strength that they may possess.

'Letitia Blacklock, of course, had quite a different personality. Inspector Craddock told me that Belle Goedler described her as really *good* – and I think Letitia *was* good. She was a woman of great integrity who found – as she put it herself – a great difficulty in understanding how people couldn't see what was dishonest. Letitia Blacklock, however tempted, would never have contemplated any kind of fraud for a moment.

'Letitia was devoted to her sister. She wrote her long accounts of everything that happened in an effort to keep her sister in touch with life. She was worried by the morbid state Charlotte was getting into.

'Finally Dr Blacklock died. Letitia, without hesitation, threw up her position with Randall Goedler and devoted herself to Charlotte. She took her to Switzerland to consult authorities there on the possibility of operating. It had been left very late – but as we know the operation was successful. The deformity was gone – and the scar this operation had left was easily hidden by a choker of pearls or beads.

'The war had broken out. A return to England was difficult and the two sisters stayed in Switzerland doing various Red Cross and other work. That's right, isn't it, Inspector?'

'Yes, Miss Marple.'

'They got occasional news from England – amongst other things, I expect, they heard that Belle Goedler could not live long. I'm sure it would be only human nature for them both to have planned and talked together of the days ahead when a big fortune would be theirs to spend. One has got to realize, I think, that this prospect meant much more to *Charlotte* than it did to Letitia. For the first time in her life, Charlotte could go about feeling herself a normal woman, a woman at whom no one looked with either repulsion or pity. She was free at last to enjoy life – and she had a whole lifetime, as it were, to crowd into her remaining years. To travel, to have a house and beautiful grounds – to have clothes and jewels, and go to plays and concerts, to gratify every whim – it was all a kind of fairy tale come true to Charlotte.

'And then Letitia, the strong healthy Letitia, got flu which turned to pneumonia and died within the space of a week! Not only had Charlotte lost her sister, but the whole dream existence she had planned for herself was cancelled. I think, you know, that she may have felt almost resentful towards Letitia. Why need Letitia have died, just then, when they had just had a letter saying Belle Goedler could not last long? Just one more month, perhaps, and the money would have been Letitia's – and hers when Letitia died . . .

'Now this is where I think the difference between the two came in. Charlotte didn't really feel that what she suddenly thought of doing was wrong – not really wrong. The money was meant to come to Letitia – it *would* have come to Letitia in the course of a few months – and she regarded herself and Letitia as one.

'Perhaps the idea didn't occur to her until the doctor or someone asked her her sister's Christian name – and then she realized how to nearly everyone they had appeared as the two Miss Blacklocks – elderly, well-bred Englishwomen, dressed much the same, with a strong family resemblance (and, as I pointed out to Bunch, one elderly woman is *so* like another). Why shouldn't it be Charlotte who had died and *Letitia* who was alive?

'It was an impulse, perhaps, more than a plan. Letitia was buried under Charlotte's name. "Charlotte" was dead, "Letitia" came to England. All the natural initiative and energy, dormant for so many years, were now in the ascendant. As Charlotte she had played second fiddle. She now assumed the airs of command, the feeling of command that had been Letitia's. They were not really so unlike in mentality – though there was, I think, a big difference *morally*.

'Charlotte had, of course, to take one or two obvious precautions. She bought a house in a part of England quite unknown to her. The only people she had to avoid were a few people in her own native town in Cumberland (where in any case she'd lived as a recluse)

509

and, of course, Belle Goedler who had known Letitia so well that any impersonation would have been out of the question. Handwriting difficulties were got over by the arthritic condition of her hands. It was really very easy because so few people had ever really known Charlotte.'

'But supposing she'd met people who'd known Letitia?' asked Bunch. 'There must have been plenty of those.'

'They wouldn't matter in the same way. Someone might say: "I came across Letitia Blacklock the other day. She's changed so much I really wouldn't have known her." But there still wouldn't be any suspicion in their minds that she wasn't Letitia. People *do* change in the course of ten years. *Her* failure to recognize *them* could always be put down to her short-sightedness; and you must remember that she knew every detail of Letitia's life in London – the people she met – the places she went. She'd got Letitia's letters to refer to, and she could quickly have disarmed any suspicion by mention of some incident, or an inquiry after a mutual friend. No, it was recognition as *Charlotte* that was the only thing she had to fear.

'She settled down at Little Paddocks, got to know her neighbours and, when she got a letter asking dear Letitia to be kind, she accepted with pleasure the visit of two young cousins she had never seen. Their acceptance of her as Aunt Letty increased her security.

'The whole thing was going splendidly. And then she made her big mistake. It was a mistake that arose solely from her kindness of heart and her naturally affectionate nature. She got a letter from an old school-friend who had fallen on evil days, and she hurried to the rescue. Perhaps it may have been partly because she was, in spite of everything, lonely. Her secret kept her in a way apart from people. And she had been genuinely fond of Dora Bunner and remembered her as a symbol of her own gay carefree days at school. Anyway, on an impulse, she answered Dora's letter in person. And very surprised Dora must have been! She'd written to *Letitia* and the sister who turned up in answer to her letter was *Charlotte*. There was never any question of pretending to be Letitia to Dora. Dora was one of the few old friends who had been admitted to see Charlotte in her lonely and unhappy days.

'And because she knew that Dora would look at the matter in exactly the same way as she did herself, she told Dora what she had done. Dora approved wholeheartedly. In her confused muddle-headed mind it seemed only right that dear Lotty should not be done out of her inheritance by Letty's untimely death. Lotty *deserved* a reward for all the patient suffering she had borne so bravely. It would have been most unfair if all that money should have gone to someone nobody had ever heard of.

'She quite understood that nothing must be allowed to get out. It was like an extra pound of butter. You couldn't talk about it but there was nothing wrong about having it. So Dora came to Little Paddocks – and very soon Charlotte began to understand that she had made a terrible mistake. It was not merely the fact that Dora Bunner, with her muddles and her mistakes and her bungling, was quite maddening to live with. Charlotte could have put up with that – because she really cared for Dora and, anyway, knew from the doctor that Dora hadn't got a very long time to live. But Dora very soon became a real danger. Though Charlotte and Letitia had called each other by their full names, Dora was the kind of person who always uses abbreviations. To her the sisters had always been Letty and Lotty. And, though she schooled her tongue resolutely to call her friend Letty, the old name often slipped out. Memories of the past, too, were rather apt to come to her tongue – and Charlotte had constantly to be on the watch to check these forgetful allusions. It began to get on her nerves.

'Still, nobody was likely to pay much attention to Dora's inconsistencies. The real blow to Charlotte's security came, as I say, when she was recognized and spoken to by Rudi Scherz at the Royal Spa Hotel.

'I think that the money Rudi Scherz used to replace his earlier defalcations at the hotel may have come from Charlotte Blacklock. Inspector Craddock doesn't believe – and I don't either – that Rudi Scherz applied to her for money with any idea of blackmail in his head.'

'He hadn't the faintest idea he knew anything to blackmail her about,' said Inspector Craddock. 'He knew that he was quite a personable young man – and he was aware by experience that personable young men sometimes can get money out of elderly ladies if they tell a hard-luck story convincingly enough.

'But she may have seen it differently. She may have thought that it was a form of insidious blackmail, that perhaps he suspected something – and that later, if there was publicity in the papers as there might be after Belle Goedler's death, he would realize that in her he had found a gold mine.

'And she was committed to the fraud now. She'd established herself as Letitia Blacklock. With the Bank. With Mrs Goedler. The only snag was this rather dubious Swiss hotel clerk, an unreliable character, and possibly a blackmailer. If only he were out of the way – she'd be safe.'

'Perhaps she made it all up as a kind of fantasy first. She'd been starved of emotion and drama in her life. She pleased herself by working out the details. How would she go about getting rid of him?

'She made her plan. And at last she decided to act on it. She told her story of a sham hold-up at a party to Rudi Scherz, explained that she wanted a stranger to act the part of the "gangster", and offered him a generous sum for his co-operation.

'And the fact that he agreed without any suspicion is what makes me quite certain that Scherz had no idea that he had any kind of hold over her. To him she was just a rather foolish old woman, very ready to part with money.

'She gave him the advertisement to insert, arranged for him to pay a visit to Little Paddocks to study the geography of the house, and showed him the spot where she would meet him and let him into the house on the night in question. Dora Bunner, of course, knew nothing about all this.

'The day came –' He paused.

Miss Marple took up the tale in her gentle voice.

'She must have spent a very miserable day. You see, it still wasn't too late to draw back . . . Dora Bunner told us that Letty was frightened that day and she must have been frightened. Frightened of what she was going to do, frightened of the plan going wrong – but not frightened enough to draw back.

'It had been fun, perhaps, getting the revolver out of Colonel Easterbrook's collar-drawer. Taking along eggs, or jam – slipping upstairs in the empty house. It had been fun getting the second door in the drawing-room oiled, so that it would open and shut noiselessly. Fun suggesting the moving of the table outside the door so that Phillipa's flower arrangements would show to better advantage. It may have all seemed like a game. But what was going to happen next definitely wasn't a game any longer. Oh, yes, she was frightened . . . Dora Bunner was right about that.'

'All the same, she went through with it,' said Craddock. 'And it all went according to plan. She went out just after six to "shut up the ducks", and she let Scherz in then and gave him the mask and cloak and gloves and the torch. Then, at 6.30, when the clock begins to chime, she's ready by that table near the archway with her hand on the cigarette-box. It's all so natural. Patrick, acting as host, has gone for the drinks. She, the hostess, is fetching the cigarettes. She's judged, quite correctly, that when the clock begins to chime, everyone will look at the clock. They did. Only one person, the devoted Dora, kept her eyes fixed on her friend. And she told us, in her very first statement, exactly what Miss Blacklock did. She said that Miss Blacklock had picked up the vase of violets.

'She'd previously frayed the cord of the lamp so that the wires were nearly bare. The whole thing only took a second. The cigarette-box, the vase and the little switch were all close together. She picked up the violets, spilt the water on the frayed place, and switched on the lamp. Water's a good conductor of electricity. The wires fused.'

'Just like the other afternoon at the Vicarage,' said Bunch. 'That's what startled you so, wasn't it, Aunt Jane?'

'Yes, my dear. I've been puzzling about those lights. I'd realized that there were two lamps, a pair, and that one had been changed for the other – probably during the night.'

'That's right,' said Craddock. 'When Fletcher examined that lamp the next morning it was, like all the others, perfectly in order, no frayed flex or fused wires.'

'I'd understood what Dora Bunner meant by saying it had been the *shepherdess* the night before,' said Miss Marple, 'but I fell into the error of thinking, as she thought, that *Patrick* had been responsible. The interesting thing about Dora Bunner was that she was quite unreliable in repeating things she had heard – she always used her imagination to exaggerate or distort them, and she was usually wrong in what she *thought* – but she was quite accurate about the things she *saw*. She saw Letitia pick up the violets –'

'And she saw what she described as a flash and a crackle,' put in Craddock.

'And, of course, when dear Bunch spilt the water from the Christmas roses on to the lamp wire I realized at once that only Miss Blacklock herself could have fused the lights because only she was near that table.'

'I could kick myself,' said Craddock. 'Dora Bunner even prattled about a burn on the table where someone had "put their cigarette down" – but nobody had even lit a cigarette ... And the violets were dead because there was no water in the vase – a slip on Letitia's part – she ought to have filled it up again. But I suppose she thought nobody would notice, and as a matter of fact Miss Bunner was quite ready to believe that she herself had put no water in the vase to begin with.'

He went on:

'She was highly suggestible, of course. And Miss Blacklock took advantage of that more than once. Bunny's suspicions of Patrick were, I think, induced by her.'

'Why pick on me?' demanded Patrick in an aggrieved tone.

'It was not, I think, a serious suggestion – but it would keep Bunny distracted from any suspicion that Miss Blacklock might be stage-managing the business. Well, we know what happened next. As soon as the lights went and everyone was exclaiming, she slipped out through the previously oiled door and up behind Rudi Scherz who was flashing his torch round the room and playing his part with gusto. I don't suppose he realized for a moment she was there behind him with her gardening gloves pulled on and the revolver in her hand. She waits till the torch reaches the spot she must aim for – the wall near which she is supposed to be standing. Then she fires rapidly twice and as he swings round startled she holds the revolver close to his body and fires again. She lets the revolver fall by his body, throws her gloves carelessly on the hall table, then back through the other door and across to where she had been standing when the lights went out. She nicked her ear – I don't quite know how –'

'Nail scissors, I expect,' said Miss Marple. 'Just a snip on the lobe of the ear lets out a lot of blood. That was very good psychology, of course. The actual blood running down over her white blouse made it seem certain that she *had* been shot at, and that it had been a near miss.'

'It ought to have gone off quite all right,' said Craddock. 'Dora Bunner's insistence that Scherz had definitely aimed at Miss Black-lock had its uses. Without meaning it, Dora Bunner conveyed the impression that she'd actually seen her friend wounded. It might have been brought in Suicide or Accidental Death. And the case would have been closed. That it was kept open is due to Miss Marple here.'

'Oh, no, no.' Miss Marple shook her head energetically. 'Any little efforts on my part were quite incidental. It was you who weren't satisfied, Mr Craddock. It was *you* who wouldn't let the case be closed.'

'I wasn't happy about it,' said Craddock. 'I knew it was all wrong somewhere. But I didn't see *where* it was wrong, till you showed me. And after that Miss Blacklock had a real piece of bad luck. I discovered that that second door had been tampered with. Until that moment, whatever we agreed *might* have happened – we'd nothing to go upon but a pretty theory. But that oiled door was *evidence*. And I hit upon it by pure chance – by catching hold of a handle by mistake.'

'I think you were *led* to it, Inspector,' said Miss Marple. 'But then I'm old-fashioned.'

'So the hunt was up again,' said Craddock. 'But this time with a difference. We were looking now for someone with a motive to kill Letitia Blacklock.'

'And there *was* someone with a motive, and Miss Blacklock knew it,' said Miss Marple. 'I think she recognized Phillipa almost at once. Because Sonia Goedler seems to have been one of the very few people who had been admitted to Charlotte's privacy. And when one is old (you wouldn't know this yet, Mr Craddock) one has a much better memory for a face you've seen when you were young than you have for anyone you've only met a year or two ago. Phillipa must have been just about the same age as her mother was when Charlotte remembered her, and she was very like her mother. The odd thing is that I think Charlotte was very pleased to recognize Phillipa. She became very fond of Phillipa and I think, unconsciously, it helped to stifle any qualms of conscience she may have had. She told herself that when she inherited the money she was going to look after Phillipa. She would treat her as a daughter. Phillipa and Harry should live with her. She felt quite happy and beneficent about it. But once the Inspector began asking questions and finding out about ''Pip and Emma'' Charlotte became very uneasy. She didn't want to make a scapegoat of Phillipa. Her whole idea had been to make the business look like a hold-up by a young criminal and his accidental death. But now, with the discovery of the oiled door, the whole viewpoint was changed. And, except for Phillipa, there wasn't (as far as *she* knew, for she had absolutely no idea of Julia's identity) anyone with the least possible motive for wishing to kill her. She did her best to shield Phillipa's identity. She was quick-witted enough to tell you when you asked her that Sonia was small and dark, and she took the old snapshots out of the album, so that you shouldn't notice any resemblance, at the same time as she removed snapshots of Letitia herself.'

'And to think I suspected Mrs Swettenham of being Sonia Goedler,' said Craddock disgustedly.

'My poor mamma,' murmured Edmund. 'A woman of blameless life – or so I have always believed.'

'But of course,' Miss Marple went on, 'it was Dora Bunner who was the real danger. Every day Dora got more forgetful and more talkative. I remember the way Miss Blacklock looked at her the day we went to tea there. Do you know why? Dora had just called her Lotty again. It seemed to us a mere harmless slip of the tongue. But it frightened Charlotte. And so it went on. Poor Dora could not stop herself talking. That day we had coffee together in the Bluebird, I had the oddest impression that Dora was talking about *two* people, not one – and so, of course, she was. At one moment she spoke of her friend as not pretty but having so much character – but almost at the same moment she described her as a pretty light-hearted girl. She'd talk of Letty as so clever and so successful – and then say what a sad life she'd had; and then there was that quotation about stern affliction bravely borne – which really didn't seem to fit Letitia's life at all. Charlotte must, I think, have overheard a good deal that morning she came into the café. She certainly must have heard Dora mention about the lamp having been changed – about its being the shepherd and not the shepherdess. And she realized then what a very real danger to her security poor devoted Dora Bunner was.

'I'm afraid that that conversation with me in the café really sealed Dora's fate – if you'll excuse such a melodramatic expression. But I think it would have come to the same in the end . . . Because life couldn't be safe for Charlotte while Dora Bunner was alive. She loved Dora – she didn't want to kill Dora – but she couldn't see any other way. And I expect (like Nurse Ellerton that I was telling you about, Bunch) she persuaded herself that it was really almost a *kindness*. Poor Bunny – not long to live anyway and perhaps a painful end. The queer thing is that she did her best to make Bunny's last day a happy day. The birthday party – and the special cake . . .'

'Delicious Death,' said Phillipa with a shudder.

'Yes – yes, it was rather like that . . . she tried to give her friend a delicious death . . . The party, and all the things she liked to eat, and trying to stop people saying things to upset her. And then the tablets, whatever they were, in the aspirin bottle by her own bed so that Bunny, when she couldn't find the new bottle of aspirin she'd just bought, would go there to get some. And it would look, as it did look, that the tablets had been meant for *Letitia* . . .

'And so Bunny died in her sleep, quite happily, and Charlotte felt safe again. But she missed Dora Bunner – she missed her affection and her loyalty, she missed being able to talk to her about the old days . . . She cried bitterly the day I came up with that note from Julian – and her grief was quite genuine. She'd killed her own dear friend . . .'

'That's horrible,' said Bunch. 'Horrible.'

'But it's very human,' said Julian Harmon. 'One forgets how human murderers are.'

'I know,' said Miss Marple. 'Human. And often very much to be pitied. But very dangerous, too. Especially a weak kindly murderer like Charlotte Blacklock. Because, once a weak person gets *really* frightened, they get savage with terror and they've no self-control at all.'

'Murgatroyd?' said Julian.

'Yes, poor Miss Murgatroyd. Charlotte must have come up to the cottage and heard them rehearsing the murder. The window was open and she listened. It had never occurred to her until that moment that there was anyone else who could be a danger to her. Miss Hinchliffe was urging her friend to remember what she'd seen and until that moment Charlotte hadn't realized that anyone could have seen anything at all. She'd assumed that everybody would automatically be looking at Rudi Scherz. She must have held her breath outside the window and listened. Was it going to be all right? And then, just as Miss Hinchliffe rushed off to the station Miss Murgatroyd got to a point which showed that she had stumbled on the truth. She called after Miss Hinchliffe: "She wasn't *there* . . ."

'I asked Miss Hinchliffe, you know, if that was the way she said it ... Because if she'd said "*She* wasn't there" it wouldn't have meant the same thing.'

'Now that's too subtle a point for me,' said Craddock.

Miss Marple turned her eager pink and white face to him.

'Just think what's going on in Miss Murgatroyd's mind ... One does see things, you know, and not know one sees them. In a railway accident once, I remember noticing a large blister of paint at the side of the carriage. I could have *drawn* it for you afterwards. And once, when there was a flying bomb in London – splinters of glass everywhere – and the shock – but what I remember best is a woman standing in front of me who had a big hole half-way up the leg of her stockings and the stockings didn't match. So when Miss Murgatroyd stopped thinking and just tried to remember what she *saw*, she remembered a good deal.

'She started, I think, near the mantelpiece, where the torch must have hit first – then it went along the two windows and there were people in between the windows and her. Mrs Harmon with her knuckles screwed into her eyes for instance. She went on in her mind following the torch past Miss Bunner with her mouth open and her eyes staring – past a blank wall and a table with a lamp and a cigarette-box. And then came the shots – and quite suddenly she remembered a most incredible thing. She'd seen the wall where, later, there were the two bullet holes, the wall where Letitia Blacklock had been standing when she was shot, and at the moment when the revolver went off and Letty was shot *Letty hadn't been there* ...

'You see what I mean now? She'd been thinking of the three women Miss Hinchliffe had told her to think about. If one of them hadn't been there, it would have been the *personality* she'd have fastened upon. She'd have said – in effect – "*That's* the one! *She* wasn't there!" But it was a *place* that was in her mind – a place where someone should have been – but the place wasn't filled – there wasn't anybody there. The place was there – but the person wasn't. And she couldn't take it in all at once. "How extraordinary, Hinch," she said. "She wasn't *there*." ... So that could only mean Letitia Blacklock ...'

'But you knew before that, didn't you?' said Bunch. 'When the lamp fused. When you wrote down those things on the paper.'

'Yes, my dear. It all came together then, you see – all the various isolated bits – and made a coherent pattern.'

Bunch quoted softly:

'*Lamp?* Yes. *Violets?* Yes. *Bottle of Aspirin.* You meant that Bunny had been going to buy a new bottle that day, and so she ought not to have needed to take Letitia's?'

'Not unless her own bottle had been taken or hidden. It had to appear as though Letitia Blacklock was the one meant to be killed.'

'Yes, I see. And then "Delicious Death". The cake – but more than the cake. The whole party set-up. A happy day for Bunny before she died. Treating her rather like a dog you were going to destroy. That's what I find the most horrible thing of all – the sort of – of spurious kindness.'

'She *was* quite a kindly woman. What she said at the last in the kitchen was quite true. "I didn't want to kill anybody." What she wanted was a great deal of money that didn't belong to her! And before that desire – (and it had become a kind of obsession – the money was to pay her back for all the suffering life had inflicted on her) – everything else went to the wall. People with a grudge against the world are always dangerous. They seem to think life owes them something. I've known many an invalid who has suffered far worse and been cut off from life much more than Charlotte Blacklock – and they've managed to lead happy contented lives. It's what's in *yourself* that makes you happy or unhappy. But, oh dear, I'm afraid I'm straying away from what we were talking about. Where were we?'

'Going over your list,' said Bunch. 'What did you mean by "Making enquiries"? Inquiries about what?'

Miss Marple shook her head playfully at Inspector Craddock.

'You ought to have seen that, Inspector Craddock. You showed me that letter from Letitia Blacklock to her sister. It had the word "enquiries" in it twice – each time spelt with an *e*. But in the note I asked Bunch to show you, Miss Blacklock had written "inquiries" with an *i*. People don't often alter their spelling as they get older. It seemed to me very significant.'

'Yes,' Craddock agreed. 'I ought to have spotted that.'

Bunch was continuing. '*Severe affliction bravely borne*. That's what Bunny said to you in the café and of course Letitia hadn't had any affliction. *Iodine*. That put you on the track of goitre?'

'Yes, dear. Switzerland, you know, and Miss Blacklock giving the impression that her sister had died of consumption. But I remembered then that the greatest authorities on goitre and the most skilful surgeons operating on it are Swiss. And it linked up with those really rather preposterous pearls that Letitia Blacklock always wore. Not really her *style* – but just right for concealing the scar.'

'I understand now her agitation the night the string broke,' said Craddock. 'It seemed at the time quite disproportionate.'

'And after that, it *was* Lotty you wrote, not Letty as we thought,' said Bunch.

'Yes, I remembered that the sister's name was Charlotte, and that Dora Bunner had called Miss Blacklock Lotty once or twice – and that each time she did so she had been very upset afterwards.'

'And what about Berne and Old Age Pension?'

'Rudi Scherz had been an orderly in a hospital in Berne.'

'And Old Age Pension.'

'Oh, my dear Bunch, I mentioned that to you in the Bluebird though I didn't really see the application then. How Mrs Wotherspoon drew Mrs Bartlett's Old Age Pension as well as her own – though Mrs Bartlett had been dead for years – simply because one old woman is so like another old woman – yes, it all made a pattern and I felt so worked up I went out to cool my head a little and think what could be done about proving all this. Then Miss Hinchliffe picked me up and we found Miss Murgatroyd . . .'

Miss Marple's voice dropped. It was no longer excited and pleased. It was quiet and remorseless.

'I knew then something had *got* to be done. Quickly! But there still wasn't any *proof*. I thought out a possible plan and I talked to Sergeant Fletcher.'

'And I have had Fletcher on the carpet for it!' said Craddock. 'He'd no business to go agreeing to your plans without reporting first to me.'

'He didn't like it, but I talked him into it,' said Miss Marple. 'We went up to Little Paddocks and I got hold of Mitzi.'

Julia drew a deep breath and said, 'I can't imagine how you ever got her to do it.'

'I worked on her, my dear,' said Miss Marple. 'She thinks far too much about herself anyway, and it will be good for her to have done something for others. I flattered her up, of course, and said I was sure if she'd been in her own country she'd have been in the Resistance movement, and she said, "Yes, indeed." And I said I could see she had got just the temperament for that sort of work. She was brave, didn't mind taking risks, and could act a part. I told her stories of deeds done by girls in the Resistance movements, some of them true, and some of them, I'm afraid, invented. She got tremendously worked up!'

'Marvellous,' said Patrick.

'And then I got her to agree to do her part. I rehearsed her till she was word-perfect. Then I told her to go upstairs to her room and not come down until Inspector Craddock came. The worst of these excitable people is that they're apt to go off half-cocked and start the whole thing before the time.'

'She did it very well,' said Julia.

'I don't quite see the point,' said Bunch. 'Of course, I wasn't there —' she added apologetically.

'The point was a little complicated — and rather touch and go. The idea was that Mitzi, whilst admitting, as though casually, that blackmail *had* been in her mind, was now so worked up and terrified that she was willing to come out with the truth. She'd seen, through the keyhole of the dining-room, Miss Blacklock in the hall with a revolver behind Rudi Scherz. She'd seen, that is, *what had actually taken place*. Now the only danger was that Charlotte Blacklock might have realized that, as the key was in the keyhole, Mitzi couldn't possibly have seen anything at all. But I banked on the fact that you don't think of things like that when you've just had a bad shock. All she could take in was that Mitzi had seen her.'

Craddock took over the story.

'But — and this was essential — I pretended to receive this with scepticism, and I made an immediate attack as though unmasking my batteries at last upon someone who had not been previously suspected. I accused Edmund —'

'And very nicely *I* played *my* part,' said Edmund. 'Hot denial. All according to plan. What wasn't according to plan, Phillipa, my love, was you throwing in your little chirp and coming out into the open as "Pip". Neither the Inspector nor I had any idea you were Pip. *I* was going to be Pip! It threw us off our stride for the moment, but the Inspector made a masterly comeback and made some perfectly filthy insinuations about my wanting a rich wife which will probably stick in your subconscious and make irreparable trouble between us one day.'

'I don't see why that was necessary.'

'Don't you? It meant that, *from Charlotte Blacklock's point of view*, the only person who suspected or knew the truth was *Mitzi*. The suspicions of the police were elsewhere. They had treated Mitzi for the moment as a liar. But if Mitzi were to persist, they might listen to her and take her seriously. So Mitzi had got to be silenced.'

'Mitzi went straight out of the room and back to the kitchen — just like I had told her,' said Miss Marple. 'Miss Blacklock came out after her almost immediately. Mitzi was apparently alone in the kitchen. Sergeant Fletcher was behind the scullery door. And I was in the broom cupboard in the kitchen. Luckily I'm very thin.'

Bunch looked at Miss Marple.

'What did you expect to happen, Aunt Jane?'

'One of two things. Either Charlotte would offer Mitzi money to hold her tongue — and Sergeant Fletcher would be a witness to that offer; or else — or else I thought she'd try to kill Mitzi.'

'But she couldn't hope to get away with *that*? She'd have been suspected at once.'

'Oh, my dear, she was past reasoning. She was just a snapping terrified cornered rat. Think what had happened that day. The scene between Miss Hinchliffe and Miss Murgatroyd. Miss Hinchliffe driving off to the station. As soon as she comes back Miss Murgatroyd will explain that Letitia Blacklock wasn't in the room that night. There's just a few minutes in which to make sure Miss Murgatroyd can't tell anything. No time to make a plan or set a stage. Just crude murder. She greets the poor woman and strangles her. Then a quick rush home, to change, to be sitting by the fire when the others come in, as though she'd never been out.

'And then came the revelation of Julia's identity. She breaks her pearls and is terrified they may notice her scar. Later, the Inspector telephones that he's bringing everyone there. No time to think, to rest. Up to her neck in murder now, no mercy killing — or undesirable young man to be put out of the way. Crude plain murder. Is she safe? Yes, so far. And then comes Mitzi — yet *another* danger. Kill Mitzi, stop her tongue! She's beside herself with fear. Not human any longer. Just a dangerous animal.'

'But why were you in the broom cupboard, Aunt Jane?' asked Bunch. 'Couldn't you have left it to Sergeant Fletcher?'

'It was safer with two of us, my dear. And, besides, I knew I could mimic Dora Bunner's voice. If anything could break Charlotte Blacklock down – that would.'

'And it did . . . !'

'Yes . . . she went to pieces.'

There was a long silence as memory laid hold of them; and then, speaking with determined lightness, to ease the strain, Julia said:

'It's made a wonderful difference to Mitzi. She told me yesterday that she was taking a post near Southampton. And she said (Julia produced a very good imitation of Mitzi's accent):

' "I go there and if they say to me you have to register with the police – you are an alien, I say to them, 'Yes, I will register! The police, they know me well. I assist the police! Without me the police never would they have made the arrest of a very dangerous criminal. I risked my life because I am brave – brave like a lion – I do not care about risks.' 'Mitzi,' they say to me, 'you are a *heroine*, you are superb.' 'Ach! it is nothing, I say.' " '

Julia stopped.

'And a great deal more,' she added.

'I think,' said Edmund thoughtfully, 'that soon Mitzi will have assisted the police in not one but hundreds of cases!'

'She's softened towards me,' said Phillipa. 'She actually presented me with the recipe for Delicious Death as a kind of wedding present. She added that I was on no account to divulge the secret to Julia, because Julia had ruined her omelette pan.'

'Mrs Lucas,' said Edmund, 'is all over Phillipa now that, since Belle Goedler's death, Phillipa and Julia have inherited the Goedler millions. She sent us some silver asparagus tongs as a wedding present. I shall have enormous pleasure in *not* asking her to the wedding!'

'And so they lived happily ever after,' said Patrick. 'Edmund and Phillipa – and Julia and Patrick?' he added, tentatively.

'Not with me, you won't live happily ever after,' said Julia. 'The remarks that Inspector Craddock improvised to address to Edmund apply far more aptly to you. You *are* the sort of young man who would like a rich wife. Nothing doing!'

'There's gratitude for you,' said Patrick. 'After all I did for that girl.'

'Nearly landed me in prison on a murder charge — that's what your forgetfulness nearly did for me,' said Julia. 'I shall never forget that evening when your sister's letter came. I really thought I was for it. I couldn't see any way out.

'As it is,' she added musingly, 'I think I shall go on the stage.'

'What? You, too?' groaned Patrick.

'Yes. I might go to Perth. See if I can get your Julia's place in the rep there. Then, when I've learnt my job, I shall go into theatre management — and put on Edmund's plays, perhaps.'

'I thought you wrote novels,' said Julian Harmon.

'Well, so did I,' said Edmund. 'I began writing a novel. Rather good it was. Pages about an unshaven man getting out of bed and what he smelt like, and the grey streets, and a horrible old woman with dropsy and a vicious young tart who dribbled down her chin — and they all talked interminably about the state of the world and wondered what they were alive for. And suddenly I began to wonder too ... And then a rather comic idea occurred to me ... and I jotted it down — and then I worked up rather a good little scene ... All very obvious stuff. But somehow I got interested ... And before I knew what I was doing I'd finished a roaring farce in three acts.'

'What's it called?' asked Patrick. '*What the Butler Saw*?'

'Well, it easily might be ... As a matter of fact I've called it *Elephants Do Forget*. What's more, it's been accepted and it's going to be produced!'

'Elephants Do Forget,' murmured Bunch. 'I thought they didn't?'

The Rev. Julian Harmon gave a guilty start.

'My goodness. I've been so interested. My *sermon*!'

'Detective stories again,' said Bunch. 'Real-life ones this time.'

'You might preach on Thou Shall Do No Murder,' suggested Patrick.

'No,' said Julian Harmon quietly. 'I shan't take that as my text.'

'No,' said Bunch. 'You're quite right, Julian. I know a much nicer text, a happy text.' She quoted in a fresh voice, '*For lo the Spring is here and the Voice of the Turtle is heard in the Land* — I haven't got it quite right — but you know the one I mean. Though why a *turtle* I can't think. I shouldn't think turtles have got nice voices at all.'

'The word *turtle*,' explained the Rev. Julian Harmon, 'is not very happily translated. It doesn't mean a reptile but the turtle dove. The Hebrew word in the original is –'

Bunch interrupted him by giving him a hug and saying:

'I know one thing – *you* think that the Ahasuerus of the Bible is Artaxerxes the Second, but between you and me it was Artaxerxes the Third.'

As always, Julian Harmon wondered why his wife should think that story so particularly funny.

'Tiglath Pileser wants to go and help you,' said Bunch. 'He ought to be a very proud cat. *He* showed us how the lights fused.'

Epilogue

'We ought to order some papers,' said Edmund to Phillipa upon the day of their return to Chipping Cleghorn after the honeymoon. 'Let's go along to Totman's.'

Mr Totman, a heavy-breathing, slow-moving man, received them with affability.

'Glad to see you back, sir. *And* madam.'

'We want to order some papers.'

'Certainly, sir. And your mother is keeping well, I hope? Quite settled down at Bournemouth?'

'She loves it,' said Edmund, who had not the faintest idea whether this was so or not but, like most sons, preferred to believe that all was well with those loved, but frequently irritating beings, parents.

'Yes, sir. Very agreeable place. Went there for my holiday last year. Mrs Totman enjoyed it very much.'

'I'm glad. About papers, we'd like –'

'And I hear you have a play on in London, sir. Very amusing, so they tell me.'

'Yes, it's doing very well.'

'Called *Elephants Do Forget*, so I hear. You'll excuse me, sir, asking you, but I always thought that they *didn't* – forget, I mean.'

'Yes – yes, exactly – I've begun to think it was a mistake calling it that. So many people have said just what you say.'

'A kind of natural history fact, I've always understood.'

'Yes – yes. Like earwigs making good mothers.'

'Do they indeed, sir? Now, that's a fact I *didn't* know.'

'About the papers –'

'*The Times*, sir, I think it was?' Mr Totman paused with pencil uplifted.

'The *Daily Worker*,' said Edmund firmly. 'And the *Daily Telegraph*,' said Phillipa. 'And the *New Statesman*,' said Edmund. 'The *Radio Times*,' said Phillipa. 'The *Spectator*,' said Edmund. 'The *Gardener's Chronicle*,' said Phillipa.

They both paused to take breath.

'Thank you, sir,' said Mr Totman. '*And* the *Gazette*, I suppose.'

'No,' said Edmund.

'No,' said Phillipa.

'Excuse me, you *do* want the *Gazette*?'

'No.'

'No.'

'You mean' – Mr Totman liked to get things perfectly clear – 'you *don't* want the *Gazette*!'

'No, we don't.'

'Certainly not.'

'You don't want the *North Benham News and Chipping Cleghorn Gazette*?'

'No.'

'You don't want me to send it along to you every week?'

'*No*.' Edmund added: 'Is that quite clear now?'

'Oh, yes, sir – yes.'

Edmund and Phillipa went out, and Mr Totman padded into his back parlour.

'Got a pencil, Mother?' he said. 'My pen's run out.'

'Here you are,' said Mrs Totman, seizing the order book. 'I'll do it. What do they want?'

'*Daily Worker, Daily Telegraph, Radio Times, New Statesman, Spectator* – let me see – *Gardener's Chronicle*.'

'*Gardener's Chronicle*,' repeated Mrs Totman, writing busily. 'And the *Gazette*.'

'They don't want the *Gazette*.'

'What?'

'They don't want the *Gazette*. They said so.'

'Nonsense,' said Mrs Totman. 'You don't hear properly. Of course they want the *Gazette*! Everybody has the *Gazette*. How else would they know what's going on round here?'

4.50 from Paddington

CHAPTER ONE

Mrs McGillicuddy panted along the platform in the wake of the porter carrying her suitcase. Mrs McGillicuddy was short and stout, the porter was tall and free-striding. In addition, Mrs McGillicuddy was burdened with a large quantity of parcels; the result of a day's Christmas shopping. The race was, therefore, an uneven one, and the porter turned the corner at the end of the platform whilst Mrs McGillicuddy was still coming up the straight.

No. 1 Platform was not at the moment unduly crowded, since a train had just gone out, but in the no-man's-land beyond, a milling crowd was rushing in several directions at once, to and from undergrounds, left-luggage offices, tearooms, inquiry offices, indicator boards, and the two outlets, Arrival and Departure, to the outside world.

Mrs McGillicuddy and her parcels were buffeted to and fro, but she arrived eventually at the entrance to No. 3 Platform, and deposited one parcel at her feet whilst she searched her bag for the ticket that would enable her to pass the stern uniformed guardian at the gate.

At that moment, a Voice, raucous yet refined, burst into speech over her head.

'The train standing at Platform 3,' the Voice told her, 'is the 4.50 for Brackhampton, Milchester, Waverton, Carvil Junction, Roxeter and stations to Chadmouth. Passengers for Brackhampton and Milchester travel at the rear of the train. Passengers for Vanequay change at Roxeter.' The Voice shut itself off with a click, and then reopened conversation by announcing the arrival at Platform 9 of the 4.35 from Birmingham and Wolverhampton.

Mrs McGillicuddy found her ticket and presented it. The man clipped it, murmured: 'On the right – rear portion.'

Mrs McGillicuddy padded up the platform and found her porter, looking bored and staring into space, outside the door of a third-class carriage.

'Here you are, lady.'

'I'm travelling first-class,' said Mrs McGillicuddy.

'You didn't say so,' grumbled the porter. His eye swept her mascu-line-looking pepper-and-salt tweed coat disparagingly.

Mrs McGillicuddy, who *had* said so, did not argue the point. She was sadly out of breath.

The porter retrieved the suitcase and marched with it to the adjoining coach where Mrs McGillicuddy was installed in solitary splendour. The 4.50 was not much patronized, the first-class clientele preferring either the faster morning express, or the 6.40 with dining-car. Mrs McGillicuddy handed the porter his tip which he received with disappointment, clearly considering it more applicable to third-class than to first-class travel. Mrs McGillicuddy, though prepared to spend money on comfortable travel after a night journey from the North and a day's feverish shopping, was at no time an extravagant tipper.

She settled herself back on the plush cushions with a sigh and opened her magazine. Five minutes later, whistles blew, and the train started. The magazine slipped from Mrs McGillicuddy's hand, her head dropped sideways, three minutes later she was asleep. She slept for thirty-five minutes and awoke refreshed. Resettling her hat which had slipped askew she sat up and looked out of the window at what she could see of the flying countryside. It was quite dark now, a dreary misty December day – Christmas was only five days ahead. London had been dark and dreary; the country was no less so, though occasionally rendered cheerful with its constant clusters of lights as the train flashed through towns and stations.

'Serving last tea now,' said an attendant, whisking open the corridor door like a jinn. Mrs McGillicuddy had already partaken of tea at a large department store. She was for the moment amply nourished. The attendant went on down the corridor uttering his monotonous cry. Mrs McGillicuddy looked up at the rack where her various parcels reposed, with a pleased expression. The face towels had been excellent value and just what Margaret wanted, the space gun for Robby and the rabbit for Jean were highly satisfactory, and that evening coatee was just the thing she herself needed, warm but dressy. The pullover for Hector, too . . . her mind dwelt with approval on the soundness of her purchases.

Her satisfied gaze returned to the window, a train travelling in the opposite direction rushed by with a screech, making the windows rattle and causing her to start. The train clattered over points and passed through a station.

Then it began suddenly to slow down, presumably in obedience to a signal. For some minutes it crawled along, then stopped, presently it began to move forward again. Another up-train passed them, though with less vehemence than the first one. The train gathered speed again. At that moment another train, also on a down-line, swerved inwards towards them, for a moment with almost alarming effect. For a time the two trains ran parallel, now one gaining a little, now the other. Mrs McGillicuddy looked from her window through the windows of the parallel carriages. Most of the blinds were down, but occasionally the occupants of the carriages were visible. The other train was not very full and there were many empty carriages.

At the moment when the two trains gave the illusion of being stationary, a blind in one of the carriages flew up with a snap. Mrs McGillicuddy looked into the lighted first-class carriage that was only a few feet away.

Then she drew her breath in with a gasp and half-rose to her feet.

Standing with his back to the window and to her was a man. His hands were round the throat of a woman who faced him, and he was slowly, remorselessly, strangling her. Her eyes were starting from their sockets, her face was purple and congested. As Mrs McGillicuddy watched fascinated, the end came; the body went limp and crumpled in the man's hands.

At the same moment, Mrs McGillicuddy's train slowed down again and the other began to gain speed. It passed forward and a moment or two later it had vanished from sight.

Almost automatically Mrs McGillicuddy's hand went up to the communication cord, then paused, irresolute. After all, what use would it be ringing the cord of the train in which *she* was travelling? The horror of what she had seen at such close quarters, and the unusual circumstances, made her feel paralysed. *Some* immediate action was necessary – but what?

The door of her compartment was drawn back and a ticket collector said, 'Ticket, please.'

Mrs McGillicuddy turned to him with vehemence.

'A woman has been strangled,' she said. 'In a train that has just passed. I saw it.'

The ticket collector looked at her doubtfully.

'I beg your pardon, madam?'

'A man strangled a woman! In a train. I saw it — through there.' She pointed to the window.

The ticket collector looked extremely doubtful.

'Strangled?' he said disbelievingly.

'Yes, *strangled*! I saw it, I tell you. You must *do* something at once!'

The ticket collector coughed apologetically.

'You don't think, madam, that you may have had a little nap and — er —' he broke off tactfully.

'I have had a nap, but if you think this was a dream, you're quite wrong. I *saw* it, I tell you.'

The ticket collector's eyes dropped to the open magazine lying on the seat. On the exposed page was a girl being strangled whilst a man with a revolver threatened the pair from an open doorway.

He said persuasively: 'Now don't you think, madam, that you'd been reading an exciting story, and that you just dropped off, and awaking a little confused —'

Mrs McGillicuddy interrupted him.

'*I saw it*,' she said. 'I was as wide awake as you are. And I looked out of the window into the window of the train alongside, and a man was strangling a woman. And what I want to know is, what are you going to do about it?'

'Well — madam —'

'You're going to do *something*, I suppose?'

The ticket collector sighed reluctantly and glanced at his watch.

'We shall be in Brackhampton in exactly seven minutes. I'll report what you've told me. In what direction was the train you mention going?'

'This direction, of course. You don't suppose I'd have been able to see this if a train had flashed past going in the other direction?'

The ticket collector looked as though he thought Mrs McGillicuddy was quite capable of seeing anything anywhere as the fancy took her. But he remained polite.

'You can rely on me, madam,' he said. 'I will report your statement. Perhaps I might have your name and address — just in case . . .'

Mrs McGillicuddy gave him the address where she would be

staying for the next few days and her permanent address in Scotland, and he wrote them down. Then he withdrew with the air of a man who has done his duty and dealt successfully with a tiresome member of the travelling public.

Mrs McGillicuddy remained frowning and vaguely unsatisfied. Would the ticket collector report her statement? Or had he just been soothing her down? There were, she supposed vaguely, a lot of elderly women travelling around, fully convinced that they had unmasked communist plots, were in danger of being murdered, saw flying saucers and secret space ships, and reported murders that had never taken place. If the man dismissed her as one of those . . .

The train was slowing down now, passing over points and running through the bright lights of a large town.

Mrs McGillicuddy opened her handbag, pulled out a receipted bill which was all she could find, wrote a rapid note on the back of it with her ball-pen, put it into a spare envelope that she fortunately happened to have, stuck the envelope down and wrote on it.

The train drew slowly into a crowded platform. The usual ubiquitous Voice was intoning:

'The train now arriving at Platform 1 is the 5.38 for Milchester, Waverton, Roxeter, and stations to Chadmouth. Passengers for Market Basing take the train now waiting at No. 3 platform. No. 1 bay for stopping train to Carbury.'

Mrs McGillicuddy looked anxiously along the platform. So many passengers and so few porters. Ah, there was one! She hailed him authoritatively.

'Porter! Please take this at once to the Stationmaster's office.'

She handed him the envelope, and with it a shilling.

Then, with a sigh, she leaned back. Well, she had done what she could. Her mind lingered with an instant's regret on the shilling . . . Sixpence would really have been enough . . .

Her mind went back to the scene she had witnessed. Horrible, quite horrible . . . She was a strong-nerved woman, but she shivered. What a strange – what a fantastic thing to happen to her, Elspeth McGillicuddy! If the blind of the carriage had not happened to fly up . . . But that, of course, was Providence.

Providence had willed that she, Elspeth McGillicuddy, should be a witness of the crime. Her lips set grimly.

Voices shouted, whistles blew, doors were banged shut. The 5.38

drew slowly out of Brackhampton station. An hour and five minutes later it stopped at Milchester.

Mrs McGillicuddy collected her parcels and her suitcase and got out. She peered up and down the platform. Her mind reiterated its former judgment: Not enough porters. Such porters as there were seemed to be engaged with mail bags and luggage vans. Passengers nowadays seemed always expected to carry their own cases. Well, she couldn't carry her suitcase and her umbrella and all her parcels. She would have to wait. In due course she secured a porter.

'Taxi?'

'There will be something to meet me, I expect.'

Outside Milchester station, a taxi-driver who had been watching the exit came forward. He spoke in a soft local voice.

'Is it Mrs McGillicuddy? For St Mary Mead?'

Mrs McGillicuddy acknowledged her identity. The porter was recompensed, adequately if not handsomely. The car, with Mrs McGillicuddy, her suitcase, and her parcels drove off into the night. It was a nine-mile drive. Sitting bolt upright in the car, Mrs McGillicuddy was unable to relax. Her feelings yearned for expression. At last the taxi drove along the familiar village street and finally drew up at its destination; Mrs McGillicuddy got out and walked up the brick path to the door. The driver deposited the cases inside as the door was opened by an elderly maid. Mrs McGillicuddy passed straight through the hall to where, at the open sitting-room door, her hostess awaited her; an elderly frail old lady.

'Elspeth!'

'Jane!'

They kissed and, without preamble or circumlocution, Mrs McGillicuddy burst into speech.

'Oh, Jane!' she wailed. 'I've just seen a *murder*!'

CHAPTER TWO

True to the precepts handed down to her by her mother and grand-mother – to wit: that a true lady can neither be shocked nor surprised – Miss Marple merely raised her eyebrows and shook her head, as she said:

'*Most* distressing for you, Elspeth, and surely *most* unusual. I think you had better tell me about it *at once.*'

That was exactly what Mrs McGillicuddy wanted to do. Allowing her hostess to draw her nearer to the fire, she sat down, pulled off her gloves and plunged into a vivid narrative.

Miss Marple listened with close attention. When Mrs McGilli-cuddy at last paused for breath, Miss Marple spoke with decision.

'The best thing, I think, my dear, is for you to go upstairs and take off your hat and have a wash. Then we will have supper – during which we will not discuss this *at all.* After supper we can go into the matter thoroughly and discuss it from every aspect.'

Mrs McGillicuddy concurred with this suggestion. The two ladies had supper, discussing, as they ate, various aspects of life as lived in the village of St Mary Mead. Miss Marple commented on the general distrust of the new organist, related the recent scandal about the chemist's wife, and touched on the hostility between the school-mistress and the village institute. They then discussed Miss Marple's and Mrs McGillicuddy's gardens.

'Paeonies,' said Miss Marple as she rose from table, 'are most unaccountable. Either they do – or they don't do. But if they *do* establish themselves, they are with you for life, so to speak, and really most beautiful varieties nowadays.'

They settled themselves by the fire again, and Miss Marple brought out two old Waterford glasses from a corner cupboard, and from another cupboard produced a bottle.

'No coffee to-night for you, Elspeth,' she said. 'You are already over-excited (and no wonder!) and probably would not sleep. I prescribe a glass of my cowslip wine, and later, perhaps, a cup of camomile tea.'

Mrs McGillicuddy acquiescing in these arrangements, Miss Marple poured out the wine.

'Jane,' said Mrs McGillicuddy, as she took an appreciative sip, '*you* don't think, do you, that I dreamt it, or imagined it?'

'Certainly not,' said Miss Marple with warmth.

Mrs McGillicuddy heaved a sigh of relief.

'That ticket collector,' she said, '*he* thought so. Quite polite, but all the same —'

'I think, Elspeth, that that was quite natural under the circumstances. It sounded — and indeed was — a most unlikely story. And you were a complete stranger to him. No, I have no doubt at all that you saw what you've told me you saw. It's very extraordinary — but not at all impossible. I recollect myself being interested when a train ran parallel to one on which I was travelling, to notice what a vivid and intimate picture one got of what was going on in one or two of the carriages. A little girl, I remember once, playing with a teddy bear, and suddenly she threw it deliberately at a fat man who was asleep in the corner and he bounced up and looked most indignant, and the other passengers looked *so* amused. I saw them all quite vividly. I could have described afterwards exactly what they looked like and what they had on.'

Mrs McGillicuddy nodded gratefully.

'That's just how it was.'

'The man had his back to you, you say. So you didn't see his face?'

'No.'

'And the woman, you can describe her? Young, old?'

'Youngish. Between thirty and thirty-five, I should think. I couldn't say closer than that.'

'Good-looking?'

'That again, I couldn't say. Her face, you see, was all contorted and —'

Miss Marple said quickly:

'Yes, yes, I quite understand. How was she dressed?'

'She had on a fur coat of some kind, a palish fur. No hat. Her hair was blonde.'

'And there was nothing distinctive that you can remember about the man?'

538

Mrs McGillicuddy took a little time to think carefully before she replied.

'He was tallish – and dark, I think. He had a heavy coat on so that I couldn't judge his build very well.' She added despondently, 'It's not really very much to go on.'

'It's something,' said Miss Marple. She paused before saying: 'You feel quite sure, in your own mind, that the girl *was* – dead?'

'She was dead, I'm sure of it. Her tongue came out and – I'd rather not talk about it . . .'

'Of course not. Of course not,' said Miss Marple quickly. 'We shall know more, I expect, in the morning.'

'In the morning?'

'I should imagine it will be in the morning papers. After this man had attacked and killed her, he would have a body on his hands. What would he do? Presumably he would leave the train quickly at the first station – by the way, can you remember if it was a corridor carriage?'

'No, it was not.'

'That seems to point to a train that was not going far afield. It would almost certainly stop at Brackhampton. Let us say he leaves the train at Brackhampton, perhaps arranging the body in a corner seat, with her face hidden by the fur collar to delay discovery. Yes – I think that that is what he would do. But of course it will be discovered before very long – and I should imagine that the news of a murdered woman discovered on a train would be almost certain to be in the morning papers – we shall see.'

II

But it was not in the morning papers.

Miss Marple and Mrs McGillicuddy, after making sure of this, finished their breakfast in silence. Both were reflecting.

After breakfast, they took a turn round the garden. But this, usually an absorbing pastime, was to-day somewhat half-hearted. Miss Marple did indeed call attention to some new and rare species she had acquired for her rock-garden but did so in an almost absent-minded manner. And Mrs McGillicuddy did not, as was customary, counter-attack with a list of her own recent acquisitions.

539

'The garden is not looking at all as it should,' said Miss Marple, but still speaking absent-mindedly. 'Doctor Haydock has absolutely forbidden me to do any stooping or kneeling – and really, what can you do if you *don't* stoop or kneel? There's old Edwards, of course – but *so* opinionated. And all this jobbing gets them into bad habits, lots of cups of tea and so much pottering – not any real *work*.'

'Oh, I know,' said Mrs McGillicuddy. 'Of course, there's no question of my being *forbidden* to stoop, but really, especially after meals – and having put on weight' – she looked down at her ample proportions – 'it does bring on heartburn.'

There was a silence and then Mrs McGillicuddy planted her feet sturdily, stood still, and turned on her friend.

'*Well?*' she said.

It was a small insignificant word, but it acquired full significance from Mrs McGillicuddy's tone, and Miss Marple understood its meaning perfectly.

'I know,' she said.

The two ladies looked at each other.

'I think,' said Miss Marple, 'we might walk down to the police station and talk to Sergeant Cornish. He's intelligent and patient, and I know him very well, and he knows me. I think he'll listen – and pass the information on to the proper quarter.'

Accordingly, some three-quarters of an hour later, Miss Marple and Mrs McGillicuddy were talking to a fresh-faced grave man between thirty and forty who listened attentively to what they had to say.

Frank Cornish received Miss Marple with cordiality and even deference. He set chairs for the two ladies, and said: 'Now what can we do for you, Miss Marple?'

Miss Marple said: 'I would like you, please, to listen to my friend Mrs McGillicuddy's story.'

And Sergeant Cornish had listened. At the close of the recital he remained silent for a moment or two.

Then he said:

'That's a very extraordinary story.' His eyes, without seeming to do so, had sized Mrs McGillicuddy up whilst she was telling it.

On the whole, he was favourably impressed. A sensible woman, able to tell a story clearly; not, so far as he could judge, an over-imaginative or a hysterical woman. Moreover, Miss Marple, so it

540

seemed, believed in the accuracy of her friend's story and he knew all about Miss Marple. Everybody in St Mary Mead knew Miss Marple; fluffy and dithery in appearance, but inwardly as sharp and as shrewd as they make them.

He cleared his throat and spoke.

'Of course,' he said, 'you may have been mistaken — I'm not saying you *were*, mind — but you *may* have been. There's a lot of horse-play goes on — it mayn't have been serious or fatal.'

'I know what I saw,' said Mrs McGillicuddy grimly.

'And you won't budge from it,' thought Frank Cornish, 'and I'd say that, likely or unlikely, you may be right.'

Aloud he said: 'You reported it to the railway officials, and you've come and reported it to me. That's the proper procedure and you may rely on me to have inquiries instituted.'

He stopped. Miss Marple nodded her head gently, satisfied. Mrs McGillicuddy was not quite so satisfied, but she did not say anything. Sergeant Cornish addressed Miss Marple, not so much because he wanted her ideas, as because he wanted to hear what she would say.

'Granted the facts are as reported,' he said, 'what do you think has happened to the body?'

'There seems to be only two possibilities,' said Miss Marple without hesitation. 'The most *likely* one, of course, is that the body was left in the train, but that seems improbable now, for it would have been found some time last night, by another traveller, or by the railway staff at the train's ultimate destination.'

Frank Cornish nodded.

'The only other course open to the murderer would be to push the body out of the train on to the line. It must, I suppose, be still on the track somewhere as yet undiscovered — though that does seem a little unlikely. But there would be, as far as I can see, no other way of dealing with it.'

'You read about bodies being put in trunks,' said Mrs McGillicuddy, 'but no-one travels with trunks nowadays, only suitcases, and you couldn't get a body into a suitcase.'

'Yes,' said Cornish. 'I agree with you both. The body, if there is a body, ought to have been discovered by now, or will be very soon. I'll let you know any developments there are — though I dare say you'll read about them in the papers. There's the possibility, of course, that the woman, though savagely attacked, was not actually dead. She may have been able to leave the train on her own feet.'

'Hardly without assistance,' said Miss Marple. 'And if so, it will have been noticed. A man, supporting a woman whom he says is ill.'

'Yes, it will have been noticed,' said Cornish. 'Or if a woman was found unconscious or ill in a carriage and was removed to hospital, that, too, will be on record. I think you may rest assured that you'll hear about it all in a very short time.'

But that day passed and the next day. On that evening Miss Marple received a note from Sergeant Cornish.

In regard to the matter on which you consulted me, full inquiries have been made, with no result. No woman's body has been found. No hospital has administered treatment to a woman such as you describe, and no case of a woman suffering from shock or taken ill, or leaving a station supported by a man has been observed. You may take it that the fullest inquiries have been made. I suggest that your friend may have witnessed a scene such as she described but that it was much less serious than she supposed.

CHAPTER THREE

'Less serious? Fiddlesticks!' said Mrs McGillicuddy. 'It was murder!'

She looked defiantly at Miss Marple and Miss Marple looked back at her.

'Go on, Jane,' said Mrs McGillicuddy. 'Say it was all a mistake! Say I imagined the whole thing! That's what you think now, isn't it?'

'Anyone *can be* mistaken,' Miss Marple pointed out gently. 'Anybody, Elspeth – even you. I think we must bear that in mind. But I still think, you know, that you were most probably *not* mistaken . . . You use glasses for reading, but you've got very good far sight – and what you saw impressed you very powerfully. You were definitely suffering from shock when you arrived here.'

'It's a thing I shall never forget,' said Mrs McGillicuddy with a shudder. 'The trouble is, I don't see what I can do about it!'

'I don't think,' said Miss Marple thoughtfully, 'that there's anything more you can do about it.' (If Mrs McGillicuddy had been alert to the tones of her friend's voice, she might have noticed a very faint stress laid on the *you*.) 'You've reported what you saw — to the railway people and to the police. No, there's nothing more you can do.'

'That's a relief, in a way,' said Mrs McGillicuddy, 'because as you know, I'm going out to Ceylon immediately after Christmas — to stay with Roderick, and I certainly do not want to put that visit off — I've been looking forward to it so much. Though of course I *would* put it off if I thought it was my duty,' she added conscientiously.

'I'm sure you would, Elspeth, but as I say, I consider you've done everything you possibly could do.'

'It's up to the police,' said Mrs McGillicuddy. 'And if the police choose to be stupid—'

Miss Marple shook her head decisively.

'Oh, no,' she said, 'the police aren't stupid. And that makes it interesting, doesn't it?'

Mrs McGillicuddy looked at her without comprehension and Miss Marple reaffirmed her judgment of her friend as a woman of excellent principles and no imagination.

'One wants to know,' said Miss Marple, 'what really happened.'

'She was killed.'

'Yes, but *who* killed her, and *why*, and what happened to her body? Where is it now?'

'That's the business of the police to find out.'

'Exactly — and they *haven't* found out. That means, doesn't it, that the man was clever — very clever. I can't imagine, you know,' said Miss Marple, knitting her brows, '*how* he disposed of it . . . You kill a woman in a fit of passion — it must have been unpremeditated, you'd never choose to kill a woman in such circumstances just a few minutes before running into a big station. No, it must have been a quarrel — jealousy — something of that kind. You strangle her — and there you are, as I say, with a dead body on your hands and on the point of running into a station. What *could* you do except as I said at first, prop the body up in a corner as though asleep, hiding the face, and then yourself leave the train as quickly as possible. I don't see any other possibility – and yet there must have been one . . .'

Miss Marple lost herself in thought.

Mrs McGillicuddy spoke to her twice before Miss Marple answered.

'You're getting deaf, Jane.'

'Just a little, perhaps. People do not seem to me to enunciate their words as clearly as they used to do. But it wasn't that I did not hear you. I'm afraid I wasn't paying attention.'

'I just asked about the trains to London to-morrow. Would the afternoon be all right? I'm going to Margaret's and she isn't expecting me before teatime.'

'I wonder, Elspeth, if you would mind going up by the 12.15? We could have an early lunch.'

'Of course and –' Miss Marple went on, drowning her friend's words:

'And I wonder, too, if Margaret would mind if you didn't arrive for tea – if you arrived about seven, perhaps?'

Mrs McGillicuddy looked at her friend curiously.

'What's on your mind, Jane?'

'I suggest, Elspeth, that I should travel up to London with you, and that we should travel down again as far as Brackhampton in the train you travelled by the other day. You would then return to London from Brackhampton and I would come on here as you did. *I*, of course, would pay the *fares*,' Miss Marple stressed this point firmly.

Mrs McGillicuddy ignored the financial aspect.

'What on earth do you expect, Jane?' she asked. 'Another murder?'

'Certainly not,' said Miss Marple shocked. 'But I confess I should like to see for myself, under your guidance, the – the – really it is most difficult to find the correct term – the *terrain* of the crime.'

So accordingly on the following day Miss Marple and Mrs McGillicuddy found themselves in two opposite corners of a first-class carriage speeding out of London by the 4.50 from Paddington. Paddington had been even more crowded than on the preceding Friday – as there were now only two days to go before Christmas, but the 4.50 was comparatively peaceful – at any rate, in the rear portion.

On this occasion no train drew level with them, or they with

544

another train. At intervals trains flashed past them towards London. On two occasions trains flashed past them the other way going at high speed. At intervals Mrs McGillicuddy consulted her watch doubtfully.

'It's hard to tell just when – we'd passed through a station I know . . .' But they were continually passing through stations.

'We're due in Brackhampton in five minutes,' said Miss Marple.

A ticket collector appeared in the doorway. Miss Marple raised her eyes interrogatively. Mrs McGillicuddy shook her head. It was not the same ticket collector. He clipped their tickets, and passed on staggering just a little as the train swung round a long curve. It slackened speed as it did so.

'I expect we're coming into Brackhampton,' said Mrs McGillicuddy.

'We're getting into the outskirts, I think,' said Miss Marple.

There were lights flashing past outside, buildings, an occasional glimpse of streets and trams. Their speed slackened further. They began crossing points.

'We'll be there in a minute,' said Mrs McGillicuddy, 'and I can't really see this journey has been any good *at all*. Has it suggested anything to you, Jane?'

'I'm afraid not,' said Miss Marple in a rather doubtful voice.

'A sad waste of good money,' said Mrs McGillicuddy, but with less disapproval than she would have used had she been paying for herself. Miss Marple had been quite adamant on that point.

'All the same,' said Miss Marple, 'one likes to see with one's own eyes where a thing happened. This train's just a few minutes late. Was yours on time on Friday?'

'I think so. I didn't really notice.'

The train drew slowly into the busy length of Brackhampton station. The loudspeaker announced hoarsely, doors opened and shut, people got in and out, milled up and down the platform. It was a busy crowded scene.

Easy, thought Miss Marple, for a murderer to merge into that crowd, to leave the station in the midst of that pressing mass of people, or even to select another carriage and go on in the train wherever its ultimate destination might be. Easy to be one male passenger amongst many. But not so easy to make a body vanish into thin air. That body must be *somewhere*.

Mrs McGillicuddy had descended. She spoke now from the platform, through the open window.

'Now take care of yourself, Jane,' she said. 'Don't catch a chill. It's a nasty treacherous time of year, and you're not so young as you were.'

'I know,' said Miss Marple.

'And don't let's worry ourselves any more over all this. We've done what we could.'

Miss Marple nodded, and said:

'Don't stand about in the cold, Elspeth. Or you'll be the one to catch a chill. Go and get yourself a good hot cup of tea in the Restaurant Room. You've got time, twelve minutes before your train back to town.'

'I think perhaps I will. Good-bye, Jane.'

'Good-bye, Elspeth. A happy Christmas to you. I hope you find Margaret well. Enjoy yourself in Ceylon, and give my love to dear Roderick — if he remembers me at all, which I doubt.'

'Of course he remembers you — very well. You helped him in some way when he was at school — something to do with money that was disappearing from a locker — he's never forgotten it.'

'Oh, *that*!' said Miss Marple.

Mrs McGillicuddy turned away, a whistle blew, the train began to move. Miss Marple watched the sturdy thickset body of her friend recede. Elspeth could go to Ceylon with a clear conscience — she had done her duty and was freed from further obligation.

Miss Marple did not lean back as the train gathered speed. Instead she sat upright and devoted herself seriously to thought. Though in speech Miss Marple was woolly and diffuse, in mind she was clear and sharp. She had a problem to solve, the problem of her own future conduct; and, perhaps strangely, it presented itself to her as it had to Mrs McGillicuddy, as a question of duty.

Mrs McGillicuddy had said that they had both done all that they could do. It was true of Mrs McGillicuddy but about herself Miss Marple did not feel so sure.

It was a question, sometimes, of using one's special gifts . . . But perhaps that was conceited . . . After all, what *could* she do? Her friend's words came back to her, 'You're not so young as you were . . .'

Dispassionately, like a general planning a campaign, or an

accountant assessing a business, Miss Marple weighed up and set down in her mind the facts for and against further enterprise. On the credit side were the following:

1. My long experience of life and human nature.
2. Sir Henry Clithering and his godson (now at Scotland Yard, I believe), who was so very nice in the Little Paddocks case.
3. My nephew Raymond's second boy, David, who is, I am almost sure, in British Railways.
4. Griselda's boy Leonard who is so very knowledgeable about maps.

Miss Marple reviewed these assets and approved them. They were all very necessary, to reinforce the weaknesses on the debit side – in particular her own bodily weakness. 'It is not,' thought Miss Marple, 'as though I could go here, there and everywhere, making inquiries and finding out things.'

Yes, that was the chief objection, her own age and weakness. Although, for her age, her health was good, yet she *was* old. And if Dr Haydock had strictly forbidden her to do practical gardening he would hardly approve of her starting out to track down a murderer. For that, in effect, was what she was planning to do – and it was there that her loophole lay. For if heretofore murder had, so to speak, been forced upon her, in this case it would be that she herself set out deliberately to seek it. And she was not sure that she wanted to do so . . . She was old – old and tired. She felt at this moment, at the end of a tiring day, a great reluctance to enter upon any project at all. She wanted nothing at all but to march home and sit by the fire with a nice tray of supper, and go to bed, and potter about the next day just snipping off a few things in the garden, tidying up in a very mild way, without stooping, without exerting herself . . .

'I'm too old for any more adventures,' said Miss Marple to herself, watching absently out of the window the curving line of an embankment . . .

A curve . . .

Very faintly something stirred in her mind . . . Just after the ticket collector had clipped their tickets . . .

It suggested an idea. Only an idea. An entirely different idea . . .

547

A little pink flush came into Miss Marple's face. Suddenly she did not feel tired at all!

'I'll write to David to-morrow morning,' she said to herself.

And at the same time another valuable asset flashed through her mind.

'Of course. My faithful Florence!'

II

Miss Marple set about her plan of campaign methodically and making due allowance for the Christmas season which was a definitely retarding factor.

She wrote to her great-nephew, David West, combining Christmas wishes with an urgent request for information.

Fortunately she was invited, as on previous years, to the vicarage for Christmas dinner, and here she was able to tackle young Leonard, home for the Christmas season, about maps.

Maps of all kinds were Leonard's passion. The reason for the old lady's inquiry about a large-scale map of a particular area did not rouse his curiosity. He discoursed on maps generally with fluency, and wrote down for her exactly what would suit her purpose best. In fact, he did better. He actually found that he had such a map amongst his collection and he lent it to her, Miss Marple promising to take great care of it and return it in due course.

III

'Maps,' said his mother, Griselda, who still, although she had a grown-up son, looked strangely young and blooming to be inhabiting the shabby old vicarage. 'What does she want with maps? I mean, what does she want them *for*?'

'I don't know,' said young Leonard, 'I don't think she said exactly.'

'I wonder now . . .' said Griselda. 'It seems very fishy to me . . . At her age the old pet ought to give up that sort of thing.'

Leonard asked what sort of thing, and Griselda said elusively:

'Oh, poking her nose into things. Why *maps*, I wonder?'

In due course Miss Marple received a letter from her great-nephew David West. It ran affectionately:

'Dear Aunt Jane, – Now what are you up to? I've got the information you wanted. There are only two trains that can possibly apply – the 4.33 and the 5 o'clock. The former is a slow train and stops at Haling Broadway, Barwell Heath, Brackhampton and then stations to Market Basing. The 5 o'clock is the Welsh express for Cardiff, Newport and Swansea. The former might be overtaken somewhere by the 4.50, although it is due in Brackhampton five minutes earlier and the latter passes the 4.50 just before Brackhampton.

In all this do I smell some village scandal of a fruity character? Did you, returning from a shopping spree in town by the 4.50, observe in a passing train the mayor's wife being embraced by the Sanitary Inspector? But why does it matter which train it was? A week-end at Porthcawl perhaps? Thank you for the pullover. Just what I wanted. How's the garden? Not very active this time of year, I should imagine.

Yours ever,
  David'

Miss Marple smiled a little, then considered the information thus presented to her. Mrs McGillicuddy had said definitely that the carriage had not been a corridor one. Therefore – not the Swansea express. The 4.33 was indicated.

Also some more travelling seemed unavoidable. Miss Marple sighed, but made her plans.

She went up to London as before on the 12.15, but this time returned not by the 4.50, but by the 4.33 as far as Brackhampton. The journey was uneventful, but she registered certain details. The train was not crowded – 4.33 was before the evening rush hour. Of the first-class carriages only one had an occupant – a very old gentleman reading the *New Statesman*. Miss Marple travelled in an empty compartment and at the two stops, Haling Broadway and Barwell Heath, leaned out of the window to observe passengers entering and leaving the train. A small number of third-class passengers got in at Haling Broadway. At Barwell Heath several third-class passengers got out. Nobody entered or left a first-class carriage except the old gentleman carrying his *New Statesman*.

As the train neared Brackhampton, sweeping around a curve of line, Miss Marple rose to her feet and stood experimentally with her back to the window over which she had drawn down the blind.

Yes, she decided, the impetus of the sudden curving of the line and the slackening of speed did throw one off one's balance back against the window and the blind might, in consequence, very easily fly up. She peered out into the night. It was lighter than it had been when Mrs McGillicuddy had made the same journey – only just dark, but there was little to see. For observation she must make a daylight journey.

On the next day she went up by the early morning train, purchased four linen pillow-cases (tut-tutting at the price!) so as to combine investigation with the provision of household necessities, and returned by a train leaving Paddington at twelve fifteen. Again she was alone in a first-class carriage. 'This taxation,' thought Miss Marple, 'that's what it is. No one can afford to travel first class except business men in the rush hours. I suppose because they can charge it to expenses.'

About a quarter of an hour before the train was due at Brackhampton, Miss Marple got out the map with which Leonard had supplied her and began to observe the countryside. She had studied the map very carefully beforehand, and after noting the name of a station they passed through, she was soon able to identify where she was just as the train began to slacken for a curve. It was a very considerable curve indeed. Miss Marple, her nose glued to the window, studied the ground beneath her (the train was running on a fairly high embankment) with close attention. She divided her attention between the country outside and the map until the train finally ran into Brackhampton.

That night she wrote and posted a letter addressed to Miss Florence Hill, 4 Madison Road, Brackhampton . . . On the following morning, going to the County library, she studied a Brackhampton directory and gazetteer, and a County history.

Nothing so far had contradicted the very faint and sketchy idea that had come to her. What she had imagined was possible. She would go no further than that.

But the next step involved action – a good deal of action – the kind of action for which she, herself, was physically unfit. If her

theory were to be definitely proved or disproved, she must at this
point have help from some other source. The question was – who?
Miss Marple reviewed various names and possibilities rejecting them
all with a vexed shake of the head. The intelligent people on whose
intelligence she could rely were all far too busy. Not only had they
all got jobs of varying importance, their leisure hours were usually
apportioned long beforehand. The unintelligent who had time on
their hands were simply, Miss Marple decided, no good.

She pondered in growing vexation and perplexity.

Then suddenly her forehead cleared. She ejaculated aloud a name.
'Of course!' said Miss Marple. '*Lucy Eyelesbarrow!*'

CHAPTER FOUR

The name of Lucy Eyelesbarrow had already made itself felt in
certain circles.

Lucy Eyelesbarrow was thirty-two. She had taken a First in Mathematics at Oxford, was acknowledged to have a brilliant mind and
was confidently expected to take up a distinguished academic career.

But Lucy Eyelesbarrow, in addition to scholarly brilliance, had a
core of good sound common sense. She could not fail to observe
that a life of academic distinction was singularly ill rewarded. She
had no desire whatever to teach and she took pleasure in contacts
with minds much less brilliant than her own. In short, she had a
taste for people, all sorts of people – and not the same people the
whole time. She also, quite frankly, liked money. To gain money
one must exploit shortage.

Lucy Eyelesbarrow hit at once upon a very serious shortage – the
shortage of any kind of skilled domestic labour. To the amazement
of her friends and fellow-scholars, Lucy Eyelesbarrow entered the
field of domestic labour.

Her success was immediate and assured. By now, after a lapse
of some years, she was known all over the British Isles. It was quite
customary for wives to say joyfully to husbands, 'It will be all right.
I *can* go with you to the States. *I've got Lucy Eyelesbarrow!*' The
point of Lucy Eyelesbarrow was that once she came into a house,

all worry, anxiety and hard work went out of it. Lucy Eyelesbarrow did everything, saw to everything, arranged everything. She was unbelievably competent in every conceivable sphere. She looked after elderly parents, accepted the care of young children, nursed the sickly, cooked divinely, got on well with any old crusted servants there might happen to be (there usually weren't), was tactful with impossible people, soothed habitual drunkards, was wonderful with dogs. Best of all she never minded *what* she did. She scrubbed the kitchen floor, dug in the garden, cleaned up dog messes, and carried coals!

One of her rules was never to accept an engagement for any long length of time. A fortnight was her usual period – a month at most under exceptional circumstances. For that fortnight you had to pay the earth! *But*, during that fortnight, your life was heaven. You could relax completely, go abroad, stay at home, do as you pleased, secure that all was going well on the home front in Lucy Eyelesbarrow's capable hands.

Naturally the demand for her services was enormous. She could have booked herself up if she chose for about three years ahead. She had been offered enormous sums to go as a permanency. But Lucy had no intention of being a permanency, nor would she book herself for more than six months ahead. And within that period, unknown to her clamouring clients, she always kept certain free periods which enabled her either to take a short luxurious holiday (since she spent nothing otherwise and was handsomely paid and kept) or to accept any position at short notice that happened to take her fancy, either by reason of its character, or because she 'liked the people'. Since she was now at liberty to pick and choose amongst the vociferous claimants for her services, she went very largely by personal liking. Mere riches would not buy you the services of Lucy Eyelesbarrow. She could pick and choose and she did pick and choose. She enjoyed her life very much and found in it a continual source of entertainment.

Lucy Eyelesbarrow read and re-read the letter from Miss Marple. She had made Miss Marple's acquaintance two years ago when her services had been retained by Raymond West, the novelist, to go and look after his old aunt who was recovering from pneumonia. Lucy had accepted the job and had gone down to St Mary Mead. She had liked Miss Marple very much. As for Miss Marple, once she had caught a glimpse out of her bedroom window of Lucy Eyelesbarrow really trenching for sweet peas in the proper way, she had leaned back on her pillows with a sigh of relief, eaten the tempting little meals that Lucy Eyelesbarrow brought to her, and listened, agreeably surprised, to the tales told by her elderly irascible maidservant of how 'I taught that Miss Eyelesbarrow a crochet pattern what she'd never heard of! Proper grateful, she was.' And had surprised her doctor by the rapidity of her convalescence.

Miss Marple wrote asking if Miss Eyelesbarrow could undertake a certain task for her – rather an unusual one. Perhaps Miss Eyelesbarrow could arrange a meeting at which they could discuss the matter.

Lucy Eyelesbarrow frowned for a moment or two as she considered. She was in reality fully booked up. But the word *unusual*, and her recollection of Miss Marple's personality, carried the day and she rang up Miss Marple straight away explaining that she could not come down to St Mary Mead as she was at the moment working, but that she was free from 2 to 4 on the following afternoon and could meet Miss Marple anywhere in London. She suggested her own club, a rather nondescript establishment which had the advantage of having several small dark writing-rooms which were usually empty.

Miss Marple accepted the suggestion and on the following day the meeting took place.

Greetings were exchanged; Lucy Eyelesbarrow led her guest to the gloomiest of the writing-rooms, and said: 'I'm afraid I'm rather booked up just at present, but perhaps you'll tell me what it is you want me to undertake?'

'It's very simple, really,' said Miss Marple. 'Unusual, but simple. I want you to find a body.'

For a moment the suspicion crossed Lucy's mind that Miss Marple was mentally unhinged, but she rejected the idea. Miss Marple was eminently sane. She meant exactly what she had said.

'What kind of a body?' asked Lucy Eyelesbarrow with admirable composure.

'A woman's body,' said Miss Marple. 'The body of a woman who was murdered – strangled actually – in a train.'

Lucy's eyebrows rose slightly.

'Well, that's certainly unusual. Tell me about it.'

Miss Marple told her. Lucy Eyelesbarrow listened attentively, without interrupting. At the end she said:

'It all depends on what your friend saw – or thought she saw –?' She left the sentence unfinished with a question in it.

'Elspeth McGillicuddy doesn't imagine things,' said Miss Marple. 'That's why I'm relying on what she said. If it had been Dorothy Cartwright, now – it would have been *quite* a different matter. Dorothy always has a good story, and quite often believes it herself, and there is usually a kind of *basis* of truth but certainly no more. But Elspeth is the kind of woman who finds it very hard to make herself believe that anything at all extraordinary or out of the way *could* happen. She's almost unsuggestible, rather like granite.'

'I see,' said Lucy thoughtfully. 'Well, let's accept it all. Where do I come in?'

'I was very much impressed by you,' said Miss Marple, 'and you see, I haven't got the physical strength nowadays to get about and do things.'

'You want me to make inquiries? That sort of thing? But won't the police have done all that? Or do you think they have been just slack?'

'Oh, no,' said Miss Marple. 'They haven't been slack. It's just that I've got a theory about the woman's body. It's got to be *somewhere*. If it wasn't found in the train, then it must have been pushed or thrown out of the train – but it hasn't been discovered anywhere on the line. So I travelled down the same way to see if there was anywhere where the body could have been thrown off the train and yet wouldn't have been found on the line – and there was. The railway line makes a big curve before getting into Brackhampton, on the edge of a high embankment. If a body were thrown out there, when the train was leaning at an angle, I *think* it would pitch right down the embankment.'

'But surely it would still be found – even there?'

'Oh, yes. It would have to be taken away ... But we'll come to that presently. Here's the place – on this map?'

Lucy bent to study where Miss Marple's finger pointed.

'It is right in the outskirts of Brackhampton now,' said Miss Marple, 'but originally it was a country house with extensive park and grounds and it's still there, untouched – ringed round with building estates and small suburban houses. It's called Rutherford

Hall. It was built by a man called Crackenthorpe, a very rich manufacturer, in 1884. The original Crackenthorpe's son, an elderly man, is living there still with, I understand, a daughter. The railway encircles quite half of the property.'

'And you want me to do – what?'

Miss Marple replied promptly.

'I want you to get a post there. Everyone is crying out for efficient domestic help – I should not imagine it would be difficult.'

'No, I don't suppose it would be difficult.'

'I understand that Mr Crackenthorpe is said locally to be somewhat of a miser. If you accept a low salary, I will make it up to the proper figure which should, I think, be rather more than the current rate.'

'Because of the difficulty?'

'Not the difficulty so much as the danger. It might, you know, be *dangerous*. It's only right to warn you of that.'

'I don't know,' said Lucy pensively, 'that the idea of danger would deter me.'

'I didn't think it would,' said Miss Marple. 'You're not that kind of person.'

'I dare say you thought it might even attract me? I've encountered very little danger in my life. But do you really believe it might be dangerous?'

'Somebody,' Miss Marple pointed out, 'has committed a very successful crime. There has been no hue-and-cry, no real suspicion. Two elderly ladies have told a rather improbable story, the police have investigated it and found nothing in it. So everything is nice and quiet. I don't think that this somebody, whoever he may be, will care about the matter being raked up – especially if you are successful.'

'What do I look for exactly?'

'Any signs along the embankment, a scrap of clothing, broken bushes – that kind of thing.'

Lucy nodded.

'And then?'

'I shall be quite close at hand,' said Miss Marple. 'An old maidservant of mine, my faithful Florence, lives in Brackhampton. She has looked after her old parents for years. They are now both dead, and she takes in lodgers – all most respectable people. She has arranged for me to have rooms with her. She will look after me most devotedly, and I feel I should like to be close at hand. I would suggest that you mention you have an elderly aunt living in the neighbourhood, and that you want a post within easy distance of her, and also that you stipulate for a reasonable amount of spare time so that you can go and see her often.'

Again Lucy nodded.

'I *was* going to Taormina the day after to-morrow,' she said. 'The holiday can wait. But I can only promise three weeks. After that, I am booked up.'

'Three weeks should be ample,' said Miss Marple. 'If we can't find out anything in three weeks, we might as well give up the whole thing as a mare's nest.'

Miss Marple departed, and Lucy, after a moment's reflection, rang up a Registry Office in Brackhampton, the manageress of which she knew very well. She explained her desire for a post in the neighbourhood so as to be near her 'aunt'. After turning down, with a little difficulty and a good deal of ingenuity, several more desirable places, Rutherford Hall was mentioned.

'That sounds exactly what I want,' said Lucy firmly.

The Registry Office rang up Miss Crackenthorpe, Miss Crackenthorpe rang up Lucy.

Two days later Lucy left London en route for Rutherford Hall.

II

Driving her own small car, Lucy Eyelesbarrow drove through an imposing pair of vast iron gates. Just inside them was what had originally been a small lodge which now seemed completely derelict, whether through war damage, or merely through neglect, it was difficult to be sure. A long winding drive led through large gloomy clumps of rhododendrons up to the house. Lucy caught her breath in a slight gasp when she saw the house which was a kind of miniature Windsor Castle. The stone steps in front of the door could have done with attention and the gravel sweep was green with neglected weeds.

She pulled an old-fashioned wrought-iron bell, and its clamour sounded echoing away inside. A slatternly woman, wiping her hands on her apron, opened the door and looked at her suspiciously.

'Expected, aren't you?' she said. 'Miss Something-barrow, she told me.'

'Quite right,' said Lucy.

The house was desperately cold inside. Her guide led her along a dark hall and opened a door on the right. Rather to Lucy's surprise, it was quite a pleasant sitting-room, with books and chintz-covered chairs.

'I'll tell her,' said the woman, and went away shutting the door after having given Lucy a look of profound disfavour.

After a few minutes the door opened again. From the first moment Lucy decided that she liked Emma Crackenthorpe.

She was a middle-aged woman with no very outstanding characteristics, neither good-looking nor plain, sensibly dressed in tweeds and pullover, with dark hair swept back from her forehead, steady hazel eyes and a very pleasant voice.

She said: 'Miss Eyelesbarrow?' and held out her hand.

Then she looked doubtful.

'I wonder,' she said, 'if this post is really what you're looking for? I don't want a housekeeper, you know, to supervise things. I want someone to do the work.'

Lucy said that that was what most people needed.

Emma Crackenthorpe said apologetically:

'So many people, you know, seem to think that just a little light dusting will answer the case – but I can do all the light dusting myself.'

'I quite understand,' said Lucy. 'You want cooking and washing-up, and housework and stoking the boiler. That's all right. That's what I do. I'm not at all afraid of work.'

'It's a big house, I'm afraid, and inconvenient. Of course we only live in a portion of it – my father and myself, that is. He is rather an invalid. We live quite quietly, and there is an Aga stove. I have several brothers, but they are not here very often. Two women come in, a Mrs Kidder in the morning, and Mrs Hart three days a week to do brasses and things like that. You have your own car?'

'Yes. It can stand out in the open if there's nowhere to put it. It's used to it.'

'Oh, there are any amount of old stables. There's no trouble about that.' She frowned a moment, then said, 'Eyelesbarrow – rather an

557

unusual name. Some friends of mine were telling me about a Lucy Eyelesbarrow — the Kennedys?'

'Yes. I was with them in North Devon when Mrs Kennedy was having a baby.'

Emma Crackenthorpe smiled.

'I know they said they'd never had such a wonderful time as when you were there seeing to everything. But I had the idea that you were terribly expensive. The sum I mentioned —'

'That's quite all right,' said Lucy. 'I want particularly, you see, to be near Brackhampton. I have an elderly aunt in a critical state of health and I want to be within easy distance of her. That's why the salary is a secondary consideration. I can't afford to do nothing. If I could be sure of having some time off most days?'

'Oh, of course. Every afternoon, till six, if you like?'

'That seems perfect.'

Miss Crackenthorpe hesitated a moment before saying: 'My father is elderly and a little — difficult sometimes. He is very keen on economy, and he says things sometimes that upset people. I wouldn't like —'

Lucy broke in quickly:

'I'm quite used to elderly people, of all kinds,' she said. 'I always manage to get on well with them.'

Emma Crackenthorpe looked relieved.

'Trouble with father!' diagnosed Lucy. 'I bet he's an old tartar.'

She was apportioned a large gloomy bedroom which a small electric heater did its inadequate best to warm, and was shown round the house, a vast uncomfortable mansion. As they passed a door in the hall a voice roared out:

'That you, Emma? Got the new girl there? Bring her in. I want to look at her.'

Emma flushed, glanced at Lucy apologetically.

The two women entered the room. It was richly upholstered in dark velvet, the narrow windows let in very little light, and it was full of heavy mahogany Victorian furniture.

Old Mr Crackenthorpe was stretched out in an invalid chair, a silver-headed stick by his side.

He was a big gaunt man, his flesh hanging in loose folds. He had a face rather like a bulldog, with a pugnacious chin. He had thick dark hair flecked with grey, and small suspicious eyes.

'Let's have a look at you, young lady.'

Lucy advanced, composed and smiling.

'There's just one thing you'd better understand straight away. Just because we live in a big house doesn't mean we're rich. We're *not* rich. We live simply – do you hear? – *simply!* No good coming here with a lot of high-faluting ideas. Cod's as good a fish as turbot any day, and don't you forget it. I don't stand for waste. I live here because my father built the house and I like it. After I'm dead they can sell it up if they want to – and I expect they will want to. No sense of family. This house is well built – it's solid, and we've got our own land around us. Keeps us private. It would bring in a lot if sold for building land but not while *I'm* alive. You won't get me out of here until you take me out feet first.'

He glared at Lucy.

'Your home is your castle,' said Lucy.

'Laughing at me?'

'Of course not. I think it's very exciting to have a real country place all surrounded by town.'

'Quite so. Can't see another house from here, can you? Fields with cows in them – right in the middle of Brackhampton. You hear the traffic a bit when the wind's that way – but otherwise it's still country.'

He added, without pause or change of tone, to his daughter:

'Ring up that damn' fool of a doctor. Tell him that last medicine's no good at all.'

Lucy and Emma retired. He shouted after them:

'And don't let that damned woman who sniffs dust in here. She's disarranged all my books.'

Lucy asked:

'Has Mr Crackenthorpe been an invalid long?'

Emma said, rather evasively:

'Oh, for years now . . . This is the kitchen.'

The kitchen was enormous. A vast kitchen range stood cold and neglected. An Aga stood demurely beside it.

Lucy asked times of meals and inspected the larder. Then she said cheerfully to Emma Crackenthorpe:

'I know everything now. Don't bother. Leave it all to me.'

Emma Crackenthorpe heaved a sigh of relief as she went up to bed that night.

'The Kennedys were quite right,' she said. 'She's wonderful.'

Lucy rose at six the next morning. She did the house, prepared vegetables, assembled, cooked and served breakfast. With Mrs Kidder she made the beds and at eleven o'clock they sat down to strong tea and biscuits in the kitchen. Mollified by the fact that Lucy 'had no airs about her', and also by the strength and sweetness of the tea, Mrs Kidder relaxed into gossip. She was a small spare woman with a sharp eye and tight lips.

'Regular old skinflint *he* is. What she has to put up with! All the same, she's not what I call down-trodden. Can hold her own all right when she has to. When the gentlemen come down she sees to it there's something decent to eat.'

'The gentlemen?'

'Yes. Big family it was. The eldest, Mr Edmund, he was killed in the war. Then there's Mr Cedric, he lives abroad somewhere. He's not married. Paints pictures in foreign parts. Mr Harold's in the City, lives in London – married an earl's daughter. Then there's Mr Alfred, he's got a nice way with him, but he's a bit of a black-sheep, been in trouble once or twice – and there's Miss Edith's husband, Mr Bryan, ever so nice, he is – she died some years ago, but he's always stayed one of the family, and there's Master Alexander, Miss Edith's little boy. He's at school, comes here for part of the holidays always; Miss Emma's terribly set on him.'

Lucy digested all this information, continuing to press tea on her informant. Finally, reluctantly, Mrs Kidder rose to her feet.

'Seem to have got along a treat, we do, this morning,' she said wonderingly. 'Want me to give you a hand with the potatoes, dear?'

'They're all done ready.'

'Well, you are a one for getting on with things! I might as well be getting along myself as there doesn't seem anything else to do.'

Mrs Kidder departed and Lucy, with time on her hands, scrubbed the kitchen table which she had been longing to do, but which she had put off so as not to offend Mrs Kidder whose job it properly was. Then she cleaned the silver till it shone radiantly. She cooked lunch, cleared it away, washed it up, and at two-thirty was ready to start exploration. She had set out the tea things ready on a tray, with sandwiches and bread and butter covered with a damp napkin to keep them moist.

She strolled round the gardens which would be the normal thing to do. The kitchen garden was sketchily cultivated with a few vegetables. The hot-houses were in ruins. The paths everywhere were overgrown with weeds. A herbaceous border near the house was the only thing that showed free of weeds and in good condition and Lucy suspected that that had been Emma's hand. The gardener was a very old man, somewhat deaf, who was only making a show of working. Lucy spoke to him pleasantly. He lived in a cottage adjacent to the big stableyard.

Leading out of the stableyard a back drive led through the park which was fenced off on either side of it, and under a railway arch into a small back lane.

Every few minutes a train thundered along the main line over the railway arch. Lucy watched the trains as they slackened speed going round the sharp curve that encircled the Crackenthorpe property. She passed under the railway arch and out into the lane. It seemed a little-used track. On the one side was the railway embankment, on the other was a high wall which enclosed some tall factory buildings. Lucy followed the lane until it came out into a street of small houses. She could hear a short distance away the busy hum of main road traffic. She glanced at her watch. A woman came out of a house nearby and Lucy stopped her.

'Excuse me, can you tell me if there is a public telephone near here?'

'Post office just at the corner of the road.'

Lucy thanked her and walked along until she came to the Post Office which was a combination shop and post office. There was a telephone box at one side. Lucy went into it and made a call. She asked to speak to Miss Marple. A woman's voice spoke in a sharp bark.

'She's resting. And I'm not going to disturb her!! She needs her rest – she's an old lady. Who shall I say called?'

'Miss Eyelesbarrow. There's no need to disturb her. Just tell her that I've arrived and everything is going on well and that I'll let her know when I've any news.'

She replaced the receiver and made her way back to Rutherford Hall.

CHAPTER FIVE

'I suppose it will be all right if I just practise a few iron shots in the park?' asked Lucy.

'Oh, yes, certainly. Are you fond of golf?'

'I'm not much good, but I like to keep in practice. It's a more agreeable form of exercise than just going for a walk.'

'Nowhere to walk outside this place,' growled Mr Crackenthorpe. 'Nothing but pavements and miserable little band boxes of houses. Like to get hold of my land and build more of them. But they won't until I'm dead. And I'm not going to die to oblige anybody. I can tell you that! Not to oblige *anybody*!'

Emma Crackenthorpe said mildly:

'Now, Father.'

'*I* know what they think — and what they're waiting for. All of 'em. Cedric, and that sly fox Harold with his smug face. As for Alfred, I wonder he hasn't had a shot at bumping me off himself. Not sure he didn't, at Christmas-time. That was a very odd turn I had. Puzzled old Quimper. He asked me a lot of discreet questions.'

'Everyone gets these digestive upsets now and again, Father.'

'All right, all right, say straight out that I ate too much! That's what you mean. And *why* did I eat too much? Because there was too much food on the table, far too much. Wasteful and extravagant. And that reminds me — you, young woman. Five potatoes you sent in for lunch — good-sized ones too. Two potatoes are enough for anybody. So don't send in more than four in future. The extra one was wasted to-day.'

'It wasn't wasted, Mr Crackenthorpe. I've planned to use it in a Spanish omelette to-night.'

'Urgh!' As Lucy went out of the room carrying the coffee tray she heard him say, 'Slick young woman, that, always got all the answers. Cooks well, though — and she's a handsome kind of girl.'

Lucy Eyelesbarrow took a light iron out of the set of golf clubs she had had the forethought to bring with her, and strolled out into the park, climbing over the fence.

She began playing a series of shots. After five minutes or so, a ball, apparently sliced, pitched on the side of the railway embankment. Lucy went up and began to hunt about for it. She looked back towards the house. It was a long way away and nobody was in the least interested in what she was doing. She continued to hunt for the ball. Now and then she played shots from the embankment down into the grass. During the afternoon she searched about a third of the embankment. Nothing. She played her ball back towards the house.

Then, on the next day, she came upon something. A thorn bush growing about half-way up the bank had been snapped off. Bits of it lay scattered about. Lucy examined the tree itself. Impaled on one of the thorns was a torn scrap of fur. It was almost the same colour as the wood, a pale brownish colour. Lucy looked at it for a moment, then she took a pair of scissors out of her pocket and snipped it carefully in half. The half she had snipped off she put in an envelope which she had in her pocket. She came down the steep slope searching about for anything else. She looked carefully at the rough grass of the field. She thought she could distinguish a kind of track which someone had made walking through the long grass. But it was very faint – not nearly so clear as her own tracks were. It must have been made some time ago and it was too sketchy for her to be sure that it was not merely imagination on her part.

She began to hunt carefully down in the grass at the foot of the embankment just below the broken thorn bush. Presently her search was rewarded. She found a powder compact, a small cheap enamelled affair. She wrapped it in her handkerchief and put it in her pocket. She searched on but did not find anything more.

On the following afternoon, she got into her car and went to see her invalid aunt. Emma Crackenthorpe said kindly, 'Don't hurry back. We shan't want you until dinner-time.'

'Thank you, but I shall be back by six at the latest.'

No. 4 Madison Road was a small drab house in a small drab street. It had very clean Nottingham lace curtains, a shining white doorstep and a well-polished brass door handle. The door was opened by a tall, grim-looking woman, dressed in black with a large knob of iron-grey hair.

She eyed Lucy in suspicious appraisal as she showed her in to Miss Marple.

Miss Marple was occupying the back sitting-room which looked out on to a small tidy square of garden. It was aggressively clean with a lot of mats and doilies, a great many china ornaments, a rather big Jacobean suite and two ferns in pots. Miss Marple was sitting in a big chair by the fire busily engaged in crocheting.

Lucy came in and shut the door. She sat down in the chair facing Miss Marple.

'Well!' she said. 'It looks as though you were right.'

She produced her finds and gave details of their finding.

A faint flush of achievement came into Miss Marple's cheeks.

'Perhaps one ought not to feel so,' she said, 'but it *is* rather gratifying to form a theory and get proof that it is correct!'

She fingered the small tuft of fur. 'Elspeth said the woman was wearing a light-coloured fur coat. I suppose the compact was in the pocket of the coat and fell out as the body rolled down the slope. It doesn't seem distinctive in any way, but it may help. You didn't take all the fur?'

'No, I left half of it on the thorn bush.'

Miss Marple nodded approval.

'Quite right. You are very intelligent, my dear. The police will want to check exactly.'

'You are going to the police – with these things?'

'Well – not quite yet . . .' Miss Marple considered: 'It would be better, I think, to find the body first. Don't you?'

'Yes, but isn't that rather a tall order? I mean, granting that your estimate is correct. The murderer pushed the body out of the train, then presumably got out himself at Brackhampton and at some time – probably that same night – came along and removed the body. But what happened after that? He may have taken it *anywhere*.'

'Not *anywhere*,' said Miss Marple. 'I don't think you've followed the thing to its logical conclusion, my dear Miss Eyelesbarrow.'

'Do call me Lucy. Why not anywhere?'

'Because, if so, he might much more easily have killed the girl in some lonely spot and driven the body away from there. You haven't appreciated –'

Lucy interrupted.

'Are you saying – do you mean – that this was a premeditated crime?'

'I didn't think so at first,' said Miss Marple. 'One wouldn't –

naturally. It seemed like a quarrel and a man losing control and strangling the girl and then being faced with the problem which he had to solve within a few minutes. But it really is too much of a coincidence that he should kill the girl in a fit of passion, and then look out of the window and find the train was going round a curve exactly at a spot where he could tip the body out, *and* where he could be sure of finding his way later and removing it! If he'd just thrown her out there by chance, he'd have done no more about it, and the body would, long before now, have been found.'

She paused. Lucy stared at her.

'You know,' said Miss Marple thoughtfully, 'it's really quite a clever way to have planned a crime – and I think it was very carefully planned. There's something so anonymous about a train. If he'd killed her in the place where she lived, or was staying, somebody might have noticed him come or go. Or if he'd driven her out in the country somewhere, someone might have noticed the car and its number and make. But a train is full of strangers coming and going. In a non-corridor carriage, alone with her, it was quite easy – especially if you realize that he knew exactly what he was going to do next. He knew – he *must* have known – all about Rutherford Hall – its geographical position, I mean, its queer isolation – an island bounded by railway lines.'

'It is exactly like that,' said Lucy. 'It's an anachronism out of the past. Bustling urban life goes on all around it, but doesn't touch it. The tradespeople deliver in the mornings and that's all.'

'So we assume, as you said, that the murderer comes to Rutherford Hall that night. It is already dark when the body falls and no one is likely to discover it before the next day.'

'No, indeed.'

'The murderer would come – how? In a car? Which way?'

Lucy considered.

'There's a rough lane, alongside a factory wall. He'd probably come that way, turn in under the railway arch and along the back drive. Then he could climb the fence, go along at the foot of the embankment, find the body, and carry it back to the car.'

'And then,' continued Miss Marple, 'he took it to some place he had already chosen beforehand. This was all thought out, you know. And I don't think, as I say, that he would take it away from Rutherford Hall, or if so, not very far. The obvious thing, I suppose, would be to bury it somewhere?' She looked inquiringly at Lucy.

'I suppose so,' said Lucy considering. 'But it wouldn't be quite as easy as it sounds.'

Miss Marple agreed.

'He couldn't bury it in the park. Too hard work and very noticeable. Somewhere where the earth was turned already?'

'The kitchen garden, perhaps, but that's very close to the gardener's cottage. He's old and deaf — but still it might be risky.'

'Is there a dog?'

'No.'

'Then in a shed, perhaps, or an outhouse?'

'That would be simpler and quicker . . . There are a lot of unused old buildings; broken down pigsties, harness rooms, workshops that nobody ever goes near. Or he might perhaps thrust it into a clump of rhododendrons or shrubs somewhere.'

Miss Marple nodded.

'Yes, I think that's *much* more probable.'

There was a knock on the door and the grim Florence came in with a tray.

'Nice for you to have a visitor,' she said to Miss Marple, 'I've made you my special scones you used to like.'

'Florence always made the most delicious tea cakes,' said Miss Marple.

Florence, gratified, creased her features into a totally unexpected smile and left the room.

'I think, my dear,' said Miss Marple, 'we won't talk any more about murder during tea. Such an *unpleasant* subject!'

II

After tea, Lucy rose.

'I'll be getting back,' she said. 'As I've already told you, there's no one actually living at Rutherford Hall who could be the man we're looking for. There's only an old man and a middle-aged woman, and an old deaf gardener.'

'I didn't say he was actually *living* there,' said Miss Marple. 'All I mean is, that he's someone who knows Rutherford Hall very well. But we can go into that after you've found the body.'

'You seem to assume quite confidently that I *shall* find it,' said Lucy. 'I don't feel nearly so optimistic.'

'I'm sure you will succeed, my dear Lucy. You are such an efficient person.'

'In some ways, but I haven't had any experience in looking for bodies.'

'I'm sure all it needs is a little common sense,' said Miss Marple encouragingly.

Lucy looked at her, then laughed. Miss Marple smiled back at her.

Lucy set to work systematically the next afternoon.

She poked round outhouses, prodded the briars which wreathed the old pigsties, and was peering into the boiler room under the greenhouse when she heard a dry cough and turned to find old Hillman, the gardener, looking at her disapprovingly.

'You be careful you don't get a nasty fall, miss,' he warned her. 'Them steps isn't safe, and you was up in the loft just now and the floor there ain't safe neither.'

Lucy was careful to display no embarrassment.

'I expect you think I'm very nosy,' she said cheerfully. 'I was just wondering if something couldn't be made out of this place – growing mushrooms for the market, that sort of thing. Everything seems to have been let go terribly.'

'That's the master, that is. Won't spend a penny. Ought to have two men and a boy here, I ought, to keep the place proper, but won't hear of it, he won't. Had all I could do to make him get a motor mower. Wanted me to mow all that front grass by hand, he did.'

'But if the place could be made to pay – with some repairs?'

'Won't get a place like this to pay – too far gone. And he wouldn't care about that, anyway. Only cares about saving. Knows well enough what'll happen after he's gone – the young gentlemen'll sell up as fast as they can. Only waiting for him to pop off, they are. Going to come into a tidy lot of money when he dies, so I've heard.'

'I suppose he's a very rich man?' said Lucy.

'Crackenthorpe's Fancies, that's what they are. The old gentleman started it, Mr Crackenthorpe's father. A sharp one he was, by all accounts. Made his fortune, and built this place. Hard as nails, they say, and never forgot an injury. But with all that, *he* was open-handed. Nothing of the miser about him. Disappointed in both his sons, so the story goes. Give 'em an education and brought 'em up to be gentlemen – Oxford and all. But they were too much of gentlemen to want to go into the business. The younger one married an actress and then smashed himself up in a car accident when he'd been drinking. The elder one, our one here, his father never fancied so much. Abroad a lot, he was, bought a lot of heathen statues and had them sent home. Wasn't so close with his money when he was young – come on him more in middle age, it did. No, they never did hit it off, him and his father, so I've heard.'

Lucy digested this information with an air of polite interest. The old man leant against the wall and prepared to go on with his saga. He much preferred talking to doing any work.

'Died before the war, the old gentleman did. Terrible temper he had. Didn't do to give him any cause, he wouldn't stand for it.'

'And after he died, this Mr Crackenthorpe came and lived here?'

'Him and his family, yes. Nigh grown up they was by then.'

'But surely . . . Oh, I see, you mean the 1914 war.'

'No, I don't. Died in 1928, that's what I mean.'

Lucy supposed that 1928 qualified as 'before the war' though it was not the way she would have described it herself.

She said: 'Well, I expect you'll be wanting to go on with your work. You mustn't let me keep you.'

'Ar,' said old Hillman without enthusiasm, 'not much you can do this time of day. Light's too bad.'

Lucy went back to the house, pausing to investigate a likely-looking copse of birch and azalea on her way.

She found Emma Crackenthorpe standing in the hall reading a letter. The afternoon post had just been delivered.

'My nephew will be here tomorrow – with a school-friend. Alexander's room is the one over the porch. The one next to it will do for James Stoddart-West. They'll use the bathroom just opposite.'

'Yes, Miss Crackenthorpe. I'll see the rooms are prepared.'

'They'll arrive in the morning before lunch.' She hesitated. 'I expect they'll be hungry.'

'I bet they will,' said Lucy. 'Roast beef, do you think? And perhaps treacle tart?'

'Alexander's very fond of treacle tart.'

The two boys arrived on the following morning. They both had well-brushed hair, suspiciously angelic faces, and perfect manners.

Alexander Eastley had fair hair and blue eyes, Stoddart-West was dark and spectacled.

They discoursed gravely during lunch on events in the sporting world, with occasional references to the latest space fiction. Their manner was that of elderly professors discussing palaeolithic implements. In comparison with them, Lucy felt quite young.

The sirloin of beef vanished in no time and every crumb of treacle tart was consumed.

Mr Crackenthorpe grumbled: 'You two will eat me out of house and home.'

Alexander gave him a blue-eyed reproving glance.

'We'll have bread and cheese if you can't afford meat, Grandfather.'

'Afford it? I can *afford* it. I don't like waste.'

'We haven't wasted any, sir,' said Stoddart-West, looking down at his place which bore clear testimony of that fact.

'You boys both eat twice as much as I do.'

'We're at the body-building stage,' Alexander explained. 'We need a big intake of proteins.'

The old man grunted.

As the two boys left the table, Lucy heard Alexander say apologetically to his friend:

'You mustn't pay any attention to my grandfather. He's on a diet or something and that makes him rather peculiar. He's terribly mean, too. I think it must be a complex of some kind.'

Stoddart-West said comprehendingly:

'I had an aunt who kept thinking she was going bankrupt. Really, she had oodles of money. Pathological, the doctor said. Have you got that football, Alex?'

After she had cleared away and washed up lunch, Lucy went out. She could hear the boys calling out in the distance on the lawn. She herself went in the opposite direction, down the front drive and from there she struck across to some clumped masses of rhododendron bushes. She began to hunt carefully, holding back the leaves and peering inside. She moved from clump to clump systematically, and was raking inside with a golf club when the polite voice of Alexander Eastley made her start.

'Are you looking for something, Miss Eyelesbarrow?'

'A golf ball,' said Lucy promptly. 'Several golf balls in fact. I've

569

been practising golf shots most afternoons and I've lost quite a lot of balls. I thought that to-day I really must find some of them.'

'We'll help you,' said Alexander obligingly.

'That's very kind of you. I thought you were playing football.'

'One can't go *on* playing footer,' explained Stoddart-West. 'One gets too hot. Do you play a lot of golf?'

'I'm quite fond of it. I don't get much opportunity.'

'I suppose you don't. You do the cooking here, don't you?'

'Yes.'

'Did you cook the lunch to-day?'

'Yes. Was it all right?'

'Simply wizard,' said Alexander. 'We get awful meat at school, all dried up. I love beef that's pink and juicy inside. That treacle tart was pretty smashing, too.'

'You must tell me what things you like best.'

'Could we have apple meringue one day? It's my favourite thing.'

'Of course.'

Alexander sighed happily.

'There's a clock golf set under the stairs,' he said. 'We could fix it up on the lawn and do some putting. What about it, Stodders?'

'Good-oh!' said Stoddart-West.

'He isn't really Australian,' explained Alexander courteously. 'But he's practising talking that way in case his people take him out to see the Test Match next year.'

Encouraged by Lucy, they went off to get the clock golf set. Later, as she returned to the house, she found them setting it out on the lawn and arguing about the position of the numbers.

'We don't want it like a clock,' said Stoddart-West. 'That's kid's stuff. We want to make a course of it. Long holes and short ones. It's a pity the numbers are so rusty. You can hardly see them.'

'They need a lick of white paint,' said Lucy. 'You might get some to-morrow and paint them.'

'Good idea.' Alexander's face lit up. 'I say, I believe there are some old pots of paint in the Long Barn – left there by the painters last hols. Shall we see?'

'What's the Long Barn?' asked Lucy.

Alexander pointed to a long stone building a little way from the house near the back drive.

'It's quite old,' he said. 'Grandfather calls it a Leak Barn and says its Elizabethan, but that's just swank. It belonged to the farm that was here originally. My great-grandfather pulled it down and built this awful house instead.'

He added: 'A lot of grandfather's collection is in the barn. Things he had sent home from abroad when he was a young man. Most of them are pretty awful, too. The Long Barn is used sometimes for whist drives and things like that. Women's Institute stuff. And Conservative Sales of Work. Come and see it.'

Lucy accompanied them willingly.

There was a big nail-studded oak door to the barn.

Alexander raised his hand and detached a key on a nail just under some ivy to the right hand of the top of the door. He turned it in the lock, pushed the door open and they went in.

At a first glance Lucy felt that she was in a singularly bad museum. The heads of two Roman emperors in marble glared at her out of bulging eyeballs, there was a huge sarcophagus of a decadent Greco-Roman period, a simpering Venus stood on a pedestal clutching her falling draperies. Besides these works of art, there were a couple of trestle tables, some stacked-up chairs, and sundry oddments such as a rusted hand mower, two buckets, a couple of moth-eaten car seats, and a green painted iron garden seat that had lost a leg.

'I think I saw the paint over here,' said Alexander vaguely. He went to a corner and pulled aside a tattered curtain that shut it off.

They found a couple of paint pots and brushes, the latter dry and stiff.

'You really need some turps,' said Lucy.

They could not, however, find any turpentine. The boys suggested bicycling off to get some, and Lucy urged them to do so. Painting the clock golf numbers would keep them amused for some time, she thought.

The boys went off, leaving her in the barn.

'This really could do with a clear up,' she had murmured.

'I shouldn't bother,' Alexander advised her. 'It gets cleaned up if it's going to be used for anything, but it's practically never used this time of year.'

'Do I hang the key up outside the door again? Is that where it's kept?'

'Yes. There's nothing to pinch here, you see. Nobody would want those awful marble things and, anyway, they weigh a ton.'

Lucy agreed with him. She could hardly admire old Mr Cracken-thorpe's taste in art. He seemed to have an unerring instinct for selecting the worst specimen of any period.

She stood looking round her after the boys had gone. Her eyes came to rest on the sarcophagus and stayed there.

That sarcophagus . . .

The air in the barn was faintly musty as though unaired for a long time. She went over to the sarcophagus. It had a heavy close-fitting lid. Lucy looked at it speculatively.

Then she left the barn, went to the kitchen, found a heavy crowbar, and returned.

It was not an easy task, but Lucy toiled doggedly.

Slowly the lid began to rise, prised up by the crowbar.

It rose sufficiently for Lucy to see what was inside . . .

CHAPTER SIX

A few minutes later Lucy, rather pale, left the barn, locked the door and put the key back on the nail.

She went rapidly to the stables, got out her car and drove down the back drive. She stopped at the post office at the end of the road. She went into the telephone box, put in the money and dialled.

'I want to speak to Miss Marple.'

'She's resting, miss. It's Miss Eyelesbarrow, isn't it?'

'Yes.'

'I'm not going to disturb her and that's that, miss. She's an old lady and she needs her rest.'

'You must disturb her. It's urgent.'

'I'm not —'

'Please do what I say at once.'

When she chose, Lucy's voice could be as incisive as steel. Florence knew authority when she heard it.

Presently Miss Marple's voice spoke.

'Yes, Lucy?'

Lucy drew a deep breath.

'You were quite right,' she said. 'I've found it.'

'A woman's body?'

'Yes. A woman in a fur coat. It's in a stone sarcophagus in a kind of barn-cum-museum near the house. What do you want me to do? I ought to inform the police, I think.'

'Yes. You must inform the police. At once.'

'But what about the rest of it? About you? The first thing they'll want to know is *why* I was prying up a lid that weighs tons for apparently no reason. Do you want me to invent a reason? I can.'

'No. I think, you know,' said Miss Marple in her gentle serious voice, 'that the only thing to do is to tell the exact truth.'

'About you?'

'About everything.'

A sudden grin split the whiteness of Lucy's face.

'That will be quite simple for me,' she said. 'But I imagine they'll find it quite hard to believe!'

She rang off, waited a moment, and then rang and got the police station.

'I have just discovered a dead body in a sarcophagus in the Long Barn at Rutherford Hall.'

'What's that?'

Lucy repeated her statement and anticipating the next question gave her name.

She drove back, put the car away and entered the house.

She paused in the hall for a moment, thinking.

Then she gave a brief sharp nod of the head and went to the library where Miss Crackenthorpe was sitting helping her father to do *The Times* crossword.

'Can I speak to you a moment Miss Crackenthorpe?'

Emma looked up, a shade of apprehension on her face. The apprehension was, Lucy thought, purely domestic. In such words do useful household staff announce their imminent departure.

'Well, speak up, girl, speak up,' said old Mr Crackenthorpe irritably.

Lucy said to Emma:

'I'd like to speak to you alone, please.'

'Nonsense,' said Mr Crackenthorpe. 'You say straight out here what you've got to say.'

'Just a moment, Father.' Emma rose and went towards the door.

'All nonsense. It can wait,' said the old man angrily.

'I'm afraid it can't wait,' said Lucy.

Mr Crackenthorpe said, 'What impertinence!'

Emma came out into the hall. Lucy followed her and shut the door behind them.

'Yes?' said Emma. 'What is it? If you think there's too much to do with the boys here, I can help you and –'

'It's not that at all,' said Lucy. 'I didn't want to speak before your father because I understand he is an invalid and it might give him a shock. You see, I've just discovered the body of a murdered woman in that big sarcophagus in the Long Barn.'

Emma Crackenthorpe stared at her.

'In the sarcophagus? A murdered woman? It's impossible!'

'I'm afraid it's quite true. I've rung up the police. They will be here at any minute.'

A slight flush came into Emma's cheeks.

'You should have told me first – before notifying the police.'

'I'm sorry,' said Lucy.

'I didn't hear you ring up –' Emma's glance went to the telephone on the hall table.

'I rang up from the post office just down the road.'

'But how extraordinary. Why not from here?'

Lucy thought quickly.

'I was afraid the boys might be about – might hear – if I rang up from the hall here.'

'I see . . . Yes . . . I see . . . They are coming – the police, I mean?'

'They're here now,' said Lucy, as with a squeal of brakes a car drew up at the front door and the front-door bell pealed through the house.

II

'I'm sorry, very sorry – to have asked this of you,' said Inspector Bacon.

His hand under her arm, he led Emma Crackenthorpe out of the barn. Emma's face was very pale, she looked sick, but she walked firmly erect.

'I'm quite sure that I've never seen the woman before in my life.'

'We're very grateful to you, Miss Crackenthorpe. That's all I wanted to know. Perhaps you'd like to lie down?'

'I must go to my father. I telephoned Dr Quimper as soon as I heard about this and the doctor is with him now.'

Dr Quimper came out of the library as they crossed the hall. He was a tall genial man, with a casual off-hand cynical manner that his patients found very stimulating.

He and the inspector nodded to each other.

'Miss Crackenthorpe has performed an unpleasant task very bravely,' said Bacon.

'Well done, Emma,' said the doctor, patting her on the shoulder. 'You can take things. I've always known that. Your father's all right. Just go in and have a word with him, and then go into the dining-room and get yourself a glass of brandy. That's a prescription.'

Emma smiled at him gratefully and went into the library.

'That woman's the salt of the earth,' said the doctor, looking after her. 'A thousand pities she's never married. The penalty of being the only female in a family of men. The other sister got clear, married at seventeen, I believe. This one's quite a handsome woman really. She'd have been a success as a wife and mother.'

'Too devoted to her father, I suppose,' said Inspector Bacon.

'She's not really as devoted as all that – but she's got the instinct some women have to make their menfolk happy. She sees that her father likes being an invalid, so she lets him be an invalid. She's the same with her brothers. Cedric feels he's a good painter, what's his name – Harold – knows how much she relies on his sound judgment – she lets Alfred shock her with his stories of his clever deals. Oh, yes, she's a clever woman – no fool. Well, do you want me for anything? Want me to have a look at your corpse now Johnstone has done with it' (Johnstone was the police surgeon) 'and see if it happens to be one of my medical mistakes?'

'I'd like you to have a look, yes, Doctor. We want to get her identified. I suppose it's impossible for old Mr Crackenthorpe? Too much of a strain?'

'Strain? Fiddlesticks. He'd never forgive you or me if you didn't let him have a peep. He's all agog. Most exciting thing that's happened to him for fifteen years or so – *and* it won't cost him anything!'

'There's nothing really much wrong with him then?'

'He's seventy-two,' said the doctor. 'That's all, really, that's the matter with him. He has odd rheumatic twinges – who doesn't? So he calls it arthritis. He has palpitations after meals – as well he may – he puts them down to "heart". But he can always do anything he wants to do! I've plenty of patients like that. The ones who are really ill usually insist desperately that they're perfectly well. Come on, let's go and see this body of yours. Unpleasant, I suppose?'

'Johnstone estimates she's been dead between a fortnight and three weeks.'

'Quite unpleasant, then.'

The doctor stood by the sarcophagus and looked down with frank curiosity, professionally unmoved by what he had named the 'unpleasantness'.

'Never seen her before. No patient of mine. I don't remember ever seeing her about in Brackhampton. She must have been quite good-looking once – hm – *somebody* had it in for her all right.'

They went out again into the air. Doctor Quimper glanced up at the building.

'Found in the what – what do they call it? – the Long Barn – in a sarcophagus! Fantastic! Who found her?'

'Miss Lucy Eyelesbarrow.'

'Oh, the latest lady help? What was *she* doing, poking about in sarcophagi?'

'That,' said Inspector Bacon grimly, 'is just what I am going to ask her. Now, about Mr Crackenthorpe. Will you – ?'

'I'll bring him along.'

Mr Crackenthorpe, muffled in scarves, came walking at a brisk pace, the doctor beside him.

'Disgraceful,' he said. 'Absolutely disgraceful! I brought back that sarcophagus from Florence in – let me see – it must have been in 1908 – or was it 1909?'

'Steady now,' the doctor warned him. 'This isn't going to be nice, you know.'

'No matter how ill I am, I've got to do my duty, haven't I?'

A very brief visit inside the Long Barn was, however, quite long enough. Mr Crackenthorpe shuffled out into the air again with remarkable speed.

'Never saw her before in my life!' he said. 'What's it mean?

576

Absolutely disgraceful. It wasn't Florence – I remember now – it was Naples. A very fine specimen. And some fool of a woman has to come and get herself killed in it!'

He clutched at the folds of his overcoat on the left side.

'Too much for me . . . My heart . . . Where's Emma? Doctor . . .'

Doctor Quimper took his arm.

'You'll be all right,' he said. 'I prescribe a little stimulant. Brandy.'

They went back together towards the house.

'Sir. Please, sir.'

Inspector Bacon turned. Two boys had arrived, breathless, on bicycles. Their faces were full of eager pleading.

'Please, sir, can we see the body?'

'No, you can't,' said Inspector Bacon.

'Oh, sir, *please*, sir. You never know. We might know who she was. Oh, please, sir, do be a sport. It's not fair. Here's a murder, right in our own barn. It's the sort of chance that might never happen again. Do be a sport, sir.'

'Who are you two?'

'I'm Alexander Eastley, and this is my friend James Stoddart-West.'

'Have you ever seen a blonde woman wearing a light-coloured dyed squirrel coat anywhere about the place?'

'Well, I can't remember exactly,' said Alexander astutely. 'If I were to have a look –'

'Take 'em in, Sanders,' said Inspector Bacon to the constable who was standing by the barn door. 'One's only young once!'

'Oh, sir, thank you, sir.' Both boys were vociferous. 'It's *very* kind of you, sir.'

Bacon turned away towards the house.

'And now,' he said to himself grimly, 'for Miss Lucy Eyelesbarrow!'

III

After leading the police to the Long Barn, and giving a brief account of her actions, Lucy had retired into the background, but she was under no illusion that the police had finished with her.

She had just finished preparing potatoes for chips that evening when word was brought to her that Inspector Bacon required her presence. Putting aside the large bowl of cold water and salt in which the chips were reposing, Lucy followed the policeman to where the inspector awaited her. She sat down and awaited his questions composedly.

She gave her name – and her address in London, and added of her own accord:

'I will give you some names and addresses of references if you want to know all about me.'

The names were very good ones. An Admiral of the Fleet, the Provost of an Oxford College, and a Dame of the British Empire. In spite of himself Inspector Bacon was impressed.

'Now, Miss Eyelesbarrow, you went into the Long Barn to find some paint. Is that right? And after having found the paint you got a crowbar, forced up the lid of this sarcophagus and found the body. What were you looking for in the sarcophagus?'

'I was looking for a body,' said Lucy.

'You were looking for a body – and you found one! Doesn't that seem to you a very extraordinary story?'

'Oh, yes, it is an extraordinary story. Perhaps you will let me explain it to you.'

'I certainly think you had better do so.'

Lucy gave him a precise recital of the events which had led up to her sensational discovery.

The inspector summed it up in an outraged voice.

'You were engaged by an elderly lady to obtain a post here and to search the house and grounds for *a dead body*? Is that right?'

'Yes.'

'Who is this elderly lady?'

'Miss Jane Marple. She is at present living at 4 Madison Road.'

The inspector wrote it down.

'You expect me to believe this story?'

Lucy said gently:

'Not, perhaps, until after you have interviewed Miss Marple and got her confirmation of it.'

'I shall interview her all right. She must be cracked.'

Lucy forbore to point out that to be proved right is not really a proof of mental incapacity. Instead she said:

'What are you proposing to tell Miss Crackenthorpe? About *me*, I mean?'

'Why do you ask?'

'Well, as far as Miss Marple is concerned I've *done* my job, I've found the body she wanted found. But I'm still engaged by Miss Crackenthorpe, and there are two hungry boys in the house and probably some more of the family will soon be coming down after all this upset. She needs domestic help. If you go and tell her that I only took this post in order to hunt for dead bodies she'll probably throw me out. Otherwise I can get on with my job and be useful.'

The inspector looked hard at her.

'I'm not saying anything to *anyone* at present,' he said. 'I haven't verified your statement yet. For all I know you may be making the whole thing up.'

Lucy rose.

'Thank you. Then I'll go back to the kitchen and get on with things.'

CHAPTER SEVEN

'We'd better have the Yard in on it, is that what you think, Bacon?'

The Chief Constable looked inquiringly at Inspector Bacon. The inspector was a big stolid man – his expression was that of one utterly disgusted with humanity.

'The woman wasn't a local, sir,' he said. 'There's some reason to believe – from her underclothing – that she might have been a foreigner. Of course,' added Inspector Bacon hastily, 'I'm not letting on about that yet awhile. We're keeping it up our sleeves until after the inquest.'

The Chief Constable nodded.

'The inquest will be purely formal, I suppose?'

'Yes, sir. I've seen the Coroner.'

'And it's fixed for – when?'

'Tomorrow. I understand the other members of the Crackenthorpe family will be here for it. There's just a chance *one* of them might be able to identify her. They'll all be here.'

He consulted a list he held in his hand.

'Harold Crackenthorpe, he's something in the City – quite an important figure, I understand. Alfred – don't quite know what he does. Cedric – that's the one who lives abroad. Paints!' The inspector invested the word with its full quota of sinister significance. The Chief Constable smiled into his moustache.

'No reason, is there, to believe the Crackenthorpe family are connected with the crime in any way?' he asked.

'Not apart from the fact that the body was found on the premises,' said Inspector Bacon. 'And of course it's just possible that this artist member of the family might be able to identify her. What beats me is this extraordinary rigmarole about the train.'

'Ah, yes. You've been to see this old lady, this – er –' (he glanced at the memorandum lying on his desk) 'Miss Marple?'

'Yes, sir. And she's quite set and definite about the whole thing. Whether she's barmy or not, I don't know, but she sticks to her story – about what her friend saw and all the rest of it. As far as all that goes, I dare say it's just make-believe – sort of thing old ladies do make up, like seeing flying saucers at the bottom of the garden, and Russian agents in the lending library. But it seems quite clear that she *did* engage this young woman, the lady help, and told her to look for a body – which the girl did.'

'*And* found one,' observed the Chief Constable. 'Well, it's all a very remarkable story. Marple, Miss Jane Marple – the name seems familiar somehow . . . Anyway, I'll get on to the Yard. I think you're right about its not being a local case – though we won't advertise the fact just yet. For the moment we'll tell the Press as little as possible.'

II

The inquest was a purely formal affair. No one came forward to identify the dead woman. Lucy was called to give evidence of finding the body and medical evidence was given as to the cause of death – strangulation. The proceedings were then adjourned.

It was a cold blustery day when the Crackenthorpe family came out of the hall where the inquest had been held. There were five of them all told, Emma, Cedric, Harold, Alfred, and Bryan Eastley, the husband of the dead daughter Edith. There was also Mr Wimborne, the senior partner of the firm of solicitors who dealt with the Crackenthorpes' legal affairs. He had come down specially from London at great inconvenience to attend the inquest. They all stood for a moment on the pavement, shivering. Quite a crowd had assembled; the piquant details of the 'Body in the Sarcophagus' had been fully reported in both the London and the local Press.

A murmur went round: 'That's them . . .'

Emma said sharply: 'Let's get away.'

The big hired Daimler drew up to the kerb. Emma got in and motioned to Lucy. Mr Wimborne, Cedric and Harold followed. Bryan Eastley said: 'I'll take Alfred with me in my little bus.' The chauffeur shut the door and the Daimler prepared to roll away.

'Oh, stop!' cried Emma. 'There are the boys!'

The boys, in spite of aggrieved protests, had been left behind at Rutherford Hall, but they now appeared grinning from ear to ear.

'We came on our bicycles,' said Stoddart-West. 'The policeman was very kind and let us in at the back of the hall. I hope you don't mind, Miss Crackenthorpe,' he added politely.

'She doesn't mind,' said Cedric, answering for his sister. 'You're only young once. Your first inquest, I expect?'

'It was rather disappointing,' said Alexander. 'All over so soon.'

'We can't stay here talking,' said Harold irritably. 'There's quite a crowd. And all those men with cameras.'

At a sign from him, the chauffeur pulled away from the kerb. The boys waved cheerfully.

'All over so soon!' said Cedric. 'That's what *they* think, the young innocents! It's just beginning.'

'It's all very unfortunate. *Most* unfortunate,' said Harold. 'I suppose –'

He looked at Mr Wimborne who compressed his thin lips and shook his head with distaste.

'I hope,' he said sententiously, 'that the whole matter will soon be cleared up satisfactorily. The police were very efficient. However, the whole thing, as Harold says, has been most unfortunate.'

He looked, as he spoke, at Lucy, and there was distinct disapproval in his glance. 'If it had not been for this young woman,' his eyes seemed to say, 'poking about where she had no business to be – none of this would have happened.'

581

This statement, or one closely resembling it, was voiced by Harold Crackenthorpe.

'By the way – er – Miss – er – er Eyelesbarrow, just what *made* you go looking in that sarcophagus?'

Lucy had already wondered just when this thought would occur to one of the family. She had known that the police would ask it first thing; what surprised her was that it seemed to have occurred to no one else until this moment.

Cedric, Emma, Harold and Mr Wirnborne all looked at her.

Her reply, for what it was worth, had naturally been prepared for some time.

'Really,' she said in a hesitating voice. 'I hardly know . . . I *did* feel that the whole place needed a thorough clearing out and cleaning. And there was' – she hesitated – 'a very peculiar and disagreeable smell . . .'

She had counted accurately on the immediate shrinking of everyone from the unpleasantness of this idea . . .

Mr Wimborne murmured: 'Yes, yes, of course . . . about three weeks the police surgeon said . . . I think, you know, we must all try and not let our minds *dwell* on this thing.' He smiled encouragingly at Emma who had turned very pale. 'Remember,' he said, 'this wretched young woman was nothing to do with any of *us*.'

'Ah, but you can't be so sure of that, can you?' said Cedric.

Lucy Eyelesbarrow looked at him with some interest. She had already been intrigued by the rather startling differences between the three brothers. Cedric was a big man with a weather-beaten rugged face, unkempt dark hair and a jocund manner. He had arrived from the airport unshaven, and though he had shaved in preparation for the inquest, he was still wearing the clothes in which he had arrived and which seemed to be the only ones he had; old grey flannel trousers, and a patched and rather threadbare baggy jacket. He looked the stage Bohemian to the life and proud of it.

His brother Harold, on the contrary, was the perfect picture of a City gentleman and a director of important companies. He was tall with a neat erect carriage, had dark hair going slightly bald on the temples, a small black moustache, and was impeccably dressed in a dark well-cut suit and a pearl-grey tie. He looked what he was, a shrewd and successful business man.

He now said stiffly:

'Really, Cedric, that seems a *most* uncalled for remark.'

'Don't see why? She was in our barn after all. What did she come there for?'

Mr Wimborne coughed, and said:

'Possibly some – er – assignation. I understand that it was a matter of local knowledge that the key was kept outside on a nail.'

His tone indicated outrage at the carelessness of such procedure. So clearly marked was this that Emma spoke apologetically.

'It started during the war. For the ARP wardens. There was a little spirit stove and they made themselves hot cocoa. And afterwards, since there was really nothing there anybody could have wanted to take, we went on leaving the key hanging up. It was convenient for the Women's Institute people. If we'd kept it in the house it might have been awkward – when there was no one at home to give it them when they wanted it to get the place ready. With only daily women and no resident servants . . .'

Her voice trailed away. She had spoken mechanically, giving a wordy explanation without interest, as though her mind was elsewhere.

Cedric gave her a quick puzzled glance.

'You're worried, sis. What's up?'

Harold spoke with exasperation:

'Really, Cedric, can you ask?'

'Yes, I do ask. Granted a strange young woman has got herself killed in the barn at Rutherford Hall (sounds like a Victorian melodrama) and granted it gave Emma a shock at the time – but Emma's always been a sensible girl – I don't see why she goes on being worried *now*. Dash it, one gets used to everything.'

'Murder takes a little more getting used to by some people than it may in your case,' said Harold acidly. 'I dare say murders are two a penny in Majorca and –'

'Ibiza, not Majorca.'

'It's the same thing.'

'Not at all – it's quite a different island.'

Harold went on talking:

'My point is that though murder may be an everyday commonplace to *you*, living amongst hot-blooded Latin people, nevertheless in England we take such things seriously.' He added with increasing irritation, 'And really, Cedric, to appear at a public inquest in those clothes –'

'What's wrong with my clothes? They're comfortable.'

'They're unsuitable.'

'Well, anyway, they're the only clothes I've got with me. I didn't pack my wardrobe trunk when I came rushing home to stand in with the family over this business. I'm a painter and painters like to be comfortable in their clothes.'

'So you're still trying to paint?'

'Look here, Harold, when you say trying to paint –'

Mr Wimborne cleared his throat in an authoritative manner.

'This discussion is unprofitable,' he said reprovingly. 'I hope, my dear Emma, that you will tell me if there is any further way in which I can be of service to you before I return to town?'

The reproof had its effect. Emma Crackenthorpe said quickly:

'It was most kind of you to come down.'

'Not at all. It was advisable that someone should be at the inquest to watch the proceedings on behalf of the family. I have arranged for an interview with the inspector at the house. I have no doubt that, distressing as all this has been, the situation will soon be clarified. In my own mind, there seems little doubt as to what occurred. As Emma has told us, the key to the Long Barn was known locally to hang outside the door. It seems highly probable that the place was used in the winter months as a place of assignation by local couples. No doubt there was a quarrel and some young man lost control of himself. Horrified at what he had done, his eye lit on the sarcophagus and he realized that it would make an excellent place of concealment.'

Lucy thought to herself, 'Yes, it sounds most plausible. That's just what one might think.'

Cedric said, 'You say a local couple – but nobody's been able to identify the girl locally.'

'It's early days yet. No doubt we shall get an identification before long. And it is possible, of course, that the *man* in question was a local resident, but that the girl came from elsewhere, perhaps from some other part of Brackhampton. Brackhampton's a big place – it's grown enormously in the last twenty years.'

'If I were a girl coming to meet my young man, I'd not stand for being taken to a freezing cold barn miles from anywhere,' Cedric objected. 'I'd stand out for a nice bit of cuddle in the cinema, wouldn't you, Miss Eyelesbarrow?'

'Do we need to go into all this?' Harold demanded plaintively.

And with the voicing of the question the car drew up before the front door of Rutherford Hall and they all got out.

CHAPTER EIGHT

On entering the library Mr Wimborne blinked a little as his shrewd old eyes went past Inspector Bacon whom he had already met, to the fair-haired, good-looking man beyond him.

Inspector Bacon performed introductions.

'This is Detective-Inspector Craddock of New Scotland Yard,' he said.

'New Scotland Yard – hm.' Mr Wimborne's eyebrows rose.

Dermot Craddock, who had a pleasant manner, went easily into speech.

'We have been called in on the case, Mr Wimborne,' he said. 'As you are representing the Crackenthorpe family, I feel it is only fair that we should give you a little confidential information.'

Nobody could make a better show of presenting a very small portion of the truth and implying that it was the whole truth than Inspector Craddock.

'Inspector Bacon will agree, I am sure,' he added, glancing at his colleague.

Inspector Bacon agreed with all due solemnity and not at all as though the whole matter were prearranged.

'It's like this,' said Craddock. 'We have reason to believe, from information that has come into our possession, that the dead woman is not a native of these parts, that she travelled down here from London and that she had recently come from abroad. Probably (though we are not sure of that) from France.'

Mr Wimborne again raised his eyebrows.

'Indeed,' he said. 'Indeed?'

'That being the case,' explained Inspector Bacon, 'the Chief Constable felt that the Yard was better fitted to investigate the matter.'

'I can only hope,' said Mr Wimborne, 'that the case will be solved quickly. As you can no doubt appreciate, the whole business has been a source of much distress to the family. Although not *personally* concerned in any way, they are –'

He paused for a bare second, but Inspector Craddock filled the gap quickly.

'It's not a pleasant thing to find a murdered woman on your property? I couldn't agree with you more. Now I should like to have a brief interview with the various members of the family –'

'I really cannot see –'

'What they can tell me? Probably nothing of interest – but one never knows. I dare say I can get most of the information I want from you, sir. Information about this house and the family.'

'And what can that possibly have to do with an unknown young woman coming from abroad and getting herself killed here?'

'Well, that's rather the point,' said Craddock. '*Why* did she come here? Had she once had some connection with this house? Had she been, for instance, a servant here at one time? A lady's maid, perhaps. Or did she come here to meet a former occupant of Rutherford Hall?'

Mr Wimborne said coldly that Rutherford Hall had been occupied by the Crackenthorpes ever since Josiah Crackenthorpe built it in 1884.

'That's interesting in itself,' said Craddock. 'If you'd just give me a brief outline of the family history –'

Mr Wimborne shrugged his shoulders.

'There is very little to tell. Josiah Crackenthorpe was a manufacturer of sweet and savoury biscuits, relishes, pickles, etc. He accumulated a vast fortune. He built this house. Luther Crackenthorpe, his eldest son, lives here now.'

'Any other sons?'

'One other son, Henry, who was killed in a motor accident in 1911.'

'And the present Mr Crackenthorpe has never thought of selling the house?'

'He is unable to do so,' said the lawyer dryly. 'By the terms of his father's will.'

'Perhaps you'll tell me about the will?'

586

'Why should I?'

Inspector Craddock smiled.

'Because I can look it up myself if I want to, at Somerset House.'

Against his will, Mr Wimborne gave a crabbed little smile.

'Quite right, Inspector. I was merely protesting that the information you ask for is quite irrelevant. As to Josiah Crackenthorpe's will, there is no mystery about it. He left his very considerable fortune in trust, the income from it to be paid to his son Luther for life, and after Luther's death the capital to be divided equally between Luther's children, Edmund, Cedric, Harold, Alfred, Emma and Edith. Edmund was killed in the war, and Edith died four years ago, so that on Luther Crackenthorpe's decease the money will be divided between Cedric, Harold, Alfred, Emma and Edith's son Alexander Eastley.'

'And the house?'

'That will go to Luther Crackenthorpe's eldest surviving son or his issue.'

'Was Edmund Crackenthorpe married?'

'No.'

'So the property will actually go – ?'

'To the next son – Cedric.'

'Mr Luther Crackenthorpe himself cannot dispose of it?'

'No.'

'And he has no control of the capital.'

'No.'

'Isn't that rather unusual? I suppose,' said Inspector Craddock shrewdly, 'that his father didn't like him.'

'You suppose correctly,' said Mr Wimborne. 'Old Josiah was disappointed that his eldest son showed no interest in the family business – or indeed in business of any kind. Luther spent his time travelling abroad and collecting *objets d'art*. Old Josiah was very unsympathetic to that kind of thing. So he left his money in trust for the next generation.'

'But in the meantime the next generation have no income except what they make or what their father allows them, and their father has a considerable income but no power of disposal of the capital.'

'Exactly. And what all this has to do with the murder of an unknown young woman of foreign origin I cannot imagine!'

'It doesn't seem to have anything to do with it,' Inspector Crad-

587

dock agreed promptly, 'I just wanted to ascertain all the facts.'

Mr Wimborne looked at him sharply, then, seemingly satisfied with the result of his scrutiny, rose to his feet.

'I am proposing now to return to London,' he said. 'Unless there is anything further you wish to know?'

He looked from one man to the other.

'No, thank you, sir.'

The sound of the gong rose fortissimo from the hall outside.

'Dear me,' said Mr Wimborne. 'One of the boys, I think, must have been performing.'

Inspector Craddock raised his voice, to be heard above the clamour, as he said:

'We'll leave the family to have lunch in peace, but Inspector Bacon and I would like to return after it – say at two fifteen – and have a short interview with every member of the family.'

'You think that is necessary?'

'Well . . .' Craddock shrugged his shoulders. 'It's just an off chance. *Somebody* might remember something that would give us a clue to the woman's identity.'

'I doubt it, Inspector. I doubt it very much. But I wish you good luck. As I said just now, the sooner this distasteful business is cleared up, the better for everybody.'

Shaking his head, he went slowly out of the room.

II

Lucy had gone straight to the kitchen on getting back from the inquest, and was busy with preparations for lunch when Bryan Eastley put his head in.

'Can I give you a hand in any way?' he asked. 'I'm handy about the house.'

Lucy gave him a quick, slightly preoccupied glance. Bryan had arrived at the inquest direct in his small MG car, and she had not as yet had much time to size him up.

What she saw was likeable enough. Eastley was an amiable-looking young man of thirty-odd with brown hair, rather plaintive blue eyes and an enormous fair moustache.

'The boys aren't back yet,' he said, coming in and sitting on the end of the kitchen table. 'It will take 'em another twenty minutes on their bikes.'

Lucy smiled.

'They were certainly determined not to miss anything.'

'Can't blame them. I mean to say – first inquest in their young lives and right in the family so to speak.'

'Do you mind getting off the table, Mr Eastley? I want to put the baking dish down there.'

Bryan obeyed.

'I say, that fat's corking hot. What are you going to put in it?'

'Yorkshire pudding.'

'Good old Yorkshire. Roast beef of old England, is that the menu for today?'

'Yes.'

'The funeral baked meats, in fact. Smells good.' He sniffed appreciatively. 'Do you mind my gassing away?'

'If you came in to help I'd rather you helped.' She drew another pan from the oven. 'Here – turn all these potatoes over so that they brown on the other side . . .'

Bryan obeyed with alacrity.

'Have all these things been fizzling away in here while we've been at the inquest? Supposing they'd been all burnt up.'

'Most improbable. There's a regulating number on the oven.'

'Kind of electric brain, eh, what? Is that right?'

Lucy threw a swift look in his direction.

'Quite right. Now put the pan in the oven. Here, take the cloth. On the second shelf – I want the top for the Yorkshire pudding.'

Bryan obeyed, but not without uttering a shrill yelp.

'Burnt yourself?'

'Just a bit. It doesn't matter. What a dangerous game cooking is!'

'I suppose you never do your own cooking?'

'As a matter of fact I do – quite often. But not this sort of thing. I can boil an egg – if I don't forget to look at the clock. And I can do eggs and bacon. And I can put a steak under the grill or open a tin of soup. I've got one of those little electric whatnots in my flat.'

'You live in London?'

'If you call it living – yes.'

His tone was despondent. He watched Lucy shoot in the dish with the Yorkshire pudding mixture.

'This is awfully jolly,' he said and sighed.

Her immediate preoccupations over, Lucy looked at him with more attention.

'What is — this kitchen?'

'Yes. Reminds me of our kitchen at home — when I was a boy.'

It struck Lucy that there was something strangely forlorn about Bryan Eastley. Looking closely at him, she realized that he was older than she had at first thought. He must be close on forty. It seemed difficult to think of him as Alexander's father. He reminded her of innumerable young pilots she had known during the war when she had been at the impressionable age of fourteen. She had gone on and grown up into a post-war world — but she felt as though Bryan had not gone on, but had been passed by in the passage of years. His next words confirmed this. He had subsided on to the kitchen table again.

'It's a difficult sort of world,' he said, 'isn't it? To get your bearings in, I mean. You see, one hasn't been trained for it.'

Lucy recalled what she had heard from Emma.

'You were a fighter pilot, weren't you?' she said. 'You've got a DFC.'

'That's the sort of thing that puts you wrong. You've got a gong and so people try to make it easy for you. Give you a job and all that. Very decent of them. But they're all admin. jobs, and one simply isn't any good at that sort of thing. Sitting at a desk getting tangled up in figures. I've had ideas of my own, you know, tried out a wheeze or two. But you can't get the backing. Can't get the chaps to come in and put down the money. If I had a bit of capital —'

He brooded.

'You didn't know Edie, did you? My wife. No, of course you didn't. She was quite different from all this lot. Younger, for one thing. She was in the WAAF. She always said her old man was crackers. He is, you know. Mean as hell over money. And it's not as though he could take it with him. It's got to be divided up when he dies. Edie's share will go to Alexander, of course. He won't be able to touch the capital until he's twenty-one, though.'

'I'm sorry, but will you get off the table again? I want to dish up and make gravy.'

At that moment Alexander and Stoddart-West arrived with rosy faces and very much out of breath.

'Hallo, Bryan,' said Alexander kindly to his father. 'So this is where you've got to. I say, what a smashing piece of beef. Is there Yorkshire pudding?'

'Yes, there is.'

'We have awful Yorkshire pudding at school — all damp and limp.'

'Get out of my way,' said Lucy. 'I want to make the gravy.'

'Make lots of gravy. Can we have two sauce-boats full?'

'Yes.'

'Good-oh!' said Stoddart-West, pronouncing the word carefully.

'I don't like it pale,' said Alexander anxiously.

'It won't be pale.'

'She's a smashing cook,' said Alexander to his father.

Lucy had a momentary impression that their roles were reversed. Alexander spoke like a kindly father to his son.

'Can we help you, Miss Eyelesbarrow?' asked Stoddart-West politely.

'Yes, you can. James, go and sound the gong. Alexander, will you carry this tray into the dining-room? And will you take the joint in, Mr Eastley? I'll bring the potatoes and the Yorkshire pudding.'

'There's a Scotland Yard man here,' said Alexander. 'Do you think he will have lunch with us?'

'That depends on what your aunt arranged.'

'I don't suppose Aunt Emma would mind . . . She's very hospitable. But I suppose Uncle Harold wouldn't like it. He's being very sticky over this murder.' Alexander went out through the door with the tray, adding a little additional information over his shoulder. 'Mr Wimborne's in the library with the Scotland yard man now. But he isn't staying to lunch. He said he had to get back to London. Come on, Stodders. Oh, he's gone to do the gong.'

At that moment the gong took charge. Stoddart-West was an artist. He gave it everything he had, and all further conversation was inhibited.

Bryan carried in the joint, Lucy followed with vegetables — returning to the kitchen to get the two brimming sauce-boats of gravy.

Mr Wimborne was standing in the hall putting on his gloves as Emma came quickly down the stairs.

'Are you really sure you won't stop for lunch, Mr Wimborne? It's all ready.'

'No, I've an important appointment in London. There is a restaurant car on the train.'

'It was very good of you to come down,' said Emma gratefully. The two police officers emerged from the library.

Mr Wimborne took Emma's hand in his.

'There's nothing to worry about, my dear,' he said. 'This is Detective-Inspector Craddock from New Scotland Yard who has come to take charge of the case. He is coming back at two-fifteen to ask you for any facts that may assist him in his inquiry. But, as I say, you have nothing to worry about.' He looked towards Craddock. 'I may repeat to Miss Crackenthorpe what you have told me?'

'Certainly, sir.'

'Inspector Craddock has just told me that this almost certainly was not a local crime. The murdered woman is thought to have come from London and was probably a foreigner.'

Emma Crackenthorpe said sharply:

'A foreigner. Was she French?'

Mr Wimborne had clearly meant his statement to be consoling. He looked slightly taken aback. Dermot Craddock's glance went quickly from him to Emma's face.

He wondered why she had leaped to the conclusion that the murdered woman was French, and why that thought disturbed her so much?

CHAPTER NINE

The only people who really did justice to Lucy's excellent lunch were the two boys and Cedric Crackenthorpe who appeared completely unaffected by the circumstances which had caused him to return to England. He seemed, indeed, to regard the whole thing as a rather good joke of a macabre nature.

This attitude, Lucy noted, was most unpalatable to his brother Harold. Harold seemed to take the murder as a kind of personal insult to the Crackenthorpe family and so great was his sense of outrage that he ate hardly any lunch. Emma looked worried and unhappy and also ate very little. Alfred seemed lost in a train of thought of his own and spoke very little. He was quite a good-looking man with a thin dark face and eyes set rather too close together.

After lunch the police officers returned and politely asked if they could have a few words with Mr Cedric Crackenthorpe.

Inspector Craddock was very pleasant and friendly.

'Sit down, Mr Crackenthorpe. I understand you have just come back from the Balearics? You live out there?'

'Have done for the past six years. In Ibiza. Suits me better than this dreary country.'

'You get a good deal more sunshine than we do, I expect,' said Inspector Craddock agreeably. 'You were home not so very long ago, I understand – for Christmas, to be exact. What made it necessary for you to come back again so soon?'

Cedric grinned.

'Got a wire from Emma – my sister. We've never had a murder on the premises before. Didn't want to miss anything – so along I came.'

'You are interested in criminology?'

'Oh, we needn't put it in such highbrow terms! I just like murders – Whodunnits and all that! With a Whodunnit parked right on the family doorstep, it seemed the chance of a lifetime. Besides, I thought poor Em might need a spot of help – managing the old man and the police and all the rest of it.'

'I see. It appealed to your sporting instincts and also to your family feelings. I've no doubt your sister will be very grateful to you – although her two other brothers have also come to be with her.'

'But not to cheer and comfort,' Cedric told him. 'Harold is terrifically put out. It's not at all the thing for a City magnate to be mixed up with the murder of a questionable female.'

Craddock's eyebrows rose gently.

'Was she – a questionable female?'

'Well, you're the authority on that point. Going by the facts, it seemed to me likely.'

'I thought perhaps you might have been able to make a guess at who she was?'

'Come now, Inspector, you already know – or your colleagues

will tell you, that I haven't been able to identify her.'

'I said a guess, Mr Crackenthorpe. You might never have *seen* the woman before – but you might have been able to make a guess at who she was – or who she might have been?'

Cedric shook his head.

'You're barking up the wrong tree. I've absolutely no idea. You're suggesting, I suppose, that she may have come to the Long Barn to keep an assignation with one of us? But we none of us live here. The only people in the house were a woman and an old man. You don't seriously believe that she came here to keep a date with my revered Pop?'

'Our point is – Inspector Bacon agrees with me – that the woman may once have had some association with this house. It may have been a considerable number of years ago. Cast your mind back, Mr Crackenthorpe.'

Cedric thought a moment or two, then shook his head.

'We've had foreign help from time to time, like most people, but I can't think of any likely possibility. Better ask the others – they'd know more than I would.'

'We shall do that, of course.'

Craddock leaned back in his chair and went on:

'As you have heard at the inquest, the medical evidence cannot fix the time of death very accurately. Longer than two weeks, less than four – which brings it somewhere around Christmas-time. You have told me you came home for Christmas. When did you arrive in England and when did you leave?'

Cedric reflected.

'Let me see . . . I flew. Got here on the Saturday before Christmas – that would be the 21st.'

'You flew straight from Majorca?'

'Yes. Left at five in the morning and got here midday.'

'And you left?'

'I flew back on the following Friday, the 27th.'

'Thank you.'

Cedric grinned.

'Leaves me well within the limit, unfortunately. But really, Inspector, strangling young women is *not* my favourite form of Christmas fun.'

'I hope not, Mr Crackenthorpe.'

594

Inspector Bacon merely looked disapproving.

'There would be a remarkable absence of peace and good will about such an action, don't you agree?'

Cedric addressed this question to Inspector Bacon who merely grunted. Inspector Craddock said politely:

'Well, thank you, Mr Crackenthorpe. That will be all.'

'And what do you think of him?' Craddock asked as Cedric shut the door behind him.

Bacon grunted again.

'Cocky enough for anything,' he said. 'I don't care for the type myself. A loose-living lot, these artists, and very likely to be mixed up with a disreputable class of woman.'

Craddock smiled.

'I don't like the way he dresses, either,' went on Bacon. 'No respect – going to an inquest like that. Dirtiest pair of trousers I've seen in a long while. And did you see his tie? Looked as though it was made of coloured string. If you ask me, he's the kind that would easily strangle a woman and make no bones about it.'

'Well, he didn't strangle this one – if he didn't leave Majorca until the 21st. And that's a thing we can verify easily enough.'

Bacon threw him a sharp glance.

'I notice that you're not tipping your hand yet about the actual date of the crime.'

'No, we'll keep that dark for the present. I always like to have something up my sleeve in the early stages.'

Bacon nodded in full agreement.

'Spring it on 'em when the time comes,' he said. 'That's the best plan.'

'And now,' said Craddock, 'we'll see what our correct City gentleman has to say about it all.'

Harold Crackenthorpe, thin-lipped, had very little to say about it. It was most distasteful – a very unfortunate incident. The newspapers, he was afraid . . . Reporters, he understood, had already been asking for interviews . . . All that sort of thing . . . Most regrettable . . .

Harold's staccato unfinished sentences ended. He leaned back in his chair with the expression of a man confronted with a very bad smell.

The inspector's probing produced no result. No, he had no idea who the woman was or could be. Yes, he had been at Rutherford Hall for Christmas. He had been unable to come down until Christmas Eve – but had stayed on over the following week-end.

'That's that, then,' said Inspector Craddock, without pressing his questions further. He had already made up his mind that Harold Crackenthorpe was not going to be helpful.

He passed on to Alfred, who came into the room with a nonchalance that seemed just a trifle overdone.

Craddock looked at Alfred Crackenthorpe with a faint feeling of recognition. Surely he had seen this particular member of the family somewhere before? Or had it been his picture in the paper? There was something discreditable attached to the memory. He asked Alfred his occupation and Alfred's answer was vague.

'I'm in insurance at the moment. Until recently I've been interested in putting a new type of talking machine on the market. Quite revolutionary. I did very well out of that as a matter of fact.'

Inspector Craddock looked appreciative – and no one could have had the least idea that he was noticing the superficially smart appearance of Alfred's suit and gauging correctly the low price it had cost. Cedric's clothes had been disreputable, almost threadbare, but they had been originally of good cut and excellent material. Here there was a cheap smartness that told its own tale. Craddock passed pleasantly on to his routine questions. Alfred seemed interested – even slightly amused.

'It's quite an idea, that the woman might once have had a job here. Not as a lady's maid; I doubt if my sister has ever had such a thing. I don't think anyone has nowadays. But, of course, there is a good deal of foreign domestic labour floating about. We've had Poles – and a temperamental German or two. As Emma definitely didn't recognize the woman, I think that washes your idea out, Inspector, Emma's got a very good memory for a face. No, if the woman came from London . . . What gives you the idea she came from London, by the way?'

He slipped the question in quite casually, but his eyes were sharp and interested.

Inspector Craddock smiled and shook his head.

Alfred looked at him keenly.

'Not telling, eh? Return ticket in her coat pocket, perhaps, is that it?'

'It could be, Mr Crackenthorpe.'

'Well, granting she came from London, perhaps the chap she came to meet had the idea that the Long Barn would be a nice place to do a quiet murder. He knows the set up here, evidently. I should go looking for *him* if I were you, Inspector.'

'We are,' said Inspector Craddock, and made the two little words sound quiet and confident.

He thanked Alfred and dismissed him.

'You know,' he said to Bacon, 'I've seen that chap somewhere before . . .'

Inspector Bacon gave his verdict.

'Sharp customer,' he said. 'So sharp that he cuts himself sometimes.'

II

'I don't suppose you want to see me,' said Bryan Eastley apologetically, coming into the room and hesitating by the door. 'I don't exactly belong to the family —'

'Let me see, you are Mr Bryan Eastley, the husband of Miss Edith Crackenthorpe, who died five years ago?'

'That's right.'

'Well, it's very kind of you, Mr Eastley, especially if you know something that you think could assist us in some way?'

'But I don't. Wish I did. Whole thing seems so ruddy peculiar, doesn't it? Coming along and meeting some fellow in that draughty old barn, in the middle of winter. Wouldn't be my cup of tea!'

'It is certainly very perplexing,' Inspector Craddock agreed.

'Is it true that she was a foreigner? Word seems to have got round to that effect.'

'Does that fact suggest anything to you?' The inspector looked at him sharply, but Bryan seemed amiably vacuous.

'No, it doesn't, as a matter of fact.'

'Maybe she was French,' said Inspector Bacon, with dark suspicion.

Bryan was roused to slight animation. A look of interest came into his blue eyes, and he tugged at his big fair moustache.

'Really? Gay Paree?' He shook his head. 'On the whole it seems to make it even more unlikely, doesn't it? Messing about in the barn, I mean. You haven't had any other sarcophagus murders, have you? One of these fellows with an urge – or a complex? Thinks he's Caligula or someone like that?'

Inspector Craddock did not even trouble to reject this speculation. Instead he asked in a casual manner:

'Nobody in the family got any French connections, or – or – relationships that you know of?'

Bryan said that the Crackenthorpes weren't a very gay lot.

'Harold's respectably married,' he said. 'Fish-faced woman, some impoverished peer's daughter. Don't think Alfred cares about women much – spends his life going in for shady deals which usually go wrong in the end. I dare say Cedric's got a few Spanish señoritas jumping through hoops for him in Ibiza. Women rather fall for Cedric. Doesn't always shave and looks as though he never washes. Don't see why that should be attractive to women, but apparently it is – I say, I'm not being very helpful, am I?'

He grinned at them.

'Better get young Alexander on the job. He and James Stoddart-West are out hunting for clues in a big way. Bet you they turn up something.'

Inspector Craddock said he hoped they would. Then he thanked Bryan Eastley and said he would like to speak to Miss Emma Crackenthorpe.

III

Inspector Craddock looked with more attention at Emma Crackenthorpe than he had done previously. He was still wondering about the expression that he had surprised on her face before lunch.

A quiet woman. Not stupid. Not brilliant either. One of those comfortable pleasant women whom men were inclined to take for granted, and who had the art of making a house into a home, giving it an atmosphere of restfulness and quiet harmony. Such, he thought, was Emma Crackenthorpe.

Women such as this were often underrated. Behind their quiet exterior they had force of character, they were to be reckoned with. Perhaps, Craddock thought, the clue to the mystery of the dead woman in the sarcophagus was hidden away in the recesses of Emma's mind.

Whilst these thoughts were passing through his head, Craddock was asking various unimportant questions.

'I don't suppose there is much that you haven't already told Inspector Bacon,' he said. 'So I needn't worry you with many questions.'

'Please ask me anything you like.'

'As Mr Wimborne told you, we have reached the conclusion that the dead woman was not a native of these parts. That may be a relief to you – Mr Wimborne seemed to think it would be – but it makes it really more difficult for us. She's less easily identified.'

'But didn't she have anything – a handbag? Papers?'

Craddock shook his head.

'No handbag, nothing in her pockets.'

'You've no idea of her name – of where she came from – anything at all?'

Craddock thought to himself: She wants to know – she's very anxious to know – who the woman is. Has she felt like that all along, I wonder? Bacon didn't give me that impression – and he's a shrewd man . . .

'We know nothing about her,' he said. 'That's why we hoped one of you could help us. Are you sure you can't? Even if you didn't recognize her – can you think of anyone she might be?'

He thought, but perhaps he imagined it, that there was a very slight pause before she answered.

'I've absolutely no idea,' she said.

Imperceptibly, Inspector Craddock's manner changed. It was hardly noticeable except as a slight hardness in his voice.

'When Mr Wimborne told you that the woman was a foreigner, why did you assume that she was French?'

Emma was not disconcerted. Her eyebrows rose slightly.

'Did I? Yes, I believe I did. I don't really know why – except that one always tends to think foreigners *are* French until one finds out what nationality they really are. Most foreigners in this country are French, aren't they?'

'Oh, I really wouldn't say that was so, Miss Crackenthorpe. Not nowadays. We have so many nationalities over here, Italians, Germans, Austrians, all the Scandinavian countries –'

'Yes, I suppose you're right.'

'You don't have some special reason for thinking that this woman was likely to be French?'

She didn't hurry to deny it. She just thought a moment and then shook her head almost regretfully.

'No,' she said. 'I really don't think so.'

Her glance met his placidly, without flinching. Craddock looked towards Inspector Bacon. The latter leaned forward and presented a small enamel powder compact.

'Do you recognize this, Miss Crackenthorpe?'

She took it and examined it.

'No. It's certainly not mine.'

'You've no idea to whom it belonged?'

'No.'

'Then I don't think we need worry you any more – for the present.'

'Thank you.'

She smiled briefly at them, got up, and left the room. Again he may have imagined it, but Craddock thought she moved rather quickly, as though a certain relief hurried her.

'Think she knows anything?' asked Bacon.

Inspector Craddock said ruefully:

'At a certain stage one is inclined to think everyone knows a little more than they are willing to tell you.'

'They usually do, too,' said Bacon out of the depth of his experience. 'Only,' he added, 'it quite often isn't anything to do with the business in hand. It's some family peccadillo or some silly scrape that people are afraid is going to be dragged into the open.'

'Yes, I know. Well, at least –'

But whatever Inspector Craddock had been about to say never got said, for the door was flung open and old Mr Crackenthorpe shuffled in in a high state of indignation.

'A pretty pass, when Scotland Yard comes down and doesn't have the courtesy to talk to the head of the family first! Who's the master of this house, I'd like to know? Answer me that? Who's the master here?'

'You are, of course, Mr Crackenthorpe,' said Craddock soothingly and rising as he spoke. 'But we understood that you had already told Inspector Bacon all you know, and that, your health not being good, we must not make too many demands upon it. Dr Quimper said –'

'I dare say – I dare say. I'm not a strong man ... As for Dr Quimper, he's a regular old woman – perfectly good doctor, understands my case – but inclined to wrap me up in cottonwool. Got a bee in his bonnet about food. Went on at me Christmas-time when I had a bit of a turn – what did I eat? When? Who cooked it? Who served it? Fuss, fuss, fuss! But though I may have indifferent health, I'm well enough to give you all the help that's in my power. Murder in my own house – or at any rate in my own barn! Interesting building, that. Elizabethan. Local architect says not – but fellow doesn't know what he's talking about. Not a day later than 1580 – but that's not what we're talking about. What do you want to know? What's your present theory?'

'It's a little too early for theories, Mr Crackenthorpe. We are still trying to find out who the woman was.'

'Foreigner, you say?'

'We think so.'

'Enemy agent?'

'Unlikely, I should say.'

'You'd say – you'd say! They're everywhere, these people. Infiltrating! Why the Home Office lets them in beats me. Spying on industrial secrets, I'd bet. That's what she was doing.'

'In Brackhampton?'

'Factories everywhere. One outside my own back gate.'

Craddock shot an inquiring glance at Bacon who responded.

'Metal Boxes.'

'How do you know that's what they're really making? Can't swallow all these fellows tell you. All right, if she wasn't a spy, who do you think she was? Think she was mixed up with one of my precious sons? It would be Alfred, if so. Not Harold, he's too careful. And Cedric doesn't condescend to live in this country. All right, then, she was Alfred's bit of skirt. And some violent fellow followed her down here, thinking she was coming to meet him and did her in. How's that?'

Inspector Craddock said diplomatically that it was certainly a theory. But Mr Alfred Crackenthorpe, he said, had not recognized her.

'Pah! Afraid, that's all! Alfred always was a coward. But he's a

601

liar, remember, always was! Lie himself black in the face. None of my sons are any good. Crowd of vultures, waiting for me to die, that's their real occupation in life,' he chuckled. '*And* they can wait. I won't die to oblige *them*! Well, if that's all I can do for you . . . I'm tired. Got to rest.'

He shuffled out again.

'Alfred's bit of skirt?' said Bacon questioningly. 'In my opinion the old man just made that up,' he paused, hesitated. 'I think, personally, Alfred's quite all right – perhaps a shifty customer in some ways – but not our present cup of tea. Mind you – I did just wonder about that Air Force chap.'

'Bryan Eastley?'

'Yes. I've run into one or two of his type. They're what you might call adrift in the world – had danger and death and excitement too early in life. Now they find life tame. Tame and unsatisfactory. In a way, we've given them a raw deal. Though I don't really know what we could do about it. But there they are, all past and no future, so to speak. And they're the kind that don't mind taking chances – the ordinary fellow plays safe by instinct, it's not so much morality as prudence. But these fellows aren't afraid – playing safe isn't really in their vocabulary. If Eastley were mixed up with a woman and wanted to kill her . . .' He stopped, threw out a hand hopelessly. 'But why should he want to kill her? And if you do kill a woman, why plant her in your father-in-law's sarcophagus? No, if you ask me, none of this lot had anything to do with the murder. If they had, they wouldn't have gone to all the trouble of planting the body on their own back door step, so to speak.'

Craddock agreed that that hardly made sense.

'Anything more you want to do here?'

Craddock said there wasn't.

Bacon suggested coming back to Brackhampton and having a cup of tea – but Inspector Craddock said that he was going to call on an old acquaintance.

CHAPTER TEN

Miss Marple, sitting erect against a background of china dogs and presents from Margate, smiled approvingly at Inspector Dermot Craddock.

'I'm so glad,' she said, 'that you have been assigned to the case. I hoped you would be.'

'When I got your letter,' said Craddock, 'I took it straight to the AC. As it happened he had just heard from the Brackhampton people calling us in. They seemed to think it wasn't a local crime. The AC was very interested in what I had to tell him about you. He'd heard about you, I gather, from my godfather.'

'Dear Sir Henry,' murmured Miss Marple affectionately.

'He got me to tell him all about the Little Paddocks business. Do you want to hear what he said next?'

'Please tell me if it is not a breach of confidence.'

'He said, "Well, as this seems a completely cockeyed business, all thought up by a couple of old ladies who've turned out, against all probability, to be right, and since you already know one of these old ladies, I'm sending you down on the case." So here I am! And now, my dear Miss Marple, where do we go from here? This is not, as you probably appreciate, an official visit. I haven't got my henchmen with me. I thought you and I might take down our back hair together first.'

Miss Marple smiled at him.

'I'm sure,' she said, 'that no one who only knows you officially would ever guess that you could be so human, and better-looking than ever – don't blush . . . Now, what, exactly, have you been told so far?'

'I've got everything, I think. Your friend, Mrs McGillicuddy's original statement to the police at St Mary Mead, confirmation of her statement by the ticket collector, and also the note to the stationmaster at Brackhampton. I may say that all the proper inquiries were made by the people concerned – the railway people and the

603

police. But there's no doubt that you outsmarted them all by a most fantastic process of guesswork.'

'*Not* guesswork,' said Miss Marple. 'And I had a great advantage. I *knew* Elspeth McGillicuddy. Nobody else did. There was no obvious confirmation of her story, and if there was no question of any woman being reported missing, then quite naturally they would think it was just an elderly lady imagining things – as elderly ladies often do – but not Elspeth McGillicuddy.'

'Not Elspeth McGillicuddy,' agreed the inspector. 'I'm looking forward to meeting her, you know. I wish she hadn't gone to Ceylon. We're arranging for her to be interviewed there, by the way.'

'My own process of reasoning was not really original,' said Miss Marple. 'It's all in Mark Twain. The boy who found the horse. He just imagined where he would go if he were a horse and he went there and there was the horse.'

'You imagined what you'd do if you were a cruel and cold-blooded murderer?' said Craddock looking thoughtfully at Miss Marple's pink and white elderly fragility. 'Really, your mind –'

'Like a sink, my nephew Raymond used to say,' Miss Marple agreed, nodding her head briskly. 'But as I always told him, sinks are necessary domestic equipment and actually very hygienic.'

'Can you go a little further still, put yourself in the murderer's place, and tell me just where he is now?'

Miss Marple sighed.

'I wish I could. I've no idea – no idea at all. But he must be someone who has lived in, or knows all about, Rutherford Hall.'

'I agree. But that opens up a very wide field. Quite a succession of daily women have worked there. There's the Women's Institute – and the ARP Wardens before them. They all know the Long Barn and the sarcophagus and where the key was kept. The whole set up there is widely known locally. *Anybody* living round about might hit on it as a good spot for his purpose.'

'Yes, indeed. I *quite* understand your difficulties.'

Craddock said: 'We'll never get anywhere until we identify the body.'

'And that, too, may be difficult?'

'Oh, we'll get there – in the end. We're checking up on all the reported disappearances of a woman of that age and appearance. There's no one outstanding who fits the bill. The MO puts her down as about thirty-five, healthy, probably a married woman, has had at least one child. Her fur coat is a cheap one purchased at a London store. Hundreds of such coats were sold in the last three months, about sixty per cent of them to blonde women. No sales girl can recognize the photograph of the dead woman, or is likely to if the purchase were made just before Christmas. Her other clothes seem mainly of foreign manufacture mostly purchased in Paris. There are no English laundry marks. We've communicated with Paris and they are checking up there for us. Sooner or later, of course, someone will come forward with a missing relative or lodger. It's just a matter of time.'

'The compact wasn't any help?'

'Unfortunately, no. It's a type sold by the hundred in the Rue de Rivoli, quite cheap. By the way, you ought to have turned that over to the police at once, you know – or rather Miss Eyelesbarrow should have done so.'

Miss Marple shook her head.

'But at that moment there wasn't any question of a crime having been committed,' she pointed out. 'If a young lady, practising golf shots, picks up an old compact of no particular value in the long grass, surely she doesn't rush straight off to the police with it?' Miss Marple paused, and then added firmly: 'I thought it *much* wiser to find the body first.'

Inspector Craddock was tickled.

'You don't seem ever to have had any doubts but that it would be found?'

'I was sure it would. Lucy Eyelesbarrow is a most efficient and intelligent person.'

'I'll say she is! She scares the life out of me, she's so devastatingly efficient! No man will ever dare marry that girl.'

'Now you know, I wouldn't say *that*. . . It would have to be a special type of man, of course.' Miss Marple brooded on this thought a moment. 'How is she getting on at Rutherford Hall?'

'They're completely dependent on her as far as I can see. Eating out of her hand – literally as you might say. By the way, they know nothing about her connection with you. We've kept that dark.'

'She has no connection *now* with me. She has done what I asked her to do.'

'So she could hand in her notice and go if she wanted to?'

'Yes.'

'But she stops on. Why?'

'She has not mentioned her reasons to me. She is a very intelligent girl. I suspect that she has become interested.'

'In the problem? Or in the family?'

'It may be,' said Miss Marple, 'that it is rather difficult to separate the two.'

Craddock looked hard at her.

'Oh, no – oh, dear me, no.'

'Have you got anything particular in mind?'

'I think you have.'

Miss Marple shook her head.

Dermot Craddock sighed. 'So all I can do is to "prosecute my inquiries" – to put it in jargon. A policeman's life is a dull one!'

'You'll get results, I'm sure.'

'Any ideas for me? More inspired guesswork?'

'I was thinking of things like theatrical companies,' said Miss Marple rather vaguely. 'Touring from place to place and perhaps not many home ties. One of those young women would be much less likely to be missed.'

'Yes. Perhaps you've got something there. We'll pay special attention to that angle.' He added, 'What are you smiling about?'

'I was just thinking,' said Miss Marple, 'of Elspeth McGillicuddy's face when she hears we've found the body!'

II

'Well!' said Mrs McGillicuddy. '*Well!*'

Words failed her. She looked across at the nicely spoken pleasant young man who had called upon her with official credentials and then down at the photograph that he handed her.

'That's her all right,' she said. 'Yes, that's her. Poor soul. Well, I must say I'm glad you've found her body. Nobody believed a word I said! The police, or the railway people or anyone else. It's very galling not to be believed. At any rate, nobody could say I didn't do all I possibly could.'

The nice young man made sympathetic and appreciative noises.

'Where did you say the body was found?'

'In a barn at a house called Rutherford Hall, just outside Brack-hampton.'

'Never heard of it. How did it get there, I wonder?'

The young man didn't reply.

'Jane Marple found it, I suppose. Trust Jane.'

'The body,' said the young man, referring to some notes, 'was found by a Miss Lucy Eyelesbarrow.'

'Never heard of her either,' said Mrs McGillicuddy. 'I still think Jane Marple had something to do with it.'

'Anyway, Mrs McGillicuddy, you definitely identify this picture as that of the woman whom you saw in a train?'

'Being strangled by a man. Yes, I do.'

'Now, can you describe this man?'

'He was a tall man,' said Mrs McGillicuddy.

'Yes?'

'And dark.'

'Yes?'

'That's all I can tell you,' said Mrs McGillicuddy. 'He had his back to me. I didn't see his face.'

'Would you be able to recognize him if you saw him?'

'Of course I shouldn't! He had his back to me. I never saw his face.'

'You've no idea at all as to his age?'

Mrs McGillicuddy considered.

'No – not really. I mean, I don't *know*. . . He wasn't, I'm almost sure – very young. His shoulders looked – well, set, if you know what I mean.' The young man nodded. 'Thirty and upward, I can't get closer than that. I wasn't really looking at him, you see. It was *her* – with those hands round her throat and her face – all blue . . . You know, sometimes I dream of it even now . . .'

'It must have been a distressing experience,' said the young man sympathetically.

He closed his notebook and said:

'When are you returning to England?'

'Not for another three weeks. It isn't necessary, is it, for me?'

He quickly reassured her.

'Oh, no. There's nothing you could do at present. Of course, if we make an arrest –'

It was left like that.

The mail brought a letter from Miss Marple to her friend. The writing was spiky and spidery and heavily underlined. Long practice made it easy for Mrs McGillicuddy to decipher. Miss Marple wrote a very full account to her friend who devoured every word with great satisfaction.

She and Jane had shown them all right!

CHAPTER ELEVEN

'I simply can't make you out,' said Cedric Crackenthorpe.

He eased himself down on the decaying wall of a long derelict pigsty and stared at Lucy Eyelesbarrow.

'What can't you make out?'

'What you're doing here?'

'I'm earning my living.'

'As a skivvy?' he spoke disparagingly.

'You're out of date,' said Lucy. 'Skivvy, indeed! I'm a Household Help, a Professional Domestician, or an Answer to Prayer, mainly the latter.'

'You can't like all the things you have to do – cooking and making beds and whirring about with a hoopla or whatever you call it, and sinking your arms up to the elbows in greasy water.'

Lucy laughed.

'Not the details, perhaps, but cooking satisfies my creative instincts, and there's something in me that really revels in clearing up mess.'

'I live in a permanent mess,' said Cedric. 'I like it,' he added defiantly.

'You look as though you did.'

'My cottage in Ibiza is run on simple straightforward lines. Three plates, two cups and saucers, a bed, a table and a couple of chairs. There's dust everywhere and smears of paint and chips of stone – I sculpt as well as paint – and nobody's allowed to touch a thing. I won't have a woman near the place.'

'Not in any capacity?'

'What do you mean by that?'

'I was assuming that a man of such artistic tastes presumably had some kind of love life.'

'My love life, as you call it, is my own business,' said Cedric with dignity. 'What I won't have is woman in her tidying-up interfering *bossing* capacity.'

'How I'd love to have a go at your cottage,' said Lucy. 'It would be a challenge!'

'You won't get the opportunity.'

'I suppose not.'

Some bricks fell out of the pigsty. Cedric turned his head and looked into its nettle-ridden depths.

'Dear old Madge,' he said. 'I remember her well. A sow of most endearing disposition and prolific mother. Seventeen in the last litter, I remember. We used to come here on fine afternoons and scratch Madge's back with a stick. She loved it.'

'Why has this whole place been allowed to get into the state it's in? It can't only be the war?'

'You'd like to tidy this up, too, I suppose? What an interfering female you are. I quite see now why you *would* be the person to discover a body! You couldn't even leave a Greco-Roman sarcophagus alone.' He paused and then went on. 'No, it's not only the war. It's my father. What do you think of him, by the way?'

'I haven't had much time for thinking.'

'Don't evade the issue. He's as mean as hell, and in my opinion a bit crazy as well. Of course he hates all of us – except perhaps Emma. That's because of my grandfather's will.'

Lucy looked inquiring.

'My grandfather was the man who madea-da-monitch. With the Crunchies and the Cracker Jacks and the Cosy Crisps. All the afternoon tea delicacies and then, being far-sighted, he switched on very early to Cheesies and Canapés so that now we cash in on cocktail parties in a big way. Well, the time came when father intimated that he had a soul above Crunchies. He travelled in Italy and the Balkans and Greece and dabbled in art. My grandfather was peeved. He decided my father was no man of business and a rather poor judge of art (quite right in both cases), so left all his money in trust for his grandchildren. Father had the income for life, but he couldn't touch the capital. Do you know what he did? He stopped spending money. He came here and began to save. I'd say that by now he's accumulated nearly as big a fortune as my grandfather left. And in the meantime all of us, Harold, myself, Alfred and Emma haven't got a penny of grandfather's money. I'm a stony-broke painter. Harold went into business and is now a prominent man in the City – he's the one with the money-making touch, though I've heard rumours that he's in Queer Street lately. Alfred – well, Alfred is usually known in the privacy of the family as Flash Alf –'

'Why?'

'What a lot of things you want to know! The answer is that Alf is the black sheep of the family. He's not actually been to prison yet, but he's been very near it. He was in the Ministry of Supply during the war, but left it rather abruptly under questionable circumstances. And after that there were some dubious deals in tinned fruits – and trouble over eggs. Nothing in a big way – just a few doubtful deals on the side.'

'Isn't it rather unwise to tell strangers all these things?'

'Why? Are you a police spy?'

'I might be.'

'I don't think so. You were here slaving away before the police began to take an interest in us. I should say –'

He broke off as his sister Emma came through the door of the kitchen garden.

'Hallo, Em? You're looking very perturbed about something?'

'I am. I want to talk to you, Cedric.'

'I must get back to the house,' said Lucy, tactfully.

'Don't go,' said Cedric. 'Murder has made you practically one of the family.'

'I've got a lot to do,' said Lucy. 'I only came out to get some parsley.'

She beat a rapid retreat to the kitchen garden. Cedric's eyes followed her.

'Good-looking girl,' he said. 'Who is she really?'

'Oh, she's quite well known,' said Emma. 'She's made a speciality of this kind of thing. But never mind Lucy Eyelesbarrow, Cedric, I'm terribly worried. Apparently the police think that the dead woman was a foreigner, perhaps French. Cedric, you don't think that she could possibly be – *Martine*?'

For a moment or two Cedric stared at her as though uncomprehending.

'Martine? But who on earth – oh, you mean *Martine*?'

'Yes. Do you think –'

'Why on earth should it be *Martine*?'

'Well, her sending that telegram was odd when you come to think of it. It must have been roughly about the same time. . . . Do you think that she may, after all, have come down here and –'

'Nonsense. Why should Martine come down here and find her way into the Long Barn? What for? It seems wildly unlikely to me.'

'You don't think, perhaps, that I ought to tell Inspector Bacon – or the other one?'

'Tell him what?'

'Well – about Martine. About her letter.'

'Now don't you go complicating things, sis, by bringing up a lot of irrelevant stuff that has nothing to do with all this. I was never very convinced about that letter from Martine, anyway.'

'I was.'

'You've always been good at believing impossible things before breakfast, old girl. My advice to you is, sit tight, and keep your mouth shut. It's up to the police to identify their precious corpse. And I bet Harold would say the same.'

'Oh, I know Harold would. And Alfred, also. But I'm worried, Cedric, I really *am* worried. I don't know what I ought to do.'

'Nothing,' said Cedric promptly. 'You keep your mouth shut, Emma. Never go half-way to meet trouble, that's my motto.'

Emma Crackenthorpe sighed. She went slowly back to the house uneasy in her mind.

As she came into the drive, Doctor Quimper emerged from the house and opened the door of his battered Austin car. He paused when he saw her, then leaving the car he came towards her.

'Well, Emma,' he said. 'Your father's in splendid shape. Murder suits him. It's given him an interest in life. I must recommend it for more of my patients.'

Emma smiled mechanically. Dr Quimper was always quick to notice reactions.

'Anything particular the matter?' he asked.

Emma looked up at him. She had come to rely a lot on the kindness and sympathy of the doctor. He had become a friend on whom to lean, not only a medical attendant. His calculated brusqueness did not deceive her — she knew the kindness that lay behind it.

'I am worried, yes,' she admitted.

'Care to tell me? Don't if you don't want to.'

'I'd like to tell you. Some of it you know already. The point is I don't know what to do.'

'I should say your judgment was usually most reliable. What's the trouble?'

'You remember — or perhaps you don't — what I once told you about my brother — the one who was killed in the war?'

'You mean about his having married — or wanting to marry — a French girl? Something of that kind?'

'Yes. Almost immediately after I got that letter, he was killed. We never heard anything of or about the girl. All we knew, actually, was her christian name. We always expected her to write or to turn up, but she didn't. We never heard *anything* — until about a month ago, just before Christmas.'

'I remember. You got a letter, didn't you?'

'Yes. Saying she was in England and would like to come and see us. It was all arranged and then, at the last minute, she sent a wire that she had to return unexpectedly to France.'

'Well?'

'The police think that this woman who was killed — was French.'

'They do, do they? She looked more of an English type to me, but one can't really judge. What's worrying you then, is that just possibly the dead woman might be your brother's girl?'

'Yes.'

'I think it's most unlikely,' said Dr Quimper, adding: 'But all the same, I understand what you feel.'

'I'm wondering if I ought not to tell the police about — about it all. Cedric and the others say it's quite unnecessary. What do you think?'

'Hm.' Dr Quimper pursed his lips. He was silent for a moment or two, deep in thought. Then he said, almost unwillingly, 'It's much *simpler*, of course, if you say nothing. I can understand what your brothers feel about it. All the same —'

'Yes?'

Quimper looked at her. His eyes had an affectionate twinkle in them.

'I'd go ahead and tell 'em,' he said. 'You'll go on worrying if you don't. I know you.'

Emma flushed a little.

'Perhaps I'm foolish.'

'You do what you want to do, my dear – and let the rest of the family go hang! I'd back your judgment against the lot of them any day.'

CHAPTER TWELVE

'Girl! You, girl! Come in here.'

Lucy turned her head, surprised. Old Mr Crackenthorpe was beckoning to her fiercely from just inside a door.

'You want me, Mr Crackenthorpe?'

'Don't talk so much. Come in here.'

Lucy obeyed the imperative finger. Old Mr Crackenthorpe took hold of her arm and pulled her inside the door and shut it.

'Want to show you something,' he said.

Lucy looked round her. They were in a small room evidently designed to be used as a study, but equally evidently not used as such for a very long time. There were piles of dusty papers on the desk and cobwebs festooned from the corners of the ceiling. The air smelt damp and musty.

'Do you want me to clean this room?' she asked.

Old Mr Crackenthorpe shook his head fiercely.

'No, you don't! I keep this room locked up. Emma would like to fiddle about in here, but I don't let her. It's *my* room. See these stones? They're geological specimens.'

Lucy looked at a collection of twelve or fourteen lumps of rock, some polished and some rough.

'Lovely,' she said kindly. 'Most interesting.'

'You're quite right. They are interesting. You're an intelligent girl. I don't show them to everybody. I'll show you some more things.'

'It's very kind of you, but I ought really to get on with what I was doing. With six people in the house —'

'Eating me out of house and home ... That's all they do when they come down here! *Eat.* They don't offer to pay for what they eat, either. Leeches! All waiting for me to die. Well, I'm not going to die just yet — I'm not going to die to please *them.* I'm a lot stronger than even Emma knows.'

'I'm sure you are.'

'I'm not so old, either. She makes out I'm an old man, treats me as an old man. You don't think I'm old, do you?'

'Of course not,' said Lucy.

'Sensible girl. Take a look at this.'

He indicated a large faded chart which hung on the wall. It was, Lucy saw, a genealogical tree; some of it done so finely that one would have to have a magnifying glass to read the names. The remote forebears, however, were written in large proud capitals with crowns over the names.

'Descended from Kings,' said Mr Crackenthorpe. 'My mother's family tree, that is — not my father's. He was a vulgarian! Common old man! Didn't like me. I was a cut above him always. Took after my mother's side. Had a natural feeling for art and classical sculpture — *he* couldn't see anything in it — silly old fool. Don't remember my mother — died when I was two. Last of her family. They were sold up and she married my father. But you look there — Edward the Confessor — Ethelred the Unready — whole lot of them. And that was before the Normans came. *Before the Normans* — that's something isn't it?'

'It is indeed.'

'Now I'll show you something else.' He guided her across the room to an enormous piece of dark oak furniture. Lucy was rather uneasily conscious of the strength of the fingers clutching her arm. There certainly seemed nothing feeble about old Mr Crackenthorpe today. 'See this? Came out of Lushington — that was my mother's people's place. Elizabethan, this is. Takes four men to move it. You don't know what I keep inside it, do you? Like me to show you?'

'Do show me,' said Lucy politely.

'Curious, aren't you? All women are curious.' He took a key from his pocket and unlocked the door of the lower cupboard. From this he took out a surprisingly new-looking cash box. This, again, he unlocked.

'Take a look here, my dear. Know what these are?'

He lifted out a small paper-wrapped cylinder and pulled away the paper from one end. Gold coins trickled out into his palm.

'Look at these, young lady. Look at 'em, hold 'em, touch 'em. Know what they are? Bet you don't! You're too young. Sovereigns – that's what they are. Good golden sovereigns. What we used before all these dirty bits of paper came into fashion. Worth a lot more than silly pieces of paper. Collected them a long time back. I've got other things in this box, too. Lots of things put away in here. All ready for the future. Emma doesn't know – nobody knows. It's our secret, see, girl? D'you know why I'm telling you and showing you?'

'Why?'

'Because I don't want you to think I'm a played-out sick old man. Lots of life in the old dog yet. My wife's been dead a long time. Always objecting to everything, she was. Didn't like the names I gave the children – good Saxon names – no interest in that family tree. I never paid any attention to what she said, though – and she was a poor-spirited creature – always gave in. Now you're a spirited filly – a very nice filly indeed. I'll give you some advice. Don't throw yourself away on a young man. Young men are fools! You want to take care of your future. You *wait* . . .' His fingers pressed into Lucy's arm. He leaned to her ear. 'I don't say more than that. *Wait.* Those silly fools think I'm going to die soon. I'm not. Shouldn't be surprised if I outlived the lot of them. And then we'll see! Oh, yes, then we'll see. Harold's got no children. Cedric and Alfred aren't married. Emma – Emma will never marry now. She's a bit sweet on Quimper – but Quimper will never think of marrying Emma. There's Alexander, of course. Yes, there's Alexander . . . But, you know, I'm fond of Alexander . . . Yes, that's awkward. I'm fond of Alexander.'

He paused for a moment, frowning, then said:

'Well, girl, what about it? What about it, eh?'

'Miss Eyelesbarrow . . .'

Emma's voice came faintly through the closed study door. Lucy seized gratefully at the opportunity.

'Miss Crackenthorpe's calling me. I must go. Thank you so much for all you have shown me . . .'

615

'Don't forget . . . our secret . . .'

'I won't forget,' said Lucy, and hurried out into the hall not quite certain as to whether she had or had not just received a conditional proposal of marriage.

II

Dermot Craddock sat at his desk in his room at New Scotland Yard. He was slumped sideways in an easy attitude, and was talking into the telephone receiver which he held with one elbow propped up on the table. He was speaking in French, a language in which he was tolerably proficient.

'It was only an idea, you understand,' he said.

'But decidedly it is an idea,' said the voice at the other end, from the Prefecture in Paris. 'Already I have set inquiries in motion in those circles. My agent reports that he has two or three promising lines of inquiry. Unless there is some family life – or a lover, these women drop out of circulation very easily and no one troubles about them. They have gone on tour, or there is some new man – it is no one's business to ask. It is a pity that the photograph you sent me is so difficult for anyone to recognize. Strangulation it does not improve the appearance. Still, that cannot be helped. I go now to study the latest reports of my agents on this matter. There will be, perhaps, something. *Au revoir, mon cher.*'

As Craddock reiterated the farewell politely, a slip of paper was placed before him on the desk. It read:

> *Miss Emma Crackenthorpe.*
> *To see Detective-Inspector Craddock.*
> *Rutherford Hall case.*

He replaced the receiver and said to the police constable:

'Bring Miss Crackenthorpe up.'

As he waited, he leaned back in his chair, thinking.

So he had not been mistaken – there was something that Emma Crackenthorpe knew – not much, perhaps, but something. And she had decided to tell him.

He rose to his feet as she was shown in, shook hands, settled her in a chair and offered her a cigarette which she refused. Then there was a momentary pause. She was trying, he decided, to find just the words she wanted. He leaned forward.

'You have come to tell me something, Miss Crackenthorpe? Can I help you? You've been worried about something, haven't you? Some little thing, perhaps, that you feel probably has nothing to do with the case, but on the other hand, just might be related to it. You've come here to tell me about it, haven't you? It's to do, perhaps, with the identity of the dead woman. You think you know who she was?'

'No, no, not quite that. I think really it's most unlikely. But –'

'But there is some possibility that worries you. You'd better tell me about it – because we may be able to set your mind at rest.'

Emma took a moment or two before speaking. Then she said:

'You have seen three of my brothers. I had another brother, Edmund, who was killed in the war. Shortly before he was killed, he wrote to me from France.'

She opened her handbag and took out a worn and faded letter. She read from it:

'I hope this won't be a shock to you, Emmie, but I'm getting married – to a French girl. It's all been very sudden – but I know you'll be fond of Martine – and look after her if anything happens to me. Will write you all the details in my next – by which time I shall be a married man. Break it gently to the old man, won't you? He'll probably go up in smoke.'

Inspector Craddock held out a hand. Emma hesitated, then put the letter into it. She went on, speaking rapidly.

'Two days after receiving this letter, we had a telegram saying Edmund was *Missing, believed killed.* Later he was definitely reported killed. It was just before Dunkirk – and a time of great confusion. There was no Army record, as far as I could find out, of his having been married – but as I say, it was a confused time. I never heard anything from the girl. I tried, after the war, to make some inquiries, but I only knew her Christian name and that part of France had been occupied by the Germans and it was difficult to find out anything, without knowing the girl's surname and more about her. In the end I assumed that the marriage had never taken place and that the girl had probably married someone else before the end of the war, or might possibly herself have been killed.'

Inspector Craddock nodded. Emma went on.

'Imagine my surprise to receive a letter just about a month ago, signed *Martine Crackenthorpe*.'

'You have it?'

Emma took it from her bag and handed it to him. Craddock read it with interest. It was written in a slanting French hand – an educated hand.

Dear Mademoiselle,

I hope it will not be a shock to you to get this letter. I do not even know if your brother Edmund told you that we were married. He said he was going to do so. He was killed only a few days after our marriage and at the same time the Germans occupied our village. After the war ended, I decided that I would not write to you or approach you, though Edmund had told me to do so. But by then I had made a new life for myself, and it was not necessary. But now things have changed. For my son's sake I write this letter. He is your brother's son, you see, and I – I can no longer give him the advantages he ought to have. I am coming to England early next week. Will you let me know if I can come and see you? My address for letters is 126 Elvers Crescent, N. 10. I hope again this will not be the great shock to you.

I remain with assurance of my excellent sentiments,
    Martine Crackenthorpe

Craddock was silent for a moment or two. He reread the letter carefully before handing it back.

'What did you do on receipt of this letter, Miss Crackenthorpe?'

'My brother-in-law, Bryan Eastley, happened to be staying with me at the time and I talked to him about it. Then I rang up my brother Harold in London and consulted him about it. Harold was rather sceptical about the whole thing and advised extreme caution. We must, he said, go carefully into this woman's credentials.'

Emma paused and then went on:

'That, of course, was only common sense and I quite agreed. But if this girl – woman – was really the Martine about whom Edmund had written to me, I felt that we must make her welcome. I wrote to the address she gave in her letter, inviting her to come down to Rutherford Hall and meet us. A few days later I received a telegram

618

from London: *Very sorry forced to return to France unexpectedly. Martine.* There was no further letter or news of any kind.'

'All this took place — when?'

Emma frowned.

'It was shortly before Christmas. I know, because I wanted to suggest her spending Christmas with us — but my father would not hear of it — so I suggested she could come down the week-end after Christmas while the family would still be there. I think the wire saying she was returning to France came actually a few days before Christmas.'

'And you believe that this woman whose body was found in the sarcophagus might be this Martine?'

'No, of course I don't. But when you said she was probably a foreigner — well, I couldn't help wondering . . . if perhaps . . .'

Her voice died away.

Craddock spoke quickly and reassuringly.

'You did quite right to tell me about this. We'll look into it. I should say there is probably little doubt that the woman who wrote to you actually *did* go back to France and is there now alive and well. On the other hand, there *is* a certain coincidence of dates, as you yourself have been clever enough to realize. As you heard at the inquest, the woman's death according to the police surgeon's evidence must have occurred about three to four weeks ago. Now don't worry, Miss Crackenthorpe, just leave it to us.' He added casually, 'You consulted Mr Harold Crackenthorpe. What about your father and your other brothers?'

'I had to tell my father, of course. He got very worked up,' she smiled faintly. 'He was convinced it was a put-up thing to get money out of us. My father gets very excited about money. He believes, or pretends to believe, that he is a very poor man, and that he must save every penny he can. I believe elderly people do get obsessions of that kind sometimes. It's not true, of course, he has a very large income and doesn't actually spend a quarter of it — or used not to until these days of high income tax. Certainly he has a large amount of savings put by.' She paused and then went on. 'I told my other two brothers also. Alfred seemed to consider it rather a joke, though he, too, thought it was almost certainly an imposture. Cedric just wasn't interested — he's inclined to be self-centred. Our idea was that the family would receive Martine, and that our lawyer, Mr

Wimborne, should also be asked to be present.'

'What did Mr Wimborne think about the letter?'

'We hadn't got as far as discussing the matter with him. We were on the point of doing so when Martine's telegram arrived.'

'You have taken no further steps?'

'Yes. I wrote to the address in London with *Please forward* on the envelope, but I have had no reply of any kind.

'Rather a curious business . . . Hm . . .'

He looked at her sharply.

'What do you yourself think about it?'

'I don't know what to think.'

'What were your reactions at the time? Did you think the letter was genuine – or did you agree with your father and brothers? What about your brother-in-law, by the way, what did he think?'

'Oh, Bryan thought that the letter was genuine.'

'And you?'

'I – wasn't sure.'

'And what were your feelings about it – supposing that this girl really *was* your brother Edmund's widow?'

Emma's face softened.

'I was very fond of Edmund. He was my favourite brother. The letter seemed to me exactly the sort of letter that a girl like Martine would write under the circumstances. The course of events she described was entirely natural. I assumed that by the time the war ended she had either married again or was with some man who was protecting her and the child. Then perhaps, this man had died, or left her, and it then seemed right to her to apply to Edmund's family – as he himself had wanted her to do. The letter seemed genuine and natural to me – but, of course, Harold pointed out that if it was written by an imposter, it would be written by some woman who had known Martine and who was in possession of all the facts, and so would write a thoroughly plausible letter. I had to admit the justice of that – but all the same . . .'

She stopped.

'You wanted it to be true?' said Craddock gently.

She looked at him gratefully.

'Yes, I wanted it to be true. I would be so glad if Edmund had left a son.'

Craddock nodded.

'As you say, the letter, on the face of it, sounds genuine enough. What *is* surprising is the sequel; Martine Crackenthorpe's abrupt departure for Paris and the fact that you have never heard from her since. You had replied kindly to her, were prepared to welcome her. Why, even if she had to return to France, did she not write again? That is, presuming her to be the genuine article. If she were an imposter, of course, it's easier to explain. I thought perhaps that you might have consulted Mr Wimborne, and that he might have instituted inquiries which alarmed the woman. That, you tell me, is not so. But it's still possible that one or other of your brothers may have done something of the kind. It's possible that this Martine may have had a background that would not stand investigation. She may have assumed that she would be dealing only with Edmund's affectionate sister, not with hard-headed suspicious business men. She may have hoped to get sums of money out of you for the child (hardly a child now – a boy presumably of fifteen or sixteen) without many questions being asked. But instead she found she was going to run up against something quite different. After all, I should imagine that serious legal aspects would arise. If Edmund Crackenthorpe left a son, born in wedlock, he would be one of the heirs to your grand-father's estate?'

Emma nodded.

'Moreover, from what I have been told, he would in due course inherit Rutherford Hall and the land round it – very valuable building land, probably, by now.'

Emma looked slightly startled.

'Yes, I hadn't thought of that.'

'Well, I shouldn't worry,' said Inspector Craddock. 'You did quite right to come and tell me. I shall make enquiries, but it seems to me highly probable that there is no connection between the woman who wrote the letter (and who was probably trying to cash in on a swindle) and the woman whose body was found in the sarcophagus.'

Emma rose with a sigh of relief.

'I'm so glad I've told you. You've been very kind.'

Craddock accompanied her to the door.

Then he rang for Detective-Sergeant Wetherall.

'Bob, I've got a job for you. Go to 126 Elvers Crescent, N. 10. Take photographs of the Rutherford Hall woman with you. See what you can find out about a woman calling herself Mrs Crackenthorpe

621

– Mrs Martine Crackenthorpe, who was either living there, or calling for letters there, between the dates of, say, 15th to the end of December.'

'Right, sir.'

Craddock busied himself with various other matters that were waiting attention on his desk. In the afternoon he went to see a theatrical agent who was a friend of his. His inquiries were not fruitful.

Later in the day when he returned to his office he found a wire from Paris on his desk.

Particulars given by you might apply to Anna Stravinska of Ballet Maritski. Suggest you come over. Dessin, Prefecture.

Craddock heaved a big sigh of relief, and his brow cleared.

At last! So much, he thought, for the Martine Crackenthorpe hare . . . He decided to take the night ferry to Paris.

CHAPTER THIRTEEN

'It's so very kind of you to have asked me to take tea with you,' said Miss Marple to Emma Crackenthorpe.

Miss Marple was looking particularly woolly and fluffy – a picture of a sweet old lady. She beamed as she looked round her – at Harold Crackenthorpe in his well-cut dark suit, at Alfred handing her sandwiches with a charming smile, at Cedric standing by the mantelpiece in a ragged tweed jacket scowling at the rest of his family.

'We are very pleased that you could come,' said Emma politely.

There was no hint of the scene which had taken place after lunch that day when Emma had exclaimed: 'Dear me, I quite forgot. I told Miss Eyelesbarrow that she could bring her old aunt to tea today.'

'Put her off,' said Harold brusquely. 'We've still got a lot to talk about. We don't want strangers here.'

'Let her have tea in the kitchen or somewhere with the girl,' said Alfred.

'Oh, no, I couldn't do that,' said Emma firmly. 'That would be very rude.'

'Oh, let her come,' said Cedric. 'We can draw her out a little about the wonderful Lucy. I should like to know more about that girl, I must say. I'm not sure that I trust her. Too smart by half.'

'She's very well connected and quite genuine,' said Harold. 'I've made it my business to find out. One wanted to be sure. Poking about and finding the body the way she did.'

'If we only knew who this damned woman was,' said Alfred.

Harold added angrily:

'I must say, Emma, that I think you were out of your senses, going and suggesting to the police that the dead woman might be Edmund's French girl friend. It will make them convinced that she came here, and that probably one or other of *us* killed her.'

'Oh, no, Harold. Don't exaggerate.'

'Harold's quite right,' said Alfred. 'Whatever possessed you, I don't know. I've a feeling I'm being followed everywhere I go by plain-clothes men.'

'I told her not to do it,' said Cedric. 'Then Quimper backed her up.'

'It's no business of his,' said Harold angrily. 'Let him stick to pills and powders and National Health.'

'Oh, do stop quarrelling,' said Emma wearily. 'I'm really glad this old Miss Whatshername is coming to tea. It will do us all good to have a stranger here and be prevented from going over and over the same things again and again. I must go and tidy myself up a little.'

She left the room.

'This Lucy Eyelesbarrow,' said Harold, and stopped. 'As Cedric says, it *is* odd that she should nose about in the barn and go opening up a sarcophagus – really a Herculean task. Perhaps we ought to take steps. Her attitude, I thought, was rather antagonistic at lunch –'

'Leave her to me,' said Alfred. 'I'll soon find out if she's up to anything.'

'I mean, *why* open up that sarcophagus?'

'Perhaps she isn't really Lucy Eyelesbarrow at all,' suggested Cedric.

'But what would be the point –?' Harold looked thoroughly upset. 'Oh, damn!'

They looked at each other with worried faces.

'And here's this pestilential old woman coming to tea. Just when we want to *think*.'

'We'll talk things over this evening,' said Alfred. 'In the meantime, we'll pump the old aunt about Lucy.'

So Miss Marple had duly been fetched by Lucy and installed by the fire and she was now smiling up at Alfred as he handed her sandwiches with the approval she always showed towards a good-looking man.

'Thank you so much . . . may I ask . . . ? Oh, egg and sardine, yes, that will be very nice. I'm afraid I'm always rather greedy over my tea. As one gets on, you know . . . And, of course, at night only a very light meal . . . I have to be careful.' She turned to her hostess once more. 'What a beautiful house you have. And so many beautiful things in it. Those bronzes, now, they remind me of some my father bought – at the Paris Exhibition. Really, your grandfather did? In the classical style, aren't they? Very handsome. How delightful for you having your brothers with you? So often families are scattered – India, though I suppose that is all done with now – and Africa – the west coast, such a bad climate.'

'Two of my brothers live in London.'

'That is very nice for you.'

'But my brother Cedric is a painter and lives in Ibiza, one of the Balearic Islands.'

'Painters are so fond of islands, are they not?' said Miss Marple. 'Chopin – that was Majorca, was it not? But he was a musician. It is Gauguin I am thinking of. A sad life – misspent, one feels. I myself never really care for paintings of native women – and although I know he is very much admired – I have never cared for that lurid mustard colour. One really feels quite bilious looking at his pictures.'

She eyed Cedric with a slightly disapproving air.

'Tell us about Lucy as a child, Miss Marple,' said Cedric.

She smiled up at him delightedly.

'Lucy was always so clever,' she said. 'Yes, you were, dear – now don't interrupt. Quite remarkable at arithmetic. Why, I remember when the butcher overcharged me for top side of beef . . .'

Miss Marple launched full steam ahead into reminiscences of Lucy's childhood and from there to experiences of her own in village life.

The stream of reminiscence was interrupted by the entry of Bryan and the boys rather wet and dirty as a result of an enthusiastic search for clues. Tea was brought in and with it came Dr Quimper who raised his eyebrows slightly as he looked round after acknowledging his introduction to the old lady.

'Hope your father's not under the weather, Emma?'

'Oh, no – that is, he was just a little tired this afternoon –'

'Avoiding visitors, I expect,' said Miss Marple with a roguish smile. 'How well I remember my own dear father. "Got a lot of old pussies coming?" he would say to my mother. "Send my tea into the study." Very naughty about it, he was.'

'Please don't think –' began Emma, but Cedric cut in.

'It's always tea in the study when his dear sons come down. Psychologically to be expected, eh, Doctor?'

Dr Quimper, who was devouring sandwiches and coffee cake with the frank appreciation of a man who has usually too little time to spend on his meals, said:

'Psychology's all right if it's left to the psychologists. Trouble is, everyone is an amateur psychologist nowadays. My patients tell *me* exactly what complexes and neuroses they're suffering from, without giving me a chance to tell them. Thanks, Emma, I will have another cup. No time for lunch today.'

'A doctor's life, I always think, is so noble and self-sacrificing,' said Miss Marple.

'You can't know many doctors,' said Dr Quimper. 'Leeches they used to be called, and leeches they often are! At any rate, we do get paid nowadays, the State sees to that. No sending in of bills that you know won't ever be met. Trouble is that all one's patients are determined to get everything they can "out of the Government," and as a result, if little Jenny coughs twice in the night, or little Tommy eats a couple of green apples, out the poor doctor has to come in the middle of the night. Oh, well! Glorious cake, Emma. What a cook you are!'

'Not mine. Miss Eyelesbarrow's.'

'You make 'em just as good,' said Quimper loyally.

'Will you come and see Father?'

She rose and the doctor followed her. Miss Marple watched them leave the room.

'Miss Crackenthorpe is a very devoted daughter, I see,' she said.

'Can't imagine how she sticks the old man myself,' said the outspoken Cedric.

'She has a very comfortable home here, and father is very much attached to her,' said Harold quickly.

'Em's all right,' said Cedric. 'Born to be an old maid.'

There was a faint twinkle in Miss Marple's eye as she said:

'Oh, do you think so?'

Harold said quickly:

'My brother didn't use the term old maid in any derogatory sense, Miss Marple.'

'Oh, I wasn't offended,' said Miss Marple. 'I just wondered if he was right. I shouldn't say myself that Miss Crackenthorpe would be an old maid. She's the type, I think, that's quite likely to marry late in life – and make a success of it.'

'Not very likely living here,' said Cedric. 'Never sees anybody she could marry.'

Miss Marple's twinkle became more pronounced than ever.

'There are always clergymen – and doctors.'

Her eyes, gentle and mischievous, went from one to another.

It was clear that she had suggested to them something that they had never thought of and which they did not find overpleasing.

Miss Marple rose to her feet, dropping as she did so, several little woolly scarves and her bag.

The three brothers were most attentive picking things up.

'So kind of you,' fluted Miss Marple. 'Oh, yes, and my little blue muffler. Yes – as I say – so kind to ask me here. I've been picturing, you know, just what your home was like – so that I can visualize dear Lucy working here.'

'Perfect home conditions – with murder thrown in,' said Cedric.

'Cedric!' Harold's voice was angry.

Miss Marple smiled up at Cedric.

'Do you know who you remind me of? Young Thomas Eade, our bank manager's son. Always out to shock people. It didn't do in banking circles, of course, so he went to the West Indies . . . He came home when his father died and inherited quite a lot of money. So nice for him. He was always better at spending money than making it.'

Lucy took Miss Marple home. On her way back a figure stepped out of the darkness and stood in the glare of the headlights just as she was about to turn into the back lane. He held up his hand and Lucy recognized Alfred Crackenthorpe.

'That's better,' he observed, as he got in. 'Brr, it's cold! I fancied I'd like a nice bracing walk. I didn't. Taken the old lady home all right?'

'Yes. She enjoyed herself very much.'

'One could see that. Funny what a taste old ladies have for any kind of society, however dull. And, really, nothing could be duller than Rutherford Hall. Two days here is about as much as I can stand. How do you manage to stick it out, Lucy? Don't mind if I call you Lucy, do you?'

'Not at all. I don't find it dull. Of course with me it's not a permanency.'

'I've been watching you – you're a smart girl, Lucy. Too smart to waste yourself cooking and cleaning.'

'Thank you, but I prefer cooking and cleaning to the office desk.'

'So would I. But there are other ways of living. You could be a freelance.'

'I am.'

'Not this way. I mean, working for yourself, pitting your wits against –'

'Against what?'

'The powers that be! All the silly pettifogging rules and regulations that hamper us all nowadays. The interesting thing is there's always a way round them if you're smart enough to find it. And you're smart. Come now, does the idea appeal to you?'

'Possibly.'

Lucy manoeuvred the car into the stableyard.

'Not going to commit yourself?'

'I'd have to hear more.'

'Frankly, my dear girl, I could use you. You've got the sort of manner that's invaluable – creates confidence.'

'Do you want me to help you sell gold bricks?'

'Nothing so risky. Just a little by-passing of the law – no more.'

His hand slipped up her arm. 'You're a damned attractive girl, Lucy. I'd like you as a partner.'

'I'm flattered.'

'Meaning nothing doing? Think about it. Think of the fun. The pleasure you'd get out of outwitting all the sober-sides. The trouble is, one needs capital.'

'I'm afraid I haven't got any.'

'Oh, it wasn't a touch! I'll be laying my hands on some before long. My revered Papa can't live for ever, mean old brute. When he pops off, I lay my hands on some real money. What about it, Lucy?'

'What are the terms?'

'Marriage if you fancy it. Women seem to, no matter how advanced and self-supporting they are. Besides, married women can't be made to give evidence against their husbands.'

'Not so flattering!'

'Come off it, Lucy. Don't you realize I've fallen for you?'

Rather to her surprise Lucy was aware of a queer fascination. There was a quality of charm about Alfred, perhaps due to sheer animal magnetism. She laughed and slipped from his encircling arm.

'This is no time for dalliance. There's dinner to think about.'

'So there is, Lucy, and you're a lovely cook. What's for dinner?'

'Wait and see! You're as bad as the boys!'

They entered the house and Lucy hurried to the kitchen. She was rather surprised to be interrupted in her preparations by Harold Crackenthorpe.

'Miss Eyelesbarrow, can I speak to you about something?'

'Would later do, Mr Crackenthorpe? I'm rather behind hand.'

'Certainly. Certainly. After dinner?'

'Yes, that will do.'

Dinner was duly served and appreciated. Lucy finished washing up and came out into the hall to find Harold Crackenthorpe waiting for her.

'Yes, Mr Crackenthorpe?'

'Shall we come in here?' He opened the door of the drawing-room and led the way. He shut the door behind her.

'I shall be leaving early in the morning,' he explained, 'but I want to tell you how struck I have been by your ability.'

'Thank you,' said Lucy, feeling a little surprised.

'I feel that your talents are wasted here – definitely wasted.'

'Do you? I don't.'

At any rate, *he* can't ask me to marry him, thought Lucy. He's got a wife already.

'I suggest that having very kindly seen us through this lamentable crisis, you call upon me in London. If you will ring up and make an appointment, I will leave instructions with my secretary. The truth is that we could use someone of your outstanding ability in the firm. We could discuss fully in what field your talents would be most ably employed. I can offer you, Miss Eyelesbarrow, a very good salary indeed with brilliant prospects. I think you will be agreeably surprised.'

His smile was magnanimous.

Lucy said demurely:

'Thank you, Mr Crackenthorpe, I'll think about it.'

'Don't wait too long. These opportunities should not be missed by a young woman anxious to make her way in the world.'

Again his teeth flashed.

'Good night, Miss Eyelesbarrow, sleep well.'

'Well,' said Lucy to herself, 'well ... this is all very interesting ...'

On her way up to bed, Lucy encountered Cedric on the stairs.

'Look here, Lucy, there's something I want to say to you.'

'Do you want me to marry you and come to Ibiza and look after you?'

Cedric looked very much taken aback, and slightly alarmed.

'I never thought of such a thing.'

'Sorry. My mistake.'

'I just wanted to know if you've a timetable in the house?'

'Is that all? There's one on the hall table.'

'You know,' said Cedric, reprovingly, 'you shouldn't go about thinking everyone wants to marry you. You're quite a good-looking girl but not as good-looking as all that. There's a name for that sort of thing – it grows on you and you get worse. Actually, you're the last girl in the world I should care to marry. The last girl.'

'Indeed?' said Lucy. 'You needn't rub it in. Perhaps you'd prefer me as a stepmother?'

'What's that?' Cedric stared at her stupefied.

'You heard me,' said Lucy, and went into her room and shut the door.

CHAPTER FOURTEEN

Dermot Craddock was fraternizing with Armand Dessin of the Paris Prefecture. The two men had met on one or two occasions and got on well together. Since Craddock spoke French fluently, most of their conversation was conducted in that language.

'It is an idea only,' Dessin warned him, 'I have a picture here of the corps de ballet – that is she, the fourth from the left – it says anything to you, yes?'

Inspector Craddock said that actually it didn't. A strangled young woman is not easy to recognize, and in this picture all the young women concerned were heavily made up and were wearing extravagant bird headdresses.

'It *could* be,' he said. 'I can't go further than that. Who was she? What do you know about her?'

'Almost less than nothing,' said the other cheerfully. 'She was not important, you see. And the Ballet Maritski – it is not important, either. It plays in suburban theatres and goes on tour – it has no real names, no stars, no famous ballerinas. But I will take you to see Madame Joilet who runs it.'

Madame Joilet was a brisk business-like Frenchwoman with a shrewd eye, a small moustache, and a good deal of adipose tissue.

'Me, I do not like the police!' She scowled at them, without camouflaging her dislike of the visit. 'Always, if they can, they make me embarrassments.'

'No, no, Madame, you must not say that,' said Dessin, who was a tall thin melancholy-looking man. 'When have I ever caused you embarrassments?'

'Over that little fool who drank the carbolic acid,' said Madame Joilet promptly. 'And all because she has fallen in love with the chef d'orchestre – who does not care for women and has other tastes. Over that you made the big brouhaha! Which is not good for my beautiful ballet.'

630

'On the contrary, big box-office business,' said Dessin. 'And that was three years ago. You should not bear malice. Now about this girl, Anna Stravinska.'

'Well, what about her?' said Madame cautiously.

'Is she Russian?' asked Inspector Craddock.

'No, indeed. You mean, because of her name? But they all call themselves names like that, these girls. She was not important, she did not dance well, she was not particularly good-looking. *Elle était assez bien, c'est tout.* She danced well enough for the corps de ballet – but no solos.'

'Was she French?'

'Perhaps. She had a French passport. But she told me once that she had an English husband.'

'She told you that she had an English husband? Alive – or dead?'

Madame Joilet shrugged her shoulders.

'Dead, or he had left her. How should I know which? These girls – there is always some trouble with men –'

'When did you last see her?'

'I take my company to London for six weeks. We play at Torquay, at Bournemouth, at Eastbourne, at somewhere else I forget and at Hammersmith. Then we come back to France, but Anna – she does not come. She sends a message only that she leaves the company, that she goes to live with her husband's family – some nonsense of that kind. I did not think it is true, myself. I think it more likely that she has met a man, you understand.'

Inspector Craddock nodded. He perceived that that was what Madame Joilet would invariably think.

'And it is no loss to me. I do not care. I can get girls just as good and better to come and dance, so I shrug the shoulders and do not think of it any more. Why should I? They are all the same, these girls, mad about men.'

'What date was this?'

'When we return to France? It was – yes – the Sunday before Christmas. And Anna she leaves two – or is it three – days before that? I cannot remember exactly ... But the end of the week at Hammersmith we have to dance without her – and it means rearranging things ... It was very naughty of her – but these girls – the moment they meet a man they are all the same. Only I say to everybody. "Zut, I do not take her back, that one!"'

'Very annoying for you.'

'Ah! Me – I do not care. No doubt she passes the Christmas holiday with some man she has picked up. It is not my affair. I can find other girls – girls who will leap at the chance of dancing in the Ballet Maritski and who can dance as well – or better than Anna.'

Madame Joilet paused and then asked with a sudden gleam of interest:

'Why do you want to find her? Has she come into money?'

'On the contrary,' said Inspector Craddock politely. 'We think she may have been murdered.'

Madame Joilet relapsed into indifference.

'*Ça se peut*! It happens. Ah, well! She was a good Catholic. She went to Mass on Sundays, and no doubt to confession.'

'Did she ever speak to you, Madame, of a son?'

'A son? Do you mean she had a child? That, now, I should consider most unlikely. These girls, all – *all* of them know a useful address to which to go. M. Dessin knows that as well as I do.'

'She may have had a child before she adopted a stage life,' said Craddock. 'During the war, for instance.'

'*Ah! dans la guerre*. That is always possible. But if so, I know nothing about it.'

'Who amongst the other girls were her closest friends?'

'I can give you two or three names – but she was not very intimate with anyone.'

They could get nothing else useful from Madame Joilet.

Shown the compact, she said Anna had one of that kind, but so had most of the other girls. Anna had perhaps bought a fur coat in London – she did not know. 'Me, I occupy myself with the rehearsals, with the stage lighting, with all the difficulties of my business. I have not time to notice what my artists wear.'

After Madame Joilet, they interviewed the girls whose names she had given them. One or two of them had known Anna fairly well, but they all said that she had not been one to talk much about herself, and that when she did, it was, so one girl said, mostly lies.

'She liked to pretend things – stories about having been the mistress of a Grand Duke – or of a great English financier – or how she worked for the Resistance in the war. Even a story about being a film star in Hollywood.'

Another girl said:

'I think that really she had had a very tame bourgeois existence. She liked to be in ballet because she thought it was romantic, but she was not a good dancer. You understand that if she were to say, "My father was a draper in Amiens," that would not be romantic! So instead she made up things.'

'Even in London,' said the first girl, 'she threw out hints about a very rich man who was going to take her on a cruise round the world, because she reminded him of his dead daughter who had died in a car accident. *Quelle blague!*'

'She told *me* she was going to stay with a rich lord in Scotland,' said the second girl. 'She said she would shoot the deer there.'

None of this was helpful. All that seemed to emerge from it was that Anna Stravinska was a proficient liar. She was certainly not shooting deer with a peer in Scotland, and it seemed equally unlikely that she was on the sun deck of a liner cruising round the world. But neither was there any real reason to believe that her body had been found in a sarcophagus at Rutherford Hall. The identification by the girls and Madame Joilet was very uncertain and hesitating. It looked something like Anna, they all agreed. But really! All swollen up – it might be anybody!

The only fact that was established was that on the 19th of December Anna Stravinska had decided not to return to France, and that on the 20th December a woman resembling her in appearance had travelled to Brackhampton by the 4.33 train and had been strangled.

If the woman in the sarcophagus was *not* Anna Stravinska, where was Anna now?

To that, Madame Joilet's answer was simple and inevitable.

'With a man!'

And it was probably the correct answer, Craddock reflected ruefully.

One other possibility had to be considered – raised by the casual remark that Anna had once referred to having an English husband.

Had that husband been Edmund Crackenthorpe?

It seemed unlikely, considering the word picture of Anna that had been given him by those who knew her. What was much more probable was that Anna had at one time known the girl Martine sufficiently intimately to be acquainted with the necessary details.

It *might* have been Anna who wrote that letter to Emma Crackenthorpe and, if so, Anna would have been quite likely to have taken
fright at any question of an investigation. Perhaps she had even
thought it prudent to sever her connection with the Ballet Maritski.
Again, where was she now?

And again, inevitably, Madame Joilet's answer seemed the most
likely.

With a man . . .

II

Before leaving Paris, Craddock discussed with Dessin the question
of the woman named Martine. Dessin was inclined to agree with
his English colleague that the matter had probably no connection
with the woman found in the sarcophagus. All the same, he agreed,
the matter ought to be investigated.

He assured Craddock that the Sûreté would do their best to discover if there actually was any record of a marriage between Lieuten-
ant Edmund Crackenthorpe of the 4th Southshire Regiment and a
French girl whose Christian name was Martine. Time – just prior
to the fall of Dunkirk.

He warned Craddock, however, that a definite answer was doubtful. The area in question had not only been occupied by the Germans
at almost exactly that time, but subsequently that part of France had
suffered severe war damage at the time of the invasion. Many buildings and records had been destroyed.

'But rest assured, my dear colleague, we shall do our best.'

With this, he and Craddock took leave of each other.

III

On Craddock's return Sergeant Wetherall was waiting to report with
gloomy relish:

'Accommodation address, sir – that's what 126 Elvers Crescent
is. Quite respectable and all that.'

'Any identifications?'

'No, nobody could recognize the photograph as that of a woman

who had called for letters, but I don't think they would anyway —
it's a month ago, very near, and a good many people use the place.
It's actually a boarding-house for students.'

'She might have stayed there under another name.'

'If so, they didn't recognize her as the original of the photograph.'

He added:

'We circularized the hotels — nobody registering as Martine
Crackenthorpe anywhere. On receipt of your call from Paris, we
checked up on Anna Stravinska. She was registered with other
members of the company in a cheap hotel off Brook Green. Mostly
theatricals there. She cleared out on the night of Thursday 19th after
the show. No further record.'

Craddock nodded. He suggested a line of further inquiries —
though he had little hope of success from them.

After some thought, he rang up Wimborne, Henderson and Car-
stairs and asked for an appointment with Mr Wimborne.

In due course, he was ushered into a particularly airless room
where Mr Wimborne was sitting behind a large old-fashioned desk
covered with bundles of dusty-looking papers. Various deed boxes
labelled *Sir John ffouldes, dec., Lady Derrin, George Rowbottom,
Esq.*, ornamented the walls; whether as relics of a bygone era or as
part of present-day legal affairs, the inspector did not know.

Mr Wimborne eyed his visitor with the polite wariness characteristic of a family lawyer towards the police.

'What can I do for you, Inspector?'

'This letter . . .' Craddock pushed Martine's letter across the table.
Mr Wimborne touched it with a distasteful finger but did not pick
it up. His colour rose very slightly and his lips tightened.

'Quite so,' he said; '*quite* so! I received a letter from Miss Emma
Crackenthorpe yesterday morning, informing me of her visit to Scotland Yard and of — ah — all the circumstances. I may say that I am
at a loss to understand — quite at a loss — why I was not consulted
about this letter at the time of its arrival! *Most extraordinary*! I
should have been informed immediately . . .'

Inspector Craddock repeated soothingly such platitudes as seemed
best calculated to reduce Mr Wimborne to an amenable frame of
mind.

'I'd no idea that there was ever any question of Edmund's having
married,' said Mr Wimborne in an injured voice.

Inspector Craddock said that he supposed – in war time – and left it to trail away vaguely.

'War time!' snapped Mr Wimborne with waspish acerbity. 'Yes, indeed, we were in Lincoln's Inn Fields at the outbreak of war and there was a direct hit on the house next door, and a great number of our records were destroyed. Not the really important documents, of course; they had been removed to the country for safety. But it caused a great deal of confusion. Of course, the Crackenthorpe business was in my father's hands at that time. He died six years ago. I dare say *he* may have been told about this so-called marriage of Edmund's – but on the face of it, it looks as though that marriage, even if contemplated, never took place, and so, no doubt, my father did not consider the story of any importance. I must say, all this sounds very fishy to me. This coming forward, after all these years, and claiming a marriage and a legitimate son. Very fishy indeed. What proofs had she got, I'd like to know?'

'Just so,' said Craddock. 'What would her position, or her son's position be?'

'The idea was, I suppose, that she would get the Crackenthorpes to provide for her and for the boy.'

'Yes, but I meant, what would she and the son be entitled to, legally speaking – if she could prove her claim?'

'Oh, I see.' Mr Wimborne picked up his spectacles which he had laid aside in his irritation, and put them on, staring through them at Inspector Craddock with shrewd attention. 'Well, at the moment, nothing. But if she could prove that the boy was the son of Edmund Crackenthorpe, born in lawful wedlock, then the boy would be entitled to his share of Josiah Crackenthorpe's trust on the death of Luther Crackenthorpe. More than that, he'd inherit Rutherford Hall, since he's the son of the eldest son.'

'Would anyone want to inherit the house?'

'To live in? I should say, certainly not. But that estate, my dear Inspector, is worth a considerable amount of money. Very considerable. Land for industrial and building purposes. Land which is now in the heart of Brackhampton. Oh, yes, a very considerable inheritance.'

'If Luther Crackenthorpe dies, I believe you told me that Cedric gets it?'

'He inherits the real estate – yes, as the eldest living son.'

'Cedric Crackenthorpe, I have been given to understand, is not interested in money?'

Mr Wimborne gave Craddock a cold stare.

'Indeed? I am inclined, myself, to take statements of such a nature with what I might term a grain of salt. There are doubtless certain unworldly people who are indifferent to money. I myself have never met one.'

Mr Wimborne obviously derived a certain satisfaction from this remark.

Inspector Craddock hastened to take advantage of this ray of sunshine.

'Harold and Alfred Crackenthorpe,' he ventured, 'seem to have been a good deal upset by the arrival of this letter?'

'Well they might be,' said Mr Wimborne. 'Well they might be.'

'It would reduce their eventual inheritance?'

'Certainly. Edmund Crackenthorpe's son − always presuming there is a son − would be entitled to a fifth share of the trust money.'

'That doesn't really seem a very serious loss?'

Mr Wimborne gave him a shrewd glance.

'It is a totally inadequate motive for murder, if that is what you mean.'

'But I suppose they're both pretty hard up,' Craddock murmured.

He sustained Mr Wimborne's sharp glance with perfect impassivity.

'Oh! So the police have been making inquiries? Yes, Alfred is almost incessantly in low water. Occasionally he is very flush of money for a short time − but it soon goes. Harold, as you seem to have discovered, is at present somewhat precariously situated.'

'In spite of his appearance of financial prosperity?'

'Façade. All façade! Half these city concerns don't even know if they're solvent or not. Balance sheets can be made to look all right to the inexpert eye. But when the assets that are listed aren't really assets − when those assets are trembling on the brink of a crash − where are you?'

'Where, presumably, Harold Crackenthorpe is, in bad need of money.'

'Well, he wouldn't have got it by strangling his late brother's widow,' said Mr Wimborne. 'And nobody's murdered Luther Crackenthorpe which is the only murder that would do the family any good. So, really, Inspector, I don't quite see where your ideas are leading you?'

The worst of it was, Inspector Craddock thought, that he wasn't very sure himself.

CHAPTER FIFTEEN

Inspector Craddock had made an appointment with Harold Crackenthorpe at his office, and he and Sergeant Wetherall arrived there punctually. The office was on the fourth floor of a big block of City offices. Inside everything showed prosperity and the acme of modern business taste.

A neat young woman took his name, spoke in a discreet murmur through a telephone, and then, rising, showed them into Harold Crackenthorpe's own private office.

Harold was sitting behind a large leather-topped desk and was looking as impeccable and self-confident as ever. If, as the inspector's private knowledge led him to surmise, he was close upon Queer Street, no trace of it showed.

He looked up with a frank welcoming interest.

'Good morning, Inspector Craddock. I hope this means that you have some definite news for us at last?'

'Hardly that, I am afraid, Mr Crackenthorpe. It's just a few more questions I'd like to ask.'

'More questions? Surely by now we have answered everything imaginable.'

'I dare say it feels like that to you, Mr Crackenthorpe, but it's just a question of our regular routine.'

'Well, what is it this time?' He spoke impatiently.

'I should be glad if you could tell me exactly what you were doing on the afternoon and evening of 20th December last – say between the hours of 3 p.m. and midnight.'

Harold Crackenthorpe went an angry shade of plum-red.

'That seems to be a most extraordinary question to ask me. What does it mean, I should like to know?'

Craddock smiled gently.

'It just means that I should like to know where you were between the hours of 3 p.m. and midnight on Friday, 20th December.'

'Why?'

'It would help to narrow things down.'

'Narrow them down? You have extra information, then?'

'We hope that we're getting a little closer, sir.'

'I'm not at all sure that I ought to answer your question. Not, that is, without having my solicitor present.'

'That, of course, is entirely up to you,' said Craddock. 'You are not bound to answer any questions, and you have a perfect right to have a solicitor present before you do so.'

'You are not — let me be quite clear — er — warning me in any way?'

'Oh, no, sir.' Inspector Craddock looked properly shocked. 'Nothing of that kind. The questions I am asking you, I am asking several other people as well. There's nothing directly personal about this. It's just a matter of necessary eliminations.'

'Well, of course — I'm anxious to assist in any way I can. Let me see now. Such a thing isn't easy to answer off hand, but we're very systematic here. Miss Ellis, I expect, can help.'

He spoke briefly into one of the telephones on his desk and almost immediately a streamlined young woman in a well-cut black suit entered with a notebook.

'My secretary, Miss Ellis, Inspector Craddock. Now, Miss Ellis, the inspector would like to know what I was doing on the afternoon and evening of — what was the date?'

'Friday, 20th December.'

'Friday, 20th December. I expect you will have some record.'

'Oh, yes.' Miss Ellis left the room, returned with an office memorandum calendar and turned the pages.

'You were in the office on the morning of 20th December. You had a conference with Mr Goldie about the Cromartie merger, you lunched with Lord Forthville at the Berkeley —'

'Ah, it was that day, yes.'

'You returned to the office about 3 o'clock and dictated half a dozen letters. You then left to attend Sotheby's sale rooms where you were interested in some rare manuscripts which were coming up for sale that day. You did not return to the office again, but I have a note to remind you that you were attending the Catering Club dinner that evening.' She looked up interrogatively.

'Thank you, Miss Ellis.'

Miss Ellis glided from the room.

'That is all quite clear in my mind,' said Harold. 'I went to Sotheby's that afternoon but the items I wanted there went for too high a price. I had tea in a small place in Jermyn Street – Russell's, I think, it was called. I dropped into a News Theatre for about half an hour or so, then went home – I live at 43 Cardigan Gardens. The Catering Club dinner took place at seven-thirty at Caterer's Hall, and after it I returned home to bed. I think that should answer your questions.'

'That's all very clear, Mr Crackenthorpe. What time was it when you returned home to dress?'

'I don't think I can remember exactly. Soon after six, I should think.'

'And after your dinner?'

'It was, I think, half-past eleven when I got home.'

'Did your manservant let you in? Or perhaps Lady Alice Crackenthorpe –'

'My wife, Lady Alice, is abroad in the South of France and has been since early December. I let myself in with my latch key.'

'So there is no one who can vouch for your returning home when you say you did?'

Harold gave him a cold stare.

'I dare say the servants heard me come in. I have a man and wife. But, really, Inspector –'

'Please, Mr Crackenthorpe, I know these kind of questions are annoying, but I have nearly finished. Do you own a car?'

'Yes, a Humber Hawk.'

'You drive it yourself?'

'Yes. I don't use it much except at week-ends. Driving in London is quite impossible nowadays.'

'I presume you use it when you go down to see your father and sister in Brackhampton?'

'Not unless I am going to stay there for some length of time. If I just go down for the night – as, for instance, to the inquest the other day – I always go by train. There is an excellent train service and it is far quicker than going by car. The car my sister hires meets me at the station.'

'Where do you keep your car?'

'I rent a garage in the mews behind Cardigan Gardens. Any more questions?'

'I think that's all for now,' said Inspector Craddock, smiling and rising. 'I'm very sorry for having to bother you.'

When they were outside, Sergeant Wetherall, a man who lived in a state of dark suspicions of all and sundry, remarked meaningly:

'He didn't *like* those questions – didn't like them at all. Put out, he was.'

'If you have not committed a murder, it naturally annoys you if it seems someone thinks that you have,' said Inspector Craddock mildly. 'It would particularly annoy an ultra respectable man like Harold Crackenthorpe. There's nothing in that. What we've got to find out now is if anyone actually saw Harold Crackenthorpe at the sale that afternoon, and the same applies to the tea-shop place. He could easily have travelled by the 4.33, pushed the woman out of the train and caught a train back to London in time to appear at the dinner. In the same way he could have driven his car down that night, moved the body to the sarcophagus and driven back again. Make inquiries in the mews.'

'Yes, sir. Do you think that's what he did do?'

'How do I know?' asked Inspector Craddock. 'He's a tall dark man. He *could* have been on that train and he's got a connection with Rutherford Hall. He's a possible suspect in this case. Now for Brother Alfred.'

II

Alfred Crackenthorpe had a flat in West Hampstead, in a big modern building of slightly jerry-built type with a large courtyard in which the owners of flats parked their cars with a certain lack of consideration for others.

The flat was the modern built-in type, evidently rented furnished. It had a long plywood table that let down from the wall, a divan bed, and various chairs of improbable proportions.

Alfred Crackenthorpe met them with engaging friendliness but was, the inspector thought, nervous.

'I'm intrigued,' he said. 'Can I offer you a drink, Inspector

Craddock?' He held up various bottles invitingly.

'No, thank you, Mr Crackenthorpe.'

'As bad as that?' He laughed at his own little joke, then asked what it was all about.

Inspector Craddock said his little piece.

'What was I doing on the afternoon and evening of 20th December. How should I know? Why, that's – what – over three weeks ago.'

'Your brother Harold has been able to tell us very exactly.'

'Brother Harold, perhaps. Not Brother Alfred.' He added with a touch of something – envious malice possibly: 'Harold is the successful member of the family – busy, useful, fully employed – a time for everything, and everything at that time. Even if he were to commit a – murder, shall we say? – it would be carefully timed and exact.'

'Any particular reason for using that example?'

'Oh, no. It just came into my mind – as a supreme absurdity.'

'Now about yourself.'

Alfred spread out his hands.

'It's as I tell you – I've no memory for times or places. If you were to say Christmas Day now – then I *should* be able to answer you – there's a peg to hang it on. I know where I was Christmas Day. We spend that with my father at Brackhampton. I really don't know why. He grumbles at the expense of having us – and would grumble that we never came near him if we didn't come. We really do it to please my sister.'

'And you did it this year?'

'Yes.'

'But unfortunately your father was taken ill, was he not?'

Craddock was pursuing a sideline deliberately, led by the kind of instinct that often came to him in his profession.

'He was taken ill. Living like a sparrow in that glorious cause of economy, sudden full eating and drinking had its effect.'

'That was all it was, was it?'

'Of course. What else?'

'I gathered that his doctor was – worried.'

'Ah, that old fool Quimper,' Alfred spoke quickly and scornfully. 'It's no use listening to *him*, Inspector. He's an alarmist of the worst kind.'

'Indeed? He seemed a rather sensible kind of man to me.'

'He's a complete fool. Father's not really an invalid, there's nothing wrong with his heart, but he takes in Quimper completely. Naturally, when father really felt ill, he made a terrific fuss, and had Quimper going and coming, asking questions, going into everything he'd eaten and drunk. The whole thing was ridiculous!' Alfred spoke with unusual heat.

Craddock was silent for a moment or two, rather effectively. Alfred fidgeted, shot him a quick glance, and then said petulantly:

'Well, what *is* all this? Why do you want to know where I was on a particular Friday, three or four weeks ago?'

'So you do remember that it was a Friday?'

'I thought you said so.'

'Perhaps I did,' said Inspector Craddock. 'At any rate, Friday 20th is the day I am asking about.'

'Why?'

'A routine inquiry.'

'That's nonsense. Have you found out something more about this woman? About where she came from?'

'Our information is not yet complete.'

Alfred gave him a sharp glance.

'I hope you're not being led aside by this wild theory of Emma's that she might have been my brother Edmund's widow. That's complete nonsense.'

'This – Martine, did not at any rate apply to you?'

'To me? Good lord, no! That would have been a laugh.'

'She would be more likely, you think, to go to your brother Harold?'

'Much more likely. His name's frequently in the papers. He's well off. Trying a touch there wouldn't surprise me. Not that she'd have got anything. Harold's as tight-fisted as the old man himself. Emma, of course, is the soft-hearted one of the family, and she was Edmund's favourite sister. All the same, Emma isn't credulous. She was quite alive to the possibility of this woman being phoney. She had it all laid on for the entire family to be there – and a hard-headed solicitor as well.'

'Very wise,' said Craddock. 'Was there a definite date fixed for this meeting?'

'It was to be soon after Christmas – the week-end of the 27th . . .' he stopped.

'Ah,' said Craddock pleasantly. 'So I see some dates have a meaning to you.'

'I've told you – no definite date was fixed.'

'But you talked about it – when?'

'I really can't remember.'

'And you can't tell me what you yourself were doing on Friday, 20th December?'

'Sorry – my mind's an absolute blank.'

'You don't keep an engagement book?'

'Can't stand the things.'

'The Friday before Christmas – it shouldn't be too difficult.'

'I played golf one day with a likely prospect.' Alfred shook his head. 'No, that was the week before. I probably just mooched around. I spend a lot of my time doing that. I find one's business gets done in bars more than anywhere else.'

'Perhaps the people here, or some of your friends, may be able to help?'

'Maybe. I'll ask them. Do what I can.'

Alfred seemed more sure of himself now.

'I can't tell you what I was doing that day,' he said; 'but I can tell you what I *wasn't* doing. I wasn't murdering anyone in the Long Barn.'

'Why should you say that, Mr Crackenthorpe?'

'Come now, my dear Inspector. You're investigating this murder, aren't you? And when you begin to ask "Where were you on such and such a day at such and such a time?" you're narrowing down things. I'd very much like to know why you've hit on Friday the 20th between – what? Lunch-time and midnight? It couldn't be medical evidence, not after all this time. Did somebody see the deceased sneaking into the barn that afternoon? She went in and she never came out, etc.? Is that it?'

The sharp black eyes were watching him narrowly, but Inspector Craddock was far too old a hand to react to that sort of thing.

'I'm afraid we'll have to let you guess about that,' he said pleasantly.

'The police are so secretive.'

'Not only the police. I think, Mr Crackenthorpe, you *could* remember what you were doing on that Friday if you tried. Of course you may have reasons for not wishing to remember –'

'You won't catch me that way, Inspector. It's very suspicious, of course, very suspicious, indeed, that I can't remember – but there it is! Wait a minute now – I went to Leeds that week – stayed at a hotel close to the Town Hall – can't remember its name – but you'd find it easy enough. That *might* have been on the Friday.'

'We'll check up,' said the inspector unemotionally.

He rose. 'I'm sorry you couldn't have been more cooperative, Mr Crackenthorpe.'

'Most unfortunate for *me*! There's Cedric with a safe alibi in Ibiza, and Harold, no doubt, checked with business appointments and public dinners every hour – and here am I with no alibi at all. Very sad. And all so silly. I've already told you I don't murder people. And why should I murder an unknown woman, anyway? What for? Even if the corpse *is* the corpse of Edmund's widow, why should any of us wish to do away with her? Now if she'd been married to *Harold* in the war, and had suddenly reappeared – then it might have been awkward for the respectable Harold – bigamy and all that. But Edmund! Why we'd all have *enjoyed* making Father stump up a bit to give her an allowance and send the boy to a decent school. Father would have been wild, but he couldn't in decency refuse to do something. Won't you have a drink before you go, Inspector? Sure? Too bad I haven't been able to help you.'

III

'Sir, listen, do you know what?'

Inspector Craddock looked at his excited sergeant.

'Yes, Wetherall, what is it?'

'I've placed him, sir. That chap. All the time I was trying to fix it and suddenly it came. He was mixed up in that tinned food business with Dicky Rogers. Never got anything on him – too cagey for that. And he's been in with one or more of the Soho lot. Watches and that Italian sovereign business.'

Of course! Craddock realized now why Alfred's face had seemed vaguely familiar from the first. It had all been small-time stuff – never anything that could be proved. Alfred had always been on the outskirts of the racket with a plausible innocent reason for having been mixed up in it at all. But the police had been quite sure that a small steady profit came his way.

'That throws rather a light on things,' Craddock said.

'Think he did it?'

'I shouldn't have said he was the type to do murder. But it explains other things – the reason why he couldn't come up with an alibi.'

'Yes, that looked bad for him.'

'Not really,' said Craddock. 'It's quite a clever line – just to say firmly you can't remember. Lots of people can't remember what they did and where they were even a week ago. It's especially useful if you don't particularly want to call attention to the way you spend your time – interesting rendezvous at lorry pull-ups with the Dicky Rogers crowd, for instance.'

'So you think he's all right?'

'I'm not prepared to think anyone's all right just yet,' said Inspector Craddock. 'You've got to work on it, Wetherall.'

Back at his desk, Craddock sat frowning, and making little notes on the pad in front of him.

Murderer (he wrote) . . . A tall dark man!!!

Victim? . . . Could have been Martine, Edmund Crackenthorpe's girl-friend or widow.

Or

Could have been Anna Stravinska. Went out of circulation at appropriate time, right age and appearance, clothing, etc. No connections with Rutherford Hall as far as is known.

Could be Harold's first wife! Bigamy!

        ,,   ,,   mistress. Blackmail!

If connection with Alfred, might be blackmail. Had knowledge that could have sent him to gaol?

If Cedric – might have had connections with him abroad – Paris? Balearics?

Or

Victim could be Anna S. posing as Martine

or

Victim is unknown woman killed by unknown murderer!

'And most probably the latter,' said Craddock aloud.

He reflected gloomily on the situation. You couldn't get far with a case until you had the motive. All the motives suggested so far seemed either inadequate or far fetched.

Now if only it had been the murder of old Mr Crackenthorpe . . . Plenty of motive there . . .

Something stirred in his memory . . .

He made further notes on his pad.

Ask Dr Q. about Christmas illness.

Cedric – alibi.

Consult Miss M. for the latest gossip.

CHAPTER SIXTEEN

When Craddock got to 4 Madison Road he found Lucy Eyelesbarrow with Miss Marple.

He hesitated for a moment in his plan of campaign and then decided that Lucy Eyelesbarrow might prove a valuable ally.

After greetings, he solemnly drew out his notecase, extracting three pound notes, added three shillings and pushed them across the table to Miss Marple.

'What's this, Inspector?'

'Consultation fee. You're a consultant – on murder! Pulse, temperature, local reactions, possible deep-seated cause of said murder. I'm just the poor harassed local GP.'

Miss Marple looked at him and twinkled. He grinned at her. Lucy Eyelesbarrow gave a faint gasp and then laughed.

'Why, Inspector Craddock – you're human after all.'

'Oh, well, I'm not strictly on duty this afternoon.'

'I told you we had met before,' said Miss Marple to Lucy. 'Sir Henry Clithering is his godfather – a very old friend of mine.'

'Would you like to hear, Miss Eyelesbarrow, what my godfather said about her – the first time we met? He described her as just the finest detective God ever made – natural genius cultivated in a suitable soil. He told me never to despise the' – Dermot Craddock paused for a moment to seek for a synonym for 'old pussies' – '– er elderly ladies. He said they could usually tell you what *might* have happened, what ought to have happened, and even what actually *did* happen! And,' he said, 'they can tell you *why* it happened. He added that this particular – er – elderly lady – was at the top of the class.'

'Well!' said Lucy. 'That seems to be a testimonial all right.'

Miss Marple was pink and confused and looked unusually dithery.

'Dear Sir Henry,' she murmured. 'Always so kind. Really I'm not at all clever – just perhaps, a *slight* knowledge of human nature – living, you know, in a *village* –'

She added, with more composure:

'Of course, I am somewhat handicapped, by not actually being on the spot. It is so helpful, I always feel, when people remind you of other people – because types are alike everywhere and that is such a valuable guide.'

Lucy looked a little puzzled, but Craddock nodded comprehendingly.

'But you've been to tea there, haven't you?' he said.

'Yes, indeed. Most pleasant. I was a little disappointed that I didn't see old Mr Crackenthorpe – but one can't have everything.'

'Do you feel that if you saw the person who had done the murder, you'd know?' asked Lucy.

'Oh, I wouldn't say *that*, dear. One is always inclined to guess – and guessing would be very wrong when it is a question of anything as serious as murder. All one can do is to observe the people concerned – or who might have been concerned – and see of whom they remind you.'

'Like Cedric and the bank manager?'

Miss Marple corrected her.

'The bank manager's *son*, dear. Mr Eade himself was far more like Mr Harold – a very conservative man – but perhaps a little too fond of money – the sort of man, too, who could go a long way to avoid scandal.'

Craddock smiled, and said:

'And Alfred?'

'Jenkins at the garage,' Miss Marple replied promptly. 'He didn't exactly appropriate tools? – but he used to exchange a broken or inferior jack for a good one. And I believe he wasn't very honest over batteries – though I don't understand these things very well. I know Raymond left off dealing with him and went to the garage on the Milchester road. As for Emma,' continued Miss Marple thoughtfully, 'she reminds me very much of Geraldine Webb – always very quiet, almost dowdy – and bullied a good deal by her elderly mother. Quite a surprise to everybody when the mother died unexpectedly and Geraldine came into a nice sum of money and went and had her hair cut and permed, and went off on a cruise, and came back married to a very nice barrister. They had two children.'

The parallel was clear enough. Lucy said, rather uneasily: 'Do you think you ought to have said what you did about Emma marrying? It seemed to upset the brothers.'

Miss Marple nodded.

'Yes,' she said. 'So like men – quite unable to see what's going on under their eyes. I don't believe you noticed yourself.'

'No,' admitted Lucy. 'I never thought of anything of that kind. They both seemed to me –'

'So old?' said Miss Marple smiling a little. 'But Dr Quimper isn't much over forty, I should say, though he's going grey on the temples, and it's obvious that he's longing for some kind of home life; and Emma Crackenthorpe is under forty – not too old to marry and have a family. The doctor's wife died quite young having a baby, so I have heard.'

'I believe she did. Emma said something about it one day.'

'He must be lonely,' said Miss Marple. 'A busy hard-working doctor needs a wife – someone sympathetic – not too young.'

'Listen, darling,' said Lucy. 'Are we investigating crime, or are we match-making?'

Miss Marple twinkled.

'I'm afraid I *am* rather romantic. Because I am an old maid, perhaps. You know, dear Lucy, that, as far as I am concerned, you have fulfilled your contract. If you really want a holiday abroad before taking up your next engagement, you would have time still for a short trip.'

'And leave Rutherford Hall? Never! I'm the complete sleuth by now. Almost as bad as the boys. They spend their entire time looking for clues. They looked all through the dustbins yesterday. Most unsavoury – and they haven't really the faintest idea what they were looking for. If they come to you in triumph, Inspector Craddock, bearing a torn scrap of paper with *Martine* – if you value your life keep away from the Long Barn! on it, you'll know that I've taken pity on them and concealed it in the pigsty!'

'Why the pigsty, dear?' asked Miss Marple with interest. 'Do they keep pigs?'

'Oh, no, not nowadays. It's just – I go there sometimes.'

For some reason Lucy blushed. Miss Marple looked at her with increased interest.

'Who's at the house now?' asked Craddock.

'Cedric's there, and Bryan's down for the week-end. Harold and Alfred are coming down tomorrow. They rang up this morning. I somehow got the impression that you had been putting the cat among the pigeons, Inspector Craddock.'

Craddock smiled.

'I shook them up a little. Asked them to account for their movements on Friday, 20th December.'

'And could they?'

'Harold could. Alfred couldn't – or wouldn't.'

'I think alibis must be terribly difficult,' said Lucy. 'Times and places and dates. They must be hard to check up on, too.'

'It takes time and patience – but we manage.' He glanced at his watch. 'I'll be coming to Rutherford Hall presently to have a word with Cedric, but I want to get hold of Dr Quimper first.'

'You'll be just about right. He has his surgery at six and he's usually finished about half past. I must get back and deal with dinner.'

'I'd like your opinion on one thing, Miss Eyelesbarrow. What's the family view about this Martine business – amongst themselves?'

Lucy replied promptly.

'They're all furious with Emma for going to you about it – and with Dr Quimper who, it seemed, encouraged her to do so. Harold and Alfred think it was a try on and not genuine. Emma isn't sure. Cedric thinks it was phoney, too, but he doesn't take it as seriously as the other two. Bryan, on the other hand, seems quite sure that it's genuine.'

'Why, I wonder?'

'Well, Bryan's rather like that. Just accepts things at their face value. He thinks it was Edmund's wife – or rather widow – and that she had suddenly to go back to France, but that they'll hear from her again sometime. The fact that she hasn't written, or anything,

650

up to now, seems to him to be quite natural because he never writes letters himself. Bryan's rather sweet. Just like a dog that wants to be taken for a walk.'

'And do you take him for a walk, dear?' asked Miss Marple. 'To the pigsties, perhaps?'

Lucy shot a keen glance at her.

'So many gentlemen in the house, coming and going,' mused Miss Marple.

When Miss Marple uttered the word 'gentlemen' she always gave it its full Victorian flavour – an echo from an era actually before her own time. You were conscious at once of dashing full-blooded (and probably whiskered) males, sometimes wicked, but always gallant.

'You're such a handsome girl,' pursued Miss Marple, appraising Lucy. 'I expect they pay you a good deal of attention, don't they?'

Lucy flushed slightly. Scrappy remembrances passed across her mind. Cedric, leaning against the pigsty wall. Bryan sitting disconsolately on the kitchen table. Alfred's fingers touching hers as he helped her collect the coffee cups.

'Gentlemen,' said Miss Marple, in the tone of one speaking of some alien and dangerous species, 'are all very much alike in some ways – even if they are quite *old* . . .'

'Darling,' cried Lucy. 'A hundred years ago you would certainly have been burned as a witch!'

And she told her story of old Mr Crackenthorpe's conditional proposal of marriage.

'In fact,' said Lucy, 'they've all made what you might call advances to me in a way. Harold's was very correct – an advantageous financial position in the City. I don't think it's my attractive appearance – they must think I know something.'

She laughed.

But Inspector Craddock did not laugh.

'Be careful,' he said. 'They might murder you instead of making advances to you.'

'I suppose it might be simpler,' Lucy agreed.

Then she gave a slight shiver.

'One forgets,' she said. 'The boys have been having such fun that one almost thought of it all as a game. But it's not a game.'

'No,' said Miss Marple. 'Murder isn't a game.'

She was silent for a moment or two before she said:

'Don't the boys go back to school soon?'

'Yes, next week. They go tomorrow to James Stoddart-West's home for the last few days of the holidays.'

'I'm glad of that,' said Miss Marple gravely. 'I shouldn't like anything to happen while they're there.'

'You mean to old Mr Crackenthorpe. Do you think *he's* going to be murdered next?'

'Oh, no,' said Miss Marple. '*He'll* be all right. I meant to the boys.'

'Well, to Alexander.'

'But surely —'

'Hunting about, you know — looking for clues. Boys love that sort of thing — but it might be very dangerous.'

Craddock looked at her thoughtfully.

'You're not prepared to believe, are you, Miss Marple, that it's a case of an unknown woman murdered by an unknown man? You tie it up definitely with Rutherford Hall?'

'I think there's a definite connection, yes.'

'All we know about the murderer is that he's a tall dark man. That's what your friend says and all she can say. There are three tall dark men at Rutherford Hall. On the day of the inquest, you know, I came out to see the three brothers standing waiting on the pavement for the car to draw up. They had their backs to me and it was astonishing how, in their heavy overcoats, they looked all alike. *Three tall dark men.* And yet, actually, they're all three quite different types.' He sighed. 'It makes it very difficult.'

'I wonder,' murmured Miss Marple. 'I have been wondering — whether it might perhaps be all much *simpler* than we suppose. Murders so often are quite simple — with an obvious rather sordid motive ...'

'Do you believe in the mysterious Martine, Miss Marple?'

'I'm quite ready to believe that Edmund Crackenthorpe either married, or meant to marry, a girl called Martine. Emma Crackenthorpe showed you his letter, I understand, and from what I've seen of her and from what Lucy tells me, I should say Emma Crackenthorpe is quite incapable of making up a thing of that kind — indeed, why should she?'

'So granted Martine,' said Craddock thoughtfully, 'there *is* a motive of a kind. Martine's reappearance with a son would diminish the Crackenthorpe inheritance – though hardly to a point, one would think, to activate murder. They're all very hard up –'

'Even Harold?' Lucy demanded incredulously.

'Even the prosperous-looking Harold Crackenthorpe is not the sober and conservative financier he appears to be. He's been plunging heavily and mixing himself up in some rather undesirable ventures. A large sum of money, soon, might avoid a crash.'

'But if so –' said Lucy, and stopped.

'Yes, Miss Eyelesbarrow –'

'I know, dear,' said Miss Marple. 'The wrong murder, that's what you mean.'

'Yes. Martine's death wouldn't do Harold – or any of the others – any good. Not until –'

'Not until Luther Crackenthorpe died. Exactly. That occurred to me. And Mr Crackenthorpe, senior, I gather from his doctor, is a much better life than any outsider would imagine.'

'He'll last for years,' said Lucy. Then she frowned.

'Yes?' Craddock spoke encouragingly.

'He was rather ill at Christmas-time,' said Lucy. 'He said the doctor made a lot of fuss about it – "Anyone would have thought I'd been poisoned by the fuss he made." That's what he said.'

She looked inquiringly at Craddock.

'Yes,' said Craddock. 'That's really what I want to ask Dr Quimper about.'

'Well, I must go,' said Lucy. 'Heavens, it's late.'

Miss Marple put down her knitting and picked up *The Times* with a half-done crossword puzzle.

'I wish I had a dictionary here,' she murmured. 'Tontine and Tokay – I always mix those two words up. One, I believe, is a Hungarian wine.'

'That's Tokay,' said Lucy, looking back from the door. 'But one's a five-letter word and one's a seven. What's the clue?'

'Oh, it wasn't in the crossword,' said Miss Marple vaguely. 'It was in my head.'

Inspector Craddock looked at her very hard. Then he said goodbye and went.

CHAPTER SEVENTEEN

Craddock had to wait a few minutes whilst Quimper finished his evening surgery, and then the doctor came to him. He looked tired and depressed.

He offered Craddock a drink and when the latter accepted he mixed one for himself as well.

'Poor devils,' he said as he sank down in a worn easy-chair. 'So scared and so stupid — no sense. Had a painful case this evening. Woman who ought to have come to me a year ago. If she'd come then, she might have been operated on successfully. Now it's too late. Makes me mad. The truth is people are an extraordinary mixture of heroism and cowardice. She's suffering agony, and borne it without a word, just because she was too scared to come and find out that what she feared might be true. At the other end of the scale are the people who come and waste my time because they've got a dangerous swelling causing them agony on their little finger which they think may be cancer and which turns out to be a common or garden chilblain! Well, don't mind me. I've blown off steam now. What did you want to see me about?'

'First, I've got you to thank, I believe, for advising Miss Crackenthorpe to come to me with the letter that purported to be from her brother's widow.'

'Oh, that? Anything in it? I didn't exactly advise her to come. She wanted to. She was worried. All the dear little brothers were trying to hold her back, of course.'

'Why should they?'

The doctor shrugged his shoulders.

'Afraid the lady might be proved genuine, I suppose.'

'Do you think the letter was genuine?'

'No idea. Never actually saw it. I should say it was someone who knew the facts, just trying to make a touch. Hoping to work on Emma's feelings. They were dead wrong, there. Emma's no fool. She wouldn't take an unknown sister-in-law to her bosom without asking a few practical questions first.'

He added with some curiosity:

'But why ask *my* views? I've got nothing to do with it?'

'I really came to ask you something quite different – but I don't quite know how to put it.'

Dr Quimper looked interested.

'I understand that not long ago – at Christmas-time, I think it was – Mr Crackenthorpe had rather a bad turn of illness.'

He saw a change at once in the doctor's face. It hardened.

'Yes.'

'I gather a gastric disturbance of some kind?'

'Yes.'

'This is difficult . . . Mr Crackenthorpe was boasting of his health, saying he intended to outlive most of his family. He referred to you – you'll excuse me, Doctor . . .'

'Oh, don't mind me. I'm not sensitive as to what my patients say about me!'

'He spoke of you as an old fuss-pot.' Quimper smiled. 'He said you had asked him all sorts of questions, not only as to what he had eaten, but as to who prepared it and served it.'

The doctor was not smiling now. His face was hard again.

'Go on.'

'He used some such phrase as – "Talked as though he believed someone had poisoned me."'

There was a pause.

'Had you – any suspicion of that kind?'

Quimper did not answer at once. He got up and walked up and down. Finally, he wheeled round on Craddock.

'What the devil do you expect me to say? Do you think a doctor can go about flinging accusations of poisoning here and there without any real evidence?'

'I'd just like to know, off the record, if – that idea – did enter your head?'

Dr Quimper said evasively:

'Old Crackenthorpe leads a fairly frugal life. When the family comes down, Emma steps up the food. Result – a nasty attack of gastro-enteritis. The symptoms were consistent with that diagnosis.'

Craddock persisted.

'I see. You were quite satisfied? You were not at all – shall we say – puzzled?'

'All right. All right. Yes, I was Yours Truly Puzzled! Does that please you?'

'It interests me,' said Craddock. 'What actually did you suspect – or fear?'

'Gastric cases vary, of course, but there were certain indications that would have been, shall we say, more consistent with arsenic poisoning than with plain gastro-enteritis. Mind you, the two things are very much alike. Better men than myself have failed to recognize arsenic poisoning – and have given a certificate in all good faith.'

'And what was the result of your inquiries?'

'It seemed that what I suspected could not possibly be true. Mr Crackenthorpe assured me that he had similar attacks before I attended him – and from the same cause, he said. They had always taken place when there was too much rich food about.'

'Which was when the house was full? With the family? Or guests?'

'Yes. That seemed reasonable enough. But frankly, Craddock, I wasn't happy. I went so far as to write to old Dr Morris. He was my senior partner and retired soon after I joined him. Crackenthorpe was his patient originally. I asked about these earlier attacks that the old man had had.'

'And what response did you get?'

Quimper grinned.

'I got a flea in the ear. I was more or less told not to be a damned fool. Well' – he shrugged his shoulders – 'presumably I *was* a damned fool.'

'I wonder,' Craddock was thoughtful.

Then he decided to speak frankly.

'Throwing discretion aside, Doctor, there are people who stand to benefit pretty considerably from Luther Crackenthorpe's death.' The doctor nodded. 'He's an old man – and a hale and hearty one. He may live to be ninety odd?'

'Easily. He spends his life taking care of himself, and his constitution is sound.'

'And his sons – and daughter – are all getting on, and they are all feeling the pinch?'

'You leave Emma out of it. She's no poisoner. These attacks only happen when the others are there – not when she and he are alone.'

'An elementary precaution – if she's the one,' the inspector thought, but was careful not to say aloud.

He paused, choosing his words carefully.

'Surely – I'm ignorant on these matters – but supposing just as a hypothesis that arsenic *was* administered – hasn't Crackenthorpe been very lucky not to succumb?'

'Now there,' said the doctor, 'you *have* got something odd. It is exactly that fact that leads me to believe that I have been, as old Morris puts it, a damned fool. You see, it's obviously not a case of small doses of arsenic administered regularly – which is what you might call the classic method of arsenic poisoning. Crackenthorpe has never had any chronic gastric trouble. In a way, that's what makes these sudden violent attacks seem unlikely. So, assuming they are not due to natural causes, it looks as though the poisoner is muffing it every time – which hardly makes sense.'

'Giving an inadequate dose, you mean?'

'Yes. On the other hand, Crackenthorpe's got a strong constitution and what might do in another man, doesn't do him in. There's always personal idiosyncrasy to be reckoned with. But you'd think that by now the poisoner – unless he's unusually timid – would have stepped up the dose. Why hasn't he?'

'That is,' he added, 'if there *is* a poisoner which there probably isn't! Probably all my ruddy imagination from start to finish.'

'It's an odd problem,' the inspector agreed. 'It doesn't seem to make sense.'

II

'Inspector Craddock!'

The eager whisper made the inspector jump.

He had been just on the point of ringing the front-door bell. Alexander and his friend Stoddart-West emerged cautiously from the shadows.

'We heard your car, and we wanted to get hold of you.'

'Well, let's come inside.' Craddock's hand went out to the door bell again, but Alexander pulled at his coat with the eagerness of a pawing dog.

'We've found a clue,' he breathed.

'Yes, we've found a clue,' Stoddart-West echoed.

'Damn that girl,' thought Craddock unamiably.

'Splendid,' he said in a perfunctory manner. 'Let's go inside the house and look at it.'

'No,' Alexander was insistent. 'Someone's sure to interrupt. Come to the harness room. We'll guide you.'

Somewhat unwillingly, Craddock allowed himself to be guided round the corner of the house and along to the stable yard. Stoddart-West pushed open a heavy door, stretched up, and turned on a rather feeble electric light. The harness room, once the acme of Victorian spit and polish, was now the sad repository of everything that no one wanted. Broken garden chairs, rusted old garden implements, a vast decrepit mowing-machine, rusted spring mattresses, hammocks, and disintegrated tennis nets.

'We come here a good deal,' said Alexander. 'One can really be private here.'

There were certain tokens of occupancy about. The decayed mattresses had been piled up to make a kind of divan, there was an old rusted table on which reposed a large tin of chocolate biscuits, there was a hoard of apples, a tin of toffees, and a jigsaw puzzle.

'It really *is* a clue, sir,' said Stoddart-West eagerly, his eyes gleaming behind his spectacles. 'We found it this afternoon.'

'We've been hunting for days. In the bushes —'

'And inside hollow trees —'

'And we went through the ash bins —'

'There were some jolly interesting things there, as a matter of fact —'

'And then we went into the boiler house —'

'Old Hillman keeps a great galvanized tub there full of waste paper —'

'For when the boiler goes out and he wants to start it again —'

'Any odd paper that's blowing about. He picks it up and shoves it in there —'

'And that's where we found it —'

'Found WHAT?' Craddock interrupted the duet.

'*The clue*. Careful, Stodders, get your gloves on.'

Importantly, Stoddart-West, in the best detective story tradition, drew on a pair of rather dirty gloves and took from his pocket a Kodak photographic folder. From this he extracted in his gloved fingers with the utmost care a soiled and crumpled envelope which he handed importantly to the inspector.

Both boys held their breath in excitement.

Craddock took it with due solemnity. He liked the boys and he was ready to enter into the spirit of the thing.

The letter had been through the post, there was no enclosure inside, it was just a torn envelope – addressed to Mrs Martine Crackenthorpe, 126 Elvers Crescent, N.10.

'You see?' said Alexander breathlessly. 'It shows she *was* here – Uncle Edmund's French wife, I mean – the one there's all the fuss about. She must have actually been here and dropped it somewhere. So it looks, doesn't it –'

Stoddart-West broke in:

'It looks as though *she* was the one who got murdered – I mean, don't you think, sir, that it simply *must* have been her in the sarcophagus?'

They waited anxiously.

Craddock played up.

'Possible, very possible,' he said.

'This *is* important, isn't it?'

'You'll test it for fingerprints, won't you, sir?'

'Of course,' said Craddock.

Stoddart-West gave a deep sigh.

'Smashing luck for us, wasn't it?' he said. 'On our last day, too.'

'Last day?'

'Yes,' said Alexander. 'I'm going to Stodders' place tomorrow for the last few days of the holidays. Stodders' people have got a smashing house – Queen Anne, isn't it?'

'William and Mary,' said Stoddart-West.

'I thought your mother said a –'

'Mum's French. She doesn't really know about English architecture.'

'But your father said it was built –'

Craddock was examining the envelope.

Clever of Lucy Eyelesbarrow. How had she managed to fake the post mark? He peered closely, but the light was too feeble. Great fun for the boys, of course, but rather awkward for him. Lucy, drat her, hadn't considered that angle. If this were genuine, it would enforce a course of action. There . . .

Beside him a learned architectural argument was being hotly pursued. He was deaf to it.

'Come on, boys,' he said, 'we'll go into the house. You've been very helpful.'

CHAPTER EIGHTEEN

Craddock was escorted by the boys through the back door into the house. This was, it seemed, their common mode of entrance. The kitchen was bright and cheerful. Lucy, in a large white apron, was rolling out pastry. Leaning against the dresser, watching her with a kind of dog-like attention, was Bryan Eastley. With one hand he tugged at his large fair moustache.

'Hallo, Dad,' said Alexander kindly. 'You out here again?'

'I like it out here,' said Bryan, and added: 'Miss Eyelesbarrow doesn't mind.'

'Oh, I don't mind,' said Lucy. 'Good evening, Inspector Craddock.'

'Coming to detect in the kitchen?' asked Bryan with interest.

'Not exactly. Mr Cedric Crackenthorpe is still here, isn't he?'

'Oh, yes, Cedric's here. Do you want him?'

'I'd like a word with him — yes, please.'

'I'll go and see if he's in,' said Bryan. 'He may have gone round to the local.'

He unpropped himself from the dresser.

'Thank you so much,' said Lucy to him. 'My hands are all over flour or I'd go.'

'What are you making?' asked Stoddart-West anxiously.

'Peach flan.'

'Good-oh,' said Stoddart-West.

'Is it nearly supper-time?' asked Alexander.

'No.'

'Gosh! I'm terribly hungry.'

'There's the end of the ginger cake in the larder.'

The boys made a concerted rush and collided in the door.

'They're just like locusts,' said Lucy.

'My congratulations to you,' said Craddock.

'What on – exactly?'

'Your ingenuity – over this!'

'Over what!'

Craddock indicated the folder containing the letter.

'Very nicely done,' he said.

'What *are* you talking about?'

'This, my dear girl – this.' He half-drew it out.

She stared at him uncomprehendingly.

Craddock felt suddenly dizzy.

'Didn't you fake this clue – and put it in the boiler room, for the boys to find? Quick – tell me.'

'I haven't the faintest idea what you're talking about,' said Lucy. 'Do you mean that –?'

Craddock slipped the folder quickly back in his pocket as Bryan returned.

'Cedric's in the library,' he said. 'Go on in.'

He resumed his place on the dresser. Inspector Craddock went to the library.

II

Cedric Crackenthorpe seemed delighted to see the inspector.

'Doing a spot more sleuthing down here?' he asked. 'Got any further?'

'I think I can say we are a little further on, Mr Crackenthorpe.'

'Found out who the corpse was?'

'We've not got a definite identification, but we have a fairly shrewd idea.'

'Good for you.'

'Arising out of our latest information, we want to get a few statements. I'm starting with you, Mr Crackenthorpe, as you're on the spot.'

'I shan't be much longer. I'm going back to Ibiza in a day or two.'

'Then I seem to be just in time.'

'Go ahead.'

'I should like a detailed account, please, of exactly where you were and what you were doing on Friday, 20th December.'

Cedric shot a quick glance at him. Then he leaned back, yawned, assumed an air of great nonchalance, and appeared to be lost in the effort of remembrance.

'Well, as I've already told you, I was in Ibiza. Trouble is, one day there is so like another. Painting in the morning, siesta from three p.m. to five. Perhaps a spot of sketching if the light's suitable. Then an apéritif, sometimes with the mayor, sometimes with the doctor, at the café in the Piazza. After that some kind of a scratch meal. Most of the evening in Scotty's Bar with some of my lower-class friends. Will that do you?'

'I'd rather have the truth, Mr Crackenthorpe.'

Cedric sat up.

'That's a most offensive remark, Inspector.'

'Do you think so? You told me, Mr Crackenthorpe, that you left Ibiza on 21st December and arrived in England that same day?'

'So I did. Em! Hi, Em?'

Emma Crackenthorpe came through the adjoining door from the small morning-room. She looked inquiringly from Cedric to the inspector.

'Look here, Em. I arrived here for Christmas on the Saturday before, didn't I? Came straight from the airport?'

'Yes,' said Emma wonderingly. 'You got here about lunch time.'

'There you are,' said Cedric to the inspector.

'You must think us very foolish, Mr Crackenthorpe,' said Craddock pleasantly. 'We can check on these things, you know. I think, if you'll show me your passport –'

He paused expectantly.

'Can't find the damned thing,' said Cedric. 'Was looking for it this morning. Wanted to send it to Cook's.'

'I think you could find it, Mr Crackenthorpe. But it's not really necessary. The records show that you actually entered this country on the evening of 19th December. Perhaps you will now account to me for your movements between that time until lunch-time on 21st December when you arrived here.'

Cedric looked very cross indeed.

'That's the hell of life nowadays,' he said angrily. 'All this red tape and form-filling. That's what comes of a bureaucratic state. Can't go where you like and do as you please any more! Somebody's always asking questions. What's all this fuss about the 20th, anyway? What's special about the 20th?'

'It happens to be the day we believe the murder was committed. You can refuse to answer, of course, but –'

'Who says I refuse to answer? Give a chap time. And you were vague enough about the date of the murder at the inquest. What's turned up new since then?'

Craddock did not reply.

Cedric said, with a sidelong glance at Emma:

'Shall we go into the other room?'

Emma said quickly: 'I'll leave you.' At the door, she paused and turned.

'This is serious, you know, Cedric. If the 20th *was* the day of murder, then you must tell Inspector Craddock exactly what you were doing.'

She went through into the next room and closed the door behind her.

'Good old Em,' said Cedric. 'Well, here goes. Yes, I left Ibiza on the 19th all right. Planned to break the journey in Paris, and spend a couple of days routing up some old friends on the Left Bank. But, as a matter of fact, there was a very attractive woman on the plane ... Quite a dish. To put it plainly, she and I got off together. She was on her way to the States, had to spend a couple of nights in London to see about some business or other. We got to London on the 19th. We stayed at the Kingsway Palace in case your spies haven't found that out yet! Called myself John Brown – never does to use your own name on these occasions.'

'And on the 20th?'

Cedric made a grimace.

'Morning pretty well occupied by a terrific hangover.'

'And the afternoon. From three o'clock onwards?'

'Let me see. Well, I mooned about, as you might say. Went into the National Gallery – that's respectable enough. Saw a film. *Rowenna of the Range*. I've always had a passion for Westerns. This was a corker ... Then a drink or two in the bar and a bit of a sleep in my room, and out about ten o'clock with the girl-friend and a round of various hot spots – can't even remember most of their names – Jumping Frog was one, I think. She knew 'em all. Got pretty well plastered and to tell the truth, don't remember much more till I woke up the next morning – with an even worse hangover. Girl-friend hopped off to catch her plane and I poured cold water over my head, got a chemist to give me a devils' brew, and then started off for this place, pretending I'd just arrived at Heathrow. No need to upset Emma, I thought. You know what women are – always hurt if you don't come straight home. I had to borrow money from her to pay the taxi. I was completely cleaned out. No use asking the old man. He'd never cough up. Mean old brute. Well, Inspector, satisfied?'

'Can any of this be substantiated, Mr Crackenthorpe? Say between 3 p.m. and 7 p.m.'

'Most unlikely, I should think,' said Cedric cheerfully. 'National Gallery where the attendants look at you with lack-lustre eyes and a crowded picture show. No, not likely.'

Emma re-entered. She held a small engagement book in her hand.

'You want to know what everyone was doing on 20th December, is that right, Inspector Craddock?'

'Well – er – yes, Miss Crackenthorpe.'

'I have just been looking in my engagement book. On the 20th I went into Brackhampton to attend a meeting of the Church Restoration Fund. That finished about a quarter to one and I lunched with Lady Adington and Miss Bartlett who were also on the committee, at the Cadena Café. After lunch I did some shopping, stores for Christmas, and also Christmas presents. I went to Greenford's and Lyall and Swift's, Boots', and probably several other shops. I had tea about a quarter to five in the Shamrock Tea Rooms and then went to the station to meet Bryan who was coming by train. I got home about six o'clock and found my father in a very bad temper. I had left lunch ready for him, but Mrs Hart who was to come in in the afternoon and give him his tea had not arrived. He was so angry that he had shut himself in his room and would not let me in or speak to me. He does not like my going out in the afternoon, but I make a point of doing so now and then.'

'You're probably wise. Thank you, Miss Crackenthorpe.'

He could hardly tell her that as she was a woman, height five foot seven, her movements that afternoon were of no great importance. Instead he said:

'Your other two brothers came down later, I understand?'

'Alfred came down late on Saturday evening. He tells me he tried to ring me on the telephone that afternoon I was out – but my father, if he is upset, will never answer the telephone. My brother Harold did not come down until Christmas Eve.'

'Thank you, Miss Crackenthorpe.'

'I suppose I mustn't ask' – she hesitated – 'what has come up new that prompts these inquiries?'

Craddock took the folder from his pocket. Using the tips of his fingers, he extracted the envelope.

'Don't touch it, please, but do you recognize this?'

'But . . .' Emma stared at him, bewildered. 'That's my handwriting. That's the letter I wrote to Martine.'

'I thought it might be.'

'But how did you get it? Did she –? Have you found her?'

'It would seem possible that we have – found her. This empty envelope was found *here*.'

'In the house?'

'In the grounds.'

'Then – she *did* come here! She . . . You mean – it was Martine there – in the sarcophagus?'

'It would seem very likely, Miss Crackenthorpe,' said Craddock gently.

It seemed even more likely when he got back to town. A message was awaiting him from Armand Dessin.

'One of the girl-friends has had a postcard from Anna Stravinska. Apparently the cruise story was true! She has reached Jamaica and is having, in your phrase, a wonderful time!'

Craddock crumpled up the message and threw it into the wastepaper basket.

III

'I must say,' said Alexander, sitting up in bed, thoughtfully consuming a chocolate bar, 'that this has been the most smashing day ever. Actually finding a real *clue*!'

His voice was awed.

'In fact the whole holidays have been smashing,' he added happily. 'I don't suppose such a thing will ever happen again.'

'I hope it won't happen again to me,' said Lucy who was on her knees packing Alexander's clothes into a suitcase. 'Do you want *all* this space fiction with you?'

'Not those two top ones. I've read them. The football and my football boots, and the gum-boots can go separately.'

'What difficult things you boys do travel with.'

'It won't matter. They're sending the Rolls for us. They've got a smashing Rolls. They've got one of the new Mercedes-Benzes too.'

'They must be rich.'

'Rolling! Jolly nice, too. All the same, I rather wish we weren't leaving here. Another body might turn up.'

'I sincerely hope not.'

'Well, it often does in books. I mean somebody who's seen something or heard something gets done in, too. It might be you,' he added, unrolling a second chocolate bar.

'Thank you!'

'I don't want it to be you,' Alexander assured her. 'I like you very much and so does Stodders. We think you're out of this world as a cook. Absolutely lovely grub. You're very sensible, too.'

This last was clearly an expression of high approval. Lucy took it as such, and said: 'Thank you. But I don't intend to get killed just to please you.'

'Well, you'd better be careful, then,' Alexander told her.

He paused to consume more nourishment and then said in a slightly offhand voice:

'If Dad turns up from time to time, you'll look after him, won't you?'

'Yes, of course,' said Lucy, a little surprised.

'The trouble with Dad is,' Alexander informed her, 'that London life doesn't suit him. He gets in, you know, with quite the wrong type of women.' He shook his head in a worried manner.

'I'm very fond of him,' he added; 'but he needs someone to look after him. He drifts about and gets in with the wrong people. It's a great pity Mum died when she did. Bryan needs a proper home life.'

He looked solemnly at Lucy and reached out for another chocolate bar.

'Not a fourth one, Alexander,' Lucy pleaded. 'You'll be sick.'

'Oh, I don't think so. I ate six running once and I wasn't. I'm not the bilious type.' He paused and then said:

'Bryan likes you, you know.'

'That's very nice of him.'

'He's a bit of an ass in some ways,' said Bryan's son; 'but he was a jolly good fighter pilot. He's awfully brave. And he's awfully good-natured.'

He paused. Then, averting his eyes to the ceiling, he said rather self-consciously:

'I think, really, you know, it would be a good thing if he married again ... Somebody decent ... I shouldn't, myself, mind at all having a stepmother ... not, I mean, if she was a decent sort ...'

With a sense of shock Lucy realized that there was a definite point in Alexander's conversation.

'All this stepmother bosh,' went on Alexander, still addressing the ceiling, 'is really quite out of date. Lots of chaps Stodders and I know have stepmothers – divorce and all that – and they get on quite well together. Depends on the stepmother, of course. And of course, it does make a bit of confusion taking you out and on Sports Day, and all that. I mean if there are two sets of parents. Though again it helps if you want to cash in!' He paused, confronted with the problems of modern life. 'It's nicest to have your own home and your own parents – but if your mother's dead – well, you see what I mean? If she's a decent sort,' said Alexander for the third time.

Lucy felt touched.

'I think *you're* very sensible, Alexander,' she said. 'We must try and find a nice wife for your father.'

'Yes,' said Alexander noncommittally.

He added in an offhand manner:

'I thought I'd just mention it. Bryan likes you very much. He told me so ...'

'Really,' thought Lucy to herself. 'There's too much match-making round here. First Miss Marple and now Alexander!'

For some reason or other, pigsties came into her mind.

She stood up.

'Good night, Alexander. There will be only your washing things and pyjamas to put in in the morning. Good night.'

'Good night,' said Alexander. He slid down in bed, laid his head

667

on the pillow, closed his eyes, giving a perfect picture of a sleeping angel; and was immediately asleep.

CHAPTER NINETEEN

'Not what you'd call conclusive,' said Sergeant Wetherall with his usual gloom.

Craddock was reading through the report on Harold Crackenthorpe's alibi for 20th December.

He had been noticed at Sotheby's about three-thirty, but was thought to have left shortly after that. His photograph had not been recognized at Russell's teashop, but as they did a busy trade there at teatime, and he was not an *habitué*, that was hardly surprising. His manservant confirmed that he had returned to Cardigan Gardens to dress for his dinner-party at a quarter to seven – rather late, since the dinner was at seven-thirty, and Mr Crackenthorpe had been somewhat irritable in consequence. Did not remember hearing him come in that evening, but, as it was some time ago, could not remember accurately and, in any case, he frequently did not hear Mr Crackenthorpe come in. He and his wife liked to retire early whenever they could. The garage in the mews where Harold kept his car was a private lock-up that he rented and there was no-one to notice who came and went or any reason to remember one evening in particular.

'All negative,' said Craddock, with a sigh.

'He was at the Caterers' Dinner all right, but left rather early before the end of the speeches.'

'What about the railway stations?'

But there was nothing there, either at Brackhampton or at Paddington. It was nearly four weeks ago, and it was highly unlikely that anything would have been remembered.

Craddock sighed, and stretched out his hand for the data on Cedric. That again was negative, though a taxi-driver had made a doubtful recognition of having taken a fare to Paddington that day some time in the afternoon 'what looked something like that bloke. Dirty trousers and a shock of hair. Cussed and swore a bit because fares

668

had gone up since he was last in England.' He identified the day because a horse called Crawler had won the two-thirty and he'd had a tidy bit on. Just after dropping the gent, he'd heard it on the radio in his cab and had gone home forthwith to celebrate.

'Thank God for racing!' said Craddock, and put the report aside.

'And here's Alfred,' said Sergeant Wetherall.

Some nuance in his voice made Craddock look up sharply. Wetherall had the pleased appearance of a man who has kept a titbit until the end.

In the main the check was unsatisfactory. Alfred lived alone in his flat and came and went at unspecified times. His neighbours were not the inquisitive kind and were in any case office workers who were out all day. But towards the end of the report, Wetherall's large finger indicated the final paragraph.

Sergeant Leakie, assigned to a case of thefts from lorries, had been at the Load of Bricks, a lorry pull-up on the Waddington-Brackhampton Road, keeping certain lorry drivers under observation. He had noticed at an adjoining table, Chick Evans, one of the Dicky Rogers mob. With him had been Alfred Crackenthorpe whom he knew by sight, having seen him give evidence in the Dicky Rogers case. He'd wondered what they were cooking up together. Time, 9.30 pm, Friday, 20th December. Alfred Crackenthorpe had boarded a bus a few minutes later, going in the direction of Brackhampton. William Baker, ticket collector at Brackhampton station, had clipped ticket of gentleman whom he recognized by sight as one of Miss Crackenthorpe's brothers, just before departure of eleven-fifty-five train for Paddington. Remembers day as there had been story of some batty old lady who swore she had seen somebody murdered in a train that afternoon.

'Alfred?' said Craddock as he laid the report down. 'Alfred? I wonder.'

'Puts him right on the spot, there,' Wetherall pointed out.

Craddock nodded. Yes, Alfred could have travelled down by the 4.33 to Brackhampton committing murder on the way. Then he could have gone out by bus to the Load of Bricks. He could have left there at nine-thirty and would have had plenty of time to go to Rutherford Hall, move the body from the embankment to the sarcophagus, and get into Brackhampton in time to catch the 11.55 back to London. One of the Dicky Rogers gang might even have helped move the body, though Craddock doubted this. An unpleasant lot, but not killers.

'Alfred?' he repeated speculatively.

II

At Rutherford Hall there had been a gathering of the Crackenthorpe family. Harold and Alfred had come down from London and very soon voices were raised and tempers were running high.

On her own initiative, Lucy mixed cocktails in a jug with ice and then took them towards the library. The voices sounded clearly in the hall, and indicated that a good deal of acrimony was being directed towards Emma.

'Entirely *your* fault, Emma,' Harold's bass voice rang out angrily. 'How you could be so short-sighted and foolish beats me. If you hadn't taken that letter to Scotland Yard – and started all this –'

Alfred's high-pitched voice said: 'You must have been out of your senses!'

'Now don't bully her,' said Cedric. 'What's done is done. Much more fishy if they'd identified the woman as the missing Martine and we'd all kept mum about having heard from her.'

'It's all very well for you, Cedric,' said Harold angrily. 'You were out of the country on the 20th which seems to be the day they are inquiring about. But it's very embarrassing for Alfred and myself. Fortunately, I can remember where I was that afternoon and what I was doing.'

'I bet you can,' said Alfred. 'If you'd arranged a murder, Harold, you'd arrange your alibi very carefully, I'm sure.'

'I gather you are not so fortunate,' said Harold coldly.

'That depends,' said Alfred. 'Anything's better than presenting a cast-iron alibi to the police if it isn't really cast-iron. They're so clever at breaking these things down.'

'If you are insinuating that I killed the woman –'

'Oh, do stop, all of you,' cried Emma. 'Of course none of you killed the woman.'

'And just for your information, I *wasn't* out of England on the 20th,' said Cedric. '*And* the police are wise to it! So we're all under suspicion.'

'If it hadn't been for Emma —'

'Oh, don't begin again, Harold,' cried Emma.

Dr Quimper came out of the study where he had been closeted with old Mr Crackenthorpe. His eye fell on the jug in Lucy's hand.

'What's this? A celebration?'

'More in the nature of oil on troubled waters. They're at it hammer and tongs in there.'

'Recriminations?'

'Mostly abusing Emma.'

Dr Quimper's eyebrows rose.

'Indeed?' He took the jug from Lucy's hand, opened the library door and went in.

'Good evening.'

'Ah, Dr Quimper, I should like a word with you.' It was Harold's voice, raised and irritable. 'I should like to know what you meant by interfering in a private and family matter, and telling my sister to go to Scotland Yard about it.'

Dr Quimper said calmly:

'Miss Crackenthorpe asked my advice. I gave it to her. In my opinion she did perfectly right.'

'You dare to say —'

'Girl!'

It was old Mr Crackenthorpe's familiar salutation. He was peering out of the study door just behind Lucy.

Lucy turned rather reluctantly.

'Yes, Mr Crackenthorpe?'

'What are you giving us for dinner to-night? I want curry. You make a very good curry. It's ages since we've had curry.'

'The boys don't care much for curry, you see.'

'The boys — the boys. What do the boys matter? I'm the one who matters. And, anyway, the boys have gone — good riddance. I want a nice hot curry, do you hear?'

'All right, Mr Crackenthorpe, you shall have it.'

'That's right. You're a good girl, Lucy. You look after me and I'll look after you.'

Lucy went back to the kitchen. Abandoning the fricassée of chicken which she had planned, she began to assemble the preparations for curry. The front door banged and from the window she saw Dr Quimper stride angrily from the house to his car and drive away.

Lucy sighed. She missed the boys. And in a way she missed Bryan, too.

Oh, well. She sat down and began to peel mushrooms.

At any rate she'd give the family a rattling good dinner.

Feed the brutes!

III

It was 3 a.m. when Dr Quimper drove his car into the garage, closed the doors and came in pulling the front door behind him rather wearily. Well, Mrs Josh Simpkins had a fine healthy pair of twins to add to her present family of eight. Mr Simpkins had expressed no elation over the arrival. 'Twins,' he had said gloomily. 'What's the good of they? Quads now, they're good for something. All sorts of things you get sent, and the Press comes round and there's pictures in the paper, and they do say as Her Majesty sends you a telegram. But what's twins except two mouths to feed instead of one? Never been twins in our family, nor in the missus's either. Don't seem fair, somehow.'

Dr Quimper walked upstairs to his bedroom and started throwing off his clothes. He glanced at his watch. Five minutes past three. It had proved an unexpectedly tricky business bringing those twins into the world, but all had gone well. He yawned. He was tired — very tired. He looked appreciatively at his bed.

Then the telephone rang.

Dr Quimper swore, and picked up the receiver.

'Dr Quimper?'

'Speaking.'

'This is Lucy Eyelesbarrow from Rutherford Hall. I think you'd better come over. Everybody seems to have taken ill.'

'Taken ill? How? What symptoms?'

Lucy detailed them.

'I'll be over straight away. In the meantime . . .' He gave her short sharp instructions.

Then he quickly resumed his clothes, flung a few extra things into his emergency bag, and hurried down to his car.

It was some three hours later when the doctor and Lucy, both of them somewhat exhausted, sat down by the kitchen table to drink large cups of black coffee.

'Ha,' Dr Quimper drained his cup, set it down with a clatter on the saucer. 'I needed that. Now, Miss Eyelesbarrow, let's get down to brass tacks.'

Lucy looked at him. The lines of fatigue showed clearly on his face making him look older than his forty-four years, the dark hair on his temples was flecked with grey, and there were lines under his eyes.

'As far as I can judge,' said the doctor, 'they'll be all right now. But how come? That's what I want to know. Who cooked the dinner?'

'I did,' said Lucy.

'And what was it? In detail.'

'Mushroom soup. Curried chicken and rice. Syllabubs. A savoury of chicken livers and bacon.'

'*Canapés Diane*,' said Dr Quimper unexpectedly.

Lucy smiled faintly.

'Yes, *Canapés Diane*.'

'All right – let's go through it. Mushroom soup – out of a tin, I suppose?'

'Certainly not. I made it.'

'You made it. Out of what?'

'Half a pound of mushrooms, chicken stock, milk, a roux of butter and flour, and lemon juice.'

'Ah. And one's supposed to say "It must have been the mushrooms."'

'It wasn't the mushrooms. I had some of the soup myself and I'm quite all right.'

'Yes, *you're* quite all right. I hadn't forgotten that.'

Lucy flushed.

'If you mean –'

'I don't mean. You're a highly intelligent girl. You'd be groaning upstairs, too, if I'd meant what you thought I meant. Anyway, I know all about you. I've taken the trouble to find out.'

'Why on earth did you do that?'

Dr Quimper's lips were set in a grim line.

'Because I'm making it my business to find out about the people who come here and settle themselves in. You're a *bona fide* young woman who does this particular job for a livelihood *and* you seem never to have had any contact with the Crackenthorpe family previous to coming here. So you're not a girl-friend of either Cedric, Harold or Alfred — helping them to do a bit of dirty work.'

'Do you really think —?'

'I think quite a lot of things,' said Quimper. 'But I have to be careful. That's the worst of being a doctor. Now let's get on. Curried chicken. Did you have some of that?'

'No. When you've cooked a curry, you've dined off the smell, I find. I tasted it, of course. I had soup and some syllabub.'

'How did you serve the syllabub?'

'In individual glasses.'

'Now, then, how much of all this is cleared up?'

'If you mean washing up, everything was washed up and put away.'

Dr Quimper groaned.

'There's such a thing as being over-zealous,' he said.

'Yes, I can see that, as things have turned out, but there it is, I'm afraid.'

'What *do* you have still?'

'There's some of the curry left — in a bowl in the larder. I was planning to use it as a basis for mulligatawny soup this evening. There's some mushroom soup left, too. No syllabub and none of the savoury.'

'I'll take the curry and the soup. What about chutney? Did they have chutney with it?'

'Yes. In one of those stone jars.'

'I'll have some of that, too.'

He rose. 'I'll go up and have a look at them again. After that, can you hold the fort until morning? Keep an eye on them all? I can have a nurse round, with full instructions, by eight o'clock.'

'I wish you'd tell me straight out. Do you think it's food poisoning — or — or — well, poisoning.'

'I've told you already. Doctors can't think — they have to be sure. If there's a positive result from these food specimens I can go ahead. Otherwise —'

'Otherwise?' Lucy repeated.

Dr Quimper laid a hand on her shoulder.

'Look after two people in particular,' he said. 'Look after Emma. I'm not going to have anything happen to Emma . . .'

There was emotion in his voice that could not be disguised. 'She's not even begun to live yet,' he said. 'And you know, people like Emma Crackenthorpe are the salt of the earth . . . Emma – well, Emma means a lot to me. I've never told her so, but I shall. Look after Emma.'

'You bet I will,' said Lucy.

'And look after the old man. I can't say that he's ever been my favourite patient, but he *is my* patient, and I'm damned if I'm going to let him be hustled out of the world because one or other of his unpleasant sons – or all three of them, maybe – want him out of the way so that they can handle his money.'

He threw her a sudden quizzical glance.

'There,' he said. 'I've opened my mouth too wide. But keep your eyes skinned, there's a good girl, and incidentally keep your mouth shut.'

V

Inspector Bacon was looking upset.

'Arsenic?' he said. 'Arsenic?'

'Yes. It was in the curry. Here's the rest of the curry – for your fellow to have a go at. I've only done a very rough test on a little of it, but the result was quite definite.'

'So there's a poisoner at work?'

'It would seem so,' said Dr Quimper dryly.

'And they're all affected, you say – except that Miss Eyelesbarrow.'

'Except Miss Eyelesbarrow.'

'Looks a bit fishy for her . . .'

'What motive could she possibly have?'

'Might be barmy,' suggested Bacon. 'Seem all right, they do, sometimes, and yet all the time they're right off their rocker, so to speak.'

'Miss Eyelesbarrow isn't off her rocker. Speaking as a medical man. Miss Eyelesbarrow is as sane as you or I are. If Miss Eyelesbarrow is feeding the family arsenic in their curry, she's doing it for a reason. Moreover, being a highly intelligent young woman, she'd be careful *not* to be the only one unaffected. What she'd do, what any intelligent poisoner would do, would be to eat a very little of the poisoned curry, and then exaggerate the symptoms.'

'And then you wouldn't be able to tell?'

'That she'd had less than the others? Probably not. People don't all react alike to poisons anyway – the same amount will upset some people more than others. Of course,' added Dr Quimper cheerfully, 'once the patient's dead, you can estimate fairly closely how much was taken.'

'Then it might be . . .' Inspector Bacon paused to consolidate his idea. 'It might be that there's one of the family now who's making more fuss than he need – someone who you might say is mucking in with the rest so as to avoid causing suspicion? How's that?'

'The idea has already occurred to me. That's why I'm reporting to you. It's in your hands now. I've got a nurse on the job that I can trust, but she can't be everywhere at once. In my opinion, nobody's had enough to cause death.'

'Made a mistake, the poisoner did?'

'No. It seems to me more likely that the idea was to put enough in the curry to cause signs of food poisoning – for which probably the mushrooms would be blamed. People are always obsessed with the idea of mushroom poisoning. Then one person would probably take a turn for the worse and die.'

'Because he'd been given a second dose?'

The doctor nodded.

'That's why I'm reporting to you at once, and why I've put a special nurse on the job.'

'She knows about the arsenic?'

'Of course. She knows and so does Miss Eyelesbarrow. You know your own job best, of course, but if I were you, I'd get out there and make it quite clear to them all that they're suffering from arsenic poisoning. That will probably put the fear of the Lord into our murderer and he won't dare to carry out his plan. He's probably been banking on the food-poisoning theory.'

The telephone rang on the inspector's desk. He picked it up and said:

'OK. Put her through.' He said to Quimper, 'It's your nurse on the phone. Yes, hallo – speaking . . . What's that? Serious relapse . . . Yes . . . Dr Quimper's with me now . . . If you'd like a word with him . . .'

He handed the receiver to the doctor.

'Quimper speaking . . . I see . . . Yes . . . Quite right . . . Yes, carry on with that. We'll be along.'

He put the receiver down and turned to Bacon.

'Who is it?'

'It's Alfred,' said Dr Quimper. 'And he's dead.'

CHAPTER TWENTY

Over the telephone, Craddock's voice came in sharp disbelief.

'Alfred?' he said. '*Alfred?*'

Inspector Bacon, shifting the telephone receiver a little, said: 'You didn't expect that?'

'No, indeed. As a matter of fact, I'd just got him taped for the murderer!'

'I heard about him being spotted by the ticket collector. Looked bad for him all right. Yes, looked as though we'd got our man.'

'Well,' said Craddock flatly, 'we were wrong.'

There was a moment's silence. Then Craddock asked:

'There was a nurse in charge. How did she come to slip up?'

'Can't blame her. Miss Eyelesbarrow was all in and went to get a bit of sleep. The nurse had five patients on her hands, the old man, Emma, Cedric, Harold and Alfred. She couldn't be everywhere at once. It seems old Mr Crackenthorpe started creating in a big way. Said he was dying. She went in, got him soothed down, came back again and took Alfred in some tea with glucose. He drank it and that was that.'

'Arsenic again?'

'Seems so. Of course it could have been a relapse, but Quimper doesn't think so and Johnstone agrees.'

'I suppose,' said Craddock, doubtfully, 'that Alfred was *meant* to be the victim?'

Bacon sounded interested. 'You mean that whereas Alfred's death wouldn't do anyone a penn'orth of good, the old man's death would benefit the lot of them? I suppose it *might* have been a mistake – somebody *might* have thought the tea was intended for the old man.'

'Are they sure that that's the way the stuff was administered?'

'No, of course they aren't sure. The nurse, like a good nurse, washed up the whole contraption. Cups, spoons, teapot – everything. But it seems the only feasible method.'

'Meaning,' said Craddock thoughtfully, 'that one of the patients wasn't as ill as the others? Saw his chance and doped the cup?'

'Well, there won't be any more funny business,' said Inspector Bacon grimly. 'We've got two nurses on the job now, to say nothing of Miss Eyelesbarrow, and I've got a couple of men there too. You coming down?'

'As fast as I can make it!'

II

Lucy Eyelesbarrow came across the hall to meet Inspector Craddock. She looked pale and drawn.

'You've been having a bad time of it,' said Craddock.

'It's been like one long ghastly nightmare,' said Lucy. 'I really thought last night that they were *all* dying.'

'About this curry –'

'It was the curry?'

'Yes, very nicely laced with arsenic – quite the Borgia touch.'

'If that's true,' said Lucy. 'It must – it's got to be – one of the family.'

'No other possibility?'

'No, you see I only started making that damned curry quite late – after six o'clock – because Mr Crackenthorpe specially asked for curry. And I had to open a new tin of curry powder – so *that* couldn't have been tampered with. I suppose curry would disguise the taste?'

'Arsenic hasn't any taste,' said Craddock absently. 'Now, opportunity. Which of them had the chance to tamper with the curry while it was cooking?'

Lucy considered.

'Actually,' she said, 'anyone could have sneaked into the kitchen whilst I was laying the table in the dining-room.'

'I see. Now, who was here in the house? Old Mr Crackenthorpe, Emma, Cedric —'

'Harold and Alfred. They'd come down from London in the afternoon. Oh, and Bryan — Bryan Eastley. But he left just before dinner. He had to meet a man in Brackhampton.'

Craddock said thoughtfully, 'It ties up with the old man's illness at Christmas. Quimper suspected that that was arsenic. Did they all seem equally ill last night?'

Lucy considered. 'I think old Mr Crackenthorpe seemed the worst. Dr Quimper had to work like a maniac on him. He's a jolly good doctor, I will say. Cedric made by far the most fuss. Of course, strong healthy people always do.'

'What about Emma?'

'She has been pretty bad.'

'Why Alfred, I wonder?' said Craddock.

'I know,' said Lucy. 'I suppose it was *meant* to be Alfred?'

'Funny — I asked that too!'

'It seems, somehow, so pointless.'

'If I could only get at the motive for all this business,' said Craddock. 'It doesn't seem to tie up. The strangled woman in the sarcophagus was Edmund Crackenthorpe's widow, Martine. Let's assume that. It's pretty well proved by now. There *must* be a connection between that and the deliberate poisoning of Alfred. It's all here, in the family somewhere. Even saying one of them's mad doesn't help.'

'Not really,' Lucy agreed.

'Well, look after yourself,' said Craddock warningly. 'There's a poisoner in this house, remember, and one of your patients upstairs probably isn't as ill as he pretends to be.'

Lucy went upstairs again slowly after Craddock's departure. An imperious voice, somewhat weakened by illness, called to her as she passed old Mr Crackenthorpe's room.

'Girl — girl — is that you? Come here.'

Lucy entered the room. Mr Crackenthorpe was lying in bed well propped up with pillows. For a sick man he was looking Lucy thought, remarkably cheerful.

'The house is full of damned hospital nurses,' complained Mr Crackenthorpe. 'Rustling about, making themselves important, taking my temperature, not giving me what I want to eat – a pretty penny all that must be costing. Tell Emma to send 'em away. You could look after me quite well.'

'Everybody's been taken ill, Mr Crackenthorpe,' said Lucy. 'I can't look after everybody, you know.'

'Mushrooms,' said Mr Crackenthorpe. 'Damned dangerous things, mushrooms. It was that soup we had last night. You made it,' he added accusingly.

'The mushrooms were quite all right, Mr Crackenthorpe.'

'I'm not blaming you, girl, I'm not blaming you. It's happened before. One blasted fungus slips in and does it. Nobody can tell. I know you're a good girl. You wouldn't do it on purpose. How's Emma?'

'Feeling rather better this afternoon.'

'Ah, and Harold?'

'He's better too.'

'What's this about Alfred having kicked the bucket?'

'Nobody's supposed to have told you that, Mr Crackenthorpe.'

Mr Crackenthorpe laughed, a high, whinnying laugh of intense amusement. 'I hear things,' he said. 'Can't keep things from the old man. They try to. So Alfred's dead, is he? *He* won't sponge on me any more, and he won't get any of the money either. They've all been waiting for *me* to die, you know – Alfred in particular. Now *he's* dead. I call that rather a good joke.'

'That's not very kind of you, Mr Crackenthorpe,' said Lucy severely.

Mr Crackenthorpe laughed again. 'I'll outlive them all,' he crowed. 'You see if I don't, my girl. You see if I don't.'

Lucy went to her room, she took out her dictionary and looked up the word 'tontine.' She closed the book thoughtfully and stared ahead of her.

III

'Don't see why you want to come to me,' said Dr Morris, irritably.

'You've known the Crackenthorpe family a long time,' said Inspector Craddock.

'Yes, yes, I knew all the Crackenthorpes. I remember old Josiah

680

Crackenthorpe. He was a hard nut – shrewd man, though. Made a lot of money,' he shifted his aged form in his chair and peered under bushy eyebrows at Inspector Craddock. 'So you've been listening to that young fool, Quimper,' he said. 'These zealous young doctors! Always getting ideas in their heads. Got it into *his* head that somebody was trying to poison Luther Crackenthorpe. Nonsense! Melodrama! Of course, he had gastric attacks. I treated him for them. Didn't happen very often – nothing peculiar about them.'

'Dr Quimper,' said Craddock, 'seemed to think there was.'

'Doesn't do for a doctor to go thinking. After all, I should hope I could recognize arsenical poisoning when I saw it.'

'Quite a lot of well-known doctors haven't noticed it,' Craddock pointed out. 'There was' – he drew upon his memory – 'the Greenbarrow case, Mrs Teney, Charles Leeds, three people in the Westbury family, all buried nicely and tidily without the doctors who attended them having the least suspicion. Those doctors were all good, reputable men.'

'All right, all right,' said Doctor Morris, 'you're saying that I could have made a mistake. Well, *I* don't think I did.' He paused a minute and then said, 'Who did Quimper think was doing it – if it was being done?'

'He didn't know,' said Craddock. 'He was worried. After all, you know,' he added, 'there's a great deal of money there.'

'Yes, yes, I know, which they'll get when Luther Crackenthorpe dies. And they want it pretty badly. That is true enough, but it doesn't follow that they'd kill the old man to get it.'

'Not necessarily,' agreed Inspector Craddock.

'Anyway,' said Dr Morris, 'my principle is not to go about suspecting things without due cause. Due cause,' he repeated. 'I'll admit that what you've just told me has shaken me up a bit. Arsenic on a big scale, apparently – but I still don't see why you come to *me*. All I can tell you is that *I* didn't suspect it. Maybe I should have. Maybe I should have taken those gastric attacks of Luther Crackenthorpe's much more seriously. But you've got a long way beyond that now.'

Craddock agreed. 'What I really need,' he said, 'is to know a little more about the Crackenthorpe family. Is there any queer mental strain in them – a kink of any kind?'

The eyes under the bushy eyebrows looked at him sharply. 'Yes,

I can see your thoughts might run that way. Well, old Josiah was sane enough. Hard as nails, very much all there. His wife was neurotic, had a tendency to melancholia. Came of an inbred family. She died soon after her second son was born. I'd say, you know, that Luther inherited a certain – well, instability, from her. He was commonplace enough as a young man, but he was always at logger-heads with his father. His father was disappointed in him and I think he resented that and brooded on it, and in the end got a kind of obsession about it. He carried that on into his married life. You'll notice, if you talk to him at all, that he's got a hearty dislike for all his own sons. His daughters he was fond of. Both Emma and Edie – the one who died.'

'Why does he dislike the sons so much?' asked Craddock.

'You'll have to go to one of these new-fashioned psychiatrists to find that out. I'd just say that Luther has never felt very adequate as a man himself, and that he bitterly resents his financial position. He has possession of an income but no power of appointment of capital. If he had the power to disinherit his sons he probably wouldn't dislike them as much. Being powerless in that respect gives him a feeling of humiliation.'

'That's why he's so pleased at the idea of outliving them all?' said Inspector Craddock.

'Possibly. It is the root, too, of his parsimony, I think. I should say that he's managed to save a considerable sum out of his large income – mostly, of course, before taxation rose to its present giddy heights.'

A new idea struck Inspector Craddock. 'I suppose he's left his savings by will to someone? That he *can* do.'

'Oh, yes, though God knows who he has left it to. Maybe to Emma, but I should rather doubt it. She'll get her share of the old man's property. Maybe to Alexander, the grandson.'

'He's fond of him, is he?' said Craddock.

'Used to be. Of course he was his daughter's child, not a son's child. That may have made a difference. And he had quite an affec-tion for Bryan Eastley, Edie's husband. Of course I don't know Bryan well, it's some years since I've seen any of the family. But it struck me that he was going to be very much at a loose end after the war. He's got those qualities that you need in wartime; courage, dash, and a tendency to let the future take care of itself. But I don't think he's got any *stability*. He'll probably turn into a drifter.'

'As far as you know there's no peculiar kink in any of the younger generation?'

'Cedric's an eccentric type, one of those natural rebels. I wouldn't say he was perfectly normal, but you might say, who is? Harold's fairly orthodox, not what I call a very pleasant character, cold-hearted, eye to the main chance. Alfred's got a touch of the delinquent about him. He's a wrong 'un, always was. Saw him taking money out of a missionary box once that they used to keep in the hall. That type of thing. Ah, well, the poor fellow's dead, I suppose I shouldn't be talking against him.'

'What about . . .' Craddock hesitated. 'Emma Crackenthorpe?'

'Nice girl, quiet, one doesn't always know what she's thinking. Has her own plans and her own ideas, but she keeps them to herself. She's more character than you might think from her general appearance.'

'You knew Edmund, I suppose, the son who was killed in France?'

'Yes. He was the best of the bunch I'd say. Good-hearted, gay, a nice boy.'

'Did you ever hear that he was going to marry, or had married, a French girl just before he was killed?'

Dr Morris frowned. 'It seems as though I remember something about it,' he said, 'but it's a long time ago.'

'Quite early on in the war, wasn't it?'

'Yes. Ah, well, I dare say he'd have lived to regret it if he had married a foreign wife.'

'There's some reason to believe that he did do just that,' said Craddock.

In a few brief sentences he gave an account of recent happenings.

'I remember seeing something in the papers about a woman found in a sarcophagus. So it was at Rutherford Hall.'

'And there's reason to believe that the woman was Edmund Crackenthorpe's widow.'

'Well, well, that seems extraordinary. More like a novel than real life. But who'd want to kill the poor thing – I mean, how does it tie up with arsenical poisoning in the Crackenthorpe family?'

'In one of two ways,' said Craddock; 'but they are both very far-fetched. Somebody perhaps is greedy and wants the whole of Josiah Crackenthorpe's fortune.'

'Damn fool if he does,' said Dr Morris. 'He'll only have to pay the most stupendous taxes on the income from it.'

CHAPTER TWENTY-ONE

'Nasty things, mushrooms,' said Mrs Kidder.

Mrs Kidder had made the same remark about ten times in the last few days. Lucy did not reply.

'Never touch 'em myself,' said Mrs Kidder, 'much too dangerous. It's a merciful Providence as there's only been one death. The whole lot might have gone, and you, too, miss. A wonderful escape, you've had.'

'It wasn't the mushrooms,' said Lucy. 'They were perfectly all right.'

'Don't you believe it,' said Mrs Kidder. 'Dangerous they are, mushrooms. One toadstool in among the lot and you've had it.

'Funny,' went on Mrs Kidder, among the rattle of plates and dishes in the sink, 'how things seem to come all together, as it were. My sister's eldest had measles and our Ernie fell down and broke 'is arm, and my 'usband came out all over with boils. All in the same week! You'd hardly believe it, would you? It's been the same thing here,' went on Mrs Kidder, 'first that nasty murder and now Mr Alfred dead with mushroom-poisoning. Who'll be the next, I'd like to know?'

Lucy felt rather uncomfortably that she would like to know too.

'My husband, he doesn't like me coming here now,' said Mrs Kidder, 'thinks it's unlucky, but what I say is I've known Miss Crackenthorpe a long time now and she's a nice lady and she depends on me. And I couldn't leave poor Miss Eyelesbarrow, I said, not to do everything herself in the house. Pretty hard it is on you, miss, all these trays.'

Lucy was forced to agree that life did seem to consist very largely of trays at the moment. She was at the moment arranging trays to take to the various invalids.

'As for them nurses, they never do a hand's turn,' said Mrs Kidder. 'All they want is pots and pots of tea made strong. And meals prepared. Wore out, that's what I am.' She spoke in a tone of great satisfaction, though actually she had done very little more than her normal morning's work.

Lucy said solemnly, 'You never spare yourself, Mrs Kidder.'

Mrs Kidder looked pleased. Lucy picked up the first of the trays and started off up the stairs.

'What's *this*?' said Mr Crackenthorpe disapprovingly.

'Beef tea and baked custard,' said Lucy.

'Take it away,' said Mr Crackenthorpe. 'I won't touch that stuff. I told that nurse I wanted a beef steak.'

'Dr Quimper thinks you ought not to have beef steak just yet,' said Lucy.

Mr Crackenthorpe snorted. 'I'm practically well again. I'm getting up tomorrow. How are the others?'

'Mr Harold's much better,' said Lucy. 'He's going back to London tomorrow.'

'Good riddance,' said Mr Crackenthorpe. 'What about Cedric — any hope that he's going back to his island tomorrow?'

'He won't be going just yet.'

'Pity. What's Emma doing? Why doesn't she come and see me?'

'She's still in bed, Mr Crackenthorpe.'

'Women always coddle themselves,' said Mr Crackenthorpe. 'But you're a good strong girl,' he added approvingly. 'Run about all day, don't you?'

'I get plenty of exercise,' said Lucy.

Old Mr Crackenthorpe nodded his head approvingly. 'You're a good strong girl,' he said, 'and don't think I've forgotten what I talked to you about before. One of these days you'll see what you'll see. Emma isn't always going to have things her own way. And don't listen to the others when they tell you I'm a mean old man. I'm careful of my money. I've got a nice little packet put by and I know who I'm going to spend it on when the time comes.' He leered at her affectionately.

Lucy went rather quickly out of the room, avoiding his clutching hand.

The next tray was taken in to Emma.

'Oh, thank you, Lucy. I'm really feeling quite myself again by now. I'm hungry, and that's a good sign, isn't it? My dear,' went on Emma as Lucy settled the tray on her knees, 'I'm really feeling very upset about your aunt. You haven't had any time to go and see her, I suppose?'

'No, I haven't, as a matter of fact.'

'I'm afraid she must be missing you.'

'Oh, don't worry, Miss Crackenthorpe. She understands what a terrible time we've been through.'

'Have you rung her up?'

'No, I haven't just lately.'

'Well, do. Ring her up every day. It makes such a difference to old people to get news.'

'You're very kind,' said Lucy. Her conscience smote her a little as she went down to fetch the next tray. The complications of illness in a house had kept her thoroughly absorbed and she had had no time to think of anything else. She decided that she would ring Miss Marple up as soon as she had taken Cedric his meal.

There was only one nurse in the house now and she passed Lucy on the landing, exchanging greetings.

Cedric, looking incredibly tidied up and neat, was sitting up in bed writing busily on sheets of paper.

'Hallo, Lucy,' he said, 'what hell brew have you got for me to-day? I wish you'd get rid of that god-awful nurse, she's simply too arch for words. Calls me "we" for some reason. "And how are we this morning? Have we slept well? Oh, dear, we're very naughty, throwing off the bedclothes like that."' He imitated the refined accents of the nurse in a high falsetto voice.

'You seem very cheerful,' said Lucy. 'What are you busy with?'

'Plans,' said Cedric. 'Plans for what to do with this place when the old man pops off. It's a jolly good bit of land here, you know. I can't make up my mind whether I'd like to develop some of it myself, or whether I'll sell it in lots all in one go. Very valuable for industrial purposes. The house will do for a nursing home or a school. I'm not sure I shan't sell half the land and use the money to do something rather outrageous with the other half. What do you think?'

'You haven't got it yet,' said Lucy, dryly.

'I shall have it, though,' said Cedric. 'It's not divided up like the other stuff. I get it outright. And if I sell it for a good fat price the money will be capital, not income, so I shan't have to pay taxes on it. Money to burn. Think of it.'

'I always understood you rather despised money,' said Lucy.

'Of course I despise money when I haven't got any,' said Cedric. 'It's the only dignified thing to do. What a lovely girl you are, Lucy, or do I just think so because I haven't seen any good-looking women for such a long time?'

'I expect that's it,' said Lucy.

'Still busy tidying everyone and everything up?'

'Somebody seems to have been tidying you up,' said Lucy, looking at him.

'That's that damned nurse,' said Cedric with feeling. 'Have you had the inquest on Alfred yet? What happened?'

'It was adjourned,' said Lucy.

'Police being cagey. This mass poisoning does give one a bit of a turn, doesn't it? Mentally, I mean. I'm not referring to more obvious aspects.' He added: 'Better look after yourself, my girl.'

'I do,' said Lucy.

'Has young Alexander gone back to school yet?'

'I think he's still with the Stoddart-Wests. I think it's the day after tomorrow that school begins.'

Before getting her own lunch Lucy went to the telephone and rang up Miss Marple.

'I'm so terribly sorry I haven't been able to come over, but I've been really very busy.'

'Of course, my dear, of course. Besides, there's nothing that can be done just now. We just have to wait.'

'Yes, but what are we waiting for?'

'Elspeth McGillicuddy ought to be home very soon now,' said Miss Marple. 'I wrote to her to fly home at once. I said it was her duty. So don't worry too much, my dear.' Her voice was kindly and reassuring.

'You don't think . . .' Lucy began, but stopped.

'That there will be any more deaths? Oh, I hope not, my dear. But one never knows, does one? When anyone is really wicked, I mean. And I think there is great wickedness here.'

'Or madness,' said Lucy.

'Of course I know that is the modern way of looking at things. I don't agree myself.'

Lucy rang off, went into the kitchen and picked up her tray of lunch. Mrs Kidder had divested herself of her apron and was about to leave.

'You'll be all right, miss, I hope?' she asked solicitously.

'Of course I shall be all right,' snapped Lucy.

She took her tray not into the big, gloomy dining-room but into the small study. She was just finishing her meal when the door opened and Bryan Eastley came in.

'Hallo,' said Lucy, 'this is very unexpected.'

'I suppose it is,' said Bryan. 'How is everybody?'

'Oh, much better. Harold's going back to London tomorrow.'

'What do you think about it all? Was it really arsenic?'

'It was arsenic all right,' said Lucy.

'It hasn't been in the papers yet.'

'No, I think the police are keeping it up their sleeves for the moment.'

'Somebody must have a pretty good down on the family,' said Bryan. 'Who's likely to have sneaked in and tampered with the food?'

'I suppose I'm the most likely person really,' said Lucy.

Bryan looked at her anxiously. 'But you didn't, did you?' he asked. He sounded slightly shocked.

'No. I didn't,' said Lucy.

Nobody could have tampered with the curry. She had made it — alone in the kitchen, and brought it to table, and the only person who could have tampered with it was one of the five people who sat down to the meal.

'I mean – why should you?' said Bryan. 'They're nothing to you, are they? I say,' he added, 'I hope you don't mind my coming back here like this?'

'No, no, of course I don't. Have you come to stay?'

'Well, I'd like to, if it wouldn't be an awful bore to you.'

'No. No, we can manage.'

'You see, I'm out of a job at the moment and I – well, I get rather fed up. Are you really sure you don't mind?'

'Oh, I'm not the person to mind, anyway. It's Emma.'

'Oh, Emma's all right,' said Bryan. 'Emma's always been very nice to me. In her own way, you know. She keeps things to herself a lot, in fact, she's rather a dark horse, old Emma. This living here and looking after the old man would get most people down. Pity

688

she never married. Too late now, I suppose.'

'I don't think it's too late, at all,' said Lucy.

'Well...' Bryan considered. 'A clergyman perhaps,' he said hopefully. 'She'd be useful in the parish and tactful with the Mothers' Union. I do mean the Mothers' Union, don't I? Not that I know what it really is, but you come across it sometimes in books. And she'd wear a hat in church on Sundays,' he added.

'Doesn't sound much of a prospect to me,' said Lucy, rising and picking up the tray.

'I'll do that,' said Bryan, taking the tray from her. They went into the kitchen together. 'Shall I help you wash up? I do like this kitchen,' he added. 'In fact, I know it isn't the sort of thing that people do like nowadays, but I like this whole house. Shocking taste, I suppose, but there it is. You could land a plane quite easily in the park,' he added with enthusiasm.

He picked up a glass-cloth and began to wipe the spoons and forks.

'Seems a waste, its coming to Cedric,' he remarked. 'First thing he'll do is to sell the whole thing and go breaking off abroad again. Can't see, myself, why England isn't good enough for anybody. Harold wouldn't want this house either, and of course it's much too big for Emma. Now, if only it came to Alexander, he and I would be as happy together here as a couple of sand boys. Of course it would be nice to have a woman about the house.' He looked thoughtfully at Lucy. 'Oh, well, what's the good of talking? If Alexander were to get this place it would mean the whole lot of them would have to die first, and that's not really likely, is it? Though from what I've seen of the old boy he might easily live to be a hundred, just to annoy them all. I don't suppose he was much cut up by Alfred's death, was he?'

Lucy said shortly, 'No, he wasn't.'

'Cantankerous old devil,' said Bryan Eastley cheerfully.

CHAPTER TWENTY-TWO

'Dreadful, the things people go about saying,' said Mrs Kidder. 'I don't listen, mind you, more than I can help. But you'd hardly believe it.' She waited hopefully.

'Yes, I suppose so,' said Lucy.

'About that body that was found in the Long Barn,' went on Mrs Kidder, moving crablike backwards on her hands and knees, as she scrubbed the kitchen floor, 'saying as how she'd been Mr Edmund's fancy piece during the war, and how she come over here and a jealous husband followed her, and did her in. It is a likely thing as a foreigner would do, but it wouldn't be likely after all these years, would it?'

'It sounds most unlikely to me.'

'But there's worse things than that, they say,' said Mrs Kidder. 'Say anything, people will. You'd be surprised. There's those that say Mr Harold married somewhere abroad and that she come over and found out that he's committed bigamy with that lady Alice, and that she was going to bring 'im to court and that he met her down here and did her in, and hid her body in the sarcoffus. Did you ever!'

'Shocking,' said Lucy vaguely, her mind elsewhere.

'Of course I didn't listen,' said Mrs Kidder virtuously, 'I wouldn't put no stock in such tales myself. It beats me how people think up such things, let alone say them. All I hope is none of it gets to Miss Emma's ears. It might upset her and I wouldn't like that. She's a very nice lady, Miss Emma is, and I've not heard a word against her, not a word. And of course Mr Alfred being dead nobody says anything against him now. Not even that it's a judgment, which they well might do. But it's awful, miss, isn't it, the wicked talk there is.'

Mrs Kidder spoke with immense enjoyment.

'It must be quite painful for you to listen to it,' said Lucy.

'Oh, it is,' said Mrs Kidder. 'It is indeed. I says to my husband, I says, however can they?'

The bell rang.

'There's the doctor, miss. Will you let 'im in, or shall I?'

'I'll go,' said Lucy.

But it was not the doctor. On the doorstep stood a tall, elegant woman in a mink coat. Drawn up to the gravel sweep was a purring Rolls with a chauffeur at the wheel.

'Can I see Miss Emma Crackenthorpe, please?'

It was an attractive voice, the R's slightly blurred. The woman was attractive too. About thirty-five, with dark hair and expensively and beautifully made up.

'I'm sorry,' said Lucy, 'Miss Crackenthorpe is ill in bed and can't see anyone.'

'I know she has been ill, yes; but it is very important that I should see her.'

'I'm afraid,' Lucy began.

The visitor interrupted her. 'I think you are Miss Eyelesbarrow, are you not?' She smiled, an attractive smile. 'My son has spoken of you, so I know. I am Lady Stoddart-West and Alexander is staying with me now.'

'Oh, I see,' said Lucy.

'And it is really important that I should see Miss Crackenthorpe,' continued the other. 'I know all about her illness and I assure you this is not just a social call. It is because of something that the boys have said to me – that my son has said to me. It is, I think, a matter of grave importance and I would like to speak to Miss Crackenthorpe about it. Please, will you ask her?'

'Come in.' Lucy ushered her visitor into the hall and into the drawing-room. Then she said, 'I'll go up and ask Miss Crackenthorpe.'

She went upstairs, knocked on Emma's door and entered.

'Lady Stoddart-West is here,' she said. 'She wants to see you very particularly.'

'Lady Stoddart-West?' Emma looked surprised. A look of alarm came into her face. 'There's nothing wrong, is there, with the boys – with Alexander?'

'No, no,' Lucy reassured her. 'I'm sure the boys are all right. It seemed to be something the boys have told her or said to her.

'Oh. Well . . .' Emma hesitated. 'Perhaps I ought to see her. Do I look all right, Lucy?'

'You look very nice,' said Lucy.

Emma was sitting up in bed, a soft pink shawl was round her shoulders and brought out the faint rose-pink of her cheeks. Her dark hair had been neatly brushed and combed by Nurse. Lucy had placed a bowl of autumn leaves on the dressing-table the day before. Her room looked attractive and quite unlike a sick room.

'I'm really quite well enough to get up,' said Emma. 'Dr Quimper said I could tomorrow.'

'You look really quite like yourself again,' said Lucy. 'Shall I bring Lady Stoddart-West up?'

'Yes, do.'

Lucy went downstairs again. 'Will you come up to Miss Crackenthorpe's room?'

She escorted the visitor upstairs, opened the door for her to pass in and then shut it. Lady Stoddart-West approached the bed with outstretched hand.

'Miss Crackenthorpe? I really do apologize for breaking in on you like this. I have seen you, I think, at the sports at the school.'

'Yes,' said Emma, 'I remember you quite well. Do sit down.'

In the chair conveniently placed by the bed Lady Stoddart-West sat down. She said in a quiet low voice:

'You must think it very strange of me coming here like this, but I have reason. I think it is an important reason. You see, the boys have been telling me things. You can understand that they were very excited about the murder that happened here. I confess I did not like it at the time. I was nervous. I wanted to bring James home at once. But my husband laughed. He said that obviously it was a murder that had nothing to do with the house and the family, and he said that from what he remembered from his boyhood, and from James's letters, both he and Alexander were enjoying themselves so wildly that it would be sheer cruelty to bring them back. So I gave in and agreed that they should stay on until the time arranged for James to bring Alexander back with him.'

Emma said: 'You think we ought to have sent your son home earlier?'

'No, no, that is not what I mean at all. Oh, it is difficult for me, this! But what I have to say must be said. You see, they have picked up a good deal, the boys. They told me that this woman — the murdered woman — that the police have an idea that she may be a

692

French girl whom your eldest brother – who was killed in the war – knew in France. That is so?'

'It is a possibility,' said Emma, her voice breaking slightly, 'that we are forced to consider. It may have been so.'

'There is some reason for believing that the body is that of this girl, this Martine?'

'I have told you, it is a possibility.'

'But why – why should they think that she was Martine? Did she have letters on her – papers?'

'No. Nothing of that kind. But you see, I had had a letter, from this Martine.'

'You had had a letter – from *Martine?*'

'Yes. A letter telling me she was in England and would like to come and see me. I invited her down here, but got a telegram saying she was going back to France. Perhaps she did go back to France. We do not know. But since then an envelope was found here addressed to her. That seems to show that she had come down here. But I really don't see . . .' She broke off.

Lady Stoddart-West broke in quickly:

'You really do not see what concern it is of mine? That is very true. I should not in your place. But when I heard this – or rather, a garbled account of this – I had to come to make sure it was really so because, if it is –'

'Yes?' said Emma.

'Then I must tell you something that I had never intended to tell you. You see, *I am Martine Dubois.*'

Emma stared at her guest as though she could hardly take in the sense of her words.

'You!' she said. 'You are Martine?'

The other nodded vigorously. 'But, yes. It surprises you, I am sure, but it is true. I met your brother Edmund in the first days of the war. He was indeed billeted at our house. Well, you know the rest. We fell in love. We intended to be married, and then there was the retreat to Dunkirk, Edmund was reported missing. Later he was reported killed. I will not speak to you of that time. It was long ago and it is over. But I will say to you that I loved your brother very much . . .

'Then came the grim realities of war. The Germans occupied France. I became a worker for the Resistance. I was one of those who was assigned to pass Englishmen through France to England. It was in that way that I met my present husband. He was an Air Force officer, parachuted into France to do special work. When the war ended we were married. I considered once or twice whether I should write to you or come and see you, but I decided against it. It could do no good, I thought, to rake up old memories. I had a new life and I had no wish to recall the old.' She paused and then said: 'But it gave me, I will tell you, a strange pleasure when I found that my son James's greatest friend at his school was a boy whom I found to be Edmund's nephew. Alexander, I may say, is very like Edmund, as I dare say you yourself appreciate. It seemed to me a very happy state of affairs that James and Alexander should be such friends.'

She leaned forward and placed her hand on Emma's arm. 'But you see, dear Emma, do you not, that when I heard this story about the murder, about this dead woman being suspected to be the Martine that Edmund had known, that I had to come and tell you the truth. Either you or I must inform the police of the fact. Whoever the dead woman is, she is not Martine.'

'I can hardly take it in,' said Emma, 'that you, *you* should be the Martine that dear Edmund wrote to me about.' She sighed, shaking her head, then she frowned perplexedly. 'But I don't understand. Was it you, then, who wrote to me?'

Lady Stoddart-West shook a vigorous head. 'No, no, of course I did not write to you.'

'Then . . .' Emma stopped.

'Then there was someone pretending to be Martine who wanted perhaps to get money out of you? That is what it must have been. But who can it be?'

Emma said slowly: 'I suppose there were people at the time, who knew?'

The other shrugged her shoulders. 'Probably, yes. But there was no one intimate with me, no one very close to me. I have never spoken of it since I came to England. And why wait all this time? It is curious, very curious.'

Emma said: 'I don't understand it. We will have to see what Inspector Craddock has to say.' She looked with suddenly softened eyes at her visitor. 'I'm so glad to know you at last, my dear.'

'And I you . . . Edmund spoke of you very often. He was very fond of you. I am happy in my new life, but all the same, I don't quite forget.'

Emma leaned back and heaved a sigh. 'It's a terrible relief,' she said. 'As long as we feared that the dead woman might be Martine – it seemed to be tied up with the family. But now – oh, it's an absolute load off my back. I don't know who the poor soul was but she can't have had anything to do with *us*!'

CHAPTER TWENTY-THREE

The streamlined secretary brought Harold Crackenthorpe his usual afternoon cup of tea.

'Thanks, Miss Ellis, I shall be going home early today.'

'I'm sure you ought really not to have come at all, Mr Crackenthorpe,' said Miss Ellis. 'You look quite pulled down still.'

'I'm all right,' said Harold Crackenthorpe, but he did feel pulled down. No doubt about it, he'd had a very nasty turn. Ah, well, that was over.

Extraordinary, he thought broodingly, that Alfred should have succumbed and the old man should have come through. After all, what was he – seventy-three – seventy-four? Been an invalid for years. If there was one person you'd have thought would have been taken off, it would have been the old man. But no. It had to be Alfred. Alfred who, as far as Harold knew, was a healthy wiry sort of chap. Nothing much the matter with him.

He leaned back in his chair sighing. That girl was right. He didn't feel up to things yet, but he had wanted to come down to the office. Wanted to get the hang of how affairs were going. Touch and go. All this – he looked round him – the richly appointed office, the pale gleaming wood, the expensive modern chairs, it all looked prosperous enough, and a good thing too! That's where Alfred had always gone wrong. If you looked prosperous, people thought you were prosperous. There were no rumours going around as yet about his financial stability. All the same, the crash couldn't be delayed very long. Now, if only his father had passed out instead of Alfred, as surely, surely he ought to have done. Practically seemed to thrive on arsenic! Yes, if his father had succumbed – well, there wouldn't have been anything to worry about.

Still, the great thing was not to seem worried. A prosperous appearance. Not like poor old Alfred who always looked seedy and shiftless, who looked in fact exactly what he was. One of those small-time speculators, never going all out boldly for the big money. In with a shady crowd here, doing a doubtful deal there, never quite rendering himself liable to prosecution but going very near the edge. And where had it got him? Short periods of affluence and then back to seediness and shabbiness, once more. No broad outlook about Alfred. Taken all in all, you couldn't say Alfred was much loss. He'd never been particularly fond of Alfred and with Alfred out of the way the money that was coming to him from that old curmudgeon, his grandfather, would be sensibly increased, divided not into five shares but into four shares. Very much better.

Harold's face brightened a little. He rose, took his hat and coat and left the office. Better take it easy for a day or two. He wasn't feeling too strong yet. His car was waiting below and very soon he was weaving through London traffic to his house.

Darwin, his manservant, opened the door.

'Her ladyship has just arrived, sir,' he said.

For a moment Harold stared at him. Alice! Good heavens, was it today that Alice was coming home? He'd forgotten all about it. Good thing Darwin had warned him. It wouldn't have looked so good if he'd gone upstairs and looked too astonished at seeing her. Not that it really mattered, he supposed. Neither Alice nor he had any illusions about the feeling they had for each other. Perhaps Alice was fond of him – he didn't know.

All in all, Alice was a great disappointment to him. He hadn't been in love with her, of course, but though a plain woman she was quite a pleasant one. And her family and connections had undoubtedly been useful. Not perhaps as useful as they might have been, because in marrying Alice he had been considering the position of hypothetical children. Nice relations for his boys to have. But there hadn't been any boys, or girls either, and all that had remained had been he and Alice growing older together without much to say to each other and with no particular pleasure in each other's company.

She stayed away a good deal with relations and usually went to the Riviera in the winter. It suited her and it didn't worry him.

He went upstairs now into the drawing-room and greeted her punctiliously.

'So you're back, my dear. Sorry I couldn't meet you, but I was held up in the City. I got back as early as I could. How was San Raphael?'

Alice told him how San Raphael was. She was a thin woman with sandy-coloured hair, a well-arched nose and vague, hazel eyes. She talked in a well-bred, monotonous and rather depressing voice. It had been a good journey back, the Channel a little rough. The Customs, as usual, very trying at Dover.

'You should come by air,' said Harold, as he always did. 'So much simpler.'

'I dare say, but I don't really like air travel. I never have. Makes me nervous.'

'Saves a lot of time,' said Harold.

Lady Alice Crackenthorpe did not answer. It was possible that her problem in life was not to save time but to occupy it. She inquired politely after her husband's health.

'Emma's telegram quite alarmed me,' she said. 'You were all taken ill, I understand.'

'Yes, yes,' said Harold.

'I read in the paper the other day,' said Alice, 'of forty people in a hotel going down with food poisoning at the same time. All this refrigeration is dangerous, I think. People keep things too long in them.'

'Possibly,' said Harold. Should he, or should he not mention arsenic? Somehow, looking at Alice, he felt himself quite unable to do so. In Alice's world, he felt, there was no place for poisoning by arsenic. It was a thing you read about in the papers. It didn't happen to you or your own family. But it had happened in the Crackenthorpe family . . .

He went up to his room and lay down for an hour or two before dressing for dinner. At dinner, tête-à-tête with his wife, the conversation ran on much the same lines. Desultory, polite. The mention of acquaintances and friends at San Raphael.

'There's a parcel for you on the hall table, a small one,' Alice said.

'Is there? I didn't notice it.'

'It's an extraordinary thing but somebody was telling me about a murdered woman having been found in a barn, or something like that. She said it was at Rutherford Hall. I suppose it must be some other Rutherford Hall.'

'No,' said Harold, 'no, it isn't. It was in our barn, as a matter of fact.'

'Really, Harold! A murdered woman in the barn at Rutherford Hall — and you never told me anything about it.'

'Well, there hasn't been much time, really,' said Harold, 'and it was all rather unpleasant. Nothing to do with us, of course. The Press milled around a good deal. Of course we had to deal with the police and all that sort of thing.'

'Very unpleasant,' said Alice. 'Did they find out who did it?' she added, with rather perfunctory interest.

'Not yet,' said Harold.

'What sort of woman was she?'

'Nobody knows. French, apparently.'

'Oh, *French*,' said Alice, and allowing for the difference in class, her tone was not unlike that of Inspector Bacon. 'Very annoying for you all,' she agreed.

They went out from the dining-room and crossed into the small study where they usually sat when they were alone. Harold was feeling quite exhausted by now. 'I'll go up to bed early,' he thought.

He picked up the small parcel from the hall table, about which his wife had spoken to him. It was a small neatly waxed parcel, done up with meticulous exactness. Harold ripped it open as he came to sit down in his usual chair by the fire.

Inside was a small tablet box bearing the label, 'Two to be taken nightly.' With it was a small piece of paper with the chemist's heading in Brackhampton. 'Sent by request of Doctor Quimper' was written on it.

Harold Crackenthorpe frowned. He opened the box and looked at the tablets. Yes, they seemed to be the same tablets he had been having. But surely, surely Quimper had said that he needn't take any more? 'You won't want them, now.' That's what Quimper had said.

'What is it, dear?' said Alice. 'You look worried.'

'Oh, it's just — some tablets. I've been taking them at night. But I rather thought the doctor said don't take any more.'

His wife said placidly: 'He probably said don't forget to take them.'

'He may have done, I suppose,' said Harold doubtfully.

He looked across at her. She was watching him. Just for a moment or two he wondered – he didn't often wonder about Alice – exactly what she was thinking. That mild gaze of hers told him nothing. Her eyes were like windows in an empty house. What did Alice think about him, feel about him? Had she been in love with him once? He supposed she had. Or did she marry him because she thought he was doing well in the City, and she was tired of her own impecunious existence? Well, on the whole, she'd done quite well out of it. She'd got a car and a house in London, she could travel abroad when she felt like it and get herself expensive clothes, though goodness knows they never looked like anything on Alice. Yes, on the whole she'd done pretty well. He wondered if she thought so. She wasn't really fond of him, of course, but then he wasn't really fond of her. They had nothing in common, nothing to talk about, no memories to share. If there had been children – but there hadn't been any children – odd that there were no children in the family except young Edie's boy. Young Edie. She'd been a silly girl, making that foolish, hasty war-time marriage. Well, he'd given her good advice.

He'd said: 'It's all very well, these dashing young pilots, glamour, courage, all that, but he'll be no good in peace time, you know. Probably be barely able to support you.'

And Edie had said, what did it matter? She loved Bryan and Bryan loved her, and he'd probably be killed quite soon. Why shouldn't they have some happiness? What was the good of looking to the future when they might well be bombed any minute. And after all, Edie had said, the future doesn't really matter because some day there'll be all grandfather's money.

Harold squirmed uneasily in his chair. Really, that will of his grandfather's had been iniquitous! Keeping them all dangling on a string. The will hadn't pleased anybody. It didn't please the grand-children and it made their father quite livid. The old boy was absolutely determined not to die. That's what made him take so much care of himself. But he'd have to die soon. Surely, surely he'd have to die soon. Otherwise – all Harold's worries swept over him once more making him feel sick and tired and giddy.

Alice was still watching him, he noticed. Those pale, thoughtful eyes, they made him uneasy somehow.

'I think I shall go to bed,' he said. 'It's been my first day out in the City.'

'Yes,' said Alice, 'I think that's a good idea. I'm sure the doctor told you to take things easily at first.'

'Doctors always tell you that,' said Harold.

'And don't forget to take your tablets, dear,' said Alice. She picked up the box and handed it to him.

He said good night and went upstairs. Yes, he needed the tablets. It would have been a mistake to leave them off too soon. He took two of them and swallowed them with a glass of water.

CHAPTER TWENTY-FOUR

'Nobody could have made more of a muck of it than I seem to have done,' said Dermot Craddock gloomily.

He sat, his long legs stretched out, looking somehow incongruous in faithful Florence's somewhat over-furnished parlour. He was thoroughly tired, upset and dispirited.

Miss Marple made soft, soothing noises of dissent. 'No, no, you've done very good work, my dear boy. Very good work indeed.'

'I've done very good work, have I? I've let a whole family be poisoned. Alfred Crackenthorpe's dead and now Harold's dead too. What the hell's going on here. That's what I should like to know.'

'Poisoned tablets,' said Miss Marple thoughtfully.

'Yes. Devilishly cunning, really. They looked just like the tablets that he'd been having. There was a printed slip sent in with them "by Doctor Quimper's instructions." Well, Quimper never ordered them. There were chemist's labels used. The chemist knew nothing about it, either. No. That box of tablets came from Rutherford Hall.'

'Do you actually *know* it came from Rutherford Hall?'

'Yes. We've had a thorough check up. Actually, it's the box that held the sedative tablets prescribed for Emma.'

'Oh, I see. For Emma . . .'

'Yes. It's got her fingerprints on it and the fingerprints of both the nurses and the fingerprint of the chemist who made it up. Nobody else's, naturally. The person who sent them was careful.'

'And the sedative tablets were removed and something else substituted?'

'Yes. That of course is the devil with tablets. One tablet looks exactly like another.'

'You are so right,' agreed Miss Marple. 'I remember so very well in my young days, the *black* mixture and the *brown* mixture (the cough mixture that was) and the white mixture, and Doctor So-and-So's *pink* mixture. People didn't mix those up nearly as much. In fact, you know, in my village of St Mary Mead we still like that kind of medicine. It's a bottle they always want, not tablets. What were the tablets?' she asked.

'Aconite. They were the kind of tablets that are usually kept in a poison bottle, diluted one in a hundred for outside application.'

'And so Harold took them, and died,' Miss Marple said thoughtfully. Dermot Craddock uttered something like a groan.

'You mustn't mind my letting off steam to you,' he said. 'Tell it all to Aunt Jane; that's how I feel!'

'That's very, very nice of you,' said Miss Marple, 'and I do appreciate it. I feel towards you, as Sir Henry's godson, quite differently from the way I feel to any ordinary detective inspector.'

Dermot Craddock gave her a fleeting grin. 'But the fact remains that I've made the most ghastly mess of things all along the line,' he said. 'The Chief Constable down here calls in Scotland Yard, and what do they get? They get me making a prize ass of myself!'

'No, no,' said Miss Marple.

'Yes, yes. I don't know who poisoned Alfred, I don't know who poisoned Harold, and, to cap it all, I haven't the least idea who the original murdered woman was! This Martine business seemed a perfectly safe bet. The whole thing seemed to tie up. And now what happens? The real Martine shows up and turns out, most improbably, to be the wife of Sir Robert Stoddart-West. So, who's the woman in the barn now? Goodness knows. First I go all out on the idea she's Anna Stravinska, and then *she's* out of it –'

He was arrested by Miss Marple giving one of her small peculiarly significant coughs.

'But is she?' she murmured.

Craddock stared at her. 'Well, that postcard from Jamaica –'

'Yes,' said Miss Marple; 'but that isn't really evidence, is it? I mean, anyone can get a postcard sent from almost anywhere, I suppose. I remember Mrs Brierly, such a very bad nervous breakdown. Finally, they said she ought to go to the mental hospital for observation, and she was so worried about the children knowing about it and so she wrote fourteen postcards and arranged that they should be posted from different places abroad, and told them that Mummy was going abroad on a holiday.' She added, looking at Dermot Craddock, 'You see what I mean.'

'Yes, of course,' said Craddock, staring at her. 'Naturally we'd have checked that postcard if it hadn't been for the Martine business fitting the bill so well.'

'So convenient,' murmured Miss Marple.

'It tied up,' said Craddock. 'After all, there's the letter Emma received signed Martine Crackenthorpe. Lady Stoddart-West didn't send that, but *somebody* did. Somebody who was going to pretend to be Martine, and who was going to cash in, if possible, on being Martine. You can't deny *that*.'

'No, no.'

'And then, the envelope of the letter Emma wrote to her with the London address on it. Found at Rutherford Hall, showing she'd actually been there.'

'But the murdered woman *hadn't* been there!' Miss Marple pointed out. 'Not in the sense *you* mean. *She* only came to Rutherford Hall *after she was dead*. Pushed out of a train on to the railway embankment.'

'Oh, yes.'

'What the envelope really proves is that the murderer was there. Presumably he took that envelope off her with her other papers and things, and then dropped it by mistake – or – I wonder now, was it a mistake? Surely Inspector Bacon, and your men too, made a thorough search of the place, didn't they, and didn't find it. It only turned up later in the boiler house.'

'That's understandable,' said Craddock. 'The old gardener chap used to spear up any odd stuff that was blowing about and shove it in there.'

'Where it was very convenient for the boys to find,' said Miss Marple thoughtfully.

'You think we were meant to find it?'

'Well, I just wonder. After all, it would be fairly easy to know where the boys were going to look next, or even to suggest to them ... Yes, I do wonder. It stopped you thinking about Anna Stravinska any more, didn't it?'

Craddock said: 'And you think it really may be her all the time?'

'I think *someone* may have got alarmed when you started making inquiries about her, that's all ... I think somebody didn't want those inquiries made.'

'Let's hold on to the basic fact that someone was going to impersonate Martine,' said Craddock. 'And then for some reason – didn't. Why?'

'That's a very interesting question,' said Miss Marple.

'Somebody sent a note saying Martine was going back to France, then arranged to travel down with the girl and kill her on the way. You agree so far?'

'Not exactly,' said Miss Marple. 'I don't think, really, you're making it simple enough.'

'Simple!' exclaimed Craddock. 'You're mixing me up,' he complained.

Miss Marple said in a distressed voice that she wouldn't think of doing anything like *that*.

'Come, tell me,' said Craddock, 'do you or do you not think you know who the murdered woman was?'

Miss Marple sighed. 'It's so difficult,' she said, 'to put it the right way. I mean, I don't know *who* she was, but at the same time I'm fairly sure who she *was*, if you know what I mean.'

Craddock threw up his head. 'Know what you mean? I haven't the faintest idea.' He looked out through the window. 'There's your Lucy Eyelesbarrow coming to see you,' he said. 'Well, I'll be off. My *amour propre* is very low this afternoon and having a young woman coming in, radiant with efficiency and success, is more than I can bear.'

CHAPTER TWENTY-FIVE

'I looked up tontine in the dictionary,' said Lucy.

The first greetings were over and now Lucy was wandering rather aimlessly round the room, touching a china dog here, an antimacassar there, the plastic work-box in the window.

'I thought you probably would,' said Miss Marple equably.

Lucy spoke slowly, quoting the words. 'Lorenzo Tonti, Italian banker, originator, 1653, of a form of annuity in which the shares of subscribers who die are added to the profit shares of the survivors.' She paused. 'That's it, isn't it? That fits well enough, and you were thinking of it even *then* before the last two deaths.'

She took up once more her restless, almost aimless prowl round the room. Miss Marple sat watching her. This was a very different Lucy Eyelesbarrow from the one she knew.

'I suppose it was asking for it really,' said Lucy. 'A will of that kind, ending so that if there was only one survivor left he'd get the lot. And yet – there was quite a lot of money, wasn't there? You'd think it would be enough shared out . . .' She paused, the words trailing off.

'The trouble is,' said Miss Marple, 'that people are greedy. Some people. That's so often, you know, how things start. You don't start with murder, with wanting to do murder, or even thinking of it. You just start by being greedy, by wanting more than you're going to have.' She laid her knitting down on her knee and stared ahead of her into space. 'That's how I came across Inspector Craddock first, you know. A case in the country. Near Medenham Spa. That began the same way, just a weak amiable character who wanted a great deal of money. Money that that person wasn't entitled to, but there seemed an easy way to get it. Not murder then. Just something so easy and simple that it hadn't seemed wrong. That's how things begin . . . But it ended with three murders.'

'Just like this,' said Lucy. 'We've had three murders now. The woman who impersonated Martine and who would have been able to claim a share for her son, and then Alfred, and then Harold. And now it only leaves two, doesn't it?'

'You mean,' said Miss Marple, 'there are only Cedric and Emma left?'

'Not Emma. Emma isn't a tall dark man. No. I mean Cedric and Bryan Eastley. I never thought of Bryan because he's fair. He's got a fair moustache and blue eyes, but you see – the other day . . .' She paused.

'Yes, go on,' said Miss Marple. 'Tell me. Something has upset you very badly, hasn't it?'

'It was when Lady Stoddart-West was going away. She had said good-bye and then suddenly turned to me just as she was getting into the car and asked: "Who was that tall dark man who was standing on the terrace as I came in?"

'I couldn't imagine who she meant at first, because Cedric was still laid up. So I said, rather puzzled, "You don't mean Bryan Eastley?" and she said, "Of course, that's who it was, Squadron Leader Eastley. He was hidden in our loft once in France during the Resistance. I remembered the way he stood, and the set of his shoulders," and she said, "I should like to meet him again," but we couldn't find him.'

Miss Marple said nothing, just waited.

'And then,' said Lucy, 'later I looked at him . . . He was standing with his back to me and I saw what I ought to have seen before. That even when a man's fair his hair looks dark because he plasters it down with stuff. Bryan's hair is a sort of medium brown, I suppose, but it can *look* dark. So you see, it might have been *Bryan* that your friend saw in the train. It might . . .'

'Yes,' said Miss Marple. 'I had thought of that.'

'I suppose you think of everything!' said Lucy bitterly.

'Well, dear, one has to really.'

'But I can't see what Bryan would get out of it. I mean the money would come to Alexander, not to him. I suppose it would make an easier life, they could have a bit more luxury, but he wouldn't be able to tap the capital for his schemes, or anything like that.'

'But if anything happened to Alexander before he was twenty-one, then Bryan would get the money as his father and next of kin,' Miss Marple pointed out.

Lucy cast a look of horror at her.

'He'd never do *that*. No father would ever do that just – just to get the money.'

Miss Marple sighed. 'People do, my dear. It's very sad and very terrible, but they do.

'People do very terrible things,' went on Miss Marple. 'I know a woman who poisoned three of her children just for a little bit of insurance money. And then there was an old woman, quite a nice old woman apparently, who poisoned her son when he came home on leave. Then there was that old Mrs Stanwich. That case was in the papers. I dare say you read about it. Her daughter died and her son, and then she said she was poisoned herself. There *was* poison in the gruel, but it came out, you know, that she'd put it there herself. She was just planning to poison the last daughter. That wasn't exactly for money. She was jealous of them for being younger than she was and alive, and she was afraid – it's a terrible thing to say but it's true – they would enjoy themselves after she was gone. She'd always kept a very tight hold on the purse strings. Yes, of course she was a little peculiar, as they say, but I never see myself that *that's* any real excuse. I mean you can be a little peculiar in so many different ways. Sometimes you just go about giving all your possessions away and writing cheques on bank accounts that don't exist, just so as to benefit people. It shows, you see, that behind being peculiar you have quite a nice disposition. But of course if you're peculiar and behind it you have a bad disposition – well, there you are. Now, does that help you at all, my dear Lucy?'

'Does what help me?' asked Lucy, bewildered.

'What I've been telling you,' said Miss Marple. She added gently, 'You mustn't worry, you know. You really mustn't worry. Elspeth McGillicuddy will be here any day now.'

'I don't see what that has to do with it.'

'No, dear, perhaps not. But *I* think it's important myself.'

'I can't help worrying,' said Lucy. 'You see, I've got interested in the family.'

'I know, dear, it's very difficult for you because you are quite strongly attracted to both of them, aren't you, in very different ways.'

'What do you mean?' said Lucy. Her tone was sharp.

'I was talking about the two sons of the house,' said Miss Marple. 'Or rather the son and the son-in-law. It's unfortunate that the two more unpleasant members of the family have died and the two more attractive ones are left. I can see that Cedric Crackenthorpe *is* very attractive. He is inclined to make himself out worse than he is and has a provocative way with him.'

'He makes me fighting mad sometimes,' said Lucy.

'Yes,' said Miss Marple, 'and you enjoy that, don't you? You're a girl with a lot of spirit and you enjoy a battle. Yes, I can see where that attraction lies. And then Mr Eastley is a rather plaintive type, rather like an unhappy little boy. That, of course, is attractive, too.'

'And one of them's a murderer,' said Lucy bitterly, 'and it may be either of them. There's nothing to choose between them really. There's Cedric, not caring a bit about his brother Alfred's death or about Harold's. He just sits back looking thoroughly pleased making plans for what he'll do with Rutherford Hall, and he keeps saying that it'll need a lot of money to develop it in the way he wants to do. Of course I know he's the sort of person who exaggerates his own callousness and all that. But that could be a cover, too. I mean everyone says that you're more callous than you really are. But you mightn't be. You might be even more callous than you seem!'

'Dear, dear Lucy, I'm so sorry about all this.'

'And then Bryan,' went on Lucy. 'It's extraordinary, but Bryan really seems to want to live there. He thinks he and Alexander could find it awfully jolly and he's full of schemes.'

'He's always full of schemes of one kind or another, isn't he?'

'Yes, I think he is. They all *sound* rather wonderful – but I've got an uneasy feeling that they'd never really work. I mean, they're not practical. The *idea* sounds all right – but I don't think he ever considers the actual working difficulties.'

'They are up in the air, so to speak?'

'Yes, in more ways than one. I mean they are usually literally up in the air. They are all air schemes. Perhaps a really good fighter pilot never does quite come down to earth again . . .'

She added: 'And he likes Rutherford Hall so much because it reminds him of the big rambling Victorian house he lived in when he was a child.'

'I see,' said Miss Marple thoughtfully. 'Yes, I see . . .'

Then, with a quick sideways glance at Lucy, she said with a kind of verbal pounce, 'But that isn't all of it, is it, dear? There's something else.'

'Oh, yes, there's something else. Just something that I didn't realize until just a couple of days ago. Bryan could actually have been on that train.'

'On the 4.33 from Paddington?'

'Yes. You see Emma thought she was required to account for *her* movements on 20th December and she went over it all very carefully – a committee meeting in the morning, and then shopping in the afternoon and tea at the Green Shamrock, and then, she said, *she went to meet Bryan at the station*. The train she met was the 4.50 from Paddington, but he could have been on the earlier train and pretended to come by the later one. He told me quite casually that his car had had a biff and was being repaired and so he had to come down by train – an awful bore, he said, he hates trains. He seemed quite natural about it all . . . It may be quite all right – but I wish, somehow, he hadn't come down by train.'

'Actually on the train,' said Miss Marple thoughtfully.

'It doesn't really prove anything. The awful thing is all this suspicion. Not to *know*. And perhaps we never shall know!'

'Of course we shall know, dear,' said Miss Marple briskly. 'I mean – all this isn't going to stop just at this point. The one thing I *do* know about murderers is that they can never let well alone. Or perhaps one should say – ill alone. At any rate,' said Miss Marple with finality, 'they can't once they've done a second murder. Now don't get too upset, Lucy. The police are doing all they can, and looking after everybody – and the great thing is that Elspeth McGillicuddy will be here very soon now!'

CHAPTER TWENTY-SIX

'Now, Elspeth, you're quite clear as to what I want you to do?'

'I'm clear enough,' said Mrs McGillicuddy, 'but what I say to you is, Jane, that it seems very *odd*.'

'It's not odd at all,' said Miss Marple.

'Well, I think so. To arrive at the house and to ask almost immediately whether I can – er – go upstairs.'

'It's very cold weather,' Miss Marple pointed out, 'and after all, you might have eaten something that disagreed with you and – er – have to ask to go upstairs. I mean, these things happen. I remember poor Louisa Felby came to see me once and she had to ask to go upstairs five times during one little half-hour. That,' added Miss Marple parenthetically, 'was a bad Cornish pasty.'

'If you'd just tell me what you're driving at, Jane,' said Mrs McGillicuddy.

'That's just what I don't want to do,' said Miss Marple.

'How irritating you are, Jane. First you make me come all the way back to England before I need –'

'I'm sorry about that,' said Miss Marple; 'but I couldn't do anything else. Someone, you see, may be killed at any moment. Oh, I know they're all on their guard and the police are taking all the precautions they can, but there's always the outside chance that the murderer might be too clever for them. So you see, Elspeth, it was your duty to come back. After all, you and I were brought up to do our duty, weren't we?'

'We certainly were,' said Mrs McGillicuddy, 'no laxness in our young days.'

'So that's quite all right,' said Miss Marple, 'and that's the taxi now,' she added, as a faint hoot was heard outside the house.

Mrs McGillicuddy donned her heavy pepper-and-salt coat and Miss Marple wrapped herself up with a good many shawls and scarves. Then the two ladies got into the taxi and were driven to Rutherford Hall.

II

'Who can this be driving up?' Emma asked, looking out of the window, as the taxi swept past it. 'I do believe it's Lucy's old aunt.'

'What a bore,' said Cedric.

He was lying back in a long chair looking at *Country Life* with his feet reposing on the side of the mantelpiece.

'Tell her you're not at home.'

'When you say tell her I'm not at home, do you mean that I should go out and *say* so? Or that I should tell Lucy to tell her aunt so?'

'Hadn't thought of that,' said Cedric. 'I suppose I was thinking of our butler and footman days, if we ever had them. I seem to remember a footman before the war. He had an affair with the kitchen maid and there was a terrific rumpus about it. Isn't there one of those old hags about the place cleaning?'

But at that moment the door was opened by Mrs Hart, whose afternoon it was for cleaning the brasses, and Miss Marple came in, very fluttery, in a whirl of shawls and scarves, with an uncompromising figure behind her.

'I do hope,' said Miss Marple, taking Emma's hand, 'that we are not intruding. But you see, I'm going home the day after tomorrow, and I couldn't bear not to come over and see you and say goodbye, and thank you again for your goodness to Lucy. Oh, I forgot. May I introduce my friend, Mrs McGillicuddy, who is staying with me?'

'How d'you do,' said Mrs McGillicuddy, looking at Emma with complete attention and then shifting her gaze to Cedric, who had now risen to his feet. Lucy entered the room at this moment.

'Aunt Jane, I had no idea . . .'

'I had to come and say goodbye to Miss Crackenthorpe,' said Miss Marple, turning to her, 'who has been so very, very kind to you, Lucy.'

'It's Lucy who's been very kind to us,' said Emma.

'Yes, indeed,' said Cedric. 'We've worked her like a galley slave. Waiting on the sick room, running up and down the stairs, cooking little invalid messes . . .'

Miss Marple broke in. 'I was so very, very sorry to hear of your illness. I do hope you're quite recovered now, Miss Crackenthorpe?'

'Oh, we're quite well again now,' said Emma.

'Lucy told me you were all very ill. So dangerous, isn't it, food poisoning? Mushrooms, I understand.'

'The cause remains rather mysterious,' said Emma.

'Don't you believe it,' said Cedric. 'I bet you've heard the rumours that are flying round, Miss – er –'

'Marple,' said Miss Marple.

'Well, as I say, I bet you've heard the rumours that are flying round. Nothing like arsenic for raising a little flutter in the neighbourhood.'

'Cedric,' said Emma, 'I wish you wouldn't. You know Inspector Craddock said . . .'

'Bah,' said Cedric, 'everybody knows. Even you've heard something, haven't you?' he turned to Miss Marple and Mrs McGillicuddy.

'I myself,' said Mrs McGillicuddy, 'have only just returned from abroad – the day before yesterday,' she added.

'Ah, well, you're not up on our local scandal then,' said Cedric. 'Arsenic in the curry, that's what it was. Lucy's aunt knows all about it, I bet.'

'Well,' said Miss Marple, 'I did just hear – I mean, it was just a *hint*, but of course I didn't want to embarrass you in any way, Miss Crackenthorpe.'

'You must pay no attention to my brother,' said Emma. 'He just likes making people uncomfortable.' She gave him an affectionate smile as she spoke.

The door opened and Mr Crackenthorpe came in, tapping angrily with his stick.

'Where's tea?' he said, 'why isn't tea ready? You! Girl!' he addressed Lucy, 'why haven't you brought tea in?'

'It's just ready, Mr Crackenthorpe. I'm bringing it in now. I was just setting the table ready.'

Lucy went out of the room again and Mr Crackenthorpe was introduced to Miss Marple and Mrs McGillicuddy.

'Like my meals on time,' said Mr Crackenthorpe. 'Punctuality and economy. Those are my watchwords.'

'Very necessary, I'm sure,' said Miss Marple, 'especially in these times with taxation and everything.'

Mr Crackenthorpe snorted. 'Taxation! Don't talk to me of those robbers. A miserable pauper – that's what I am. And it's going to get worse, not better. You wait, my boy,' he addressed Cedric, 'when you get this place ten to one the Socialists will have it off you and turn it into a Welfare Centre or something. *And* take all your income to keep it up with!'

Lucy reappeared with a tea tray, Bryan Eastley followed her carrying a tray of sandwiches, bread and butter and cake.

'What's this? What's this?' Mr Crackenthorpe inspected the tray. 'Frosted cake? We having a party today? Nobody told me about it.'

A faint flush came into Emma's face.

'Dr Quimper's coming to tea, Father. It's his birthday today and –'

'Birthday?' snorted the old man. 'What's he doing with a birthday? Birthdays are only for children. I never count my birthdays

711

and I won't let anyone else celebrate them either.'

'Much cheaper,' agreed Cedric. 'You save the price of candles on your cake.'

'That's enough from you, boy,' said Mr Crackenthorpe.

Miss Marple was shaking hands with Bryan Eastley. 'I've heard about you, of course,' she said, 'from Lucy. Dear me, you remind me *so* of someone I used to know at St Mary Mead. That's the village where I've lived for so many years, you know. Ronnie Wells, the solicitor's son. Couldn't seem to settle somehow when he went into his father's business. He went out to East Africa and started a series of cargo boats on the lake out there. Victoria Nyanza, or is it Albert, I mean? Anyway, I'm sorry to say that it wasn't a success, and he lost *all* his capital. Most unfortunate! Not any relation of yours, I suppose? The likeness is so great.'

'No,' said Bryan, 'I don't think I've any relations called Wells.'

'He was engaged to a very nice girl,' said Miss Marple. 'Very sensible. She tried to dissuade him, but he wouldn't listen to her. He was wrong of course. Women have a lot of sense, you know, when it comes to money matters. Not high finance, of course. No woman can hope to understand *that*, my dear father said. But everyday LSD – that sort of thing. What a delightful view you have from this window,' she added, making her way across and looking out.

Emma joined her.

'Such an expanse of parkland! How picturesque the cattle look against the trees. One would never dream that one was in the middle of a town.'

'We're rather an anachronism, I think,' said Emma. 'If the windows were open now you'd hear far off the noise of the traffic.'

'Oh, of course,' said Miss Marple, 'there's noise everywhere, isn't there? Even in St Mary Mead. We're now quite close to an airfield, you know, and really the way those jet planes fly over! Most frightening. Two panes in my little greenhouse broken the other day. Going through the sound barrier, or so I understand, though what it means I never have known.'

'It's quite simple, really,' said Bryan, approaching amiably. 'You see, it's like this.'

Miss Marple dropped her handbag and Bryan politely picked it up. At the same moment Mrs McGillicuddy approached Emma and murmured, in an anguished voice – the anguish was quite genuine since Mrs McGillicuddy deeply disliked the task which she was now performing:

'I wonder – could I go upstairs for a moment?'

'Of course,' said Emma.

'I'll take you,' said Lucy.

Lucy and Mrs McGillicuddy left the room together.

'Very cold, driving today,' said Miss Marple in a vaguely explanatory manner.

'About the sound barrier,' said Byran, 'you see it's like this . . . Oh, hallo, there's Quimper.'

The doctor drove up in his car. He came in rubbing his hands and looking very cold.

'Going to snow,' he said, 'that's my guess. Hallo, Emma, how are you? Good lord, what's all this?'

'We made you a birthday cake,' said Emma. 'D'you remember? You told me today was your birthday.'

'I didn't expect all this,' said Quimper. 'You know it's years – why, it must be – yes sixteen years since anyone's remembered my birthday.' He looked almost uncomfortably touched.

'Do you know Miss Marple?' Emma introduced him.

'Oh, yes,' said Miss Marple, 'I met Dr Quimper here before and he came and saw me when I had a very nasty chill the other day and he was most kind.'

'All right again now, I hope?' said the doctor.

Miss Marple assured him that she was quite all right now.

'You haven't been to see *me* lately, Quimper,' said Mr Crackenthorpe. 'I might be dying for all the notice you take of me!'

'I don't see you dying yet awhile,' said Dr Quimper.

'I don't mean to,' said Mr Crackenthorpe. 'Come on, let's have tea. What're we waiting for?'

'Oh, please,' said Miss Marple, 'don't wait for my friend. She would be most upset if you did.'

They sat down and started tea. Miss Marple accepted a piece of bread and butter first, and then went on to a sandwich.

'Are they –?' she hesitated.

'Fish,' said Bryan. 'I helped make 'em.'

Mr Crackenthorpe gave a cackle of laughter.

'Poisoned fishpaste,' he said. 'That's what they are. Eat 'em at your peril.'

'Please, Father!'

'You've got to be careful what you eat in this house,' said Mr Crackenthorpe to Miss Marple. 'Two of my sons have been murdered like flies. Who's doing it — that's what I want to know.'

'Don't let him put you off,' said Cedric, handing the plate once more to Miss Marple. 'A touch of arsenic improves the complexion, they say, so long as you don't have too much.'

'Eat one yourself, boy,' said old Mr Crackenthorpe.

'Want me to be official taster?' said Cedric. 'Here goes.'

He took a sandwich and put it whole into his mouth. Miss Marple gave a gentle, ladylike little laugh and took a sandwich. She took a bite, and said:

'I do think it's so brave of you all to make these jokes. Yes, really, I think it's very brave indeed. I do admire bravery so much.'

She gave a sudden gasp and began to choke. 'A fish bone,' she gasped out, 'in my throat.'

Quimper rose quickly. He went across to her, moved her backwards towards the window and told her to open her mouth. He pulled out a case from his pocket, selecting some forceps from it. With quick professional skill he peered down the old lady's throat. At that moment the door opened and Mrs McGillicuddy, followed by Lucy, came in. Mrs McGillicuddy gave a sudden gasp as her eyes fell on the tableau in front of her, Miss Marple leaning back and the doctor holding her throat and tilting up her head.

'But that's *him*,' cried Mrs McGillicuddy. 'That's the man in the train . . .'

With incredible swiftness Miss Marple slipped from the doctor's grasp and came towards her friend.

'I *thought* you'd recognize him, Elspeth!' she said. 'No. Don't say another word.' She turned triumphantly round to Dr Quimper. 'You didn't know, did you, Doctor, when you strangled that woman in the train, that somebody *actually saw you do it*? It was my friend here. Mrs McGillicuddy. She *saw* you. Do you understand? *Saw you with her own eyes*. She was in another train that was running parallel with yours.'

'What the hell?' Dr Quimper made a quick step towards Mrs McGillicuddy but again, swiftly, Miss Marple was between him and her.

'Yes,' said Miss Marple. 'She saw you, and *she recognizes you*,

714

and she'll swear to it in court. It's not often, I believe,' went on Miss Marple in her gentle plaintive voice, 'that anyone actually sees a murder committed. It's usually circumstantial evidence of course. But in this case the conditions were very unusual. There was actually *an eye witness to murder.*'

'You devilish old hag,' said Dr Quimper. He lunged forward at Miss Marple but this time it was Cedric who caught him by the shoulder.

'So *you're* the murdering devil, are you?' said Cedric as he swung him round. 'I never liked you and I always thought you were a wrong 'un, but lord knows, I never suspected you.'

Bryan Eastley came quickly to Cedric's assistance. Inspector Craddock and Inspector Bacon entered the room from the farther door.

'Dr Quimper,' said Bacon, 'I must caution you that . . .'

'You can take your caution to hell,' said Dr Quimper. 'Do you think anyone's going to believe what a couple of old women say? Who's ever heard of all this rigmarole about a train!'

Miss Marple said: 'Elspeth McGillicuddy reported the murder to the police at once on the 20th December and gave a description of the man.'

Dr Quimper gave a sudden heave of the shoulders. 'If ever a man had the devil's own luck,' said Dr Quimper.

'But –' said Mrs McGillicuddy.

'Be quiet, Elspeth,' said Miss Marple.

'Why should I want to murder a perfectly strange woman?' said Dr Quimper.

'She wasn't a strange woman,' said Inspector Craddock. '*She was your wife.*'

CHAPTER TWENTY-SEVEN

'So you see,' said Miss Marple, 'it really turned out to be, as I began to suspect, very, very simple. The simplest kind of crime. So many men seem to murder their wives.'

Mrs McGillicuddy looked at Miss Marple and Inspector Craddock.

'I'd be obliged,' she said, 'if you'd put me a little more up to date.'

'He saw a chance, you see,' said Miss Marple, 'of marrying a rich wife, Emma Crackenthorpe. Only he couldn't marry her because he had a wife already. They'd been separated for years but she wouldn't divorce him. That fitted in very well with what Inspector Craddock told me of this girl who called herself Anna Stravinska. *She* had an English husband, so she told one of her friends, and it was also said she was a very devout Catholic. Dr Quimper couldn't risk marrying Emma bigamously, so he decided, being a very ruthless and cold-blooded man, that he would get rid of his wife. The idea of murdering her in the train and later putting her body in the sarcophagus in the barn was really rather a clever one. He meant it to tie up, you see, with the Crackenthorpe family. Before that he'd written a letter to Emma which purported to be from the girl Martine whom Edmund Crackenthorpe had talked of marrying. Emma had told Dr Quimper all about her brother, you see. Then, when the moment arose he encouraged her to go to the police with her story. He wanted the dead woman identified as Martine. I think he may have heard that inquiries were being made by the Paris police about Anna Stravinska, and so he arranged to have a postcard come from her from Jamaica.

'It was easy for him to arrange to meet his wife in London, to tell her that he hoped to be reconciled with her and that he would like her to come down and "meet his family". We won't talk about the next part of it, which is very unpleasant to think about. Of course he was a greedy man. When he thought about taxation, and how much it cuts into income, he began thinking that it would be nice to have a good deal more capital. Perhaps he'd already thought of that before he decided to murder his wife. Anyway, he started spreading rumours that someone was trying to poison old Mr Crackenthorpe so as to get the ground prepared, and then he ended by administering arsenic to the family. Not too much, of course, for he didn't want old Mr Crackenthorpe to die.'

'But I still don't see how he managed,' said Craddock. 'He wasn't in the house when the curry was being prepared.'

'Oh, but there wasn't any arsenic in the curry *then*,' said Miss Marple. 'He added it to the curry afterwards when he took it away to be tested. He probably put the arsenic in the cocktail jug earlier.

Then, of course, it was quite easy for him, in his role of medical attendant, to poison off Alfred Crackenthorpe and also to send the tablets to Harold in London, having safeguarded himself by telling Harold that he wouldn't need any more tablets. Everything he did was bold and audacious and cruel and greedy, and I am really very, very sorry,' finished Miss Marple, looking as fierce as a fluffy old lady can look, 'that they have abolished capital punishment because I do feel that if there is anyone who ought to hang, it's Dr Quimper.'

'Hear, hear,' said Inspector Craddock.

'It occurred to me, you know,' continued Miss Marple, 'that even if you only see anybody from the back view, so to speak, nevertheless a back view *is* characteristic. I thought that if Elspeth were to see Dr Quimper in exactly the same position as she'd seen him in the train in, that is, with his back to her, bent over a woman whom he was holding by the throat, then I was almost sure she would recognize him, or would make some kind of startled exclamation. That is why I had to lay my little plan with Lucy's kind assistance.'

'I must say,' said Mrs McGillicuddy, 'it gave me quite a turn. I said, "That's him" before I could stop myself. And yet, you know, I hadn't actually seen the man's face and—'

'I was terribly afraid that you were going to say so, Elspeth,' said Miss Marple.

'I was,' said Mrs McGillicuddy. 'I was going to say that of course I hadn't seen his *face*.'

'That,' said Miss Marple, 'would have been quite fatal. You see, dear, he thought you really *did* recognize him. I mean, *he* couldn't know that you hadn't seen his face.'

'A good thing I held my tongue then,' said Mrs McGillicuddy.

'I wasn't going to let you say another word,' said Miss Marple.

Craddock laughed suddenly. 'You two!' he said. 'You're a marvellous pair. What next, Miss Marple? What's the happy ending? What happens to poor Emma Crackenthorpe, for instance?'

'She'll get over the doctor, of course,' said Miss Marple, 'and I dare say if her father were to die — and I don't think he's quite so robust as he thinks he is — that she'd go on a cruise or perhaps to stay abroad like Geraldine Webb, and I dare say something might come of it. A *nicer* man than Dr Quimper, I hope.'

'What about Lucy Eyelesbarrow? Wedding bells there too?'

'Perhaps,' said Miss Marple, 'I shouldn't wonder.'

'Which of 'em is she going to choose?' said Dermot Craddock.
'Don't you know?' said Miss Marple.
'No, I don't,' said Craddock. 'Do you?'
'Oh, yes, I think so,' said Miss Marple.
And she twinkled at him.

BY THE SAME AUTHOR
MISS MARPLE
The Complete Short Stories

At last – all 20 Miss Marple short stories
in a single volume!

Miss Marple made her first appearance in a book in 1930,
and her twelfth and final novel was published shortly after
Agatha Christie's death almost 50 years later. In the
intervening years Miss Marple also featured in 20 short
stories, published in a number of different collections. But
never before have they been available together.

In this complete volume, Miss Marple uses her unique
insight to deduce the truth about a series of unsolved crimes
– cases of a girl framed for theft, some disappearing blood-
stains, the cryptic last message of a poisoned man, a woman
killed within days of writing her will, a spiritualist who
predicts death, a mortally wounded stranger in a church, a
Christmas tragedy . . .

In all 20 ingenious crimes, every one guaranteed to keep
you guessing until the turn of the final page.

*'The plots are so good that one marvels . . . most of them
would have made a full length thriller' Daily Mirror*

ISBN 0-00-649962-7